D0040906

Angels to Watch Over Me

Angels to Watch Over Me

Angels to Watch Over Me
by Pamela Griffin

Crossroads
by Tracie Peterson and Jennifer Peterson

A Question of Balance
by Veda Boyd Jones

A Class of Her Own
by Janice Thompson

HeavenSent
FROM
Crossings

Angels to Watch Over Me
Copyright © 2001 by Pamela Griffin

Crossroads
Copyright © 1997 by Barbour Publishing, Inc.

A Question of Balance
Copyright © 1996 by Barbour and Company, Inc.

A Class of Her Own
Copyright © 2002 by Janice Thompson

This edition was especially created in 2004 for Crossings by arrangement with Barbour Publishing, Inc.

Published by Crossings Book Club, 401 Franklin Avenue, Garden City, New York 11530.

ISBN: 1-58288-084-0

Printed in the United States of America

Angels to Watch Over Me

ANGELS TO WATCH OVER ME

BY PAMELA GRIFFIN

Many thanks to my crit buds, Tracey B., Tamela H.M., Jill S., and Mom—for pitching in their time and effort at a moment's notice. You gals are the best! Also thanks to Lynn C. for answering my many questions, and to my pastor for his help. I could have never written this without my Guardian and Lord, whose angels watched over this prodigal daughter, even when I wasn't aware of it.

*S*hae!"

Hearing the troubled voice of her young sister, Marcia "Shae" Stevens whipped her head sideways and lost her balance on the top platform of the stepladder where she precariously perched. She grabbed for one of the nearby shelves and just prevented herself from toppling to the floor.

"Tiffany! What's wrong?" Shae tightened her fingers around the feather duster in her other hand and studied the guilt-ridden faces of her sister and her sister's best friend and accomplice, Liz Reihlander. Shae glanced at the chubby redhead, whose gaze seemed permanently fixed on the polished planks of the wooden floor, then looked back to her fourteen-year-old sister, Tiffany.

Tiffany's eyes darted nervously around the storage room, flicking only briefly to Shae before flying away again. Shae's heart began to beat faster with dread.

Oh, what mischief had the two cooked up this time?

"I gotta go. My mom said I had to be home by five." Liz turned and fled the room.

Tiffany's eyes followed her, as if she'd been betrayed.

"Okay, Tiff, let's have it." Shae tried to keep her voice controlled. She had learned long ago that blowing up after hearing Tiffany's confessions from past shenanigans had done nothing but cause more problems. After taking the three steps down the ladder, Shae looked to Tiffany's hand, which tightly clutched a piece of yellow paper. "Is that for me?"

Tiffany bit her lip, hazel eyes widening with apprehension. "We were only having a little fun. We never thought anything like this would really happen. Honest!"

"The paper, Tiffany."

Reluctantly, Tiffany handed her the soiled and crumpled note. At a glance Shae could see it was a business telegram.

Miss Stevens,
We are pleased to inform you that you have won the contest for "A
Dream Date with Keith Travers" sponsored by Teen Planet
Magazine. We will contact you on the twentieth of this month to
discuss the arrangements.

Sincerely,
Frederick W. Smith
Star Artists Management

Shae barely quenched the smile threatening to take over her mouth as she scanned the paper. She fingered the hole at the bottom of her worn plaid flannel shirt, wondering how to deal with this new development. It wouldn't do for her to treat the matter too lightly. Tiffany got away with far too much as it was.

"A little young to be going on a date with Keith Travers, aren't you, Tiffany?" Shae said in what she hoped was a formidable tone of voice. "Well, you'll just have to call and tell them it was all a big mistake and you're sorry."

Tiffany's rosy color faded until it matched the flocked ivory petunias on the pine green wallpaper. With growing alarm, Shae's hand tightened on the letter. "There's more you're not telling me, isn't there?"

"We entered your name in the contest!" Tiffany blurted. "You had to be at least eighteen to enter."

The blood drained from Shae's face. The faint trace of amusement she'd felt at the childish prank disappeared as swiftly as a wave crashing on the beach and receding into the sea. She remembered how insistent the girls had been about taking her picture months ago with Liz's new camera. "That's why you took the pictures of me by the ocean?"

"Yes, but—oh, Shae . . ."

"There's more?" Shae asked, eyes flying wide with disbelief.

"The pictures, uh . . . they didn't turn out. And there wasn't time to take more. So we, um . . . we sent one in of Samantha."

"Now let me get this straight." Shae put a hand to a forehead that was beginning to throb. "You entered my name and Samantha's picture in a contest for a date with Keith Travers—the famous recording artist—and now you've found out you won?"

Tiffany nodded miserably. "And we also had to write and tell them about your hobbies and other stuff."

"Great! Just what I needed, Tiffany!" Shae threw down the feather duster and marched out of the room, her younger sister following like a whipped puppy. "Well, you'll just have to get on the phone and—wait a minute! What was the date on that note?"

Remembering she still gripped the yellow paper, Shae brought it up to her eyes and let out a horrified gasp. "The twentieth—that's today! Oh, Tiff. Why didn't you give this to me earlier? You probably got this before today, didn't you?"

Tiffany gave a reluctant nod.

"I thought so. You've really landed a whopper this time. I only hope it's not too late to call—though it's strange they haven't confirmed the date yet. Their office hours should be over soon," Shae rambled, her panicked thoughts tumbling from her mouth.

She had to think clearly, stay in control, stay on top of things and not let this new mountain topple on her head. "Do you have the number to reach them? No? Well then, we'll have to call information first, since all we have is their address. I want you to know, Tiffany Lauren Stevens—this is coming out of your allowance!"

Shae rubbed dirty hands on equally dirty jeans and reached for the phone. Tiffany slumped against the wall next to the curved receiving desk, faint wrinkles creasing her brow. Shae punched a few buttons and waited for an operator to come on the line. After reaching the state and city she needed, she took a calming breath.

"Los Angeles Directory Assistance? Yes, please. I'd like the number of Star Artists . . ."

The brisk wind sneaked in and toyed with papers and tourist guides on the polished oak counter as the front door to the inn opened. Two men walked inside, one wearing dark sunglasses despite the overcast day.

"Never mind, Operator," Shae managed in a small voice. "Thank you." Dropping the humming receiver into its cradle, she eyed the newcomers with dread. She would have recognized the taller of the two anywhere. After all, his glossy likeness was plastered on her sister's wall.

His dark-spectacled gaze briefly looked her over and just as quickly dismissed her. He scanned the old-fashioned room, a look of boredom on his handsome features. The shorter man walked to where Shae stood clutching the edge of the counter with white-knuckled fingers. Balding and fat, he studied her with piggish eyes, an unlit cigar stuck in his mouth. "We're looking for the home of Shae Stevens. This is the address we were given."

Shae swallowed, trying to find her voice. "I . . . I'm sorry." The words came out in a high-pitched squeak, and she cleared her throat. "I'm afraid there's been a mistake."

She darted a look at Tiffany, who'd been inching her way backward out of the room with wide eyes pinned to Keith Travers. Tiffany caught Shae's warning gaze and wilted against the wainscoting.

"This isn't the home of Shae Stevens?" Bald Man asked sharply. Keith stopped his disinterested study of the antique furnishings and joined the other man at the arched counter.

"Um, no. I–I mean, yes," Shae stammered, strongly aware of Keith's dark gaze planted on her. "But . . . well, the fact is you've been led here under false pretenses. I'm really sorry. I–I was trying to call just now and tell you . . . I only just found out about all this . . . but I had no idea you'd come here. . . ."

"We'd like to discuss this with Miss Stevens. I assume you work for her," Bald Man said critically, eyeing her casual attire.

"Um, no. Actually, I am her . . . I mean she's me." She gave a nervous little laugh that held no humor. "I'm Shae Stevens."

"What!" He pulled a photograph from the inside pocket of his business suit. Shae caught a glimpse of the gorgeous blue-eyed, blond Samantha Reihlander.

"You're Shae Stevens?"

Keith Travers's baritone voice was rich, like creamy cappuccino. He slowly pulled off designer sunglasses, and it was all Shae could do not to gape as his piercing blue eyes studied her. Pictures definitely didn't do this man justice.

Opting for levity in the midst of this nightmare being played out by the four of them, Shae offered a wobbly smile. "Last time I looked, that was my name."

❦

Frowning, Keith took in the smooth olive complexion devoid of makeup. Dirt smudged one high cheekbone and her forehead. A blue bandanna covered her hair, and only by the wisps that had escaped near her temple could he tell she was a brunette. A pair of silver-rimmed wire glasses sat perched on her slightly upturned nose, and through them he saw thickly-lashed, almond-shaped dark eyes—wide and staring.

He bunched his brows. "Is this some kind of joke? You're a little old to be playing games like this, aren't you? And certainly too old to be reading teen magazines, I'd think."

She visibly stiffened. "I assure you, Mr. Travers, this wasn't my idea, but rather the mischief of two young girls who've had way too much time on their hands. I promise you they'll be properly dealt with." While addressing him, she darted a glance toward the teen hugging the wall. "I hope this little misunderstanding hasn't inconvenienced you too much. Please believe me when I say I'm sorry."

Intermingled feelings of interest and curiosity swamped Keith when he saw the quivering, stuttering girl had disappeared to be replaced by a self-assured woman with a fiery sparkle in her chocolate-colored eyes.

"Inconvenienced! Lady, you have no idea—"

"Let it go, Freddie." Keith stopped his manager's beginning tirade with an upraised hand. His glance went to the trembling girl who looked as if she'd gladly melt into the wall if given the chance. Except for the eyes, she was a replica of Shae. He could pretty well guess what had happened. Little sister played a prank on big sister. How often had he and his older brother caused pandemonium in his family's lives with similar escapades?

"We accept your apology."

"We do?" Freddie looked at Keith in stunned disbelief. "I mean—yeah, sure. We do."

"Oh, I'm so relieved!" Shae gave them a dazzling smile. Keith noted even her face and eyes seemed to light up from within.

Freddie grumbled something and turned from the counter. "Come on, Travers. We gotta get back to California and look through the entries again. I had a feeling all along it was a mistake to accept a winner from the East Coast. Only cold and fog, fog and cold—can't expect nothin' more from a place like this. Next time the winner is coming to us, like is always done in these kinds of contests. But no-o-o-o—you had to change all the rules and fly all the way out here. . . ." His complaints trailed off as he stomped out the door.

"Don't mind him," Keith said. "He's been a bear ever since he quit smoking."

"Under the circumstances, I'd say more like a teddy bear. Thank you both for being so understanding."

"Believe me, Miss Stevens, I understand more than you think I do." His gaze lighted on Tiffany, and he gave her a smile and a wink. "Bye, now."

❧

Now what did he mean by that?

Puzzled, Shae forced her gaze away from the door the singer had exited and looked at Tiffany. Stars shone in the teen's eyes, all former anxiety seeming to have vanished. "Oh, Shae, did you see that? Keith Travers actually smiled at me . . . and he winked at me too! I'll never forget this day as long as I live. . . ."

Pulling her mouth into a severe frown, Shae crossed her arms and stared at her swooning sister. "You certainly won't, young lady. Thanks to Mr. Travers's generosity, things went a lot better than I expected. But that doesn't excuse the fact that you lied and interfered in other people's lives."

Tiffany gave no indication she'd heard, her expression showing she was still in la-la land.

Shae let out a weary sigh. "As of this moment you're grounded for two weeks—make that a month. And you can spend that time helping out at the inn instead of loafing around and dreaming up more mischief. You can start by helping Gretta in the kitchen. Right now—go."

Tiffany glided toward the designated area, the dreamy smile still on her face. Not even Shae's sharp words or the reality of being grounded seemed to have any effect on her at the moment. Shae watched as her sister walked smack into the wooden door frame.

She shook her head. Raising a younger sibling, especially a teenaged girl, was harder than she had assumed it would be. Had she been so hard to control when she'd been Tiffany's age?

Instant heaviness settled over Shae like a suffocating shroud, as memory taunted. Escape. She needed escape. Rushing up the stairs to her room, she ripped the bandanna from her head. Maybe a good jog in the brisk sea air would be just the thing.

She tore out the mammoth-sized hair clasp, brushed her thick mass of hair, and secured it with a rubber band. After changing into a pine green sweat suit, she pulled on a pair of high-topped sneakers and a windbreaker. Studying her reflection, she wiped away the dirt with a tissue. Huge eyes stared back through the lenses of her glasses, looking vulnerable and uncertain. The men's earlier appraisal made her feel that she'd been found wanting. And for some reason, that bothered her.

Though she wasn't vain, Shae had always tried to look her best around others, and to be caught looking like such a mess, and by Keith Travers to boot, had given her feminine ego—what little of it there was—quite a jolt. She knew Keith was considered a heartthrob to many of her gender—teenagers and women alike. And who wouldn't wonder? What with those unbelievably bright blue eyes of his and that wheat blond hair waving about his neck, almost touching his collarbone . . . not to mention that million-dollar smile. . . .

"Marcia Shae Stevens—stop it right now!" she angrily confronted her reflection. "You're no better than those moony-eyed teenagers. What would your mother say?" A haunted look came into the dark eyes staring back.

Yes . . . what would Mother say?

She backed up, turned, and fled the room. Darting down the stairs, out the door, and into the cloudy day, she ran as if racing the wind while trying to escape the ghosts of her past.

⤳

After a good brisk run, Shae returned to the inn feeling better. Yet once she opened the door she knew her improved disposition wasn't meant to last.

Hillary Collins paced the polished wooden floor, her high heels only silenced as they passed over wide Oriental scatter rugs. Catching sight of Shae, she stopped. Shae could see in a moment that Hillary had been crying, and heavily. Her face was blotchy, her eyes red.

"Is it Robert?" Shae asked softly, moving to stand beside the distraught woman.

Hillary nodded. "Oh, Shae. He's in jail!" She practically collapsed against her, throwing thin arms around her shoulders.

Relieved to see the front desk empty of curious onlookers, Shae shepherded Hillary into the office. After helping her friend onto a cushioned chair, Shae closed the door. "Tell me."

"He got pulled over for a DUI on the mainland." Hillary sniffled. "He must have gotten belligerent—you know how he can be when he's been drinking. Ever since I became a Christian last winter, his drinking has gotten worse. Oh, Shae . . . I just don't know what to do anymore!" She broke down into a fresh torrent of tears.

Shae sighed. Robert and Hillary were the inn's floor show. Robert played the piano, and his wife sang. Shae had known about his drinking problem, but he usually kept it under control and didn't let it affect his performances.

Hillary lifted smudged eyes to Shae. "Will you pray with me, Shae? Please?"

"Of course," Shae murmured, though she wasn't sure it would do any good. The possibility of her prayers being heard was slim. Yet she wanted to help her friend, and God might listen since the request didn't involve Shae.

She took Hillary's cold hands and offered a shaky prayer, hoping

Hillary couldn't tell how rusty she was. Afterward, she opened her eyes, affecting a small smile. "Don't worry about tonight. I'll find a replacement. You go and get Robert out of jail. Do you need bail money?"

"Well, I did just pay rent and a few other bills. But I can't take your money, Shae. I'll get the rest somehow. . . ." Her voice dwindled away, uncertain, scared.

Shae ignored her and went to the wall safe. "How much more do you need?"

"The bail bondsman said it would take a thousand—but I only need to pay 10 percent up front."

Shae's eyebrows went up at Hillary's meek answer, but then again it wasn't Robert's first time in jail. She fiddled with the knob and opened the door to the safe, pulling a few bills from the padded, zippered case inside. "You're lucky I haven't gone to the bank yet. Here. No, I insist. Take it. I'm not in lack, and you need it right now. You can pay me back when you're able."

"Thank you. I don't know where we'd be without you." Hillary's voice sounded relieved and tortured at the same time.

"I think our paths crossed for a reason, Hillary. God takes care of His own, you know." These last words came out wooden, learned by rote, but Hillary didn't seem to notice. Shae quickly slammed the door of the safe.

"You're right, Shae. And I believe you're my own guardian angel He sent to watch out for me." Still teary-eyed, Hillary took the proffered bills with a grateful smile and hug, then left the office. Her soft words resounded in Shae's ears, mocking her.

And what angel had looked out for her parents that night over seven years ago? Where had God been when they needed Him? But then—the disaster hadn't been God's fault. The blame was hers. All hers.

Shae sank onto her chair and dropped her forehead into her hands. Was God standing in the clouds, angry and waiting to bang a huge, deserved anvil on her head?

She attended her local church because she knew it was required of a Christian. She said and did what she thought was right, helped others, never broke the Ten Commandments . . . Still Shae had little hope that heaven would one day be her eternal home. But the thought of going to hell terrified her. She visited it each night in her dreams. . . .

With an angry, muffled exclamation, she straightened and snatched up the slim telephone book at her elbow to scan its pages for a replacement act. Things were certainly bad enough in the present without dwelling on the past. Or the future.

~&

"You've gotta be kidding! It's important we get back to LA as soon as possible." Freddie's face reddened as he chewed on the stump of his unlit cigar.

"Sorry, Mister. Fog's too thick. Won't be going anywhere 'til it clears. Too dangerous."

Both Keith and Freddie looked out at the wall of dense white fog smothering an unusually calm ocean and heading in their direction. "There must be someone with a boat who's willing to try it. I'd pay them well."

The old sailor crossed his arms and wryly observed them from eyes the color of the sea. "Not likely you'd find anyone round these parts. Old Man McClury's got a rowboat. But he wouldn't risk it. Too smart. He might be willing to rent it out to you. But you'd be on your own."

Freddie let out a harsh expletive. Even Keith was getting irritated with the crusty boatman's sarcasm. No one in his right mind would take a small rowboat over twelve miles of foggy ocean.

"Listen, Freddie," Keith said, "your ranting and raving isn't helping any. We might as well face it—we're stuck here for the night. I vote we head back to that inn and see if there are any vacancies. I'm beat."

"We should've taken the ferry," Freddie mumbled. "At least then we'd be on the mainland now."

"Ferries don't run in fog," the boatman shot back. "Planes either."

"Yeah, so we heard." After throwing a nasty look at the unruffled local, Freddie turned to Keith. "Let's find a telephone book and call a taxi."

Keith nodded, relieved Freddie had finally given in. They had chartered a flight from Providence, but the planes at the small island airport were now grounded due to the oncoming bad weather. Unfortunately, they'd left their overnight bags in an airport locker on the mainland. Chartering a small boat had been Freddie's last-ditch effort to get there.

Once the cab arrived, Freddie slid beside Keith on the backseat, grumbling something about New England's lousy weather and being trapped on a remote island. Yet Keith was relieved at this turn of events. He wasn't ready for more wearying hours of travel yet, having recently completed a concert tour, and would enjoy a short break on Block Island. Besides, he had other interests in this part of the country—that is, if he didn't lose his nerve. Interests Freddie knew nothing about.

Soon they again found themselves in front of the renovated Victorian inn—one of many scattered throughout the island's lone city of New Shoreham. They took the four steps to the wraparound porch of the three-story building that boasted dark gray siding and white gingerbread trim. In the old-fashioned lobby, a young girl with a blond ponytail checked them in and gave them their room keys, all the while casting surreptitious glances at Keith. "Say, Mister, did you know you look a lot like—"

"Yeah, Kid. He hears it all the time," Freddie interrupted. "Is there a dining room in this joint?"

The blond nodded. "Down that hall and to your left. You're just in time for the floor show."

"Whoopee."

At Freddie's sardonic reply, the girl stared, clearly puzzled.

"Lighten up, Freddie," Keith muttered under his breath.

Following her directions, they found themselves in a large room with a stage against one wall and linen-covered square tables in front. Stubby candles glowed from within smoky, netted glass globes on the center of each table. The dark wooden decor looked as if it would fit right in a hundred years previously, except for the dim lights glowing from strategic places along the high-beamed ceiling. Long picture windows covered one side, giving a view of the fog-covered ocean.

"Charming," Freddie drawled.

"Will you cut it out already? We're stuck here, so we might as well make the most of it." Keith surveyed the large room, hoping to catch a glimpse of Shae Stevens. The no-frills woman intrigued him, though he couldn't begin to understand why. She was nothing like the glamour girls he knew.

They sat at a back table in the corner, so the small crowd of diners wouldn't easily notice them. A middle-aged woman wearing a navy uniform ambled their way with menus. The two men scanned the plastic covers, made their order, and the waitress bustled away.

"Only five choices for entrées? Say what kind of place is this?" Freddie complained to his dinner partner. "And I didn't see any alcohol on the menu. Don't tell me everyone around here is a teetotaler."

"Shh. The floor show is about to begin," Keith said as a lovely young woman took the stage, moved toward the piano, and sat on the matching bench.

The overhead lights went out, and a blue spotlight beamed down on her. The woman's waist-length hair shone a glossy blue-black, swaying gently to and fro, as her slim hands began to roam the ivory keys. Her winter-white dress sparkled in the light.

Keith studied her over his lowered sunglasses a moment, then resumed scanning the dim room. Judging from her appearance, Shae Stevens was probably a maid and wouldn't be working in the dining room, but one never knew.

The woman at the piano began to sing, and Keith's attention again turned her way. He noticed even Freddie perked up. She sang a few show tunes from the forties and fifties, her soft voice ringing with a clear bell-like quality. The last note from a sad love song barely died away before Freddie turned to Keith, an excited gleam in his eye.

"Maybe it's not such a bad thing we got stuck here after all, Travers," he said over the burst of loud clapping in the room. "We've been looking for a replacement backup singer for your new CD. She's perfect. Understated—yet the lady can carry a tune and then some. And she definitely has stage presence. Whattaya think?"

Keith, who was often skeptical of Freddie's ideas, nodded slowly. *Yes, she could fill Lil's shoes. Providing she was willing, of course.* He watched as she stood, acknowledged the audience's applause with a graceful bow and hurried backstage.

Freddie shot to his feet. "Come on. Let's find her before she gets away."

"But we haven't eaten yet!"

"You can eat later. We don't want to lose her."

"Freddie, I haven't eaten since this morning. . . ."

But Keith spoke to empty air. His manager was already three tables away and heading for the door. With a frustrated groan, Keith snatched up his water glass and downed its contents, then plucked two large wheat rolls from the basket the waitress had set on the table before writing down their order. Taking a huge bite of one roll, he stood and followed Freddie.

After searching a few of the public rooms, they again found themselves at the reception counter, the same blond again giving Keith the eye while he finished off his last roll.

"We'd like to speak to the lady who sang for the floor show," Freddie said.

The blond chewed her lip. "I guess that would be Hillary Collins, but I thought I saw her leave earlier. Short blond hair, deep sultry voice?"

"No, no, no!" Freddie bellowed. "The lady had long dark hair and a sweet voice that could charm the birds from the trees."

"But . . . I'm sorry. I . . . I don't know who—"

Freddie let out a few choice words. "Don't you even know who you hire for your entertainment?"

"I only work here p—part-time." The girl's lip quivered and her eyes filled with tears. Keith was about to admonish Freddie, when a familiar voice spoke from behind.

"Is there a problem, Katie?"

The girl's eyes widened. "Miss Stevens."

The men turned simultaneously. Keith's jaw dropped as he came face-to-face with Shae and realized she was the girl for whom they'd been searching. From their back table, Keith hadn't been able to see her clearly. Yet even if he would have had a front row seat, center stage, he doubted he would've recognized her.

Her face was dramatically made up—minus the glasses—smoky blue enhancing dark eyes that sparkled like black star sapphires. Pink blusher swept the high cheekbones, and her lips were a bright cherry red. Blue-black hair fell in a dark curtain to her waist.

A white lace dress hugged her slim curves, and a scalloped, straight neckline barely revealed the tips of her round shoulders. Sprinkled with rhinestones, the dress caught the light and matched the sparkle in her eyes. A choker of tiny white diamonds encircled her neck, and matching earrings dangled from her ears.

Keith blinked, stunned. *She looks like a bride.* And then, remarkably, it was as if the present faded away and she was standing amid myriad colorful flowers beside the ocean, wearing another white dress and looking up at him with eyes of love—as if she'd become his bride. . . .

He shook his head to clear it. What was wrong with him? Was he hallucinating? Unlike some in his profession, he didn't do drugs—though he had tampered with them the first two and a half years of his career. An episode he now regretted, as he did so many other events in his life. Still, his former drug abuse and drinking didn't explain how he could be seeing things that weren't there now.

The day had been long and filled with surprises. Maybe he was just tired and hungry. Definitely hungry. He turned to Freddie and tried to concentrate on what his manager was saying.

"So you're the nightingale. Hmm . . . Tell me, Miss Stevens, besides acting as a maid, a desk clerk, and entertainment for this inn, what other duties do you perform?"

"What?" She blinked, evidently still as flustered as Keith, and turned her gaze away from him to Freddie.

"I asked what you do here."

"Oh. I own and manage The Roosting Place. I was on my way to my room to change when I heard the commotion." Her words sounded nervous as she looked at Keith. "I must say I'm surprised to see you again, Mr. Travers. I didn't expect you back."

Katie let out a squeal. "Then you are Keith Travers—I knew it! Wait 'til Amber hears about this. And you're staying here for the night—Keith Travers is staying at The Roosting Place!"

Shae lifted her brow in surprise, and he nodded. "The fog trapped us."

She turned toward the desk. "Katie, not a word of this to anyone while these men are our guests. Is that understood?"

Katie nodded grudgingly, never taking her eyes off Keith, who still looked at Shae.

"Have you eaten yet, Miss Stevens?" Freddie asked after a moment, a smug note to his voice.

"No."

"Good. Maybe you'd like to eat with us then? We have some business we'd like to discuss. Don't we, Travers? *Travers!*"

"Huh?" Keith forced himself to look away. Freddie was smiling that Cheshire cat grin and had that all too familiar gleam in his eye. Keith held back a groan. Knowing his manager, this didn't look good.

*A*s they neared the dining room, Shae moved in the opposite direction. "Tiffany and I usually take our meals privately." She stopped and looked at them. "Unless, of course, you'd prefer to eat in the dining room?"

"No, no. Lead the way, Miss Stevens. Wherever you usually eat is fine with us," Freddie almost crooned.

Shae continued down the hall and opened a door. "This is it."

She almost laughed aloud at his expression when they entered a kitchen. He'd obviously been expecting a little more grandeur, to say the least. A rotund, middle-aged woman stood over the industrial-sized stove, stirring something in a huge pot. She smiled at them and nodded, then turned back to her work.

"This is Gretta, one of the best cooks on the island, as I'm sure you'll soon agree. I know all of Germany must miss her delicious strudels. Gretta, these are our guests: Mr. Smith and Mr. Travers," Shae said, inclining her head toward each man as she gave the introductions.

Gretta's ears turned red from the compliments, but she smiled and nodded. "*Guten abend.* Please, you must sit down and I will serve you, *ja?*"

Shae led them past an accordion screen that acted as a partition in secluding a room for dining. Tiffany sat at the table, a forkful of sauerkraut halfway to her mouth. She raised her head to see who'd joined her. The fork fell with a loud clatter to her plate. Her eyes widened, saucer-like, a stupefied expression covering her face.

"Tiffany, you remember Mr. Travers and Mr. Smith. They're our guests at The Roosting Place tonight."

"They're staying here!" Tiffany squeaked.

Shae ignored her, turning to the men. "And this, as I'm sure you've probably guessed by now, is one of the girls responsible for your coming east. My sister Tiffany."

Keith pocketed his sunglasses and moved to stand in front of the girl, taking her limp hand in a gentle handshake. "It's a pleasure to meet you, Tiffany."

Tiffany stared at the hand he'd held as if she'd never seen it before, then up into his eyes. Shae was afraid Tiffany would faint any moment, as goofy as she was acting.

"Tiff, if you're finished with dinner, you'd better head upstairs and start your homework. I seem to remember something you said about a science report being due Friday. We three have some business to discuss—"

"Oh! Then you're going to do it!" Tiffany straightened in her chair, a smile beaming across her face.

"Do what?"

"You're going on a date with him after all—even if you don't look like Samantha. Wait 'til I tell Liz!"

Shae's face suffused with heat. "Tiffany, I—"

"Yes, she is, Tiffany. And if you want the truth," Keith leaned down conspiratorially toward the gawking teenager, "I think she's much cuter than Samantha."

Shae looked at him, dumbfounded, her face growing even hotter. "I am?"

"Yes. You're really quite pretty."

"No, no! I mean, I'm going on a date with you?"

Tiffany squealed with delight. "Great—it worked! Liz said it would, but I wasn't sure after what happened today."

"What are you talking about?" Shae demanded.

"Nothing. I'd better go do my homework." She pushed away from the table. "Night, Shae! Night, Mr. Travers!" she called back in a singsong voice, miraculously shedding her awkwardness with Keith like a snake sheds its skin.

"Tiffany!" But she was already out the door. Shae whirled to face Keith. "Really! I wish you wouldn't have encouraged her. She's impossible as it is. You shouldn't have told her that."

"Why not? You did win the contest."

"But . . . that was under false pretenses. You thought I was Samantha, remember? Besides, I don't date."

Keith's brows lifted in surprise. "Why not?"

"Because I . . . well, I—"

"Look, it's just one date. There'll be a reporter along acting as chaperon. He has to write the story for the teen magazine that started the contest in the first place. And there'll be a photographer there too."

"A photographer?" Shae swallowed, trying not to panic. Years had elapsed since those days. No one would recognize her now.

"Yeah, all part of the publicity. Not that any part of this contest was my idea, mind you," Keith added dryly, his gaze cutting to Freddie before capturing hers again. "But if this date has to be, I'd rather it be with you than anyone else. Please say you'll reconsider."

Shae blinked. Was this a dream? Was the famous Keith Travers actually begging her for a date? It must be a dream. Reality wasn't this fantastic. "Well, perhaps just one date wouldn't hurt. . . ."

Keith's smile grew wide, sending shock waves to her heart.

Or would it?

"*Ach*, sit down, sit down." Gretta hustled in with steaming platters of sauerkraut and sausages. "Why are you just standing there, staring at one another across the table?"

Shae and Keith exchanged embarrassed smiles and sat. Freddie also pulled up a chair. Automatically, Shae bowed her head in prayer. "For what we are about to receive, Lord, we are truly thankful. Amen."

Lifting her eyes, realizing what she'd just done, Shae was shocked to see Keith gazing at her, his expression soft. A scowl covered Freddie's lined face.

Diving into his food, he began, "I told you there was some business we wanted to discuss with you, Miss Stevens. We've been looking for a backup—"

"Another time, Freddie," Keith broke in. "It can wait 'til tomorrow. Let's not bring up business now." He took a heaping bite of sauerkraut. "Hey, this is good!"

Opening his mouth again, Freddie stared at Keith. The singer shook his head, his eyes issuing a warning, making Shae wonder.

Freddie closed his mouth, his brows pulled down in a scowl. "Sure, okay, swell. We'll talk in the morning."

⟡

Not long after the sun had risen above the ocean, while eating a breakfast of white cornmeal johnnycakes, crisp bacon, scrambled eggs, and apple strudel, Freddie dove into the subject with as much relish as he dove into his food. "Miss Stevens, we have something we'd like to discuss with you, concerning a job. . . ."

Exasperated, Keith discreetly waved one hand at table level and shook his head, trying to get his manager's attention. Freddie ignored him and forked up another helping of egg.

"One of Travers's backup singers will soon be leaving the band," he said, mouth full. "We've been searching for someone to take her place, and after hearing your performance last night, we think you would work out."

"You were there?" Shae's voice was a mere whisper, and Keith wondered if Freddie noticed how wide her eyes had gone.

"Yes, we saw the whole thing. You have an adequate voice, Miss Stevens, and with a little work we think you could fit in—"

Shae awkwardly stood, knocking her leg against the back of the chair, almost toppling it over. "No thank you, Mr. Smith. I'm really not interested. Excuse me."

Throwing down her napkin, she made her escape—there was no other word to describe it. As though she were a prisoner who'd just realized the guard's back was turned and the shackles were loose.

Frustrated, Keith turned to Freddie, "Why'd you have to open your big mouth? I was trying to tell you to stop."

"Who'd have known she'd react like that? You'd have thought I had offered her sister's head to her on a platter the way she ran outta here. And did you see the look in her eyes? What's with her?"

"I'm not sure. But I had an idea something like this would happen from the way she acted last night when we brought up the contest. One reason I would have preferred to talk to her about the job myself." Keith sighed, his gaze briefly going to the door through which she'd exited. "I think where Shae Stevens is concerned we're going to have to tread lightly."

"Well, I don't like it." Freddie's expression turned grim. "I'll admit, at first I was glad that you'd finally found someone who interested you." He held up his hand to stop Keith's automatic denial. "Yes, she does—don't feed me any lines. I've seen that look in other men's eyes before, usually before they head for the altar. Like I said, at first I thought 'why not?' Other artists have taken the plunge, and it hasn't affected the sales of their CDs or the amount of concert tickets sold."

"I don't want to talk about this right now," Keith said, annoyed.

"Hear me out, Travers." Freddie leaned forward. "It's bothered me that you haven't shown any interest in a woman for a long time—it's not good for your image. Except for the publicity dates I arrange, you pretty much stay to yourself."

Keith didn't answer. The women he'd been associated with weren't exactly marriage material.

"But with this Shae character," Freddie continued, "I just don't know. She's one weird dame. You don't suppose she's wanted by the law and is hiding out on this island?" Freddie stabbed another forkful of egg and held it horizontally, propping his elbow on the table. He shook the fork. "It makes sense, ya know. Rhode Island is the smallest state in the country, and this is certainly one of the littlest islands I ever saw. What better place for a hideout?"

Keith gave a disbelieving snort, but Freddie pensively went on as if he hadn't heard him.

"Maybe she killed off her husband and is afraid someone will recognize her. Or maybe she's had several and killed them all—like that movie I saw last week. She seems to be loaded. That's probably where she got the dough. And that would also explain why she's so nervous about dating—she doesn't want it to happen again—"

"Or maybe the *real* problem is that you watch too many of those brain-warping psycho-flicks," Keith responded dryly. He gave Freddie a disgusted look and rose from the table. "I'm going out for some air."

Keith found Shae on the front porch, the salty, cold breeze blowing tendrils into her face, despite the fact that a red velvet band held back her hair. He sank to the top step beside her. Whitecaps ruffled the grayish blue sea, the waves giving a loud hiss as they hit the beach. Wispy clouds, like trailing strips of gauze, floated in a pale blue sky.

"Sorry about the way I acted in there," she said, staring out over the expanse of water.

"You have my manager really worried. He's now convinced you're a psychopathic killer who's just bumped off another wealthy husband and is afraid of being discovered."

Shae's head zipped his way, her eyes widening. She laughed, though Keith thought it held a nervous ring. "And how did he reach that conclusion?"

"You don't know Freddie. Once he lets that imagination of his start to work, watch out!" He studied her profile when she didn't answer. "I wouldn't worry about it. He's harmless."

She absentmindedly nodded, and they passed a few moments in silence, staring at the view.

"Bumping off wealthy husbands, huh?" She gave a dry chuckle. "If I liked to tease I might have fun with that."

"Maybe you should. It's about time someone put Freddie in his place." Relieved that her mood had lightened, Keith took a chance. "You know, you really do have a beautiful voice. Can you tell me why you're not interested in being my backup singer?"

Instantly she stiffened. Afraid she would bolt again, he quickly added, "It's okay if you don't want to. I shouldn't have brought it up a second time."

She lowered her lashes. "Please don't take this wrong, Mr. Travers, but I don't really care for today's music."

"I see." Sensing there was more, he asked, "And is that the only reason?"

Shae kept her gaze on her hands. "Yes."

Her word came out faint, and Keith was sure she was holding something back. "Okay." He let out a weary breath. Strike two. "So, where would you like to go for our date?"

"What?" That got her attention.

"Anything special you'd like to do for our date?"

Her face matched her dusky-rose sweater. "You mean *we* choose? I thought the magazine staff would arrange everything."

"No. Nothing specific was made out. Just a contest for a date—that's all. Normally the magazine's PR rep would have contacted you, but Freddie insisted on screening the winner, and he usually gets his way. Not always, though. Once or twice I've had something to say about it."

Shae tilted her head, lines of confusion marring her brow. "If he believes I'm a psychopath, what makes you think he'll let me go on a date with you?"

Keith chuckled. "I wouldn't worry about it. Like I said—once in awhile I get the final word. And I happen to think you're pretty normal."

She nodded, looked away.

"So, is there anything special you'd like to do? Rent a yacht, or go sailing maybe? Then dinner at a nice restaurant or something like that? Or we could do something on the mainland if you'd prefer."

"I'd like to think about it. When would the date take place?"

"Tomorrow too soon?"

Shae's eyes widened and her mouth opened in shocked protest.

"Just kidding." Keith grinned, leaning back on his elbows. "Freddie will have to make arrangements with *Teen Planet* to send a reporter and photographer. It probably would be next week at the earliest. Okay with you?"

"I think so. The inn practically runs itself, what with all the help I have. The only problems I've had lately concern the floor show—but I'm usually able to find a replacement. Last night was the first time I couldn't—not enough advance notice."

"You mean you don't usually perform?"

"No."

The reply was clipped, and Keith noted the shuttered look that slammed over her face. Again, he decided to change the subject. "I guess we'll be staying on your island awhile. I sure could use the vacation. Can you board us?"

"Of course. There are plenty of rooms and few reservations—tourist season doesn't really start for a few weeks yet. But, Mr. Travers—"

"Call me Keith. If we're going to be dating, it would seem strange for you to call me anything else."

"Uh, Keith," she said with a nervous laugh, "I should warn you, the entire teenage population of our island probably knows you're here by now. Katie's a good worker, but she's got a big mouth. It might not be safe for you to stay here."

He nodded, thoughtful. "Hmm. You could be right. So I guess we should keep one step ahead of them."

Shae looked at him, clearly puzzled. "What do you mean?"

"Invite the girls and a reporter from your local paper to a private party you'll be throwing at the inn."

"Huh?"

"Maybe if we give them what they want, they won't look for it and in turn will leave me alone."

Shae snorted. "I doubt that'll work."

"Why not?"

She slowly shook her head. "You really have no idea how popular you are to those girls, do you? They idolize you. My own sister has been walking around in a trance ever since you got here."

Keith winced at the word "idolize" but mulled over Shae's warning. Yet this was a small coastal town, a lot like his childhood home, and not a large metropolis. He knew it could work, if given the chance. Tiffany wasn't all that bad. Three or four more like her he could handle. Freddie was the only problem, but Keith could take care of him. Spending a few hours with the girls, along with the promise of backstage concert tickets—if they allowed him a few weeks of breathing space and privacy. The lure was too great.

"I think they act that way only because they see me onstage under bright lights, or my face bigger than life, smiling down at them from posters," he explained. "When they see I'm just a normal person, like they are, and we all have a nice visit—maybe even lunch, sandwiches or something—they'll relax and might not look at me like star material. Deep down, they're just a bunch of friendly girls looking for acceptance from someone in the adult world."

"I'm not sure I think them normal, or you either, if you believe that tripe you just dished out. And Freddie is worried about me?" Shae gave a short laugh, though she didn't sound amused. "I suppose I'll need to take out extra insurance—and maybe you should, too—if you're serious about doing this. The seasonal hurricanes we have would be a mild problem compared to the explosive whirlwind that's sure to hit the inn."

His finger lifted and gently traced the line in her forehead. Her eyes widened at his touch. "You worry too much, Shae. Trust me—it'll work out. I have a feeling about this. Now, go tell your sister to invite her friends over after school, and I'll contact the paper."

"A feeling, huh?" Her words came out hoarse. "Tell me, are you on medication? Does your therapist know you've escaped?"

"I'll send him an invitation too." Keith winked and stood. "Let's synchronize our watches for four o'clock. Until then, Comrade." He gave her a mock salute and headed back inside, ignoring her skeptical stare.

3

*D*on't open that door! They're like a pack of wild animals—just look what they did to my clothes!"

"Didn't you have a nice visit?" Shae couldn't resist asking.

"You were out there—you saw! I never got a chance to open my mouth and say 'hi.' As soon as they saw me they tackled me!"

"I'm sure they were just trying to be friendly. Let's see, how did you put it? Oh, yes, I remember. They're probably just 'looking for acceptance from someone in the adult world.'"

Keith groaned. "I thought you didn't like to tease."

"Oh, but I'm having too much fun! Shall I serve the sandwiches now?" she asked innocently, eyes wide.

"Okay, Shae. You win. I was wrong—dead wrong." He reached down and plucked off a button that hung by a thread from a shirt he'd purchased only that morning.

Shae's mouth thinned as she watched Keith's actions. "Maybe not. Someone needs to set them straight. Actually, it might work after all." She turned, her hand going to the knob and rotating the lock.

"No! Don't open that door!"

She looked over her shoulder into his panicked eyes. "Trust me, Comrade," she said, echoing his words of yesterday. "They're just a bunch of friendly girls, remember?"

She slipped out of the small, closet-like room they used for personal storage and into the family parlor, firmly closing the door behind her. Before it connected with the jamb, she thought she heard him groan again. She did hear the click of the lock as it was shot back into position.

Looking at the sea of expectant faces, she straightened her shoulders. Friendly girls—ha! What on earth could she say to this wild-eyed throng of fourteen teenagers? How could they have known Tiffany would invite every girl in her class, and not just the three or four expected? It had been a miracle that Shae, Katie, and Gretta had been able to wrest Keith from their clutches.

"Where is he, Miss Stevens?"

"We want Keith Travers," a bold young brunette with braces on her teeth demanded. "Bring him out here!"

"Yeah, Shae. What's the big deal? Are you trying to keep him all to yourself?"

Shae looked in the direction of the voice until she spotted the red-headed culprit. "Liz, I'm surprised at you. At all of you! Most of you come from good homes and were raised better than the wild animals I saw a few minutes ago. What got into you?"

"But that's Keith Travers!" Tamela, a pretty blond with multiple ear piercings, chimed in. There was a stir of agreement, and others begged to see him.

"Yes, that's Keith Travers. And yes, he's been given a talent that must be remarkable, judging from your interest in him. But it doesn't change the fact that he's a person—just like you or me."

Some of the girls looked at one another, evidently not sure what to say in the face of such logic.

"But, Shae, that's dumb."

Trust her sister to argue. Shae ignored Tiffany and continued her speech. "Most of you know what the Bible says about worshipping idols. Right? Well that's what you're doing to Mr. Travers. You're worshipping him as a god—but he's only a man."

"But he's *sooo* good-looking!" A short girl with glitter on her face and neon pink streaks in her hair intoned.

Shae held back a smile at the teen's impassioned words. "Yes, he is. But so is Trent Harmon, the druggist's son—at least that's what some of you have told me . . . and Will Blakely who works on the docks. Yet I'll bet you don't tackle them when they come see you."

"But, Shae, they're ordinary people. Keith Travers is, well—Keith Travers!" a plump girl with freckles jumped in.

"Who is a person—created by God—like Trent and William. And he deserves the same kind of respect you give your friends. You girls put too much value on looks. It's what's inside that counts."

"Aw, my mom says the same thing."

"Well, she's right, Jill."

"It doesn't matter. Keith's still got it all!" the girl with the glittery face exclaimed.

"Admiration is one thing," Shae said patiently. "But idolatry is just plain wrong, as I'm sure you know if you've read your Bibles. Think what happened to the people in the Old Testament who worshipped other gods. Would you want something like that to happen to you? God is serious when He tells us not to do something that's wrong." Shae's last sentences trembled as a flicker of the past returned, and her mother's voice faintly echoed those same words in her mind.

"Aw, Shae, lighten up," Tiffany said, rolling her eyes. "We were just having a little fun."

Shae studied her sister. At least she hadn't been one of those who'd mobbed Keith. " 'Fun'?" she challenged. "If you went to a party, and once you walked in the room you were attacked by a group of people—would you want to stay? Or let's say you were the host, as Keith was, and your guests turned on you the moment they walked through the door. Would you consider that 'fun'? Would you have them over again?"

She watched in relief as her quiet words started to get through to the throng. Several of the girls glanced at each other, uncertain. Some looked down, shame written on their faces.

"We're sorry, Shae," Liz mumbled. "Please tell Mr. Travers we apologize."

A click sounded behind Shae, and she glanced over her shoulder. Keith opened the door a crack, sticking his head out. "Did I hear my name mentioned?"

Fourteen faces turned to him, most with stars still in their eyes— but no one moved a muscle. With wary steps, he went to stand beside Shae. Fourteen pairs of eyes looked in shock at the demolished shirt he wore over his turtleneck. Most of the buttons were ripped away, the collar torn half off, and a slit parted the side halfway to the armpit.

"Did you want to say something, Liz?" Shae prompted.

The girl with braces elbowed Liz in the ribs. "Ow! All right, just don't do that again, Tracey," Liz whispered loudly in warning. She faced Keith's expectant gaze, turned fiery red and just stared.

"Aw, man. What Liz is trying to say is we're really sorry, Mr. Travers," Tracey said. "We didn't mean to jump on you or tear your clothes, and we promise we won't do it again."

"Yes—please stay!" the others joined in. "We're really sorry. Please stay!"

The clamor of the girls' cries covered Keith's low voice as he spoke into Shae's ear. "Since you won't be my backup singer, remind me to ask Freddie to offer you a job as my bodyguard. You were wonderful."

A tingle crept up Shae's spine at his words and the brush of his warm breath against her skin. Keith turned to the girls and gave them one of his famous smiles.

"How about some sandwiches?"

A medley of agreement and relieved laughter trickled through the room, and Gretta suddenly appeared with a tray of club sandwiches and chips. Even the reporter, who sat in a far corner of the room, smiled and mopped his forehead with a handkerchief.

Looking worried, Keith jerked his head sideways, motioning to the middle-aged man. "What about him?" he murmured to Shae. "Think he'll expound on this episode? And will he wait to release the story until after I return to California, like I asked? Somehow I don't think free concert tickets will buy his silence."

"I don't think you'll have any problem where Mr. Franklin is concerned."

"How can you be so sure?"

Shae smiled secretly. "The ringleader, Tracey—the tall brunette with the braces who tackled you—is his daughter. I imagine he'll be very cooperative under the circumstances."

Keith's smile matched her own. Tiffany shyly walked up to him, her guitar in hand. "Will you sing for us, Mr. Travers? My sister's never heard you sing, and we'd all love it if you would."

A loud chorus of agreement filled the room. Keith turned to Shae in surprise. "You've never heard me sing?"

Shae's face grew hot as all eyes turned her way, and she gave her sister a narrowed look. *Thanks a lot, Tiff.*

"Oh, don't take it personally," Tiffany quickly inserted. "She prefers slower music—like gospel stuff—and says she's too old for the 'bubblegum rock' we listen to. Besides, she's not thrilled with what she calls our 'worldly music' anyway."

If the floor had opened up and swallowed her, Shae would have been greatly relieved. But it stubbornly remained fixed and solid beneath her feet and she still stood next to Keith. Amusement danced in his eyes as he watched her.

"Oh! I didn't mean that the way it sounded. What I meant to say was—"

"I think you've said plenty, Tiffany," Shae interrupted.

Keith tilted his head, as if in thought, then faced Shae's sister. "I'll sing—but I'd like to sing something different than what you're used to hearing from me."

"Uh, okay—I guess." Tiffany shrugged.

Keith strode to the baby grand in the opposite corner of the room and perched on the edge of the glossy bench. Interlacing his fingers, he flexed them to loosen them.

"I didn't know you played piano," Tiffany said, surprised.

He looked at her, then his eyes cut to Shae. "There's probably a lot about me you don't know."

Shae's stomach flipped at his words, which seemed directed only to her. His gaze remained fixed on her a moment longer, then he lowered it to the keyboard and positioned his hands on the yellowed keys. His fingers began to float over the ivories in a familiar tune. Stunned, Shae listened as he sang what had been her grandmother's favorite hymn, "The Old Rugged Cross."

The music reached deep into her soul, as though trying to pull away the cobwebs there and let the light infiltrate what had become a dark tomb. Hot tears sprang to her eyes, and she hastily wiped them away. Goose bumps popped out on her arms at the haunting timbre of his voice. After the final note died, a surrealistic hush settled over the room.

"Wow, that was really great, Mr. Travers. I've never heard you sing like that before."

Tiffany's awed remark punctured the quiet atmosphere as successfully as a needle pricking a latex balloon, and everyone began to talk at once. Even the reporter snapped out of his trance and busily began writing in his notepad.

"Will you sing another one?"

"Sing 'Your Love Alone'—it's my favorite," someone piped up.

Pivoting around on the bench, Keith reached for the guitar. The rest of the hour he spent granting requests, giving a private mini-concert. Shae smiled, looking on. The songs were a little immature for her taste, but the girls seemed to like them. Yet nothing compared with his rendition of "The Old Rugged Cross."

After the sandwiches and chips had been consumed, someone suggested hot buttered popcorn, which Gretta hastened to make. The girls sat cross-legged on the floor around Keith, listening to his stories, laughing at his jokes, and obviously having one of the best times of their young lives.

When it was time to go, they did so reluctantly, saying shy good-byes and promising they would grant him the rest and privacy he needed for the remainder of his stay. Shae had a feeling they would have done so even without the promise of free concert tickets and backstage passes. She knew they'd come to the inn that afternoon expecting to see an idol, but left having gained a friend. Keith Travers was really a pretty amazing guy—much different from the egotist Shae had expected.

❧

Keith let out a relieved breath, plopping onto the sofa. "That went well."

"Hmm, yes." Shae eyed the disorganized room, her lips twisting in a grimace. "I suppose I shouldn't leave this mess for Millie."

"I'll help," Tiffany volunteered, though very halfheartedly.

"No. You have a science report to finish. It's due tomorrow, re-member."

"Thanks for reminding me!" Tiffany shot up from her place on the couch. "I better go start writing it."

"Tiffany Lauren Stevens! Do you mean to tell me you haven't even started yet?" Shae exclaimed.

But Tiffany had already darted out the door. Shae turned to Keith. "I don't know what I'm going to do with that girl."

He straightened from picking a few kernels of popcorn off the floor and tossed them on the coffee table. "I wouldn't worry about it I remember burning the midnight oil, trying to get a report finished that should have been done over a period of days, yet was accomplished in a few hours."

"Yeah, thanks. You're a lot of help," Shae remarked wryly while collecting empty paper cups, plates, and bowls and stacking them. "I can imagine what kind of grades you must've made."

Remembering, he grimaced. "Let's just say they weren't always in the first three letters of the alphabet."

Shaking her head, she threw the party ware into a large rubber trash can Gretta had brought in, and sat on the couch beside him to retrieve a few empty cups that had found their way under the coffee table. "By the way, where was Freddie today? I was surprised he didn't show for the party."

"I didn't think he'd agree with the idea, so I sent him to collect our luggage at the airport in Providence. He should be returning soon."

She straightened, bunching her brows in puzzlement. "Just who's the boss—him or you?"

"Ours is a very strange working relationship."

"Obviously."

Her gaze went to the ceiling, her mind clearly going on another track. "Three years ago when I became Tiffany's guardian, I never thought it would be so hard to take care of her. Boy, was I wrong."

In rapid succession, Keith tossed four wadded yellow napkins into the trash bin, sinking every one of them. "You've taken on a big responsibility for one so young. How old are you anyway? Twenty-four?"

She wrinkled her nose at him. "Actually I'm twenty-two. So tell me, Keith, did you major in basketball in high school? Is that how you passed senior year?" She motioned to the garbage can across the room.

He grinned. "You found me out. But seriously, Shae, you can't be only twenty-two. You're kidding, right?"

"I don't know if I should be offended by that remark or not. A woman likes to be told she looks younger than her age—unless of course, she's under the age of eighteen," she joked.

"But that means you were only nineteen when you became Tiffany's guardian! Fess up—you're pulling my leg."

"No, I was twenty. I have a birthday coming up." She leaned forward to sweep the popcorn kernels he'd thrown onto the table into an empty bowl. "So, Keith, besides being a famous high school basketball star, as well as a singer and musician, what other secrets does your life hold?"

"I'm beginning to wonder the same about you."

She looked up, startled. "What do you mean?

"You don't like to talk about yourself, and I'm curious as to why. Most of the women I know love the subject."

She gave an airy wave of her hand. "There's nothing too spectacular about me." Her voice had a false ring to it.

"I wouldn't be so sure about that," he drawled. When she didn't respond, he shrugged. "Okay. Mind if I ask some questions?"

"Tiffany told me she sent in my personal history for the contest. Read that—I'm sure it tells all about me."

He smiled. "Well, I'm relieved to know it was your history and not Samantha's. We share a lot of the same hobbies. But the form just glossed over the basics. It didn't get into the real nitty-gritty. Besides, it's much more interesting to talk to a person face-to-face than to read a piece of paper about them. Don't you agree?"

She shrugged, her eyes darting to the doorway.

"First question. How did you come to own this inn?"

She visibly relaxed and set down the bowl. "It belonged to my grandmother. She left it to Tiffany, me, and my brother, Tommy, who's younger than me by seven months. Tommy was born prematurely but evidently thinks he's older, considering the bossy way he treats me sometimes." A sparkle lit her eyes. "I don't mind too much, though, since he lives in Connecticut. He's what you'd call a silent partner. And Tiff won't be able to make any decisions concerning the inn until she's older."

"So your parents are deceased?"

"Yes." The word came out faint, clipped.

"Sorry about that." Keith decided to switch to a lighter topic before he lost her. "Okay. Next question. Did you mean what you said to the girls, when you told them you thought I was good-looking?"

The tense expression left her face and she laughed. "Oh, come on, Don't tell me the famous Keith Travers needs his ego stroked?"

"Just answer the question."

"I find you easy to look at," she admitted with an impish grin.

"Good. I'm glad to hear it."

"Why?"

"Huh-uh. I'm asking the questions, remember?"

She rolled her eyes. "I'm not sure I like this game anymore."

Might as well go for the gold. "Why don't you like to discuss your talent?"

Shae's features sobered into a mask of caution. "I don't know what you mean." She plucked at the bottom of her long satin shirt.

"Why do you run away when someone brings up your singing?"

"Now I know I don't like this game anymore." She tried to rise, but he grasped her arm.

"Please, Shae, just listen a minute." His words came quietly. "I think you would be a great asset to the band, and I wish you'd give it some serious thought. I have a feeling there's more behind your refusal than what you're telling me—and I'd really like to understand. Maybe we could even come up with a solution. Is it because of the travel and the time you would have to spend away from here and your sister? Or does it have something to do with your parents and grandmother? Would they have not approved?"

Her eyes grew panicked. "Leave it be, Keith," she said, her words raspy as she broke loose from his light grip.

Alarmed and a bit stunned by her reaction, he shook his head. "What? What did I say? I don't understand."

"Look, I don't want to talk about it. So please, just drop the subject. Okay?" Tears glistened in her eyes as she clumsily stood. Little black pools appeared underneath her lashes, and she hastily wiped them away with a curled forefinger.

Feeling like pond scum, though he wasn't exactly sure what he'd done wrong, Keith shook his head. "Shae, whatever I said to upset you—I'm sorry."

"Forget it. It's okay, and I'd rather not talk about it anymore." She plucked a tissue from a box, wiped off her fingers, and blotted underneath her eyes. "I think I'll turn in now. It's been a long day."

"It's not even seven o'clock. You haven't had dinner."

"I'm not hungry. And I feel another migraine coming on. You and Freddie will have to eat without me. Night, Keith."

"Night . . . I wish you'd tell me what's bothering you," he added under his breath, watching her trudge away. Keith shook his head in confusion. He was getting as aggressive as Freddie. What had compelled him to push like that? Settling his neck against the top of the sofa, he stared at the ceiling.

Strike three, Travers. You're out.

❧

Shae darted up the stairs, calling herself ten kinds of a fool for losing it like that in front of Keith. His words had brought up old memories, memories better left forgotten. As if she ever could forget.

Pressing her fingertips to her temples, she made little circles, trying to relieve the tension. The headaches were coming more frequently than they used to. Probably because of all the stress she was under—playing a combination of big sister, mother, and warden to her irrepressible sister—though so far the month-long sentence of being grounded hadn't commenced. Add to that the everyday duties of trying to run an inn while dealing with Robert and Hillary's marital problems, and now unexpectedly boarding a teen idol with a penchant for tossing out personal questions—it was a wonder she wasn't a candidate for a padded cell.

Shae sighed and pushed open her door. The welcome sight of her antique four-poster bed greeted her. Not bothering to undress, she grabbed the nearby bottle of pain reliever tablets off her bedside table. Popping two, she washed them down with a glass of water before lying on the chenille spread.

Keith Travers might be gorgeous, but he was just too pushy for Shae's peace of mind. She would have to watch herself.

❧

Keith woke and dressed in a pair of blue jeans and a chunky ivory sweater. It was good to have his things again. The sun's rays beamed through the pale gray-and-white pinstriped curtains of the old-fashioned room, cheering him. He smiled back at the inn's logo of the smiling Rhode Island rooster on the plastic-wrapped cup in the bathroom. At last he could enjoy much-needed privacy and a quiet vacation. With Shae. Despite his failure with her last night, Keith was optimistic this morning.

After zipping through his daily grooming, he hurried to the kitchen, deciding to forgo the continental breakfast being served in the dining room. Disappointment deflated his bubble when he saw Shae wasn't in the family's dining nook. Tiffany stared at him, her eyes still a little dazed.

"Morning, Mr. Travers."

He managed a smile. "My friends call me Keith, Tiffany."

A pleasantly shocked expression covered her face. Gretta set a full plate and a glass of juice on the table in front of Keith. Thanking her, he began buttering a muffin. "So how'd the science report go?"

Tiffany's face crumpled into a grimace. "Don't even ask. I'll be lucky to pass this semester. I never knew biology could be so hard." She glanced at her neon-colored wristwatch. "Oh, no. I'm late!"

She took a swift gulp of orange juice and jumped up from the table, banging her leg against the edge. The juice in Keith's glass rocked and sloshed over. He grabbed a napkin and sponged up the liquid before it could seep through the crack and onto the floor.

Tiffany's face turned as pink as her fuzzy top. "Oops. Sorry— gotta run." She plucked up her bookbag from a nearby chair.

"Wait!"

She glanced over her shoulder at him, looking uncertain. "Yeah?"

"Is Shae not feeling well? I was hoping to talk to her."

"She already ate. I think she's in the old storage room, dusting. Later!"

Keith stared after her. Dusting a storage room?

Tiffany zipped out the door, narrowly missing Gretta, who carried a large platter of sausage links to one of the waitresses for the breakfast buffet.

"Oh—*meine Himmel!*" The woman exclaimed as she spun around, platter held high, to avoid the hurtling teenager.

Keith shook his head in amusement. Tiffany's boundless energy reminding him of his young sisters. Sobering at the thought of his family, he grabbed another apple cinnamon muffin and left the table, heading in the direction of what he hoped was "the old storage room."

After going down one wrong hall and finding nothing but a linen closet and two locked doors, he backtracked and ran across Millie, the cleaning lady. At his question, she peered at him oddly over her half glasses, but motioned to a hallway on the right. Thanking her, Keith strode to the other end of the inn. Seeing a door open a crack, he peeked inside.

Shae, wearing a long-sleeved blue flannel shirt and a pair of dirty jeans, had her back to him. She perched atop a step stool, meticulously dusting a shelf of breakables with a feather duster. Again her hair was pinned up and covered by the blue bandanna she'd worn the first day he'd come to the inn.

The curtains in the room were drawn, the only light coming from a small fixture in the ceiling. The entire back wall was bracketed with wooden shelves. On each one sat delicate figurines of ceramic, crystal, and porcelain. He walked closer, the wide scatter rug muffling his steps.

"I thought the old saying famous for hired help was 'I don't do windows.' How come Millie isn't doing that?"

Shae jerked and teetered on the step. Hurriedly Keith reached up, placing a hand on each side of her waist to steady her.

"I . . . I didn't hear you come in." She turned her head and looked at him over her shoulder, her eyes wide behind her glasses.

"Obviously. Sorry I scared you."

"I'm okay."

Not wanting to, but knowing he should, Keith removed his hands from her sides. She took the three steps down the ladder, clutching the feather duster.

"Did you need to see me about something?" she asked, not looking at him.

"Not really. Hey, this is nice." His gaze had lit on one of the figurines—a crystalline angel with golden wings—and he reached toward it, intending to examine it closer.

"Don't touch that!"

Her sharp command stilled his arm. Shocked, he studied her. "Sorry—I only wanted to get a look at the bottom and see the markings. It looks like a collector's piece."

"Yes . . . yes it is. I didn't mean to yell. I'm just a little high-strung today. Had a bad night." Shae nervously ran her fingers through the ostrich feathers of the duster. Dust motes filled the air and she sneezed.

"Bless you," he said, not sure what to say next. Why did she always make him feel like a gawky kid? "You have some nice pieces. Are those Hummels? My aunt collects them too."

"Yes. They were my mother's."

The dead tone of her voice made him wonder, but he'd already decided he wouldn't put her through another episode like last night. Uneasy, he fished for something to say. Spotting a telephone on a white painted desk in a corner of the room reminded him he had business to take care of. "Any chance I can use the phone? I need to make a local call."

"Of course. But doesn't the one in your room work?" she asked, all business again.

"Uh, to tell the truth, I never checked."

"Oh." Shae studied him, her brow lifted curiously, then shrugged. "Sure, you're welcome to use that phone. I'll wait outside." She moved toward the door.

"You don't have to go, Shae," he said hurriedly, not wanting her to leave. "It's no big deal. I only felt that since I'm in the area, I should at least call Mom and say hi."

Shae turned and stared. A frown tilted her mouth downward, and Keith wondered what he'd done wrong now.

"Did you say it was a local call?" she asked.

"Yeah. At least I'm pretty sure it is. She lives on the mainland. If it's not, I'll reimburse you."

She crossed her arms. "Do you mean to tell me, Keith Travers, that you've been here three whole days and haven't contacted your mom, who actually lives in the area? And you're planning to visit her with a *phone call?*"

Keith frowned. "My parents and I didn't exactly part on good terms. They were dead set against me pursuing a singing career."

Her mouth fell open. "You mean you haven't talked to them in four years?"

"I send them a postcard now and then."

"And I'll bet they're just thrilled! After all, a postcard does so much to take the place of actually being there."

Keith's mouth thinned. "Look, Shae, what's it to you? I don't get why you're so concerned whether I see my parents or not."

Sadness washed across her face, making Keith wish he could retrieve his curt words. "I've found you don't really appreciate them 'til they're gone, Keith," she whispered, her eyes filled with pain. "Once that happens, the time for togetherness and for words never spoken—that should have been said—is gone too. And you can never get it back."

"Shae—"

"Don't let that happen, Keith. No misunderstanding is worth it." She hurried past him and out the door.

Keith watched her go, feeling as though a lead weight had dropped on him. Turning his attention to the phone, he picked up the receiver and stopped. He couldn't talk to his mom now. Shae's words bore down hard on his conscience, making him feel like a lowlife. He thought about some of the decisions he'd made these past four years and grimaced. Maybe he was.

Upset, he let the receiver fall back into its cradle with a loud clunk.

$\bigcirc\!\!\!\!4$

*S*hae went over the day's correspondence, pulling her brows together in a frown. Sighing, she wrote a check for the electric bill and put it with the envelopes addressed to the meat and fish markets. Thanks to their parents, she and Tiffany were well-off. There was enough to cover their needs, with a substantial part put away for Tiffany to go to college. Yet if prices continued to escalate, Shae might have to increase room rates, and she didn't want to do that.

She laid the pen down and leaned back in her chair. Closing her eyes, she put her fingers to her temple and tried to massage away the tension. The tension that had taken root since Tiffany had informed Shae that she was a contest winner five days ago.

"You look like you could use a break."

Her eyes flew open and lit upon Keith. He stood in the entrance. "Hope you don't mind—the door was open," he said, motioning to it. "I came to ask if you'd like to take a walk with me. You look as if you could use a breather, and even innkeepers take lunch breaks, right?"

Shae's gaze flew to the antique wooden clock on the wall. Already past noon! Where had the day gone?

Keith pulled a wrapped sandwich from his coat pocket. "I'll even provide lunch," he said with a contagious grin.

Shae arched a brow. "From what I've seen of your eating habits the past several days, you give new meaning to the term 'eating on the run.'"

"When you have to keep up with Freddie, it's the only way to survive. Well, how about it? Consider it a peace offering."

Shae hesitated. She was hungry, and the fresh air might do her

43

head some good. "Just let me get my jacket." On second thought, she took off her glasses, slid them into the upright brass holder, then turned to retrieve her windbreaker.

Outside, they strolled down a winding bicycle path cut through the trees, about a hundred feet from the ocean. Above the wind rustling the branches, she could hear waves gently break on the beach. Dark green shrubs—bayberry and others—dotted the un- spoiled beauty of the island. The fresh, salty air was just what Shae needed to clear her head, and she inhaled deeply.

Keith regaled her with entertaining stories of his youth and, after awhile, Shae relaxed, even taking part in the easy conversation. After one particular comment, she halted on the trail and gaped at him, fighting back a smile.

"What's so funny?" He looked at her with pretended offense.

"You can't be serious. You don't actually expect me to believe you took home economics in high school, do you?" She shook her head. "I just can't picture the star player dribbling a basketball while wearing an apron—though it would make an interesting photo for your fan club." She chuckled.

"Ha ha. Very funny." His brows drew together. "What's so strange about my learning to cook? There are world famous gourmet chefs who are men, you know."

"Ah, I see." She nodded like a wise sage. "Then a possible career in the culinary department was your only reason at the time?"

He broke away from her gaze, looking a bit sheepish. "Well, no. I was told by a guy during registration that it was an easy credit and a great way to meet girls."

"Yes, I can believe that," she countered dryly. "But surely the great Keith Travers didn't have problems communicating with the opposite sex?"

"Hey, I had feelings of insecurity too. It was my first year at a new school—I didn't know anyone yet."

"Hmm, maybe," Shae said with a thoughtful tilt of her head. They began strolling again. "Somehow, though, I'd pictured you as the type to escort the homecoming queen to the prom." She darted him a glance and noticed his reddening face. She laughed. "You did—didn't you?"

"Well, yeah. But only because the captain of the football team—who was a good friend of mine as well as being her boyfriend—ended up in the hospital with a broken hip," he explained hurriedly. "I was the only one he could trust with her, since I had a steady of my own. I took them both."

Shae smiled sweetly, fully enjoying her game. "And were you also on the football team, Keith?"

A pause. "Yeah."

"Top ten?"

He nodded, beginning to look uncomfortable again.

"Aha!" She said, lifting her index finger like a scientist who'd just made a startling new discovery. "Now let's see, the way the popularity cliques work . . . hmm . . . my guess is your girl was on the cheerleading squad. Right?"

He rolled his eyes. "She was the captain."

Shae burst into gales of laughter. "Oh, yeah, Keith. I can see why you were so insecure."

He shook his head with a defeated grin. "Okay, Miss Smarty," he said when she'd quieted down and they resumed their walk, "now it's your turn. You don't look like you were a wallflower. My guess is you were on the drill team, and . . . in your senior year you were voted 'most likely to succeed.' Did I hit the mark?"

Shae swung her startled gaze to him. "Not about my being on the drill team. I was in the choral department for two years."

"Doesn't surprise me a bit. And I'll bet you usually had the lead in the school's musicals."

She flushed and looked away, which answered his remark. "And the other—about being voted most likely to succeed?"

"Yes," she said quickly. "But they were wrong. I wouldn't call being an innkeeper a huge success."

"Maybe not. But I don't think that's where your destiny really lies, Shae."

"Oh, look! Did you see that? I think it's a marsh hawk. They're endangered, you know."

Keith looked to where she pointed, but could see no evidence of the bird in question.

"So even your school years are off-limits, huh?" he muttered, half to himself.

She bristled. "I don't know what you're talking about."

"I thought you needed glasses to see. Are you sure it was a hawk and not a tree branch? Maybe it broke and fell, or the wind was tossing it around."

"That's silly. Branches don't look anything like birds. Besides, branches don't fly through the air. My vision may be blurry, but I'm not blind."

Without thought, Keith stopped walking and turned, lowering his face until it was inches from hers. The darks of her eyes widened to the size of the cocoa-colored marbles he'd had as a kid.

"And do you see me as a blur, Shae?" he whispered in a low voice. "Can you see me clearly when I get close like this?"

"I . . . I see you okay."

He watched as she caught her lower lip between her teeth. Hurriedly he straightened, wondering what had prompted him to pull such a crazy stunt. He was the one acting like a deranged psychopath, and the last thing he wanted was to startle her away. Yet when he was around her, he couldn't seem to think clearly. *Chill, Travers.*

"Hungry?" he asked with forced lightness. "Let's eat the sandwiches on the way back."

Shae gave a brief nod, and he retrieved two squares wrapped in wax paper from his pocket, handing one to her. Her hands shook a bit as she unwrapped the sandwich. She took a small bite, pulled it away and looked at the bread, puzzled. "Peanut butter and jelly? I thought Gretta was against such plain fare."

"I made them."

"You?"

"There's something about a peanut butter and jelly sandwich that takes a person back to his childhood," he explained.

The glint of mischief was back in her eyes. "Well, I guess I shouldn't be too surprised, being as you took home economics, I mean. Your teacher taught you well, Keith. This is delicious." She took another bite as if to prove her remark.

"You really don't believe I took the course, do you? Took it and passed with flying colors, I might add—though it wasn't as easy as Jim told me it would be."

"Of course I believe you, Keith. Why would you lie?" Her voice danced with merriment.

"All right, Miss Know-it-all, I'll prove it to you. If Gretta will allow me to invade her domain one night, I'll make you a gourmet meal you'll never forget. And never again will you think to doubt the word of Keith Travers."

"You're on. But be warned—I intend to hold you to it. A night of grilled cheese sandwiches and soup might be nice for a change."

"Ha, ha—very funny. You'll see. I'll make you eat those words, Shae Stevens."

"Oh, but I'm sure they couldn't compare to your cooking talents, Keith. I'll just stick to food, thanks."

"I think what you need is a good spanking." He narrowed his eyes and steadily approached her. Giving a laughing yelp of protest, she dodged away and took off down the path. Keith gave chase. After letting her take the lead for a short time, he closed in and grabbed her arm. She squealed but didn't try to break away when he pulled her around to face him.

Out of breath, they stared at one another. Shae's face was rosy from running, and her eyes sparkled with a life of their own. Perspiration dotted her upper lip.

"You have jelly on the corner of your mouth," he panted, his voice low.

The tip of her tongue flicked to the purple spot, licking it away. His eyes stayed riveted to her mouth. He had never wanted to kiss anyone so badly. Forcing himself to look away, Keith pushed a shaky hand through his hair, sweeping it off his forehead. "I think we'd better head back."

Needing to touch her, he allowed himself to reach for her hand and was thankful she didn't pull away. They didn't speak a word the entire walk back. When they reached the side of the inn, Keith stopped, Shae's hand still enfolded in his.

She looked at him, questions in her eyes.

Unable to help himself, he lifted her hand to his lips and kissed the tips of her curled fingers lightly. He loved watching her eyes soften in wonder.

"I'd better let you get back to work now. I know you're busy." A movement from a top window caught his eye, and he looked up to see a curtain flutter into place.

Shae followed his gaze. The dazed expression left her features, and her mouth drew into a grim line. "Tiffany's room," she muttered. "I'll talk to you later, Keith. I have some business to attend to."

Reluctantly, he let go of her hand and watched her march to the front of the inn.

~&

Shae knocked on her sister's door, then pushed it open without waiting for an answer. Tiffany lay on her back on the twin bed, her arms underneath the pillow. Her gaze was fastened to the ceiling, and a big smile spread over her face. The flowered curtain at the window was cracked slightly.

Shae approached the foot of the bed and crossed her arms. "Why aren't you in school, Tiff?"

"It's spring break."

"Oh," Shae muttered with a defeated breath. "I'd forgotten that was coming up."

Tiffany jumped up to a kneeling position and clutched her pillow, her eyes dancing. "He kissed your hand!" She threw the pillow in the air and caught it with a delighted little laugh.

Memory of Keith's lips on her skin made Shae tingle all over again. She forced herself to stay mad and address the issue at hand. "So, you *were* spying!"

"Hey, it's not a crime to look out your own window." Tiffany shrugged. "Besides I'm grounded, remember?"

For the first time Shae wished she could revoke the month-long sentence.

"Anyway, Liz was right—she said it would happen, but I didn't believe it. Wait 'til I tell her! It'll cost me my new CD, but it's worth it."

Shae gritted her teeth. "That's the second time you've mentioned

Liz being right concerning my situation with Keith. I want to know what you're talking about, and I want to know this minute."

Tiffany shrugged. "Okay. I guess I can tell you now. When Keith came back to the inn, Liz said she'd bet the bad weather wasn't the only thing that brought him back. After we found out we—I mean you—had won the contest, Liz had a feeling that when Keith met you, he'd take you out anyway, and might even fall for you even if you weren't Samantha. I wasn't sure after your first meeting. I mean, face it, Shae, you weren't looking your best."

"Thanks for the compliment."

"Awww, Shae. You know what I mean. You were all dirty from cleaning and had that awful plaid shirt on—and your hair hidden by that bandanna you wear, and not one speck of makeup on, and those dumb glasses—"

"If you keep it up, little sister, you'll turn my head with your flattery."

Tiffany grinned. "You're really a knockout when you try. But until Keith came into the picture you just haven't cared much about trying."

"Oh, I don't know. . . ."

"I'm not talking about when you play hostess. I'm talking about just any old day. Look at you—I think that's the first time I've seen you wear a pretty ribbon in your hair instead of pulling it back with just a rubber band. And you're wearing lipstick too!"

Shae blushed, but stood her ground. "I often wear something on my lips."

"Lip balm doesn't count. Hey, don't get so defensive—I think it's great. It's about time you had something to attract you—like a man in your life. And Keith Travers definitely fits that bill!"

"Why, Tiff? Why the sudden interest in my social calendar?"

"But that's just it! You don't have a social calendar. Besides working at the inn, you're life is just one big zero. Soon—if I ever pass biology that is—I'll be off to college and start a career and maybe even get married. And what will you do, Shae? Just puddle around The Roosting Place until you get old like Grandma? At least she had a life first."

"That's piddle, not puddle."

Tiffany rolled her eyes. "Whatever."

"I appreciate your concern for my welfare, little sister, but I assure you there's no need."

"I know. Like I said—Liz was right."

"Oh—you're impossible!"

Exasperated, Shae turned to leave. Keith's handsome face smiled down at her from a poster, bigger than life. She felt herself turn an embarrassed red, as if he'd actually heard their conversation. Ridiculous! Averting her eyes, she left the room.

❧

"There you are. What're you watching?"

Keith entered the dark private family parlor where Shae sat on the sofa in front of the TV, her legs drawn up beneath her while she munched on a bowl of popcorn. "A movie on the life of Jesus."

"Sounds good. Okay if I join you?"

Her heart gave a nervous little lurch, but she nodded. He sank to the cushion beside her while reaching into her small bowl for a large handful of popcorn.

"Help yourself," she said dryly.

"Thanks. I will."

"There's more in the kitchen if you'd like your own bowl."

"No thanks, I'll just eat out of yours." He threw a few kernels into his mouth. "Hmm. Needs more salt. More butter wouldn't hurt either."

"Right. I forgot you were a connoisseur of foods."

He threw her a grin. "By the way, I talked to Gretta. Tomorrow night plan for the meal of your life—say at seven? I guarantee, you won't forget it."

"That reminds me, I need to write antacid on the grocery list." She gave him an impish smile.

"You just don't quit, do you? Well, you'll see. Meanwhile, I'm going to the kitchen and doctor this popcorn." He stood and reached for her bowl, which she firmly held.

"No thanks. I like it this way."

"That's because your taste buds have grown used to it. Wait until you taste mine." He jerked the bowl out of her hands with a firm tug and strode out the door.

Shae blew a stray wisp of hair from her temple. She was hungry, and now he'd taken her popcorn—some nerve! Still, he did have an endearing boyish quality about him.

Soon Keith returned, triumphantly bearing a huge bowl of buttery popcorn that smelled delicious. Shae smothered the smile that had stuck to her face while she'd been thinking of him—the entire time he'd been gone.

"Wait 'til you taste this!" He sat back down beside her.

"I've heard a starving person will eat anything."

"Just for that, maybe I shouldn't let you have any." He held the bowl out of her reach.

"Ke-eith," she groaned. "I haven't eaten since that sandwich at lunch."

"Apologize."

"Okay, you win. I'm sorry," she muttered, the tantalizing aroma making her mouth water.

He replaced the bowl on his lap and casually looped his arm around her, his hand resting on her shoulder. Large butterflies ran relays in her stomach.

"Did I miss much?" he asked.

"Just commercials." Her voice sounded funny. She ate some of the popcorn so she wouldn't have to talk. It was good. After a few more handfuls, she glanced his way. "How did you manage to make the butter stick to each kernel?"

"Do you like it?" he asked, grinning.

"I have to admit, this is some of the best popcorn I've eaten. When I make it, not all the popcorn gets buttered—even when I shake the bowl. So, how did you do it?"

"Trade secret." He winked.

"Kee-eith!"

"Shh. The movie's starting."

Determined to discover his secret later, Shae watched the opening credits of the historical drama and contentedly munched her popcorn. Gretta came in with two soft drinks and set them down on the coffee table. Shae thanked her and invited her to watch, but she declined with a smile and quickly left. Strange. Gretta loved movies based on Christ's life.

Shrugging to herself, Shae settled against the cushion. She and Keith bantered during commercials, quieting once the movie came back on.

Toward the end, she sniffled when Jesus raised Lazarus from the dead. Tears dripped down her cheeks when He was betrayed and arrested. She cried quietly when they beat Him and nailed Him to the cross. The moisture sped down her cheeks at the end of the movie after He'd risen and the music from the "Hallelujah Chorus" filled the room; she used the sleeve of her sweater to blot the wetness. But when the actor who had the role of Jesus looked lovingly into the camera while the background music reached its crescendo, and said "Lo, I am with you always, even until the end of the world," she really lost it. She buried her face in her hands—and wailed through the entire list of credits.

❦

Keith helplessly looked around the darkened room lit only by the flickering TV. At last seeing the dim outline of what he was searching for, he hurried to a lamp table in the far corner, plucked a couple of tissues from a box, then changed his mind and picked up the whole thing. Returning to Shae's side, he stuck the box in her hand. She thanked him and began to swipe at her eyes with the tissues.

"I–I'm sorry." She hiccupped softly. "Th–this is the second time I've cried around you. But those kinds of m–movies get me every time." She pulled another tissue from the box, dabbed the tears from her cheeks, took a deep breath and gave him a trembling smile. "You must think I'm a silly, hopeless female—and you're right. I probably look like a raccoon by now." She gave a shaky laugh. "I don't know why I don't just quit wearing this stupid mascara."

His heart beginning to hammer, Keith lifted his hand and stroked her glistening cheek with the back of his fingers. "Actually, I think you're pretty wonderful . . . I think you're quite beautiful . . . and I think I'm going to kiss you."

Her eyes widened. Before she could say anything more, Keith lowered his mouth to hers.

A car salesman came on the screen, trying to convince anyone who would listen that he had the best deal in town. Keith shut him out, concentrating only on the woman in his arms. Shae tasted like buttered popcorn, his new favorite flavor. She clung to his shirt as if she were drowning, and he was her life preserver. Keith moved his lips to her cheek then upward to her temple. She exhaled softly, her warm breath fanning his skin. Feeling his pulse race, he lowered his head to reclaim her lips, and she inched her arms up around his neck.

"Hey, what's going on—why's it so dark in here?"

Suddenly they were immersed in a bath of artificial light. Shae pulled away, and Keith shot his gaze toward the door and the intruder. Freddie walked into the room. "Looks like I got here just in time," he drawled, the ever present unlit cigar clamped between his teeth.

Shae jumped up from the couch, red suffusing her face. "I'm going to bed. G'night, Freddie—night, Keith." Before he could say a word, she fled from the room.

"You have all the finesse of a bull in a china shop," Keith muttered.

"What's that supposed to mean?"

"Never mind." Keith sighed and whisked a hand through his hair, brushing it away from his forehead. "What did you want anyway? Couldn't it have waited 'til morning?"

"I didn't intend to intrude on your little love scene. But maybe it's good that I did." Freddie's eyes narrowed. "I'd advise you to stay away from her, Travers. She's a strange bird—"

"Watch it," Keith warned. "Be careful how you talk about Shae."

"Oh, so that's how it is," Freddie grumbled. "Like I said, I'm in favor of you finding a love interest—but not with a woman who might have psychotic tendencies. . . ."

Infuriated, Keith stood and raised both hands upright at his sides at chest level. "I refuse to hash this out again. Our conversation is over. She's not what your deranged mind has dreamed up, but I don't suppose anything will convince you of that. Good night."

Keith stomped up the stairs to his room, tired of Freddie thinking he owned him just because Keith signed a piece of paper years ago. Yet he was just as angry with himself as he was with his manager. He hadn't meant to kiss Shae yet, though he was elated by her warm response to him. But he meant what he told Freddie. She was special, and Keith was determined to treat their budding relationship with care. That is, if he was ever given the chance again.

5

*S*hae tried to focus on the printed page of the ledger she used for recording reservations, but her eyes felt scratchy. She leaned back in the chair and massaged her closed eyelids with her fingertips. Sleep had eluded her until the wee hours of morning, until she'd at last fallen into exhausted slumber for three hours before her alarm raided disturbing dreams.

"You okay?"

Her eyes flew open at the familiar voice, and her heart tripped. Keith stood in the doorway, dressed to go out. Brown corduroy jeans covered his long legs, and an ivory ribbed turtleneck enhanced the bronzed glow of his skin. Wheat blond hair brushed the collar of his dark brown bomber jacket. The usual pair of designer sunglasses covered his eyes. He looked like he belonged on the cover of an outdoor magazine.

Shae remembered to breathe. "I guess I've just been working too hard. My eyes feel a little tired."

"Where are your glasses?"

"I left them upstairs. Sometimes when I do book work without them, my eyes start to hurt." She shrugged. "It's really no big deal. I'll live."

"Hmm. I think what you need is some fresh air and sunshine. Wanna come with me?"

"Where to?"

He gave her one of his heart-stopping smiles. "I need to pick up some things for tonight's meal. Have you forgotten?"

No. She hadn't forgotten. She hadn't forgotten anything. Just being in his presence was doing crazy things to her insides. And after last night, she didn't think it wise to be alone with him more than was necessary.

How many others had he kissed? Immediately Shae retracted the mental question, deciding she'd rather not know. She didn't need to know. She wouldn't be another conquest, adding herself to the long line of women that must be in his past. Strong values had been instilled in her since childhood, and even for the famous Keith Travers, Shae wouldn't give them up.

"Shae?"

She blinked. *It's just an outing to the store. Not a weekend getaway,* she reminded her foolish brain. "Sure, I'll go with you." She rose from the chair and grabbed her jacket slung over the back.

"By the way, do you have a car?"

"It's only a few blocks to the market, Keith. Walking distance."

"I know, but we're going to the other side of the island."

She quit pushing her arm through the jacket sleeve and stared. "Why?"

"Because the ingredients I'm looking for, the market doesn't have. I called and found them at a larger grocer's though."

"Doesn't have?" She eyed him with suspicion. "What are you looking for, Keith? Cow's tongue? Pig's feet? Snails?"

He grinned. "Actually, they are considered delicacies."

She let out a little moan and continued shrugging into her windbreaker. "I think I'd better get a large box of that antacid."

"Trust me, Shae. I think you'll be pleasantly surprised."

Hoping he was right, but doubting it, she stopped at the front desk for her car keys and led him around the side of the inn to the small, private garage. She tossed him the keys. "You drive—my eyes hurt."

He slipped behind the wheel. Shae got in on the other side and laid her head against the seat. Blissfully, she closed her eyes.

Soon Keith turned onto another road. The sun poured into the passenger side window, ruthlessly attacking her shut eyelids. Shae sat up and groped through the glove compartment, finding a pair of dark sunglasses with one of the temples missing. They hadn't been like that the last time she'd worn them. No doubt Tiffany was responsible for their present condition. But even broken sunglasses were better then none at all. Shae rammed them onto her nose and laid her head back again.

It seemed she'd just fallen asleep when her arm was grasped and she was gently shaken. She mumbled incoherently, pushing Keith's hand away.

"Wake up, Shae. We're here."

At his soft, insistent words, she opened her eyes, but they still felt gritty. "I'm not much company. Maybe I should just stay in the car while you go in," she murmured, tilting her head against the window.

"Actually, I've enjoyed your company. When you snore, it sounds almost musical."

"I do not snore!" His teasing words had the effect of a dousing of icy water. Sitting upright, she turned and glared at him through the crooked dark glasses, daring him to say otherwise.

His lips flickering at the corners as though holding back a smile, he pulled off his sunglasses and concentrated hard on cleaning them with the bottom of his shirt. Finally he looked her way with a hopeful expression. "Come with me, Shae . . . please?"

"Oh, all right," she muttered. How could she resist those gorgeous eyes? She imagined he would probably have a lucrative business selling ice cream to Eskimos, or saunas to the Arabs in the Syrian Desert, if he chose to do so.

Keith put his sunglasses back on and got out of the car. Reluctantly, Shae removed her broken ones, set them on the dashboard, and followed him into the grocery store. She watched as he searched the narrow aisles, selecting various items. As they were heading to the checkout, she gave him a puzzled glance.

"Is this meal vegetarian? You didn't buy any meat or fish."

"Trust me, Shae."

She rolled her eyes in exasperation, tired of hearing those words. Noticing a box of antacid on the end aisle next to the cash register, she grabbed it and put it with the other items. "For the guests," she said innocently when Keith cast a suspicious glance her way. "I was serious when I said I needed to restock. I'll pay you back."

Keith shrugged it off. "Don't worry about it."

Their turn came up. He pulled an eel-skin wallet out of his back pocket and riffled through it. "I'll have to use a credit card," he told the blond cashier after she'd rung up the items. "I seem to be out of cash."

She barely looked at him or the card as she slid it and the charge slip into the old metal contraption and moved the handle back and forth with a snap. She pulled out the slip, marked on it, then placed it in front of Keith for him to sign, her bored gaze lifting to his.

Blue-violet eyes grew wide, her pink lips parting in a look of disbelief. She stared down at the paper with his signature and gasped. "It *is* you! I can't believe it." Her eyes lifted to his, adoration now written in them. "Will you sign this for me?"

Keith smiled. "I think I already have."

"Oh, not the charge slip," she laughed, pushing it away as if it were of little importance. She pulled a thick pad of paper from her green smock. "This. I'd like your autograph. Address it to Kitty, please. . . . Keith Travers on our little island—I still can't believe it. I waited on Keith Travers! Oh, wait 'til the other girls hear—they'll never believe me. Too bad I don't have a camera. . . ."

Keith hurriedly signed the pad while the cashier rambled on, gushing over him. He began to look uneasy when a couple of curious women shoppers stopped what they were doing to listen to the enamored cashier's words. Even the bag boy moved at a snail's pace, staring at Keith while clumsily sacking the purchases. The bottle of sparkling cider missed the bag and hit the counter with a bang.

"Oh, thank you! Thank you so much!" Kitty clutched the paper to her heart, her hands trembling.

"Uh, can I have my card back now?" Keith asked, his eyes darting around the area.

"Oh, of course. Silly me! Here." She handed him the card. Snatching it out of her hand, he plucked up the sack of groceries.

"Look! It *is* him—it's Keith Travers!" came a squeal from several aisles away.

"Oh, no," Keith groaned. He grabbed Shae's hand, pulling her with him as he sped to the glass door. His shoulder accidentally brushed a teetering display of straw containers stacked by the entrance. Shae winced when she heard muffled thuds as the baskets fell and rolled over the tile floor behind them. Keith didn't stop, but flew through the door—almost running down an elderly gentleman and his wife as they approached the store.

"Oh!" the woman exclaimed, putting a hand to her bosom.

"Sorry!" Keith yelled over his shoulder, not stopping until he reached the car. He yanked open the driver's door, jumped inside, and slammed it shut, Shae following suit on the passenger side. She looked over her shoulder at the store's entrance.

Kitty had run out and was waving a slip of paper above her head "Wait, you forgot your receipt!" Three teenaged girls ran past, their eyes eagerly scanning the parking area. When they saw Shae's car, they gave a shout and scampered toward it.

"Hold on!" Keith jammed the key into the ignition, started the car, and took off with a squeal of burning rubber as the tires spun on black tarmac. Shae turned on the seat and looked behind her at the three disappointed faces. One of the teens burst into tears when she realized her idol had gotten away.

"Guess I was wrong to trust Tiffany's friends," Keith said in a clipped tone.

"Those three weren't at the party. In fact, I've never seen them before. They must be tourists." When he didn't answer, just gave an abrupt nod, Shae tried for levity, hoping to break the tension. "I'd hate to be the next customer in Kitty's aisle. There's no telling when she'll come down to earth." When Keith still didn't respond, she queried softly, "Is it always like that?"

"Always," he bit out, then groaned. "Sometimes I can't even go outside my apartment to get the paper without finding one of them camped on my lawn, even though I do live in a high security area. No one can get through the gate without punching in a code," he explained, "but it doesn't seem to do any good. I've moved six times in four years—and they always still seem to find me. I had thought on this small island I wouldn't have that kind of problem, but I guess Freddie is right. I can't go anywhere without the hassle." He hit the steering wheel with the flat of his hand.

Not certain what to say, Shae kept quiet and let him spill.

"Privacy is a luxury I can't even remember," he gritted. "I like what I do—sing and write songs—but sometimes I wonder if it's worth it. You know what I'm saying?" He shot a glance her way, a frown marring his brow.

"Believe me, Keith. I understand better than you realize," she said under her breath, then wished she hadn't.

He let out a frustrated sigh, obviously not hearing her words. "I'm sorry, Shae. I know you weren't feeling good to begin with. Just once, I'd like to go somewhere without being recognized."

"You could always wear a dark wig," she joked.

"Believe me, I've thought about it."

"Maybe you're singing for the wrong audience." The words tumbled out of her mouth before she thought twice.

Keith briefly looked her way, his brows bunched in a puzzled frown. "What do you mean?"

Shae squirmed in her seat. Yes, what did she mean? Memory of the day he'd sung "The Old Rugged Cross" hit her. She remembered, too, the feeling in the atmosphere and the awed faces in the room.

"God gave you a wonderful talent, Keith. Maybe He wants you to use it for Him."

Yeah, you're one to talk, Marcia Shae. Wincing, she tried to block out the sardonic thought. She wouldn't blame Keith if he threw those same words in her face, as many times as he'd tried to convince her to sing.

A nerve near his jaw tensed and there was an uncomfortable pause before he responded. "My granny said the same thing. She was one of the strongest believers I've known."

Shae blinked. He had used the word *believers*—a word used by those of the Christian faith. Did that mean . . . ?

Keith glanced sideways and studied her fixed gaze. "Well, aren't you going to ask me?"

"Ask you what?" Shae's mouth felt dry.

"If I'm a Christian. I've seen the look in your eyes when you've prayed at mealtimes. I'm surprised you haven't said anything yet."

"Okay," she whispered. "Are you?"

He gave a self-deprecating laugh. "Well, I walked right into that one." His face sobered, looked sad. "I was. I accepted Jesus as my Savior at a youth camp when I was twelve. But, well, I guess the draw to the limelight was too strong." He sighed and shook his head.

"You don't sound too happy with your life," Shae said, somewhat surprised.

"Could be because I'm not. One day, the limelight doesn't shine so brightly anymore, and you look around and wonder how you got where you did. At least, that's what happened to me." He gave her a sober glance. "I'm twenty-five, Shae. I've achieved in four years what most men dream of in a lifetime—wealth, success, and fame. But still that void is always there, sucking me dry."

Shae squirmed at the turn of conversation. She understood about that void all too well. "So tell me how you got started in the business." She forced a bright tone to her voice, one she didn't feel.

He threw her a puzzled look, a flicker of hurt in his eyes. Shae inwardly cringed, not wanting to seem unfeeling, but she just couldn't talk about voids and God right now.

"When I wasn't playing sports, I spent every spare moment I had in bands all through junior high and high school," he said after awhile. "Music was my first love. I remember writing and singing songs when I was eleven and hoping someday I'd be a musician. I learned guitar and piano when I was a just a squirt—thanks to Mom's influence. The sax, too—though that only lasted two years. I got into school sports because that's what Dad wanted, though I can't say I didn't enjoy playing them."

He shrugged. "After high school, I won a regional music contest and was offered a recording contract. Against my parents' wishes I took it. I'd just turned twenty-one, so there wasn't much they could do to stop me. Star Artists offered me a better contract after that one expired, and here I am. I guess you could say I'm like the modern-day prodigal—only I haven't gone home."

"You still could, you know."

"What?"

"Go home."

Silence.

"Keith, I've been thinking about where I want to go on our date."

"Yeah?" he asked warily.

"I'd like to meet your family." What she really wanted was for him to be reunited with them.

"I don't think that's a good idea, Shae," he said after another span of thick silence. "Remember, someone from the magazine will be there. I don't want to make a three-ring media circus out of what should be a quiet family gathering."

She sighed. "Yeah, I see your point. But I still think you should visit them while you're in Rhode Island—especially since you said they live in the area. Just think how they would feel if they discovered you were here and didn't even bother to visit."

"I'll think about it."

Nothing more was said during the drive back to the inn. Shae studied his grim countenance, wondering if she'd gone too far. How could she get him to realize just how important it was to be part of a family unit with a mother and father who cared? The times of togetherness, the unconditional love, the support that only parents could give their children . . . All these were lost to her now. She supposed the old adage was true that people didn't appreciate what they had until it was gone. How she wished she could turn the hands of time backward and be given a second chance.

Idly, she stared out the window at the pastel-painted summer cottages and renovated historical homes they passed. Her favorite on this street, the gray one with white trim and the crow's nest, didn't even make her smile like it usually did.

When they reached the inn, Keith pulled in front, but didn't turn off the motor. "There's still something I need to take care of," he said, not looking at her.

Shae stepped out and took the stairs to the wraparound porch. She stood at the rail, watching the car disappear down the coastal road. Had she blown it?

❧

Shae studied the contents of her closet, trying to decide what to wear. She hadn't talked to Keith since he'd returned a few hours earlier, but since he hadn't informed her otherwise, she assumed tonight's dinner was still on. Anxiety made her hands shake as she slid a dress along the rod.

The private phone on her bedside table emitted a shrill ring, demanding attention. She thought about ignoring it, then blew out an irritated breath, ran across the room to grab it on the fifth ring, and gave a halfhearted "Hello?"

"How's one of my favorite sisters doing? You're not an easy person to get ahold of. Where were you earlier?"

"Tommy?" Smiling, she sank onto her four-poster bed. "It's good to hear from you. How's Linda?"

"Badgering me about taking a vacation. That's why I called. I thought we might come down next week—say Wednesday? Think you can spare a room?"

"Of course. You know better than to ask."

"How's Tiffany?"

Shae groaned. "Don't ask."

"Up to her usual tricks, huh?"

"You won't believe the latest."

"Save it 'til I get there, Sis. There's something I need to talk to you about. I'd better go for now, though. Long distance rates are still too high for my tastes. See you next Wednesday!"

"Yeah, bye." Shae replaced the phone, uneasy, then mentally chastised herself. Just because Tommy wanted to discuss something with her didn't necessarily mean it was something negative. But he had sounded so strange. Determined to forget her brother for now, Shae again approached her walk-in closet.

An hour later she studied the person in the mirror, wearing the royal blue silk dress. Who was that girl staring back? She seemed so calm, so confident—nothing like Shae really felt. Turning her back on the illusory image, she went downstairs.

Keith stood waiting on the landing, looking far too handsome in a blue cotton shirt that matched his eyes and a pair of gray slacks. A contemporary tie in swirls of blues hung neatly from his collar. When he caught sight of her, his eyes lit up and glowed with approval. Shae's heart beat a little faster.

"Very nice," he murmured, making her cheeks grow warm. He put a hand to her elbow and steered her toward a room they kept reserved for private parties.

"I thought we were eating in the kitchen or the dining room," she said, hating the nervous warble in her voice.

"Gretta told me about this room, and I thought it would be more appropriate. Relax, Shae, I won't bite."

More appropriate? For what? She followed him into the cozy room, her pulse rate increasing in tempo like a rapidly ticking metronome atop a piano. A linen and lace cloth lay draped over a round table. Two elegant place settings sat across from one another. A short crystal vase with blue and white flowers stood in the center.

Shae remained near the door, uncertain.

Keith had pulled out a chair and now looked at her. "Wouldn't you like to sit down and eat?"

"I wasn't planning on standing." Nervousness put a bite to her words.

A confused vee formed between his brows. "Shae, I don't know what happened in the last few hours to make you look at me like the big bad wolf that's ready to eat you. But let's try to have a nice evening anyway. Okay?"

She knew she was acting silly, but couldn't seem to help it. First dates were scary enough, she'd heard. But when the date was with someone like Keith, who'd taken out so many glamorous, popular women in his lifetime . . . Shae clenched her hands in determination. This wasn't an actual date. She'd eaten with him other times, though usually in the presence of others. The only difference tonight was that they were dressed up and using good china instead of stoneware. And they were alone.

She swallowed and, with what she hoped passed for a normal smile, moved toward him and sat down. "Something smells great."

"That's music to my ears, coming from you," Keith said, taking the chair across from her. To her surprise, he bowed his head and said the blessing for both of them. The words were rusty, as if he hadn't prayed in awhile, but they sounded sincere.

Shae bit the inside of her cheek, knowing she needed to clear the air before they went any further. "Keith, about this afternoon, I'm sorry. I know I wasn't very nice."

He gave her a soft smile. "Forget it. I'm sorry too. Now eat!" he quietly commanded with a boyish smirk.

She couldn't help but grin. His smiles were infectious.

As the meal progressed, his easygoing attitude soon helped relax her. She toyed with a forkful of crab quiche and cocked her brow. "Say, Keith, didn't I hear something once that real men don't eat—"

"Don't say it," he said, rolling his eyes.

She chuckled and popped one of the peppery fried smelts in her mouth. "Hey, this is good."

"You sound surprised," he said in mock indignation. "But don't worry, I won't say I told you so. Even if I did." His smile was smug.

She chose to ignore him and focus on the food.

"Try some of the shrimp paste," he encouraged, handing her a platter with a bowl of dip surrounded by herb crackers.

She took an oval cracker and dipped it into the paste. It was delicious—everything was. Even the garden salad—made with three kinds of lettuce, grated carrots, and bits of green peppers—was a treat to the taste buds. Chocolate mousse followed, creamy and rich. After scraping her dish with her spoon and draining the last drop of sparkling cider from her glass, Shae sat back, giving a contented sigh.

"Well, Keith, when I'm wrong I admit it. Remind me to send a thank-you card to your home economics teacher. Did you really learn all this in high school?"

He nodded. "I've learned a lot since then too. I told myself being a bachelor doesn't mean I'm going to be stuck with a life of frozen dinners and takeouts. You'd be amazed at how easy a cookbook is to follow when you've had the training."

"I guess I took the wrong classes—I should have taken home ec. I can't even boil an egg." She giggled. "I tried once, but the water boiled over, the egg cracked, and all that filmy white stuff inside poked out the middle."

Keith smiled, his expression tender and his eyes full of something Shae didn't understand. Her heart began to race. Quickly she lowered her gaze to her empty dish and stared, feeling her muscles begin to tighten again.

After about a minute of silence, he threw his napkin to the table and stood. "How about a walk by the ocean?"

She thought about her two-inch heels. "I'm not dressed for it."

"Well then, want to check out the floor show?"

"I know it forward and backward."

"Okaaay. Shall we see what's on TV?"

Remembering what happened the last time they'd watched television together, Shae gave a quick shake of her head. "No, thanks. The meal was superb and I thoroughly enjoyed it, but if you'll excuse me, I think I'll turn in early."

"I don't think so."

Her eyes widened at this unexpected response. He crossed his arms over his chest, his stance nonchalant yet almost formidable at the same time.

Her heart skipped a beat. "Excuse me?"

"I don't know why you're suddenly uncomfortable to be in my company, but I intend to find out what's going on in that imagination of yours if it takes all night. Ladies first," he said, motioning to the door.

"Where to?"

"To your family parlor, to discuss this like two mature adults. After you?" Again he gestured to the door with a sweep of his hand.

Shae wondered if Keith would chase her up the stairs if she headed that way. As stubborn as he was, he probably would. She grimaced. With Keith around digging up her buried secrets, she didn't stand a chance. Yet she determined he would *never* uncover her darkest one.

6

Shae preceded Keith into the parlor and sank to the far end of the couch. He watched her move a small beaded throw pillow on the cushion beside her, preventing him from sitting there. Perched on the edge of the sofa, she reminded him of a wary bird poised for flight. Her back was ramrod straight, her hands clasped tightly in her lap, and her eyes had the look of one hunted.

He gave a world-weary sigh. "Shae—"

She raised a hand to stop him. "Allow me to save you the trouble of delving into my inner mind and bringing out all my close-kept secrets. I know for some strange reason you insist on knowing all the answers about me—though I can't begin to understand why—and that you won't stop until you get them.

"So, okay, Keith, here it is. Brace yourself. The terrible truth is I've never dated—not even in high school—and this is the first time I've shared dinner, alone, with a man. So go ahead and laugh. I wouldn't blame you one bit."

"You never dated?" Keith shook his head, flabbergasted. She was so pretty, sweet, and fun to be with, as well as highly intelligent. Were the men on this island blind, stupid, or both?

Shae flicked her long hair over one shoulder in a nervous gesture. "It wasn't that my parents didn't allow it—though they said I had to wait until I was sixteen. It's just that we were so busy. Moving all the time, never really settling down, always on the go. I . . . I didn't always live on the island."

She paused, tightly clasped her hands on her lap, and stared at them. Keith waited patiently, afraid to say anything that might make her clam up again. He took a seat a couple of feet away from her on the couch, respecting her wish for distance.

"Occasionally I would go with a boy and other friends to a pizza place," she continued. "My parents allowed group dates. But I never got the chance to get to know someone well, because of all the moves. Then after . . . after they died . . . for awhile I just didn't care about anything anymore. Later my grandmother had a stroke and there wasn't time to form any new relationships what with running the inn and taking care of Tiffany and everything else to do. . . ."

"You poor kid." He reached over to lay a hand on her clenched ones, but Shae snatched them away before he could make contact. She shot to her feet and faced him, her chin lifted proudly.

"I didn't tell you this to gain your pity, Keith." Her voice and emotions were in control again. "I just felt I owed you an explanation for my strange behavior tonight. And I am *not* a kid!"

"Bad choice of words, sorry," he muttered. He thought a moment. "That's why I had such a hard time convincing you to go on the contest date with me, isn't it?"

She nodded.

Something else dawned on him. "Why, I'll bet you'd never been kissed before either!"

Her face grew rosier. "A few quick pecks on the lips by a fifteen-year-old boy were all I experienced. Until you came along."

"Then last night . . ."

As if a lightbulb flashed on inside his head, chasing away the darkness of ignorance, Keith suddenly understood. Because of her inexperience, she must think his repeated attempts at getting to know her were a ploy to use her for selfish purposes—ultimately to hurt her in the end. *That's* probably why she'd been so distant. She was afraid to get close.

"Shae, now I have a confession to make. Please, sit down."

Her brow crinkled in an uncertain frown. Slowly, she sank to the cushion beside him and grabbed the pillow, cradling it to her breast, as though it were a shield.

"Contrary to what you've heard or read about me, I haven't chosen to date anyone for over a year," he said in a low voice. When she would have interrupted, he held up a hand to stop her. "Doubtless you've heard of different women, whom I've been seen with on dates. But my manager arranged all of them for publicity. They were not my own idea."

He averted his gaze, feeling uneasy and a bit ashamed with what he was about to tell her. "When I first got into the business, I was bowled over by instant fame. I let it get to my head and sowed a few wild oats, went a little crazy. But the women I knew were hard, and those kinds of relationships soured fast." He glanced at her. "Shae, the other night when I kissed you "

Her face reddened, and she dropped her gaze. Slowly, he slid toward her, relieved when she didn't flinch from him.

"I haven't kissed anyone like that, feeling it deep within my heart, since I went steady with Heather in high school."

"The captain of the cheerleading squad?" she whispered.

"Yeah. Though I like to think I'm more mature now than the boy I was then." He stared down at her hand and covered it with his. "I want to thank you for opening up and sharing some of your past with me. I know it wasn't easy, but it helps me understand you a little better now."

Shae looked at him then, gave a small nod and an even smaller smile. She seemed so vulnerable that it was all Keith could do not to take her in his arms and hold her. Powerless to resist, he put a finger underneath her chin, moved toward her, and touched his lips to hers in a brief, gentle kiss. It took every bit of determination he had to move away. The last thing he wanted was to scare her. Shallow waters were safest.

She opened wide, dark, ocean-deep eyes—ones he could easily drown in.

Keith swallowed and his voice came out a little husky. "I think we should call it a night, before I get hopelessly lost in those chocolate-colored eyes of yours and forget myself." He lightly stroked the back of his fingers over her cheek and managed a slight grin. "Chocolate always was one of my weaknesses."

Not willing to test his self-control further, he rose from the couch with a soft good night, leaving her staring after him in bewilderment.

The next Sunday Shae was surprised when Keith woke early and accompanied her to church. He had exhibited an interest the previous afternoon at dinner, but she didn't think he'd really go. Not considering the way he'd been acting this past week. He'd spent little time with her, only seeing her during meals. And though those times had been pleasant, his attitude toward her apparently had altered. She wondered if the change had to do with her confession about never having dated. Although Keith's sudden distance was a relief, Shae also couldn't help but feel strangely disappointed.

From her place on the back pew of the historic church building, Shae noticed two young girls whisper and dart interested glances over their shoulders in his direction. Poor Keith. She wondered how he managed any semblance of a normal life.

After the service, he grabbed her arm and steered her out of the small church and to the car. The day was beautiful. The sun shone from a clear sky, and the sweet scent of wildflowers scattered over the grassy hills mixed with the ocean breeze. In the distance, between the budding trees and summer cottages, Shae could see a sliver of the Atlantic—cerulean blue today, instead of a stormy greenish gray.

However, yesterday's storm seemed to have invaded the confines of the car. Keith was quiet, and Shae sensed he was angry. He seemed morose, far away. Nothing like his usual self.

"It's not my fault," she said, breaking the silence.

"What?" He gave her a distracted glance.

"You looked at me as if I'd instigated the whole thing."

"What whole thing?"

"Today's message. I can't help it that Pastor Williams chose the topic of the prodigal son."

Keith didn't respond. Shae turned her upper body around in the bucket seat to get a better look at him. "You don't honestly believe I called him last night and asked him to change his message when I found out you were coming?"

He released a weary breath. "Of course not. I'm just going through a bit of a mental battle."

"Because of those girls back there?"

His brow creased. "What girls?"

Wow. He must have been deeply immersed in the message not to notice the interested stares he'd been getting.

"Never mind." Shae looked out the window, focusing on the scenery as they drove home. They passed a popular sandy beach, and Shae spotted several hardier souls throwing a football around and running along the sun-bleached dunes, though the temperature barely wavered above fifty. It had been an unusually cold spring.

"Freddie got in touch with *Teen Planet*," Keith said. "We've set the date up for a week from this Thursday. Okay with you?"

"Sure. My brother and his wife are coming to the island this week. They usually stay awhile, so there won't be any problem with me taking off a full day for the, uh, date." She still had a problem saying the word.

"Great." He glanced her way. "Did you tell your brother about me?"

"I didn't think you'd want your whereabouts known."

He softly snorted. "Don't you think he may begin to wonder when he sees me sitting on your porch?"

"Why should he? I own the inn, and you are my guest."

They rolled to a stop at a traffic light, and he turned to face her. "Is that all I am to you, Shae? Just a guest at The Roosting Place? I thought we'd gone beyond that."

His probing, flame-blue eyes melted her to her seat. This was getting dangerous as well as confusing. Hadn't he spent almost the entire past week practically ignoring her?

She shrugged and looked out the window. The car took off with a jerk, making the tires squeal.

Shae darted a glance in his direction, noting his tense jaw. "Even if I'd wanted to tell Tommy about you being here, there wasn't time," she explained. "It was a short call. My brother is a miser when it comes to money."

Keith gave a curt nod. Uncomfortable, Shae looked back out the window. When they reached the inn, she wrenched open her door and hurried from the car before he turned off the ignition.

"It's not over yet, Shae," Keith murmured as he watched her retreating figure in the rearview mirror. "I'm not going anywhere for awhile."

The relief Keith felt days ago that he'd successfully talked Freddie into putting off the contest date, so that Keith could extend his vacation, evaporated as frustration seized his emotions. He'd honestly thought he and Shae had reached an understanding. This past week he had done his level best to take their relationship slow and not push, not crowding her, and had foolishly thought he was making headway. So why was she holding back again? Keith knew she felt something for him. He'd seen it in her eyes. And since he'd come to this island, he couldn't stop thinking about her, couldn't stop wanting to be with her, even searching her out to do things with him that first week. Like a lovesick puppy.

Keith shook his head and shifted his gaze to the windshield and the blue sea—as changeable as Shae.

Perhaps it was time to switch tactics. Instead of treading carefully maybe he should pursue. That something from her past haunted her was obvious. And he was almost sure that *something* had to do with her parents. Was that what held her back from him?

He let out a mirthless chuckle. The situation was really ironic when he thought about it. Countless females threw themselves over each other to get to him. Yet the one woman Keith was interested in seemed bent on running the opposite direction.

Years ago he'd made a point to keep an emotional distance from women, though Heather had wanted to marry him right after high school. But Keith hadn't felt the same way. He didn't want any ties while trying to boost his singing career.

Thinking about those first years away from home, he felt shame flood through him, heating his face. He had eventually wised up and entered a drug rehab shortly after a good friend died from an overdose, and not long after that he'd sworn off promiscuous women. Yet could God ever forgive him for his temporary insanity? Was He really holding His arms open, waiting to forgive? Or did He have His back turned to Keith, as Keith imagined? Because he'd been raised in a Christian home, Keith knew the story of the prodigal son, had heard it many times when he was a kid. But he hadn't really understood the story then and wasn't sure he quite believed it now. . . .

While the mental and spiritual battle raged on inside him, Keith stared at the ocean and wondered if the expanse was too great to go to the other side.

~&

Shae darted a nervous glance Keith's way. Sunday morning she'd bolted from this car. Today was Wednesday. During that time Keith had completely avoided her, not even sharing in their meals, as he had done since he'd come to the inn. Shae had missed their dinner conversations—missed Keith—and that scared her. She didn't want to think of Keith as more than a guest. It was too dangerous.

"You're awfully quiet," Keith's voice broke into her musings.

She shrugged. "Not much to say."

Ha! What a joke. Her mind fairly screamed with questions she wanted answers to—answers only he could give. Why did he want to know so much about her? Why couldn't he leave her alone? Why had he ignored her? And then, after days of ignoring her, why did he suddenly appear and invite her on a picnic? Concentrating on the scenery, she tensed. Her eyes widened when she realized where they were headed.

To the left, dark brown clay bluffs stretched for miles along the south side of the island and sharply dropped 150 feet to the pale beaches below. Crimson and yellow wildflowers dotted the sparse shrubs, and wild grasses grew throughout the area. In the distance, an old red brick lighthouse with an A-shaped roof and octagonal tower stood sentinel against the powder-gray sky.

Keith drove a little farther then stopped the car. "This is as good a place as any. Let's eat." He reached behind him for the hamper.

Shae didn't move, barely breathed. "Who told you about this place?"

"No one needed to tell me, Shae. Mohegan's Bluffs is one of the biggest attractions on the island. I saw the write-up in a tourist brochure at the inn."

She chewed on her lip. "Let's go somewhere else. Please, Keith. It's . . . it's too cold to eat by the ocean, and I didn't bring a jacket."

"You can wear mine." He shrugged out of his bomber jacket and handed it to her.

"There are better places to have a picnic."

"I like it here," he countered stubbornly. "There's something about the ocean that speaks to you."

"Block Island has countless views of the ocean. We're completely surrounded by water. Why don't we go to Old Harbor, or the beach next to the inn—"

"I'm hungry now, and this is a great spot—one I haven't seen until today." Keith grinned. "Besides, I don't want to spend any more time driving around when that food in the hamper is begging for me to eat it." He got out of the car, putting an end to further argument.

Shae clutched the door handle tightly, wishing he hadn't taken the car keys. If she had the choice, she would drive off and leave him here. But she obviously had no choice.

Gritting her teeth, she got out of the car and slammed the door. She shrugged into Keith's jacket, smelling of spicy cologne, and trailed behind him. He had already spread a blanket on the ground. As Shae approached, he motioned her to it. She remained standing.

"Just listen to the soothing sound of that ocean," Keith said. "It's so peaceful here. Something I've really missed in my fast-paced life."

"It looks as if it might storm. I think we should go home."

"Storm? I don't think so. Not a thundercloud for miles." He handed her a sandwich. "Here. Eat up."

With a loud sigh, Shae knelt at the edge of the blanket and sat on her calves. She took the sandwich and paper cup he gave her, but didn't unwrap it. Just stared at a nearby clump of vegetation.

"Tiffany tells me you used to come here with your parents."

Her head shot up, anger eating away her unease. Tiffany!

"Oh? And what else did she tell you?" Shae squeezed the cup in her hand. It made a popping noise, and tea spilled out, sloshing over her fingers and onto her lap.

"Hey! You gotta be careful with those flimsy things. Here." Keith handed her a couple of napkins. "Good thing it wasn't hot coffee."

Shae automatically took the napkins, barely cognizant of the fact that her jeans leg was soaked. "What else did Tiffany tell you?" she demanded.

"That her times here were some of the best memories she had of her family," Keith said quietly after studying her a moment. "That your parents often took you to visit the lighthouse over there, and the beaches below—"

Shae rocketed to her feet. "That's it. I want to go home."

"I haven't finished eating yet."

"You know what? I really don't care."

Shae turned on her heel and stomped to the car. She'd only made it a few yards before she felt his hand on her shoulder, pulling her around to face him.

"What are you running from, Shae? I want to help. Please don't shut me out."

She shook his hand off, glaring at him. "Just because you're a big hotshot celebrity doesn't give you the right to interfere in my business. You act like some kind of shrink! Next thing you know you'll be wanting me to play some kind of word association game or some crazy thing like that."

"That might not be a bad idea," he said, as though considering.

"Oh, puh-leease. Give me a break." Shae spun on her heel, continued to the car, wrenched open her door, and got inside.

Keith slid behind the wheel, but made no move to put the key into the ignition. "Black."

Shae tensed. "Excuse me?"

"I'll say a word, and you quickly say the first word that comes to mind."

"You must be joking," Shae said, widening her eyes in disbelief. "Didn't you hear a word I said back there?"

"Black."

"What is it with all these games you keep coming up with? First twenty questions, then guessing games, now this!"

"Black."

Shae threw up her hands in disgust. "Okay, okay. If I humor you and play your stupid game, then can we go?"

"Black."

"White!" She looked daggers at him.

"Heaven," he shot back calmly.

"Hell."

"Bad."

"Good," she gritted between clenched teeth, throwing her head back against the seat.

"Life."

"Death."

"God."

"Powerful."

"Devil."

"Angel."

"Father."

"Mother."

"Sister."

"Brother."

"Daughter."

"Killer." The word slipped out, startling them both. Shae gaped, blinked. "I . . . I don't know why I said that. I—" She threw open her door and jumped outside.

Walk, just walk. Escape. She needed escape. He was getting too close. She had to calm down, get back in control. But she couldn't think straight, couldn't reason. This place. That day. Her legs moved automatically, the grasses swishing against her jeans. Her vision blurred with tears, making it harder to see.

"Shae!"

She heard him coming up behind her and increased her pace until she was almost at a run. Without her realizing it, her feet carried her toward the bluffs. He caught up to her, gripping her arm before she'd reached the barrier. "Shae—"

"Why can't you leave me alone?" she cried, whirling to face him. "Why don't you just go back to California and leave me alone?"

"I can't do that. I want to help you beat this thing."

"Why?! Why do you care?"

"I just do."

Beyond frustration, she put her hands straight up at shoulder level as though to ward him off. Staring at the ground, she shook her head and backed up until her tailbone hit the barrier.

"Shae," Keith said quietly. "I don't know much about your past, but I can guarantee you're no killer."

She clenched her teeth and glared at him. "How can you say that? You don't know anything about me!"

"I know enough to know you're not capable of such a thing."

Unable to handle his persistence any longer, she felt her last vestige of control snap. "Well, you're wrong," she screamed, the words rushing from her mouth before she could stop them. "You know nothing—nothing at all! Your manager was right. I am a killer! It's because of me my parents are dead. So now you know. There—are you happy now?"

She whirled from him and raced down the road.

7

*Of*tunned, Keith stood immobile and watched Shae run from him as if the hounds of hell were chasing her. Not for a minute did he believe she'd willfully killed anyone. Killers were angry or bitter, with hard hearts and selfish motives. Shae didn't fit the type. Yet at the same time Keith didn't deny the fact that *she* believed she'd killed her parents. How and why she felt that way, he hoped to find out some time in the future. But not today.

He moved to the car and slid behind the wheel. Slipping the key into the ignition, he started the car and pulled out onto the road in the direction Shae had taken.

As he came up alongside her, he eased his foot off the gas, hitting the switch that automatically rolled down the passenger window. She had trailed to a walk, her breath coming in panting gasps.

"Get in, Shae," he said, leaning across the seat.

She gave a short, hysterical laugh. "Sure you want . . . to ride with me . . . after what I said?"

"I'm sure."

She halted, darting him a puzzled, incredulous look. He put his foot on the brake.

"Why, Keith? Why don't you hate me now?"

Hate her? Keith studied her curiously. Her dark eyes held deep wells of pain. Wet, black trails ran down each cheek. His heart wrenched at her distress.

"I'm only going to say this once, Shae, and then I'm not going to speak of it anymore unless you bring it up." He released a soft breath, hoping he wasn't making a mistake that might send her over the edge again. "I know for some reason you feel responsible for your parents' deaths—and one day I hope you'll trust me enough to tell me why. Until then, I plan to treat you as I always have. I'm a pretty good judge of character, believe it or not, and I think it's safe to say you're no murderer. Now, get inside, and I'll take you back to the inn. It's too far to walk."

Shae inhaled deeply, her eyes sliding shut a moment. At last, giving a curt nod, she opened the door and slid onto the passenger seat.

Relieved, Keith pulled the car away and headed toward the inn. The entire drive back, Shae kept her face averted, staring at the choppy ocean. The sky had grown a shade darker, and Keith was surprised when several raindrops splattered against the windshield. Soon the drops increased in quantity and strength, drumming against the car. He turned the wipers on.

"I didn't think it would rain, or I would have never suggested a picnic." He winced. *Great, Travers. You had to go and bring that up again.*

But Shae only shrugged. "New England weather," she said, her voice raspy. "Can't trust it. It'll pass soon enough."

She was right. By the time they reached the road leading to The Roosting Place, the downpour had abated.

Shae let out a groan.

"What's wrong?" Keith glanced her way.

"Tommy's car. I'd forgotten he was coming today." She pulled at her disheveled hair. "I can't face him looking like this!"

Keith nodded and turned the car onto another road.

Shae looked at him in surprise. "What are you doing?"

"Giving you time to compose yourself." He took a hand off the wheel, reached into his back pocket, and pulled out a comb, offering it to her. "I noticed there's a box of tissues on the backseat if you want to wipe your face."

When she didn't take the comb, he shot a glance her way. "Don't worry. I don't have cooties."

A grin trembled on the corners of her lips. "Thanks, Keith." Her soft words thanked him for so much more than the comb, and he gave her an understanding smile. She took the comb, put the visor down, and gasped when she saw her reflection in the mirror. Hurriedly she reached in back for the tissues and swiped one after another under her eyes, then took the comb and slowly worked it through the snarls in her thick hair.

While Shae spruced herself up, Keith drove along the road heading north toward the Great Salt Pond. From tourist brochures, he knew it was a sheltered harbor, a perfect retreat for water activities. At some point while he was here he'd like to check it out and do some boating. He missed that sport. Thinking about that made him think about his dad, and how he, Keith, and his older brother Kenneth would often take the sailboat out on summer weekends when Keith had been a kid. Life had been so simple then.

"Okay, I'm ready," Shae said, sticking the crumpled tissues into a car trash bag.

Without a word, Keith turned the car around. Soon they arrived at the inn. A slender man with black hair stood on the veranda, his hands in his pockets.

"That's Tommy," Shae said nervously. "Will I pass inspection? He's sometimes a little overbearing in the protective brother role, and I don't want him to suspect I've been upset."

Keith drove to the side of the inn, put the car in park, and turned off the ignition before looking her way. She stared back, her eyes apprehensive. Her ebony hair was smooth, framing a face that was a shade too pale. Pink bands stood out on her cheeks where she'd rubbed hard with the tissues. His heart lurched with empathy at what she must be going through. He lifted a hand and, with his thumb, wiped away an overlooked black speck near her jaw.

"Just one more thing. Smile. And remember, I'm right behind you." He gave her an encouraging grin and was relieved when the corners of her mouth lifted in response.

❧

"There you are! I was worried when you didn't meet us at the ferry. Who's this?"

Shae tried to keep the smile on her face, though it was difficult with Tommy's suspicious stare settling on her, traveling to Keith, then shooting back to her again.

Before she could reply, Tiffany came sailing out the door, a triumphant expression on her face. "See, I told you, Linda. Keith Travers is so Shae's boyfriend."

Embarrassed heat rushed to Shae's face. "Tiffany—"

"Tiff, you're too old for these kinds of games," Linda's voice grew louder as she approached the door and stepped outside. Her blue eyes lit on Keith and widened. "Oh, wow. . . ."

Shae wished she could dissolve into the ground and disappear between the tufts of wet grass. Somehow she had to make it through introductions. She felt Keith move closer, as though to offer support, and it bolstered her to speak.

"Tommy, Linda, this is Keith. Keith, my brother and my sister-in-law."

Tommy shook Keith's hand in a death grip, giving him a long, measured look. Linda talked as if she'd been medicated and didn't have proper use of her tongue or brain. Embarrassed by the behavior of her kin, Shae grimaced and suggested they all go to the family parlor.

Gretta brought coffee, and Shae gratefully cupped the hot ceramic, taking measured sips as she listened to Tommy's pointed and nosy questions. This was ridiculous. He sounded as if he were trying out for the part of Perry Mason. Just what had Tiffany told her brother to make him act this way?

Shae had to hand it to Keith. He took it well. Casually he answered each question, not once getting upset. If it had been Shae who was being grilled like a defendant on a witness stand, she wouldn't be half as congenial.

"A contest date, huh?" Tommy darted a glance Shae's way. "Sounds fishy to me. Who dreamed up something like that?"

Shae rolled her eyes. "It's perfectly legit."

"Shae's right," Tiffany piped up. "I should know. I filled out the form."

"*You* filled out the form?" Tommy's eyes narrowed as he looked from Tiffany to Keith and back to Shae.

Linda broke out of the stupor she'd been in since meeting Keith, rose from her chair, and put an arm around her husband's shoulders. "Tommy, let's talk about this later. We just got here. Shae's a smart girl. I'm sure she wouldn't get involved in anything that was in any way suspect."

Tommy hesitated, then gave her a faint smile and linked an arm around her waist. "Okay, Hon."

"I need your help with the luggage," Linda said moving with him to the door. "That suitcase sticks and I can never open it." Before they disappeared from sight, Linda looked over her shoulder, flashing a conspiratorial smile at Shae.

"Man, what's with him?" Tiffany said when they were out of earshot. "I don't think I've ever seen him give anyone the third degree like that."

Shae lifted a brow. "So just what did you tell him while we were gone?"

"Nothing, really." Tiffany perked up, sitting forward in the chair. "Hey, guess what? Tommy wants to go to Mohegan Bluffs this Sunday. I haven't been there in forever!"

"This Sunday?" Shae said faintly, setting down the coffee before she spilled it.

"Yeah. We're going after church. Oh, wow, I better call Liz and let her know. Tommy said she could come too." Tiffany bounded off the chair and out the door.

"You okay?" Keith asked quietly when the sudden silence in the room threatened to smother her.

Shae took a deep breath and nodded. "It shouldn't have come as a shock. Tommy often goes there with Tiffany when he comes to visit." Her gaze briefly lowered to her lap. "About my brother—I'm sorry about that cross-examination you got. My guess is he acted that way because I've never dated. And to hear that my first date is with you probably rattled him."

"I understand. No need to apologize. He cares about you and wants to make sure my intentions are honorable. If I were at home I'd do the same with my three sisters, though Beth is still the baby in the family and I won't have to worry about her social life for a long time."

82

Keith hesitated, looked at his coffee. "Shae, about this Sunday . . ."

She tensed.

"I wasn't going to say anything, since I thought you'd spend the day with your brother and his wife. But my guess is you won't be going with them." He looked at her. "Right?"

"Right."

"Then I'd like you to come with me. I'm going home for a visit."

Startled at the unexpected announcement, she drew a breath, her eyes widening. "Really, Keith?"

He nodded. "And it would mean a lot to me if you came along. I could use the support," he joked, though his blue eyes were serious.

She hesitated. "Are you sure your parents won't mind?"

"When my mom discovers that it was largely because of your influence that I decided to see them, I imagine she'll roll out the red carpet for you."

Shae smiled. "Then the answer is yes. I'd like to go with you and meet your family."

⤫

The evening progressed better than the afternoon had. Shae's brother was sullen, but he didn't question Keith further or stare at him as if he were a convicted felon. Linda made up for Tommy's morose attitude with her bubbly behavior, shooting Keith question after question— none of them as uncomfortable or rude as Tommy's had been.

When dinnertime came, they went to the dining room to catch the floor show. Seeing a rather large crowd, Keith slipped on his sunglasses then took them off, deciding in this dark room they made him look conspicuous. Besides, from what he could tell, the audience consisted of those from an older generation. Keith doubted anyone in this crowd had even heard of him.

Feeling at ease, he gave his order to the waitress who'd come to their table. After she left, he settled back and listened to the singer. She crooned a couple of blues songs from the forties while a man in a black tuxedo expertly accompanied her on the piano.

Keith took a sip of rich coffee. The duo was good, but he preferred Shae's bell-like soprano to this woman's husky alto. He leaned over to make a comment, when he noticed Freddie enter the dining room and survey the area with that predatory expression on his face. *Uh-oh. Now what?*

Freddie's gaze landed on Keith and he motioned him over.

"I'll be right back," Keith whispered to Shae. As he walked away, he noticed the waitress approach the table with their food, and barely withheld a groan.

"Do you have built-in radar?" he asked in a low voice when he'd reached his manager. "Is that how you can tell when I'm about to eat?"

"Come on," Freddie said, grabbing his arm. "This is more important than food."

They walked out the door, down a hallway, and slipped into an empty room. Freddie flicked on the light to expose three washers and two dryers on a white linoleum floor.

Keith shrugged his arm away. "You brought me here to do laundry?"

Freddie ignored his feeble joke. "I was on the phone with my secretary earlier, and she mentioned that you only have two months under the old contract. We need to get a new one made up."

"Yeah, okay."

Freddie's eyes narrowed. "You don't sound too sure, Travers." Without waiting for Keith's response, he added, "It was rumored Hugh Fielder from FLD Management was seen talking to you the night of the Video Music Awards. He make you any offers?"

Keith let out an irritated breath. "Yeah. But don't worry about it. I didn't like his terms—"

"Of all the—" Freddie let loose with a few choice expletives. "That rotten, no good chiseler . . . trying to steal my people when my back is turned—"

"I told you, I turned him down. So just chill."

But Freddie wouldn't be pacified. "As soon as this 'dream date' is over, we're heading back to California ASAP. I should have never let you talk me into pushing the date to a later day and staying here so long in the first place. The date is set for next Thursday. We leave on

Friday." He clamped down on his unlit cigar and turned on his heel, leaving the room.

Keith's eyes slid shut. Friday. He had known he would have to return to California soon. Yet now that a definite day had been set, an uncomfortable heaviness settled in his gut. It would be difficult to leave this relaxing island paradise. But it would be even harder to say good-bye to Shae.

❧

The next morning, shortly after breakfast, Keith knocked on Shae's open office door. "Hey, there. Want to take an hour or two off, rent a couple of bikes, and hit the trails?"

Startled, Shae studied him. Obviously, her hysterical confession at the bluffs hadn't fazed him one bit. Like he'd told her he would, Keith treated her the same as always, as if the incident had never happened. But it had.

True, she hadn't outright killed her parents, but she was responsible for their deaths. And that horrible blotch could never be erased from her life, or her records. God could never forgive her for what she'd done.

Feeling that awful blackness rise inside, Shae knew she needed escape. Sunshine. Fresh air. A change of surroundings.

"Sure," she said, rising and throwing her pen down on her open ledger, "but we don't need to rent bikes. I've got several here. I'll meet you on the porch in five minutes."

She went upstairs and changed into some old jeans, a sweatshirt, and sneakers. Before she left the inn, she told Gladys, the assistant manager, that she would be gone. Linda was in bed, not feeling well, and Tommy was taking a walk through town.

With Keith's help, Shae retrieved two bikes from the storage shed, wondering how long it had been since she'd been cycling. They pedaled down a nearby twisting trail close to the water, abreast of each other. The sea breeze was cool, the salt spray invigorating. A pale sun shone in a crystal blue sky, the ocean shimmering a darker blue below.

The path took them through a nearby copse of trees. When they approached a freshwater pond, Keith suggested they stop for a breather. Shae gladly agreed, her leg muscles beginning to ache. She climbed off her bike, leaned it against a tree trunk next to his, and joined him where he sat sprawled on the grass, against a maple, one hand dangling over his upraised knee.

For a few minutes they relaxed in undisturbed silence, listening to the rhythmic birdsong filtering through the trees. Keith reached into his pocket and pulled out a small foil bag, tore it open with his teeth, and offered it to her.

"Peanuts?"

"Thanks." Shae held out a hand, and he poured several into her palm. She smirked in amusement.

"What's so funny?" he asked suspiciously.

"I was just thinking. Have you noticed—it seems whenever we get together, food is involved?"

Keith grinned, leaning his head back against the tree trunk. "I hadn't really thought about it, but you're right. Guess it's because my manager starves me, so naturally it's uppermost in my mind."

She eyed his slim, well-built physique and healthy skin tone. "Yeah, you really look starved."

He popped a couple of peanuts into his mouth. "By the way, I called Mom, and she's excited about meeting you. We'll charter a flight from the airport to the mainland and rent a car—"

"A plane? Can't we take the ferry?" Shae asked, feeling the blackness rise again.

"A plane trip will take twelve minutes," Keith said patiently. "The ferry takes over an hour."

She looked down, brushing imaginary dirt from her jeans. "I know. But I'd prefer to take the ferry. I don't like to fly. That way we can take my car."

"Don't you think it's a little too late to get a reservation for taking the car on the ferry?"

"We can go on standby," she countered. "At least we can try. . . ."

A long pause. "Okay, Shae. If that's what you want, that's what we'll do."

She gave him a self-conscious smile. "Thanks, Keith. I appreciate it."

He didn't return her smile. His steady eyes regarded her, probing, asking questions he didn't speak. Afraid of his starting another inquisition into her past, Shae rose from the ground. "I need to be getting back. More tourists mean more work. This time of year the ferries deliver thousands of people to the island a day—though they don't all spend the night here, of course. There wouldn't be room for them, since the island is only seven miles long and three miles wide—and our town of New Shoreham is the smallest town in the nation." She gave a nervous laugh, realizing she sounded a lot like an overeager tour guide.

Keith nodded thoughtfully, watching her. "All right. Let's go."

On the trail again, he glanced her way as they pedaled out of the copse. "I'll race you," he challenged with a wide smile.

"Race me?" She barely got the words out before he took off, his feet pumping hard on the pedals.

Shae shook her head, bemused, and then began pedaling harder to catch up. Him and his endless games! He was nothing but a big kid.

As they neared the inn, she came closer to him, by this time panting for breath. She was in no shape for these long-distance bike races of his! Perspiration trickled down her face, and she was thankful she'd thought to gather her hair back in a looped ponytail before leaving the inn.

She won by a narrow margin and practically fell off her bike when she dismounted. Her legs no longer felt a part of her. Bending over, she grasped her knees, gasping for air. Keith's footsteps crunched her way.

"Congratulations. You won."

She raised her head to see him grinning, his arms crossed. To her disgust, he wasn't even breathing heavily. "Small consolation . . . if I don't live to enjoy the prize," she rasped.

"Prize?" Keith asked in mock amazement. "You expect a prize? Hmm. Okay, tell you what. Since I lost, I'll put up the bikes."

Skeptical about his jocular behavior, Shae watched as he pushed both bicycles into the shed and closed the door. She straightened as he came toward her.

"And since you're the winner," he said quietly, searching her face, "you know what you get, don't you?"

Shae felt mesmerized by the look in his eyes. "No. What?"

"This."

Placing a hand to either side of her face, he inclined his head and kissed her, stealing what little breath she'd regained. Though the kiss was feather light, her heart sped up again, and her legs threatened to fold beneath her.

"Shae!"

Tommy's gruff voice sliced through the pleasant wooziness cottoning her mind. She tore her lips from Keith's warm ones, blinking up at him, then turned to face her brother.

He stood near the inn, his stance angry. "We need to talk. Now." His dark eyes cut into Keith. "If you'll excuse us?"

Disturbed at being caught kissing Keith, but even more upset by her brother's Neanderthal behavior, Shae frowned.

"It's okay," Keith murmured behind her, speaking so only she could hear. He put a reassuring hand on her shoulder. "I'll talk to you later."

Shae watched as he strode toward the inn. When Keith neared Tommy, her brother caught his gaze, his eyes clearly issuing a warning. Keith paused then continued walking toward the front. After he disappeared from sight, Shae snapped her gaze to Tommy's.

"Just what is your problem?"

His eyes narrowed. "I might ask you the same thing. One minute you show no interest in men, the next minute you're a groupie." He said the last word as if it left a bitter taste in his mouth.

Shae's cheeks grew even hotter. "You have no idea what you're talking about. And I suggest we leave it that way. This is my life—not yours."

Wanting only to escape, she stormed toward the inn. He caught her elbow when she would have swept past. "I care, big sister, even if you don't. I don't want to see you get hurt. You have no experience in this kind of thing, and with this Keith guy, you're jumping into the major leagues instead of starting with Little League and learning how to bat first."

Shae rolled her eyes at Tommy's reference to his favorite sport. "All right, Tommy, point taken. I'll be careful. Now if that's all, I really need to get back to work—"

"No, that's not what I needed to talk to you about."

Shae's heart jumped at the change in his pitch. Low, serious, as if he had something important to say, and she wouldn't want to hear it. She looked at him. His dark eyes were solemn.

"Let's go sit on the porch and talk. We have some things we need to discuss."

8

*S*hae sank to a cushioned chair on the wraparound porch and expectantly turned to face her brother, who'd taken the seat next to her. "Well?"

"Linda's pregnant."

Shae gaped, then offered a faint grin. "Congratulations." When he didn't respond, she studied him in confusion, her smile fading. "So what's the problem? Babies are good news, right?"

He gave a curt nod, his gaze going to the trees. "There are . . . complications. You know she had a miscarriage last year . . . ," he broke off, swept an unsteady hand through his hair. "Bottom line is the doctor said that Linda needs plenty of rest, even after the baby comes. She needs someone to help out."

Shae's breath snagged in her throat. She had a feeling she knew where this was going. "So, you're going to hire a nurse?" she said hopefully. "Or a maid?"

"No." Tommy looked at her then. "I want Tiffany to come live with us."

Shae stared at him for a few seconds, then rocketed up from her chair. Moving to the railing, she kept her gaze fixed on the ocean. Tense, she clutched the white banister. "We've discussed this before, Tommy. Tiffany stays with me."

"Why, Shae? I love her, too."

Shae's grip tightened on the carved wood. How could she tell Tommy that his wife was just too immature to raise a teenager? Not that Shae was doing the greatest job of it, but Linda was two years younger than Shae and acted more like a teenybopper than an adult.

Their parents would have wanted the best for Tiffany. Shae was determined to see that wish come to fulfillment.

She turned on her heel and made her way to the door. "Case closed, Tommy. It's best for everyone concerned."

"She could die, Shae."

Tommy's quiet words halted her as she put her hand to the brass latch. Stunned, she looked at him. "What?"

"Linda. She could die."

Shae shook her head. "With the wonders of modern medicine on her side?"

"She has a weak heart. They were discussing the probability of her needing a pacemaker, but now that she's pregnant . . ."

A weak heart? Linda? Sweet, vivacious, bubbly Linda? Shae's eyes slid shut.

"Don't tell her I told you. She doesn't want anyone to know. Just please think about Tiffany coming back with us to Connecticut. She would love it on the farm. There's a good school nearby and plenty of wide-open space. Not a lot of opportunity for her to get into trouble . . ."

The pleading note in his voice combined with the worried look in his eyes stabbed into Shae. She turned her gaze toward the door. "I'll think about it," she murmured. "And, Tommy . . . I'm sorry about Linda."

She knew she should go hug him, offer some kind of comfort, but the roller coaster of emotions she'd whirled through these past weeks made her seek the solace of her locked office instead. How much more could she take? First Keith pops into her lonely life with his crazy games—knocking her off balance and causing her to tell him more than she should . . . not to mention his unexpected warm kisses catching her off guard and making her melt like a marshmallow in a flame, then Tiffany shaking up life with her unpredictable ways followed by Tommy's news of Linda. And now Tommy wanted to take her sister away from her. Hadn't she been robbed of enough in life— even if it was her own fault?

Shae dropped her face into her open hands, wondering what to do. Knowing what she should do.

꠵

Sunday dawned bright, and after early morning services, Keith and Shae hurried to catch the ferry. They hadn't been able to get a spot for Shae's car, but Keith assured her they could rent one at Port Judith.

Twenty minutes later, they sat on the third level of the sleek white ferry that chugged across the ocean. The crisp sea breeze kissed Shae's face and hair, and she deeply inhaled the familiar and loved salty smell. Seagulls screeched, and she watched them dip and sway, their white wings vivid against the washed-out blue of the sky.

During the entire trip over to the mainland, Keith was talkative—more so than usual—and he gestured with his hands a lot. The usual sunglasses were in place, and so far his anonymity was protected. However, once they hit Port Judith and rented a car for the day, he became more pensive, frowning as he drove. He gripped the steering wheel, his knuckles white.

"Keith?" He looked her way, and she offered an encouraging smile. "Everything will be fine, I'm sure. You said your mother was happy to hear from you and was looking forward to today."

Keith nodded, turning his gaze back to the windshield, but the grim look remained. "It isn't Mom I'm worried about. It's Dad." He puckered his cheeks, blowing out a noisy breath. "Like I said, we didn't exactly part on good terms. I basically left home, but he pretty much threw me out at the same time. Said if I wanted to ruin my life, he wouldn't stand by and watch." His low, emotional words clearly revealed to Shae just how much he loved his dad.

"Four years is a long time," she said gently. "I'm sure by now he's forgotten the trouble between you and is looking forward to the visit as much as your mom is."

Keith didn't look her way . . . didn't say anything.

"Tell me again about your sisters," Shae said, changing the subject, hoping to get his mind off the problem.

Keith was quiet a moment, clearly lost in thought. "Abby, the oldest, is a little boy-crazy. She should be fresh out of high school by now, if I remember right. And Candy wears braces, which are a real issue with her from what Mom wrote me several years back. Try not to notice them. Bethie's the youngest. She collects Barbie dolls and every accessory that goes with them." He chuckled. "She's probably got the complete town by now."

"They sound like a nice group of girls."

"They are. I have a brother too—Kenneth—but he had duty this weekend. He's in the Navy, stationed in Virginia Beach. One of these days I'd sure like to see him again."

"I hope that happens for you, Keith. I really do. Family is so important."

He gave a vague nod, thoughtful once more. "Shae, there's something I suppose I should tell you. Generally when someone wins a contest, it's up to them to meet with the company holding the contest. When I found out the winner was from Rhode Island and only a short distance from my hometown, I insisted on coming. Freddie wasn't too happy about it. But like I said, I sometimes get the final word."

"Then you'd planned to visit your family all along?" she asked in mild shock.

"Yeah, though I chickened out several times since I've been here." He briefly looked her way. "Your advice that morning I found you dusting really had an impact on me, though—made me think. Thank you for that."

Shae smiled. "I'm glad I could help."

"More than you know."

The drive was long, but Shae didn't mind. She enjoyed being with Keith. Now that much of her past had been laid before this man—and he hadn't rejected her—it was easier to relax around him. He still didn't know everything, nor did she plan to tell him. There was no reason to. He would be leaving for California soon.

The thought invaded like a thundercloud on a clear day.

❧

Keith turned onto a narrow residential street lined with colorful clapboard houses and pulled the car to a stop in front of a yellow one. Hollyhocks climbed the front wall and porch rail. Flowered curtains fluttered in the open windows. In the yard, a giant elm stood sentinel, a tire swing hanging from its lower branch.

Keith sucked in his lower lip. This was it.

The door flew open and a blond girl holding a toddler on one hip ran out to greet them. "Keith! You really came!"

Before he was all the way out of the car, he was engulfed in a bear hug, baby and all. When his sister pulled away, he looked down at her in shock. "Abby? Wow! You look great. I'm glad to see you put on some weight—you always were too skinny. But why are you baby-sitting on Sunday?"

Abby laughed and hefted the slipping baby higher on her hip. "I'm not, Dummy. This is Ricky." She looked at the chubby baby, then at Keith. "Say hi to your nephew."

"My nephew," Keith echoed, dumbfounded.

"Sure. Didn't you get Mom's letters? I married Matt three years ago—"

"Ab-by!" A desperate masculine shout bellowed from within the house, interrupting her.

"Oops. Sandra must need a diaper change. I'd recognize that frantic tone in Matt's voice any day. I still haven't convinced him to help with that chore, though he does with all the others," Abby explained hurriedly, as she walked back up the stairs. "Come on in. Don't be a lug and stand out here all day." She disappeared into the house.

"Are you okay?" Shae asked softly, putting a hand to his arm.

Keith nodded, but he wasn't sure if he was. Why didn't he remember reading about Abby getting married? Three years ago . . . must have been during his first European tour. His stint with drugs and drinking had probably aided in his forgetfulness too. Or maybe he was just dense. He honestly didn't remember reading about Abby's marriage.

Making an effort to compose himself, he threw a faint grin Shae's way and walked with her up the sidewalk. Before they reached the door, a tiny woman wearing a huge smile rushed out to greet them.

"Keith!" She hurtled into his arms.

"Mom?" He hugged her close. After a long moment, she pulled away, her blue eyes watery. Gray hairs had replaced most of the blond ones, and her face had more wrinkles. With a pang of worry, he noted she looked tired. "You okay?" he asked, putting an arm around her shoulders.

"I am now that you came."

Keith smiled, wiped her tears away with his thumb then looked at Shae. "This is Shae Stevens, Mom. The girl I told you about."

His mom turned to Shae, taking one of Shae's hands in both of hers. "What a pleasure to meet you! Keith told me that his being here is largely due to you. I want to thank you from the bottom of my heart, though there are no words to express how grateful I am for this day—" She broke off, her words wobbly.

"Don't mind my family. They're all a bit overemotional," Keith said with a wink to Shae.

"Oh, you!" Keith's mother playfully struck her son's shoulder. "Well, come on inside. Dinner won't be for another thirty minutes, but I've got chips and pretzels, and I can open a can of salted nuts—"

"Mom," Keith said softly, "don't fuss. We'll be fine until dinner." He sobered. "Dad around?"

"He's reading the paper. You know how your father likes to keep informed."

Keith reached for Shae's hand as they walked into the cozy mulberry and tan den scattered with appliqués and doilies of all sizes. His father looked up from where he sat in a recliner, a pair of reading glasses perched on the end of his nose. He stood, setting down the newspaper, and eyed Keith with weary blue eyes.

"Hello, Keith," he said, no sign of animosity in his tone.

"Dad." Keith barely got the greeting out. His father had aged, though he must only be in his early fifties. Yet the wheat-colored hair was almost white, and numerous lines Keith didn't remember covered most of his face. He looked as if life had beaten him.

He extended a gnarled hand, and Keith took it in an awkward handshake. Both men tried to hold emotion back, but failed, and his father pulled Keith into a strong embrace. "It's good to have you home, Son."

The low, emphatic words unleashed a few drops of wetness, and Keith swiped a hand over his cheeks to rid them of tears while he pulled away. "It's good to be home, Dad."

A young teenager, whom Keith guessed to be Tiffany's age, strode into the room. She flashed a faint tin smile, braces covering her teeth. "Hi," she said a little nervously.

"Candy!" Keith moved to hug his sister. "You've hardly changed. Except your hair is curlier and lighter than it was." He was relieved to find someone who had stayed pretty much the same since he'd left. "Too much sun, or are you using hair color? It's pretty," he added hastily, seeing her cheeks and forehead go pink.

"I'm Beth."

"Bethie?" he whispered, his eyes going wide. "But when I left, you were playing with Barbie dolls and had freckles and braids." His gaze swept over her and he noted the curves underneath the striped T-shirt and baggy jeans. On second glance at her face he noticed she was wearing makeup too.

She wrinkled her nose in a saucy way. "Get real, Keith. I'm too old to play with dolls now."

"Yes, I can see that." His voice was strained. "So, how old are you?"

"I turned fourteen last winter. You do remember my birthday is a week before Christmas, don't you?" she asked tartly.

"Bethany Anne Travers—we'll have none of that," his father said. "Apologize to your brother."

She sighed and rolled her eyes. "Sorry, Keith. I'm really glad you found time to visit. I need to go back to the kitchen and finish making the salad now. Later."

She pranced from the room, and Keith sank onto the couch, every part of him feeling the shock. Shae took a place beside him. "You okay?" she asked, looping her hand around his arm and leaning close.

"I don't know." Keith sat perched on the edge of the sofa, staring at the floor, his forearms resting on his thighs. "So much has changed."

"Beth has developed an attitude this past year," his father explained. "Don't mind her, Son."

The front door banged open, and a beautiful woman with wheat blond hair and bright blue eyes rushed into the room, followed by a dark-haired man who eyed Keith with awe. He already knew who the girl was. He only had three sisters. But if he hadn't known for certain, Keith would've never believed the elegant young woman standing in front of him in the chic designer suit was Candy.

"Keith!" She ran to him, knelt on the floor and hugged him hard.

"Hi, Candy," he murmured, giving her a limp hug back. "You've changed. You're a real knockout now."

"Uh, thanks—I think," Candy said uncertainly, her straight white teeth, minus the braces, flashing in a pretty smile. "I want you to meet Carl." She looked with adoration at the man beside her. "We are going to be married at the end of the year. I hope you can come to the wedding, Keith."

Keith soundlessly formed the word "married," then shook his head. "Yeah, sure," he said, not really knowing what he was saying. Too much was happening too fast, and he needed to get away. "If you guys will excuse me for a minute, I'll be right back."

He offered Shae a faint smile then strode from the sofa and onto the back porch. Inhaling the pungent air fragrant with the scent of his mother's rosebushes, he closed his eyes. Well, at least one thing hadn't changed—his mother's love of roses.

Walking around to the side of the house where the old oak stood, he studied the high leafy branches. He almost gave a sigh of relief to see the old tree house—rotting, and minus wooden planks—but still there. Seeing his childhood refuge brought comfort. He almost wished he were a kid again and could escape into the private world he and Kenneth had shared. What fun they'd had! Pretending to be pirates hiding treasure . . . frequently peering between branches and looking for enemy ships dotting the wide ocean.

Keith shook his head. How time flew. It seemed like only yesterday they'd been troublesome boys playing pranks. Like the soap that turned the skin black. That had happened on a Sunday morning, and the family had been late to church because of it. Keith and Kenneth hadn't been able to sit down for some time after that.

A finger tapped his shoulder, breaking into his reverie, and he turned. Feminine arms wrapped around his neck, and a curvy body pressed close while a pair of soft lips landed on his in a kiss that sizzled. Bewildered by the past twenty minutes, as well as the present few seconds, Keith did nothing, feeling powerless to stop the kiss that might have lasted a few seconds or an eternity for all he knew. When she pulled away, he looked down into a pair of sea-green eyes.

"Welcome home, Keith."

"Heather."

She tried to kiss him again, but he stepped back.

Heather's brows drew down into a frown. "Aren't you happy to see me?"

"Sure," Keith said uneasily. "You've changed."

And she had, though he probably would have recognized her. The ponytail and cheerleading outfits were gone, of course, but the woman standing in front of him looked like she could have stepped off the cover of a high fashion magazine. A long-sleeved green top hugged full curves and was cut low enough to leave little to the imagination and high enough to give a glimpse of her tanned midriff. Slim-fitting pants revealed she was still model-thin. She wore three-inch stacked heels, making her legs seem even longer. Sunny blond hair swirled around her shoulders in the latest style.

She was beautiful, but Keith wasn't tempted.

As if Heather could read his mind, her eyes hardened. "What's the matter, Keith? Now that you're a big celebrity, I'm not good enough for you anymore?" She stepped toward him and looked up coyly, her hand going to his chest. "Why don't you give me a chance? I've missed you. Maybe I don't have as much experience as those glamorous stars you've dated. But I'm willing to learn." She trailed a coral fingernail down the middle of his chest.

Grabbing her hand hard, he stopped its trek.

"Ow! You're hurting me." She looked up and bit her lower lip when she saw his angry gaze.

"You're a little old to play with fire, aren't you, Heather?"

"What do you mean?"

"Stop trying to act like something you're not. And why are you wearing *that*? It's not even your style."

She smiled. "Do you like it? I wore it especially for you."

"No. It makes you look cheap."

She pouted. "What's wrong with you, anyway? We're not innocent kids playing at love anymore. We're supposed to be two adults. So why don't you treat me like one?" She moved closer. "You might even find you like it."

Keith gripped her upper arms, pushing her back. "I didn't come home to rekindle a high school romance. There's someone else in my life."

He saw the hurt flash in her eyes and felt instant remorse for his gruff behavior. They had known each other for years, played on the same street, grown up together.

"Heather, I know I left without saying good-bye, and I'm sorry. It wasn't very nice of me. But we had already drifted apart—"

"Who is she?"

He blew out a breath. "It doesn't really matter, okay? It's been over four years. There were no promises made between us."

"Is she here today? Is that her car out front?"

"Keith?"

His mother's voice came clearly to them before she rounded the corner. Keith quickly stepped away from his former girlfriend.

"Oh, hello, Heather. I didn't know you were here."

"Hi, Mrs. Travers."

"Why don't you come in and say hello to everyone? It's been awhile since we've seen you," his mother said, to Keith's chagrin. The last thing he wanted was for Heather and Shae to meet. He had enough problems trying to gain Shae's trust. This could spoil everything.

Keith firmly took Heather's upper arm, pointing her in the direction of her house. "I think Heather has to go home now—"

"Oh, don't be silly, Keith," she purred, smiling up at him. "I can come in for a minute just to say hi. Besides, I'd love to meet your *girlfriend*."

"Well, then, that's settled," his mother said. "Come along, Heather."

Heather broke away from his grasp, and Keith watched the two women walk ahead of him. Shaking his head in dismay, he had little choice but to follow.

9

$\mathcal{S}$hae politely pretended to listen to Carl give an elaborate account of the house he and Candy had found, her mind all the while wondering what had happened to Keith. He'd been gone a long time.

The back door opened, and she looked up. A voluptuous blond glided in beside Keith's mom. Keith followed. Shae's eyes widened. The coral dots in the pattern of his gray sweater matched his lips. Was he wearing lipstick? Taking another look at the blond, Shae solved the mystery.

Her heart seemed to freeze into a chunk of ice. Tommy had warned her she was playing in the major leagues. Shae knew how popular Keith was with women. If she hadn't listened, it was her own fault.

"Heather," Candy said, obviously uneasy, "what are you doing here?"

Heather. The cheerleading captain. Of course.

"Just wanted to say hi to my old friends." She turned narrowed green eyes on Shae. "Hello. I don't believe we've met."

"Shae Stevens." Her voice came out strained.

"Heather Fontaine." With graceful ease, she covered the distance and perched on a chair across from the couch. "So tell me, Shae, how did you meet Keith? Are you one of his fans?"

Keith strode their way. "Heather, I don't think—"

Candy shot up from the couch. "Keith, can I talk to you a minute? Excuse us." She grabbed his arm and escorted him from the room as though she were a jailer taking a prisoner to his cell.

Shae looked on in confusion. *What was that all about?*

Carl cleared his throat and asked Keith's father if he'd like to check out his new car. Agreeing, the older man hastily stood, and the pair left the room.

Heather's gaze roamed Shae's face, hair, and rose-colored silk dress, and she gave her a smile that didn't quite reach her eyes. "I hope you didn't think my question rude, Shae. But, well, you see, I've known Keith a long time. As a matter of fact, we went steady in high school all through our junior and senior years, and I've really been looking forward to seeing him again—"

Abby rounded the corner, carrying Ricky. "Heather! It's been ages." She gave her a quick hug. "Come and see the baby. Come on. She looks just like a little doll when she's asleep."

Heather rose and went with Abby, though it was obvious she didn't want to. Keith strode back into the room, minus the lipstick on his mouth and wearing a sheepish expression on his face.

Shae dropped her gaze to a pile of boating magazines on the table. He sank to the cushion beside her. "Shae, about Heather—"

"Dinner's ready!" Keith's mom singsonged from the open kitchen door. "Where is everybody?"

"Mr. Travers and Carl went to check out Carl's new car," Shae said in a monotone. "I think the ladies are looking at the baby."

"Oh. Well, come along you two. I'll get the others." The woman whisked out the front door.

Keith put a hand over Shae's clasped ones resting on her knees. "Shae, as I was saying . . ."

Beth breezed into the room from the kitchen. "Have either of you two seen Abby?"

Shae pulled her hands away from Keith and motioned to the hallway beyond. Once the girl headed that direction, Keith spoke again. "I'm not sure what you're thinking, but I can guess. Shae, it's not how it looks—"

The front door swung open and Keith's mom, dad, and Carl piled inside. "Come on you two," Keith's mom said, gesturing with her arm. "Don't want the food to get cold."

Keith blew out a short, irritated breath. "We'll talk later. This isn't over."

Shae turned her head and looked directly into his eyes. "Yes, Keith. I think maybe it is."

❧

Silence shrouded the car. Keith had tried several times to explain about Heather, but each time Shae focused her attention out her window at the passing scenery. Although the last time he'd tried to explain, she did give a brief nod—not encouraging, but at least it showed she was listening. Frustrated, he concentrated on the road and mentally reviewed the disastrous day.

Not all bad, he relented. Being reunited with his family—especially his father—had been worth any embarrassment or frustration Keith had suffered. After dinner, his dad had taken him aside and they'd had a long talk. Though no mention was made of Keith's career, his father treated Keith as though no harsh words had ever been spoken between them—even suggesting that the next time Keith made it to Rhode Island they go sailing.

And Keith planned to visit again. As often as he could. The shock of seeing the changes in his family made Keith realize he didn't want to miss out on their lives any more than he had to. He shouldn't have been surprised at the differences, since he, too, had changed in four years. Yet he'd kept a mental picture of the way they'd been when he left, expecting to see that same picture today.

Loud inhaling followed by a melodic hum alerted Keith that Shae had fallen asleep. He smiled. She really did have a musical snore.

At the docks they took back the rental and barely made it to the ferry in time for its scheduled departure. Once aboard, Keith turned to Shae. "Did you have a good nap?"

Her eyes narrowed in suspicion. "Fair. Why do you ask?"

"Oh, no reason." She was still testy, and Keith decided now was not the time for banter.

Instead he filled the hour talking about his family and was relieved when she joined in the conversation, seeming to relax. Soon they docked at Old Harbor. By the time they reached The Roosting Place, the sky flamed in the west with deep ribbons of orange, melon, and coral. Keith would have liked to enjoy the sunset with Shae, or what he could see of it over the trees, but she dashed up the porch steps and into the inn before he could suggest it. Frustrated, Keith lingered on the porch and eyed the partially open door, wondering what he could say to fix things between them.

"Tiffany!"

At Shae's agonized shout, Keith rushed into the inn. No one was in the lobby, except Katie, who stood behind the desk, her eyes wide.

"Where's Shae?" he asked.

She pointed down the hallway that led to the old storage room. As he approached it, he saw the door standing ajar.

Inside, Tiffany stood on the second rung of the stepladder, her face a mask of shock. She stared down at Shae, who knelt beside the ladder and picked up something off the floor. On closer scrutiny, Keith could see it was the crystal angel that he'd tried to examine his first week at the inn.

"Oh, no!" Shae moaned.

"I'm sorry, Shae. I didn't mean to. I just wanted to look at it. And then when you came in here all mad, like you did, it slipped out of my hand. . . ." Tiffany's words trailed away as Shae's gaze snapped upward.

"It's chipped, Tiffany. The wing is chipped."

"I'm really sorry," the girl said in a voice trembling with tears. "I . . . I never meant to break it."

"You had no right to come in here without permission," Shae bit out, rising to her feet and cradling the angel.

Seeing that Tiffany was shaking all over, Keith strode into the room. "Shae, calm down. It was an accident."

Shae turned on him, her dark eyes full of pain and anger. "Stay out of it, Keith."

"She was my mother too!" Tiffany screeched, tears rolling down her face. "I may have been a little girl when she died, but I loved her just as much!" With a loud sob, she jumped down from the stepladder and made a beeline for the door.

Shae's eyes closed, and she took a shaky breath.

Keith moved toward her. "Are you okay?"

She looked his way. He was struck by the childlike vulnerability clouding her face. Moved with compassion, he reached out to touch her, but she drew back. "Really, I'm fine. I'm tired. It's just been a long day."

His gaze lowered to the angel she still cradled to her breast. "Want me to see if I can fix that? I used to be pretty handy with a glue gun."

She gave a little shake of her head, a faint troubled smile on her lips. "It's just a piece of glass, right? Don't worry about it. It's not that big a deal." Her words didn't mesh with the tone of her voice. She stepped around him. "I've got work to do before I turn in. Thanks for taking me to meet your family."

At the reminder, he grimaced. "I'm just sorry about what happened with Heather. I had no idea she would show—"

"Really, Keith. It's okay." She looked at him again. "I understand." With jerky steps she hurried out the door.

Keith noticed she didn't replace the angel on the shelf, but instead took it with her.

❧

Huge celestial beings, their wings spanning across the sky, loomed over the little family who laughed and frolicked on the sandy beach not far from the lighthouse. Shae called out, but they couldn't seem to hear. As she watched, the angels' faces became grotesque, frightening. She screamed. But no sound issued from her mouth.

Her mother looked up and spotted her, smiling, motioning for her to join them. Shae seemed to be the only one capable of seeing the menacing angels overhead. She watched, horrified, as one of them took its mighty sword and struck her father down. Shae soundlessly screamed again and tried to run to help. But her way was littered with shards of broken crystal—her feet, barefoot and bleeding. She looked up and helplessly watched as the angel struck her mother down from behind . . .

"Shae!"

Insistent hands shook her. Her eyes flickered open, but the room was dark and she couldn't see well. Her heart banged against her rib cage. Her throat felt raw and raspy. The fragrance of spicy cologne filled her nostrils.

"Keith?" she whispered.

"It's me. You were having a nightmare."

Remembering, she shuddered and held to his arms.

"Are you okay?" he asked gently.

"I . . . I think so." With his help, she inched up to a sitting position against the pillow and noticed she lay on the couch in the family parlor. To her left, snow filled the TV screen with soft static. "It was the dream again."

She stiffened. Why had she told him that?

He sank to the edge of the cushion, near her legs. The blue-white glow from the television made it easy to see the concern written in his eyes. "Do you want to tell me about it?"

For a moment she considered, then shook her head. She'd never told anyone about the nightmare. "It was just a silly dream."

"Not silly enough to keep you from screaming out."

Her eyes widened. "I screamed?"

He nodded. "Several times. If I hadn't been walking by the door, I wouldn't have heard you. You had it closed."

Embarrassed, Shae dropped her gaze to the blanket. She crossed her arms over her sweatshirt, hugging herself.

"I'm a good listener," Keith said softly. "Sometimes it helps to talk."

Shae gave a short nod. She felt drained, helpless. What was left of her defenses began to crumble under his gentle concern, his strength, and his protection. He knew the worst and hadn't ridiculed her or run away—though he didn't know the details. She'd never told a soul any of it—not even her grandmother. For over seven intolerable years she'd carried the burden alone. . . .

"Please, Shae, let me help," he said, putting a light hand on the blanket that covered her upraised knee. "Don't shut me out. I care."

At his soft plea, she closed her eyes and nodded. Before she could change her mind, the whole horrible dream spilled from her mouth. Afterward he took her in his arms and held her head close to his chest for a long time. The reassuring steady thud of his heartbeat calmed her trembling.

"It was just a dream," he murmured, smoothing a hand over her hair. "Just a dream."

Shae closed her eyes. It was much more than that. It was her penance. Something she deserved. But for him to understand, she would have to tell him what happened that day . . . and suddenly, she wanted to, though she didn't understand why.

Her gaze went to the crystal figurine on the coffee table. Light from the TV sparked off its gown and wings. She shuddered.

"Shae?" Keith asked, worried.

She took a shaky breath. Lying with her head against his chest like this, one of his arms wrapped around her back, his hand stroking her hair, made it easier. Much easier than facing him.

"I . . . I've had the dream since the accident," she began, her voice a raspy whisper, "since after the picnic at the bluffs. I was a little older than Tiffany at the time." She took an unsteady breath. "I had turned into a rebel. My parents weren't around much, and I was angry. I took up with the wrong crowd and got into drinking and partying. We three kids stayed here with Grandma that summer, and when my parents suddenly showed up one week we were thrilled. I had thought we'd go home with them when they left—that they'd come to get us."

Shae swallowed hard. "At the picnic they told us they were off to Europe in the morning and that we were to stay behind. I got really mad, screamed a lot of things—things I didn't really mean." She felt the tears burn her nose. "I yelled that I wished they were dead. That they only cared about their career, and that if they really cared about us they would take another flight and stay longer than just three days. Then I ran from the beach and up the stairs to the road. A friend of mine was driving by. I hitched a ride with her, and she lit up a joint to calm me down."

Keith's arm tightened around Shae's trembling back, giving her the courage she needed to go on.

"When I got to the inn, I couldn't think straight I was so high. I'd told my friend what happened, and she supported me—making me even angrier with my parents. I ran to my room. On my bureau was a crystal angel Mama had given me—a twin to the one Tiffany broke. Mama told me when she gave it to me that it was a reminder—that whenever we were apart, each of us would have the angel to remind us God and His angels were watching over us—holding our family together. I picked it up and hurled it at the wall. I–It shattered. Later Mama came to talk to me, but I w–wouldn't listen, and we got into a fight."

Shae sobbed brokenly, putting a hand to her face. "Th–they changed their plans to s–spend more time with me. Their plane crashed—and they died."

Keith stilled his hand on her hair and cupped her head. "Oh, Shae, I'm sorry. So very sorry . . ."

"If it h–hadn't been for me, they would've taken that earlier flight. They'd s–still be alive today. It's my fault they're dead."

"Shae, that's not true."

"Yes, it is. I killed them."

Shae's soft, pitiful words threatened to rip his heart. He pulled away from her and cradled her tear-smudged face, lifting it to see into her eyes. "You did not kill them, Shae. What happened was an accident, something over which you had no control. It's understandable that you wanted more time with them—and most children have tantrums and say and do things they don't mean. You can't go on blaming yourself for what happened. It's not your fault."

She didn't answer, only looked at him with those dark, wounded eyes. Keith could see that she didn't believe a word he said. Drawing her close again, he closed his eyes, searching for something to say to convince her. But this went too deep for him. She needed more help than he could give.

Hoping God would still listen to him, despite all he'd done, Keith sent a silent prayer upward for Shae.

⁓❧

Shae riffled the corner pages of the ledger and stared out the window, thinking. Last night, when she confided in Keith after the horrible nightmare, she'd temporarily forgotten the upsetting incident with Heather. Since then, she'd mulled it over. Remembering Keith's chagrined explanations in the car on the way back to Port Judith then reflecting on how Heather had approached Shae—immediately making it a point to imply that she and Keith had something going—Shae was more inclined to believe Keith innocent. Or was she just so naïve concerning men that she didn't know better?

The rapid click of high heels startled her, and she turned her head and watched as Hillary rushed through the open door. One look at her anxious expression told Shae it was going to be a bad day.

"Shae, I don't know what to do. Robert didn't come home last night. I called his friends and found out he went to the mainland again. And I don't know what he does there, or who to contact to get ahold of him."

Alarm prickled through Shae. "I'm sure he'll be back soon."

"When he's gone there before, he's usually back before morning," Hillary worriedly continued, as though she hadn't heard. "And it's four o'clock now."

Shae's eyes flew to the clock. Four o'clock! She'd have to get on the phone fast if she were to find a replacement for tonight's floor show. "Hillary, go home. He may be trying to call. I'll find someone else. But, Hillary," her voice held gentle warning, "this can't continue. Please explain it to Robert when you talk to him. I have an inn to run."

Hillary nodded, tears swimming in her eyes. Shae rose from behind her desk and went to her, giving the distraught woman a hug. "It'll be okay. There's probably a simple explanation for everything."

After Hillary left, Shae set to work. Fifteen minutes later she folded her arms on top of her desk and laid her head down on them, too discouraged to go on.

"That bad, huh?"

Hearing Keith's warm baritone, Shae lifted her head and gave a dry laugh. "Hillary can't perform tonight—Robert's missing. And unless I hire fifteen-year-old Phillip Starnes with his amazing tuba, or Billy Grafton and his dancing dog, Fluffy, then I haven't got an act."

"So I take it that means you'll have to provide the entertainment tonight."

She gave a weary nod, her eyes going to the crystal angel now sitting on her desk. "I'm just not sure I can sing after last night."

A long pause. "Would you like some help?"

Surprised, Shae looked at him. "Help?"

"I'll sing with you. We'll make it a duet."

Her eyes widened. "Aren't you afraid your cover will be blown? That you'll be recognized and stampeded?"

"No," he said calmly. "From what I've seen, the audience that frequents your nightclub is mostly of an older generation. I think I'll be safe. Besides, none of the tourists that have stayed here seemed to recognize me."

"Well, that's true," she said uncertainly. "But won't Freddie mind?"

"He's in his room with his laptop, answering E-mail and making calls. He won't know. Besides, he doesn't *own* me, Shae. I don't have to get his permission."

Mulling his clipped words over, she rubbed her temples.

"Headache?" he asked more softly.

She nodded. "Not a bad one. Just started an hour ago."

"Why don't you go upstairs, lie down, and I'll bring you some tea. I've heard chamomile is great when you need to relax."

Despite the constant dull thudding at her temples, Shae managed a smile. "I appreciate the offer, Keith, but there just isn't time. The show starts in less than three hours. I'll pop a couple of aspirin or something." She considered his other offer. Remembering how supportive he'd been last night, and how comforting his support had felt, Shae regarded him. "But I would like you to sing with me."

His eyes lit up. "I look forward to it."

~

Not long before show time, Keith searched for Shae but couldn't find her. He approached Katie at the desk. "Have you seen Shae?"

"In the kitchen, I think."

Keith thanked her and headed that way. He found Shae standing by the sink, tossing a half-squeezed lemon into the disposal.

"What are you doing?"

She held up a glass full of something that looked like milky water. "Lemon water. It helps clear my throat, so I can sing better. Want some?"

Keith stared doubtfully at the concoction. "Er, no thanks." He pulled a small aerosol spray bottle from his pocket. "I use this—it's specially designed for singers."

She lifted the glass in a toast. "Oh. Well, bottoms up."

Wondering how she could stand to chug such sour stuff, he took another look at her deep blue, sequined cocktail dress. "Sorry. All I have to wear is this," he said, motioning to his blue cotton shirt and gray pants. "I didn't exactly come prepared."

She pulled the empty glass away from her mouth and set it on the counter. "No problem. At least we match. That's what's important." Her brow furrowed. "And of course it's important that our voices blend well. I hadn't thought of that when I agreed to this. What if we don't click?"

Keith smiled. "Well, if you're ready, let's go find out."

They went to the dining room and hurried backstage. Shae suddenly whirled to face him, as if something had just occurred to her. "Keith, do you know any show tunes from the golden years of music? That's basically what we sing here, though we do one or two modern songs too." She named a few of the more modern ones.

Keith shook his head. "Don't know any of them. Sorry."

"Hmm." Averting her gaze, Shae screwed her mouth up in a thoughtful expression. She snapped her fingers, looking up. "What about 'You Light Up My Life'? Know that one?"

"I remember my mom listening to it when I was a kid." Keith frowned. "Not sure I know the words, though."

Shae hurried to a table against the wall that held a receptacle of sheet music. Thumbing through the large box, she grinned, triumphantly pulling a paper out. "There. Think you could learn the words in the time before we go on?"

"I've been in trickier situations." He took the music. "But are we only going to sing one song, or do a set?"

Shae stuck out her lower lip, blowing out a loud breath that stirred her hair at her temple. "I hadn't thought of that. I'm usually so much better prepared. . . ."

"Want me to sing one or two of my songs?"

She gave him a faint smile. "No offense, Keith. But they rock a bit too much for this place."

"I could do 'The Old Rugged Cross,'" he joked.

She shook her head, then stared, her brow slowly wrinkling in thought. "You know, that might not be such a bad idea."

"Here?" Keith said incredulously. "In a nightclub?"

"I own the place, remember? And what the manager says, goes." She grinned.

"Your customers might not like it."

She shrugged. "They're lucky to be getting any music at all—especially with how this day has gone. Besides, as you pointed out, our crowds are usually older. I say we give it a shot."

"Okay, if you're sure. And if we're doing something like that anyway, maybe for a third number we can sing 'Angels to Watch over Us.' Got the sheet music for that? It's a gospel song from about fifteen years ago, I think. It was a favorite of Mom's. I remember some of the words, but not all of them."

Shae stiffened and turned away. "No. Sorry." She pulled out another sheet and handed it over sideways without facing him. "How about this one?"

Keith studied her, not sure if he was just imagining Shae's sudden withdrawal, or if it was the stress of the moment. Probably it was the situation that made her shoulders tremble and her voice come out funny. Memory of her nightmare flashed through his mind, and he mentally kicked himself. Of course she wouldn't want to sing a song like that right now!

He slowly pulled her into a gentle hug. "Buck up, Partner," he whispered, "we can do this."

She nodded against his chest.

Thirty minutes later, they took the stage amid polite applause. No one announced them, and for that Keith was grateful. He'd been pretty certain he wouldn't be recognized when he'd first offered to sing with Shae, but it was still a relief that no face in the crowd lit with recognition. Although it was hard to see anyone in the dark area with the bright lights of the stage blinding him.

He and Shae had practiced backstage earlier, but here at the microphone, with Shae playing the piano and Keith sitting beside her, he was amazed at just how harmoniously their voices blended. Judging from the enthusiastic audience response, the crowd was pleased as well. They sang two more numbers, and afterward Keith took the piano to sing the gospel hymn, hoping Shae wasn't mistaken and it would be received well. After the last note trailed in the air, there were a few seconds of nerve-wracking silence, followed by a loud wave of applause. Keith let out a relieved breath, faced the crowd, and inclined his head in a bow while Shae did the same, also saying a soft "thank you" into the mike.

Once backstage, he pulled her into a tight hug, which she returned. "You did great," he said. "We belong together, Shae. Our voices blend so well—"

"Young man? Young man!" A plump middle-aged woman in a green suit dress waddled up to Keith, another woman with her. Wetness glimmered on the first woman's cheeks, and she smiled at him. "I just wanted to tell you how much your last song moved me. It was lovely. I haven't heard that song since my father sang it."

Keith smiled. "Thank you. I'm glad you enjoyed it."

"Do you sing? I mean professionally."

"Uh," Keith looked to Shae, "now and then."

"Well, you have a wonderful voice. God gave you a remarkable talent, and I hope you continue using it for Him."

Keith just stared, managed a nod.

She pulled a card from her clasped purse. "I'm Theda London. I'm a pastor's wife, and I would love for you to come sing at our church this summer—in Connecticut."

"I'm sorry. I'm leaving for California Friday. I'm only visiting Rhode Island."

"Oh, what a shame. Well, if you're ever in town . . ."

Keith thanked the woman again, and after she left, he turned to Shae. She looked up at him. "I didn't know you were leaving Friday."

Keith grimaced. "I was going to wait for a better time to tell you. There are several things I want to say—"

"Shae!"

At Hillary's frantic cry, they turned in her direction as she rushed toward them. A panic-stricken look filled her eyes. "I just heard. Robert is in the hospital—he . . . he had a car accident. He's in emergency surgery now. Oh, Shae, what am I going to do?"

"You're going to go to him." Shae looped an arm around Hillary. "And I'll go with you."

Hillary shook her head. "He's on the mainland, Shae. And the last ferry has left by now."

"I can try to charter a flight at the airport," Keith said.

"The airport?" Shae echoed hollowly.

"Thank you, Keith," Hillary sniffled. "I just can't seem to think straight. I don't know what to do." She turned teary eyes Shae's way. "You're the only friend I've got on the island. Will you come with me? I'm so scared."

Keith noticed how Shae's face had paled. He put a hand to the middle of her back. "I'll come too."

She stared at him, then slowly nodded, terror in her eyes.

10

*S*hae tried to push down her panic as she stared at the small plane. The reverberations on the tarmac, coming from the loud engine, matched the pounding of her heart. How could she go through with this? She'd flown many times before, but not since her parents died. Twice she'd almost declined and returned to the inn, but each time Shae had glanced at Hillary's distraught face and kept silent. Yet Keith understood.

Shae looked his way now. He stared at her with sympathetic concern etched on his features and held out a hand. She took it, clutching it hard, desperately soaking up every ounce of support he offered. She was doubly relieved she had told him everything. Well, almost everything. There was no reason to tell him the rest. He would be gone in a few days.

Saddened by the thought, Shae wrinkled her brow.

"Watch your step," the pilot warned when Shae slipped on the stair leading up to the metal monster that she was willfully allowing to devour her. . . .

"I'm right behind you," Keith said close to her ear, helping her into the plane.

The takeoff was bumpy, and Shae gripped Keith's arm with both hands, feeling her heart lurch. Unable to stop herself, she took one brief look out the small window at the dark ocean below—too far below for her peace of mind. The same ocean that had sucked her parents into its great belly.

Shae's eyelids slammed shut. She wouldn't look. Her fingernails made creases in Keith's jacket. Somehow, she had to find the strength to be there for Hillary—but she couldn't think about anything like that now, when she felt so weak inside.

Keith had said the trip to the mainland only took a little over ten minutes, but it seemed more like eons to Shae. When the plane finally set down with a powerful jolt, shaking her in her seat as if it would try to destroy her yet, her eyes flew open. She watched with horrified fascination as they sped down the runway. When they came to a stop and deplaned, her legs trembled so badly she found it difficult to walk, and again Keith stayed beside her, this time putting an arm around her waist until she'd regained some composure.

"I'm proud of you," he said for her ears alone. "I know that wasn't easy."

Shae nodded, gave him a faint smile then looked at Hillary. Now that she'd safely made it through the ordeal, Shae needed to focus on her friend. "You okay, Hillary?"

The woman gave a slight nod, staring at the ground. "They wouldn't tell me much," she murmured. Frightened eyes turned Shae's way. "Oh, Shae. What if he doesn't make it? What will I do without him?"

Shae moved from Keith and put an arm around Hillary's shoulders. "Let's not think about things like that right now. I'm with you, and I'll stay tonight as long as you need me."

After a long taxi ride, they arrived at the hospital. Coming out of the dark night into the glaring lights of the pristine building temporarily blinded Shae. Keith, as he usually did when in public, slipped on his sunglasses, and for a moment Shae wished she also had a pair. The events of the past few hours had brought on her headache again. At least she'd had the foresight to exchange the scratchy sequined dress for a comfortable sweatshirt and pants before leaving the inn. They approached the information desk, where a harried nurse glanced up.

"I'm Mrs. Collins," Hillary said, a tremor in her voice. "I was told my husband is in surgery. He . . . he had an accident."

The nurse directed them to the small waiting area outside surgery. Hillary sank onto one of the cushioned chairs while Shae informed the nurse behind the computer at the nurses' station that Mrs. Collins had arrived, and asked if there was any news. The nurse shook her head.

Keith went to a nearby table where an automatic coffeemaker sat and poured three cups of hot coffee. He handed Hillary a cup, and she took it with a soft "thank you."

The minute hand on the big face of the round clock above the nurses' counter seemed to creep by as though taking its last breath. Except for their presence, the waiting area was clear. Nurses hurried about their duties, their white shoes creaking softly down immaculate corridors. From beyond the nurses' station, the muted ding-ding of a bell issued a quiet alert.

Keith thumbed through a magazine. Hillary sat forward and stared into space, ignoring her coffee, and Shae sat quietly beside her, glancing at her watch now and then to be sure the clock was right.

"What's taking so long?" Hillary moaned. "It's been over two hours since I got the phone call."

Shae put an arm around her shoulders, not knowing what to say. After the minute hand had crept halfway to the other side of the round clock, a tall man in scrubs appeared in the corridor. His face was lined and weary as he approached. "Mrs. Collins?"

Hillary stood, her face blanched by fear, and went to meet him, Shae by her side. "I'm Mrs. Collins."

His brown eyes were solemn. "I'm Dr. Brent. Your husband is being transferred to recovery. He's a lucky man, Mrs. Collins. His heart stopped once on the operating table, but we were able to resuscitate him. We stopped the internal bleeding, but the next few hours are crucial. As for his facial . . ." He broke off, obviously ill at ease when he noted how Hillary folded against Shae. "The lacerations were extensive and will require plastic surgery at a later date—"

"P–plastic surgery," Hillary repeated.

"Yes," he said more gently. "I won't lie to you—his chances of making it are slim, but we're doing everything we can. And Mrs. Collins, if you believe in prayer, I'd recommend it. If your husband does pull through, it's going to be a long haul on the road ahead."

"Wh–when can I see him?" she breathed.

"As soon as he has been moved to the ICU," the doctor promised. After a few more words describing Robert's other injuries, he left them, promising to keep her informed.

Shae held onto Hillary, who went limp against her. "Let's sit down," she suggested softly, steering her back to the chair and taking a place beside her. "Is there any family that should be notified?"

Hillary shook her head. "Robert is a foster child, and never talked about his family." Her voice came dull. "My parents live in Portsmouth, but I doubt they'd care. They never did like Robert."

"Still you should call them," Shae said, putting a gentle hand to her back. "I'm sure they care about you and would want to be here for you." In Shae's opinion, Hillary needed something to do, to occupy her mind. Such things helped when the grief was overwhelming.

Hillary nodded and walked woodenly to the phone on a nearby table. Keith took the empty chair next to Shae. "I heard the doctor from here. He has the type of voice that carries. How's she doing?"

"Not good. About as well as can be expected." Shae put her hands to her temples and rubbed with circular motions.

"Headache back?"

She nodded.

"Let me."

Shae was surprised when she felt his hand slip under her hair and circle the nape of her neck, his fingers beginning a slow, firm massage. She closed her eyes and relaxed.

"You've been under a lot of stress. You need rest. Have you eaten today?"

Shae thought back. Had she? "Breakfast. I had breakfast."

"As soon as they allow Hillary to see her husband, we're going to the cafeteria to get you some food."

"I can't leave her now," Shae protested.

"If you don't take care of yourself, you won't be any good for your friend. Especially if they have to put you in one of those hospital beds."

Shae gave a reluctant nod.

Later, after a nurse finally informed Hillary that she could see Robert, Shae told Hillary she'd be back soon and walked with Keith to the elevator. Inside the small enclosure, two young girls stopped chattering and eyed Keith. They began to whisper to one another, and Shae caught a few of their words.

"Is it him?"

"I don't know—ask him."

"Me! Why don't you?"

When the elevator doors whooshed open, Keith hurried out with Shae, turned the corner, and ducked into a gift shop, behind a tall revolving book rack. "That was close," he breathed.

"Maybe it's not safe for you to be here," Shae said. "I've witnessed firsthand how girls react when they find out who you are—well, let's just say a hospital isn't a place for that to happen."

Keith let out a harsh breath. "You're right."

"Excuse me, Sir," a woman's voice said from behind the counter. "We're closing now."

Keith nodded, scanning the aisles. He grabbed a blue bandanna from a rack and laid it on the counter. "Do I still have time to buy this?"

The woman nodded and rang up his purchase. Shae wondered, but didn't question, her gaze going to a nearby shelf of magazines. On the cover of one, Keith's face smiled at her. She strode across the carpet to get a better look. Curious, she pulled the publication out and read the caption beside it: *Pop Rock Star Offers Himself As Dream Date. Who Will Be The Lucky Girl?*

Sudden heat rushing to her face, Shae curiously flipped through the pages until she found the four-page full-color section on Keith. She skimmed the article, frowning.

"Don't believe everything you read," Keith's low voice suddenly came from behind her, near her ear. "I've heard he's really an okay kinda guy."

Startled, Shae jumped and dropped the magazine, another wave of heat flooding her face. Hastily, she bent and plucked it up from the floor, stuffing it back in its slot. She turned, her gaze going to the glass door.

"Will you help me tie this?"

She looked at him then. Keith wore the bandanna over his head, biker style, and was trying to knot it in the back.

"Sure." She stepped around him and tied the scarf, tucking his blond hair underneath so it wouldn't show.

"Shae," he muttered, "seriously—about that magazine spread . . . a lot of things are often blown out of proportion for publicity's sake. . . ."

She forced her tone to be light, though she was still a little embarrassed at being caught poring over an article concerning him. "Oh. So you really weren't a wild playboy who liked to party every night and date a different woman every month?"

Keith groaned. "Okay, the first few years in the business I was a jerk and a snob. I'll be the first to admit it. But I don't play fast anymore. I got tired of that lifestyle—"

"Hey, I was just teasing. Don't worry about it. And concerning what you said about publicity—believe me, I understand." She gave a pat to the head covering. "There. All finished."

He turned. "How do I look?"

Grinning, she cocked her brow. "You really want to know? A couple of gold hoops in each ear, and maybe some tattoos to add to the outfit of that bandanna and your sunglasses and leather jacket—and you won't have to worry about anyone chasing after you, Keith. Except maybe to throw you out." She chuckled. "You look like a highly suspicious character."

"Thanks," he said drolly. "But if it shields my identity, then so be it. Let's get out of here."

After a quick bite at the cafeteria, Keith and Shae returned to the waiting area where Hillary sat, staring at the curtains. Her face was set in a frozen mask, and she twisted her wedding ring on her finger.

"Hillary?"

The blond turned her way, her eyes hurt and angry. "I found out he had a woman with him, Shae. He'd been drinking. He broke through a guardrail and sent the car hurtling down the embankment. He flew through the windshield—wasn't wearing his seat belt. The woman is in critical condition."

"Oh, Hillary," Shae breathed, sinking to the chair beside her, not knowing what to say.

Hillary gave a short laugh that sounded more like a sob. Her gaze drifted to her hand again. "If he survives, he's in a lot of trouble with the law."

Shae put the sack with the croissant she'd brought for Hillary on the lamp table next to her, knowing food would be the furthest thing from her mind. Sitting beside her, Shae put an arm around her friend. Sometimes quiet support was best.

❦

After an uncomfortable night sprawled upright in a chair, sleeping with the back of his neck against its hard rim, Keith opened his eyes. He was relieved for the comfort of his sunglasses, which helped dim the bright light coming through a slit in the curtain. The next thing he noticed was that Shae was missing. She'd slept with her head against his shoulder almost all night, and though that part of him was stiff, Keith didn't really mind. He'd go through it again, to have her beside him.

Shae Stevens was a very special woman, different from anyone he'd ever known. Now he had more than one reason for visiting Rhode Island on a regular basis. He only hoped that she was in favor of the idea. She still seemed as though she were holding a part of herself back from him, and he wanted to know everything concerning her. At first his desire had stemmed from curiosity, then the need to help her in whatever way he could as a friend, but now he knew his feelings went deeper than any of those reasons. He was in love.

Keith uncurled from his position and straightened his cramped body, spotting Hillary across from him, riffling through a magazine.

"How's your husband?"

She looked up. "The same. He's still in ICU. There's been no change in his condition."

"Sorry to hear that." Keith hunched his shoulders then brought them down, trying to get out the kinks. "Where's Shae?"

"She ran into an old friend in the rest room this morning. Her mother had surgery a few days ago. Shae went to visit her."

Keith nodded and stood. "I'll be back. I need to stretch my legs."

He left the ICU waiting room, where they'd relocated in the middle of the night, and strode the hospital corridors. While he roamed the area, he thought about Shae, ignoring the wide-eyed looks cast in his direction. Curious, he studied his reflection in a dark office window as he walked past, stopped, and took off his sunglasses so he could see more clearly. The bandanna had inched up and blond hair snaked out over his collar. Giving a disgusted snort, he started to tuck it back in.

Three teenagers came around the corridor, one of them carrying a basket of flowers. They slowed their steps as their eyes turned his way, and they began to whisper to one another. One of them bravely piped up, "Aren't you Keith Travers?"

"*No comprende,*" he answered hurriedly, wondering why they weren't in school. He slipped his shades back on, ducked into a nearby elevator, and took it to the next floor. As he walked the spotless corridors, he noticed most of the room doors were open wide, for any visitors that happened by, he supposed.

Hands in his jacket pockets, Keith wondered about the future and if he should renew his contract. His mind again went to what that pastor's wife had told him the night before, about how he should use his voice for God. Her words exactly echoed what his granny had told him many years ago, stunning Keith. Was God trying to get his attention? But why would He after all Keith had done?

He turned the corner into another corridor, startled to hear soft singing coming from a nearby room. Lifting the bandanna off one ear to try to hear more clearly, he was even more surprised to discover the voice belonged to Shae. In dazed curiosity, he halted beside the entrance of a patient's room and leaned his shoulder against the wall.

That tune . . . he knew it. He'd heard it before. And then it hit him. It was the song he'd suggested they sing last night, the song Shae had said she didn't have the music to.

From the way her voice shook, Keith could tell it was a struggle for her to sing. After the last sweet note trembled in the air, an elderly woman's frail voice floated into the corridor. "Thank you, Marcia. Thank you for giving a dying old woman one last request. Your mother and father . . . they would've been proud. You've done credit to their name. . . ."

Keith wrinkled his brow. *Marcia?* He puzzled over the woman's strange words, at the same time recalling everything he'd learned about Shae these past weeks. Her parents' tragic death . . . her nightmares and guilt . . . her hesitancy to talk about herself . . . Marcia. Marcia Stevens.

The truth hit with a powerful blow. Keith turned his back to the wall, leaning against it, and closed his eyes in shock.

At last, he'd found the missing piece of the puzzle.

∽❧

Shae overtly studied Keith across the table in the hospital cafeteria. When she'd left Mrs. Braxton and had returned to Hillary with the intent to take her friend to breakfast and force food down her throat if she had to, Shae noticed Keith's strange behavior. When she'd suggested they go to the cafeteria, he looked at her as if he'd never seen her before.

Since being here, he'd seemed distant, unfocused, hardly speaking a word to either of them. For the extroverted Keith, that was tantamount to a world crisis. Even Hillary seemed to notice his preoccupied behavior as he toyed with his food, for she gave him a puzzled glance, then looked at Shae with lifted brows.

Shae shrugged her shoulders at her friend's silent inquiry. She had no idea what was bothering him.

Picking up a forkful of sausage, she stuck it in her mouth and chewed. She tried to make it go down past the lump in her throat, but she may as well have been eating putty for all the taste she got out of it. Pushing her plate away, she noted with relief that Hillary had managed to eat, though nowhere near her normal appetite. Shae took a sip of juice. It helped ease the lump, but not much. At least the headache wasn't as bad as last night. She glanced at her watch.

"Hillary, I hate to leave you, but I have to get back to the inn, and the ferry will be leaving soon." She blotted her mouth with a napkin. "I really wish there was someone who could be here for you until your mom gets here. . . ."

Hillary gave a weak smile. "I'll be fine."

Shae rose to give the blond a hug. "Call me with any news?"

Hillary nodded. "Thank you, Shae. You've been a true friend."

Shae looked at Keith, who was staring at her with a slight frown. She wished she could see his eyes behind the shades. Maybe then she could determine just what he was thinking. "Ready?"

He nodded, and after another quick good-bye to Hillary, Shae walked with him to the front where they called a taxi.

Once in the back of the cab, which smelled of old vinyl and grease, Keith removed his sunglasses, closed his eyes, and rubbed the bridge of his nose. When several minutes elapsed with only silence between them, Shae looked at him uneasily. "Is something bothering you, Keith? You've been acting strange all morning."

He turned to her, his blue eyes steady. "Were you ever planning to tell me who you really are?" His voice came out low, almost sad.

"What . . . what do you mean?" Her heart began beating a mile a minute.

"Marcia, I know."

Feeling the world cave in, she closed her eyes.

*H*ow did you find out?" Shae asked, her voice hoarse, panicked.

Keith watched in concern as her face went a shade pale. Maybe he shouldn't have spoken; maybe that had been a mistake. Yet, since leaving his post by her friend's hospital door, Keith had been able to think of little else but the discovery he had happened on.

"Pure chance. I was walking through the hospital and heard you sing to your friend." He fiddled with the temples of his sunglasses. "What I don't understand is why the big secret?"

Shae let out a humorless laugh. "You shouldn't have to ask that, Keith, knowing what you know about me. Knowing that I'm responsible for my parents' deaths—for robbing the world of two of the most popular gospel singers of the decade."

He shook his head. "It wasn't your fault. You can't predict the future, Shae, you couldn't have known what would happen."

Seeing the cabdriver frequently peer into the rearview mirror, Keith grimaced his way. "Do you mind?"

The cabbie looked back out the windshield.

"Nothing you say can ever convince me of that," Shae replied quietly, staring at the back of the seat in front of her. "I've lived with the pain and guilt for over seven long years. What makes you think I can let go of it now?"

Her gaze swung his way. "You ask why I protected my anonymity? Why the big secret? Well, I'll tell you. It's because I didn't want the reporters to find out who I am. As I'm sure you know, they can be very sneaky about getting you to say things you don't mean, things you don't want the public to know." Angry tears shone in her eyes. "You would have made a great reporter, Keith. You've found out more about me in three weeks than most people who've known me my whole life."

"Shae . . ."

"And now let me anticipate your next question, for I'm sure you have one," she interrupted, her voice growing a little hysterical and raising a notch. "Why wouldn't I want the public to know? Because I would've never been able to stand the hate or revulsion or anger or pity in people's eyes if they somehow found out that it was because of me that Trey and Marilyn Stevens' plane got caught in a bad storm and crashed in the middle of the Atlantic Ocean."

The taxi swerved, the cabbie's wide eyes flashing to the rearview mirror again.

"I think we'd better have this conversation elsewhere," Keith muttered, noticing they had neared the docks. "Pull over here," he told the cabdriver.

After paying the cabbie, Keith led Shae to a nearby bench.

"We'll miss the ferry," she mumbled.

"No, we won't. It won't be here for another twenty minutes, and the dock is about a five-minute walk from here. And anyway, if we do miss it, we can always take the next one."

Shae didn't say a word, just slumped onto the bench like a marionette whose strings had been cut loose. She stared at the ground, frowning. Keith heaved a quiet breath of frustration, and sank beside her.

"I wish I knew what to say to convince you you're wrong about all this. Shae, but I don't seem to have the words."

She gave a humorless little sound, bordering on a laugh. "Well, that's a first!"

Wondering how he could reach her and make her see the truth, Keith studied her profile. Her long hair hung like a black silk drape, covering part of her jaw. Her eyes were downcast, hands stuffed into the pockets of her sweatshirt.

This sullen woman was far removed from the bright-faced child with the braids and braces who sang every year on her parents' annual

Christmas television specials. Now that Keith thought about it, a boy had been on there too—Tommy, probably—but the show had mainly focused on Shae and her parents. Keith remembered lying on his stomach on the floor in front of the television, his chin propped in his hands, and watching the specials with the rest of his family. After one of Shae's solos, his mom would go on and on about what a lovely voice the Stevens' little girl had, and how she would probably be as famous as her parents someday. But at the time, Keith had done what most typical adolescent boys would do. Just shrugged it off, uninterested.

But now he was interested. Very interested. *Oh, God, how can I help her?* he thought in frustration.

It's not your place to do that, Son. Direct her to Me.

Keith blinked when the gentle and unexpected words filtered through his mind. Shock that God would still want to use Keith— much less talk to him after all he'd willfully done wrong—brought emotion to Keith's throat that he awkwardly swallowed down. And with it came the vivid realization that God had never turned His back on Keith, even when Keith had been at his worst. But rather, Keith had turned his back on God. God was just waiting for Keith's return, like the father of the prodigal, like Keith's earthly father had done. Waiting and hoping . . .

"Shae," Keith began, a slight tremor to his voice, "forgive me for being a hypocrite."

She turned and looked at him then, her face full of wary surprise. "What do you mean?"

"All this time I've been trying to help you with your problems, trying to get you to see the truth—and failing badly at it, too, I might add—when I've been just as blind about my own problems. I've been running from the truth, just like you—unable and maybe a little afraid to accept it." He sighed. "And I seem to remember reading something in the Bible, a long time ago, about a blind man unable to lead a blind man because they'd both fall into a ditch."

She shook her head in obvious confusion. "I don't get what you're saying."

"What I'm saying is that I think you need to talk to someone about your fears. But I also think that person should be someone more qualified to do it. Like Pastor Williams."

Shae stared a moment then gave a short nod. "To tell the truth, I'd thought about it once or twice. Especially since I know that his profession binds him under a confidentiality type clause and that he wouldn't relate anything I told him to anyone else." She bit her upper lip. "But like I said, Keith, before you came along, I hadn't told anyone any of it. I just couldn't. Not even Grandma. Not even Tommy."

"But now that you've told one person—me—maybe it won't be as hard to open up a second time and talk to your pastor."

"Maybe." She grew thoughtful again. "Keith," she said looking down nervously, "please don't tell anyone what you've learned. About who I am, I mean. Some of Grandma's old friends know, of course, but there aren't many of them left on the island. I'd just rather no one knew the truth."

"I understand, and I hope you know I'd never do anything to hurt you. Though I may not agree with you in this, I'll keep your secret. You can trust me."

"Thanks," Shae said very softly, still not looking at him. She glanced at her watch. "I think we'd better make tracks for the ferry."

"Yeah, I guess so."

They rose from the bench and began walking to the spot where the ferry would dock. "Keith?"

"Yeah?" He sent a glance her way.

"About the other night, when I had the nightmare. I just want you to know that your being there with me helped a lot." She turned her head and gave a glimmer of a smile. "So you see, you didn't fail in everything concerning me."

"Thank you for telling me that, Shae."

Her admission meant more to him than she could know. It meant that she was opening up to him—a deliberate action on her part, without her being coerced into it. Smiling, he held his hand out to her, and she took it.

Shae hung up the phone and frowned. Robert was still in ICU. Hillary was holding up well under the circumstances, and Shae was glad Hillary's mother was there to support her daughter through this crisis. Tears had been in Hillary's voice when she'd told Shae that her mother had said she'd been praying for Hillary and Robert for the past few months now. Maybe God would somehow work in their lives and bring them to a turning point through this accident.

Turning point. Shae sighed. She had also reached a turning point of sorts, now that Keith knew everything about her. Speaking the truth aloud had forced her to dwell on the past more often than she cared to. Yet it made her realize that she did need some kind of help from somewhere if she was going to successfully live in the present. . . .

"Hey, Shae," Tiffany said, breezing into the office. "So, what are you wearing?"

Puzzled, Shae cast a fleeting look at her cream-colored cotton skirt and white blouse. "The same kind of thing I usually wear when I'm working."

Tiffany rolled her eyes. "You can be so dense sometimes. I'm talking about for the date tomorrow. You know, the one with Keith."

Shae froze. *The date!* With all the turmoil that had rocked her world this past week, the dream date coming up so soon had completely slipped her mind. Her gaze went to the pile of unanswered correspondence, bills, and the like. She'd taken too much time away from work as it was, and tomorrow she'd be gone all day with Keith. "Oh, I don't know. Probably a pair of jeans and a sweatshirt I guess."

Tiffany gaped in horror. "You have got to be kidding. This is Keith Travers we're talking about, Shae. Not some average guy down the street. And remember, your picture is going to be in a national magazine! You can't just go looking like you're out for a jog or something."

Shae released an irritated sigh. "Well then, what do you suggest?"

Tiffany pondered. "Something romantic, but casual. Something you can dress up if you had to—that is, if you're going anywhere fancy."

Shae thought over her words. She and Keith had decided they would do a little of what both liked on their date. First, because of

Shae's love of antiques and historic houses, they would visit The Breakers in Newport. Freddie had made special arrangements for a private morning tour. Then they would lunch at a dockside restaurant, window-shop at Old Harbor, and afterward charter a boat and go fishing. The evening would conclude with a romantic dinner by sunset. Or as romantic as you could get with a photographer and reporter breathing down your neck and eyeing your every move, telling you just how to pose and do things. Shae still remembered those days.

She studied her sister's excited features, relieved that they were talking again. Since the incident with the crystal angel, Tiffany had steered clear of her older sister, and Shae had never brought up that night, just wanting to forget about it.

Rising from the desk, deciding the work could wait, Shae smiled. "Okay, Tiff. What say you and I go raid my closet?"

"Cool." Tiffany beamed her a smile and walked upstairs with Shae.

Fifteen minutes later, Shae sighed, throwing the hanger with the ivory, lace-edged casual dress onto the fast-growing pile on her bed. "Okay, so what's wrong with this one?"

"It's just blah." Tiffany scoured through Shae's closet, sliding clothes down the rack with a sense of purpose. "Besides, the material is all wrong. You'll need something that won't get ruined by salt spray. And, Shae, that color is just not you."

Crossing her arms at her sister's emphatic statement, Shae arched an eyebrow. "So just when did you become Miss Fashion Wardrobe Consultant?"

Tiffany shrugged. "I've always been interested in clothes, you know that." She paused. "I've even thought about designing them—when I'm older anyway." Suddenly she beamed and pulled something from the rack. "Perfect! And underneath you can wear knee-length pants for the fishing thing if you want."

Shae eyed the rose-red durable blouse with the breast pockets and the black cotton skirt with small rose swirls on it. "I don't know, Tiffany. Short sleeves? I get cold really easily."

Tiffany scrunched her brow in thought. "Wear Mama's black lace shawl that Daddy bought for her—the one with the silver threads. I think I saw it in Grandma's closet."

"Mama's shawl?" Shae's voice came out hoarse.

Tiffany's gaze dropped to the floor. "Oh, yeah, that's right. You don't want to have anything to do with them anymore. It was just a suggestion," she mumbled.

Dismayed, Shae studied her sister. "Is that what you think? That I don't want to have anything to do with Mama and Daddy?"

"Well, sure. Why else would you want our identity kept such a secret? Liz said—" Tiffany clapped a hand over her mouth.

"Some secret," Shae said wryly, feeling a trace of panic.

"Oh, Liz won't tell—honest! She was too young to remember them, and I don't think her parents listened to gospel music anyway. So it's no big deal to her. Besides, she's known for years."

Shae nodded vaguely. "But it is a big deal to you, isn't it, Tiff?"

"Sure." Tiffany eyed her as though she couldn't believe Shae would ask such a dumb question. "Even though I was only seven when they died and don't remember as much about them as you or Tommy, I loved them too, Shae. And I want people to know who my parents were. I'm tired of hiding it. Tommy doesn't hide it."

Shae averted her gaze to the pile of clothes on the bed.

In a sudden, very grown-up gesture, Tiffany went to her and gave her a one-armed hug. "Please don't be sad that I'm going to go live with them. I'll still come and visit."

Shae offered her a weak smile. "You're really looking forward to going, aren't you?"

"Well, sure. I mean Tommy's got a stable full of horses and everything. And you know how I like horses. And, well, then I can be myself. I won't have to worry about slipping up, or hiding who I am anymore because of who my parents were. And it will be really cool when the baby comes. It's so awesome that I'm going to be an aunt—and that I can help Linda with the baby and all."

"But what about Liz? I thought you two were close."

"She's coming to visit in August. Tommy said she could, and her parents already said okay."

"Poor Tommy," Shae said, her smile growing. "I wonder if he has any idea what he's in for."

Tiffany grinned. "Then you're okay with it? About me going?"

"I won't lie to you, Tiff. It hurts to see you go. I've never been separated from you, so this is going to be hard on me. Things certainly won't be the same around here once you're gone. But I want what's best for all concerned." She ruffled Tiffany's hair, which was almost as long as hers now. "Besides, maybe being in a family environment and having more responsibility will help keep you out of trouble. One can hope."

Tiffany wrinkled her nose at her, and Shae laughed.

The next morning, Shae hurried down the stairs to the family parlor, a bit apprehensive. Tiffany had taken extra time to braid Shae's hair in a French braid, then looped it underneath and tied it with a rose ribbon to match the outfit. Shae dreaded being in the presence of the media, though Keith had assured her several times at dinner last night that she in no way resembled the gawky kid with braces the world remembered. Shae had just looked at him.

She nervously entered the parlor, where Keith and the man from *Teen Planet* waited. Keith's eyes widened when he saw her, and she managed a smile. "Hi."

"Hi. You look great."

The freckle-faced stranger with the expensive camera around his neck turned from staring out the window and groaned. "Didn't you even think to discuss what you'd both be wearing? Those colors clash, and since the pictures will be in color, I must insist you wear something else," he said to Shae.

She looked down at her red blouse, uncertain, then her gaze went to Keith's burgundy shirt. She should have stuck with her first choice and not let Tiffany talk her into this.

"I'll change." Keith clipped any further comment by the photographer with a cold look toward the man. "She's perfect."

While Keith was gone, the aloof photographer introduced himself to Shae as Cameron, and said he would be doing both the write-up and taking pictures. Shae exhaled a soft breath of relief. He looked like little more than a kid and showed no sign of recognizing her.

Keith entered the room about five minutes later, wearing a navy blue cotton shirt. Cameron pulled his mouth into a wry twist. "I guess that'll have to do. Okay, first I want a picture like you two have just met. Shake hands or hug or something." He lifted his camera, looked through the viewfinder, and blew out an exasperated breath. "Can't you smile, Miss Stevens? At least look like you're glad to be with the famous Keith Travers. There's probably thousands of women wishing they were in your shoes today."

Shae gritted her teeth and offered the best smile she could under the circumstances. Keith took her hand.

Flash!

Shae sensed by the fiery glint in Keith's eyes and the hardening of his jaw that he was barely holding himself back from punching the guy's lights out.

"Perfect," Cameron announced. "Just a couple more." Flash! Flash! He clicked the camera shutter in rapid succession. "Okay, that's enough for now. Well, come on. Busy day ahead."

Keith quirked an eyebrow at Cameron's departing figure. "It appears we've been given permission to leave," he said dryly to Shae. "If the day passes without me decking that guy, I'll be surprised."

Shae chuckled. "That would make an interesting blurb for a magazine spread: 'Flash! Pop Rock Star Hammers Obnoxious Reporter With Own Camera. The Truth Exposed.'"

Keith groaned, his eyes briefly sliding shut.

Shae sobered and put a hand to his arm. "Seriously, Keith, don't worry about Cameron's behavior on my account. I've had my share of reporters in the past, and though some were nice, a lot of them were their own breed. I remember Daddy getting mad when an article would misquote something he said. And Mama never could stand it when photographers popped up out of nowhere and hounded us while we were having family time."

Keith suddenly beamed a smile so wide that Shae looked at him confused. "What? Why are you looking at me like that?"

"This is the first time I've heard you casually mention your parents since I've known you. It's a good sign." He took her hand and squeezed. "I guess we better go before Attila comes looking for us."

Shae gave a distracted nod, his words making her think. She was surprised to discover it had been easy to talk to Keith about her parents; the words had just tumbled out without her noticing them. And she wasn't sure that was such a "good sign" at all. At some point this past week she'd started considering Keith as much more than a friend. And that was dangerous. She would need to watch herself.

Tomorrow he would leave for California. And Shae would again be alone.

12

*O*utside, a dark blue luxury car awaited them. Freddie sat behind the wheel, wearing what looked like a chauffeur's uniform. Lifting her brow at the incongruous sight, Shae glanced at Keith as he opened the door to the back.

He shrugged. "Freddie rented it for the day. He also plans to be our official driver."

"But where did he get that outfit?"

"Who knows?"

As soon as the car took off, Cameron, who sat in the front passenger seat, twisted his body to face them, snapping pictures and firing questions at both Keith and Shae. Keith suggested that Cameron turn around and fasten his seat belt, since it was safer—especially with Freddie driving. Cameron gave him an incredulous look, but did face front and buckle up. However, the questions didn't stop, and Keith shook his head.

"Gotta be a rookie," he muttered so only Shae could hear.

Soon discovering that Freddie's aggressive personality matched his driving, Shae felt thankful for the one-hour reprieve they would have on the ferry. When they arrived at the mainland they drove into the old settlement of Newport, with its quaint homes and cobbled streets dating back to the colonial era, then on to Cliff Walk. Shae felt as if she'd been swept into another time. She'd visited this seaport before, but the grandeur never ceased to take her breath away.

Mansions of the millionaires, left over from the gilded age of the late nineteenth century, lay spread out along the curved, rocky coast. They went to The Breakers, the Italian Renaissance style palazzo that once belonged to the famous Vanderbilts. With its many arches, colonnades, and tall chimneys, the opulent manor sat on a sea of green lawn at the end of the stretch of land. Trees sheltered three of its sides, cutting it off from the other mansions.

They entered the great hall through a curtained archway, and Shae looked up, stunned. The ceiling loomed above and had been painted to resemble a cloud-covered sky, giving the room an even greater sense of expansiveness. Everywhere one looked was intricate scroll-work, alabaster, marble, mosaics, and antique wood. The ceiling, walls, railings, pillars, furniture, chandeliers—nothing looked simple. A red-carpeted grand staircase led to spacious balconies that opened to other rooms. One wall, made mostly of glass, gave a fantastic view of the ocean waves crashing onto the rocks.

"The breakers of the ocean are what Mr. Vanderbilt named the house for—hence, The Breakers," the tour guide informed them. "The Breakers is one of the grandest mansions on Cliff Walk. Seventy rooms wrap around the great hall, the room in which we are now standing . . ."

"Imagine what the cleaning bill for a place like this would be," Keith whispered in an aside to Shae. "Millie would be set for life."

Shae giggled. The tour guide cast a curious glance her way, but continued her monologue. After their tour, they exited the manor, and Keith turned to Shae.

"How about a stroll down Cliff Walk?"

She looked over the expanse of green lawns, down the ribbon of sandy trail that went on for three miles, mansions as magnificent as The Breakers on one side of the path, the restless ocean on the other. "Maybe not, Keith. I feel kind of dizzy after all that. And besides," she shot a furtive glance Cameron's way, "somehow I don't think it would be much fun with him breathing down our necks and ordering us around, like he did in there."

Keith gave a short nod. "Okay then—how about lunch?"

"I'm game."

They piled into the car and headed for a nearby wharf and a restaurant that had been recommended to Shae. Colorful sailboats, sleek motorboats, and huge yachts and fishing boats dotted the rippling sea, which almost reflected the overcast sky and had turned a greenish gray.

Cameron took pictures of Keith and Shae while they ate at the outdoor restaurant, stopping every now and then to dig into his fried shrimp and smelts. With her fork, Shae twisted a piece of the succulent white meat from her lobster tail, dipping it into a silver salver of melted butter. "It's too bad there were no boat races today. You would have loved seeing them."

Keith looked up from his plate. "I'm from Rhode Island too, remember. I've seen quite a few boat races." His tone questioned her, sounded strange.

"Oh, yeah, right." Feeling heat rise to her face, Shae bent her head to take a bite of rice pilaf. Who could concentrate on what to say with Cameron constantly snapping pictures? He must have shot at least two rolls of film already.

On their return to Old Harbor, the sky had darkened and the sea lashed against the pilings of the dock. Shae noticed disappointment cloud Keith's features. "Looks like sailing is out."

"Maybe not," Shae murmured. "It might clear."

"Maybe. Oh, well. Ready for the shopping district? Or is that a loaded question to ask a woman?" He gave her a teasing grin.

Shae laughed. "Always."

Yet before they could head to the long line of renovated historical buildings and shops, Cameron shouted to them. "Wait! I want to get a few shots of you over there—by that yacht."

Keith barely suppressed a groan, and Shae rolled her eyes. The wind had picked up, and she could hardly see how Cameron's idea would make a good shot, but she followed Keith to the wharf. At least they weren't overly conspicuous, since tourists were scattered throughout the area, also taking pictures with their cameras. And although the sky was murky, a few others besides Keith wore sunglasses.

"Point to the yacht," Cameron instructed Keith, "as if you're explaining things to her. And you," he turned to Shae, "look up at him as if you're hanging on his every word."

Muttering something about overzealous cameramen, Keith complied. Cameron took several side shots, and Shae tried to keep her eyes open, though salt spray stung them.

"Okay," Cameron said finally, "on to the next item on the agenda."

Keith shook his head in disgust. Shae hoped this "dream date" would soon end, but on second thought maybe she didn't. Keith was leaving in the morning. This was her last day to spend in his company, and she wanted to make every minute count.

They strode the sidewalks of the shopping district, with its rows of two- and three-story brown and white historic buildings packed closely together. Cameron dogged Keith and Shae's every step. Freddie was waiting in the car, with the complaint that his bunions were hurting him. Keith shot a glance over his shoulder, then turned to Shae, mischief turning his lips up at the corners.

"Are you game to start having some real fun on this date?"

Shae nodded, wondering what he was up to.

"On the count of three." He took a few more steps, darted another glance over his shoulder. "One, two . . ." He grabbed her hand. "Three—Run!"

They dashed down the sidewalk, skirting surprised tourists and ignoring Cameron's protests behind them to stop. For the first time that day, Shae's heart felt light as she sped with Keith around the corner of a building as though they were truant children escaping an overbearing schoolmaster.

They flew through the narrow space, single file, and around the back of the store, then came along the other side. Keith peeked around the building in the direction from which they'd come.

"All clear." He scoped the area around him. "Let's duck into that ice cream shop."

They scampered to the brown brick structure, ignoring the curious stares from passersby, and hurried through the door. Keith shot a glance out the window. "I think we lost him." He threw a boyish grin at Shae, one that she couldn't help answering with a smile of her own.

"Won't you get in trouble for this?" she asked.

"At this point, I don't care. Do you?"

"No," she admitted. "It's nice to be able to breathe again, without being told how to pose, or having to worry about embarrassing candid shots." She cocked her head with a teasing grin. "So now I guess we can add hide-and-seek to your list of games, huh?"

"Let's just hope Cameron's not that great at the seeking part." He looked beyond her to the counter. "As long as we're here—how about some ice cream?"

"Why doesn't it surprise me that you would suggest food?"

Keith laughed and bought two chocolate silk ice creams. They ate the messy treat, licking the drips along the sides of the waffle cones like two little kids. Afterward they left the shop to browse the area, all the while keeping a watch out for Cameron. At a department store, Shae pulled Keith inside, wanting to see a new line of straw hats. He patiently waited while she tried different ones on, and gave her a one-line appraisal of each.

"That one makes you look as if you're wearing a whole flower garden on your head. . . . That one looks like a flying saucer. . . . Whoever made that one must have lost his equilibrium. . . . Now, you look like you're wearing an overturned bowl sitting on a plate."

Shae rolled her eyes and pulled off the straw bonnet. She reached for the last hat, a breezy number with a wide rim and scarlet band. "Well, Mr. Fashion Expert?"

"Hmm." He smiled. "I like it."

Shae liked it too.

Hat decided on, Keith dragged Shae to the electronics section. She watched while he scanned the shelves and fiddled with the dials and buttons of the store's demo models.

"Don't you have a stereo?" she finally asked.

"Yeah, sure," Keith muttered as he switched on the Dolby sound. "But they're always coming out with something better, and I'm not against upgrading."

Shae rolled her eyes. She preferred antiques to new products. And as for any electronic gadgets she had, her motto was: If it works, keep it.

After fiddling with the stereo another minute, Keith rose. "Maybe we should look into buying you a computer while you're here. If they have them, that is. It would cut down on your workload."

"No, thanks. I'm not that electronically inclined. Besides, even if I did agree to shell out big bucks for something like that, how would we carry it out of here? On our backs?"

He grinned. "You have a point."

At the checkout, Shae pulled out her wallet, but Keith insisted on buying her the hat, to remember their day together. After leaving the store, they crossed the street to the next block when fat raindrops suddenly splattered them.

"Uh-oh," Keith muttered, turning his head up to the boiling grayish black clouds. He'd barely gotten the words out of his mouth before the sky unleashed a torrent.

"Quick, under that awning!"

Shae clapped a hand to her new bonnet and scampered with him to shelter, glad she'd rejected Tiffany's advice about the shawl and had worn her windbreaker instead. Keith linked his arm around her waist, drawing her close in the narrow space and trying to prevent rain from hitting her.

She craned her head to look up at him. His rain-darkened hair hung in dripping strands, and he futilely wiped rivulets of water from his dark lenses with two fingers, then gave up and pulled the shades off.

"Guess the sunset dinner by the ocean is off, huh?" Shae quipped softly.

Keith moved his head to look at her. "I'll make it up to you next time."

Her heart jumped. "Next time?"

"I'm coming back, Shae, you can depend on it," he said quietly. His eyes searched hers. "That is, if it's okay with you?"

She managed a nod, lost in the blue of his eyes and wishing he would kiss her.

As though reading Shae's mind, Keith moved to face her and wound his other arm around her waist. "I'm so glad your little sister sent in that contest form. It's changed my life," he whispered before dipping his head to hers.

Her heart hammering, Shae slid her arms around his neck and kissed him back while the rain beat down all around them, and her hat tumbled backward to the ground.

And she knew, beyond any doubt, she'd lost her heart to this man.

Once the downpour stopped, Keith took Shae's hand and headed with her back to the rental car. A few buildings across the street they ran into Cameron, who glowered at them, his expression as forbidding as the dark skies. From his dry clothing and hair, Keith surmised he'd found shelter during the storm.

"Was that fun?" Cameron asked sarcastically.

"Much," Keith said with a grin.

"You can be certain that your manager will hear about your stunt."

"I'll save you the trouble," Keith said, his voice light. "I'll confess my crime and turn myself in. Only please don't suggest a bread and water diet."

Cameron snorted. "This is all just one big joke to you, isn't it, Travers? Well, we'll see who gets the last laugh." His voice sounded almost smug.

"What did he mean by that?" Shae whispered when he marched ahead of them.

"Who knows?" Keith shrugged, not all that worried. "How about an early dinner?"

Shae laughed. "You and your stomach."

They dined indoors on broiled sea bass, in a secluded corner away from the curious stares of others. Though Cameron kept up with his relentless photo shoot, Keith noticed that Shae seemed more relaxed. Their little breakout from Cameron must have done her some good. It certainly had done Keith good. Remembering the feel of her in his arms, he wished this date would soon end, so they could return to The Roosting Place and he could be alone with Shae to tell her what was on his heart.

At last they headed back to the inn. Freddie dropped Keith and Shae off, then took Cameron to the island's airport. The ocean's waves splashed upon the shore, and night insects began their chirring. Yellow light glowed from the windows, casting Keith and Shae in a soft pool of illumination. Before she could go inside, he grabbed her wrist.

"Stay and watch the sunset with me."

Shae's forehead wrinkled. "What sunset? The sky is gray and getting darker."

"So, we'll pretend."

She shook her head, smiling. "You really are just a big kid, aren't you?"

"Guess the secret's out. And I tried so hard to keep it."

Shae's brow arched. "Oh, yeah—speaking of secrets, you never did tell me about how you got the butter to stay on the popcorn."

Keith let out a great laugh. Shae pulled her hand from his, crossed her arms and stared.

He winked. "Family secret."

"Last time you said it was a trade secret."

"It's both. My grandpa was in the popcorn business."

"Humph." Shae turned on her heel. "I've got to check at the desk and make sure everything went smoothly while I was gone."

"Come back?" His words were low.

She paused without turning around, gave a brief nod, and hurried up the steps and through the door. Keith stuck his hands in his jacket pockets and stared at the spot where she'd been.

"Now that the dream date is over, I want you to leave my sister alone."

Tommy's grave voice sailed from a nearby copse of trees, and Keith turned in surprise. He watched as the tall man stepped out of the shadows and approached, his steps squishing in the grass.

"I'm not kidding, Travers. Just head on home to California, and don't come back."

Keith eyed him, trying to tamp his irritation. He reminded himself that with his three sisters, and in a similar situation, he might have acted the same way. "I care about Shae. I would never hurt her."

Tommy snorted. "Is that what you told the others too?" He shook his head. "You're bad news. I've heard about you and your exploits. Life has hurt Shae enough. She doesn't need a big star playboy musician making things worse."

Keith grimaced. "What makes you so sure you know just what Shae needs?"

"I may not know everything she needs, but I know for sure it isn't you!" Tommy said between clenched teeth, jabbing an accusatory finger toward Keith while spitting the last word.

"Why? Because of who your parents were? Because you don't want her to get involved in the music business like them?"

A look of perplexity crossed Tommy's features. "She told you about that?" At Keith's abrupt nod, Tommy's expression darkened. "All the more reason for you to stay away, Travers. If she's telling you her secrets, that means she's starting to trust you. And we both know what a riot that is, don't we?"

Keith ignored the sardonic words and regarded the man across from him, his gaze steady. "I love her, and I think she loves me."

"You don't even know what the word means," Tommy shot back. "And as for Shae, neither does she. This dating thing is new to her. She's got stars in her eyes concerning you, is all. Once you fade from her life, she'll forget you exist and find someone better suited to her. I guarantee it. I know my sister better than anyone."

His blood beginning to simmer, Keith turned away. "I doubt you know her at all," he muttered before heading down the road. He wasn't sure where he was going, but at this point he knew he'd better get away before he did something stupid. Like punch Shae's brother in the nose.

As he walked, the glimmer of uncertainty Tommy had lit burst into flame. Tommy *was* Shae's brother. He'd known her his whole life, so it stood to reason that he would understand her better than someone who'd known her only a short time—like Keith. Did Shae's feelings run shallow, whereas Keith's ran deep? Was getting to know Keith just a novel experience for Shae, one that she'd file away in a scrapbook of memories and later forget? Though at first she'd been a little dazed around him, she'd never acted starstruck in his company. Yet, considering her history, that didn't come as much of a surprise.

Keith didn't want a fan to love him, he wanted a woman—one who would love Keith the person, not Keith the singer. A woman like Shae. No, not a woman like Shae. Only Shae. Yet except for today's kiss, she hadn't exactly encouraged Keith concerning a relationship between them . . . and that kiss might have just been a spur-of-the-moment thing with her, a curiosity fueled by her innocence, nothing serious on her part . . .

Annoyed with himself for not being sure of the answers and irritated with Tommy for putting the questions there in the first place, Keith swiped a hand through his hair and continued down the road.

∾

Shae twisted the wrench over the nut under the handle, stopping the faucet's slow drips. One of her guests had previously called the desk, complaining about the problem, and though Shae wasn't great when it came to home improvement, she did know how to fix a leak. Besides, it was too late to call anyone else.

The relieved tourist thanked her, and Shae put the wrench back in the toolbox and hurried to the porch, anxious to spend more time with Keith. Now that she knew he planned to return to Block Island, she wasn't as wary of him as she'd been before. He seemed to feel as deeply about her as she'd come to feel concerning him.

She opened the door and stepped outside. Tommy sat on a chair on the veranda, but there was no sign of anyone else.

"Where's Keith?" she asked.

Tommy shrugged. "He took off walking down the road."

"Just like that?" Shae looked at her brother in surprise. "Did he say where he was going?"

"No. But then guys like him usually don't. Once they get bored, or when something more interesting attracts their attention, they take off. He probably went to go check out one of the island's livelier nightclubs—one that serves alcohol."

Shae crossed her arms. "You're just prejudiced against Keith because of his profession. He quit that lifestyle—he told me so." Frowning, she stepped to the edge of the porch stairs and stared past the lawn to the road, barely discernable now that darkness had come.

"Most guys like that will say anything to get what they want," Tommy said, his voice low, "anything they think you want to hear. No, Shae. I speak from experience. You can't trust that type. I've met enough dishonest people to recognize one when I see him."

Shae thought of the many times Keith had asked her to trust him. He had seemed so sincere. And though at first she'd pushed him away, later she *had* opened her heart and trusted him with her innermost secrets, a part of herself no one knew about.

She shook her head. "No, Tommy, you're wrong about him." Her words sounded vague to her own ears.

Yet what if Tommy were right? Shae was inexperienced when it came to men. She recalled the scandalous bits of information about Keith's history she'd read in the magazine at the hospital's gift shop. But what if it wasn't just history? What if it described his present life too?

Troubled, Shae spun around and moved toward the door. "I'm going to call it a night," she muttered, wanting to escape the doubt Tommy was feeding her mind. She needed to be alone, to try to separate the facts from the fiction.

"Night, Sis. I know it's hard for you to face the truth, but you'll get through this. You're strong."

Shae held back a wry laugh. *Strong?* Right now, she felt as if she were beginning to crumble inside.

~&

Shae awoke to a clear day, much calmer than the night's thunderstorms. A beautiful eastern sky of lilac and mauve, with splashes of pink, heralded the sun's appearance. Strange that the day promised such beauty when her heart felt as if another storm brewed inside. She took a sip of coffee and continued to stare at the secluded beach from the window of her dining nook.

"Hi. Want some company?"

The familiar voice jarred her thoughts, and she turned. Keith stood in the entrance, wearing his bomber jacket and holding his overnight bag in one hand. The sight brought a lump to her throat. "Leaving so soon?"

Nodding, he dropped the bag to the floor. "Freddie is checking us out now." He took a seat at the table.

"Oh." She toyed with the handle of her mug. "Guess you're anxious to get back to the glamour of the big city, huh?"

He shrugged. "I'll be glad to start recording that new CD, though I did enjoy taking a break away from it all." His gaze seemed to impale her. "And I imagine you'll be happy to have things back to normal after I'm gone. No more worries of some girl possibly recognizing me and creating havoc in your inn. And no one to badger you with unwanted questions about your life." He sounded almost bitter, though his tone was light.

Shae stared into her cup. "It has been an interesting experience. One I won't soon forget."

A long pause. "Neither will I."

At his low, intense words, she raised her head. His eyes seemed to question while at the same time compel her to draw closer. Confused, she averted her gaze to the window.

"Beautiful day for travel."

Keith blew out a long breath. "Shae, we need to talk."

She tightened her grip on the mug. *Here it comes. Tommy was right. He's going to tell me it was fun while it lasted, but now that his vacation is over, so are we.* Remembering Keith's words at the store about upgrading, she really shouldn't be surprised.

"I don't think there's anything left to talk about," she said hurriedly. Taking a large swig of her coffee, she scalded her tongue. "Mmm," she moaned, clapping a hand over her mouth.

"You okay?"

Shae gave a brisk nod and heard him walk to the sink, the creak of the cupboard door opening and water gurgling into a tumbler. He came to her side and hunkered down to her level, handing her the glass.

"This will help."

Shae didn't want to look at him but couldn't resist. His eyes were gentle, troubled. The crazy idea of throwing herself into his arms and begging him not to leave her flitted across her mind, but instead she focused on the glass, taking it from him.

"Thanks." She took a sip of water, holding it in her mouth a few seconds to ease her throbbing tongue, then swallowed.

"I'll never forget these past weeks with you," Keith said quietly. "Both the good times and the bad."

Shae forced down the emotion threatening to overwhelm her. His words sounded like a permanent good-bye. Well, if that's what he wanted, so be it. She forced a smile. "And I've also enjoyed your stay at our island paradise, Keith. It'll be a memory I'll long treasure. Something to tell my grandchildren someday."

He flinched and stood, gripping the edge of the table. "Then I guess there's nothing more to say."

"Guess not." Her gaze returned to her mug. The seconds ticked by, but still he didn't go. When she thought she wouldn't be able to stand the silence any longer, he spoke.

"Shae . . ."

The door opened and Freddie appeared. "There you are. Time to leave. Plane's waiting."

Shae forced herself to rise and hold out her hand for Keith to shake. "Good-bye, Keith. It was a pleasure to serve you and your manager as my guests. I wish you a safe trip and much more success."

Keith stared at her a moment, then took her hand. But instead of shaking it, he brought it to his lips and kissed the inside of her curled fingers, sending spirals of electricity swirling through her.

"Good-bye, Shae." His eyes were steady when he looked at her again. "I hope you find everything in life that makes you happy." He turned, picked up his bag and followed Freddie out the door—and out of her life. Forever.

Shae collapsed to her chair and folded her arms on the table, burying her head against them.

*B*leary-eyed, Shae tried to focus. For the second time in a row, the long column of figures didn't add up. Disgusted, she tossed her pencil next to the adding machine with a muffled exclamation. The past two weeks, she'd thrown herself into her work, doing as much as she could to keep her mind off her problems. As a result, her concentration was wearing thin. If that wasn't bad enough, the nightmares were almost a nocturnal ritual now, and Keith had been transported into them too.

"Shae?" Katie poked her head in the office. "Got a minute? Pastor Williams is here to see you."

"Pastor Williams?" Shae said in surprise. She threw a disparaging glance at the aggravating book work and rose from her chair. "Sure. I'll be right there."

He stood in the lobby, his hazel eyes brightening when he saw her. "It's good to see you again, Shae. Is there someplace we can go to talk?"

Curious, she nodded and led him to the front parlor. He took a seat on the sofa, declining her offer of refreshment, and she sat across from him in an antique chair she'd recently acquired.

"How have you been?" he asked. "I know things have been rough for you now that Tiffany's gone to live with your brother."

Shae nodded. "Yes, even with tourist season at its peak the days seem quiet without her. But I'm holding out. I did find a new permanent act for the floor show, so that's a burden removed." She looked at her hands. "Hillary decided to stay on the mainland near Robert and see him through this. He's still in a coma, you know."

"I know. I visited the hospital yesterday." He hesitated. "Have you heard from Keith?"

Her head shot up. "No. Why should I have?"

His expression was puzzled. "Well, I thought . . . You know he came to see me the night before he left, don't you?"

Shae's heart tripped. "No, I didn't. What about?"

A gentle smile lit his face. "Sorry, Shae. That's confidential. But he did suggest I visit you after he'd gone." Shae averted her gaze, and his words became quiet. "Actually, I'd already planned to, but my schedule has been so full. Then when you didn't show up for church services twice in a row, I grew concerned and shuffled my appointments around to come today."

Shae nodded, looking at her hands. "Did he tell you everything about me?" Her voice was bitter, resigned.

"No. But he did hint that you might have something you want to discuss."

Shae's gaze lifted to Pastor Williams. With his boyish features and earnest smile, this dark-haired man looked too young to be in the ministry. But his anointed messages had touched many lives, and she knew God had called him to this vocation. She swallowed, knowing it was time.

"He's right. There is something I want to share with you." And over the next ten minutes, she told him everything, about the dreams, about her identity, about her guilt. After she finished, he studied her, a hint of sorrow and concern clouding his eyes. He seemed to think a moment.

"Shae, do you have a Bible handy?"

"I think I have one in here." She located a pocket-sized New Testament in the drawer of the end table beside her. "How's this?"

"Perfect." He thumbed through the pages. "Listen to this. It's from Romans 8: 'Therefore, there is now no condemnation for those who are in Christ Jesus, because through Christ Jesus the law of the Spirit of life set me free from the law of sin and death.'" He looked at her. "God is greater than the condemnation you feel in your heart, Shae. He knows you didn't mean those things you said to your parents, and He doesn't want you to remain in bondage to guilt for past mistakes."

"But if I hadn't been such a rebel and they hadn't changed their plans to spend more time with me, they would still be alive today," she insisted.

"How do you know that?"

"What?" Shae blinked, startled by the unexpected question.

"How do you know when the time would have come for them to meet their maker?" He stroked his jaw in thought when she remained silent. "Tell me, Shae, did you force your parents to change their travel plans?"

"Of course not. I was just a kid. I didn't have that kind of power over them."

"Exactly. They made their own choices."

She looked down. "But I screamed horrible words at them. I said I wished they were dead . . . and, then they were."

He squeezed her hand. "Shae, you didn't cause that airplane to crash. You don't have that kind of power either. Don't get me wrong, the words we speak are important and powerful—but do you really think an all-loving God would allow the temper tantrum of an immature sixteen year old to be the weapon that took His children?"

"When you say it that way, it sounds silly," Shae admitted, uncertain. "But why did they have to die? Why like that? They were good people who loved and served God."

Removing his hand, the pastor leaned back against the cushion and let out a long breath. "We don't understand everything, Shae. Our finite minds don't have the capacity to grasp it all—though God does often reveal His truths to us. And we do know there is a devil who steals from God's children, if given the chance. Yet we have to go on trusting God, who knows all, to be God, and we must hold fast to our faith in Him."

Shae released a weary sigh. "I understand all you're saying, Pastor, but I still find it hard to believe God could love me, though I try to be a Christian and do good things to make up for that day."

"Oh, Shae. No matter how many brownie points you try to chalk up to earn your way into heaven, it's an impossible task. If we could earn our way there, then Jesus wouldn't have had to die. He took every sin—every terrible thing Marcia Shae Stevens ever did or will do—to the cross with Him. Accept His grace, Shae. God is all-loving—He isn't able to be anything else. And He's all-forgiving. He doesn't hold the past against you. You are forgiven. Now you need to let go of it and forgive yourself.

"The forty-third chapter of Isaiah says He blots out your transgressions and won't remember your sins anymore. Shae, once you tell God you're sorry, He doesn't even remember what you did."

She attempted a smile, but it fell short and tears clouded her eyes instead. "I wish I could believe you, Pastor. I really do. . . ."

He looked directly into her eyes. "I'd like you to come in for counseling."

"Counseling?" She bit her lip. "For how long?"

"Until we get to the root of the problem," he answered without hesitancy. "It might take weeks—even months. But if I felt it wasn't important, I wouldn't have suggested it."

She nodded. "Okay, if you think it will help."

"I don't *think* it will help, Shae. I *know* it will. You need to learn who you are in Christ—to reprogram your mind to God's way of thinking. Marcia Shae Stevens is very special to God. There's no one else like her in His eyes."

His soft, emphatic words unleashed several tears, and they rolled down her cheeks.

He patted her hand. "I want you to read the entire chapter of 1 John before you come. It's often called the love chapter." He smiled. "Soon you'll see why."

❧

Shae sat in her dining nook, sipping her coffee. Katie walked in, a magazine in her hands, a wary look in her eyes. "Seen the new issue of *Teen Planet*?"

Shae shook her head. "Is it out?"

"Yeah, you could say that." The young girl dropped the magazine in front of Shae and left the room. Shae studied the doorway where she'd exited. Katie seemed edgy, and Shae was sure it had something to do with what was inside the glossy pages.

Taking a steadying breath, she flipped through the magazine until she found the spread. Her heart lurched at the photos of her and Keith together at The Breakers, on the ferry, at the restaurant, by the yacht—bringing back vivid memories of that day. With a bittersweet smile, she lightly swept a finger down his face. She turned the page and her heart stopped.

There, in a full-color three-by-five shot, stood Shae and Keith, their arms wrapped around each other, kissing beneath the awning. Underneath the photo was the caption: "Is Dream Date New Love Interest?"

Closing her eyes, Shae groaned and pushed the magazine away. Now she understood Cameron's smug comment about getting the last laugh. And she *would* be the laughingstock of the island—especially when it was discovered that Keith dumped her the next day. Shae didn't think she could stand to read the article.

She was halfway through the article when the phone rang. Her eyes on the print, Shae reached for the wall and groped for the receiver. "Hello?" she mumbled.

"Happy birthday, Sis!"

"Tommy?"

"Who else?" he said, amusement evident in his tone. "We wanted to come and see you, but Linda wasn't feeling well."

Shae pushed the magazine away. "How's she doing?"

"Some days are better than most. How are your headaches?"

"Haven't had one in weeks," she said with a grateful smile.

"Hi, Shae! Happy birthday. Did you see the new issue of *Teen Planet?*" Tiffany's voice came clearly over the line.

"Tiff! It's so good to hear your voice."

"But did you see it?"

Shae heaved a sigh. "Yeah, I saw."

"Wow! That must have been some date," Tiffany said.

"So, what are you doing for your birthday?" Tommy quickly interrupted.

"Actually, I'd forgotten it was my birthday."

"What—you're kidding!" This from Tiffany.

"Listen, Shae, I won't have this," Tommy said. "Not at all. Take the day off and have some fun. Tiffany had a great idea earlier. You always did like the gardens in Portsmouth."

Shae bunched her brows. "Why should I go all the way to Portsmouth when I live in the middle of a vacation paradise?"

"True. But you need to get off that island sometimes. Now is as good a day as any."

Shae nodded, thoughtful. Maybe her brother was right.

"Well, we'd better let you go. Phone rates, you know."

"Tommy, can I talk to Shae a minute?"

"Well, all right. Make it short. Bye, Shae."

A click, then, "Shae?"

"I'm here, Tiffany. What did you want to talk about?"

There was a pause. When Tiffany finally spoke, her voice was soft. "Thank you for sending me Mama's angel. I promise every time I look at it, I'll remember that God and His angels are watching over our family and keeping us together, even though we're apart—just like your note said."

Happy tears filled Shae's eyes. "You're more than welcome, Tiff. I love you, Kiddo."

"Love you too . . . oh, and Shae, one more thing. Um . . . If Tommy tells you anything about me dying the neighbor's poodle neon blue—it really wasn't my fault. The stupid dog stepped in a pan of paint. Honest!"

Shae laughed—she couldn't help herself. "I'll remember that."

She hung up, feeling much better. Her gaze went out the window, to the sunny day. Maybe a trip to the gardens was in order. It would be fun to do something different, and she hadn't been there in years. Katie could take care of the desk, and Shae had hired a new assistant to help out during the busy season too.

Making her decision, she grabbed the magazine and went to her room to get her keys, first stuffing the magazine in the bottom of her bureau drawer. Though what had been written was pure garbage, she just couldn't throw away photographs of their day together.

Shae ambled down the meandering path, hands in her windbreaker pockets, and enjoyed the breezy day. Everywhere she looked, a green, prickly animal stared back amid the trees. She had always loved the gardens and marveled at the skill of the person who'd crafted these amazing sculptures from greenery. Her gaze lifted to a tall cone-shaped boxwood, pruned to represent a spiral, and she smiled, watching as a cardinal landed on top.

Strolling past bushes resembling a bear, an elephant, and other animals and geometric shapes, she allowed her mind to wander to Keith—as it did most of the time now. Where was he? What was he doing? Did he ever think about her?

Shae thought over the weeks they'd shared. At first, she had to admit, she'd been a little starstruck around Keith, even if she had been somewhat of a celebrity once too. Yet at some point, the giddy feeling disappeared, and love took over. Not the superficial love a girl has for someone who is popular, attractive, and fun to be with. But the genuine love one has for another—knowing and understanding his faults, yet accepting and loving him, regardless.

And he has his share of faults, Shae thought, with a grim little smile. By no stretch of the imagination could Keith Travers be labeled perfect. He was entirely too pushy, too nosy, and too stubborn. And yet if he'd never walked into her life she might still be in hiding, beaten down by fear and guilt. For his persistence, she was grateful, though she hadn't been at the time.

Shae continued to stare up at the bush sheared to resemble a giraffe. Her smile turned dreamy when she thought of Keith's good qualities, his sensitivity, his boyish charm . . . but wait. Why was she doing this to herself? He was gone from her life—all the way across the country—and Shae hadn't heard from him once these past two months, not that she'd expected to. She had obviously only been a curiosity to Keith, a mystery—which, once it was solved, no longer appealed. Besides, as far as she knew, he hadn't recommitted his life to God. And she could never get serious about a man who didn't serve and love the Lord like she now did. She didn't want the same problems Hillary faced.

Shae forced herself to erect a wall around her heart and block out any emotions concerning Keith. Mentally she kicked herself for sightlessly staring at the animal-shaped bush for the past five minutes while daydreaming about him.

"It's over. Done with," she firmly told the green giraffe while crossing her wrists and swooping her hands flat out to the sides in a completion sign. "He's out of my life for good, and it's time to go on."

"Do you always talk to the shrubbery?"

A silent bomb exploded inside Shae's head when she heard the low words behind her. It couldn't be. Her imaginings must have gone a step further, and now she was hearing voices. She turned, dazed.

He pushed a hand through his hair, sweeping it from his forehead. The usual pair of designer sunglasses covered his eyes, but she could almost imagine their riveting blue gaze on her now.

"Keith," she managed in a breathy whisper.

"Is that all the welcome I get?" His tone was light, though he sounded uncertain. "Of course, after hearing you talk to your woodland friend here, I guess I shouldn't be surprised. I assume you were talking about me?"

She gave a slight nod, her heart pounding.

Keith let out a weary sigh. "Shae, we need to talk."

He was right. There was so much left unexplained. "Okay. There's a bench over there." She led the way, needing to sit down before she fell down.

"Actually, I was hoping for someplace more private. Like the inn," he said, taking a seat beside her.

She studied the nearly deserted gardens and raised her brows in confusion. "Private? I don't see anyone around."

Nodding toward the bushes surrounding them, Keith gave a wry grin. "It's been said the walls have ears. I wonder if that saying applies to bushes shaped like animals too. Especially after hearing you talk to one."

Heat flashed to her face, and she lifted her chin. "Exactly how long were you watching me?"

"Long enough."

Her stomach gave a little flip. "But . . . how did you find me? How did you know I was here?"

"When my plane landed on the mainland, I called the inn." He paused. "I've missed you, Shae."

She averted her gaze, didn't respond.

"Did you miss me? Even a little?"

A small girl with a red balloon barreled around the corner and scurried down the path past them, laughing and squealing while her harried mother ran after in hot pursuit with a toddler in her arms. Keith blew out a loud breath, obviously frustrated at the interruption.

"Okay. Maybe we should go to the inn," Shae relented. "Did you drive to the gardens?"

"I took a taxi, hoping for a ride back with you."

"Actually, I splurged and took a taxi too. No room for my car on the ferry."

Keith stood and extended his hand. "Shall we?"

Shae allowed him to help her up, but once she was on her feet, she pulled her hand from his. Keith stared but didn't say a word.

In the back of the cab, he filled in the time talking of inconsequential things. Remembering their last taxi ride together, Shae was glad the conversation wasn't personal, but still she wondered what Keith had to tell her that would bring him back to the island.

Once they boarded the ferry, Shae could no longer hold back her curiosity. "So, tell me. Why are you here?"

He stared out at the sea a long time before answering. "I was hoping you wouldn't have to ask that question."

Shae's heart gave a jolt. What did that mean? That he didn't want her to know his business? She looked out over the ocean. "Did Freddie come with you?"

"No. We've parted ways."

Shae's eyes widened as she swung her gaze to him. He continued to study the sea. "How come?" she asked.

"Let's just say we didn't see eye to eye. After a great deal of soul-searching, I chose not to renew my contract."

Shae didn't move a muscle, didn't even breathe. What was he saying?

"I've had a lot of questions," Keith mused. "I talked to Pastor Williams before I left the island last time. He cleared up a lot of things for me. Did he come see you?" He glanced her way.

She nodded. "He mentioned you came to see him, but he wouldn't tell me what you talked about."

Keith hesitated. "I was having a hard time believing God could forgive me for those years I turned away from Him. Choosing to live in a life of sin, even though I'd been raised otherwise."

"And?"

His mouth lifted in a wry grin. "And Pastor Williams pointed out the story of the prodigal son, among other things. But I still struggled with the issue. A month ago, I went to God and laid it all on the line. I told Him I was a worthless sinner who knew better than to sin, but had done it anyway. And I told Him if He still wanted me, He could have me."

Shae only stared.

Keith looked her way and chuckled. "Surprised?"

She gave a slight nod, then shook her head no. Keith laughed again.

"What about your singing?"

"I've quit the secular music business, Shae. I see now it was pulling me down."

Shae blinked, trying to absorb it all. "But . . . what will you do now?"

"I guess a lot of that depends on you."

"What do you mean?" she asked, her voice a little breathless.

"We'll talk about it more when we get to the inn."

She opened her mouth to speak, but he laid a finger alongside her lips, shaking his head. "Patience, Shae."

❧

To Shae, it seemed to take forever to reach The Roosting Place. Once there, Keith put a hand to her elbow, stopping her from going inside.

Curious, she looked up at him. He smiled secretly and escorted her around to the back of the inn, to the secluded beach beside the ocean.

Shae gaped, blinked.

A table had been set on the sand, replete with a melon-colored tablecloth, silver, and china. Two chairs sat opposite one another. In the background, the cobalt blue ocean sluggishly lapped against the beach, and overhead, the sky shone turquoise.

"Happy birthday," Keith said softly.

Shae swallowed hard, tears springing to her eyes. "How . . .?"

"Tiffany managed to get ahold of me a couple of weeks ago, and we set this up. Katie helped."

She put a hand to her mouth, overwhelmed. Keith gently steered her to a chair and held it out while she slid onto it. "You did all this for me?" she managed to squeak.

Keith smiled as he took the place across from her. "Of course. And I'd do it again just to see that look on your face."

Shae offered him a wavery smile, still feeling as if she were dreaming. From the back door, Gretta suddenly appeared bearing a platter and a wide smile. "*Alles Gute zum Geburtstag, Fräulein* Stevens—a happy birthday."

"Thank you, Gretta. And thank you for the part you played in this."

Gretta blushed, the tips of her ears going red. "You enjoy this birthday dinner, *ja*?" She set two bowls of what looked like cream of celery soup on the table. "I will be back with more."

Before they began, Keith took Shae's hands and offered a blessing for the food, also asking God to bless Shae on her birthday. His fluent prayer sounded nothing like the rough one he'd stumbled through months ago when he'd cooked dinner for her.

A delicious meal of baked bluefish stuffed with dill cheese, along with buttered peas, baby carrots, and green salad followed. Throughout the dinner, Keith kept the conversation light, and though Shae would have liked to know what he meant by his last remark on the ferry, she tried her best to exhibit the patience for which he'd asked.

Taking her last bite of chocolate nut parfait, Shae let her eyes slide shut at the delightful mixture of walnuts, creamy chocolate, and vanilla cookie crumbs. "Better than any birthday cake," she said, her mouth half full.

Keith smiled. "I'm glad you enjoyed the meal. Take a walk with me along the beach?"

Shae nodded, tossing her napkin to the table. She pulled off her sandals, holding them in one hand. They plodded through the sand, side by side, but not touching. In the waning light, the gulls cawed to one another, playing games of swooping and diving. The ocean whispered its secrets, as it sloshed against the shore at rapid intervals. The wonderful smells of wildflowers and saltwater filled her senses.

"Shae, I have a proposition for you," Keith said at last.

She tensed. *A proposition?*

"As I told you, I've left the secular music industry for good. And now I want to try getting into the Christian music world—with you. Ever since we sang the duet at the inn, I've felt we should pair up. We'd make a great team. I'd write the songs, and together we'd sing them."

Shae considered a long moment. "My immediate response would be to say no—after having come from that kind of life and losing my parents to it. But I promise I *will* consider it and pray about it, Keith. If that's what God wants me to do—sing for Him—then I'm willing."

He halted and turned to face her. "Really?" His tone sounded as though he hadn't expected her to come that close to agreeing.

She nodded, smiling. "Really. Pastor Williams has been counseling with me. Through him and the sessions, God has delivered me from the fear I've had. I know now I belong to Him—really belong to Him. In fact, God never left me. I'm the one who walked away."

Shae tilted her head in thought as she stared up at his dazed expression. "I guess we both did the same thing, Keith. You walked away from God physically, and I walked away from Him emotionally. But like you, I've come home. And I'm no longer afraid for the world to find out who I am—" She broke off as Keith pulled her to him and hugged her hard.

"Oh, Shae, I'm so glad," he breathed into her hair. "I'm proud of you—that you've shown courage to deal with the past."

She nodded, barely able to breathe because he was holding her so tightly. Yet it felt wonderful to be in his arms again. He loosened his hold and looked down at her.

"I have one more surprise." He grinned. "I seem to remember promising you a sunset. I can't think of a better place than New Harbor. Come with me?"

She smiled. "I'd like that."

They drove the few miles across the island to its west side where the Great Salt Pond was located. Keith removed his sunglasses, came around to her door, and helped her out. "I know the deal was a sunset dinner by the ocean, but I didn't see how we'd drag the table over here."

Shae laughed. "Don't worry about it, Keith. This is fine."

Together they walked to the dock. Soon, a horizontal flame of red mixed with orange slashed the sky directly above the horizon, a dark band of clouds above it. Myriad boats dotted the harbor, their black silhouettes identical in color to the surrounding land. The calm sea acted as a mirror for the sky, shimmering crimson.

"It's beautiful," Shae murmured, awed with their creator.

"I have a birthday present for you," Keith said, gaining her attention.

Shae turned to him, surprised. "Another one?"

"Yeah, only this one is just from me." He held out his fists at chest level, pointing them downward. "Which hand?"

She chuckled at his endless games and tapped his right hand.

"Nope. Guess again."

Grinning, she shook her head, and tapped the other. He turned his hand upward and opened it. A piece of saltwater taffy lay in his palm.

"Oh, my favorite!" she enthused, grabbing the treat. She tore off the wax paper, stuffed it into her pocket, and popped the pink candy into her mouth.

"Okay, now try the other hand," he said when she'd finished the sweet.

"Keith, if you don't stop feeding me, you're going to make me fat," she complained. "I gained five pounds when you were here last time."

"That's okay. I'll still love you."

Her heart jumped, but she tried not to make much of his light words. It was all part of the banter, she reminded herself.

"Go on. Try the other one."

She rolled her eyes and tapped his right hand. Keith turned it over and opened his fingers. A diamond solitaire sat in his palm.

Shae only stared, unable to think, unable to form words, unable to breathe.

"Marry me, Shae," he said quietly. "Make my life complete."

When she didn't answer right away, he continued. "Now that I've found God again, my life has improved. But I still lack something. Someone with whom I can share life's joys and sorrows. Someone I can love. I want you to be that someone, Shae . . . I feel as if I've waited for you a lifetime. Marry me—tomorrow, this weekend. Whenever you say—only please make it soon."

With trembling fingers, Shae tentatively touched the ring in his hand, then turned her eyes upward to his. "Oh, Keith . . . I do love you."

His brows bunched in an anxious frown. "But?"

"But I can't marry you that soon. We've both recently recommitted our lives to God. We need time to get to know Him again, as well as taking the time to learn more about each other. Until today, I wasn't sure if I'd ever see you again."

Keith stared down at the solitaire for a moment, then looked up at her. "Will you still wear my ring?"

Shae laughed. "Of course I will. I didn't say I wouldn't marry you—just not yet."

"So is that a yes?"

She nodded, a wide smile on her face. "Yes."

Grinning, he picked up the solitaire and with infinite care slid it onto her third finger. He bent his head and kissed her slowly, sending pleasurable heat tingling through her, and she wrapped her arms around his neck.

"Though my first inclination is to try to persuade you to change your mind and marry me the first chance we get," he said quietly after pulling away a fraction, "you're right. You're one smart woman, Marcia Shae Stevens."

His hand lifted to the side of her face, his fingers slipping beneath her hair. "Only promise me one thing, okay?"

"What?"

"The exact moment you know when the time is right, let me in on it?"

Shae smiled. "Believe me, Keith, you'll be the first to know."

He gave her another melting kiss before they turned and watched the last of the sunset.

*E*PILOGUE

*T*he evening was hot, the skies shimmering a pale robin's egg blue. A crowd of thousands cheered, standing in front of an outdoor stage, where a band had just exited after playing their last song. Wearing a huge smile, a scrawny man with wild red hair and freckles approached the microphone and signaled for silence. The noise died down.

"We have a treat for you," he said into the mike. "I'm sure you've heard of Keith Travers and Marcia Stevens—the daughter of famous gospel singers Trey and Marilyn Stevens. Well, they're with us tonight, and have agreed to sing a few songs. . . ."

Backstage, Shae straightened her airy, eyelet blouse, making sure it was properly fastened and none of the buttons had popped open. The waistband of her silky broomstick skirt felt tight too. When she'd last checked the scales, they'd shown she'd put on a whopping ten pounds! She would have to force herself to moderate her food—even if she had to chain the refrigerator door shut. And definitely no more of the sweets Keith loved to share with her.

Feeling uncomfortable, Shae wished for the hundredth time that she'd bought new clothes—some that fit. The last thing she wanted to do right now was to go onstage in front of all those people. How did she ever let Keith talk her into this? She gave a wry grin. She'd always been a sucker for those mesmerizing eyes of his, and the feel of his warm hands and kisses made her melt every time. . . . Okay, so she knew how he'd talked her into it. But could she go through with the performance?

Tightening her hold on the full glass of lemon water, Shae anxiously studied the raised platform where the announcer was finishing up their introduction. Keith came up behind her, looping his arms around her waist. "Hey there, Gorgeous. Feeling okay?"

"No, I'm terrified. I've never sung for a crowd this size."

"I understand. I get that queasy feeling too. You'll do fine. Otherwise okay?"

She nodded. He took the glass from her hand and set it down, then brushed a quick kiss over her lips.

"It gives me great pleasure to introduce the new singing team of Keith Travers and Marcia Shae Stevens!"

Hearing their cue, Keith and Shae took the steps leading to the platform and sat on stools a roadie had put center stage. Keith held his guitar ready, the only accompaniment they had since the rest of their band wasn't with them. He gave her a reassuring wink as they waited for the applause to die down.

Shae's hands were clammy, and her heart raced. She looked out over the crowd and up into the sky, where pinpoints of white stars were barely visible.

"For you, Mama and Daddy," she whispered. "I love you."

Together, she and Keith sang the title song from their new CD that had topped the charts only two weeks after its release. The same song that her father had written and her parents had sung over a decade ago:

Though the road before me is long and winding,
And the way lay covered in snares,
Though the path is full of potholes,
And my life's loaded with worries and cares,
Though it seems like the night's never-ending,
And I'll never again see the dawn,
I look up and remember God's promise,
That He'll never leave me alone.

And He sends His angels to watch over us,
To guard us, protect us, help us, uphold us
And I know, no matter how bad it seems,
The heavenly troops are under His command.

Though the way is littered with broken promises,
From those who aren't perfect—like me,
Though detours sometimes lure me astray,
From the narrow path where I always should be,
Though sometimes the way I choose is rocky,
And I fall on my face in shame,
He'll always be there to turn back to,
And He'll never turn me away.

So if I stick to the road before me,
No matter how hard it may be,
I'm assured at the end He will be there,
And His heavenly Kingdom I'll see,
Then I'll look back on the road I had chosen,
Two sets of footprints making it clear,
That He never left or forgot me,
But He walked with me and always stayed near.

So if you, too, are weary,
Of the long road we all must take,
I want to encourage you, friend,
The rewards are well worth the wait,
And when the road seems too steep to climb,
Just look up and see the cross,
For He's already taken your burdens,
And He has paid the final cost.
(© 1998 PMG)

Before the final notes died away, thunderous applause filled the outdoor arena in Dallas, Texas, where several Christian bands had gathered to hold a summer music festival. Shae opened teary eyes and smiled at Keith, who gave her a soft wink. Mentally, she prepared for the next number. Keith faced the crowd, holding up his hand to get their attention.

Suspicious, Shae studied him. Now what was he up to?

"I just want to thank you for your support," he said when the noise died down. His voice amplified over the huge outdoor speakers. "That song means a lot to both of us."

He sent a glance Shae's way and smiled before turning back to the audience. "God has blessed me with a partner like Marcia. And before we sing our next song, I want to share something with all of you. Something I just found out today . . ."

Alarmed, Shae shook her head, trying to catch his eye. Keith paid no attention.

"I'm going to be a father!"

A few seconds of silence then the buzz of murmured conversation filled the arena as people turned to their neighbors. But no one smiled. Keith looked at Shae, his brows raised in question.

Thoroughly exasperated with him, she rolled her eyes. "Well, you've told them that much. Now, you'd better tell them the rest before they start throwing things at us. Like rotten tomatoes."

Understanding dawned, and he grinned. "Maybe I should let them stew awhile. Get it? Stewed tomatoes?"

"Ke–eith!" Shae groaned softly, though she couldn't help but smile.

He chuckled and turned back to the microphone. "Did I forget to mention we were secretly married three months ago?"

At this announcement, the crowd went wild.

Keith threw Shae a sheepish grin, and she shook her head. "I can't believe you did that—though knowing you, I guess I shouldn't be surprised." Her words came soft, so the microphone wouldn't pick them up, though with the loud applause, she doubted anyone would hear.

He reached for her hand. "I'm sorry, Shae, I know we'd agreed to release the wedding announcement to the press next week. But I just had to tell someone about the baby. Am I forgiven?"

A hint of mischief tilted her lips. "Only if you tell me how you got the butter to stay on the popcorn."

Keith let out a great laugh and pulled her to him. "I love you, Marcia Shae Travers. You are definitely the woman for me!"

He kissed her while the crowd sent up another roar of approval, and Shae forgot all about buttered popcorn.

CROSSROADS

BY TRACIE PETERSON AND

JENNIFER PETERSON

$$1$$

"Hi, Daddy! How's Dallas?" Leslie Heyward cradled the cordless phone between her head and her shoulder as she stirred a pot of boiling spaghetti. "Oh, yeah, Travis is doing fine. Do you want to talk to him? Hang on."

Putting her spoon down, she covered the mouthpiece and called to her five-year-old brother in the next room. She was answered by an immediate crash of what Leslie's trained ear knew to be Legos, and a pounding of pajama-clad feet.

"What?" panted a tiny blond-haired boy. His voice betrayed his annoyance with the interruption.

"Here, Travis. Talk to Daddy." Leslie handed the boy the phone. He awkwardly positioned it against his small head. Leslie bent down to hold it for him, and as he heard his father's voice, his blue eyes sparkled with delight and his attitude instantly changed.

"Daddy!" he cried. "Daddy, did you get me something?" Leslie couldn't help but smile. "Daddy, I built a big airplane, like the one you and Mommy flyed on! It's a 7-2-4-7-9-50. It's *real* big. But I broke part of it when I got up."

Travis intently studied the floor as he listened and began to nod slowly. "Yeah, I think I can have it fixed before you get home. I'll have to work hard. It'll probably take twenty-fifty hours. But I'll try. I love you, Daddy. Can I talk to Mama?"

Travis squinted his eyes as if trying to summon his mother to the phone. When he heard her voice, his face instantly relaxed. "Mama!" he squealed. "Mama, I've been good. Haven't I, Leslie?" Leslie smiled and nodded her approval. "See? Leslie said I been good. Did you get me something?"

He became quiet, and then broke out into a huge grin. "But, Mama, tell me *now*. I promise I'll pretend to be surprised. Please tell me! Okay. I love you, Mama. Here's Leslie."

Leslie took the phone, and Travis scampered back to his room. Leslie repositioned the receiver and stirred the noodles once more.

"He really has been an angel, Mom. I haven't had any problems. But tell me about your trip! How's the second honeymoon going? Is Dad still romantic enough after twenty-five years?"

Turning off the heat, Leslie picked up the pot and walked over to the sink. "That's just great! I hope you two enjoy your dinner. And don't forget to behave! I love you both. Travis and I are about to sit down to a late supper . . . Yeah, we got back late from the movie. We went to see that one with the animals . . . Uh-huh, the one he's been bugging us about since he saw the commercial. Well, he liked it, I guess. We may go out for ice cream later, if he wants to.

"Anyway, I guess I will let you two get on with your evening. Tell Daddy to make sure and open the doors for you . . . I love you, too, Mom. Give Dad my love. Talk to you later."

Leslie placed the phone back on the charger. After rinsing the spaghetti, she set the kitchen table for two. Placing the pasta and the sauce in the middle of the table, Leslie sneaked over to the open door of her little brother's room. Crouching near the ground, she stealthily poked her head around the corner and watched Travis rebuild his masterpiece. Suppressing a giggle, she began to crawl in on hands and knees. As Travis delicately placed the huge, multicolored configuration on the hardwood floor and began to search for an eluding component, Leslie reached out and tickled him.

Laughing and squealing, Travis tried in vain to fight off the attack. Leslie rolled over onto her back and propped him up in the air with her legs. "I'm gonna let go! Uh-oh, Travis, don't fall!" She held on to his stubby arms as he kicked his legs.

"Leslie, I saw you. You didn't sneak up on me. I saw you!"

"You did not! I'm a spy. You couldn't have seen me."

"I did! Really! Let me down, please!"

Leslie eyed the smiling child suspiciously. Narrowing her blue-green eyes, she demanded, "Why should I? You're not hungry, are you?"

"Yes! Yes, I am, Leslie." He tried his best to sound convincing.

"I don't think you are. No, Travis, I am, in fact, certain that you're not. You know why?"

"Why?"

"Because I specifically recall feeding you *yesterday*." Lowering her legs, Leslie brought the boy to the floor but quickly captured him in a tight hug.

"But Leslie, you *have* to feed me! Mama said!" Travis continued to squirm, but she held him fast.

"She did?"

"Yes," he said matter-of-factly. "Mama *and* Daddy said you had to feed me. Every day."

"Every day? They did?" Leslie feigned confusion. "Hmmm . . . well, I guess I've got to, if Mom *and* Dad said to. It's a good thing I made a bunch of spaghetti then, isn't it?"

She picked him up and carried him on her hip as she turned off his bedroom light. Travis happily chanted a song about spaghetti, and Leslie placed him on the floor. "What do you want to drink, honey?"

"Orange juice," he proclaimed, climbing into his chair. Leslie brought down a plastic glass with a lid, filled it with orange juice, and placed it in front of him.

"I'm afraid we don't have any orange juice, sir. But, we do have some orange slime that I'm sure you'll find to your liking."

"Ewww . . . slime! Cool." Leslie laughed as he took a giant gulp. "Hey, it *tastes* like orange juice." He looked down at the top of his lid, perplexed. "Leslie, is it really slime?"

"Yes, Travis, it is. I bought it especially for you this very morning." She blessed the food and then asked, "Do you like it?" She fixed his plate of pasta and sauce, carefully cutting the noodles and mixing it all together. Setting it before him, she awaited his answer with a look of intent interest.

Travis took another sip of his drink. "Yeah, I guess so. It's pretty good. Do you want some?" He extended his tiny hand. Leslie puckered her lips and shook her head violently.

"No, no, no. It says right on the bottle, 'Only for Five Year Olds Named Travis!' I can't drink it. I'm too old." Leslie spooned the meaty sauce onto her own plate of spaghetti.

"Your name isn't Travis, either," he pointed out thoughtfully.

Leslie's face assumed a puzzled look. "No, I suppose you're right. You know, you may get to be a spy yet. Hey," she whispered conspiratorially, "you wanna go out for ice cream?" Despite the fact that it was below freezing outside, ice cream was a treat always welcomed at the Heyward house. "It would be the perfect thing for spies. Who else would go eat ice cream in January?"

Travis leaned in close to her. "Okay. We'll be spies."

Leslie looked him over critically. "No, wait. You can't be a spy."

Travis looked wounded. "Why not, Leslie? I want to. Please?"

"No, no. It can't happen. You see, Travis, spies don't eat ice cream in pajamas. Spaghetti, maybe. Ice cream, never." Leslie put her fork on the table. "I guess we'll just have to stay home."

"I can change, Leslie! Then we can go! Please? Let me change," Travis pleaded.

"I suppose that would work. Yes, that should work nicely. Okay. We can still go get ice cream. Just make sure you finish your spaghetti and your slime. Then we'll go pick out a spy outfit for you."

Travis looked pleased with himself. "Good. Thank you, Leslie. I'll be a good spy. I promise."

Leslie felt her heart swell with love for the little boy. "I know you will, honey. I trust you. Now hurry and finish up."

Leslie managed to twirl the last of her pasta onto her fork and eat it without getting it all over her white T-shirt. Travis's pajama top was another story.

Leslie scrutinized him for a moment. "Any of that food make it into your mouth, Travis?"

The little boy grinned a messy spaghetti smile and nodded. Strings of pasta fell from his pajama top as he replied, "Uh-huh, see?" He opened up his mouth, displaying for her the contents.

"Sorry I asked."

She cleared the table and sent Travis off to wash, which of course she had to complete when he returned still wearing a spaghetti sauce mustache. Within minutes, however, Travis was clad in black sweats. He insisted on wearing sunglasses. Leslie agreed that they did, indeed, complete his spy motif and loaded him into her teal Toyota. It was a good night, she thought. Turning on the car radio, Travis insisted on the *1812 Overture*, and they drove off to the ice cream shop, singing along with the orchestra.

⸙

Leslie turned off the engine and looked over at the sleeping boy in the passenger's seat. Gently, she unbuckled his seat belt and then undid her own. Pulling him onto her lap, she cradled his limp body in her arms and managed to get out of the small car. Fumbling for her house key, she awkwardly unlocked the front door and switched on the lights.

Familiarity greeted her like an old friend. She had shared this house with her parents for all of her twenty-four years, and in that time she had known nothing but happiness. Travis stirred in her arms, and she smiled, remembering the surprise he had caused with his birth. Her mother had given up on having any more children, although she and Aaron Heyward had wanted a half dozen or more. Travis had been born on her mother's fortieth birthday, and Peggy Heyward had proclaimed him the perfect gift.

Carrying her brother upstairs, Leslie readied him for bed, and after removing his sunglasses, she stood back for a moment and studied the angelic face. A small sigh escaped. He was so peaceful when he was asleep, yet twenty places at once when he was awake. She kissed him on the forehead and switched off the light.

"I wonder if I'll ever have a son," she murmured, glancing back at the door. The warm glow of the hall light fell across the boy's face like a muted spotlight. "If I do, I hope he's half as nice as you, Travis."

Downstairs, the silence of the evening seemed out of place for the house of Travis Heyward. She turned on the television and plopped down in an overstuffed chair.

Using the remote to run through several channels, she gave up. "Nothing's on," she said to no one in particular. Leaning over to the phone, she noticed she had a message. "Probably Aunt Margie," she said, playing the tape.

"Ms. Heyward, this is Detective Casey Holder with the Dallas Police Department. There's been an emergency here, and we need you to contact our office immediately. You can reach me at . . ."

Leslie's mind shut the tape out. Numb, she rewound it and played it again, just to make sure she had heard the man's voice correctly. In disbelief, she dialed the number left on the tape. It rang several times before a woman answered.

"Dallas Police Department. How may I direct your call?"

"I . . . I need to speak to Detective Holder," Leslie stammered.

"One moment. May I ask who's calling?" The woman's gravelly voice seemed unfeeling and empty. Just the way Leslie, herself, felt.

"This is Ms. Leslie Heyward. He called me while I was out and left a message that I should contact him immediately."

"Okay, I'll put you through." Leslie heard the phone ringing again and stared blindly at the television.

"Detective Holder here." A man's deep voice sharply filled her mind.

Leslie was forced back into reality. "Detective Holder, this is Leslie Heyward. You called about some emergency. Please tell me what this is about." She sounded more panicked than she wanted to, but she couldn't help herself.

"Ms. Heyward, how difficult would it be for you to come to Dallas right away?"

"What's going on? What's happened?"

"Well . . . that is to say . . ." The man paused, obviously uncomfortable with the task at hand. "Ms. Heyward, your parents were hit by a drunk driver this evening. It was head-on at about ninety miles per hour."

"Are they . . . are they okay?" she paused, trying to think. *Of course, they wouldn't be okay.* "Were they hurt badly?"

The man's voice seemed to lose its edge. "I'm sorry, Ms. Heyward. They were both killed."

Both? They're both dead?

"Ms. Heyward, are you there?"

She thought she'd spoken the words aloud. "Yes," she managed to whisper. "Are you sure that it was Peggy and Aaron Heyward who were killed?"

"Well, that's why I've called. I mean . . . I . . . well these things are never easy. We need you to come identify their belongings, and, well, we need you to bring their dental records."

"Dental records?"

"Yes, I'm afraid there was a fire and well . . . the bodies . . ." He left the rest unsaid.

"I understand," she said mechanically. "I'll leave in the morning if I can get hold of the dentist. I'll just need to get someone to watch my brother . . ." Her voice trailed off.

"Ma'am?"

"Yes, I'm sorry. Just tell me where to come. I'll be there sometime tomorrow afternoon."

"Certainly, Ms. Heyward."

❧

"Hello?"

"Aunt Margie, it's Leslie. I need you to come over here right now."

"Les, what is it? Is it Travis? Is he okay?"

"Margie, Mom and Dad were in an accident tonight."

"What? How?" The obvious disbelief in her aunt's fearful tone left Leslie realizing she should have waited to explain until they were in person.

"I don't have many of the details," Leslie stalled.

"But surely they told you how it happened—where they've taken them."

"Look, this isn't the kind of thing we should discuss over the telephone. It's such a shock and I know—"

"Leslie, you aren't leveling with me," her aunt suddenly interrupted. "Just how bad was this accident, and don't you dare try to sugarcoat it for me."

Leslie felt tears come to her eyes as she broke the news. "They were killed, Aunt Margie. I have to go to Dallas tomorrow and identify their things. It was a drunk driver, head-on. The detective said it was a collision at about ninety miles per hour. I need you to watch Travis for me. Please."

"Oh, no!" Leslie heard Margie begin to sob. "Les, no! Not Peggy."

"Aunt Margie, please. Travis is asleep, and you can use the guest room or sleep on the couch. I need you to do this. Please."

She knew the older woman was trying to compose herself. "Yes, Les, I'm on my way. You do whatever you need to do. I'll watch Travis for you. But what are we going to do about Crossroads?"

For the first time, Leslie thought about the coffee shop she co-owned with her parents. Now, it was hers. Hers. *Dear God,* she prayed, *help me make sense of it all.*

"Tomorrow is Sunday, Margie. The store will be closed anyway. I should be back Monday. Well, at least I hope I'll be back then. We'll just have to take turns running it while the other one watches Travis. I just can't do this right now. We'll figure it out later. Right now I'm too frazzled. I've got to make arrangements for the plane ticket, and then I have to call the dentist. Or should I call the dentist first? Oh, I don't know!"

"The dentist? Why the dentist?"

Leslie frowned and tried to think of a delicate way to explain. "They need the dental records for identification."

"Oh, my" was all Margie could say.

"Can you please come?" Leslie questioned one final time.

Margie sniffled. "I'm on my way. Don't go anywhere until I get there. We'll do this together. I can make calls while you're gone and tell everybody else."

"Thanks, Margie. I'll be here."

Leslie hung up the phone and began to cry softly into a pillow, trying to muffle her sobs. *I can't wake Travis,* she thought. Sheer dread flooded her mind. *How am I ever going to tell my poor baby brother?*

$$2$$

Kansas City International Airport was alive with action. The incessant hum of conversations reminded Darrin Malone of a cloud of angry bees. It was just as intimidating. Leaning closer into the partitioned phone booth, Darrin struggled to hear the busy signal on the other end of the line. He was used to it by now. After attempting to place a call for the last forty-five minutes, he had pretty much given up on Laurelin ever answering.

"Come on, Lin, hang up the phone," he pleaded to the pulsing tone. "I don't have time for this!" He placed the receiver back on the hook and sighed. Running his fingers through his dark brown hair, he contemplated just getting on the plane without calling her. Surely she'd understand. He shook his head. No, she wouldn't. Laurelin wouldn't understand because it didn't concern her. It wouldn't matter to her. "What a way to think about the woman who will be my wife!" he muttered. He dialed her number again, this time more out of guilt than consideration. Finally, the line was not occupied.

"Hello?" A perky voice filled his mind.

"Lin, it's Darrin."

"Darrin, where are you, sweetie? You *are* still going to dinner with me tonight, aren't you?"

"That's why I called. I, uh, have to fly to Dallas this morning. It's an emergency. I'm sorry, but I can't take you to dinner tonight." Darrin waited for the inevitable vituperation of his slighted fiancée.

"What? Oh, no, mister. You are *not* going anywhere tonight unless it's with me. Do you have any idea how many appointments I made for this? Nails, hair, everything! You simply cannot do this to me."

"Honey, I know. I understand, and I will make it up to you, I promise. Please understand *me*. You know I wouldn't cancel if I didn't absolutely have to. Don't take this personally. It has nothing to do with you. I will explain everything later. It shouldn't take any longer than a day, maybe two. We'll go out when I get back."

"Oh, *fabulous*, Darrin. Positively fabulous. You are so inconsiderate sometimes. I honestly don't know if I will ever be able to marry you. You just don't think about *me*." Laurelin stopped to take a breath. "So just what do you propose I do all evening? Hmmm? Did *that* fit into your plans? Did it ever occur to you that I'll be sitting around all night, watching stupid sitcoms? No, of course it didn't. I can't believe you can treat me like this and just expect me to take it."

"Look, Laurelin, I have tried to be congenial about this and respect your feelings. However, instead of being a grown-up about this, you have wasted my time with the rantings of a spoiled high school girl who doesn't get to go to the prom. It really is ridiculous. It seems I spend more and more of my time trying to justify my actions to you. Now, my flight leaves in five minutes, and I hardly think the pilot will be sympathetic when I explain that he had to hold the flight so I could listen to my fiancée act like a child. I will call you when I get to Dallas, and we can discuss this then. For now, please trudge on like the trooper I know you are, and spare me the melodramatics."

Darrin stopped and took a deep breath. No doubt he'd crossed the line, but he didn't care. There was a time and a place for everything, and Laurelin would definitely have to learn that.

"I can't believe you! You are so . . . so . . ."

"So late. Now, if you'll excuse me, I have a flight to catch. Why don't you go sit down and figure out some nasty, yet oddly witty names to call me and write them down so you don't forget them when I call you later? Good-bye."

Darrin waited for her to say the same, but instead, he was left listening to a dead line. She'd hung up on him. Again. What difference did it make? Darrin replaced the receiver and gathered up his carry-on bag. Three minutes to go. Wonderful. Dashing through the labyrinth of security, Darrin finally boarded his plane.

There was one thought on his mind—marriage to Laurelin was steadily losing its appeal.

Darrin fastened his seat belt and melted into the chair. Closing his eyes, he tried desperately to clear his mind but couldn't. His life was in utter turmoil, and he had no control. It was not a position he relished.

When had Laurelin started to irritate him so? He tried to think back to better times between them, but frankly there weren't that many to reflect on. Laurelin had been thrown at him in a rather unavoidable manner, and like a hound to the fox, she had taken it from there. They'd met at the grand opening of his antique store, Elysium. The shop was designed to carry not only the finest American antiques, but also specialized European articles. This immediately appealed to Laurelin, whose freelance interior design work could greatly benefit by having such lovely articles at her fingertips.

From that first moment, however, Darrin knew Laurelin had been after more than a good discount on antiques. She'd managed to artfully maneuver herself so completely into Darrin's life that when he found himself needing to either shut down the shop while he went to Paris or send someone in his place to inspect a new cache of antiques, Laurelin offered to keep the home fires burning.

After that, there was no stopping her. She made herself indispensable in ways that Darrin found impossible, or at least difficult, to refuse. The business was consuming his days and nights, and taking on a partner or at least an associate seemed the smart and reasonable thing to do. Laurelin made certain that Darrin was completely charmed by her looks, her manners, and her personality, and it wasn't hard to believe her capable of being all the things he wanted her to be.

He sighed, wondering why the plane delayed its takeoff. It was bad enough to carry the added burden of Laurelin's anger, but facing what he had to deal with in Dallas was enough to make him jump out of his seat and flee the plane. _Why did everything have to fall apart at the same time?_

"This is your seat," the flight attendant announced, and Darrin glanced up in time to find the attendant and an attractive, petite blond hovering beside him.

He could see that the seat in question was the only empty place in first class, and he was blocking access to it. "I'm sorry," he said and unbuckled his seat belt. Getting to his feet, he let the young woman into the window seat and returned to his position. Rebuckling the belt, he turned to find the woman looking around her with a rather startled expression of helplessness.

"Do you fly often?" he asked casually, wondering if it might just be first-time-flyer jitters.

"Not really," she whispered. "Not for a while."

He noticed that she was clutching her carry-on bag as if it might suddenly escape her hold. "Would you like me to put that in the overhead compartment for you?" he questioned, nodding to the bag.

"No!" she exclaimed, then seemed to force herself to relax. "I mean . . . that is . . . I want to keep it close."

"You'll have to put it under the seat then," he told her in a conspiratorial manner and grinned. "It's rumored that the plane can't achieve lift without the baggage properly stowed."

She looked at him with wide, reddened eyes as if trying to decide whether he was telling the truth or not. Darrin felt almost guilty for having made the joke. He shrugged and smiled again. "Sorry. I was just trying to humor you."

She nodded and loosened her hold on the bag. "I guess you're right," she murmured and slipped the bag under the seat in front of her.

The flight attendants were instructed to prepare the cabin for takeoff, and after running through their routine of seat belt instructions and nearest exits, they made their way through the cabin for one final check. Darrin had fully planned to sit back and doze for the hour-and-ten-minute flight, but with the woman at his side now softly weeping into a well-spent tissue, he couldn't begin to relax. For some reason, his heart went out to the petite blond. She looked exactly the way he felt on the inside.

Once the plane had taken off, Darrin rummaged around his own carry-on bag and produced a monogrammed handkerchief. Sheepishly, he offered it to her, his look a cross between consuming sympathy and embarrassment. "Here. This won't fall apart on you like that paper."

Surprisingly, she reached for it and dabbed at her blue-green eyes. He found they were more brilliant against the redness caused by her tears and was momentarily speechless.

"Thank you," she squeaked.

"No problem," he said, immediately composing himself. "My name is Darrin Malone. If there's anything else I can do for you, don't hesitate to ask. I'm headed for Dallas." At this, the woman's tears began anew. After a brief, yet heart-wrenching deluge, she managed to pull herself together.

"I'm going to Dallas, too. My parents were killed in a car accident down there." She paused, as if listening to herself. Then, almost as an afterthought, she offered her right hand. "I'm Leslie Heyward."

Darrin was stunned into silence. "I'm so sorry" was all he could say. His mind blurred with unspoken questions. *And I offered to help this woman? What could I possibly do to aid her?* Feeling very awkward, Darrin stared at the headrest of the seat in front of him. *Should I ask her for more details? Or would that only make her feel worse?*

As if knowing the dilemma she'd created, the woman spoke again. "They were there for their twenty-fifth wedding anniversary."

Darrin turned his gaze to the woman, surveying her jeans and pale blue sweatshirt. She looked as though she hadn't slept for at least a day or so, and her face had a soft, yet haggard appearance. Makeup less and ponytailed, Leslie Heyward was still one of the most beautiful women Darrin had ever seen.

"I had just talked to them on the phone before they left for dinner last night . . ." Her voice trailed off.

"Last night? How awful."

He watched as she fought off another round of tears. "Yes," she nodded. "I was babysitting, and we went out for ice cream. When I got home, there was a message for me to contact the police, so I did and—" She stopped abruptly. "I'm sorry. I'm rambling. It's just such a shock." She appeared almost embarrassed by her grief. "Please forgive me."

"It's no problem, Ms. Heyward, really. I don't mind listening. I can tell that you must have loved them very much."

"Please, call me Leslie. I don't feel very much like a 'Ms. Heyward' right now. Though I'm sure I'll hear a lot of it in the days to come." For several moments, neither one said anything. Then Leslie added, "Anyway, at least I know they're in heaven, and that comforts me."

"They were Christians, then?" Darrin asked.

Leslie nodded emphatically. "Yes, Mom and Dad were strong Christians. I was brought up in a very loving and supportive environment. We went to church together, and Mom led a women's Bible study group, and . . ." Tears began to streak her face again.

"It's good that you have that kind of faith," Darrin encouraged. "It will, no doubt, ease a lot of the pain to come if you know where they are."

Leslie looked up suddenly at him. "Are you a Christian?" She seemed almost pleading.

"Yes, I am." He noticed a sense of relief washing over her and decided not to add that while he considered himself a Christian, he knew he was sorely lacking in that area.

"I'm glad."

Darrin waited for some further comment, but none came. It was as if with that matter settled, Leslie had climbed back into her own private world and locked the door behind her. Darrin leaned back against the thickly cushioned seat and closed his eyes. Laurelin found his faith a pain—something to be dealt with only when absolutely necessary. Yet this stranger, this pain-filled young woman, was glad to know that he was a Christian. The comparison between the two women hit him like a load of bricks. Guiltily he remembered his mother's and grandmother's admonitions to only marry a woman of like faith.

"You'll never know a minute's peace," his grandmother had told him when he'd been nothing more than a gangly adolescent, "if you marry a woman who rejects God."

His mother's words had been similar. "You know the truth about God, Darrin," she had told him not long before dying. "And because you know the truth, God will expect you to live by that truth. Find a mate who will live that truth with you."

Darrin felt bittersweet pain at the memory. He'd somehow allowed all of his mother's and grandmother's wise words to vanish when Laurelin had arrived on the scene. *Oh, but that woman could make a man forget a great many important things*, he thought, with the weight of reality bearing down on him.

3

*T*hank you for arriving so quickly, Ms. Heyward." Leslie studied the tall man, reading the pin that identified him as Detective Holder. "Please, come right this way."

She followed his commanding form into a spacious room with bare walls, several chairs, and a large table covered with odds and ends. The fluorescent lights provided a dreamlike quality in their illumination, and Leslie moved as though she were underwater. *Maybe this is a dream*, she thought hopefully. *Please, God, let it be a dream.* The fuzzy serenity of the scene was soon shattered as she began to recognize various items on the table.

Her mother's purse—she'd shopped for hours at the outlet mall back home, trying to find one with just the right compartments in just the right places, and Leslie had spent the afternoon laughing with and at her because of her finicky nature.

A black pump that, no doubt, belonged to her mom.

Two suitcases.

Suddenly, everything became blurry, and Leslie realized she was crying softly as she touched the items that represented her parents. Turning away, she felt a strong hand on her shoulder.

"Are you going to be all right, Ms. Heyward?" It was Detective Holder. She knew his voice now.

"Yes," she managed. "I just need some water, I think." Her throat felt tight and dry. Detective Holder left the room and reentered with a small Styrofoam cup. Leslie took a long drink and tried to clear her thoughts.

"Are those the dental records we requested?" Detective Holder asked, motioning to the envelope Leslie clutched with her purse.

"Yes." She looked at the envelope as though remembering it for the first time. She put the cup down and handed it to him.

"Thank you," he said. "I'm sure this will take care of everything." He wrote something across the top and put it aside. "Now, what we need you to do is positively identify these items. The purse and shoe were apparently expelled from the car at the point of impact. We found the rental car registration inside the purse and traced the names to their hotel. The suitcases are from there. Do you think you can handle it?"

His voice was soothing, almost coddling, as though he were speaking to a child. Leslie didn't take offense. His manner was exactly what she needed at that moment, and she was grateful for his compassion.

"I think so." She walked over to the table again. "That's my mother's purse. I was with her when she bought it." She caressed the handbag, remembering the afternoon. "I think those are Mom's shoes, and that looks like their suitcases."

"You can go ahead and open it, if you think the contents will confirm it for you."

Gingerly, she snapped the clasps, and her eyes fell upon neatly folded piles of clothes. There was Mom's favorite red sweater and the tie that Travis picked out for Daddy's Christmas present. Leslie smiled as she fingered the obnoxious yellow and orange patterned material, remembering how proudly her father had worn it. Travis had insisted it was "just the thing for Dallas," and Aaron had obligingly packed it so as not to offend his son's undeveloped sense of style.

Digging deeper, she found a brown paper sack and opened it. Inside, she saw an electronic children's book about Texas. It was unmistakably intended for Travis. Slamming down the lid, she fought back tears and managed to choke out, "Yes, these things are all theirs."

She looked up, as if seeking reassurance that she had done well. Detective Holder nodded and scribbled a few words onto a clipboard. Leslie exhaled sharply. Had she been holding her breath? When the detective motioned her out of the room, she followed without question, anxious to be out of the surrealism of her parents' possessions.

"Now, if you'll have a seat in here." He opened a door across the hallway. "I'll get these dental records on their way to the coroner, and then I'll be right back to speak with you."

Numb, Leslie sat down in an oversized blue chair. She vaguely remembered from college psychology that blue was supposed to calm the mind. She hoped it would work for her but felt no immediate relief. Studying the cornflower velveteen, she tried desperately to feel the effects of its color. Her search for solace was interrupted abruptly by the entrance of Detective Holder, and her head jerked up as though she'd been slapped.

"Okay, Ms. Heyward. What I'm going to do now is explain what happened, and then I need you to tell me how you want things arranged. Okay?" He seemed genuinely concerned, his gunmetal blue eyes trying to read what she was feeling. His mouth appeared to be in a perpetual frown, as though he'd been surrounded by death and despair for too long to remember how to smile.

"Yes, please tell me what happened." She sat back, deep into the chair, seeking comfort and security in the abundant stuffing, bracing herself.

"Well, they were driving toward their hotel at around nine o'clock, Saturday night. From the other direction, a drunk driver jumped the curb and hit the rental car at approximately ninety miles per hour. Your parents and the other driver were killed instantly. They didn't suffer. In fact, they probably never even knew what happened."

Leslie nodded, glad to know they hadn't been in prolonged pain.

The detective continued. "The rental car burst into flames. Sparks and gasoline were to blame most likely. The police arrived shortly after 9:07, but by that time, the bodies were unrecognizable. They were able to salvage a few of the items, and from them, we were able to locate their hotel. That's where most of the items are from—the ones you identified in the other room."

He seemed to wince a bit before he went on. "Now, Ms. Heyward, I don't know how you feel about dealing with the remains, but I will be honest with you. I wouldn't want you, or anyone else for that matter, to see them as they are. I suggest that you go ahead and allow them to be cremated, just for the sake of preserving their memories."

"I don't, that is to say, my family doesn't have a lot of money to spend." She hated the way the words sounded. Funerals were supposed to be a final good-bye to the physical evidence of your loved ones. Leslie felt frustrated by the fact that money would need to be an issue.

"I understand. I'm sure we can work out all the details, however," the detective told her. "The Dallas Police Department will be more than happy to help you arrange for something to be done here. Frankly, a simple cremation will be the cheapest way to go. You avoid the big cost of transporting coffins . . ." His voice trailed off as though he could see how his words were hitting her. "We'll try to do what we can to help. But it is your decision, and it will be respected."

Leslie couldn't find any words. She'd never considered planning her mother and father's funeral. She'd always assumed they would be old and that one or the other of them would be left alive to help her make the decisions. Cremation was something she'd never thought about, but given the details that Detective Holder had just shared, Leslie knew he was right. Travis couldn't see them like that. He wouldn't understand that the charred and mangled bodies weren't really his parents anymore. Aunt Margie didn't need to see them that way, either. And Leslie herself knew that she certainly didn't want to have her final memories of her parents to be in that form.

"I suppose you're right, Detective Holder. It would be best to have them cremated here, and I will just fly home with the urns and try to explain it to the family. Please, just get me the paperwork, and I'll sign it."

She felt exhausted and her jean-clad legs felt like they were made of lead. Detective Holder gave her his best encouraging smile-frown and left the room.

Leslie felt overwhelmed. For the first time, she had all the information—and all the pain. Before Detective Holder's explanation, it was almost as if it hadn't happen. Now, how could she deny the cold, hard facts? She had seen her parents' things—lifeless reminders of the people who'd once been so very much alive. She had heard the police account—official, unemotional words. She had consented to their cremation. It was real. And she was alone.

Detective Holder reappeared, and Leslie looked up at him. "So now what?" she asked, feeling at a loss.

"Have you checked into a hotel yet?"

"No," she said, shaking her head. "I came right here from the airport. I didn't even think about needing a place to stay."

"That's not a problem," the man replied. "I can have you put up nearby."

"Is that absolutely necessary? I mean . . . I . . . well . . ."

He appeared to redden a bit as if embarrassed for her. "I know money's a factor, but don't worry about it. It'll be taken care of."

Leslie could only nod. "How long will I have to be here?"

"Well, this is Sunday. We'll have the coroner confirm things in the morning and get the bodies right over to a funeral home. I'll see to it that the matter is taken care of in an expeditious fashion. There's no reason you should have to wait around here for more than a day, two at the most."

Nodding her understanding, Leslie next turned to the stack of forms Detective Holder had brought with him.

~❧~

That night, after a quick call to her aunt, Leslie lay awake for a long time. The hotel bed was comfortable enough, but her mind wouldn't let her relax. What were they going to do now? Suddenly she was responsible for everything. It only proved to her how sheltered a life she'd lived. Her parents had always been good to give her the freedom to explore and come of age, but they'd also given her a stable family to count on. To be secure in. Now that was gone, and Leslie felt rather like someone had just pulled the rug from beneath her feet.

Could she possibly pick herself back up much less pull together the rest of the broken pieces of their lives? Could she take over the role of guardian to Travis?

The thought of her little brother caused a sob to escape from her throat. *Poor little guy. He has no idea what has happened.*

"Oh, God," she moaned the prayer, "how can I ever help him past this? How do you tell a five year old that his parents are never coming back to him?" She cried softly into the pillow, wishing against all other desires that this nightmare could be a mistake. What bliss it would be

188

to have the detective call her in the morning and say that the records hadn't matched and that her parents were safely alive and well.

She wiped her tears and wondered for a moment if this might be a possibility. Maybe there had been a mistake. Maybe . . .

❧

It was after ten the next morning when Leslie finally awoke with a splitting headache and swollen eyes. For a moment, it all seemed to have just been a bad dream, yet even as she focused on the room around her, Leslie knew better. She yawned and stretched, feeling little strength to climb out from under the covers. She hadn't eaten in over twenty-four hours and while her hunger was clearly absent, the weakness was not.

She considered calling room service when the telephone rang, startling her. Hesitantly she went to pick it up.

"Hello?"

"Leslie?" It was Aunt Margie.

"Hi, Margie."

"How's it going? Have you heard anything yet?"

"No, I'm afraid not. Detective Holder said he'd push things through as quickly as possible, and I have a standby seat on the 5:30 flight out of Dallas, just in case everything can be handled in time." Leslie paused and took a deep breath. "How's Travis?"

"He's fine. I haven't told him much of anything. I just mentioned that you had to take care of some business and that hopefully you would be home tonight."

"Oh, Margie, how in the world am I ever going to explain this to him? He's only five. What can life and death mean to a five year old? He probably will think that they're just dead today and that they'll be back tomorrow. I can just see having to deal with this over and over and over again, and I don't know if I have the strength to do that."

"You can find that strength in God," Margie replied. "I know after my Bill died, it was almost more than I could bear, but somehow my faith in God got me through the rough times. God will see us through this as well. He's always with us."

"Then where was He when Mom and Dad were killed?" Leslie asked bitterly.

"Standing with open arms to welcome them home," Margie answered, her voice cracking with emotion.

Leslie nodded to the empty room. She knew that Margie spoke the truth. She knew she could trust God, even though all seemed lost. "This isn't going to be easy," she murmured.

"No, but we have each other, and I hope you know that I'm here for you and Travis. Together we can help each other stay strong, and together we can help each other find healing."

"Thanks, Margie. I guess I needed to hear that."

"Would you like me to get in touch with the pastor? I can get things started for the funeral if that would be of help to you."

"It would be wonderful," Leslie said, a heavy sigh escaping her. "Plan out whatever you think would be best." She gritted her teeth together, remembering that she'd not explained to Margie about the cremation. "Margie, there's something you need to know."

"What is it?"

"Well, you knew that the bodies were burned." She stopped and tried to push aside the hideous images that came to mind. "Detective Holder said it would be best that we not see them like that, and I . . . well . . . I signed the papers to have them cremated. I didn't even see them myself."

Margie was silent for several moments before answering. "I think you did the right thing. I suppose it will be hard for Travis to understand. They say it's much easier to deal with death if you actually can say good-bye to your loved one face to face. You know, see the body, the casket, and so forth."

"Yes, I know," Leslie admitted, having recalled reading about that very thing. "But this couldn't be helped. I suppose we'll just have to make it work in some other fashion for Travis. I can't imagine that giving him all the gory details would be healthy."

"Maybe not, but don't lie to him. If he asks, tell him the truth. You don't have to get graphic in order to do that, but he'll forever feel betrayed if he finds out that you sugarcoated it or outright lied."

"I'll keep that in mind. Look, I'd better get off of here. You know, in case they try to call me."

"I understand," Margie answered. "Les?"

"Yes?"

"You aren't alone. Remember that. God is by your side every step of the way."

Leslie smiled and felt her nerves steady a bit. "Thanks, Margie. I'll remember."

4

*D*arrin Malone let the steaming water rush over his face. The powerful jets of the hotel shower mingled with the warmth, and he felt his muscles untie themselves from the knots of the day's dilemmas. All his worries swirled down the drain. For the first time in days, Darrin knew peace.

Sighing deeply, he reached out and rotated the handle to "off." He'd no sooner stepped onto the cold linoleum of the bathroom floor, than he heard a muffled pounding. Quickly, he wrapped a towel around his waist and strode out into the main room of his suite.

Knock-knock-knock!

So much for peace.

"Yes?" Darrin questioned through the door. The peephole revealed two men: one in a rather rumpled-looking suit, the other in the uniform of a Dallas police officer.

"Mr. Malone, I'm Detective Holder with the Dallas Police Department, and this is Officer Daniels. If you wouldn't mind, we'd like to speak to you for a moment about your father." Both men held their badges up to the hole and waited.

Darrin grimaced, even though he knew why they'd come. Unlocking the bolt, he opened the door and ushered the officers inside. They promptly took a seat at the table next to the windows and turned to face him.

"I'm afraid you caught me coming out of the shower. If you don't mind, I'll get dressed," he said, grabbing a pair of jeans and a flannel shirt from the opened suitcase lying on the queen bed.

"No problem." The men waited in silence.

Within minutes, Darrin reemerged, buttoning the last few buttons of his shirt. He tucked in the flannel and took a seat in the wing-backed chair across from the table set.

"Well, let's hear it." It was like a bad play that Darrin was forced to relive every few months. Always his father would drink himself into oblivion and then wrap his car around a telephone pole or drive off an embankment. Usually he escaped with little or no damage done to his own body, but always the cars were totaled. This time was different, however. This time would be the last time.

"Please tell me," Darrin added, looking up to meet the detective's guarded expression, "that no one else was involved."

"I wish I could, Mr. Malone. But it's not that simple." Detective Holder paused as though trying to choose the perfect words to describe the most imperfect of situations.

"Who else." It was more of a statement than a question, and Darrin was well aware of the angry, yet pained resignation in his voice.

"Why don't I just explain it from the beginning, Mr. Malone? That way, there won't be any holes in the account and you can fully comprehend the circumstances." Darrin nodded his approval and settled back into the burgundy material of the chair. At least this was the last time his father could cause any harm. Not that it soothed any of the wounds he had left behind, but it comforted Darrin in an odd way.

Detective Holder looked over to Officer Daniels before beginning. He opened the file he had brought along and perused its contents. He anxiously fidgeted with the file folder's edge before continuing.

"Well, Mr. Malone, it seems that Saturday night your father, Michael Malone, became intoxicated and began driving at excessive speeds. Around nine o'clock, he turned onto a four-lane divided street, and his speed reached approximately ninety miles per hour. He lost control of the vehicle and jumped the median. Another car traveling in the opposite direction was hit head-on and burst into flames instantaneously. Michael Malone died on impact, as did the passengers of the other car."

Darrin's stomach churned, and his chest tightened. He gripped the sides of the chair in order to keep from leaping to his feet. Brutal images filled his mind, and he could almost smell the smoke of burning rubber and paint.

"Who were they?" he barely whispered.

"A vacationing couple from Lawrence, Kansas."

"Young? Old?" Darrin questioned, barely keeping his voice steady. In his mind the ugly truth painted itself in even more vivid scenes. Years of living with his father's alcoholism were coming back to haunt him. Haunt him in a way that smothered his very breath.

"They were middle-aged," the detective replied hesitantly.

Darrin nodded, trying to fit imagined faces to the victims. "Are they being cared for?"

Officer Daniels nodded. "Yes, but we need to know what you want done with your father's body, Mr. Malone." He shifted in his seat before continuing. "It is not a good idea, in my opinion, nor in the opinion of the Dallas Police Department, that you see him. The dental records checked out, but the rest of the late Mr. Malone is unrecognizable. The fire spread quickly, and while the department put out the flames as fast as they could, your father's car was . . ." His voice trailed off as he realized Darrin was no longer listening.

Tears of anger stung Darrin's eyes, and he fought to keep them back. *What do I want to do with the body?* he thought. *Make him an example! Show all of those high school kids how cool it is to drink and drive. Show them what is left behind when the party's over and somebody else is left to pick up the pieces. Hah! It'd be the first time my father ever taught anybody anything worthwhile.*

"Mr. Malone?"

Darrin snapped back into reality. "What do you suggest?" he managed. His anger was the only thing protecting him from grief.

"Well, like we suggested to the family of the Kansas couple, cremation is, in our eyes, the best alternative. We would be more than happy to arrange for it to be done here and ship the urn home with you as soon as possible. Of course, your decision will be abided by. We just need an answer."

Cremation? Yes, that would make sense. After all, there was a fire. Darrin nodded in agreement. "Cremation sounds acceptable. How soon can this be over and done with?"

"We can call over first thing tomorrow morning. You shouldn't have to be here more than a couple of days." He handed the folder to Officer Daniels, who scribbled a few words across the top of the sheet.

"We thank you for your time." Officer Daniels extended his hand as the two men rose in unison. Detective Holder did likewise, and Darrin followed them to the door. "We'll be in touch."

Closing the door behind them, Darrin felt his anger renew itself. "How could you, Dad? What were you thinking? Or did you even re-member how to do that? You didn't just hurt yourself this time. You killed two innocent people, probably here on vacation to relax! Well, they're relaxing now, aren't they, Dad? Just like Mom. Only you didn't kill her as directly, now did you? You happened to use a little more discretion when you got her, didn't you? Just let news of your drunken escapades trickle back to her until it was finally too much, and her body just gave up.

"It wasn't enough to just let the cancer eat her away! You weren't happy unless you could be an intricate part of her suffering even after the separation. At least now you can't hurt anyone. At least now the world can rest easy knowing the Great Mike Malone has finally done himself in like so many before him!"

Tears streamed down his face as he yelled into the empty room, screaming at the ghost of a man who was easier to talk to in death than he ever was in life.

Darrin fell to his knees in complete emotional exhaustion. "Dear God—what do I do now? How do I rid myself of this bitterness—this rage?" He thought immediately of the verses in Ephesians 4. Verses that had made him almost get up from the church services and run without ever looking back:

Let all bitterness, and wrath, and anger, and clamor, and evil speaking, be put away from you, with all malice: And be ye kind one to another, tenderhearted, forgiving one another, even as God for Christ's sake hath forgiven you.

"But God, how do you forgive this?" he cried. "How do you for-give the taking of another life? Innocent life that was murdered by the choice of a ruthless man. My father wasn't saved. He found his savior and religion in a fifth of whiskey." Hot tears of anger flooded his face.

How many times had he tried to make his father see the truth? How many times had he prayed for his father to find salvation? Yet it was as if each and every prayer went unheard. "Why, God? Why this? Why now? There is no good thing that can possibly come out of this."

He stilled his rage for a moment and remembered the Scriptures again. *Forgiving . . . as God for Christ's sake hath forgiven you.*

"But how, God?" Darrin asked, looking at the stark white ceiling. "How can I forgive him this? How can You? He didn't want forgiveness, so what possible good can it do me to forgive him now?"

"Forgive him for *Christ's* sake," a voice seemed to whisper within his heart.

"I don't know if I can," he murmured, and those words hurt perhaps more than anything his father had done. The Bible clearly told him what he must do, but his human nature argued against it. The last thing he wanted was another battle over his father.

"I'll try." He closed his eyes and drew a deep breath. "That's all I can do. For Your sake, Jesus, I will try to forgive him."

Minutes passed, and finally he composed himself. Reaching for the remote control, he turned on the television and sat dejectedly on the end of the bed. It was as hard as a concrete bench, he thought, but somehow it didn't seem to matter.

The television hummed to life, and as the color image formed, a perky brunette appeared on the screen. "And in North Dallas, last night a drunk driver crashed into an on-coming vehicle and both cars burst into flames. The driver and the occupants of the other automobile, a couple from Kansas, were killed instantly in a mass conflagration of fire, twisted steel, and carnage."

She reads it as though it's about a sale at Neiman Marcus, Darrin thought. *Is there no compassion anywhere?* Suddenly, his eyes were filled with photos of the deceased Kansas couple and of his father.

For a moment, Darrin was speechless. Studying the picture, he felt he vaguely recalled the woman. The eyes seemed the same, but the face was different. Altered somehow. This woman was older, but . . .

And then he knew.

"No!" he cried out. They were *her* parents. They were the Heywards. The family Leslie had lost. And his father was to blame. He threw the remote across the room and listened to it clatter against the dresser.

It wasn't as if the thought hadn't crossed his mind on the flight to Dallas. He'd easily put it aside, however. His father's accidents were usually in the wee hours of the morning, and usually no one else was involved. Well, that certainly wasn't the case this time, and now he couldn't deny the truth of his earlier suspicions.

He conjured to mind the young woman who'd cried so pathetically into his handkerchief. Blue eyes, or were they green, seemed to stare back in his memory. What would she say to him now?

He couldn't shake the picture of her sitting there beside him—so tiny and frightened. So young. Then he had a horrible feeling. How young was she? The couple shown on the television looked to be in their fifties. Surely she was old enough to deal with matters, or she'd not have been on that plane.

The television was rambling on about an all-out winter car sale when Darrin got up and switched it off. He found the remote behind the dresser and placed it on the bedside nightstand. Restlessness overtook him. He had to do something. He had to find out where Leslie was and somehow do something to make it right.

No, he couldn't make it right, but he might be able to make it better. Perhaps he could help her with the arrangements or offer to pay her expenses. He went into the bathroom to comb his still-damp hair. Then an even more troubling thought came to mind.

"She won't ever want to see you once she knows the truth," he told his reflection in the mirror. "Your father killed her parents. She'll never want anything to do with you."

He hung his head and gripped the counter. "Who could blame her?"

His anger was surging anew. His own likeness to his father didn't help much, and soon the image in the mirror blurred into a reminder of his dad. It was like some kind of psychological warfare was being fought within him. *I am my father's son*, he thought, and this truth caused him even more pain.

He pushed down thoughts of the past and buried his pain deep within. "I may be his son," he reasoned, "but I'm not like him. I'm not a killer!"

5

Leslie sat tightly on the pinewood chair of one of the many dinette sets positioned around the coffee shop. *Her* coffee shop, she remembered painfully. Hers alone. Yet another responsibility. Yet another worry. But there would be plenty of time to think about all of that later.

Right now, she had to figure out a way to deal with Travis. She still hadn't told him the reason for her rush-rush trip to Texas. Nor had she offered any real explanation when she told him that he'd be spending the day with the next-door neighbors, the Richmonds. He was happy enough to comply, as their twins, Kyle and Laney, were his best friends, and the reality of a day at play with them left Travis without any need of the details.

Wearily, she brought her gaze to meet that of the haggard-looking woman who only slightly resembled her aunt. They exchanged glances for several minutes. Both gripped steaming mugs of flavored coffees, as though deriving strength from the heat. Leslie brought her cup to her lips and gingerly sipped. Anything to buy time.

She scanned the interior of Crossroads. In two hours, it would be open for business. In two short hours, she would have to face the real world again. Sighing deeply, she tried desperately to compose her thoughts.

"God was with them," Margie murmured, as if sensing Leslie's renewed apprehension.

Leslie's head snapped up.

"No, really, Les. He was good to take them home so quickly."

Leslie's emotions surged like water escaping a dam. "I'm so confused! I know that all things are supposed to work for the good of

199

those who love God, but where is the good in this? Where is the justice or the reason? How do you explain to a five-year-old boy that God saw fit to take his mommy and daddy away, but that it's really okay because everything will work out if we trust in Him? You can't, Margie. You can't! I can't even find the strength to believe it.

"There are mountains of problems we haven't even seen, let alone tackled. There are social norms that must be abided by, all the while maintaining faith in a God who robs babies of their parents for no reason at all! And I'm left to pick up the pieces, just as alone and scared as Travis. But I don't get the sugarcoated version. I am left with facts and figures and explanations and bills and fear and anger and—"

Her voice abruptly stopped, and she looked down into the creamy tan of her coffee. When she looked up, she felt a cross between shame and utter defeat. Aunt Margie's tender eyes, glistening with tears, never left Leslie's face.

"Les, you're not alone. You have me, and like it or not, you have God. A God who cares very deeply for you and for what has happened to your parents. A God whose plans, while no doubt mysterious and vexating to us, are surely unfolding as they should. He knows you're hurting, but He can't help you until you allow Him to." Aunt Margie's soft, yet stern voice filled Leslie's head, but it couldn't manage to push out the questions or the pain.

"If He cares so much, how could He let this happen?" She knew she sounded more like a little girl demanding answers about a runaway cat than a twenty-four-year-old woman, but she couldn't help herself. The hurting was too intense, and her need for understanding burned inside her mind. She needed reassurance, yet wasn't willing to accept the promises being offered.

Margie shifted forward to scrutinize her niece. "Leslie Heyward, do you really believe that God killed your parents? You know better than that! My sister raised you to know the truth. Now this is painful and this is hard for us to comprehend. Well, guess what? We don't have to! The world will not end just because you do not fully understand why God has allowed certain things to happen. I know you're hurting, Leslie. I'm hurting, too! But you cannot allow that pain to blind you from what is real. If you give up on God now, what good are you going to be to Travis? What is he going to think when his big sister doesn't even buy the rhetoric she's offering as an explanation? He's not stupid. He may be young, but often the young are the first to figure things out, especially when it comes to honesty. I don't believe for one second that you could look that boy in the face and lie. And that's just what you'll be doing if you tell him this and don't believe it."

Her face seemed to soften a bit as she relaxed against the back of the chair. "Oh, Leslie. Look inside your heart and inside your soul. There lives a God who is merciful and loving, a God who longs for you to return to His arms, and a God who desires to comfort you, not alienate you. Don't abandon your faith just because He didn't run things by you first. It doesn't work that way. Now is when you need Him the most. If you push Him away, what are you left with? Bitterness? Resentment? What kind of guide will those feelings be? Where will they lead you? How will they comfort you in the deepest darkness of the night, when your soul is bared and your defenses are shattered? Think about that before you blame God for what has happened."

Leslie sat in stunned silence. She knew the truth. It didn't erase the pain, but had she really expected it to? Well, actually, yes. She had. Even though she was a grown woman, she still believed in the Santa Claus God. If you were good, He would bless your life with wondrous things. If you believed, you would be spared pain and suffering. Bad things happened only to bad people. Injustice was punishment, not an everyday occurrence. Not to real Christians.

But what had just happened?

Bad things had happened to good people. No one could believe fervently enough or pray hard enough to avoid tragedy. Not her, not her parents, not anyone. What was she left with? A God who allowed His people to suffer at the hands of a cruel world, with nothing more than this concept of "faith" to comfort them.

But she was also left with a God who had blessed her in many ways. He had given her loving parents and a secure home. He had surprised her and her parents with the gift of a blond, blue-eyed tornado of a boy. He had allowed her to be brought to the truth at a young age and had kept her from harm's way for the better part of her twenty-four years. And now, now that she was being tested and tried, she was going to give up? Just because the presents stopped coming and the party was over?

This is real life, she scolded herself. *There is pain and suffering at every turn, and I can't explain it or stop it. But I am forced to deal with it and to help those around me by being strong. Am I so confident that I don't need God? Hah! I'm anything but confident. But still, it is so much more difficult when the pain is your own.*

"Leslie?"

Margie's words brought her back to the coffee shop and away from her troubled thoughts. She slowly shook her head and fingered the handle of her mug.

"Margie, I'm sorry. I know that what you say is the truth. I know this even in the deepest, most secret parts of my heart. I know that I'm being weak and letting my anger rule me, but this hurts so much! I don't know how I'm going to explain this to Travis because I'm not sure how to explain it to myself."

"Then don't. Accept that it has happened, acknowledge that it cannot be changed, and go on living with the faith you had before, when everything was beautiful and all was right with the world. Leslie, either God is God, or you are. And I think we both know, beyond a shadow of a doubt, the answer to that one."

The older woman smiled. "I will be here for you when you need me. I will listen to you and I will comfort you, but I will not let you lie to yourself and blame God for what has happened. I will not let you use that as an excuse to give up and go your own way. I love you, and God loves you. And don't forget that there's a five-year-old whirlwind at home who thinks the world of you, too. Search your heart, read the Bible, and pray. There's nothing more you can do. In time, you will find peace in those things. No peace comes from harboring bitterness and pain."

Silence filled the shop. Leslie's thoughts churned endlessly. They always returned to one central theme. Travis. What was she going to tell her baby brother? How was she to explain this random tragedy? How could she possibly word it so that a five year old would understand?

"Margie? How am I going to let Travis know?"

The older woman shook her head slowly. "I don't know, Leslie. All I can tell you is, don't lie, but don't offer any more than is necessary. He doesn't need to be let in on all the gory details, but this shouldn't be written off, either. This is a very important issue. It may well come back to haunt you someday, no matter how you tell him. Above all, be honest with him."

"But do I say, 'Okay, Travis, we need to talk about Mommy and Daddy. They are not coming home because they now live in heaven'? Or do I say, 'Travis, something really bad has happened to Mommy and Daddy, and I need you to be a very strong boy about this'? Should I start positive and work my way to negative, or start negative and end with something optimistic? Margie, there are thousands of books written on this subject. How can I be expected to figure something out that psychologists are still arguing over?"

"Pray for guidance, Les. Let God give you the words to say. I am not fool enough to believe that there is any one right way to break this to him. Just do your best. That's all anyone can ask of you."

"No, Margie. They can, and often do, ask for a lot more than 'your best.' Your best is never, ever good enough, especially in instances like this. There will be friends, family, church members, and whoever else you can think of who will have a recipe for success when it comes to helping Travis cope. All of them will have ideas that merit consideration, but they can't all be abided by! My best in this situation is going to be someone else's 'Avoid at All Costs' scenario. This isn't me running a race or writing a paper. This is a child's well-being—his life—at stake.

"If I don't do the right thing, my best isn't going to matter much at all. That's why this is so scary. Helping a child deal with the death of his parents is not something you can learn from a book or a television special. It may help, but in the end, you're on your own. I just don't feel strong enough to deal with this."

"I know."

Margie offered no other word, and soon the silence threatened to destroy Leslie's sanity. How could she just open the coffee shop with business as usual? How could she smile and serve and pretend that a cup of espresso could solve any problem her clientele might have on their minds? She slammed the mug down harder than she'd intended.

"It just isn't fair," she said getting to her feet. "And please don't counter with 'Life's not fair.' I think I've learned that lesson well enough." She paused, knowing that she had inflicted wounds with her words. "Look, I know we need to be strong together in this, but I feel so angry. Down deep inside," she said, pounding a slim fist against her breast. "Right here, I feel as though a hard, black lump of hatred and anger is threatening to explode. That man, that drunken fool, killed my parents—your sister."

Leslie whirled around and stared at the homey, hand-painted menu that was affixed to the wall behind the counter. "He stole them from us. He chose to drink too much. Then he chose to drive his car in a drunken stupor. He had the final say, and he took my parents away from me."

"Moving the blame from God to that man isn't going to bring them back," Margie whispered softly.

Leslie turned and stared in disbelief. "What do you want from me? First I'm angry at God and you tell me not to be—that He's still my best bud and He'll never leave me. So I try to rationalize that a loving God allows hideous actions to take place while He's ultimately in charge of everything, and you admonish me not to refix the blame? I'm sorry, but that man did make a conscious decision, and that decision ended the life of my parents. No, blaming him won't bring them back, but it does help to keep my mind on something other than my questions for God."

Margie got up and came to Leslie. Gently, she put an arm around her niece's shoulders. Leslie could feel a bit of the anger fade, remembering times when her mother had done the exact same thing. "Leslie, we have to go forward. Sitting here, wallowing in our self-pity is going to accomplish very little. You are angry. I am angry. It's something we must deal with, and I'm certain that each of us will have to deal with it in our own way."

Leslie felt tears come to her eyes. Why was it just when she figured herself to be all cried out, something would come along to prove her wrong?

Margie squeezed her shoulders. "Les, God knows you're mad. You don't have to feel guilty or try to hide it from Him. Take it to Him and talk it through."

Leslie looked quite seriously at Margie. "They'll still be dead," she whispered.

"Yes. Yes, they will." Margie's reply came accompanied with her own tears. "But they wouldn't want this for you, and you know that full well. If that's the only thread that you have to grasp onto, then take it. Do this in honor of them, even if you can't find the strength to do it for yourself. Do it for Travis. He's going to need you now more than ever. You're literally his only link to them. Oh, I know, I'm his aunt and his mother's sister, but it isn't the same. You're the one he will depend upon. Remember that."

"But don't you see," Leslie said, pulling away, "that's all I can remember. He's going to look up at me with those huge eyes and say, 'But how can I believe what you say is true anymore? You said they'd come home and they never will again.' Believe me, Margie, I've played this thing over and over in my head. He's not ready for something like this."

"Neither were you, nor, for that matter, me. But he'll deal with it, just as we have. Hiding here at the shop isn't going to make matters any easier."

"We have to keep Crossroads open," Leslie answered curtly. "We aren't made of money, and the funeral is going to cost quite a pretty penny in spite of the fact that they . . ." Her words faded. She didn't even want to say the word *cremation*.

"Les," Margie came to stand directly in front of her, "we will get through this, and we will either fall completely apart or we will be stronger. Part of it is up to us. Our choice." She paused and once again placed her hands on Leslie. This time she tenderly touched Leslie's face and held her fast. "I'll stay here and open the shop, but you need to go to Travis. What if one of the Richmond kids overhears their parents talking and says something to Travis before you get a chance to speak to him? He's going to need to hear this from you, not from neighbors or friends."

Leslie swallowed down the painful lump in her throat. "You're right."

Margie nodded. "I know you would avoid this forever if you could."

"I wish—"

Margie put her finger to Leslie's lips. "I know. But what has happened has happened. And what you have to do now won't go away. Travis needs you. Will you leave him behind? Leave him in the same way that he will probably believe his parents left him?"

"No—never." Resignation washed over Leslie. What was it Thoreau had said about resignation? Oh, yes, 'What is called resignation is confirmed desperation.' That was exactly how she felt. Desperate. Desperate to see this thing over and done with. Desperate to know that Travis would survive the loss of his parents. Desperate to know that she would survive their loss as well.

◦֎

Leslie sat comfortably in the chair that had always been called Daddy's chair and cradled Travis in her arms. He didn't understand, nor had she expected him to.

"But why did they go away?" he asked, his voice strangely void of its usual rambunctious delight.

"Because it was time for them to go," Leslie offered, knowing it was a question she hadn't answered for herself. "We can't know all the answers, Travis. It's kind of like we're reading a big, big book called *Life*. We can only know what's happening on one page at a time, and we can't skip to the end to check on how things turn out."

"Is it like when Samson died?"

Samson had been their tabby cat. A year ago, Samson had lounged lazily under the family car in order to avoid the stifling heat of a Kansas summer sun. Their mother hadn't realized he was positioned just behind the front wheel of the car when she backed out. She ran over him, killing him instantly, and then spent the next few weeks ridden with guilt.

"In a way," Leslie began, "it's like when Samson died. That was an accident, and no one wanted him to die. Mommy and Daddy died in an accident, too, and no one wanted them to die."

"Does it hurt to die?" Travis asked, his voice now starting to quiver with emotion.

"It didn't hurt Mommy and Daddy when they died. It happened so fast that the police said they didn't even know anything bad was going to happen."

"And they're never coming back?"

"Well, not to earth, anyway. But we'll see them in heaven when we go to live with Jesus," Leslie answered softly. She prayed that he could somehow take in the information and make sense of it.

"Can we go to heaven now?"

Leslie felt her eyes fill with tears. Oh, if only they could just go to heaven now. If only she could press a button and announce that God could send a celestial chariot anytime. Or better yet, request to be beamed up as those science fiction shows did all the time.

"No, Travis. We have to wait until it's time for us to go to heaven. We don't know when God will be ready for us to come to heaven, but when He is, when we die, it will be all right because going to heaven is the very best gift of all."

Travis suddenly pushed away from her and jumped out of the chair. "But I want to go now! I want to go with Mommy and Daddy." He looked enraged, and Leslie was shocked by the transformation.

"But, sweetie, we can't. God isn't ready for us to come to heaven just yet."

"Then I want Mommy and Daddy to come back here. If I can't go, then I don't want them to go."

Leslie leaned forward and tried to reach a hand to her brother, but he pulled away. "I know how you feel, Travis. I feel the same way. But now, it's you and me and Aunt Margie, and together we have to stay here and keep trusting Jesus to help us. We'll miss them a lot, but we have each other. And when we miss them together, it won't seem near as bad as missing them alone."

Travis's lower lip jutted out. He was very close to crying, yet Leslie noted the restraint he practiced. "Please come here, Travis. Let me hold you."

"No! I'm not a baby." He ran off to his room, refusing any further discussion.

Leslie got up to go after him, but just then the telephone rang. Wearily, she picked it up. "Hello? Yes, this is she."

It was the funeral home. Leslie listened intently as an ancient sounding man went over the details of the funeral arrangements. He rattled on about the chapel usage and the cost of the organist, and after that some mention was made about family cars and how many would be attending so that announcements could be printed up.

"Wait a minute," Leslie interrupted. "What kind of cost are we talking here?" She suddenly realized for the first time that Margie had said nothing of the plans she'd put in motion. Cost had never been discussed, and Leslie knew it was going to be a major factor in planning the funeral of her parents.

The man seemed hesitant to discuss money over the telephone, but Leslie finally wore him down and got an item by item total.

"Well," Leslie said, looking at the figures she'd just written, "this is costing a great deal more than we'd planned on. For the time, I'd appreciate it if you would do nothing more." She paused. "Yes, I know these things take time and planning, but apparently they take a great deal of money as well."

She listened as the man explained why money should be the very least of her concerns at a time like this. Leslie felt herself burning with anger as he hinted a lack of caring on her part was causing her to suggest that cost dictate the funeral arrangements.

Finally, she could take no more. "I'm sorry that we bothered you. We won't be needing your services after all." She hung up the phone.

"Now what do I do?" she wondered aloud. "Aunt Margie will probably be furious with me. After all, she's the one who called them." A million thoughts raced through her mind. Her mother had always said that if anything happened to them, the shoebox in the basement would have all of their papers, including the deed to the house and the shop, as well as their wills. With a sigh, Leslie knew what she had to do, but facing up to it was almost more than she could bear. Then, too, there was Travis.

She strained an ear for any sound of the boy, but he'd closed his bedroom door and Leslie could hear nothing. *Give him some time*, a voice seemed to whisper to her heart.

Leslie started up, then thought better of it and sat down on the carpeted stairs to think. It was probably a good thing there was so much for adults to do at a time like this. It kept their minds busy, as well as their hands. But what of five year olds? What did they do at times like this? Should she give Travis a series of tasks to fulfill? Make him a part of the arrangements? Or would that only make it harder for him? Should she go try to talk to him again? Or did he need to search the silence to find his own answers?

"Oh, God," she cried, burying her face in her hands, "what do I do?"

6

arrin was thankful for his many years of flying experience. When it came to boarding a plane, he was a pro. He could aimlessly wander through the routine without giving much thought to the actions he performed. There was comfort in such experience. Experience lent itself to routine, and routine allowed his mind to wander to other things, like Leslie.

After the plane touched down in Kansas City, Darrin collected his things and absentmindedly boarded one of the many airport shuttles. Grief and guilt washed over him in waves as he considered the situation in full. His mind could still hardly conceive that the nightmare of the past two days had actually happened. First, the sadness—the overwhelming loss that drenched his mind and soul. Sadness for the teary-faced woman who would have to wait for eternity in order to see her parents again. This sadness was quickly followed by shame and guilt, and then the melancholy would return. The turbulence of his emotions made him feel sick.

The shuttle pulled alongside his parking lot, and Darrin was soon behind the wheel of his car, merging with other travelers onto the interstate. He drove dejectedly through the heavy traffic and made his way toward his apartment outside Kansas City. The silence seemed too much to handle, so he switched on the radio to fill the consuming void. Mindless tunes poured out of the speakers, and for a moment, Darrin forced himself to think of nothing at all. But reality would not be ignored for long. Soon the pain and the remorse assaulted him once more and demanded to be dealt with.

"Oh, Lord," he prayed aloud, "what am I supposed to do? I know there must be something I can do to help this woman. I have to try! It's my fault—it was my father."

Money. He could offer money. That's all he was really good for. And he had plenty of it. Yes, he would find her and offer financial assistance. Surely she could use it. Paying for a double funeral wouldn't be easy. But how would he explain it? How could he justify his interest in her well-being without revealing his relationship to her grief?

Darrin expertly navigated the winding streets of the busy Kansas City neighborhood and made his way to his apartment complex. Barely fitting his sports car between two inconsiderately parked vehicles, he squeezed out of the ten-inch opening he had managed to create without touching the immaculate Cadillac on his left.

"Please don't let it have an alarm," he repeated softly, over and over. He didn't feel like dealing with the attention of a sensory-activated alarm system that would, no doubt, yield bells or sirens or robotic voices. He just wanted to be anonymous and hide inside his own world for a little longer.

All hopes of quiet contemplation were dashed as soon as his eyes fell on the red convertible Mustang. Laurelin. She was waiting in his apartment. Why had he ever given her the key? Heaving a sigh, Darrin debated whether or not he should just turn around and leave. He didn't feel like dealing with her or her plans. Not now. Not ever, really.

For the past two days, their relationship had begun to weigh heavy on his heart. Not that it hadn't bothered him for quite a while. He had just been able to mask it better. Now, with the Heywards consuming his energies, he had very little tolerance for the materialistic rantings of the lovely Ms. Firth.

She didn't even know about his father, which in and of itself would prove interesting. Before, he'd implied that his father was no longer in his world, which was true. But Darrin knew that Laurelin had believed his father to be long dead and gone to whatever place Laurelin believed people went. With the ghost of such an undesirable character threatening her pristine family tree, she might very well break off the engagement herself.

"Oh, if it were only that easy," he muttered, making his way up the flights of stairs.

❧

"Just where have you been?"

Darrin had barely unlocked the door before the vituperations of a slighted Laurelin began. He didn't bother to answer. It wouldn't matter, he knew, because until she had gotten her initial assault of words in, he would never be able to offer up even the most meager of explanations.

"Just what do you mean, leaving me alone for two days? The Andrews party was last night. I had to go alone. Alone. Me! I had to show up all alone and go home all alone and listen to everybody ask me where in the world you were and why you weren't at the party. And that was worse yet, because I didn't *know* why you weren't at the party. I couldn't very well say, 'Oh, you know, he forgot to tell me what he was doing!' You simply have no idea how difficult it was. I had to make up something that would excuse your absence from their party. Are you listening to me?"

Darrin's head was partially inside his closet as he hung up his suit jacket. "Yes, dear," he answered in monotone.

"I thought it was just going to be a quick overnight. But no, you were gone for two days. Just what was I supposed to do with myself for those two days?" Well-manicured hands rested upon slender hips, and Laurelin's brown eyes were dark and furious.

"Well, I hope you went to work at the shop," Darrin said casually, as he picked up his bag and carried it into his bedroom.

"The *shop*? Is that all you think about, Darrin Malone? How can I be expected to babysit your antiques *and* plan a fabulous wedding?" She shook her head, the short light brown hair falling perfectly into place with each pouty turn. "Darrin, I'm not a magician. I need *time*. I need you here taking care of things so I have time to think. I was too worried about you to go to the shop. Besides, I had to call the caterer, and the florist, and my mother, and . . ."

Darrin held up his hand. "Just stop. I don't want to hear about it right now. I need to talk, and you need to listen. Understand?"

Laurelin's frown deepened. "How dare you talk to me like that! I am your fiancée, not a child!"

"Then quit acting like one and sit down." She turned from him and glided to the nearest overstuffed chair.

Darrin studied her for a moment. She looked very professional, and there was no denying her beauty. She was elegant and refined, her light brown hair styled just enough to allow movement while retaining its form. Her makeup was expertly applied and accentuated her sapphire jacket and skirt. Her long legs were trim and defined and seemed to have pantyhose surgically grafted to them. He couldn't remember the last time he'd seen her in a sundress or relaxing in a pair of cutoff shorts and a T-shirt. Granted, he was first drawn to her for her impeccable taste in clothes and antiques, but now, he couldn't help but think it would be nicer to be engaged to a person instead of a fashion doll.

"Well?" Laurelin's impatient voice brought him back to reality. "What is it that's *so* important that you have to take that tone with me?"

"Look," he began. "The reason I had to fly to Dallas at the last minute was because my father had died in a car accident."

"Your *father*? I thought your father was already dead. Well, at least I thought he was out of the picture. Why in the world should it matter to you *what* happens to him? You couldn't possibly have had much of a relationship if I thought he was dead all this time."

"Ah, Lin. Your compassion is overwhelming. It's a wonder I could manage being away from your sweetness for forty-eight hours." Darrin sighed in complete exasperation. They were headed for another major fight at this rate, and that was the last thing he needed. Leaving his bags, he motioned her back to the living room. He tried to calm his nerves and rid his mind of the sarcasm he felt.

"Let me start again," he finally said as Laurelin fashionably rearranged herself on the sofa.

"What's to start?" Laurelin asked, appearing rather bored. "He's dead, and you've taken care of business there. Now I hope you'll take care of business here. I mean, really, Darrin. You've never mentioned the man except in the past tense, and now you're acting as though you've just gone through some tremendously difficult circumstance. How could it be that traumatic if you wrote him off so many years ago anyway?"

Darrin found her attitude not only distasteful, but downright aggravating. His desire to keep from arguing was rapidly disappearing.

"I'm sorry, dear. I'm sure this is difficult for you to deal with, but you must know that your vast mercy is misplaced on such a man as my father." His voice dripped sarcasm, and he rolled up his shirt sleeves like a man preparing to do battle.

"My father is, or rather was, an alcoholic. He and my mother were separated because she refused to let her only son be raised by the bottle. I grew up hating my father for what he had done. However, after my mother died, I was the one the police would come to after every drunk driving arrest and every accident. I've let you assume he was already dead because in many ways—all the ways that mattered—he was. It was wrong of me to lead you on about it, but I was naturally very disturbed and ashamed of the man. I wanted nothing more to do with him, yet it was only right that upon his death, the police would call me."

"But you hated him, right?" she asked with a tiny shake of her head. "So, it's not like this is a tug at any emotional heartstrings, right?"

Darrin had fixed his gaze upon her, but it was as if he could no longer see her. His mind seemed to play tricks on him. He could hear her voice, but all he could think of were the Heywards.

"So what's the big deal, Darrin? He's dead, and now you don't have to worry about him bothering you or us ever again. I don't see where this is really a problem. It's not like you or he loved each other or had this binding father-son relationship. He was a drunken fool, and you are better off without him. Now if that's all, can we *please* talk about the wedding?" Laurelin crossed her legs in the opposite direction and waited for Darrin's usual surrender.

Her words snapped him back to reality. "Laurelin, you never cease to amaze me. Were you born this calloused and cynical, or did you have to work up to it? I just can't understand you. You know nothing about my father except for what I have just told you. Granted, I abhorred the man, but at least I have *reasons*. You only hate him because his death managed to cut into your agenda by taking me to Dallas for two days. Time, which I might add, could have been used to your benefit, if you had chosen to act like a grown-up instead of a spoiled little girl."

He was letting his anger out, and he could tell by the look of feigned surprise that Laurelin was taking particular delight in his losing control. Instead of letting her respond, he continued as he ripped away the tie at his neck. "So, in answer to your question, no, we *cannot* talk about the wedding now, because I was not finished explaining the situation to you."

He tossed the tie across the chair and went into the kitchen for a glass of something cold. Finding a can of cola, he popped the top and took a long, steady drink. This wasn't how he wanted things to be. He needed comfort right now. He needed to find a reason to believe that things would get better. He needed . . . What did he need?

"Turn it over to God" he could almost hear his mother saying.

Oh, God, help me, he prayed and took another drink. He was surprised and grateful that Laurelin hadn't followed him into the kitchen or called out to him. Slowly he took a deep breath and walked back into the living room.

"Look, I don't want to fight with you tonight. I don't want to plan a wedding, and I don't want to listen to any complaints about my absence. Yes, my father is dead because of his own stupidity, and yes, in its own way, it is a blessing. However, my father's stupidity has also cost the lives of two other individuals. This is an important thing."

"But the crash was in Texas. That's why you had to fly to Dallas, right?"

Darrin nodded curtly and took another drink.

"So *why* is it so important? We don't know the other people, and they didn't know us. None of our friends will find out about this, if that's what's bothering you. Just keep quiet about it."

Darrin shook his head in disbelief. Who *was* this woman before him? Had she always been this way? Had he really loved her at one point and time? He knew for certain he harbored no such feelings now, and he longed to tell her so—but it wasn't the right time.

"Laurelin, the couple he killed was from Lawrence. Do you know where that is?"

"Oh, Larryville?" she said, throwing out the insulting nickname. "The one in Kansas? That little college town, right?"

"Yes, that's the one. I met their daughter on the flight down to Dallas."

"You didn't tell her did you? She doesn't know it was your father, does she?"

"No, I didn't realize how the situations were connected until I saw the pictures of her parents and my father on the evening news. She told me her parents were killed in a car accident and that she was headed to Dallas, but I figured Dallas is a big city and—"

"She isn't going to sue your father's estate is she? Is this what you've been trying to tell me all evening? Oh, this *does* change everything. I wonder . . ."

Darrin had taken more than he could deal with. Going to the front door, he opened it and motioned to her. "Just get out. Go back to your perfectly decorated apartment and wonder about it there. I can't deal with you. I don't want to deal with you. Go decorate something for someone, but don't come near me. I don't want to hear from you or see you. You disgust me. Two innocent people lost their lives, and all you care to ask me is if their bereaved daughter is going to sue. Well, whether she sues or not, I am going to help her and her remaining family in any way I possibly can. That means financially, emotionally, or whatever other way they need assistance."

Laurelin winced but still hadn't bothered to get up from the sofa. "You're going to give them money? Darrin, why? That's just asking for a lawsuit of major proportions. Look, I have a great lawyer who can tell you exactly how to handle this. Just don't do anything stupid. If you go telling this woman who you are and give her money, well, who knows what will happen? You'll probably find the whole thing on the front page of the paper.

"Darrin, you need to be responsible about this. Think of our wedding—our friends. Think about the shop and your clientele. You can't risk this getting out. I don't want *anyone* to know about it. You haven't spoken to your father for years. Don't bring him home now that he's a ghost. I don't know what I'd do if any of our friends found out, Darrin. I really don't."

"Out!" Darrin's face flushed and his heartbeat quickened. What made him think he could ever live in the same world, let alone the same house, with this woman?

Laurelin smiled coyly and walked ever-so-gracefully to the door. "Fine, Darrin. You play it your way. You're just upset, but once you calm down you'll see that I'm right."

She took up her purse and came to stop in front of him. "You just might want to think about one thing. What makes you believe that once she discovers that it was your daddy who killed her parents, she'll want anything to do with you? Or worse yet, what if the pittance you offer her isn't enough and she keeps milking this thing for years? You'll want me then. You'll need someone like me to get you out of your self-imposed nightmare. I just hope you realize it before it's too late and you've given all your assets to those hicks in Lawrence."

She reached a hand up to touch his chest. "Look, Darrin, I'm not being cruel. I'm just being realistic. You can't change anything by wallowing in self-pity and anguish over what your father did. You're nothing like him, and you don't need to attach yourself to his wrongdoings. You're like me. We're survivors. More still, we're victors."

Darrin took hold of her hand and removed it from his chest. "Lin, please just go before I say something we're both going to regret."

Laurelin shrugged. "Have it your way. But just remember, we're engaged, and your assets are important to me."

"I thought I was important to you," he said.

Laurelin smiled coquettishly. "Well, of course. That goes without saying."

"It seems a lot of truly important things go without saying," Darrin replied. He came very close to concluding their conversation by breaking their engagement, but something held him back. "Just give me some time, Lin, okay? I'll call you when I'm ready to talk about all of this."

"Well, just so long as you don't take too long," Laurelin replied. "I can't put a wedding together overnight."

As usual, she had the last word and slipped out the door before Darrin could even register a proper comment. Everything that came to mind had to do with telling her that they could take all the time they wanted, because there wasn't going to be a wedding.

$$\left(7 \right)$$

*E*xcuse me, can I get a double espresso to go?" a harried woman asked while juggling a stack of books and papers.

Leslie's head began to spin. She'd been at Crossroads for almost nine hours straight, and because it was only two blocks from the University of Kansas, the shop was nearly always packed. It was nearing midnight, and the college students were preparing for all-nighters with last minute to-go orders of double everythings, except decaffeinated anything.

She smiled at the woman. "Sure thing."

Quickly, she made her way back to the wooden counter. She filled the large paper cup with the steaming liquid and applied the lid. She mechanically punched in the price on the cash register, derived the total, and delivered the goods to the book-laden woman. "That'll be $2.58." Leslie waited while the woman rummaged around in an ancient-looking billfold.

"Here you go." She handed Leslie a five-dollar bill. "Keep it. You look like you could use a double espresso yourself." She smiled and picked up some papers that had escaped her. "Have a good night," she called over her shoulder on the way out of the shop.

"Yeah," Leslie muttered and sighed deeply. Looking around, she suddenly realized she was all alone. *Good*, she thought, glancing at her watch. *I can close early tonight.* She dragged her exhausted body over to the entrance and locked the door. She flipped the sign to SORRY, WE'RE CLOSED! and began clearing any tables she'd overlooked throughout the night.

After thirty minutes of cleaning, Leslie was more than ready to leave, yet she still had to count the money in the drawer and balance it against the receipts. That would consume as much as an hour of her time. "At least Margie's got the store in the morning," she breathed with relief.

Carefully she entered each receipt into the adding machine as her parents had taught her to do so many years ago. How old had she been? Eight? Nine? She smiled at the bittersweet memories of her patient mother, who never became frustrated or angry when Leslie failed to remember to push the plus button or lost count of the daily earnings.

Leslie reflected fondly on the first time she "took the drawer down," as her father called it, all by herself. Her parents had beamed with pride, despite the fact that they'd helped the gangly, blond ponytailed girl every step of the way. They always knew how to build up her confidence and make her feel as though the world were at her fingertips.

"Oh, Mama, Daddy. I still need you so much!" Tears caught in her long lashes and spilled onto the stacks of papers and currency. "This is so hard without you. I'm so tired, and I know Aunt Margie is, too, but we're trying. We want to keep the store, and goodness knows we need to. I haven't even gone down to the basement to find your box of papers!"

Leslie thought about the shoe box full of deeds, wills, receipts, and other important documents. Her parents never forgot to remind her about the box before leaving on a trip. It was a part of the routine. And for the longest time, she hadn't thought anything of it. Nothing would ever come of it anyhow, she'd convinced herself over the years. She'd never need to go find the box and deal with its confidential contents.

The tears fell harder now. She recalled the first time the seriousness of their instructions had finally caught up with her. *What if something did happen?* she remembered thinking. *I'm only eighteen years old. What if they die and I suddenly have to handle everything alone?* But just as quickly, she'd brushed aside her worries. Nothing was going to happen to her parents. How often did things like that occur? No, her parents were strong and healthy and very cautious people. They'd no doubt live to a ripe old age, and she'd not have to deal with "the box" until she was an old woman with kids of her own.

Leslie smiled briefly, reflecting on the naive reasoning of her youth. "I'm twenty-four, and I still don't know what to do. Everything was supposed to be so clear by now, but it's still as hazy as it was when I was a teenager! And I still can't believe that they're gone. Just like that. One minute here—the next in heaven."

But she had to believe it. As often was the case, the truth was a hard pill to swallow. It was time for her to be responsible. It was time to locate the sacred box. The box that summarized her parents' lives and that would forever change hers. She tried to mentally unearth it from the myriad of clothes and old toys her mother had stored in the basement. Perhaps it was beside the rocking horse. Yes, she seemed to recall seeing the large, brown shoebox wrapped tightly in rubber bands and sealed securely in a clear plastic bag. She would definitely have to look when she returned home.

Wiping the tears from her eyes, she walked to the women's bathroom to splash cold water on her face. The place was a mess, as usual. Paper towels had overflown the trash container and now lay strewn around the small room. One more job to do before she could go home.

When both restrooms were set in order, Leslie carried out the last of the trash and heaved it into the bin with a groan.

"Finally!" she sighed, locking the back door. She gathered up her purse and jacket and gave the shop one last lookover. Satisfied, she made her way to her parked Toyota and wearily drove home.

❧

"Hello?" Leslie called as she unlocked the front door of her house.

"In here," Margie's voice emanated from the kitchen. Leslie found her, nightgown-clad, her face wan. In her hands was a china cup with what appeared to be tea. No doubt it was a cup of Margie's favorite chamomile. "How was your day?" Margie asked.

"Long. Too long. But everything's balanced and ready for your morning arrival, Auntie dear." A weak smile played at her lips. "Tips were decent." Margie nodded approvingly, and Leslie continued. "So how was Travis?"

Margie shifted uncomfortably in her chair. "Well, Les, I don't know what to do with him. He's so quiet. Too quiet. You've seen him. He just sits in his room or on the couch. Doesn't even care if cartoons are the show *du jour* or not. I'd be lying if I told you I wasn't worried."

Leslie nodded sadly, knowing full well the extent of the little boy's sorrow. "I am, too, Margie. Maybe tomorrow I'll call Pastor Parkinson. He may have some ideas, because I'm sure out of them. I mean, I knew this would be hard for Travis to deal with, but I never thought he'd just withdraw altogether. I guess I expected him to cry a lot and be clingy. I think I could have handled that, but this is . . . well . . . it just doesn't seem natural."

"I know. This is just so very hard." Rising to her feet, Margie walked to her niece and embraced her.

Leslie felt as though the older woman were trying to draw energy and momentum from her body, but unfortunately, she had none left to offer. Her aunt was dipping into a dry well.

Margie drew away and yawned. "Well, I guess I'm off to bed. Morning will come around awfully quick as it is."

Leslie nodded. "You know, you don't have to wait up for me. I'm a big girl now and I . . ." She could see a flicker of hurt in her aunt's expression. "Oh, pay me no attention. I'm so tired I don't know if I'm coming or going. I'm going to go take a hot shower and go to bed." She gave Margie a peck on the cheek. "Thanks for caring about me."

"That's what I'm here for," the older woman replied.

Leslie found some comfort in her words. "I'll probably see you before you leave in the morning. Even if he is the picture of dejection, Travis's internal alarm clock is perpetually set at 7:30." Both emitted a strained laugh, and Margie began to walk toward the guest room. Before she was out of sight, Leslie spoke again. "I'm really glad you're here, Margie. I mean that. I don't think I could live in this house without your help and support."

The woman turned and offered a weak smile. "I know what you

mean, Les. I don't think I could be alone, either." With that, she disappeared into the darkness of the doorway.

Leslie made her way to the spacious bathroom and turned the nozzles until she had the desired temperature. Steam rose to meet her face, and she inhaled deeply. This working arrangement would, no doubt, be the death of her. She felt so old. She and Margie traded time at the shop. Margie took days so that Leslie could spend more waking hours with Travis. Leslie was more in tune with the night crowd anyway. She'd always show up around four in the afternoon, bringing Travis in tow, and she and Margie would exchange shop and child, like couriers bent on a secret mission. It seemed the easiest answer, and for six days out of the week, this was to be the routine.

Sundays had always been set aside for family, and the shop was closed, much to the grumbling of the clientele. Leslie cherished Sundays. They made it a true day of rest, usually characterized by naps after morning church service and lunch. Sometimes the afternoon lent itself to trips to the park or the museum. In the past they'd even taken day trips to Kansas City or Topeka. Leslie fondly remembered those times she'd gone along when her parents had planned some special outing for Travis.

Poor Travis.

The once vivacious boy was not dealing well with the absence of his parents, and often did nothing but surrender to fitful sleep. Leslie had tried to find books that dealt with childhood trauma and how to help children cope with losing their parents, but the pickings were very slim. Christian books often fell short of really offering anything solid for children.

She didn't know how to comfort her brother, and that seemed the most important thing right now. Nothing either woman did would console the child. It was as though his entire five-year-old being was drenched in anguish. His eyes looked hollow, and his appetite had greatly diminished. His ashen face and the ever-present dreamy look in his blue eyes broke Leslie's heart each time she saw him.

As the massaging jets of the showerhead stripped away the trials and worries of the day, Leslie tried to focus on ways to help her baby brother. She could think of nothing at all, save counseling. Professional and educated counseling. There was a great hospice organization in Topeka. Someone at church had mentioned being helped by a warm teddy bear of a man named Byron. It seemed he worked at the hospice and dealt primarily with children. It was at least worth considering. Someone had to be able to reach Travis. Somehow, he would work through this. He just had to. Leslie realized that without him, she really had nothing left of her parents, or herself.

Reluctantly, she turned the water off and stepped onto the terry cloth mat beside the tub. Slipping into her fuzzy, mulberry-colored robe, she lightly towel-dried her hair and made her way down the hall to Travis's room. She peaked her head through the cracked door and watched as he slumbered. All at once, his mouth contorted slightly, his brow wrinkled, and he tossed and turned violently. Then, he snuggled back into his covers and tightly clenched his teddy bear.

Tears sprang to Leslie's eyes once more. "Dear God, please give him peace. He's only a little guy." She thought of how they'd all called him their "Baby Guy" when he'd been born. He was tiny and feisty and so unique to the Heyward household.

"God, he can't deal with this alone. I can't deal with this alone, either, and I don't know how to comfort him when I can't even comfort myself. I know there has to be an answer. Maybe it's just that we all need time, but I love him so much," she whispered through her stifled sobs. "Please, Lord, give me back my Baby Guy."

Gingerly, she stepped into Travis's room. It was typical little boy motif, filled with building blocks, stuffed animals, and all the latest science fiction collectibles. Leslie mourned that the toys had not been played with for some time. Approaching his bedside, she eased onto her knees and looked into the troubled face of her brother. He was her entire life now. Nothing else mattered. Not the shop, not herself, not anything in this world. She loved him with her entire being. Just when she thought she had reached her limit and could no longer go on, the thought of Travis urged her forward. It was a feeling she had never thought possible.

Of course, she had loved him when her parents were still alive. But this was so much more intense. Every time she looked at him, her heart leaped into her throat, and she was forced to choke back sobs of joy, of frustration, of love. He was truly the only thing that made her remember she was alive.

Leaning closer, she softly kissed his flushed cheek. He stirred a bit and then seemed to relax. "Good night, my angel. Sissy promises to help you get better." Tears plopped onto his comforter, and Leslie inhaled a ragged breath. "I promise." Rising, she tiptoed back and noiselessly closed the door.

She leaned against the wall for a moment and sighed. There was nothing she could do. Nothing in her power would make him better. But God's power was another story. She might be helpless, but He wasn't. She had to believe that God could work through all the details.

"Just show me what to do, God," she prayed, and instantly an image of the shoebox came to mind. It was time to deal with the facts of the situation. Desperate for sleep but compelled to seek out the box, Leslie put aside her desires for bed and instead went to the basement.

❧

Darrin found his mind consumed with thoughts of Leslie, and when he could no longer restrain himself from action, he got in the car and drove to Lawrence. A quaint little town with hilly, winding streets, Lawrence had a village-style atmosphere in its downtown district. There were marvelous Victorian homes that lined narrow lanes, as well as completely modern housing architecture. Darrin found it peaceful and stimulating at the same time.

He drove down Massachusetts, the main drag through town, and turned off at Fourteenth Street. He rechecked the address one more time and headed up the steep hill that led toward the college campus. Then without warning he saw it. The large wooden sign with antique lettering: Crossroads.

He felt his chest tighten, and he pulled the car into the only available parking spot, nearly half a block away. For a moment, he just sat, staring at the shop. There were two shops really. One was Crossroads; the other was a small mom-n-pop drugstore that sported a sign in the window that read WINTER SALE. The building the two businesses shared was quaint, like the neighborhood, and seemed to have a generous number of patrons coming and going. That helped him relax a bit. Perhaps he could just slip in and out unnoticed and get a feel for the welfare of Leslie Heyward.

He approached the shop amid an onslaught of chattering girls. He waited until they'd passed into the shop before trying to follow them. Inside, the darkness instantly demanded his eyes adjust, and when they did, he found Leslie behind the counter taking orders from the talkative group.

Standing back, he just watched for several minutes. He was clearly out of place with all the young college students, but no one seemed to pay him much attention. Perhaps they thought he was a professor or instructor from the college. Perhaps they didn't care who he was. Everyone seemed quite wrapped up in their own world, and even as one table of customers seemed to rise in unison and move toward the exit, no one appeared to care that he stood idle in the middle of the room.

The girls took their coffee and rushed past him, giggling about something that one of the group had said. He watched them for a moment, then noticed that Leslie was watching him. *Did she remember him from the plane?* he wondered.

He smiled. "I don't remember being that young," he told her as he approached the counter.

A wistful look engulfed Leslie's face. "I do. And how I wish I could go back." Quickly, her expression melted into a customer-friendly grin, and she wiped away puddles of spilt coffee from the counter. She lifted her eyes to meet his face, those brilliant blue-green eyes he remembered so well. "So, what'll it be?"

Darrin breathed a sigh of relief. Apparently she didn't remember him, or if she did, she wasn't acknowledging it. "I don't know. I've never been here before. What do you suggest?"

"Well, it depends on what you like. If you're looking to stay awake all night, I'd suggest a double espresso with your favorite flavoring. If you're looking for something to warm you up from the cold, but don't want the caffeine, I'd suggest a decaf latte."

"What do you like?" he asked, taking a stool at the counter.

Leslie looked up for a moment. "I'm particularly fond of the grand-sized latte with raspberry."

"Does that come in decaf? I don't think I want to be up all night," Darrin said with a quick glance around the room. The place was nearly deserted, and he suddenly felt quite conscious of the fact.

"You can have it in decaf," Leslie told him and picked up a mug. "Is that what you'd like?"

"Sure. I'll give it a try."

"Is that for here or to go?"

"Here."

She smiled and went to work, bringing back a glass mug of rose-tinted liquid. "I hope you like it." As she handed it to him, her face assumed a look of concern. "I'd feel pretty bad if I suggested it and you turned out hating it."

Darrin took a taste and nodded. "It's good. Never thought about raspberry coffee before."

"We get all kinds here," Leslie said, busying herself with odd jobs behind the counter. "The kids can come up with some really crazy combinations."

"Kids? You don't look like much more than a kid yourself."

"Oh, aren't you the charmer?"

"I suppose you get a lot of those, too," he said, taking another drink.

Leslie laughed. "Yeah, like I said, we get all kinds."

"But seriously," Darrin began, "don't you go to the university?"

"No. I'm the owner of this shop. I graduated from there some time ago, and now I spend all my time here. Or so it seems. My name is Leslie Heyward."

"I'm Darrin," he offered, deciding against giving his last name in case she made the connection. "Well, it looks like a great place. I'll have to remember it."

"We'd love to have you back."

The small talk seemed to wear on his nerves, and yet he was drawn to the petite blond in the same way he had been on the plane. "So, when you're not here, what do you do?"

"Mostly I spend time at home with Travis. He consumes a lot of my time, especially now." The telephone rang and Leslie excused herself.

Travis? Darrin couldn't help but wonder who Travis might be. Would it be rude to come right out and ask? He sipped at the coffee and waited for her to return. But when Leslie hung up the phone, she grabbed a tray and went out to clean tables. Darrin had no choice but to turn around if he wanted to talk with her or ignore her and act like a regular customer whose attention was on coffee and not the proprietor. His heart won over and he twisted around on the stool.

"So, you were telling me about your off hours."

Leslie kept her back to him and continued wiping at the table. "I don't have many of them, but like I said, they're usually consumed with about a million things. My parents recently died—in fact, the funeral was just a few days ago. It's about all I can do to keep up."

Darrin was glad she couldn't see his expression because he was certain he had grimaced. "I'm sorry about your folks."

"Yeah, me too. It's been especially hard on Travis."

"Who's that—a boyfriend?" There, the question was finally asked.

Leslie laughed. "No. I don't have a boyfriend. When would I find the time?"

Darrin found himself relieved at her answer and, for reasons beyond his understanding, almost smiled. But her next words put aside such joyous thoughts.

"Travis is my little brother. He's only five. Guess you could say he was one of those late-life or at least mid-life surprises for my folks." She turned and straightened, the glass-ladened tray balanced expertly in her hand. "Travis isn't dealing very well with this at all. He's not talking much these days, and it's becoming pretty evident that he's going to need some professional help to get through losing his mom and dad."

Darrin felt instantly sickened. A child! A little boy named Travis was now without his parents because Darrin's own father had . . . It was too much to even consider. Why was it suddenly so much worse than before? It wasn't like he didn't know that people were affected by the Heywards' deaths, but he'd never for one moment envisioned that a child would be orphaned by the accident.

"I'm so sorry. How horrible for a little boy to be confronted with the death of his parents. I suppose you were left as his guardian?"

She nodded. "Mom and Dad had the good sense to plan it all out with a will, but I would have cared for him anyway. We're terribly close."

"I suppose something like this is never really planned for."

"No, not really, but Mom and Dad did their best to make it easy on us. They had one of those prearranged funeral plans." She smiled rather sheepishly. "I could have saved myself a great deal of worry if I'd just bothered to go through their private papers first thing. I don't know why I put it off. I guess going through those papers made their deaths more real—more final."

"I can understand that," he replied sympathetically. "So everything was arranged and taken care of, and you only had to worry about seeing that their wishes were carried out?"

"Pretty much so. Wish it could be that easy for Travis. When you're five, death has very little meaning."

"But when you're an adult watching a child deal with death, it has a great deal of meaning."

He could see Leslie's eyes sparkle with tears. "Yeah, it's really hard to watch him deteriorate like this. I love him so much. Everybody does. He's so good-natured—or at least he was. It's just not fair." As if embarrassed for her muted outburst, she offered a pain-filled smile. "Sometimes I'm not very understanding when it comes to trusting God to work this out for the best."

"I completely understand. I have my fair share of questions to ask Him. And that's on a good day!" Darrin removed a five-dollar bill from a monogrammed wallet and handed it to Leslie. She began to fumble for change in the pocket of her apron, but Darrin reached out and placed his hand on her forearm. "No, you go ahead and keep that."

He got to his feet and drained the rest of the coffee. "Thanks a lot. I really enjoyed this place."

"I'm glad. Thank *you* for listening to me. I don't seem to be getting much contact with the outside world, except for my aunt. Between our hours here and watching Travis, we don't have much time for heart-to-heart conversations." Clearing Darrin's mug from the counter and wiping the pinewood with a damp cloth, Leslie turned to face him. "Do come back."

Darrin smiled. "I plan on it. See you later."

As soon as he was out-of-doors, Darrin heaved a sigh. He felt like a wound had not only reopened, but that it had become deeper. Leslie *and* her little brother were suffering from the sins of his father. A five-year-old child was left with only an overworked, overworried sister and an aunt to care for him. A twenty-four-year-old woman was left with a business, a grieving brother, and no additional guidance. And he was left with the guilt. The guilt of knowing that, had it not been for the irresponsible acts of Michael Malone, they would be a very happy and complete family.

8

s the weeks blended together, Leslie found herself growing more and more weary of everything. She was sick of the shop and the routine there. She was tired of dealing with problems that she had no answers for and had reached an absolute limit with Travis.

In the weeks since their parents' accident, Travis had gone through a period of silence and distancing. He chose to stay in his room for hours on end, and even when Leslie tried to draw him out, he would refuse. It was a real trial to take him to church or the park or anywhere else for that matter. But during the last week he'd passed into another stage of mourning. His security level plummeted, and he demanded to have Leslie's utmost attention at every turn. He cried every time she left him, and whenever she'd return to the house, he'd cling to her for hours. This happened even when she was working late at night, and it worried her more than she could say.

She'd fully intended to seek some counseling for him, but her pastor didn't think it would require anything so professional or detailed, at least not at this point. He suggested she just give the boy time and let nature run its course. But as far as Leslie was concerned, nature's course was beginning to frighten her.

The Saturday evening crowd finally thinned out and eventually left the shop. Leslie was exhausted, partially because of being on her feet since late afternoon, and partially because Travis's nightmares often kept them both awake at night and she wasn't getting much sleep. Leslie cleaned up, counted the money, and headed for her car. She was too tired to think and knew that she shouldn't be driving, but the trip home was short and she tried to focus all her attention on the steep hill that was Fourteenth Street. She breathed a sigh of relief to find it clear of snow and ice, but nevertheless slipped the car into low gear to save wear on her brakes.

Just as she crossed the intersection at Kentucky Street, Leslie had the scare of her life. Out of nowhere a car came barreling down the street, and before Leslie could clear the intersection, it clipped the back end of her Toyota and spun her around.

"Great!" she exclaimed as she came to a stop. "This is just what I need." The shock of the accident kept her foot firmly on the brake and her hands on the wheel for several long minutes.

The driver from the other vehicle had run a red light and, after hitting Leslie, had run the front end of his car up on the sidewalk. There it sat, precariously balanced half on and half off the street. For a second, Leslie took a mental inventory. She felt all right and didn't think any real injury had come to her from the accident.

The car—well, that would take getting out to survey the damage, and since it was after midnight, Leslie was hesitant to do so. She'd just read how people were sometimes rear-ended or run into in order for the driver of the other vehicle to do further harm to the occupants of the incapacitated car. But no one in the other vehicle seemed inclined to get out and check on her. Maybe they were hurt. Maybe she should go to them and stop worrying about the consequences.

She sat there wondering what she should do, when to her relief the flashing lights of a Lawrence police car came into view behind her. "Thank you, Father," she whispered as she turned off her engine.

The police car was soon joined by another. Leslie gave her statement, trying to remember every detail. She was amazed at how much she took for granted. How fast was she going? Was the light green or had it already turned amber when she went through? Was she wearing her seat belt? Had there been any ice on the roadway?

She tried to make certain of her answers. The seat belt situation was easy—she always wore it and demanded that anyone riding in her car wear theirs as well. Aunt Margie often protested, saying that they never worried about such things when she was a child, but nevertheless she'd wear one for Leslie. She gave the answers that she thought were correct. She was certain that she wasn't going over the speed limit because she always geared down to come down the hill and she hadn't yet geared back up when she'd been hit.

The officer was noting everything, and it was while he was finishing that she noted the other driver was led away in handcuffs. His loud protests left Leslie little doubt as to his sobriety.

"It doesn't look like there's much damage here," the officer told her. "In fact, you were very lucky."

"It wasn't luck," Leslie replied, her breath coming out in puffs of steam against the cold February night. "I'm sure God was watching out for me."

The officer seemed unimpressed with her faith and, after finishing his report, gave her a copy of the insurance information from the other driver and offered to follow her to her house in order to make sure the car could operate properly. Leslie thanked him and headed the car in the direction of home. She had just reached down to turn up the heater when she noted that the dashboard clock read 1:35.

"Oh, Margie will be sick with worry," she exclaimed.

Ten minutes later she pulled into her driveway and waved to the police officer as she made her way to the house. Margie was waiting for her with a fearful expression on her face.

"Where have you been? I called the shop, but you were already gone."

"Oh, I know, and I'm so sorry. I was coming down Fourteenth when a drunk driver hit my car. He barely clipped the backside, so the damage is real limited, but it scared me. Coming home just now, I thought of Mom and Dad and how they didn't fare as well from their drunk driver."

Margie nodded. "People are so thoughtless to drink themselves into a stupor and then get behind the wheel of a car. Even if it wasn't illegal, they ought not to take people's lives into their own hands."

"Well, I'll have to call the insurance agent tomorrow. Do you think I can get ahold of him on Sunday?"

"It's hard to say, but I'd imagine there's some kind of emergency number. How do you feel? You weren't hurt were you? Whiplash sometimes doesn't show up right away."

Leslie rubbed her neck. "No, I don't think I'm hurt."

At this, both women were startled to find Travis screaming Leslie's name as he ran down the stairs. "Leslie! You're hurt!"

"No," Leslie said, lifting him in her arms. He wrapped his arms so tightly around Leslie's neck that she was nearly deprived of air. "Trav, stop squeezing so tight," she gasped and pried his arms away. "Travis, I'm okay. I had a little accident tonight, but I'm okay. God was taking good care of me."

Travis sobbed hysterically, and it was an hour before Leslie and Margie could get him calm. Leslie finally decided to let him sleep in her bed that night, even though she questioned the sensibility of it. What if he decided he needed to sleep with her every night? That would certainly never do.

She carried him upstairs, talking soothingly all the way, while Margie followed behind, snapping off lights. "Tomorrow," she told Travis, "we'll go to church and then maybe we can . . ."

"I don't want to ride in the car. The car will kill me," Travis told her adamantly. "The car killed Mommy and Daddy."

Leslie exchanged glances with Margie before answering. "No, sweetie, it wasn't the car's fault. It was the fault of the person driving the car. Remember, I told you. The man had too much alcohol to drink, and he didn't know what he was doing. He shouldn't have been driving. Just like the man tonight. He shouldn't have been driving, but because he didn't think about the consequences, he did what he wanted to anyway. Now I'm all right, and we need to get some sleep, so I want you to just stop worrying about it. Okay?"

Travis nodded sleepily but said nothing. Leslie shook her head at Margie's mournful expression and took Travis into her room. It was going to be a long night.

❧

"But Travis, I thought you understood. Remember what I told you about the car? It can't hurt anybody by itself. We're just driving to church and back. We won't be hurt, I promise." But even as the words were out of her mouth, Leslie wondered how she would ever explain it, if by some strange twist of fate, they were in another accident.

Travis had planted himself under the bed and refused to come out. Even now, as Leslie lay on her stomach and tried to coax him from his hiding place, she could see that her pleas were having little effect. He was terrified, and there was no way he was going to climb into a car again without a great deal of thought and possibly professional help.

"Come on, Trav, I'll take good care of us."

"No!" He scooted further back toward the headboard end of the bed.

Leslie sighed and glanced up at Margie, who waited in anxious worry by the door. "Margie, you go on to church. I don't think we'll be going today, but maybe you could have everyone pray for us."

Margie grimaced. "Are you sure you don't want me to stay here with you?"

"No, we'll be fine. Travis and I just need to spend some time together."

Margie left in silence, and for several minutes Leslie just lay with her cheek against the hardwood floor of Travis's room. Travis watched her without moving. The terror in his eyes made Leslie feel terrible. She felt like it was all her fault. If she'd only been more cautious telling Margie about the accident, Travis might never have heard. On the other hand, it was probably only a matter of time until his fears had taken over anyway. Better to deal with it now, she guessed.

"Hey, Trav, I know what we could do."

"What?" he asked softly.

"Well, it snowed again last night, and I was thinking maybe we could make a snowman in the yard."

"You won't make me ride in the car?"

"No," she answered. "I love you, baby. I don't want you to be afraid."

He started to cry. "I miss Mommy and Daddy."

Tears formed in Leslie's eyes. "I miss them, too. Say, would you like to walk over to the cemetery?"

"So we can see them?" Travis asked, sounding almost hopeful.

"Well, they aren't there, not really. You remember what I told you about them being in heaven, don't you?"

"You said they just left their bodies here."

"That's right." Leslie's back began to ache, so she sat up, thinking that perhaps Travis would at least come to the edge of the bed in order to better talk to her. "It's like your box of toys. You have the outside box, but the real treasure is the toys inside. Mommy and Daddy had bodies that were kind of like boxes to hold their spirits. Their spirits are the very best part, and that part has gone to heaven to live with Jesus."

Travis came out from under the bed and surprised Leslie by plopping down on her lap. "Do their spirits remember me?" he asked.

"I'm sure they do. You know, there's a lot about heaven that I don't understand or know much about, but I do know that people in heaven are never sad."

"Never? What if they fall down and get hurt?"

"You can't get hurt in heaven—there are no tears in heaven."

"Then let's go now, Sissy. I want to be in heaven with Mommy and Daddy."

Leslie hugged her brother close. Tears were streaming down her face. "Oh, baby, I want to be with them, too. I want to be with Jesus and never cry again, but it isn't time for us to go. When it's time, Jesus will come and get us, but until then, I need you here with me. I need someone to stay and help me be strong."

Travis looked up to see her tears. His lip quivered and puckered as he started to cry. Leslie reached out to wipe his tears. "We're going to make it through this, Travis. It hurts a lot right now, but it won't hurt this bad forever. We need to let God help us, though. In the Bible, God says that He loves us and that He'll be with us even when we're afraid."

"I'm 'fraid, Sissy," Travis said, snuggling against her.

Leslie nodded. "I know you are. Sometimes, I'm afraid, too. But you know what? I remember a little verse in the Bible, and it helps me to know that I'm going to be all right."

"What is it?" he asked, his breath ragged.

"Psalm 56:3," Leslie replied. " 'When I am afraid, I will trust in You.' "

"When I'm 'fraid, I'll trust in You," Travis whispered.

"Can you remember that?" Leslie asked him softly.

Travis nodded, and Leslie smiled. She only hoped she could do as well to remember it when fearful times were upon her.

9

arrin waited uncomfortably for Laurelin to show up at the apartment. He'd invited her to share dinner with him, with the determined purpose of telling her that it was over between them. The problem was, he didn't know how exactly he was going to handle the situation. Laurelin wasn't going to take rejection lightly, and there was no way she would see this as anything but rejection.

A bigger problem was that Laurelin was a great help with the store, and with several spring trips to Europe on his agenda, Darrin wasn't yet ready to be rid of the helpfulness of an assistant, especially one as savvy as Laurelin. Still, he couldn't string her along just in order to have her help at the store. She might even surprise him and ask to stay on with Elysium. Stranger things had come from Laurelin in the past.

A light-handed knock sounded at the door, and Darrin instantly recognized it as belonging to Laurelin. He opened the door and found her decked out in her full-length, arctic fox coat.

"Thanks for coming," he said, opening the door wide. "Come on in."

"Well, I must say, I haven't enjoyed your silent treatment one bit," Laurelin said, throwing off the coat to reveal a stunning winter-white pantsuit. "Nor have I enjoyed being responsible for the store all by myself. Oh, Gerda was there part-time, but she was practically useless. I don't know why you keep her. And I don't know why you call me to come over on the coldest day of the year. I swear the temperature has to be somewhere below zero."

Darrin took the coat and draped it over the back of a chair as his fiancée droned on. Laurelin had berated him quite severely once for daring to hang her coat on a hanger in his closet. He really wasn't sure what proper etiquette required in caring for arctic fox. Personally, he thought the coat looked better on the animal than on Laurelin, but he hadn't purchased it, so it really wasn't his place to complain.

"So did you order out for us?" she questioned, sniffing the air as if to identify the aroma.

Darrin smiled as he thought perhaps she should have kept the coat on. She looked like some sort of animal, sniffing the air for scent of her prey.

"What's so funny?" she suddenly asked, and Darrin realized that he'd been caught.

"Nothing, Lin. I doubt you'd see it the same way I did."

"Well," she paused as if deciding to pursue what she felt must be an insult. Then just as quickly she dismissed her concern and swept back her brown hair in a fluid, graceful move. "So, what are we eating?"

"I fixed us stir-fry," he said with an apologetic shrug. "It's pretty tasty, if I do say so myself."

"I suppose it will have to do," Laurelin replied. "Unless, of course, you'd like to take me out. I know this great new restaurant down on the plaza."

"No, I'm not going out tonight."

"Fine." She seemed to pout for a moment, but as Darrin turned to lead the way to the dining room, she followed without hesitation.

"I'm sorry I haven't been good company of late. I'm sorry, too, that I haven't called much or kept up with the parties and such. I've had a lot on my mind and felt it unfair to burden you with it," Darrin said as he took a chair opposite her.

He dished up steaming rice and then added a generous ladle of vegetables to top this before handing the plate to Laurelin. She murmured thanks as he doubled the portion for himself and then paused thoughtfully. "If you don't mind," he said, "I'd like to pray."

"Pray? *Now?*" Laurelin asked in disbelief. "Whatever for?"

"Because I feel thankful, that's why," Darrin said and bowed his head. "Father, I thank You for this food and the blessings You've bestowed. I ask You to be with me now as I share this meal with Laurelin. I ask that we might better understand Your will in our lives. In Jesus' name, amen."

Laurelin was still sitting there watching him as she had been before he'd bowed in prayer. "What in the world was that all about?"

"It's about a great deal," Darrin said, mixing the vegetables with the rice. "You've always known that I was a Christian, although I do apologize for not being a very active one. I've suddenly come to realize how very important prayer is to me, and that God needs to play a more major role in my life."

"Is *that* why you asked me over?" Her voice betrayed a tone of disbelief.

"Not completely. There are a great many things we need to discuss."

"Don't I know it," she answered rather haughtily. "You leave me virtually on hold for weeks, making an appearance when it suited you, leaving the store in limbo. Not to mention—"

Darrin held up his hand. "Lin, I don't want to fight."

"Well, neither do I," she snapped back. "But I do want some explanations."

"And you deserve to have them," Darrin answered. "That's exactly why I wanted us to get together. But not if it means that we spend the time yelling at each other. I've let that kind of communication go on too long. We need to be able to talk in a civilized manner to each other. You know what I mean? With respect and—"

"Darrin," Laurelin interrupted, putting a hand to her head, "don't try to psychoanalyze my life. I have one therapist, and I don't need another."

"I'm not trying to be your therapist. I am trying to explain, however, that I'm only coming to see the error of my ways in a great many areas."

Laurelin sat back and smiled smugly. "Well, why didn't you say so in the first place? If you've brought me here to apologize, by all means have at it."

"It isn't that I feel the need to apologize," Darrin said, feeling angry at her suggestion that he owed her something other than an explanation. He tried to calm his feelings, remembering the time he'd spent in prayer before Laurelin's arrival. "Look, Lin, I want you to understand that I've come to realize how much I've distanced myself from God. As a Christian, I know that I'm to continue my spiritual walk and growth, but I feel like the past few years have been spent taking a nap alongside the path rather than pursuing the journey."

"Whatever are you talking about? We've been seen in church nearly every Sunday. Well, at least most every Sunday until that dreadful Dallas fiasco. Speaking of which, has that woman slapped you with a lawsuit yet? Is that why you called me?"

"No, she's not suing me."

"Well, don't bet on it. I'd keep a good lawyer on retainer just the same." Laurelin dug into the food and nodded. "This isn't too bad, Darrin."

"Thank you," he answered, feeling his patience begin to wear thin. He opened his mouth to try once again to explain the need to allow God to direct his life, when Laurelin started off on her own agenda.

"You know, Darrin, I've been looking at houses, and I know you'd wanted to put it off until a year or two after we marry, but I think we ought to consider getting a place right away. I have found the most delightful house, in the perfect neighborhood. We can entertain and have brokers over and . . ."

"I'm not buying a house, Laurelin," he said flatly and went to the kitchen for the coffee pot.

"But Darrin, this place is so small, and the neighborhood is becoming so overrun with people of lower standards than ours. I think it would do your image good to relocate. I'd suggest we live in my place, but there is even less room than here, and I know we'd never be happy there."

"No, I'm sure we wouldn't," Darrin said. "Which brings me to my point."

"Look, Darrin, it wouldn't hurt you at all to consider my feelings in the matter. I want to feel proud of the place I live in. I want a home that I can entertain in and not be afraid that all the guests will be discussing my poor taste behind my back."

"Laurelin, we aren't buying a house."

She glared at him and slammed down her fork. "You simply don't care about me, do you? Is this some kind of male control issue? Because if it is, I'm not buying into it."

"And I'm not buying a house. It has nothing to do with control issues, but it has everything to do with us," Darrin replied.

"You just don't understand how important this is, do you?" She was clearly angry. "You give more consideration to a know-nothing family in Lawrence that you don't even know than you do to the woman you're supposed to marry. I don't understand you. I don't understand your lack of consideration."

"Oh, and you're the queen of consideration, yourself," Darrin countered. Once again she'd led him where he didn't want to go. How crafty she was at manipulating people into arguments.

"I don't have to take this from you, Darrin."

"You know, Lin, you're right. I'm feeling a bit angry now, and I'm going to go for a drive. When I get back, I hope you'll have the good sense to be gone."

"You can't just walk out on me like this," Lin said, getting to her feet and following Darrin into the living room.

"I can and I will," Darrin replied, pulling his coat out of the closet. "And this time, I'll have the last word."

∾

Leslie glanced up at the sound of the bells ringing on the front door. She smiled to herself as she recognized one of her regular customers. It was that nice man, David . . . no, Darrin something. She didn't know much about him except that he liked to sit at the counter and talk to her rather than take a table or join anyone else. She reached for a glass mug and began preparing a decaf raspberry latte, knowing by now that this was his usual request.

"Brrrr," he said, dusting a few snowflakes from his coat. "It's definitely winter out there."

"I see it's started to snow again," Leslie offered.

"Yes, but I don't think it's going to make anything of itself." He unzipped the coat and nodded. "I see you've learned to know me pretty well."

"I try to keep track of my regulars," Leslie said with a smile. "But if you have a taste for something different tonight, you certainly aren't obligated to this." She held up the steaming mug of coffee as if posing a question of acceptance.

"No, by all means, let me have at it. I'm half frozen." He took the coffee and downed half of it while Leslie rang up his sale.

Leslie caught the motion of another customer at the opposite end of the counter and, after putting Darrin's change down in front of him, went to see what the man wanted. It wasn't a hectic night, and for that Leslie was both grateful and concerned. The cold sometimes had the opposite desired effect, and rather than finding the shop filled with people demanding hot drinks, Leslie found that they all stayed home and refused to venture out into the frigid night.

"I need one more, only make this to go," the man said, after Leslie asked how she could serve him. She filled a paper cup, secured the lid, and took his money, all while allowing herself brief glimpses at Darrin. She couldn't help wondering who he was and why he always came alone. She always tried to imagine the lives of her customers, and some of them, most of them, were pretty ease to peg. Like the man she was waiting on just now. He wasn't all that well known to her, but what she did know was that he lived only a block away and the coffee shop afforded him a quick get-away from his crowded apartment. She knew it was crowded because usually the man was accompanied by four other people, all who claimed residence in the same student rental as he did. She didn't know his name. Didn't really care to, and yet, she knew his face and what he liked to drink in the way of coffee. Seemed a small pittance of information to summarize a man's life by.

The man took off, leaving Leslie to clean the space he'd just vacated. She waved good-bye to three women who were also regulars from the college. All three were housemothers for different campus sororities, and all came in once a week like clockwork to discuss their problems and accomplishments. They each ordered a different type of coffee and always had cinnamon scones to accompany their chats. They always stayed about an hour and a half and always left her a two-dollar tip. You didn't get any more regular than that.

But Darrin, he was different, and Leslie couldn't quite peg him. He'd only been coming in for the last few weeks, but in that short time she'd really come to enjoy his visits. Whenever he came, he always sought her out and struck up a conversation. He always wanted to know how the shop was doing—how she was doing. He seemed, too, to genuinely care about the answers, and he was overwhelmingly generous. He always left her tips that were three and four times the price of his order. She'd started to argue with him once when he'd left her a twenty after ordering a two-dollar cup of coffee, but he told her that was his way, and he wouldn't be moved to change his mind.

"So, how's business?" he asked as she cleaned her way back to his spot at the counter.

"It's been better," Leslie admitted, throwing the cloth into a bucket of bleach water that resided under the counter.

Darrin's face was still touched with a rosy glow from the cold, and Leslie liked the way his bright blue eyes seemed to sparkle with enthusiasm for her company. He was a handsome man, she thought. Handsome and considerate. She wondered if he was attached to someone somewhere, but because he never mentioned anyone, Leslie allowed herself to believe he was a free agent.

Not that it really mattered. She wasn't looking for anyone at this point in her life. There was so much trouble at home that dating wasn't an option, and considering anything beyond the day-to-day trials only made her feel desperately alone and hopeless. She knew God was there for her, but at times she longed for *someone* to be there as well.

"You aren't listening to me, are you?" Darrin questioned.

Leslie felt her face flush. "Sorry. I've just got a lot on my mind."

"Like the shop being slow?"

"That, among other things," she admitted. "You want another?" she asked, noting that his mug was nearly empty.

"Sure, it's decaf, right?"

She nodded and went to work while Darrin questioned her about her week and why business was off. "Mostly it's because of the cold. You'd think cold weather would bring out the coffee and hot chocolate drinkers, but because most of the college kids are on foot, getting out in this cold doesn't hold near the attraction that staying home and fixing your own hot drinks has. I'm sure it will pick up in time." *At least I hope it does*, she added to herself.

"But that's not all you have on your mind, is it?"

Leslie bit at her lower lip before answering. "No, I guess it ranks down second or third on the list."

"What's number one?"

Leslie noted genuine concern in his expression. His eyes seemed to reflect unspoken questions, and his attention warmed her heart. "Travis," she finally murmured.

"Your little brother?"

"That'd be the one." She tried to sound lighthearted, but it was almost impossible. "He's having a lot of trouble with the death of our parents." She noted that Darrin visibly winced and quickly moved to change the subject. "But he'll be all right. What about you? Did you have a good work week?"

"What happened with me isn't important. Tell me about Travis. Are you getting him counseling?"

"Well, we didn't go that route at first. Our pastor was kind of the old-fashioned sort who figured kids in their resilient natures would bounce back from death in a fairly reasonable fashion. He told us to let nature run its course, but as time passed by and Travis started having more and more nightmares, I figured nature wasn't running the way it should. Now, Travis won't even get into the car without hysterical, traumatic fits, and, frankly, I'm worn out from dealing with it."

Darrin appeared compassionately interested, and Leslie found herself clinging to his attentiveness like a drowning woman. He was good for her. He was like her own private counselor, showing up week after week, always asking for her to spill her heart. What was funnier yet was that Leslie felt quite content in doing just that. She didn't feel withdrawn and closed off with Darrin.

"You can't just leave him to find his own way through this," Darrin commented. "I don't think kids are as resilient as we'd like to believe. This is big-time stuff, and he needs real help."

Leslie nodded. "And he's finally getting it. I think once I told my pastor what we were up against, he understood that Travis wasn't getting any better. Now we're getting counseling, but it's like taking five steps back for every one we take forward. Travis hates talking to anyone, but he really hates it when the counselor wants to send me from the room so that he can talk to Travis alone. Travis has developed this real phobia about letting me out of his sight. He has our aunt call down here several times a night, all in order to make sure I haven't been killed."

Darrin frowned. "Do you feel confident about the counselor? I mean, is he qualified to deal with this kind of thing?"

"Oh, definitely," Leslie said, pausing to sip her coffee. "He's a Christian who specializes in dealing with children, and he centers his advice and counseling on the Bible. Of course, he doesn't just sit there and spout Bible verses. After all, Travis is only five."

"I don't think it helps adults to just sit and spout verses, as you say, either." Darrin seemed to search for the right words. "I mean . . . it's just that . . . well, the verses are great, but too often I think people are in the habit of throwing them out like coins. They see someone in need and say, 'Well, here's a verse, now get over your problem and go on with life.'"

Leslie nodded. "Oh, I quite agree. I think there are a great many Christians who have focused on memorizing the words, but not the application behind those words. I've been quoted at many a time, but once in particular I remember asking the woman what she meant by suggesting that particular verse, and she couldn't really explain it."

"I've been there, too. When my mother died from cancer, I can't tell you the number of people that came forward to say, 'Remember Romans 8:28. All things work together for good, to them that love the Lord.'"

Leslie smiled. "I've heard that more times than I care to remember." She put down her mug. "And, it isn't because I don't believe that, because I do. I believe that God is in everything. I believe that He alone holds the answers to the questions in my heart. But it doesn't make my pain any less to know that He has worked this all out for a purpose and reason. I'm glad God's in the details, but I still hurt, and He knows that."

Darrin looked at her strangely for a moment. "Yet, you find your comfort in Him, don't you?"

She felt a tingling run down her arms. The way he looked at her was so startling, almost as if he could see inside her soul and find the answer for himself. "Yes, I do," she murmured. "And, I find real comfort in His Word. Just as those people who throw out verses without application have sometimes left me frustrated and numb, I've been blessed by a handful of others who have brought genuine direction into my life by sharing Scripture. Just the other day, for example." She paused, looking at Darrin as if to weigh whether or not he really wanted to hear this.

"Go on," he urged without hesitation.

Leslie felt suddenly self-conscious. She glanced around the shop to see if she'd neglected anyone. No one seemed to care that she stood in discussion with one of the customers. Taking a deep breath, she steadied her nerves. "Well, a good friend shared some verses with me from 2 Corinthians 4. I was so moved that I memorized the words, and every day I've used them to strengthen my heart. Not because she threw them out at me and left me to consider them. But because she shared them with me and told me how they applied to her life and how she felt they would apply to my life, as well. Then she prayed with me and even cried with me. It made all the difference in the world."

"And what were the verses?" he asked softly.

Leslie closed her eyes. "'We are hard pressed on every side, but not crushed; perplexed but not in despair; persecuted but not abandoned; struck down but not destroyed. We always carry around in our body the death of Jesus, so that the life of Jesus may also be revealed in our body. For we who are alive are always being given over to death for Jesus' sake, so that His life may be revealed in our mortal body.'"

Leslie opened her eyes and found Darrin's blue eyes filled with tears. She lowered her gaze and continued. "It meant so much to hear those words and to know that God knew we would have moments of overwhelming heartache and misery, but that we wouldn't be left to bear it alone. That, in fact, it had already been carried to Calvary by His Son Jesus.

"I looked at those verses over and over, and I can still hear the voice of my friend as she shared losing her husband in a plane crash. She told me that she felt so abandoned after his death, but here was proof that she wasn't. She felt completely crushed, crushed in ways that she couldn't begin to explain. Yet here were words that addressed her very feelings, and in that she began to heal, to see that while she was hard-pressed, she wasn't truly crushed. And that while she felt destroyed, in truth she was only struck down for a time.

"She finished up by sharing the very last verses in that chapter, and I'll never forget the love in her voice as she promised me that she knew the truth of those words: 'For our light and momentary troubles are achieving for us an eternal glory that far outweighs them all. So we fix our eyes not on what is seen, but on what is unseen. For what is seen is temporary, but what is unseen is eternal.'"

"That's good advice," Darrin said, pulling out his handkerchief.

He wiped his eyes unashamedly and smiled at Leslie in such a way that she had to swallow her heart to keep it from leaping out of her throat. Who was this man, and why did he affect her the way he did?

The couple at the corner table was getting up to leave, and instantly Leslie felt the spell of the moment broken by their activity. She picked up her cloth from the bleach water and grabbed a tray. "Work calls," she told Darrin as evenly as she could manage.

It wasn't until she was bent over the table and reaching for the couple's empty mugs that she saw how her hands were shaking. A strange feeling washed over her as a thought came unbidden to her mind. Darrin was a remarkable man, and he alone was responsible for these feelings. *But what were these feelings?* Leslie wondered. *Was this what it was like to fall in love?*

She wiped the table and came back to the counter, where Darrin sat with a distant look on his face. *Apparently he isn't moved to ask the same questions of himself*, she thought sadly.

Pushing down her emotions, Leslie nodded to the clock. "I'm afraid it's closing time."

Darrin nodded and put twenty dollars on the counter. "Thanks for the conversation and for the Scripture. I'm going to check it out when I get home." He left her then, and Leslie watched after him until he had disappeared from view.

"You're welcome," she whispered to the empty room and added, "Anytime."

⑩

*A*fter locking the entrance to Crossroads, Leslie turned the knob and pushed, just to make sure. It was an old habit, but she was sure it had its merits. As she hurriedly walked to her parked car, she felt drawn to look at the stars. It was something she hadn't done for years. Remembering her father, she felt tears sting her eyes. Aaron Heyward was the first person to take the time to introduce Leslie to the sky. He pointed out constellations and planets and was always patient and understanding when her eyes were too untrained to pick out the patterns. Now that she was a grown woman, the sky was no less magical and no less wonderful. And it served as yet another example of how much her parents had given to her.

It wasn't until she had started her car that she realized what time it was. Ten till one. Not too terribly late, but late, nonetheless. She had called Margie around eleven-thirty to tell her that it was a possibility and not to wait up, but no doubt Travis would be waiting. At least nothing had gone wrong tonight. Perhaps that would ease his mind.

Leslie drove carefully down the hill, taking extra care at the Kentucky Street intersection. Within minutes, she was in the driveway of her home. She quickly gathered her purse and gloves and made her way to the door. Upon entering the warmth of the living room, Leslie was surprised to find neither a distraught Travis nor Aunt Margie. Relief washed over her. Maybe they had gone to bed early. This was definitely a good sign.

Wrestling with her coat, scarf, and purse, Leslie found a note taped to the closet door. "We went to bed early—see you in the morning. Margie."

Smiling, she placed her coat in the hall closet and set her boots by the front door. The note said "we went to bed early." That would have to imply that Travis was feeling a little better. At least he wasn't panicked about Leslie getting home. "Thank You, God," she whispered.

For a moment, she just enjoyed the silence of the night. An image of Darrin filtered into her head. She'd really like to know him better. He appeared to be a Christian and enjoy discussions that focused on spiritual matters. He also seemed to genuinely care about the things she told him. Maybe it was just her imagination, but for some reason Leslie got the distinct impression he cared about her. Almost as though she'd known him all her life.

She put such thoughts aside. Her mind was too tired to think about anything more than a hot shower and a soft bed, and there would always be tomorrow to dream about the illustrious Mr . . . Mr. Who? He'd only told her that his name was Darrin.

She pondered the matter only as long as it took to step into the shower. Exhaustion swept over her like the steaming water and lulled her into a state of relaxed disregard. She would let all her worries and troubles wash from her and go down the drain.

Her mother had given her this analogy when she had been a teenager. She could still hear her saying, "Leslie, God tells us to cast all our cares on Him, because He cares for us. When you step into a shower after a hot, dirty game of fast-pitch, you let the dirt and grime wash down the drain without ever desiring to have it back. Just do the same with worry and concern."

"I'm trying, Mama," she whispered, spying the drain with a smile. "I'm trying."

After washing her hair and preparing for bed, she stopped by Travis's room. She could see his still form snuggled under his blankets. The peaceful slumber of his body gave Leslie reason to hope. He didn't thrash about or moan as he usually did during the night. Perhaps tonight there were no nightmares. Perhaps tonight he knew peace. This convinced her not to disturb him. He needed his rest. So did she. Whispering a short prayer for him, Leslie turned and made her way to her own bed.

The next morning, Leslie awoke slowly. The house was totally quiet and peaceful. Closing her eyes tightly, she stretched out her refreshed body under the warmth of her comforter. For a moment, she debated whether or not she should drift back to sleep and enjoy one of the few peaceful times in her hectic life. No, she decided. It would be better to enjoy this time with coffee and conversation. She and Margie seldom had any real time to talk, and Leslie could think of a great many things they needed to discuss. Then, too, maybe Travis would be somewhat recovered, given his early bedtime and uninterrupted slumber. Optimistic thoughts surged through Leslie, urging her out of bed and into her robe.

Leslie hummed as she filled the coffee filter and placed it in the basket of the coffee maker. Maybe she should run down to Joe's Bakery and surprise Margie and Travis with fresh doughnuts. Travis loved it when the glazed doughnuts were warm from the oven and the glaze was still drippy. Her parents had always indulged his love of the sticky pastry, even though cleaning him up was quite a chore. Leslie had always been fond of their baked cinnamon rolls, while her mother had adored the cream puffs. Leslie's father, however, had no favorites. If it was from Joe's, he ate it.

She smiled as she recalled the mornings when her mother would sneak down to the tiny bakery before anyone had awakened. The family would gather in the kitchen and laugh as they ate and drank, enjoying each other's company. How she longed for those mornings again!

Margie padded into the kitchen, still half asleep. She seemed to be guided by the aroma of fresh coffee. "Good morning," she mumbled. "How was work last night?"

"Oh, it went all right. I was glad that I called you, though. I didn't get home until almost one." Leslie handed her aunt a porcelain mug and retrieved one for herself. She filled each with coffee and replaced the pot on the heater. "I was so surprised not to find you or Travis waiting up for me. I hope this means he's getting better."

Margie sipped her coffee and nodded. "It was odd, but he asked if he could go to sleep in my bed for a while. I guess that was around ten-thirty or so. I was exhausted, so the prospect of an early bedtime thrilled me to pieces. He wasn't with me this morning, so I assumed he woke up and went back to his own bed. Isn't he up yet?"

"Nope. I was thinking about going down to Joe's and bringing him some of those fresh glazed doughnuts that he likes so much. I was afraid to just leave without someone being up for him, though. It is odd that he's not around. It's almost eight-fifteen." Leslie poured herself more coffee and sat down at the table with Margie.

"Well, you could check on him, but let him sleep. His body and mind are so exhausted. Maybe this is the best thing for him."

"I'd better get around so I can make it to Joe's before they get cleaned out by the morning rush. I'll check in on Travis first, though. He seemed so peaceful last night that I didn't bother him. Apparently he went back to his bed before I got home," she said, emptying her mug. An unwelcome thought suddenly came to mind. "He didn't seem sick to you last night, did he? I never even thought that he might have a fever or . . ." Her words trailed off as she got to her feet. Motherhood was so new to her that she felt suddenly quite incompetent.

Margie shook her head. "No, he seemed fine. Just very set on going to bed early. I'm sure he's okay, Les. He's just a very tired little boy."

Leslie relaxed and nodded. "I'm sure you're right. I just don't want to overlook anything."

"You're doing a good job, Leslie. I can't imagine how you could do anything better. Your mom and dad would be proud of you, and so am I."

"Thanks," Leslie said, feeling bittersweet love in the praise. She yawned, stretched, then got to her feet. "I'm going to get dressed."

Upstairs, she selected a pastel blue sweater from her closet and a heavy pair of jeans. Maybe she'd convince Travis to take another walk to the cemetery with her. They'd gone twice before, and both times he seemed to find comfort in the visits. After pulling her hair into a loose ponytail, she put on a pair of thick wool boot socks and went to check on her brother.

Tiptoeing into the small boy's room, Leslie noted that he was still in the same position he'd been in the night before. His body lay completely hidden deep within his covers. Even his head was snuggled under his blankets. She approached the bed and ran a hand along the child's still form and felt goose bumps line her arm.

It didn't feel like Travis. In fact, it didn't feel like anyone. She felt no contour of his body, no arms or legs. Panicked, she turned down the comforter and saw nothing but a pillow. Frantically, she pulled the blankets from the bed, revealing a network of pillows but no Travis.

"Margie!" Leslie screamed. Looking around the room, she noticed several things missing.

The book bag he used on long car trips to fill with toys and picture books.

His favorite teddy bear. It wasn't in his bed or on the floor, like it normally was.

His coat. It was supposed to be hanging on his closet door knob. It was gone as well. "Margie, come quick!"

Leslie felt the room begin to spin. Where was he? Maybe he was just hiding. Yes, that was it. He was pretending to camp out somewhere in the house like he had done before he had become so withdrawn. Maybe he was in the basement or maybe he was in his parents' bedroom.

"Travis? Travis, answer me! Where are you?" Leslie ran out of the room, nearly flattening Margie against the wall.

"What's wrong, Leslie? What's wrong with Travis?" Margie's face was pale.

"He's gone! I don't know where he is. Oh, Margie. Maybe he's playing that camping game that he and Dad used to play. You know, where he sleeps somewhere in the house and camps out? He's got to be here somewhere. Help me find him!" Leslie tore from room to room, calling his name. "Travis! Travis, honey, please tell Sissy where you are! You're scaring Sissy."

Margie began searching in the opposite direction, but found nothing. Leslie continued yelling and exploring the house. "Travis!" She had checked everywhere. The basement, the bathrooms, the pantry, the closets. Nothing. Travis was nowhere to be found. "Travis, oh, Travis, where are you?"

Suddenly, she felt two hands on her shoulders, gently shaking her. "Leslie, calm down." For the first time, Leslie realized she was sobbing hysterically. What she perceived to be calls to Travis were incoherent screams, reverberating through the empty house. Margie's strong grip guided her back into the kitchen and to the table. "Leslie, stop crying. We need to think."

After being handed another cup of coffee, Leslie quieted herself and concentrated on swallowing the hot liquid. Margie patiently waited for her niece's nerves to come under control.

"Now, what we need to do is call the police, and then the neighbors. Maybe he went over to play with the twins without asking. Maybe he's just testing us. It may not be as bad as we think." Leslie nodded like a frightened child. Margie rose to retrieve the telephone and dialed the police department.

"Yes, I'd like to report a missing child." At this, Leslie began to cry anew, but a sharp look from Margie stifled her sobs.

"My name is Margie Dover. My nephew is missing." Pause. "No, we're not sure how long he's been gone." Again a lengthy pause filled the air with silence. "Five years old," Margie replied into the receiver. "Please, can you send someone over right away?" Margie waited for a moment and then recited the address. "We'll be watching for you. Thank you." She returned the telephone to the cradle and looked over to Leslie.

"They're sending someone over right this minute. It's going to be okay, Les. We'll find him."

"He's just a little boy, Margie. It's so cold outside. I can't believe I didn't check on him. I thought he was asleep, and he hasn't been sleeping well, and I didn't want to risk waking him, so I just went to bed and . . ."

"Les, calm down. Come pray with me, and you'll feel better." Leslie set her empty mug on the oak table and got to her feet. Dejectedly, she walked over to Margie and took her hand. Margie bowed her head, "Dear Lord, our little Travis is out there somewhere, and we know that You are with him, protecting and comforting him. Please help us find Travis, and please keep him safe from all harm. Bring peace to our hearts and guide the police in their search as well as ours. In Your Son's precious name, amen."

Leslie looked up, tears streaming from her eyes. Margie's green eyes also glistened with tears. "It'll be all right, Leslie. God is with us, and He is with Travis. We'll find him." The older woman reached out, and Leslie eagerly accepted the physical contact. Hadn't she just been reflecting on how wonderful the day had seemed?

"Now," Margie said briskly. "It's time to call our neighbors."

Leslie waited anxiously through each phone call. She could tell by Margie's responses that Travis was not to be found. After the last call, the two women simply looked at each other blankly.

A knock at the door brought both women to attention. Margie hurried to usher in the officers, while Leslie tried to still her raging nerves. *If only I'd looked in on him last night. If only I'd . . .* She couldn't help the rampant thoughts that filled her mind.

"So when did you first notice that the boy was missing?" The man's pin identified him as Officer Keats.

Leslie's attention was immediately focused on the man. "I went to check on him after I got dressed," she began. "You see, he hasn't been sleeping well since our parents died. That was about a month ago. Last night, I came home, and he wasn't waiting up for me like usual. I thought it meant he was getting better, so I didn't want to disturb him. This morning, when he still wasn't up, we decided to check on him. That's when I found the pillows."

"And did you notice if anything else was missing?"

"Yes, his favorite teddy bear was gone and his book bag and coat were also gone." Leslie struggled to maintain her calm. "I thought maybe he was hiding because he was angry with me for coming home late or perhaps he was playing a game my father had taught him. It was like camping out, only inside the house. But we searched, and we couldn't find him anywhere."

"Do you have any idea where he may have gone? Neighbors. Friends?"

Leslie and Margie shook their heads. "We've called the only ones we could think of."

"Maybe somewhere he may have felt close to his parents?"

Leslie thought for a moment, and then it dawned on her. "The cemetery. Travis and I walked there often and talked about Mom and Dad. He always talked about wanting to go to be with them in heaven, but I told him that he had to wait until Jesus decided it was time. He liked going to cemetery. It made him feel close to them."

"So you think he might have walked to the cemetery by himself?"

"It's definitely a possibility. It's only about a quarter mile away. I just hate to think of his little body battling the cold. He could have been there all night. There's no telling when he left." Just then, an officer poked his head into the kitchen.

"Hey, I found footprints in the snow leading west. They look child sized."

Leslie nodded. "Yes, the cemetery is west of here. I'm sure that's where he went. We need to get there right now. I want to go along with you." She stood up and retrieved her boots from beside the front door.

"I'll wait here in case he comes back," Margie offered. Officer Keats got to his feet.

"Ms. Heyward, you're welcome to ride with us," he said, striding out of the kitchen and to the front door. Leslie nodded and followed close behind. Forgetting to grab a coat, Leslie shivered violently as soon as she stepped outside. Poor Travis might be out in this. It couldn't be much above zero. Quickly, she got into the squad car.

"You can turn up here at the corner," she said, chattering directions without taking time for a breath.

"I think I know where this cemetery is, Ms. Heyward. Just try to calm down and relax. It'll only take a few minutes before we're there. I'm sure it was a quicker walk than a drive, but just be patient." Leslie nodded. She knew as well as any long-time resident that Lawrence had a myriad of one-way streets, making nearby locations a difficult trip by automobile. That's why it was so much easier to walk than drive.

"Oh, God," she whispered, still shivering from the cold, "please let him hurry. Please let us find Travis, and God, let him be all right."

Moments later, they had arrived at the cemetery. Leslie led them through the headstones to the graves of her parents. She strained to see footprints or anything else that might suggest Travis's approach. *But Travis would have come from the other direction*, she reminded herself. If there were footprints, they wouldn't be found in this area of the cemetery.

Now she was running, and with her she could hear the officers jogging to keep up. Warm air from her lungs streamed from her mouth and nose as she ran. Her lungs ached from the cold and her body protested the abuse, yet she continued, urgently pressing on, needing to know the truth.

They rounded the final corner, and even as they approached, a gasp escaped Leslie's throat. A strangled cry came from her mouth and she stopped without warning, nearly causing one of the officers to plow right into her from behind.

"Oh, God," she moaned unable to find the words to pray. "Oh, please God."

There on the ground in front of her parents' headstone lay the near-frozen body of Travis Heyward.

$$\textbf{\Large (11)}$$

arrin Malone had just finished locking the door of his BMW when he realized the sign at Crossroads read SORRY! WE'RE CLOSED.

"That's odd," he muttered to himself. "I wonder what's going on." Striding up to the entrance, he peered in through the windows, hoping that maybe Leslie had just decided to close early and would be inside counting the drawer or washing off the tables. But much to his dismay, the large room was empty. It was only six o'clock. Where was Leslie or her aunt?

Darrin decided to check the neighboring business. Leslie had said it was run by a man she knew from church. She had mentioned him in several of her conversations with Darrin, and he knew that the family trusted him implicitly. Walking to the door, he struggled to remember. What was his name again? Clayton? No, Blayton? Blanton. That was it. Timothy Blanton. Perhaps he had heard why the store was closed.

Hundreds of worst-case scenarios danced in his mind. Did they have to close the store for lack of customers? Did they get bought out? Was Leslie just tired, and had she decided to take a few days off? Was she too ill to care for Crossroads? His brow furrowed, and his intimidating appearance startled the owner of the nearby shop.

"Excuse me, sir. Are you all right?" A small, bald man hesitantly stepped from behind a counter filled with cookies and chewing gum.

"Well, actually, no. Are you Mr. Timothy Blanton?" The old man nodded slowly.

Darrin sensed the discomfort in the air. He knew his harsh appearance and blunt questions were, no doubt, unnerving the quiet man's routine. "I came to see if you knew why Crossroads is closed today."

Darrin noticed the man's startled look and offered a weak smile. "Don't worry, I'm not a caffeine addict or anything. I have become a good friend of the owner, Leslie Heyward. She's always there in the evenings. When the store was closed, I automatically assumed the worst. I recalled her mentioning you as a church friend and fellow entrepreneur in a couple of our conversations. That's the reason I stopped by."

Mr. Blanton noticeably relaxed, but just as quickly became somber. "Leslie was unable to be at the store today because of her brother."

"What's wrong with Travis?"

The man seemed nervous and uncertain, but continued. "I don't have all the details, you see. Margie Dover—that's her aunt—called me this morning to tell me that Crossroads would be closed today and possibly for a time longer because Travis was in the hospital. She said something about him running away last night and that they hadn't realized he was missing until this morning. Leslie is spending all her time by his side, and that's why she's unable to run the store. That's all I know."

Mr. Blanton shook his head. "That poor little boy. He just isn't dealing well with the death of his folks. She told you about that, right?" Darrin nodded. "Well, we're praying for the little guy at church, and for his sister and aunt, too. He just doesn't seem to be getting any better."

A few customers entered the small store and immediately headed for the espresso machine near the fountain drinks. "I see her customers are going into withdrawal." Darrin smiled. "Hope she isn't closed for too long. It's a good thing you're here."

Mr. Blanton nodded. "Yep. It may be good for my business, but I'd give anything to have circumstances be different."

"I understand completely. Thank you for your time. I really appreciate it."

"You her boyfriend?" Mr. Blanton seemed to scrutinize Darrin for a moment.

Darrin laughed, but felt a tinge of . . . well, he wasn't quite sure what it was he felt. "No, I've just come to care quite a bit about her and this situation."

❧

Darrin screeched into the emergency parking area of Lawrence Memorial Hospital. He ran into the hospital and up to the front desk, panting heavily and looking to all the world as though he were a man with his own emergency. As far as he was concerned, this was his emergency.

"Can I help you, sir?" A gray-haired woman smiled sweetly.

"Yes, I hope so. I'm looking for Travis Heyward. He was brought in here earlier this morning. I'd like to go up to the waiting room. I'm just not sure where he is." The older woman's fingers tapped out "HEY-WARD, T" on the keyboard in front of her. After a few seconds, a dossier appeared on the screen of the monitor.

"Ah, yes. Here he is. He's in pediatrics." She pulled out a preprinted map and showed Darrin where to go. He thanked her and briskly walked down the long corridor, his mind unable to stop the tumble of thoughts. *What if he's not doing well? How can I help? What should I say or do? Will she understand why I'm here?*

Upon sighting the pediatrics sign, Darrin let out a sigh. He was grateful he hadn't gotten lost. Hospitals were never his forté, even though he had spent so much time in them when his mother was dying. He still managed to lose his way in their maze of sterilized hallways. He wove his way around several visiting people and came upon the waiting room. There, he saw a teary-eyed Leslie. His heart broke in two.

"Leslie?" Her head snapped up.

"Darrin, what are you doing here?" Her face reflected her grief and surprise. She didn't bother to wipe away her tears. How he wished he could see her smile just half as many times as he had seen her troubled and grieving!

"I stopped by Crossroads, but the store was closed. I remembered you saying that Mr. Blanton was a church friend and was familiar with your business, so I asked him if he knew why you weren't there. He didn't know much, except for what your aunt had told him, but he was very helpful. As soon as I heard Travis was in the hospital, my car practically drove itself here." He sat down beside her. "Have you heard anything?"

Leslie shook her head. "Not really. We've been here since around ten. They've come out off and on with bits of information, like his fingers and face are frostbitten. He isn't breathing well—it's real shallow and rapid—but they haven't determined exactly what to do. He's still unconscious," she said, choking back a sob. "The doctors are so busy they don't seem to have time for me. I don't know what to do. I don't know if he's going to . . ." She couldn't finish the sentence.

Darrin reached out to touch her hand. "It'll be all right. You'll see. God will work this out, Les. You have to believe that God is in control of even this." Suddenly, he felt the urge to pray with her, to try and offer her comfort. "Would you mind if we prayed together?"

Leslie brought her bloodshot eyes to meet his. "I'd like that," she said. "I really would."

"Good." He took hold of her trembling hand and bowed his head. "Dear Father, please be with Travis. We don't know all the details, and we're not even sure what's wrong, but we know that You will protect him and keep him from harm. Heal his body, so that it may be as strong as it once was. Give Leslie peace and let her know that Your love is more powerful than all the pain and all the trials of this world. And please allow me to help them in any way You see fit. In Jesus' name, amen." He quickly squeezed her hand and felt an odd comfort when she didn't let go. She needed him there. She wanted him there. She wanted his help.

"Thank you, Darrin. I am really glad you're here. Margie stopped in for a while, but she seemed so tired and distraught that I told her she should go home. I promised to call if I got any news, but so far, there hasn't been any, and they're too busy with him to have me in the room taking up space."

Darrin looked around the empty waiting room. A small television was showing the nightly news. Magazines were spread generously over end tables and chairs. A soda machine stood brightly in the corner. The room seemed cold and lonely. Just as he remembered them.

"Can you talk about what happened?"

Leslie nodded and inhaled deeply. "Last night, I came home, and he wasn't up waiting for me. Remember I told you that he always waits up for me to make sure I really come home?"

Darrin nodded and she continued. "I found a note from Margie saying they had gone to bed early. That surprised me so much that I decided not to disturb her or Travis. Especially once I saw how still and untroubled his sleep was. At least, I thought it was him." Her tears began anew.

"This morning, when he still wasn't up at eight fifteen or so, we thought we should check on him, but we didn't want to wake him if he was finally sleeping well. I went into his room, and I folded back the covers to see his face, and all I found were pillows. We searched the house and called the police. When I was talking to them, it came to me that he might have run away to Mom and Dad's graves. We had walked there a few times in the past month, and it wasn't far away. Well, I went along with the officers to the cemetery, and there his little body was, all frozen and curled up on the ground. It was the most awful thing I've ever seen. We brought him straight to the hospital. I've been here ever since."

A middle-aged man entered the waiting room, carrying a clipboard. "Ms. Heyward?"

Leslie looked over to the doorway where the man stood. "Yes?"

"I'm Dr. Selig. I'm in charge of caring for your little brother, Travis. I wanted to speak with you about his condition." Darrin noticed her body become rigid. Something about the doctor's manner seemed to radiate bad news. "Would you please come with me?"

Leslie looked at Darrin with sheer terror in her expression. Without being asked, Darrin got to his feet and put an arm around Leslie. "Lead the way, Doc," he said, instantly taking charge.

The doctor led them to a small consultation room, just inside the double doors that marked the pediatric ward. Darrin helped Leslie to one of the rigid plastic chairs, while the doctor took his seat behind a small desk.

"I'm afraid, Ms. Heyward, the news isn't good. It seems that Travis's exposure to the elements has left him quite ill. You know about the frostbite to his extremities, but he is also suffering internally. His lungs were frozen, barely functional when you brought him in. We're doing what we can to warm his body temperature, but he's still critically under normal."

Leslie stared stone-faced at the man, and Darrin put his arm around her once again.

"What are his chances?" Darrin asked, almost regretting the words as Leslie turned to look at him in disbelief.

"We aren't confident enough of the situation at this point to really say one way or another. We fear pneumonia will set in, but more troubling at this point is the fact that his body isn't fighting as hard as we expected it to. This is sometimes attributed to depression, as you informed our nurses that he had been experiencing. At the moment, he is unstable. I'd like to give you better news, but I just can't lie to you. Your brother is gravely ill and there is a possibility that he may not survive this ordeal. Please know we are doing all that we can."

The last words appeared to be lost on Leslie. She collapsed against Darrin's body. "You can't let him die. He's all I have. You can't let him die."

Darrin held her tight, wishing, praying that he could somehow help her. "Leslie, it'll be all right." He stroked her hair, but it seemed to have no effect.

"I can't deal with this. I can't do this. I can't lose him!" She was gasping for breath.

"Ms. Heyward, you need to calm down. Take deep breaths in through your nose and out through your mouth," Dr. Selig ordered. He called for a nurse, and instantly a petite woman appeared. "Please take Ms. Heyward into the private lounge." Then turning to Darrin he added, "There's a cot there, and I think it would be prudent to have her rest a bit. I know what a shock all of this has been."

"Come on, honey. I'm Kelly. I want you to lie down and rest while I grab you a cold cloth." She helped Leslie to her feet and wrapped a well-muscled arm around her waist. "You aren't going to do yourself any good this way." Leslie didn't even seem to hear her.

They were at the door when Leslie stopped and turned to find Darrin. "Don't go," she barely whispered.

"I promise to stay. I'll be with you in just a minute," Darrin assured her.

Before they could leave the room, a nurse appeared with a stack of papers. "Ms. Heyward, the business office needs to get your insurance information."

"What?" Leslie mumbled, clearly unable to register what the woman needed.

"Health insurance," the woman repeated.

"We don't have any," Leslie replied.

The nurse holding her pushed past the other woman. "Ms. Heyward needs to lie down. I'm taking her to the private lounge, and you can talk to her there, Amy." The woman nodded and followed.

Darrin realized that without any insurance, Travis's hospital stay was going to be Leslie's total responsibility. With the cost of hospitalization, much more so intensive care and emergency-related services, Leslie could find herself stripped of all assets just in order to see her brother received proper care.

"Dr. Selig," he said, turning to catch the doctor before he slipped from the room. "I want Travis to have the best possible treatment. It doesn't matter what it costs—money isn't a problem, and I don't want it to be an issue."

The doctor looked at him indignantly. "I would never withhold care from a patient because of the financial status of his family."

"I wasn't accusing," Darrin assured, "I'm just stating the facts. That little boy is very important to us."

Selig's expression softened. "I'm sure he is. He's important to me, as well. Rest assured, I'm doing all that I can. If we feel for even one moment that we're compromising his care, he'll be airlifted to the University of Kansas Medical Center in Kansas City."

"Thank you," Darrin said. He hurried out the door, unsure of where they'd taken Leslie. He recognized the woman named Amy and went to speak with her. "Miss?"

"Yes?" The woman looked up from the same stack of papers that had accompanied her to the consultation room.

"I want to arrange for Travis Heyward's medical expenses. As Ms. Heyward said, there is no health insurance, but I will personally be responsible for the charges." He reached into his wallet and pulled out a business card. "Have all the bills sent here, to my home address."

Amy took the card and jotted down the information. "Are you a relative?" she inquired, handing him back the card.

"No," Darrin replied. "At least not yet." The statement startled him. *Where had that come from?* He had no reason to say such a thing, and yet it seemed very, very right. "Look," he finally said, tearing his thoughts away from the internal questioning, "I don't want Leslie to know about this. I don't want anyone to know that I'm taking responsibility for the bills, understand? Especially not Leslie."

The woman looked at him suspiciously. "No, I don't understand."

Darrin nodded. "It's just that she's a very proud woman. Her business isn't doing well right now, and I know that money is an issue. If you go telling her that I've agreed to take over the payments, she'll reject it in a minute. Just let it go. Let her believe that she'll be billed in the future and that everything is acceptable and under control. That way, maybe once everything is said and done, she'll realize why I did it and accept the help."

Amy smiled. "I get the picture. You must be a very good friend to offer such generous help."

Darrin frowned, thinking of the real reason he and Leslie had come to know one another. "I don't know about that," he murmured. He was suddenly consumed with guilt. None of this would be happening if not for his father's actions. Would there be no end to the sins revisited upon him?

$$12$$

*O*nly a day had passed since they'd found Travis, but Leslie felt as though it were years instead. She'd refused to leave the hospital and, instead, became a resident of the waiting room, along with several other worried parents.

"Ms. Heyward, why don't you go downstairs and get something to eat?" the nurse admonished. It was Kelly, the same woman who had calmed her down after Leslie had heard the truth behind Travis's condition and who had been caring for Travis alongside Dr. Selig. Leslie looked up from her magazine and shook her head.

"No, I'm fine. I'm not hungry. I just don't want to leave in case they find out anything more." Her protests were weak and childlike. But there was no convincing her otherwise. Kelly shrugged and walked back to the nurses' station.

"Leslie, you really should get some rest or eat something. You won't be any good to Travis if they have to put you in the hospital for not taking care of yourself." Darrin put an arm around her, and she didn't resist. She was tired. Very tired. But what if Dr. Selig discovered something new? What good would it do to have her asleep or eating?

"Darrin, I appreciate you being here. Please understand that I don't want to leave here just so I can feel better. There's a little boy in one of those rooms who doesn't have that option, and I am to blame for that." She quieted upon seeing Dr. Selig in the doorway.

"Ms. Heyward? We have some new developments that we thought we should alert you to. You were aware of his frostbite, and due to that, we were attempting to warm his body in the appropriate ways. However, it has recently come to our attention that his body temperature is drastically rising, and he now has a fever of 102 degrees. His breathing has become quite shallow and labored, and now that he has begun to regain consciousness, it's apparent that he is experiencing discomfort in his chest as well."

"What does all this mean?" Leslie interrupted, panicked.

"After listening to Travis's lungs and seeing the X-ray, it has been determined that he is developing pneumonia. We've started him on some very powerful IV antibiotics and put him on oxygen. There's nothing more we can do at the moment. I'm very sorry, Ms. Heyward. If you'd like to see him for a few moments, you might actually catch him awake. Although, I must advise you not to get your hopes up at this point. Even if he is conscious, he won't recognize you or make any sense in the things he might say."

Leslie was immediately to her feet, with Darrin close behind. They hadn't let her see Travis at all, and the waiting was driving her insane. Hurrying to keep up with Dr. Selig, Leslie scarcely paid attention to the brightly decorated children's ward. Travis was in the intensive care unit of pediatrics, and because of this, his room was located just across from the nurses' station.

They stopped outside the sliding glass doors of the room. The clipboard outside read HEYWARD, TRAVIS, along with his date of birth. The doctor perused it momentarily, and before opening the door, he turned to Leslie. "Now, you must understand, it is important that you be prepared for his appearance. Travis is a very sick little boy. The frostbite has left patches of red swollen tissue on his face. The patches resemble burns and may remain in place for several weeks. It just depends on how his recovery goes.

"His lips are swollen and chapped, and because of the pneumonia he has a bit of a grayish-blue tint around them. You need to be as calm and relaxed as possible. If he sees you upset, that, in turn, could upset him, especially given the fact that he's already disoriented from the drugs we're giving him. We just have no way of knowing what he will or won't comprehend, but we have to do what we can to encourage him. Can you handle this?" he asked, great compassion evident in his voice.

Leslie nodded, and Darrin squeezed her hand as the doctor led them inside.

At her first look at Travis, Leslie gasped, but immediately tried to compose herself. It was worse than the doctor had described. Darrin squeezed her hand reassuringly. *Oh, God,* Leslie prayed, *let me be strong for Travis.* She moved to the bedside and watched him stir. His tiny hands and feet were bandaged and elevated. His face was spotted with ugly red blisters on his nose, cheeks, and chin. Kelly checked Travis's monitors and his IV and offered Leslie a tiny smile as she left the room.

Leslie wanted to scoop her brother up and hold him close. Instead she gently took hold of his tiny bandaged hand. *Poor Travis,* she thought. *You shouldn't have to be like this. I should have helped you more. I just didn't know how.*

The small boy stirred and opened his swollen eyes. He mumbled words that were incoherent and barely audible.

"What did you say, baby? Tell Sissy again," she whispered.

"He's been muttering something almost constantly since he began regaining consciousness," Dr. Selig offered. "I'm sure it's just gibberish."

Just then Kelly popped her head back in the room. "Dr. Selig, Dr. Ward wants to speak to you on the telephone."

"I'll be right back," the doctor told Leslie, leaving her and Darrin alone with the beeping monitors and hum of the oxygen unit.

The five year old, barely able to hold his eyes open, again mumbled a series of words.

Leslie leaned down. "Tell Sissy again," she said softly. Travis seemed to struggle for a moment, as if he were fighting the cloudiness that lay between him and full consciousness. He took a breath, and this time the words came clearer. Leslie straightened up as Travis closed his eyes. She felt her heart swell with hope. "Yes, baby, that's right. You remember that," she said, stroking his fine blond hair.

"What did he say?" Darrin asked.

She smiled. "When I'm afraid, I will trust in You."

Darrin smiled. "That's in the Psalms, isn't it?"

"Yes. I told him that verse not long after Mom and Dad died. I told him to use it when he was afraid. I told him that it's what helps me get through scary times."

"Like now?" Darrin questioned. His blue eyes searched her face intensely.

She warmed under his scrutiny. "Yes. This would be the perfect example."

"And do you?" he asked, looking down at Travis, who had closed his eyes again.

She followed Darrin's gaze to her brother's damaged body. "Especially now," she whispered. "How could I ever make it through otherwise?"

The days seemed to drag by, and every day Leslie clung to the hope that this would be the day the doctor would announce Travis's marked improvement. She felt the toll on her body and spirit as one day turned into another and then another, but even more, she saw the price it demanded from her aunt. She felt badly that Margie should have to suffer so much. It seemed that her aunt had aged twenty years in the past week and Leslie longed to offer her comfort, but there was simply nothing left to give.

Leslie was grateful for Darrin's nightly appearances. She still didn't know his last name or where he went during the day, but she knew that every evening at six on the dot, he would appear and sit by her side until it was time to go home. She was coming to count on him more and more, and in some ways it scared her at the same time it comforted her. Why was he being so generous with his time?

She glanced at her watch and smiled. He'd walk through those doors any minute now. A young couple she'd come to recognize entered the waiting room. They were smiling.

"Good news?" Leslie asked hopefully.

"Yes," the mother sighed. "Danny is making wonderful progress. He may even get to go home in another few days. The doctor was particularly worried about his head injury, but the swelling has gone down."

"Thank God," Leslie said, knowing their concern for the eight year old who'd been critically injured in a car accident.

"You can say that again," the father replied. "I never found much need for that kind of mumbo jumbo, but I'm a changed man now. God really proved Himself to me over these last few days."

Leslie nodded and smiled at the sight of Darrin in the doorway behind them. "God has a way of appearing to us in the strangest ways."

"Well, we're going to get something to eat," the woman said, gathering up her things. "See you later."

Leslie waved as they maneuvered past Darrin. "Well, you're right on schedule," she said, finding his handsome face fixed on her.

"You timing me?"

She laughed. "They could hand medication out by your appearance. That's how timely you are. Every night at exactly six o'clock."

Darrin ran a hand through his brown hair. "I can't say that I knew I was exactly that reliable, but I guess I leave the store at the same time every day and it takes exactly fifty-five minutes to fight through traffic and get here."

"Get here from where?" Leslie asked, suddenly feeling relaxed enough to pursue the matter.

"Kansas City," Darrin answered. "I own an antique store called Elysium."

"How fascinating. I would have never pegged you as the type."

"Really? Why not?" Darrin asked, taking the chair beside her.

"I don't know. I guess I saw you more as a lawyer or an accountant or something like that." Leslie shrugged. "Don't ask me why. I guess you just always seemed kind of uptight. Like you had a lot on your mind."

Darrin frowned. His brows knit together in a way that Leslie had come to recognize whenever he contemplated something deeply. "I guess I have had a great deal on my mind of late. Sorry."

"Don't be. I'm the queen of preoccupation, myself." She put down the magazine she'd been trying to concentrate on. "So was it a good day at the shop?"

"Not really," Darrin said, sounding like he'd just as soon forget it. "How about here? Any news?"

"Well, nothing to write home about, but I keep hoping and praying." She stretched her jean-clad legs out in front of her and sighed.

"When did you eat last?" he asked, sounding genuinely concerned.

"Um," she stared up at the ceiling. "I had some coffee this morning."

"Just what I thought. Come on," Darrin said, getting to his feet. "We're going to grab some supper."

Just then Dr. Selig came into the waiting room. Leslie felt her breath catch, and without giving thought to what she was doing, she reached for Darrin's hand and held it tight.

"I have some good news for you, Leslie." She'd finally gotten him to drop the formal sounding Ms. Heyward. "The fever is down, and Travis appears to be responding to the antibiotics."

"Thank God," Leslie said, exhaling the breath she'd been holding.

"So what happens now?" Darrin asked.

"We'll keep up with the antibiotics and continue to monitor him. I'm not counting him out of the woods just yet, but I'd say we've turned a real corner here, and we can look forward to a full recovery."

Dr. Selig left just as quickly as he'd come, but Leslie hardly noticed. She'd thrown herself into Darrin's arms, laughing with joy and thanking God for His goodness. It was only after she'd maintained that position for several minutes that it dawned on her as to what she had done. She could feel his strong arms around her. She could smell the sweet, spicy aftershave he wore. She could hear his heart beating rapidly against the place where she rested her head. Pulling back slowly, Leslie allowed her gaze to meet the questioning expression on Darrin's face.

"Leslie?" Margie questioned from the doorway.

Leslie realized that she still clung to Darrin, and without meaning to appear so startled, she jumped back and swallowed hard. "I . . . we . . ." She laughed nervously, noting the two church friends who accompanied Margie. "The doctor brought good news!" Leslie finally declared. "Travis is showing signs of improvement. His fever is down, and he's definitely responding to the antibiotics."

Margie's face registered instant relief. "Praise the Lord," she said. Turning to her friends, she made the introductions. "Sylvia, Clare, this is Leslie's friend, Darrin." Then smiling at Darrin, Margie added, "Darrin, these are a couple of my dear friends from church. We've been praying together every day for Travis's recovery."

"I'm glad to meet you both," Darrin said, extending his hand. "I'd say the prayers are hitting the mark."

The women smiled, instantly charmed by Darrin's sincerity and broad grin. Leslie watched the exchange, glad that the attention was off her. She felt a strange embarrassment at having her aunt catch her in the arms of a man she hardly knew, yet she couldn't help but remember how good it felt to be held.

"I was just trying to talk Leslie into getting some supper," Darrin said. "Would you ladies care to join us?"

Margie shook her head. "We've just come from Buffalo Bob's, where we ate more than our share. In fact, we've a nice doggy bag down in Clare's car if you two are interested."

"Sounds okay by me," Darrin replied. "You want me to go get it, Leslie?"

"That would be fine," Leslie answered.

Clare gave him the keys to her car, along with explicit directions as to where he could find it. "The front passenger lock is kind of temperamental," she said as he turned to go, "so use the driver's side door."

"Will do," Darrin said, offering a mock salute.

When he'd gone, Margie settled back, a frown drawing lines around her mouth. "I wanted to mention something, but not with Darrin around," she began.

Leslie instantly became aware of her serious mood. "What is it?"

Margie glanced at Clare and Sylvia before continuing. "We've been praying about this, but I don't see any other way than to just come out and say it. We're running out of money, Leslie. There are mortgage payments to be met on the house and rent on the shop, not to mention the utility bills for both places, and the coffee vendor called and said they won't make another delivery unless you pay in full."

Leslie fell back against her chair in defeat. "I have to admit, the shop has been the last thing on my mind."

"It has to be reopened, and soon," Margie said. "I know you feel the need to stay close to Travis, but . . ."

"But I need to go back to work," Leslie said matter-of-factly. She looked at her aunt and saw the weariness in her expression. Margie hadn't been healthy of late. Worry had sent her blood pressure soaring, and the doctor had put her to complete bed rest at one point. Now, here she was concerning herself over the bills, and suddenly, Leslie felt as though the weight of the world had materialized back on her shoulders.

"Travis is getting better, so it's not like you don't know what's going to happen," Margie offered. "I think I can manage a few hours at the shop in the morning, so you could still come up here and be with him first thing every day."

"No, you know very well what the doctor told you. You can't work," Leslie said sternly. "At least not just yet." She sat thinking for several minutes. "No, I'll go back and just run the shop from twelve to twelve. That shouldn't be too hard on me. It'll only be temporary. If I get home by one, I can get five or six hours of sleep and still spend time with Travis before going to work."

"That won't be easy," Margie said.

"Maybe some of the young people in the church could work at Crossroads," Clare suggested.

"It's a possibility," Margie said thoughtfully.

"I can't afford to pay anyone to work." Leslie's spirit deflated a bit more.

"Here it is," Darrin said, holding up the bag of leftovers like a trophy. "It sure smells good."

"I'll bet it is," Leslie replied, putting on a smile she didn't feel. "Let's eat." She exchanged the briefest of glances with Margie, but it was enough to close the discussion on money and the shop. One way or another, Leslie would figure a way to make it all work. If she didn't, there wouldn't be any hope of keeping the shop, much less of paying Travis's hospital bills.

~&

After Darrin's request to spend a few minutes in private discussion, Leslie finally agreed to leave Margie her car and let Darrin drive her home. She settled into the luxury of the BMW, realizing for the first time just how wealthy Darrin probably was.

"Nice car," she muttered, thinking that the cost of the car alone would probably pay Travis's hospital expenses and the other bills as well.

"What's wrong?" Darrin surprised her by asking.

"What do you mean?" Leslie asked, suddenly feeling quite self-conscious.

"Come on, Les, it's me, Darrin. You were floating on a cloud when I left to get the food, but when I got back you were considerably with-drawn and pretty moody. You want to explain?" He turned into her drive and came to a stop. Shutting off the engine, he turned to face her. "So, what gives?"

Leslie felt her face grow hot. "It's nothing, really."

"Leslie." His voice was soft and patient.

She sighed. "Okay, it's just that I need to reopen Crossroads. The money situation is pretty tight. It's not a big deal, I'll take care of it. I just don't like leaving Travis."

"Why don't you hire some temporaries?" Darrin suggested.

"Who can afford that?" Leslie countered. "We're barely making it as it is, and if I can't recover the loss and pack in some real business between now and the end of the semester, I'll really be hurting by the time summer comes."

"Can I help?" Darrin asked.

Leslie grew suddenly uncomfortable. She undid her seat belt and opened the car door. "I'll be fine, really." She got out of the door and was halfway up the walk when she realized that Darrin was right behind her.

"Leslie, don't shut me out. I didn't mean to embarrass you. I know this is a tough situation. I just want to help any way I can. You know by now that I care."

That stopped Leslie in her tracks. Turning, she found his expression filled with compassion. Her heart skipped a beat when he placed his hands on her shoulders. She found that words wouldn't come.

"I don't want you to be afraid of how you're going to deal with all of this," Darrin said softly. "I just want you to know that I'm here for you."

"I know that," Leslie whispered. Her voice sounded foreign in her ears. "You've been a good friend, Darrin."

He pulled her into his arms and kissed her long and passionately. Leslie felt goose bumps travel down her spine. His lips were warm and gentle against hers, and for a moment, Leslie forgot who she was and why she was worried in the first place.

"I want to be more than friends," Darrin whispered against her cheek. Leslie began to tremble with the reality of what he'd said. "You're cold," he said, misjudging her reaction. "I shouldn't have kept you out here, but I just had to tell you how I felt."

Leslie forced herself to meet his eyes. Under the glow of her porch light, she could see they were sparked with a fire of passion. "I . . . uh . . . I don't know what to . . . say."

Darrin smiled rather roguishly. "Say that you want to be more than friends, too."

"I . . . I . . . can't," she stammered.

Darrin's expression changed instantly. "Why not?"

"I'm sorry," she said, feeling her whole world spinning out of control. "I just can't go forward with my life until I resolve the past. The accident, my parents' deaths, and now with Travis in the hospital, I just can't."

He smiled again. "Is that all?"

"It's enough," she whispered, feeling tears come to her eyes. He couldn't possibly understand how badly she'd love to give him the answer he wanted. She needed him. Needed him badly. But Travis had to come first, and the shop needed her now, more than ever.

"Look, I have to go out of town tomorrow. I'll be gone about a week. I'm supposed to fly to Paris and look over some antiques, but I'll be back on Sunday. Can I come see you then?"

"I don't know. I really meant what I said, Darrin. I have a lot of unsorted baggage to go through. A relationship is probably a bad idea right now." She wanted so much for him to understand. She prayed he wouldn't be mad.

"I know what you said," Darrin replied, reaching out to brush back a silky strand of blond hair. "I'll call you Sunday." Then before she could protest, he kissed her lightly on the mouth and left her standing on the walkway.

Leslie couldn't comprehend what was happening. There was too much going on at once, and she felt as though none of it was making much sense. Darrin waved from his car and pulled out of her drive. She found herself waving back, and even though she felt like running after him to bring him back, she stayed rooted in place and marveled at the pleasure she found in his kiss.

"Sunday," she whispered to the cold, winter night. "He's going to call me Sunday."

$$\textcircled{13}$$

arrin had barely made it into his apartment when the telephone began its annoying ring. He could tell by the answering machine that it wasn't the first call he'd received that evening. The message line showed the number at ten, and he was certain that most, if not all of the calls, would be from Laurelin.

"Hello?"

"Darrin?" It was Laurelin. "Where in the world have you been? I've been calling all night."

"Yes, I can see that from the answering machine," Darrin said, juggling the telephone and shrugging out of his coat at the same time.

"Well?" Anger edged her voice.

"Well, what?"

"Darrin don't play games with me. You've disappeared every evening for the past week and 'Well, what?' is all you have to say? I want to know what's going on. I've been working myself to death to arrange a caterer for our wedding. The menu is a nightmare, and the prices are outrageous, and you have done nothing to help me! Do you know how many months in advance you need to plan these things? Do you even care?" She barely paused to draw breath. "Oh, Darrin, this is so immature of you."

"Lin, I seriously doubt that maturity is directly proportional to the number of months in advance that one can schedule a caterer. Especially for a wedding that may never take place." He hated himself for just dumping it on her like that. Though she probably deserved to be treated in the manner in which she treated others, Darrin knew it wasn't right for him to be the one to start.

But Laurelin hardly seemed aware of his veiled threat. "Then I've had nothing but problems with Gerda and the shop. You're leaving to-morrow for Paris, and I have to stay here and try to sort through that inventory mess that she created. It just isn't fair."

"Probably not," Darrin said, still amazed that she could ignore his mention of not having the wedding. He sat down, knowing from experience that her tirade could run into the hours if she had her wind up.

"I get the distinct impression that you couldn't care less about my problems."

"Right now, I must admit they are at the bottom of my priority ladder."

"Well, good for you, Darrin," she snapped back snidely. "You go ahead and distance yourself from the conflicts and problems of our world. You've proven to me just what kind of man you are, and what kind of man you aren't. You obviously care very little about anyone but yourself."

Darrin stared up at the ceiling. *If you only knew, Lin*, he thought. Then his conscience was pricked by the fact that she should know. He should just lay it out for her and end their engagement and deal admirably with her. He'd meant to do so weeks ago, but time had gotten away from him, and he'd allowed one excuse after another to keep him from having to deal with her.

"Look, Lin," he finally said, "there's something I need to say here."

"Oh, don't even think of starting in on me. I've had it with your melodramatic, Boy Scout routine. I know you consider yourself one of the last great humanitarians, but I don't buy it. You have a business to run and a fiancée to plan a wedding with. You obviously care very little about either one, but that doesn't change the fact that I care a great deal. I don't want to be the laughingstock of Kansas City when I throw this wedding, and I don't want the business in bankruptcy. I think you'd better give this some definite thought."

"I have given this plenty of thought, Laurelin. That's why I need to say—"

"Don't tell me how much thought you've given this! Your thoughts and time have been consumed by your father's stupidity and that family in Lawrence."

Darrin was shocked that she knew about his dealings with the

Heywards. He said nothing, trying to imagine what he could say, but before an answer came to mind, Laurelin was off and running again.

She laughed in a haughty way. "You didn't think I knew, did you? Well, it wasn't that hard to figure out. I thought we'd discussed this, Darrin. I thought I'd made it clear that those people would use you and milk you out of your money. If, and I do mean if, I go through with marrying you, you are going to put a stop to this misguided philanthropic game of yours."

"It's no game, Laurelin," Darrin said, finally moved to the anger Laurelin obviously wanted to provoke. "Those people have a great many problems right now, and I intend to help in any way I can."

"It has to stop, Darrin. You aren't doing them or us any favors. I won't take second place to a group of yokels in Lawrence, Kansas, just because you feel guilty for something you didn't do. Get over it and grow up. I want to marry a man, not a mindless little boy."

"Which brings us back," he said in a very stilted manner, "to the subject of marriage."

"Hardly," Laurelin replied. "I'm not about to continue this discussion with you. Especially not in dealing with the happiest day of my life. You think about what I've said. Think about what you should be doing with your life. After you've come to your senses, give me a call. Then and only then, will we talk about our wedding."

The sound of the receiver being slammed down was no surprise to Darrin. He'd already pulled the phone away from his ear, knowing beyond a doubt what was about to follow. For some reason, hanging up first and having the last word gave Laurelin a sense of supreme power and control.

"Well, I hope you sleep better tonight, knowing that I was the last one to hang up," he said into the receiver. He shook his head and hung up the telephone. She probably would sleep better just for having had her chance to berate him. She was like that. A good airing of her soul, and Laurelin was set for another day of living.

He sighed and got up. Staring at the confines of his living room, Darrin was amazed at just how empty it was. There were the normal living room comforts. A sofa, a couple overstuffed chairs, end tables, an entertainment center. He even sported two very fine prints by

J. W. Waterhouse on the walls. But it all seemed rather meaningless just now.

Having spent the week with Leslie—having gone through such horrific trauma—he suddenly felt quite lonely not to have her here. He'd known for some time that he was falling in love with her, but there were so many problems to overcome that Darrin didn't dare to allow himself to believe that she might come to feel the same way about him. Hadn't she made it clear tonight that she didn't want a relationship?

"But she definitely responded to my kiss," he said, feeling rather confused by the entire matter.

He paced the room and fought against the urge to call her. *She's asleep by now*, he thought, glancing at the clock to see that it was already midnight. He imagined her face relaxed and peaceful in sleep. She worried so much about everything, and he longed to make it right for her. He wanted nothing more than to protect and keep her, give her the things she needed, support her against the assaults of the world. But she might never accept him, he remembered.

Once she knows who you are, he thought, *she might well hate you for the rest of your life*. But even as that dreaded idea came to mind, Darrin was certain it would never actually happen. *Leslie's not like that. She's not given over to holding someone else accountable for something they didn't do.*

"It still doesn't mean she'd actually want anything to do with me," he said to the air. "Once she finds out that my father was the one responsible for her parents' deaths, she'll probably not hate me, but she certainly won't be able to love me, either."

Frustration and despair began to take root in his heart. He loved her. There was no way he could deny those feelings. He loved her, but he was engaged to Laurelin. "Oh, God," he prayed, suddenly dropping to his knees. "I've made such a mess of things. I need to know what to do. How do I resolve this situation?" The answer seemed evident before the words were even out of his mouth.

Tell them the truth.

Darrin knew it was right. Knew it was the only answer. He had to come clean with both women. He needed to put an end to the deception with Laurelin. He didn't love her. Never really had. He'd found her helpful and savvy, but those were certainly not reasons to marry. No, he had to tell her the truth and do it very quickly. Then a thought came to him. He was leaving in the morning for Paris. There would be no chance to tell her anything until he got back.

"Okay, God," he prayed. "I know this is all my fault. I've tried to make up for my father's sins, and I've tried to take responsibility for things that had nothing to do with me. I spent a lifetime distancing myself from my father, yet now I openly accept the problems he created, and the results are eating me alive. Show me what to do, and when. Direct my steps, and show me beyond a shadow of a doubt how to deal with each problem as it develops so that I don't find myself in this mess again."

Darrin instantly thought of that night in Dallas when he'd first learned the truth about the Heywards and his father. He thought back to the Scripture God had clearly given him for comfort and inspiration. Getting up, he went to his bedroom and took up his Bible. Sitting on the edge of the bed, he thumbed through until he came to the verse in Ephesians 4: "Let all bitterness, and wrath, and anger, and clamor, and evil speaking, be put away from you, with all malice: And be ye kind one to another, tenderhearted, forgiving one another, even as God for Christ's sake hath forgiven you."

Darrin sat staring down at the page for a long time. "For Christ's sake," Darrin murmured. "God forgave for Jesus' sake, and I have to forgive for the same reasons. Not because I'm some great guy who can just overlook the bad things in my life or the wrongs people have done. But because Jesus died and paid a very real price for those things. And because I am to be like God, forgiving and giving of kindness and love."

Peace began to filter into Darrin's heart and soul. There were many things that needed to be released from his hold. He needed to forgive his father and let go of the past mistakes and injuries done to him by the man. He needed to forgive Laurelin and to ask her to forgive him as well. He'd wronged her by agreeing to marry her for all the wrong reasons. He needed to seek Leslie's forgiveness, too. Not for what his father had done, but for not telling her right up front who he was and why he initially cared.

"Help me, Father," he whispered. "Help me to set things right. Help me to pick up the pieces and put them back where they belong."

$\mathcal{L}$ eslie found herself excited at the prospect of Darrin's return to the States. He'd told her he would call on Sunday and that would be tomorrow. She couldn't help but replay the scene between them when he'd kissed her. A real fire had ignited in her heart that night, and it was hard to ignore the effects it had on her. Just as the Kansas weather had changed and spring had finally shown signs of arrival, love had begun to bloom in her frozen heart. She still suffered from the conflicting emotions, remembering what he'd said to her and what she'd said in reply. She'd put him off, but he hadn't really been persuaded by her meager attempt.

"But it was the truth," she said aloud, as she moved around the small storage room at the back of the shop.

Taking down several bags of gourmet blend coffee, she sighed. "He wants to be more than friends." She smiled. She couldn't help it. How long had she prayed that a Christian man would come into her life and speak just those words?

With less than twenty minutes until time to open the shop, Leslie suddenly remembered that she needed to call the hospital. Travis was due to come home in a few days, and she still had no idea what the cost of his care had mounted to over the last two weeks.

Stacking the coffee behind the counter, she went to the telephone and dialed the main number for the hospital. "Business office, please," she told the operator and waited patiently while the call was connected.

"Business office," a pleasant-sounding woman answered.

"Yes, this is Leslie Heyward. My brother Travis is a patient there at the hospital, and I wanted to check on the status of his bill. I just want to get an idea of what the total is at this point."

"Well, that will be rather difficult to say, especially since he's still a patient. Charges come in every day, you understand, and there won't be an account total at this point."

"Yes, I understand all that. I just wondered if you could give me an idea of what it has come to so far. You see, we don't have insurance, and I need to be checking into ways to collect the money. If I don't have some kind of idea, I'll be trying to do everything at the last minute."

"Of course, I understand. Let me see," the woman paused, and Leslie could hear the clicking of computer keys. "You said the last name was Haywood?"

"No, that should be Heyward," Leslie replied and spelled the name slowly. "Travis is the first name."

"Oh, yes, here it is. Hmmm, he spent time in intensive care, right?"

"Yes, that's right. He's in a regular room now, however."

"Well, just in keeping with what we have so far, which is current to a point of the charges submitted, I'm showing a total of $12,211."

"What?" Leslie said, stunned by the vast numbers being thrown at her.

"A little over twelve thousand dollars," the woman replied. "Of course, that doesn't include the doctor's charges. He'll bill you separately for his work."

"I had no idea," Leslie said, taking the phone over to a counter chair where she could sit down. She felt as though the wind had been knocked from her. "And you say the charges are still coming in?"

"Well, yes. After all, he's still a patient. The charges will continue to come in for several days after he's dismissed. You know how it is—several departments with a variety of tasks performed. They try to submit their charges quickly, but it takes time. You will be given a printout of all charges on the date of dismissal, but a complete listing might take as much as thirty days to compile. We'll mail you one when it's complete."

"I see," Leslie said, still unable to fathom where she was going to come up with the money. "Do you have any estimate of what I might expect if he stays another, say three or four days?"

"Well, of course, it depends on what he needs during those days, but I would just round it off to fifteen thousand. Especially given the fact that you have no idea what Dr. Selig's charges will be. I see his name listed on the chart here, but if you had any other doctors assisting him, you'll want to remember they will be mailing you charges as well."

It was more than Leslie could deal with. "Thank you for your help," she said rather curtly and got up to hang up the phone. "What am I going to do?"

She looked around her at the shop and felt despair like she'd never known before. "Fifteen thousand dollars? Oh, God, where am I going to get that kind of money? Please, God, show me what to do."

She thought of her accountant, Bill Pendleton. He was a good friend and a Christian whom she'd met at church long ago. She quickly dialed his number, and when his wife answered the phone, Leslie apologized for disrupting their Saturday and asked to speak with Bill.

"Bill, it's Leslie Heyward. I have something I need to ask you. It's pretty overwhelming and I didn't know what else to do."

"That's quite all right, Leslie. That's what I'm here for."

"Bill, I just talked to the hospital business office about Travis's expenses."

"Say, how's he doing? I heard from my mom that he might be coming home soon."

"Yes, we're hopeful of that. Maybe another three or four days if he continues to progress the way he has been."

"That's great news. So what happened with the billing office?" In the background a loud crash of some sort disrupted the peaceful conversation. "Leslie, just a minute," Bill said into the receiver. She heard him instruct his children to go into the other room, and within seconds he was back on the line. "Sorry about that. You were saying?"

"Bill, the hospital says that I can expect Travis's account to total fifteen thousand dollars, and that doesn't include Dr. Selig's services."

Bill whistled. "Wow, that's quite a chunk."

"Yes, and we have no insurance." There was dead silence on the other end of the line. "Bill, I don't know what to do about this. Will they let us make payments at the hospital? Can I take a loan for that kind of money? Should I get a second mortgage on the house?"

"Oh, boy," Bill said, obviously overwhelmed with the news. "That's a good question. Well, right off the bat I can tell you that the hospital isn't going to want to carry a fifteen-thousand-dollar balance, but I'm not sure what their rules are on such things. As for a second mortgage—it's out of the question. The bank isn't going to be too in- clined to give out money, even though you have good equity in the house. Your only source of income is the shop, and from the last state- ment you sent me, business is way off. On top of that, you're already behind in the rent, so I doubt the bank would be willing to offer you much. Certainly not fifteen thousand." He fell silent for a moment, then added, "Look, I'll do some checking into this and get back to you."

Leslie sighed. "I guess that's all I can ask of you."

"Don't let this get to you, Leslie. Take it to God in prayer, and I'll do likewise. There has to be an answer, and God hasn't let you down yet."

"I suppose you're right," she murmured.

"Let me call around, Leslie, and don't go trying to do anything on your own, okay?"

"You mean like put the shop equipment up for sale?" she said, only half joking.

"Exactly," he replied quite seriously. "If it comes to that, I'll help you make the necessary arrangements, but Leslie," he paused and his voice softened, "it doesn't necessarily have to come to that."

"Okay, Bill. If you say so." She knew the despair was evident in her tone.

"One last thing, Leslie."

"Yes?"

"Would it bother you if I shared this information with some of the other businessmen in the church? I mean, two or three or even more heads may well be better than one in this case."

"No, I don't have a problem. Everyone there knows the circumstances well enough," Leslie replied. She knew, too, that the people of her church genuinely cared about her. "Go ahead and do what you need to, and I promise to wait until I hear from you."

"Good girl."

She hung up the telephone without having gained any sense of peace or comfort from the call. Even her accountant didn't know what to do, and that wasn't a very encouraging thought.

"Dear God," she prayed. "There has got to be a way through this. I believe that, and I know with Your help, nothing is impossible. It just really feels that way. I need You to give me strength and to give me peace. Please let me rejoice in Travis's health, and don't let the financial aspects of his recovery draw my attention away from the gift You have given me. Thank You for all You have done and continue to do. Amen."

For a moment, Leslie stood perfectly still, allowing God's peace to fill her heart. It would all work out. She knew it would, because God was with her. With that knowledge, she went back to preparing Crossroads for opening.

❧

"Leslie? This is Bill." Disappointment flooded Leslie's heart. She had hoped the ringing phone would bring Darrin's voice into her house.

"Hi, Bill. Sorry I didn't talk to you at church this morning, but Margie wasn't feeling well and I wanted to get up to the hospital to see how Travis was faring."

"I understand," he said, not sounding at all comfortable with the conversation.

"What is it, Bill? Did you find out something I should know about this financial mess?"

"I talked to some of the guys at church. In fact, we chatted about half an hour together after the service. I'm afraid we didn't come up with any concrete solutions. In looking through all of your financial information, the options are quite limited. I've asked around, and unfortunately, it does seem you may well end up having to sell Crossroads. I mean you don't want to wait until it's gone under, and you can't recoup anything from the sale. I am really sorry. I didn't believe it would have to come to this, but . . ."

"I understand, Bill." Leslie felt the bottom drop out of her world. "Thank you for your help. You will come over to help me put things together—you know, decipher the paperwork and such?" Leslie's stoic voice masked the turmoil of emotions within her.

"Of course, I will, honey. Don't you worry. I want you to know that we're all here for you. I think you've done an outstanding job taking care of everything. Your mom and dad would really be proud." Leslie could almost see his face, filled with compassion and fatherly love. Bill had always been such a good friend. She knew the prospect of selling Crossroads was just as upsetting to the Pendletons as it was to her and Margie. She had grown up knowing the Pendletons as a second family, and Leslie appreciated their unconditional support.

"Thanks, Bill. Keep me posted, all right?"

"Definitely. Bye, Les."

"Good-bye, Bill." Leslie hung the telephone back on the cradle.

Leslie changed out of her Sunday clothes and pulled on jeans. All the while she kept hearing Bill's voice in her head. *Why, God?* she asked, taking out a long-sleeved white oxford blouse. *Why?*

Doing up the buttons, Leslie felt despair take deep root in her heart. Crossroads had been such an important part of her life. How could she give it up now? How could she sell a business that her parents had created and run profitably all those years, all in order to pay an outrageous hospital bill?

But it's not outrageous, she thought. The hospital and doctors had given her back Travis. Oh, she knew full well that it had come at God's hand, but they were the instruments God had chosen to use. How could she fault them for charging for their services? She would gladly pay ten times the amount they charged, if it meant Travis would live.

The rattle and crash of pans in the kitchen brought Leslie back to reality.

Margie. Leslie hadn't said much to Margie about the hospital bill nor the situation regarding how it might be paid. She'd wanted to save the older woman any upset if it turned out that their worries had been for naught. Now, however, it appeared she was going to have to give Margie the nitty-gritty details and pray it didn't cause her blood pressure to soar out of control.

"Margie," Leslie called, coming into the kitchen. Her aunt was already changed and working on Sunday lunch.

Turning to face her niece, Margie frowned. "Is something wrong, Les? Was that the hospital calling?"

"No, it wasn't the hospital, but well, actually something is wrong. That was Bill Pendleton. I had called him yesterday after talking to the hospital about Travis's bill."

Margie's face paled a bit. "How bad is it?"

Leslie tried not to appear overly concerned. "Around fifteen thousand." She held up her hand before Margie could say anything. "That's not the exact total so it could be less."

"Oh, dear."

Leslie worried that Margie herself would soon be in the hospital if she didn't sit down and relax. "Here," Leslie said, pulling out a kitchen chair. "Sit down, and I'll tell you as much as I can."

Margie did as instructed, casting a worried gaze upon Leslie. "Don't lie to me about any of it, Leslie."

"I didn't plan to," she replied. "I worry about upsetting you, so please understand that no matter what I tell you, I believe God will see us through this."

"All right," Margie replied. "I agree with that philosophy, so lay it on me."

Leslie took a deep breath. "Bill thinks we're going to have to sell Crossroads."

"Oh, no!"

"I didn't want to worry you until I knew for sure. The only way I could see to deal with it was to sell the store, but Bill wanted to talk to some other men from the church before we decided. I guess they arrived at the same conclusion. If we wait too long, the store will lose even more value and the debts against it will climb. So we need to move right away on it."

"Leslie, this is awful. What are we going to do?"

"All that we can do, Margie. Leave it in God's hands. We always said the store was a service to Him. Even the name Crossroads was given with an intention of ministry behind it. Maybe we've done our work and it's time to move on."

Leslie paused to look heavenward. "Maybe it's even time to sell the house and get something smaller. Travis and I don't need much room, and you still have your apartment. If I work a normal job with regular hours, maybe I can be there for Travis in a better way, and he can get over the emotional damage he's suffered. I just don't know, but what I do know is that I have to step forward in faith. I have to keep going."

"Yes, yes. I know. I just hate to think of you doing this alone."

"I'm not alone. I have God. Everything will work out fine. You'll see. With or without Crossroads, as long as Travis is well and we have each other, we will be fine."

⁓

After lunch, Leslie drove the familiar route to the hospital. She was excited to see Travis, knowing that each day he seemed to be growing stronger and more healthy. As she made her way through the pediatric wing, she smiled and waved at the different nurses and doctors whom she had come to know as friends. Kelly looked up and nodded a hurried greeting as she filled out some paperwork for the doctor looming over her shoulder. Amy came over and chatted on the way to Travis's room.

"Oh, he's doing *so* much better, Leslie. All the doctors are really impressed with his recovery. What a little trooper he is!" Amy's brunette ponytail bounced with each step she took. With all that energy and optimism, it was no wonder she was assigned to work with recovering children.

"Yes, I am so grateful for all that has been done to help him. You guys really are a Godsend." Leslie smiled broadly as soon as they entered Travis's room. "Ah, there he is! How's my favorite five-year-old?"

She was relieved to see that the blisters on his face were healing, though Dr. Selig assured her the skin would be tender for months to come. His hands were unbandaged, and the pink skin against his pale arms made him look like he was wearing gloves. Despite her brother's injuries, Leslie still believed him to be the most handsome boy in the world.

"Hi, Sissy," he said brightly.

After checking his IV and his various monitors, Amy nodded satisfactorily. "Well, I guess I'll leave you two alone. You seem very healthy, Mr. Heyward." The little boy beamed at the compliment, and after ruffling his blond hair, Amy left Leslie and Travis in silence.

"So, how are you feeling, honey?" Leslie pulled one of the chairs next to his bedside and gingerly held his rosy hand.

"I feel okay, Sissy." His face assumed a somber look. "I miss my toys, though."

Smiling, Leslie nodded sympathetically. "I'll bet you do. There doesn't seem to be much fun stuff for a little boy to do in here."

"Nope," Travis shook his head sternly. "And I need fun stuff. I'm a fun boy."

"You sure are, Travis. You are definitely a fun boy. But you'll be back in your fun room soon."

Travis's eyes brightened. "Really? I'll be home soon? How many days?"

"Well, Dr. Selig says that you should be able to come home in a couple days. Unless something else happens."

"Nothing else is going to happen. I'm all better."

"I know, honey. But the doctors want to make sure. You don't want to have to come back here after I get you home, right?" Travis shook his head. "Well, then, you need to listen to Dr. Selig and do everything he says. Pretty soon, I'll be able to take you home."

For a moment, Travis was quiet. His tiny brow was furrowed, and his eyes were focused on the ceiling. "Leslie, I wanna talk to you."

"Sure, baby. What about?"

" 'Bout God. And heaven. And Mama and Daddy."

"Okay. What did you want to say?"

"Well, I been thinking 'bout what you said 'bout how when Jesus wanted me to come home to heaven, He'd tell me so. And when I went out to see Mama and Daddy that night, I thought I heard Jesus."

"What did He say to you, honey?" Leslie softly stroked his arm as he tried to put words to his thoughts.

"I thought He said I could go home," Travis replied.

"Maybe He was telling you to come back home before you got sick," Leslie offered with a smile.

"I really wanted to go to heaven, Leslie." His five-year-old face appeared very serious.

"I know, sweetie. It's okay to miss Mom and Dad, but you have to understand that they are gone and waiting for us in heaven. We can't just pick up the phone and call for God to come get us and take us to heaven, too. We can pray, though. We can tell God how much it hurts, because you know what, Trav? He already knows our pain. He knows how much you hurt and how much you miss your mama and daddy."

Travis seemed to grow distant for a moment, so Leslie got up and carefully lifted him in her arms before settling into the bed herself. She lay there with him snuggled in her arms. "Don't go away, Travis," she said, her eyes growing moist. "Don't go away and leave me. I need you. I love you."

Travis hugged her tightly. "I love you, Sissy. I won't go away again."

Leslie sniffed back her tears. "I know this is hard for you to understand, but I don't want you to go away in your mind, either. I want you to talk to me when you're upset or scared. I want you to trust me to be there for you when you need me. Travis, I know I'll never be as good a parent to you as Mom and Dad, but I will take care of you. I won't let anything bad happen to you, if you'll just let me help you."

"I don't know what you mean," Travis said, pushing away from Leslie enough to look into her tear-filled eyes.

"I mean that I don't want you to hide from me or from God." Leslie reached up with one hand to touch his head. "I don't want you to hide away inside your mind. Do you understand? I don't want you to stop talking to me. I don't want you to think that you can't tell me what's going on in here." She tapped his head gently.

Travis looked at her strangely, and Leslie knew she wasn't getting through to him. "What I mean, Trav, is that when you think about Mom and Dad, it's okay to talk to me about it. If you want to remember a funny thing and laugh about it, that's okay. If you want to talk about the accident and how bad it feels that they died, then I want you to know that I will be happy to talk to you about that as well. I just want you to know that you can talk to me about anything. Even if you think that I'll think it's silly. You are important to me.

"If you're afraid of cars, then I want you to say so, and together we'll figure out a way to help you through it. If you can't sleep at night because you have bad dreams, then come to me, and I'll sit with you, and we'll pray together until you feel better. Do you understand now, Travis?"

"I think so," he said, falling back against her. "I can talk to you like I did Mommy."

Leslie felt a lump in her throat, remembering all the times she had turned to her mother in fear or despair. "Yes," she answered softly. "I'll never be able to take Mommy's place, but I don't want to take that place, either. I want to be your big sister, and I want to be your friend."

Travis nodded. "And I'll be the brother."

Leslie laughed softly and patted his back. "Yes. You will be the brother and the fun boy, and the joy in my otherwise dismal world." She hugged him tightly, feeling the blessing God had given her in Travis. Healing had truly begun for both of their spirits. Together, they stood in the middle of a crossroad, and together they had chosen a path of healing. *If only Darrin could be here*, Leslie thought, and the idea of sharing this small step forward seemed of major importance to her. Suddenly a great idea came to mind. She wouldn't wait for him to call her. She would call him. He'd given her his phone number when Travis had first been admitted to the hospital.

"Hey, Travis," she said with absolute joy filling her heart. "How about we call Darrin?"

$\mathcal{E}$ ven with the effects of jet lag lingering in his system, Darrin had decided to speak to Laurelin at the first possible opportunity. All the time he spent in Paris, he kept thinking about how on Sunday he would go to Lawrence and spend the day with Leslie. But in the back of his mind, the nagging reminder that he had to deal with Laurelin wouldn't allow him so much as a phone call to Leslie. Now Laurelin was due at the apartment any minute, and Darrin was nervously filling his time making iced tea.

He'd prayed a great deal about what he intended to tell her. He wanted to witness to her, but knew it wouldn't be well received, especially in light of the fact that he intended to break their engagement. Laurelin would expect him to have gotten his act together and be prepared to go forward with the wedding.

A knock at the door announced her arrival, and Darrin breathed a prayer before allowing her admittance.

"Hello, Lin."

Laurelin breezed into the house, wearing a complimentary spring suit of pale pink linen. "Well, hello yourself," she said with a sunny smile. "The weather outside is absolutely perfect. It's a gorgeous afternoon. Have you been outside?"

Darrin shook his head. "No, but I could see that things were showing definite signs of spring."

"So how was Paris?"

Darrin smiled. "Cold, rainy, and tiresome."

"Tiresome? Never!" Laurelin declared good-naturedly.

Darrin was surprised by her pleasant mood, yet he proceeded forward with extreme caution. He knew just how volatile this woman and her moods could be. "So," he said in a casual fashion, "would you care for some iced tea? I just brewed a pot and was getting ready to pour it over ice."

"Sounds great. Don't forget the lemon." She sauntered over to the sofa and made herself at home. "Well, in spite of the fact that you found Paris a drudge, I'd say it did wonders for you. You don't seem nearly as uptight as you were before you left."

Just then the telephone rang, and Laurelin reached over. "I'll get it."

Darrin said nothing, seeing absolutely no reason why it should hurt anything for her to answer the phone while he was busy with the tea. He could hear her speaking, but couldn't make out the words. Whoever it was, she seemed quite capable of handling the situation.

She was just hanging up when Darrin returned with two glasses in hand. "Who was on the phone?" he asked.

"Wrong number," Laurelin purred, taking the offered tea. "So we were talking about you and how you aren't nearly as testy as you were before you left."

Darrin nodded and took a seat in one of the overstuffed chairs. Laurelin frowned at him for his obvious distancing, but she said nothing.

"A lot of answers have come to me while I was gone. I suppose that's why I don't feel so 'testy' as you put it. There was plenty to do in Paris, but I spent most of my downtime, the time I could have to myself, in prayer."

Laurelin rolled her eyes. "We aren't going to talk about that again, are we?"

"I'm afraid so," Darrin said apologetically. "Because it has everything to do with what I need to say, to you."

Her hand stopped with the glass of tea midway to her lips. "What are you trying to say, Darrin?"

"I'm trying to tell you that I can't marry you, Lin. I don't love you anymore. I'm not sure I ever loved you the way I should have, but I know for sure that I can't marry you feeling the way I do."

"Well, isn't that nice," Laurelin said rather snidely. "It's someone else, isn't it? That's where you've been spending all your time, isn't it? Of all the selfish, self-centered people, you really take the cake,

Darrin Malone. I've spent a great deal of time and effort putting together this wedding, and now you sit there ever so calmly telling me
that you can't marry me because your *feelings* have changed. Well,
I'm not going to let you do this to me. Do you have any idea how
much time has gone into this? The effort on my part has been
immeasurable. I've had to do this on my own, and now you tell me
it was for nothing? Darrin, you don't deserve me." Her brown eyes
sparked.

"No, Lin, I suppose I don't. But then again, I'm not sure who
does." He watched as a smile played at her lips. She had taken it as a
compliment. Hadn't he known that she would? Darrin attempted to
remain calm. After all, he knew in his heart he was doing the right
thing. He had expected no less from Laurelin. He couldn't blame her
for being angry. But her vicious rantings always hit a nerve in him, and
he wasn't sure how long he could maintain his composure.

"Laurelin, this was not a snap decision. For a long time, things
have not been right between us. I have taken this to God in prayer,
and I feel led to tell you the truth. The truth is, I cannot and I will not
marry you. I felt like I had to keep on with the relationship because of
how convenient you were . . . with the store, with my trips, with my
life. That was not fair to you, and I apologize. I tried to convince myself we really were alike, when in reality, we were complete opposites,
in spirit, if nothing else. You don't believe like I do, and you don't
want to. I refuse to be unequally yoked with you." Darrin took a long
sip from his iced tea and awaited her reply.

"So you're leaving me because of a God thing? Darrin, that's no
reason to end a relationship. People get married all the time without
believing the same way. There's got to be something more. You don't
really believe this religion excuse and neither do I."

She leaned forward in a menacing manner. "So, who is she, Darrin? Someone you met in Paris? Another antiques dealer? Someone
who shows more promise than I do? Tell me."

Darrin rolled his eyes. "Yes, it is a 'God thing' as you so eloquently
put it. I'm sorry if you don't believe my 'excuse,' but it's the truth. I
don't feel I have anything in common with you except the shop, and
that's not enough to base a marriage on. I am not going to continue in

a relationship where I provide no more than critical insight to your wardrobe choices and decorating techniques.

"I need to feel I can confide in you, take my fears to you, and that you will meet me halfway with love and compassion. I don't feel you are prepared to do that. As a matter of fact, I don't think you ever will be. You love Laurelin Firth and her interior decorating business. You don't love me, you don't love our relationship, and you definitely don't love God. Now, how do you propose a marriage under such conditions?"

"If you wanted it bad enough, you'd make it work. You are a quitter, Darrin Malone. You have no drive, no desire. You cut your losses and run if things don't go your way. So I didn't turn out the way you thought I would. You certainly didn't seem to mind a year ago, or even six months ago. Now you're telling me you've had this epiphany, and you realize that you can't marry me because I don't believe like you. I don't buy it! You'll be a loser without me, Darrin. You remember that. If you leave me, Elysium will fall in ruins. You think Gerda will pick up my slack? And just what am I supposed to do without that job?"

"Lin, if you want it, the job is still yours. I don't expect you to rely solely on your interior decorating." Darrin stretched out his long legs and took another drink of iced tea. This wasn't going well at all. He could tell that nothing he said made any difference to her. She had just been dumped. And that didn't happen to Laurelin Firth. Her veiled threats and snide comments were meant to keep Darrin on his toes, not push him over the edge. Now, she didn't know how to react.

"You know, Lin, it occurred to me that this is the one scenario you probably haven't rehearsed. That's what bothers you so much, isn't it? I've put you into a very uncomfortable situation, and you don't know how to deal with it any other way than to be nasty and hurtful." He watched as Laurelin's face dropped in horror.

"How dare you imply that I don't know how to deal with you? You're nothing, Darrin. Nothing at all. I'm not being nasty—I'm being realistic. Something you obviously haven't taken the time to be. I know exactly how to deal with you and your childish desires. You felt smothered and trapped, like all men do when facing a marriage, and you panicked. Then, to save yourself from looking like a noncommittal little boy, you whipped up this 'believer/nonbeliever' jazz because you knew that if all else failed, you could throw Bible verses at me and look all superior. 'See? I really can't marry you. Look how many verses I know that you don't.' That's all it is. And yes, I'm angry, and I have good reason to be. But don't you ever tell me that I don't know how to deal with something. I always know how to deal with everything."

Darrin couldn't recall a time when he'd seen her so upset. She was breathing heavily from shouting for almost five minutes without a rest. Her fists were clenched, and her teeth were gritted.

"Lin, think of it as you like. No doubt that's the version our friends will receive. I really don't care. You can't touch me with your words. What I have told you is the truth. My faith is growing stronger, and I am seeing you in a different light. I don't love you anymore, and whether or not I ever did is in question, as well. It's over. No amount of screaming is going to change that. And as to whether or not there's someone else, yes, there may very well be. But that is none of your business."

Laurelin grabbed her purse and abruptly stood up. "Fine, Darrin. Have it your way. It's over. Great. And I suppose I'm the one who gets to break it to everyone. Well, thanks a lot. At least I'll have more time on my hands." Dejectedly, she shook her head. "All those wedding napkins. Wasted. What in the world am I going to do with all those napkins?"

"Look, Laurelin, I don't want this to end badly. I really feel terrible about this, because it is my fault. Will you ever be able to forgive me?" He genuinely meant it. He didn't relish the thought of a slighted Ms. Firth being in charge of his antiques while he was away, and he truly didn't want her to be hurt and angry. She couldn't help who she was, nor could he.

"It's going to take a lot of effort on my part, Darrin, but I will try. I'm not promising anything, you know." Darrin nodded.

"No, of course you're not. How could you?"

"Another thing," she said angrily, "you can keep your job and your stupid store. I'll be fine without any handouts from you."

He watched as she confidently strode to the door of his apartment. Just before walking out, she turned. "Oh, and one more thing. You might want to call Leslie."

Quickly, she slammed the door behind her, leaving Darrin's thoughts in turmoil. Leslie? How did she know about Leslie?

Suddenly, he understood. It hadn't been a wrong number when he was in the kitchen. Laurelin had spoken to Leslie. No doubt, Lin's sarcastic and superior nature had left Leslie battered. She probably hated him now.

What if she was calling about Travis? What if he was worse? *Oh, Lord*, he prayed. *Please let Travis be okay. And please don't let Leslie be angry.* Dialing the number to her home, Darrin's frustration grew. The busy signal offered him little comfort.

"Come on, Leslie, get off the telephone."

He tried for over an hour, and still the same pulsating drone came back in his ear. His worry and concern for Travis began to eat at him, so rejecting Leslie's home phone, he dialed the hospital instead.

The hospital operator sounded less than cheery, but Darrin held back any comment and asked instead to speak to the nurses' desk in pediatrics.

"Pediatrics, this is Kelly," came the voice.

"Kelly, this is Darrin Malone. Travis and Leslie Heyward's friend, remember?"

"Oh, sure. What can I do for you?"

"Well, I've had to be out of town for the past week, and I wondered how Travis was doing. I'd tried to call Leslie, but her line is busy."

"Oh, well, you just missed her. She was here up until about five minutes ago. Travis is great. He may get to go home in a couple days."

Darrin breathed a sigh of relief. "That is good news."

"Darrin, I'm real sorry, but I can't hang on. I've got two new patients coming in and—"

"That's okay, Kelly," Darrin interrupted her explanation. "I just wanted to make sure Travis was okay."

"Sure thing."

For several seconds after Kelly had hung up, Darrin just stood in place, phone in hand. Why had Leslie called if Travis was recovering so well? Was something else wrong? Or . . . He smiled to himself. Maybe she'd changed her mind about being more than friends.

He replaced the receiver and picked up his iced tea. The urge to go to Lawrence battled with the fatigue he felt from the long flight. *Maybe I'll just grab a nap and then go over,* he thought with a yawn. That sounded exactly perfect. He'd just take a quick nap and drive to Lawrence in the early evening. Maybe he could talk Leslie into going out to dinner and . . .

Suddenly he remembered that Laurelin had spoken to Leslie on the phone. *What had she said? Had she told Leslie of her relationship with me?* These thoughts haunted him as he gave in to his exhaustion. He'd straighten it all out when he woke up. After all, he had a great deal of confessing to do anyway, so he might as well add Laurelin to the list of things to tell Leslie about.

16

$\mathcal{W}$hen Darrin awoke, he was disoriented and for a moment found it impossible to remember exactly where he was and why. He felt stiff all over and, after stretching, sat up on the edge of the bed to note the time on the clock. The red numerals glared 6:02. *So much for early evening*, he thought. *By the time I get to Lawrence, it'll be at least seven or seven-thirty.*

Getting to his feet, he stretched again and went to pull back the curtains, surprised to note the color of the sky. Something about it just didn't look right. He checked his watch again and then a sudden revelation hit him. He'd slept all night! It wasn't 6:02 on Sunday evening. It was 6:02 Monday morning.

With a groan, he flipped on the television to confirm his suspicions. "Monday morning traffic is backed up on the Shawnee Mission Parkway off of I-35," a female reporter was saying. "Also a non-injury accident at State Line and seventy-fifth is requiring a detour if you're heading north into the city." The male co-anchor joked with her about the road construction detours, which apparently were requiring detours around detours, but Darrin had stopped listening.

Shutting the set off, he sat down on the sofa and ran a hand through his hair. "How could I have slept all night? Leslie will think me a real heel for not at least calling. I promised I'd call on Sunday."

He wondered silently if it was too early to call, then deciding it was, opted for a shower instead. He'd just make up for lost time and no phone call by spending all of Monday with her. And if she couldn't get away from Crossroads, he'd plop down at one of the booths or tables and spend the entire day drinking coffee. Two hours later, Darrin wheeled the BMW into a parking spot outside of Crossroads and noted the sign in the window. SORRY, WE'RE CLOSED! stared back at him as if putting a physical wall between Darrin and his mission. The trip over had given him a great deal of time to consider how he would break his news to Leslie—not that he hadn't already been considering the hows and whens ever since he'd left for Paris.

He planned first to explain Laurelin. He knew his ex-fiancée well enough to know that she probably made it very clear to Leslie what her status was in his life, at least Laurelin's version of her status. Leslie probably thought him a complete write-off, and he couldn't blame her. He'd made a real mess of things, and only now was he beginning to fear that Leslie would have nothing more to do with him based on the Laurelin issue alone.

Even so, Laurelin's position in his life paled against the reality of his father's position. He'd sent Laurelin packing, but he couldn't just remove the fact that Mike Malone was his father, nor the fact that Mike Malone had killed Leslie's father and mother. That was an issue of such major proportions that Darrin was beginning to feel inadequate to face it.

He sat parked in front of the shop for several minutes before deciding to drive by Leslie's house. If her car was in the drive, he'd stop and visit with her there. If not, he'd head over to the hospital and hope that she'd be able to give him some private time to explain his situation. Either way, Darrin felt more and more apprehensive about facing the truth. He'd come to care about her, love her in a way that he'd never expected. This was the woman he wanted to spend the rest of his life with. Yet, this was also the woman who might never accept him in her life because of the past and what his name would forever be a reminder of.

Slowing down as he drove past the Heyward house, Darrin saw no sign of Leslie's Toyota. *She must be with Travis*, he concluded and headed to the hospital. But, upon entering pediatrics, Kelly greeted him with the same news she'd given him the day before.

"Oh, Darrin, you just missed Leslie. She was here for about half an hour, and she took off. Had some kind of meeting and said she'd be back around lunchtime." She pulled a breakfast tray from a tall, four-wheeled cart and added, "Travis is eating right now, but you're welcome to go on in. He's been moved, you know. It's the third room down that hall." She pointed.

"Thanks, Kelly." Darrin went in search of Travis, hoping that he might shed some light on Leslie's absence.

"Well, hey there, partner. You remember me?" Darrin asked, coming in to find Travis negotiating a bowl of cereal.

"You're Leslie's friend," Travis stated matter-of-factly. "You're Darrin."

"That's right, but I'm your friend, too. At least I'd like to be."

Travis's face lit up, and a smile spread from ear to ear. "Do you like Legos?"

Darrin nodded. "I think they're the best toy in the world."

Travis's face grew contemplative. "They're not just toys."

Darrin realized his mistake instantly. "Oh, of course not." He pulled up a chair alongside the bed. "No, they're really a great deal more than just toys."

Travis nodded as though important information was being shared between two people in the same secret society. "I build things with them," Travis said, dribbling milk down the front of his hospital pajamas as the spoon wobbled on the way to his mouth. "I build a lot."

"I'll bet you do. Have you ever made a whole town out of Legos?" Darrin asked, trying his best to endear himself to the boy.

"Oh, sure," Travis replied. "All the time. The hard thing is to make airplanes and helicopters. I can make them with rubber bands and Legos, and the propellers can really turn."

Darrin smiled in admiration. "That's pretty creative."

"Oh, I saw it in the Lego magazine, but I know a lot of stuff about it already."

Darrin wanted to chuckle at the boy's creative confidence, but instead he decided to change the subject. "Has your sister been in today?"

"Yup," Travis said and turned his concentration on a piece of jellied toast.

"Did she say where she was going? I mean, I know she had some kind of meeting, right?" Darrin asked, hoping the boy wouldn't clam up on him now.

"Sure. She told me," Travis said. His little brows knitted together as he tried to remember. "She was going to the bank for clothes."

"The bank?" Darrin questioned. "She was going to buy clothes at the bank? Maybe she just meant she was going to get some money to buy clothes. Is she going shopping for you—is that who the clothes are for?"

Travis began shaking his head. "No. They're for bears."

Now Darrin was genuinely confused. "For bears? Leslie is buying clothes for bears?"

"That's what she said," Travis replied, seeming completely unconcerned that it made no sense in Darrin's adult world.

"Can you remember exactly what she said, Travis?"

Travis put the toast down as if exasperated with Darrin's inability to understand. "She said she was going to see some bears at the bank for clothes."

Darrin fell silent, trying to make sense of it all, while Travis, seeing that his visitor was apparently satisfied with the answer, continued to eat his breakfast.

Bears? Clothes? What does it mean, God? It just doesn't make any sense. The only thing that did make sense was that Leslie had gone to the bank. Maybe he could catch up with her there. But which bank and . . . Then a thought came to Darrin. A very awful thought.

"Travis, are you sure your sister said bears? Could it have been buyers!"

Travis shrugged. Darrin was feeling a sick dread in the pit of his stomach. Was Leslie meeting buyers for the shop because the bank planned to foreclose? Fearing the worse, he got up. "Travis, I'll be back to see you later. Can I bring you anything?"

Travis beamed a smiled. "There's a new Lego set with enough stuff to build a time machine," he said in an offhand manner. "You could bring that."

"You got it, buddy. If I can find it, it's yours."

With that Darrin fairly flew out of the hospital, pausing only long enough to call Leslie's house. With any luck at all, he'd get ahold of Leslie's aunt Margie and perhaps she would be able to tell him where Leslie had gone. If Leslie was planning to sell the shop because the bank was threatening foreclosure, he had to stop her.

Filling Margie in on the details, including the fact that he'd already arranged to pay Travis's hospital bill, Darrin was finally given the information he needed to stop Leslie from selling Crossroads. He arrived at the bank, and after insisting the receptionist interrupt the meeting, practically dragged Leslie into the hall outside the office.

Her stunned expression did little to calm his nerves. "Look, you need to stop what you're doing and come with me."

"Why? Is something wrong with Travis?" Leslie asked, looking suddenly panicked.

"No," Darrin assured her, "but you don't have to do this. I can't explain it all here, but put your people off. Tell them you've changed your mind, or that I made you a better deal, or whatever, but just put an end to this meeting and come back to Crossroads with me."

"Darrin, I'm in the middle of—"

"I know what you're in the middle of, and you don't have to sell the shop. Just come with me, and I'll explain." Darrin persisted.

"All right, Darrin," Leslie said, exasperation edging her voice, "but this better be good."

❧

Back at Crossroads, Leslie allowed Darrin to take charge and lead her to the table in the very back of the shop. He sat down opposite her, seeing the confusion written in her expression, and sighed.

"This isn't going to be easy for me, Leslie, but I have a great deal I need to tell you."

"Like about your fiancée?" Leslie asked, her blue-green eyes searching for the truth in his face.

"Ex-fiancée," he stated clearly. Then changing his mind as to the order in which he would confess his sins, Darrin continued. "Yes, I want to explain about her as well, but first and foremost, I feel I have to tell you something of much greater importance."

"All right," Leslie replied, sounding much calmer than she looked.

Darrin sighed again. *Where do I begin?* he wondered. "You don't need to worry about the shop," he finally said. "First of all, if there is a problem with the rent or the bills or whatever, I want you to know that I intend to see it taken care of."

"But—"

"No, hear me out," Darrin said, halting her questions. "I've already arranged to pay for Travis's hospital bills, and if your time away from Crossroads has caused problems with the bank, then I'll take care of that as well."

Leslie's mouth dropped open in surprise. "But, Darrin," she insisted, "Travis's bill is going to amount to more than fifteen thousand dollars. I can't let you pay that. You don't even know us, and we certainly don't know you. There's absolutely nothing to connect you to us, and certainly nothing to obligate you to seeing to our welfare."

Darrin frowned. "But there is, Leslie. You see," he paused trying to find just the right words, "what I'm going to tell you will probably change things between us forever, but I just want to tell you something first, before I explain any more about why I'm doing this. I've fallen in love with you."

The color drained from her face, and she sat back hard against the chair.

"I told you that I wanted to be more than friends, and I meant it. I meant it because I've lost my heart to you and . . ." He stopped. "This isn't what I came here to say."

"Then what?" Leslie managed to ask.

Darrin stood and paced the aisle between the table and the counter. "Leslie, my name is Darrin Malone. I live in Kansas City, and the first time I ever set eyes on you was on our flight down to Dallas."

"You were the man next to me. I remember you now," Leslie said, gasping in surprise. "I thought you looked familiar, but I could never place it. Of course, I had a lot on my mind then."

"I know," Darrin replied. "The thing is, we share a great deal and most of it you aren't even aware of, but when you understand the full details, you may never speak to me again. I'm just begging you to hear me out before you try to throw me out."

"Why would I throw you out?" Leslie asked, shaking her head in confusion.

"Because I'm Darrin Malone."

"But that doesn't mean anything to—" She stopped in midsentence. "Malone?"

"Yes," Darrin said, nodding. "I'm Darrin Malone, and my father is, or rather was, Michael Malone—the man responsible for killing your parents."

17

*D*arrin, how? I mean, why didn't you . . ." Leslie shook her head in disbelief. This couldn't be real. He couldn't be telling her that he was part of her pain. "Your father was the man who . . ." She couldn't bring herself to say the rest.

She watched through tears that threatened to spill over as Darrin began to pace nervously. Shoving his hands deep into his pockets, he struggled to continue. "I don't really know how to explain all this to you, Leslie. You see, my father and I were never close. He had always been an alcoholic, for as long as I could remember. He and my mother separated, and after she died from cancer, I was his only living relative. I grew up hating him for killing my mother through his drunken acts of stupidity, making her a nervous wreck. He was always getting into wrecks and fender-benders, but this was the first time anyone was ever injured by his carelessness, besides himself.

"I was the one the Dallas police department located to identify his body and make arrangements for burial and so on. I met you on the plane ride down, and I think you've had my heart ever since. It wasn't until later that night when the story was on the evening news that I finally figured out who you really were and who the victims of my father's foolishness were. I was overwhelmed by guilt and anger. I felt I had to make things right, no matter the cost. I found out all I could about you and your remaining family, and that's how I came to Crossroads and to you."

He paused, and Leslie could tell he was monitoring her for some response, but she was unable to say anything. The reality of Darrin's role seeped into her consciousness. She sat completely motionless and waited for him to continue.

"Then, Travis got sick, and I insisted that all his bills be sent to me. I instructed it to be done in secret because I knew you would never accept my help outright. I meant to tell you before you found out the total, but obviously, I was a little late. That's why you don't have to sell the shop."

Leslie felt tears hot on her cheeks. "So you did all this out of guilt? You never really cared for me or for Travis? Do you even *like* raspberry lattes?" She knew it sounded insignificant, but she had to know if it was a farce—if everything he had done had been to absolve his conscience.

Darrin sat down at the table. "No, no, Leslie. I do care about you and Travis and Crossroads. That's what I need you to see. It began as guilt, but I came to care about you beyond that. I would've helped you even if I hadn't known about—"

"No, you wouldn't have! I never would have met you if you hadn't been racked with guilt. You would never have come back into my life. And that really scares me. I've come to care about you quite a bit, Darrin, and I truly thought of you as a friend. I still do. I just wish you had told me the truth from the beginning."

Leslie couldn't tell what she was feeling. It was like rage, disappointment, frustration, and hurt all wrapped up into one. She loved this man. She really did. Not for the reasons she thought she would fall in love when she was a teenager, but for so much more. For the way his patience never ran out with her. For the way he would sit with her for hours on end in a hospital waiting room. For talking with her and allowing her to vent her frustrations, her worries, and her troubles. For smiling that Darrin-smile whenever he spotted her in the coffee shop. Now, she realized that the man she had lost her heart to was the son of the drunk driver who had killed her parents. This fact was supposed to change everything, at least in Darrin's eyes. But did it?

"Leslie, I need to know what you're feeling."

"How can I tell you what I'm feeling when I don't even know what it is, myself?"

"I understand, but I need to know where I stand with you." His eyes were pleading, and his face was strained with compassion.

"It's not your job to look out for me or to repair the damage he did. But . . ." Leslie stopped and sighed.

"But what?"

"I can't accept your help. It's not right. I don't want to be obligated to you . . ."

"Leslie, didn't you pray for help? Didn't you ask God to help you and protect you through this time of trial?" Leslie nodded. "Why can't I be that help? Why can't I be the one God sent to help you through this?"

"No!" she said adamantly. "I don't want to be tied any closer to you than I already am!" She looked away, as though ashamed of the implication of her feelings. Her long blond hair fell over her shoulders and framed her face. Bringing her gaze back to meet his, she watched as pain crept into his eyes.

"Leslie, talk to me. Don't hide your feelings from me. Not now. This is too important." His dark blue eyes implored her to open up. "I need to know you don't hate me. At least that. If you don't love me, fine. I just can't stand to think you despise me."

Leslie immediately felt guilt for the harshness of her words. She hated to hurt anyone. "It just wouldn't be appropriate." Her expression softened. "I can't lie to you, Darrin. Despite all my willpower and all my determination, I fell in love with you, too. But it doesn't matter what I feel for you. You have a fiancée," she offered weakly.

"Ex-fiancée. Leslie, that's over. It was over a long time ago, at least to anyone astute enough to see the warning signs. Laurelin and I were never right for each other. When you called, I was just about to explain to Laurelin that I was breaking off the engagement. Ever since the accident, God has been working me over in a major way. I came to realize that Lin and I didn't share the same faith or the same values or even the same interests. She had a way of making herself convenient, and I was desperate enough to fall into her trap. When I listened to my heart and sought God's way, instead of Darrin Malone's way, I was led to the truth. The Lord led me away from Laurelin, and He led me to you."

Leslie shook her head in exasperation. "Darrin, I don't know what to think. I don't know why you're here, and I don't know how to feel about you or about us. You said you loved me, but then you tell me that guilt and shame brought you into my life. How can we build a relationship off that?"

"We already have, but there's so much more, Leslie. I do love you. And not because I feel obligated to. I fell in love with the woman I saw day after day. The woman who struggled but managed to keep on going. The woman who confided her fears to me and who laughed with me. The woman who was not afraid to be honest and up front with me, even though she had no real idea who I was. I love you, Leslie. I hope that you can forgive me for not telling you the truth about my father and about my presence in your life. I was just so afraid you would hate me for who I was."

"What kind of person do you think I am? How could anyone blame you because of your father's deeds? You didn't hand him the drinks or the keys. You didn't demand that he drive that night or encourage him to hit my parents' car. You had nothing to do with it. I do love you. But not because you were saving me from the evils of this world. It was because you were sharing them with me. I don't want a savior, Darrin. I have one, and His name is Jesus. I don't expect you to right the wrongs of my life. That's not what I need." She placed a hand over Darrin's. "I need you to be my friend and my companion. I need you to be more. But you can't be of any good to either of us if you're trying to atone for the sins of your father. You have to let that go, and you have to forgive him. It took a lot of prayer and a lot of God's grace to allow me to forgive your father, but I did. You need to do the same."

Darrin's eyes filled with tears. "It's so hard. I try. I really do. I just thought that you'd hate me if you knew the truth. I felt so bad that he'd taken them away from you. I wanted to help you, but I didn't want you to think I was being some great martyr. The more I was with you, the more I came to love you and admire you for your strength and your faith. Even now, you still amaze me with your confidence and your trust. I can't say that I never doubted God or that in your position I would even be able to maintain my faith."

Leslie smiled sympathetically. "I know what you mean. I wish you could've heard me during the days following the accident. I was so lost. I blamed God. I blamed your father. I blamed everything. Margie helped me deal with my anger and brought me back to the truth. I can't say I did it all on my own. And I'm not saying you have to do it all on your own, either."

Darrin sat, looking deep into her eyes. "Are you saying . . ."

"Yes, Darrin, I still love you. I want to help you through your pain and your guilt. But I need to know that you didn't just befriend me because of your guilty conscience."

For the first time that evening, Leslie saw a smile play at his lips. "No, no, Ms. Heyward. I have a great many other reasons for befriending you."

Leslie was glad to feel the weight of the conversation lighten considerably. She allowed herself to counter his playful grin with one of her own. "And, pray tell, Mr. Malone, what are these great many reasons you speak of?"

"Well, Ms. Heyward, I love you and fully intend to make you my bride."

The weight was immediately back in place, and Leslie felt as though he had knocked the wind from her. "Marriage? You're talking marriage? Oh, Darrin, I need to think . . . to pray . . . to—"

"To hush." He rose to his feet and held out his arms to her. She took hold of his hand and stood as well. He encircled her with his broad arms and turned his eyes down to meet hers. Gently, he kissed her, and Leslie felt all her cares melt away. When he drew away, she wanted to pull him back, but she refrained.

"Now, Ms. Heyward, that seems to have quieted you for a bit. I think I will take you home now and allow you to consider the prospect of being my wife."

Leslie nodded, wondering if her legs would support her all the way out to the car. Why had he chosen a table so far back? "That would probably be best, Mr. Malone."

18

*L*eslie spent the rest of the day praying about Darrin and the proposal. She told Margie that there were major decisions to be made and that she needed to pray in private. Margie understood and offered to go to the hospital and keep Travis company, while Leslie secluded herself.

Leslie was grateful for Margie's love and understanding. She had always been able to count on her aunt, and this time was no exception. Even when she heard Margie return that evening, Leslie remained in her room, fasting and praying that she might seek only God's will. It would be easy to taint her actions by relying on emotions, and Leslie was determined that this wouldn't be the case.

Yet even as she sent her prayers heavenward, she knew a peace and rightness about it that gave her confidence. She loved Darrin, and for the first time in her life, she knew what it was to desire to spend the rest of her life with a man.

The next morning, Leslie knew it was time to confide in Margie. She had been so closed-mouth on the situation that no doubt Margie had stewed and fretted throughout the night. She had just finished putting breakfast together when a sleepy-eyed Margie entered the kitchen. "Good morning," Leslie called cheerily.

"Well, something certainly seems to agree with you," Margie said, stifling a yawn. "I take it you worked through your problems."

"That and more. Aunt Margie, we need to talk," Leslie said, pulling out a chair for her aunt. "I have breakfast on the table and thought we might share it and discuss the future."

"The future?"

"Exactly," Leslie said with a grin.

After they prayed, Margie looked up at Leslie with hopeful expectation. She said nothing, but Leslie could tell she wanted to.

"I have a great deal to confide in you. The first thing is that Darrin has already seen to paying off Travis's hospital bill, and he wants to help us keep the shop." Margie said nothing, and Leslie continued. "Secondly, Darrin and I are in love, and he has asked me to marry him."

"Are you serious? When did this happen?"

Leslie picked up a piece of bacon and nibbled at it. "I'm very serious, and I suppose I should start back at the beginning. It all started when I went to Dallas . . ."

Leslie told Margie everything, and when she was finished, she sat back and offered one single question. "Can you forgive Darrin's connection to Mom and Dad's death?"

Margie's brows knit together, and her face contorted into several looks before settling on a stern, authoritative expression. "That young man has nothing to be forgiven of," she said sternly.

"Oh, but he feels he does," Leslie replied. "He feels like he should have been able to do something before it all came to this. I have to admit, when he first told me, I wasn't too inclined to remain in the same room with him. Not because I blamed him, but because I kept thinking, 'This is the son of the man who killed my parents.'"

"You obviously don't feel that way now," Margie replied.

"No, I don't. I've prayed through every aspect of this situation, and while I will forever mourn the premature passing of my parents, I know that Darrin had nothing but goodness in his heart when he came to us. He didn't want to deceive us, but he knew we wouldn't take well to his offering help when the hurt was so raw and fresh. And Margie, he was right to do it the way he did. I'd have never given him the time of day if he'd walked into Crossroads and announced that he was Michael Malone's son."

"But neither would you have held him responsible for what happened. I know you too well to believe otherwise."

"You're right, but I wouldn't have wanted to associate with him. I would have politely accepted his apology, told him we absolved him of any responsibility, and bye-bye, Mr. Malone."

"So, you're going to marry him?"

"Would that bother you?" Leslie asked quite seriously.

Margie's face lit up in a grin. "Bother me? It'll only bother me if you don't allow me to help plan the wedding. Darrin's too good to let get away, and if you don't snatch him up, some more fortunate woman will."

Leslie beamed. "I'm glad you feel that way, because I intend to reel Mr. Malone in, hook, line, and sinker."

"And maybe in doing so, the past will be laid to rest once and for all," Margie commented. "Maybe Darrin will finally realize that you love him more than the memories he might invoke, memories that relate to his father."

"I hope so, Margie," Leslie said. "I hope so."

❧

At the hospital, Leslie found Travis intent on the Lego time machine Darrin had brought him. "Hey, buddy," she said, coming into the room, "the doctor tells me that you can go home tomorrow."

"Shhh," Travis said, without so much as looking up. "This is a real hard part, and I have to . . . Ahhh!" he exclaimed in disgust as a big piece broke away from the others. "Break, break, break. It always has to break."

Leslie put her hand to the small boy's shoulder. "Trav, stop acting that way. Just rest for a minute and listen to me tell you something else. Then, after you've rested, you'll probably be able to make it work the very first time you try."

Travis didn't appear to believe her, but nevertheless he waited. "Tell me what?"

Leslie smiled. "I know you don't know Darrin very well—"

"I like Darrin. He brought me these Legos and some books, and he talked to me," Travis interrupted.

Leslie smiled. "I'm glad you like him, because I like him a lot, too. In fact, I love him, and he wants to marry me."

"Marry? Like Mommy and Daddy were married?" Travis asked, suddenly frowning.

"That's right. What would you think of that?" Leslie was stunned when Travis's face puckered into a tearful expression. "What's wrong, Trav?"

"Where will I go live when you go away with him?" Travis asked, trying hard not to cry.

"Oh, baby, I would never go live anywhere without you. You're part of the package." But suddenly it dawned on her that maybe Darrin didn't realize this. What if Darrin presumed that Margie would take Travis?

"I'd get to live with you and Darrin?" Travis asked, all traces of his frown disappearing.

"Of course," Leslie muttered, still contemplating the situation. Why hadn't she thought to talk to Darrin about all of this first? She shook the discouraging thoughts away. "Travis, believe me, I would never ask you to live with anyone who didn't love you as much as I do. Will you trust me on this one?"

"Okay."

She embraced him in a tight squeeze, then tousled his hair and kissed his cheek. "I love you, Travis. You will always be my sweet baby guy."

He smiled at her, then seemed to forget the crisis of a few moments earlier and began to take up his Lego work again. "I've got to build this before Darrin comes to see me."

Leslie nodded. *And I have to talk to Darrin before he comes up here,* she thought.

❧

A call placed from Leslie to Darrin sent him to the Heyward house, where she was waiting for him. "I'm sorry if I interrupted something important," Leslie said, meeting him on the porch, "but I have something we should discuss."

The gravity of her tone made him wince. "Am I not going to like this discussion?"

Leslie smiled. "I suppose it all depends."

"On what?"

"On whether you kiss me hello and come sit with me on the porch and enjoy the sunshine of this glorious day."

He grinned. "I suppose I can bear that." He wrapped her in his arms and sighed against her ear before kissing her cheek, then her nose, then each of her eyes, and finally her mouth. "How's that for a hello?" he asked with a mischievous twinkle in his eye.

"Ummm," she said and put her head against his shoulder. "Hello. Hello. Hello," she murmured.

"So does this mean you have good news for me?" Darrin asked, pulling away to catch the dreamy expression on her face before she covered it with a more sober one.

"I want to have good news for you, but we need to cover a few bases first."

Darrin's grin broadened. "I've heard about making it to different bases, I just never thought—"

Leslie elbowed his ribs and pushed away. "Now, Darrin Malone, you know very well that that's *not* the kind of bases I'm talking about. Come on and sit down with me."

He followed her to a set of wicker porch chairs and waited until she'd chosen the settee before motioning her to scoot over and allow him to sit beside her. Leslie did as he wanted but held up her hand.

"I brought you hear to talk, not neck."

"Can't we do both?"

She laughed, and it seemed to lighten the moment. "Maybe later. But first, you listen."

"Okay, I'm all ears." Darrin leaned back and held his breath. *What could she possibly need to cover that required a special meeting like this?*

"First of all, I've given the whole matter of us over to God. I prayed and fasted and felt very confident in the answers and peace that came because of those prayers."

"But?" Darrin said, finally daring to exhale.

Leslie's expression softened and her blue-green eyes sought his with great love. "As far am I'm concerned there are no buts, however you may feel differently once I explain."

"I doubt that quite seriously, but please explain so we can move on to second base," he said with a roguish grin.

"Now stop that. This really is very serious." Her tone told him that she was exasperated with his teasing.

"Okay, Les, tell me what has you so troubled and worried."

She folded her hands and stared at her fingers for a moment. Darrin longed to reach out and brush back the blond hair that had fallen forward across her shoulder, but instead he sat back and remained silent. Whatever she wanted to say, he needed to let her know he understood the importance of the moment.

"Darrin, I went to tell Travis about us, and he started to cry," she said, then paused to look up. "He wanted to know where he'd have to go when we got married and went away."

Darrin suddenly understood Leslie's apprehension. They'd never discussed the boy, but Darrin thought it was a given—that he and Leslie would raise him. "And what did you say?" he asked softly.

Leslie bit at her lower lip and then let out a tremendous sigh. "I told him that I loved him, and that I would never ask him to live with someone who didn't love him as much as I did."

Darrin took hold of her hand. "Then it should work out just fine, because I do love him, and I wouldn't tolerate you sending him anywhere else."

Leslie's eyes widened. "You mean it? After all, this is a big deal. Raising a child isn't going to be easy."

"Never figured it would be, but I like the idea of having a great many of our own, so Travis can just start us out in style, and we'll practice on him until we get it right. Then he can play big brother to the others."

Leslie fell into Darrin's arms. "I love you so much. I just knew this was how you'd feel."

"Then why did you become so scared a minute ago?" he asked, gently stroking her arm with his finger.

"I guess because I wanted this so much. I want to marry you. I want us to be a family. Oh, Darrin, I just want you."

He chuckled and felt a warmth of satisfaction spread through him like a wash of pride. *She doesn't care about the past,* he thought. *She cares more about the future than anything laying back there.* It was exactly what he had hoped for. Prayed for.

"And I want you—and I want Travis, too," he finally said and pulled her even tighter against him. "For all time—no matter what."

"I felt like I was standing at a crossroad," Leslie whispered, placing her hand atop his arm. "One way led me down a dark and lonely path."

"And the other?"

She pulled away and turned to see his face. Her hand reached up to touch his cheek. "The other led me to you."

$\mathscr{E}$PILOGUE

$\mathscr{F}$light attendants prepare the cabin for landing," the voice of the airline captain sounded over the intercom.

Leslie rechecked her seat belt and looked up to find a nicely tanned Darrin smiling at her. "What?" she asked, glancing back down at her Hawaiian print blouse. "Did I spill something?"

"No, not that anyone could notice against *that* wild print," he said grinning. "I was just thinking of how much I love you and how happy I am that you're my wife."

"And I am very happy to be your wife, Mr. Malone. Hawaii seems to have agreed with you. You should take honeymoons more often."

"Perhaps I will," he said, leaning close, "but only if you're included in the trip."

"But of course," she replied and reached over to squeeze his hand. "I'm afraid you're stuck with me."

"When I'm afraid," Darrin quoted the Psalmist, "I will trust in You." He looked heavenward. "There's not much we can't face if we put God at the helm, eh?"

"You're right," Leslie agreed. "I'm so excited about seeing Travis. I hope he likes his birthday present. Margie said she has the party all set up for us to celebrate when we get home. It's going to be such a surprise for him."

"Six years old and in two weeks, school starts," Darrin replied. "He's got a busy year ahead of him."

"So do we," Leslie said, glancing out the window as the plane finally touched ground. She sighed. It was good to be home.

Darrin interlaced his fingers with hers. "We can handle it. So long as we work together. Remember what the counselor said? Every family has to work together as a unit. Doesn't matter if it's a blended family or one that comes together under the loving union of one man and woman. We'll work together. Even Travis recognizes that."

"Yeah, especially after the counselor used Legos to make his point," Leslie laughed.

The flight attendant announced their arrival, and the minute the seat belt sign was turned off, Leslie jumped to her feet and motioned Darrin into the aisle. "Hurry," she said. "We don't want to keep him waiting!"

They grabbed up their carry-on bags and moved out of the plane and up the terminal ramp. Leslie could scarcely contain herself and ran the final ten or fifteen feet, edging around other people and prying herself through a narrow opening where an empty wheelchair blocked one side of the hall and a backpacking youth sauntered up the other side.

Then she saw him standing beside Margie. The look of expectation causing his eyes to be wide and searching.

"Travis!" she squealed and practically flew out of the security area to where her little brother waited. "Travis!"

She picked him up and whirled around to catch the loving expression of her husband. It was still so amazing to see how God had turned the sad and tragic death of her parents into something so positive and right.

Margie laughed and greeted Darrin. "Good to have you back. How was your flight?"

Leslie didn't hear her husband's answer because Travis had wrapped his arms around her and was squeezing her neck in a bear-like grip. "Now, we're a real family, aren't we, Sissy?"

She looked up to see that Darrin, too, had heard the question. His nod reassured her. "You bet we are, Travis. You and me and Darrin, and Aunt Margie, too. We're a family, and together with God, there isn't anything we can't face."

And in her heart, she knew it was true. Life would be filled with crossroads, but with God leading the way, the path would always be certain—the choice would always be right.

A QUESTION OF BALANCE

BY VEDA BOYD JONES

Dedication
For my brothers, Michael, Secil, and Stan, with love.

Acknowledgment
*Thanks to Dr. Dian Doody, Elaine Jones, Bonnie
Hinman, and Joan Banks for their advice on this book.
And thanks to Jimmie, Landon, Morgan, and Marshall,
who explored Kansas City with me.*

1

"Do you think they're laughing at our expense?" Sarah Madison asked her two friends and nodded across the plush restaurant at the table of three men who kept looking their direction.

"Of course they are," Maggie answered, giving her auburn locks a pert shake. "Not us, specifically, but women in general," she was quick to add. "If you'd arrived on time, you'd have seen how they've been giving us the eye all evening. Men are so obvious. I think the one in the blue blazer is interested in me."

"Maggie, you think every man over eighteen is interested in you," Ellen piped in.

Maggie gave a sly smile. "When you've got it, you've got it."

"What is *it*?" Sarah asked.

"If you have to ask, you don't have it," Maggie said and chuckled.

"I think I'm glad I don't," Sarah said. "I apologize again for being late. We're swamped at the hospital." She lifted her glass toward Ellen in a toast. "To the Fabulous Five and to the birthday gal."

The three women clinked their glasses. The pact they had made in high school to celebrate each other's birthday continued even though Mary Lynn in Denver and Connie in Des Moines were missing the dinner.

"The first of the Fab Five to hit thirty," Maggie said. "How does it feel, old-timer?"

"Just like it did yesterday," Ellen said. "I'm consoled by the fact that you'll all be joining me soon."

Sarah smiled at the two women she had known practically all her life. In high school they had been inseparable. They had attended the same youth group at church and had remained close through the years.

Of the Fab Five, Sarah was the only one who had never married. During college she had dated Jeff, but he had objected when she started medical school. The last time she had seen him, he had told her he wanted a beautiful woman like her, but not a woman who would make more money than he did.

Then three years ago, she had dated Troy for several months. When he broke up with her, he had said she gave too much of herself to her patients and not enough to him.

Since that time she had been very careful to avoid an entanglement and she was determined not to be hurt again by men who could not accept her career. She kept relationships on a friendly basis, devoted her energy to her career, and the years had slipped by. Now at twenty-nine years of age, she held an important position at the research hospital working with Dr. Warner Lewis, a renowned physician. She worked with children suffering with leukemia and she found it to be rewarding but emotionally draining; she did not have anything left in her to deal with the fragile egos of men.

Oh, she went to the occasional hospital function with a date, but those were social gatherings she had to attend, and other doctors, usually Hal, escorted her. Yes, she was content in her world, knowing she was making a difference in children's lives but sometimes she could not do enough. Right now she was losing Andrea, one of her little patients and, unless a miracle occurred, Andrea would be the next leukemia victim at the hospital, probably before the week was out.

The three women ordered dinner and settled back to catch up on news. Sarah was glad to be with such comfortable companions after a stress-filled day at the hospital and she forced herself to concentrate on the conversation around her. Sarah had never been good at separating her professional duties from what little personal time she had when the lives of children hung in the balance. She needed tonight and the lighthearted fun of a birthday celebration.

"You know, Sarah, you're missing something by not having *it*."

Ah, the mysterious *it* again. "Why, Maggie?"

"Well, before you got here, Ellen and I were discussing how serious you are these days. You need some fun in your life. Some romance . . . adventure."

Sarah turned to Ellen, who was nodding her agreement.

"You could have it all, Sarah. You're beautiful and smart, but you spend too much time at that oppressive hospital. When was the last time you laughed?" Ellen asked.

Of all the women in the Fab Five, Sarah felt closest to Ellen who was almost as determined a woman as Sarah thought herself to be. Ellen set her goals and went after them.

The two friends had quarreled only once—five years ago before Ellen's marriage into Kansas City's high society. Kent, the owner and CEO of a computer software company, was twelve years older than Ellen. Sarah had thought them an odd match and asked Ellen if Kent's wealth was part of his attraction. Ellen admitted the money was an added draw and that she wanted the luxuries it could afford her, but she said she loved Kent. Sarah, though, had accused her of being bought.

"Everyone has a price," Ellen had replied.

They had made up, apologized for words that should have never been spoken, and Sarah had been her maid of honor. She was happy to admit she had been wrong. The five-year-old marriage had kept a glow in Ellen's eyes.

Maggie was the most adventurous of the Fab Five. Sarah had always admired Maggie's free spirit and wanted to be more like her. After high school, Maggie had taken off for New York to pursue a career in fashion design. She never made the big time, although she had studied under one of the best designers in the Big Apple. Unfortunately, a brief marriage had changed a happy-go-lucky Maggie into a cynical woman.

"So, you two had a little discussion about my lack of excitement and romance while I wasn't here to defend myself." Sarah did not like the determined glint in Ellen's eyes and could tell that Ellen was up to something.

"You need to get out more. Enjoy life. Have fun," Maggie said.

"I get out," Sarah said. "I just haven't met Mr. Right yet." And she was not looking for him, either for he was a fantasy, like Superman, and did not really exist.

"You'll never meet him if you don't get out of that hospital more often," Ellen said. "You need more balance in your life. Physically you keep in shape; spiritually you have a strong belief in God; intellectually you remain challenged and work toward lofty goals. Emotionally, though, you fall down."

That must have been some discussion they had had. "Do I deserve this just because I was late?" she asked.

Another burst of laughter erupted from the table of men. Three members of the Fab Five glanced across the restaurant.

~&

"Another woman's joined them." Ed motioned with his head as he picked up a hot roll from the basket with one hand and a knife with the other. "Pass the butter, Marshall." He buttered his roll while staring at the women, then dropped his knife, which clattered loudly as it hit the edge of his plate.

"I hope you're more competent with a scalpel than you are with that butter knife," Marshall Adams said. "And why all the interest? I thought you said you were a happily married man."

"I am, I am," Ed said. "But I'm still breathing."

"Not for long if you don't drop some of that extra weight," Jason chimed in and adjusted his blue blazer. He gave the redheaded woman an interested look and a wink. "How much have you put on since medical school, Ed? Fifty pounds? Who's your doctor, anyway? Hasn't he told you how unhealthy all that extra weight is?" Jason nonchalantly tapped a cigarette on the table before he put it to his lips and lit it. He inhaled with a satisfied smile.

"Look who's talking," Ed retorted, waving the smoke out of his way.

"Doctors, doctors," Marshall chided. He really wanted to say, "Boys, boys," but knew they would object. He had been the peacemaker between these two all those years ago in medical school, and his role had not changed with this meeting at the medical convention.

Marshall had been looking forward to this week in Kansas City and to seeing his old friends. The small town where he practiced was exactly where he wanted to be, but he missed the excitement of a city and the anonymity it gave him. Because of his profession, women in his home town vied for his attention. In his younger days he had enjoyed it, but now he was tired of the game. At thirty-four, he wanted to find that special woman, attractive, intelligent, honest, and true, and he wanted to do the chasing.

At least he had never deluded himself about why most women were interested in him now that he was a physician. He was more realistic than Jason. Marshall had helped him through two divorces and understood that Jason's wolfish attitude toward women was a coverup for the hurt and shattered ego he had suffered at the hands of two unscrupulous women who had wanted to be married to a doctor.

Marshall also understood Ed's obsession with food. During their college days, when most medical students had time only for their studies, Ed had held down not one, but two part-time jobs, and still sometimes had gone hungry. Now his financial position had changed and for all his appearance and sometimes rough manner, Ed was a brilliant surgeon. The money poured in, and Ed indulged his weakness for food. He was not as obese as Jason had implied, but he could stand to lose thirty pounds.

"I think the redhead's interested in me," Jason said. "She keeps glancing over here."

Marshall's gaze traveled across twenty feet of deep burgundy carpeting to the table occupied by the three women.

"There's a lot of gold flashing over there. I think at least one of them is married. And you may be right about the redhead, Jase. Women these days sure take the guesswork out of relationships."

"What do you mean?" Ed asked.

"They leave no doubt about what they want—money."

"And social status," Jason added.

"Are you speaking from personal experience?" Ed questioned, his eyebrows raised.

"Actually two experiences," Jason admitted with a frown. "But Marshall, don't you attribute any of the female pursuit to the famous Adams charm and good looks? Remember how women used to swarm around him in school, Ed?"

"Sure. Never could figure out what his attraction was."

"Wait a minute. Basically I'm a pretty nice guy. That's all it takes. Just a good, all-around personality."

"Uh-huh. Every girlfriend I ever had and both my wives said you had rugged good looks. I never could see it," Jason said.

Marshall shrugged. He glanced at the table of women again. "Yes, Jase, I do believe the redhead is interested in you." He switched the topic away from himself.

"How about that. And she doesn't even know I'm a doctor," Jason said.

Marshall nodded and studied the woman who had joined the other two. She was a stunning blond, a real knockout. When she had entered the restaurant, he had watched her walk gracefully to her table. Her long golden hair was pulled back from her face and was secured by a metal clasp; the suit she wore gave her an air of authority but also flattered her feminine shape. After she exchanged words with the others, she cast a wilting glance at the men.

"Wow. Feel the cold air from the glacier," Jason said. "I wonder if the famous Adams charm could melt her."

"Yeah, Marshall. I don't think she'd pursue you because you're a doctor." Ed laughed out loud, and all three female heads turned toward their table.

～&

"What you need, Sarah, is something out of the ordinary. I'd say you've never even asked a man out," Maggie said.

"You're right," Sarah answered, wondering where this conversation was leading. Her friends were looking her over in a very curious manner.

"It's not that hard," Maggie said. "Men love it when women show a little initiative."

"Have you taken a survey?" Sarah asked dryly.

"Personal experience. Let's face it, men can be easily manipulated. If a woman shows a man a little interest, he's down on his knees, just waiting for the leash to be put around his neck. Even you could do it."

Sarah's fork stopped halfway to her mouth. "Even me?"

"Let's face it. You're a novice at this sort of thing. But I have a little proposition. Check out the one in the tweed jacket. I dare you to ask him out."

At the word *dare*, Sarah's eyebrows shot up. In their younger days she and Maggie had dared each other to do a number of things that usually ended up getting them in trouble. But it had been years since they had been caught wading in the big fountain at the Plaza Shopping Center, the last of many dares.

Maggie waved a finger at Sarah. "If you played your cards right, you could convince that guy to go anywhere you wanted. Say to the fashion show Saturday." The clothing store where she worked as fashion coordinator was giving a benefit fashion show for Sarah's hospital. "What do you say?"

"I say you're out of your mind."

"Come on, Sarah. What have you got to lose? Except fun," Maggie added. "Give it a shot. Try something exciting for once. Don't you have the guts?"

"I have as much courage as you do. Pardon me, guts," Sarah amended.

"And that's another thing. Watch your vocabulary. Nothing turns a man off quicker than an intelligent woman."

"Now, that's one point on which we agree," Sarah said. "The minute a man learns I'm a doctor, he's intimidated." Past experience had taught her that. "I've had men actually step back from me."

"Well, there you are," Maggie said. "Ask the guy out, but don't tell him you're a doctor."

"You don't understand. I don't need a man in my life. I'm quite content the way I am. I'm proud of my profession, I've worked hard to get where I am, and I won't be defined by my relationship with a man."

"I think you protest too much," Maggie said. "Are you afraid of men, Sarah?"

Sarah took in a quick breath and glanced at Ellen, who sat intently watching the exchange. "I'm not afraid of men. I deal with them every day." This conversation had gone on long enough. She would put Maggie on the defensive. "What would be more interesting would be for you to get the man in the blue blazer to go out with you. And you can't do the asking. I dare you to get him to the fashion show."

"No problem," Maggie said. "I prefer the direct approach, but I could get him to do the asking. I'll accept the dare if you will."

"This is ridiculous," Sarah said and shook her head.

"Maybe not," Ellen said. "It might do you both good. Prove that you have different sides to your personalities than we normally see."

"Come on, Sarah. It'll be fun," Maggie coaxed. "For once you could play a dumb blond."

Not for once, but for the third time, Sarah thought as Jeff and Troy flitted through her mind. She had learned the hard way that some men preferred airheads to smart women.

"No," she said with finality in her voice. "He could be married."

"I don't see a ring," Ellen said. "And of course, if he is married, we'll call the whole thing off."

"No," Sarah repeated. "Nothing would make me take this dare."

"Oh, really? What if there were a sizable incentive?" Ellen asked.

"I can't be bought," Sarah said, then regretted her choice of words.

"Let's talk about fifty-thousand dollars to be awarded not just to your hospital, but to your clinical research."

Sarah's mouth flew open.

"Kent just told me I needed to divest us of fifty-thousand dollars . . . to charity." She studied her nails for a moment. "He doesn't care where our charitable contributions go; that's one of my jobs. I could funnel it all to leukemia research at Children's Research Hospital and hand you the check at the fashion show Saturday." She flashed a quick, catbird smile.

Sarah closed her mouth but remained speechless. Fifty-thousand dollars could mean a great deal to her lab and might save the lives of countless children. It was too late for little Andrea, but if they could find another way of combating the cancer, it might give hope for other little girls like her. They had received a research grant last year, but this year little money had trickled down from the administration. Ellen and Kent donated thousands to charity every year, and it might as well be to further leukemia research.

"But you can't tell him you're a doctor," Maggie said.

"I would never lie," Sarah said. That went against her values.

"Well, telling a guy you're a doctor is like the kiss of death to romance. You said so yourself," Maggie said. "You need to get away from the doctor/lawyer professional type of relationship. You need a man/woman relationship. If he asks where you work, say you teach health. You do teach interns, don't you?"

"That's a technicality, and you know it." She lectured interns when they went through the pediatric oncology rotation. "Besides, I can't act like what I'm not." Sarah shook her head. Was she actually considering such a crazy idea?

"Just don't act like what you are," Maggie said.

Sarah glanced over at the man in the tweed jacket. His wavy, dark hair gleamed when it caught the light of the chandelier. His good looks were of the rugged type. Even sitting down, he positively radiated power. Maybe it was the broad shoulders. She frowned at him as she considered the dare. Could her friends be right? Was she too serious and leading an unbalanced life? All work and no play and all that?

What harm could possibly come of the dare? It would be a temporary setup, so it would not disturb her neatly ordered life. This was Monday; Saturday was only five days away. It might be a way of proving to Ellen that she did not need help with her love life. Ellen never called them blind dates, but on several occasions when Sarah had gone to dinner at Ellen and Kent's, she had discovered an extra man at the table.

"To keep the numbers even," Ellen had always said.

There was also the fifty-thousand dollars, an enormous amount for a private donation. Actually, that was the only reason she would do it. Research cost money, and every dollar could make a difference.

She glanced at the man again. He caught her eye and smiled at her, a warm, gentle smile. Against her will, she felt the corners of her lips curve up in an answering gesture.

It felt odd, and she could not remember the last time she had smiled at a man like that.

"All right," she told her friends. "I'll do it."

❧

"Did you see that, Ed?" Jason asked. "She smiled at him. I knew the old Adams charm was still there." He slapped his hand on the table. "And you always get the classiest ones. How do you do it?"

"All I did was smile."

"Hey, maybe the glacier's the one," Ed said. "See if she'll go out with you before you tell her you're a doctor."

"Yeah," Jason agreed. "If the glacier will go out with you, you'll know you still have the Adams charm."

"I could do it, but I don't want to." Marshall had come here to update his skills and to renew his friendship with these men, not to get involved with a woman. Besides, a man could not ask a woman he saw across a restaurant for a date. And he did not want to be shot down in front of these men.

"You don't want to meet the classiest looking woman in the place?" Jason asked. "What happened to the old Marshall Adams?"

Maybe Marshall could convince this woman to see him, to just have a cup of coffee with him. There was something about her that intrigued him. He glanced over at the woman and smiled.

Again she returned his smile, and the expression on her face softened.

"All right. I'll give it a try," said Marshall.

❧

Sarah finished her cheesecake and laid down her fork. What had she gotten herself into? She had no idea of how to ask a man out. After all, he was sitting with two other men. Did she confront him with them listening?

The three women had gone over the ground rules of the dare: Have fun, don't tell him you're a doctor, and get him to the fashion show on Saturday. Maggie had agreed to her dare, too.

"I know you won't donate money to my bank account," she had said, "but it'll be fun. And if it will get Sarah out, I'm willing to make the sacrifice."

Sure, thought Sarah. Since Maggie was between relationships, it would also give her a man to date for a week. The blond man looked interested enough; Sarah had seen him wink at Maggie.

"They're already on dessert," Ellen whispered conspiratorially. "You're going to have to make your move soon. What are you going to do, Sarah?"

"I'm not sure. Maggie?"

"You go first, Sarah, since you need the experience. Pretend you're a siren. You can do it."

"Thanks." Her friends stared at her, waiting. Taking a deep breath, Sarah stood, smoothed down the skirt of her rust-colored suit, and straightened her jacket. She placed some bills on the table to take care of her check, hooked the strap of her purse over her shoulder, and walked purposefully toward the table of men. She could do this. She was a woman of the nineties.

Each step shortened the expanse of burgundy carpeting between the tables. She could feel the eyes of the women on her back and those of the men on her face. Suddenly, she could not do it. She veered off her straight course, headed for the door, and slipped out into the foyer. Perhaps they would all believe she had gone to the ladies' room.

She leaned against the wall and closed her eyes. For the kind of money Ellen was offering, surely she could go back in there and talk to the man.

"Dear God, please give me the courage to do this," she whispered.

At the sound of the door opening, she opened her eyes and straightened up. Her victim stood in front of her.

"Hi," he said and smiled that charming smile of his.

"Hello," Sarah replied in what she hoped was a flirty tone. Was she that out of practice that she had forgotten how to flirt? This was her opportunity, but she felt as tongue-tied as a shy teenager. "Did you enjoy your dinner?" What a silly thing to say.

"Yes, I did. And now I'd like a cup of coffee. Would you join me?" He motioned to another room off the foyer that housed the Java Room.

"Yes, I'd like that," she said, then she actually giggled in relief. She had not giggled in years; she had not even laughed lately. Maybe her friends were right. Maybe she did need more fun in her life, more balance.

"I need to tell my friends to leave without me," she said. "I'll just be a minute."

He held the door open, and the couple walked back into the restaurant. Sarah walked quickly to the table where Ellen and Maggie waited, wide-eyed.

"We're going for coffee," she announced in a low voice.

"All right!" Maggie said. "I thought you'd chickened out on us."

"Oh, please," Sarah said. She was not about to reveal that he had asked her. "See you later."

"I'll call you tomorrow," Ellen said as Sarah turned and walked back to where Marshall stood by his table. The other men grinned at her, but Marshall escorted her out of the restaurant without a backward glance at his friends.

He kept a guiding hand on her back as they crossed the foyer and entered the espresso bar. Unlike the old brightly lit, counter-type coffee shops of the past, the Java Room was lit almost entirely by candlelight. From the center of each table, a tall taper glowed. The piano held a brass candelabra and was the only light available for the pianist, a woman in a long, black dress.

"This is lovely," Sarah murmured as she sat in the chair Marshall pulled out for her. "Wow, what a classy place," she said on second thought. Maybe she should watch her language as Maggie had suggested.

Instead of taking the chair opposite her, Marshall sat in a seat at a right angle to her.

Although the room was practically filled, a waitress appeared immediately and presented a long-stemmed rose to Sarah and took their orders.

Sarah glanced around and noticed the other women had roses, too. It was a classy place, she thought.

"So, what's your name?" she asked.

"Marshall Adams from Neosho, Missouri." He hesitated a moment. She had agreed to get a coffee without knowing he was a doctor.

Surely that was enough to prove he still had the Adams charm. Now he wanted to know her better, without making up stories or avoiding the truth. "I'm here for the AMA convention. Your turn."

"Sarah Madison. I live here in Kansas City." She extended her hand and he shook it, gently but firmly. "Are you a doctor?"

At his nod, she said, "How interesting. I'm a—" she caught herself just in time. "I teach health."

"Really?" His baritone voice had her hypnotized. Kansas City's an interesting place. I'd like to see some of it while I'm here."

Great. He was walking right into her lair. "Maybe I could show you around." If she entertained him, he would feel he owed her the favor of attending that fashion show, and she would get fifty thousand for research.

"I'd like that," he said and smiled at her.

"So, you're a doctor," she said. "Where did you go to school?" It was small talk she hoped a happy-go-lucky, not-a-care-on-her-mind type of woman would ask.

"University of Chicago," he answered.

"Really? I went there," she said. "Did you have Strausburg for basic anatomy?" Now why did she ask that? She should steer him away from talk of college. But didn't health majors take anatomy? Maybe he would let that slip by.

"Yes, I did. He's an institution in himself. When were you there?"

They discovered that Sarah was a freshman when he was an intern.

"In the same university and I didn't know it. Of course, you'd have been in the education school, so our paths wouldn't have crossed. But now my luck has changed." It sounded like a line, but he meant it.

"Sarah?"

Sarah turned her head to see Hal standing beside their table. He was an occasional date, but she knew he was not the fantasy Mr. Right.

Oh, no, she thought. *He could ruin everything.*

"Hello, Hal." This restaurant and coffee bar was within a block of the convention hotel. She figured that was why Marshall and his cronies had dined there and why Hal was there now.

Hal stared pointedly at Marshall.

"Hal, this is Dr. Marshall Adams from Neosho. He's here for the convention. Marshall, Dr. Harold Mosley from Children's Research Hospital." She gave his full name and added, "He specializes in cardiology."

The two men shook hands and exchanged civilities, but eyed each other with great interest.

"Have you known Sarah long?" Hal asked.

"We both went to the University of Chicago," Marshall answered.

"Ah, old friends. I see. Sarah and I also go back quite a ways. At Children's Research—"

Sarah felt the money for the research slipping away.

2

*H*al," Sarah interrupted, "are you with these doctors? I think they're leaving." She pointed to several men who had walked up behind him.

"Yes, but I can join—"

"Actually," she said, "I wanted to spend some time with Marshall. Catch up on old times, you understand?" Why wouldn't he go away? She had been downright rude.

Hal glanced behind him then back at Sarah and Marshall. "I guess I'd better go," he said. "I'll talk to you tomorrow."

"Fine," Sarah said, but she did not take a deep breath until he and the other doctors had left. Another doctor from Children's Research was with his group, and she had been afraid he would mention something about her work, too.

She glanced at Marshall and saw he was watching her. "Sorry. He's someone I've dated now and again, but I'm not interested, and he can't get the message." She had told her friends she would not lie, and here she was telling a whopper. Or was she? On quick reflection, Sarah knew it was true. She liked Hal as a friend, enjoyed the evenings he took her to hospital functions, but he seemed determined to turn their relationship into more than a casual friendship.

Marshall nodded and held up his cup. "To Kansas City," he said as he clinked his cup with hers.

"To Neosho," she said. "Right?"

"Yes. My hometown."

"You're from there originally?"

He nodded. "When I was a youngster, I wanted desperately to get out of Neosho and move to a big city. But after medical school, when

I was deciding where I wanted to practice, I decided on a small town. I kept thinking about some place like Neosho and finally thought, why not go home?"

"What happened to 'You can't go home again?' Do you disagree with Thomas Wolfe?" Oh, no. She had done it again. She should not talk about literature.

"You can go home again, but you go back as a different person and demand to be treated as an adult and not as a child. Of course, it helped that I had M.D. after my name."

Sarah nodded in agreement. She had found the same thing was true for her, although she had always wanted to return to Kansas City. She liked cities, but then they were all she had ever known.

"Cities are like many small towns put together. Basically I stay in one small area, maybe three miles square. But if I want to do something different, it's always available just across the city."

"I know. Remember, I lived in Chicago for several years."

"That's right." They discussed the Windy City and its points of interest.

"To think, we were in the same town and didn't know it," he said.

Her heart quickened. What was wrong with her? He was only giving her what sounded like a line. But it was a sign that he was interested. Time to turn on the charm. What did women say in a situation like this?

"What's your sign?" she said then smiled brightly. She felt foolish saying it, but it was part of the game.

"My sign?" Marshall asked. He looked at her oddly, as if trying to see behind her mind.

His eyes were the bluest she had ever seen. They would make Mel Gibson's look pale. Even in the flickering candlelight, their color was brilliant.

"Your astrological sign," Sarah explained.

Marshall studied her for a brief moment. She was sending him mixed messages. When he had first seen her in the restaurant, she had given all three men a look that would have wilted lettuce, as if she were disgusted with the whole male/female game. Yet, without the slightest hesitation, and almost eagerly, she had accepted his suggestion that they go for coffee. She was an educated woman, had read Thomas Wolfe, but was also interested in astrological small talk.

"I'm a Pisces. Do you believe that stuff?" Marshall asked.

She looked directly in his eyes. "No," she said softly. She had vowed she would not lie, and she wouldn't, at least not directly.

"Then why discuss it?"

What could she say? That she was so out of practice at flirting that she did not know how to make small talk with a man? No, he would ask why she was out of practice and that would lead to her job and then to disclosing the dare, and that she could not do.

"I'm getting mixed signs from you, Sarah Madison. And I don't mean the astrological kind. I think you're an intelligent woman with whom I would like to spend some time, and then I get a flash of dumb blond. Which is it?"

Sarah's mouth dropped open. "You don't like dumb blonds?"

Marshall shook his head "no," his gaze never leaving hers.

"Men don't like intelligent women," she said.

"Now who would tell you something like that? Surely not a man."

Surely one would, she thought, *actually two*. But she did not say it out loud. Jeff had not only said it, his actions had shouted it. Troy had been a little more discreet, but his message had been clear enough.

"Actually we were discussing men at dinner, and it came up." She leaned toward him to get a closer look at his expression. "Are you sure you'd prefer an intelligent woman?"

"Any day of the year. And especially this day."

Sarah smiled. This was a man who could appreciate her for herself. And she wanted to get to know him, not on a professional level, but as a woman knows a man. Surely she could do that without revealing she was a doctor. The dare was important. She hated to admit that she could be bought, but she reminded herself the money was not for her, but for the children. There was also the competition with Maggie over who could get a man to the fashion show. Although she did not think of herself as competitive, she knew she had to be in order to make it as far as she had in a male-dominated profession.

The medical convention ended on Saturday night with the banquet. The closing speaker was none other than her boss, Dr. Warner

Lewis, and she already had a ticket for the event. Right after the fashion show she would tell Marshall about the dare, and they would laugh about it, and he would tell her how smart she was to get that much money for her research. Then they would attend the banquet together, and after that go their separate ways. No involvement, no dependency, but a good time for a week. That was exactly the way she wanted it.

Yes, she wanted to know this man, and she wanted him to know her, her real self. The self who liked sunrises and pralines and ice cream. The one who gained serenity and peace from early morning church services and cried over late night movies. The self that she rarely showed to the world. She would share that self with him, all except the part about being a doctor. Then he would go back to his small town, she would stay in her city, and they would have enjoyed a pleasant interlude.

"Marshall, may we join you?" Jason, Marshall's friend from dinner was standing by their table with a triumphant Maggie at his side.

Marshall stood. He did not want Jason and the redhead to sit with them, but a quick glance around the full room convinced him he had no choice. "Of course," he conceded. As soon as the redhead sat down, Marshall resumed his seat and cast an apologetic look at Sarah. Things were just getting interesting, and now he could feel Sarah withdrawing.

After introductions and more coffee and a rose, Maggie dominated the conversation. "Marshall, did Sarah tell you she teaches health?" she asked.

"Yes, she did," he said and wondered briefly why Maggie was interested in their conversation. "What do you do for a living, Maggie?"

"I'm a fashion coordinator for Ambassadors, a big department store chain." She sipped her chocolate latte. Hmm, this is good." In the silence, she elaborated. "I do fashion shows a lot. General PR stuff, too. I'm doing a fashion show at Sarah's hospital Saturday."

"You own a hospital, Sarah?" Jason asked.

"No, of course not. Maggie calls Children's Research Hospital mine because I work a lot of hours there without getting paid," Sarah explained, shooting daggers at Maggie for her slip. She figured she put in many unpaid hours.

"Oh, you're a volunteer?" Jason asked, but Sarah did not answer. "Hospitals couldn't operate without them. We call them Pink Ladies at Denver General."

"Doctors, would you excuse us a moment while we visit the powder room?" Sarah asked, then practically dragged Maggie off with her.

"What's the big deal, Maggie?" She accosted her as soon as they were in the ladies' room. "Why did you say my hospital?"

Maggie shrugged. "It slipped out. Sorry."

"I want that money for research, so don't mess this up. If it weren't for you, I might have persuaded Ellen to donate it without the dare. Now I have to be on my toes all the time with Marshall. He's a nice man, and I'd like to get to know him better."

"Ah-hah! You'd have never asked him out without the dare, so you owe me one," Maggie said. "Besides, Saturday's not that far away. You can tell him as soon as the check's in your hand." She looked a little sheepish and admitted, "Actually, Jason's a real nice guy. Too bad he leaves Sunday for Denver, but maybe he'll ask me out there soon."

Sarah gave her a disbelieving look.

"He might," Maggie argued, her voice going up an octave. "Forget about Jason and me. You concentrate on Marshall. He'll be glad you didn't talk shop the whole time. Trust me." She turned and led the way back to the men.

Maggie could have a point. Marshall might say he did not like dumb blonds, but he might not like women doctors, either. Some male doctors were threatened by them.

"Oh, Maggie," Sarah said before they were within hearing range of the doctors, "how did you manage to be here with Jason?"

"I accidently bumped into him in the foyer. We started talking, and he suggested coffee. I wanted to be more original than that, but it worked." She shrugged her shoulders again, a habit that was beginning to annoy Sarah.

The two men were deep in conversation and looked up guiltily as the two women approached the table. Sarah exchanged a curious look with Maggie. The men stood as the women were seated, then resumed their own chairs.

An uncomfortable silence followed. The pianist had taken a break and conversations from the other tables could be heard.

"There seem to be a lot of doctors here," Maggie said. "Is it a big convention?"

"Several thousand," Jason answered. "We were lucky to get rooms in the convention hotel. We can walk to the Convention Center for the big meetings and just go downstairs for the smaller seminars. Marshall and I were just discussing what a nice diversion it is to have two lovely women with us instead of hearing shoptalk all night as well as at the meetings."

Maggie shot Sarah an I-told-you-so look. "Well, we'll see what else we can do to keep you away from all these doctors."

"Marshall, you mentioned you wanted to see some of Kansas City," Sarah said. "Anything special?"

"You tell me. The few times I've been here were for specific events with no extra time for exploring the area. When we go to a city from Neosho, we head for Tulsa. It's closer."

"Are you a baseball fan? The Royals are in the playoffs, and to-morrow night they play here again. If they win, they'll go to the World Series."

"I love baseball." Marshall's eyes sparkled with excitement. "I've always been a Cardinals fan, but I can switch loyalties for one night. Can we get tickets this late?"

"Tickets aren't a problem. My family has a box. It's my dad's one great passion, but he and Mom are in Connecticut visiting my sister, who just made me an aunt for the third time. So, the box is mine." She was glad he liked baseball. Getting him into this special play-off game should make him feel indebted enough to attend the fashion show with her.

"Marshall obviously hasn't told you about the big game against the Goodman town team," Jason said. He lowered his voice to imitate an announcer. "He was eighteen and playing for the American Legion team. Top of the ninth, bases loaded, score one-oh in favor of the Neosho team, when Goodman's big slugger came up to bat. You may have guessed that the southpaw on the mound was none other than Marshall Adams."

Marshall groaned. "I was going to impress her with that old story when we were alone."

"Go ahead. Impress me now," Sarah said.

"Ah, it was nothing," Marshall said with false modesty. "Just three pitches and three strikes and we won the game, the league, and the trophy."

"But how did the runners get on base in the first place?" Sarah asked, effectively puncturing his balloon.

"Well, I can't remember exactly. Maybe a walk and a couple of hits. That's not the important part, Sarah," he said in an exaggerated gruff voice.

Maggie burst out laughing and Jason joined in. Sarah maintained a straight face. "You're right, of course, Marshall. Let me feel your muscle." She reached over and massaged his left bicep through his tweed jacket. "You're strong. It must take a lot of strength to throw the ball that hard," she said in a sultry voice.

Marshall leaned over and whispered in her ear. "Forget what I said earlier. I might get to like the dumb blond routine."

He was kidding, of course, Sarah thought. But as she looked into his eyes, she saw interest mixed with humor. He took her hand and held it. With his touch, her heart skipped a beat but her mind recorded his reaction to her dumb blond comment as something to think about later.

While the conversation continued around them, he held her hand, sometimes in one hand, sometimes with both hands. She hated to admit it, but she liked it very much. It was a simple gesture, not a threatening one, but she was tingling down to the tips of her toes.

"I'm sorry to break this up," she said after they had finished their coffees, "but unlike some, who can sleep until meeting time rolls around and then skip if they want, I have to be at work early tomorrow." She stood and Marshall stood with her. He was very tall. She was five foot eight and she only came to his shoulder.

"What about the game tomorrow night?" Jason asked.

"Meet at my place, and we'll go from there. Maggie can direct you. Six-thirty." She waved a good-bye.

Marshall put his arm around her shoulders as they walked out of the candlelit room into the bright foyer. Sarah carried the long-stemmed rose the waitress had given her.

"I do love the smell of roses," she said as she sniffed it, then held it under Marshall's nose.

"Mmm. It smells lovely," he agreed.

They stepped outside into a perfect September evening. The moon was almost full, and the air held a cool hint of fall.

"Did you drive?" he asked.

"My car's in the shop being fixed and won't be ready until tomorrow. I'll take a cab."

"I'll see you home," he said and motioned to a cab parked in a yellow zone. His car was parked a block away at the hotel's underground lot, but this way he could concentrate on Sarah rather than on driving.

"That's not necessary," Sarah protested.

"Don't argue, lady. This way I'll know how to get to your house tomorrow night." He settled himself in the backseat beside her, his arm quite naturally going around her, and her head quite naturally settling on his shoulder.

Sarah straightened and gave the cab driver her address, then once more snuggled close to Marshall. She could not believe she had done that, but admitted to herself that it was where she wanted to be. This dare had somehow freed her. She felt free from responsibility, free from being serious, and free to respond exactly as she wanted to to a good-looking man. She would never see him after Saturday, so would not have a complicated relationship to break.

They were nearing her neighborhood when Marshall gently tilted up her chin and kissed her.

"We're here," the cab driver announced.

Sarah sprang away from Marshall. How could she have let herself be carried away like that? She had let him kiss her with another man a couple of feet away. The cabbie was surely aware of what was going on in the backseat. Feeling free was one thing but acting like the stereotypical dumb blond was something else.

"I'd better go in," she said hastily. She grabbed her purse and waited while Marshall spoke to the driver, opened the door, and climbed out ahead of her.

"Do you think you can find my house tomorrow night?" Sarah asked as they walked to the front door of her Georgian-style home.

"Not at the moment, but I'll watch how the cab takes me to the hotel." He looked up at the massive columns that stretched two stories. "Nice house. You live here alone?"

"Yes. My family lived here when I was younger. When my folks moved out to Lake Quivera, I bought it from them."

"Lake Quivera? A suburb?"

"On the Kansas side. Private community, homes on the golf course, that sort of thing."

Sarah found the key in her purse and opened the front door. Before she could reach in to flick on the light, Marshall put his hands on her shoulders and turned her to face him. Where his kiss in the cab had been tender, questioning, searching, this kiss was assertive, masculine.

Sarah kissed him back, then she pulled away. She had just met the man, and however much she was attracted to him, she was not going to let herself become involved. He would be gone in a few days. Besides, this was their first date, and a pickup date, at that. Worse still, it was a dare. She kept losing sight of that.

"I'll see you tomorrow night. Six-thirty. Game's at eight, but it takes a while to get there and get in. We can grab a hot dog at Kauffman Stadium."

"I'm looking forward to it, Sarah." He gave her a quick peck on the lips then walked back to the waiting cab.

Marshall climbed onto the backseat and slid toward the center so he could converse easily with the driver and learn the turns he should make to get back to Sarah's. Putting his hand down on the seat next to him, he jerked it back with a little yelp and stuck his injured finger in his mouth. Sarah had left her rose, and his second finger had found a thorn.

He gingerly lifted the flower and sniffed the delicate fragrance. He would never see a rose again without thinking of Sarah. Sarah with the golden hair and the mistaken notion that men did not like intelligent women. She was the kind of woman a man could take home to meet his family.

What was he thinking? He had just met the woman. He was attracted to her, but he did not know her well enough for these serious thoughts. Besides, this had started as an experiment to see if he could get a date with a woman who did not know he was a doctor. And he had succeeded. Getting to know her better and going to a play-off ball game were added bonuses.

When the cab delivered him to the hotel, he took the back stairs to the sixth floor to avoid the milling doctors. Once in his room, he unwrapped a cellophane-covered glass, filled it with water for the rose, and set it on his bedside table.

3

$\mathcal{M}$arshall, over here," Ed's voice boomed out.

Marshall stopped just inside the door of the large meeting room and looked around until he spotted Ed, waving his big hand in the air. He could see Ed's grin and knew he would be hit with questions about Sarah. Raising his hand in acknowledgment, he took time to speak casually to a few other doctors he had met in other meetings before ambling over to his friend.

"Well? How did it go last night?" Ed's grin got bigger.

"Sarah's quite a woman. We had coffee and a nice chat. We're going to a ball game tonight."

"To the Royals' game? How'd you manage that? If they win tonight, they'll play in the series."

"Sarah has a box for the season," Marshall said, wishing Ed would lower his voice. "Jason and Maggie are going, too."

"Is Maggie the redhead who *accidentally* bumped into Jason last night?"

"Yes." Marshall glanced at his watch—10:30. He had already called the hospital to check on an elderly patient and to make sure the transfer of his caseload to another doctor was going smoothly—10:31. It was going to be a long day before he could meet Sarah at her home.

Sarah. There was something about that woman that fascinated him, although he did not know much about her. He had thought of sending her roses to replace the one he had in his room, but he did not know where she taught health. Although she hadn't said, he figured she taught in a high school, but he had no idea which one. He gathered she volunteered at Children's Research Hospital, but he did not know which days or which floor, so he dismissed that idea. Tonight he would find out more about her.

He was almost as excited about seeing the ball game as he was about seeing Sarah again. He had never seen a play-off for a World Series game. In Chicago he had ventured to the ballpark a couple of times, but free time had been hard to come by when he was in school, and later, when he was an intern and a resident, free time was nonexistent.

The speaker was counting into the microphone, so Marshall took a seat beside Ed and prepared to take notes on the latest discoveries on how bacteria form in the body.

~&

Sarah sat on the side of the hospital bed admiring Andrea's new doll. This was the fourth time in the last two months that Andrea had been in the hospital and Sarah knew she would not be leaving this time. Acute lymphocytic leukemia, which was once considered fatal, now had a 70 percent recovery rate. But the nonlymphocytic type, which Andrea had, let only 40 percent survive. This little six-year-old girl would be one of the 60 percent.

"Have you named her yet?" Sarah asked.

"I'm going to call her Sarah," Andrea announced proudly.

"Good choice, Andrea. Are you trying to get on my good side?" Sarah teased.

"Which side is your good side, Dr. Sarah?" The frail little girl looked from one side of the doctor to the other, a twinkle in her brave, brown eyes.

Sarah turned her profile for the benefit of her young patient. "This is my better side, you little scamp." She leaned down and hugged Andrea. "I've got to check on a few more patients, then I'll be back." She hung the chart at the foot of Andrea's bed, then called, "I'll see you later," over her shoulder.

Sarah stepped out of the room and took a deep breath. Andrea represented the hardest part of her job. As many times as she had told herself not to get involved with her patients, she always violated that rule and loved each one.

She checked on a couple of other patients, then stopped at the nurses' station to use the phone.

"Arlie, this is Sarah Madison. I'm fine, thanks," she answered. "Arlie, I need a favor. I'm bringing a *real* baseball fan to the game tonight, and I'd appreciate it if you'd meet him after the game."

"Sure," the deep voice answered. "You want the usual . . . an autographed picture and a small tee shirt?"

"No. This one's not a patient. The shirt would have to be extra large."

"A man, Sarah? You're bringing a date to the game?"

"Yes, Arlie. Will you meet him, please?"

"Sure. Is he a doctor?"

"Yes." Sarah twirled the phone cord with her finger and wondered what words to use, then blurted out, "He doesn't know I'm one, too. Be sure not to mention it, okay?"

"What's the deal, Sarah? I thought you always dealt honestly in all relationships. You certainly told me fast enough you weren't interested."

"Now, Arlie. You know we were destined to be just friends. And who's that woman in the picture in yesterday's paper? You two looked pretty chummy."

"We are. I want you to meet Heather. Hey, tonight after the game, I'll have some friends over, and you can meet her then. Bring your date," he added.

"Actually there's another couple doubling with us."

"Safety in numbers, Sarah?"

"Not at all. It just worked out that way," she defended herself. Arlie was too analytical. He thought he had her all figured out.

"Bring them along. The more the merrier and all that."

"Thanks, Arlie. If you need a favor sometime, call on me."

"You can bet I will," Arlie said. "See you tonight."

"See you. And I hope you hit a homer." Sarah hung up the phone with a satisfied smile on her face. Since Marshall liked baseball so much, surely he would like to meet some major league players. He would be so beholden to her, he could not refuse to attend the fashion show. That research money was as good as hers already.

"Dr. Madison," a nurse said, "Mrs. Garren is back from breakfast and is with Andrea. She's sorry she missed you earlier, but would like to speak with you when you have a moment."

"Thanks," Sarah said. "I'll go now and come back in a few minutes to finish rounds." She glanced at her watch. Only 10:40, hours before she would meet Marshall again. But she could not dwell on that now. She squared her shoulders and marched toward Room 202 to talk with the mother of the dying child.

❧

Sarah sat in the front seat of Marshall's luxurious sedan giving him directions while Jason and Maggie shared the backseat.

Marshall had turned the car into her driveway exactly on the stroke of six-thirty. The three were excited and in high spirits about the game and teased Sarah for making them wait five minutes while she changed into jeans.

Sarah had been late getting home. When she realized she would be delayed at the hospital, she called Jefferson Wright, a former patient's father, to make sure she could get into the stadium without having the special play-off tickets. She knew of the drawer at her parents' house where tickets were always kept, but she did not have time for the drive out to Lake Quivera to get them. And she still did not have a car. By the time she left the hospital the garage was closed, so she had taken a cab home.

Jefferson had assured her that he would take care of her. She should find his ticket booth, and he would make sure she got to her box without any hassle, convincing her that it truly was a who-you-know world.

Sarah directed Marshall to the stadium and took ribbing about her last-second instructions, as she would say, "Turn there . . . turn here," when they were almost past the turns.

Marshall pulled the car up outside the gate to Kauffman Stadium.

Jason whistled. "Look at that line."

"That's why we're here an hour before the game," Sarah said. "We have quite a walk from the parking lot before we get to stand in line."

Marshall followed directions from one waving parking attendant to another and finally headed into a space and parked. The foursome trouped to the stadium, joining a throng of people converging at the ticket gates.

"Box seats," Marshall read from a sign. "Over here." He had taken Sarah's hand so they would not be separated in the push of the crowd, and now he pulled her toward that line.

Sarah squinted to see the attendant taking tickets at the front of the line. "No, that's not Jefferson," she said and led them to the next line.

"Who is Jefferson, and why are we looking for him?" Marshall asked.

Sarah explained the situation and kept urging them from line to line. *This can't be happening to me,* she thought, as they checked out the third and fourth lines. With each line they passed, she became more embarrassed.

"Here he is," she called out with relief. It was the sixth ticket booth they had checked, and now they had to go to the end of the long line. Luckily the line moved fast and, within ten minutes, they were talking to Jefferson, who handed Sarah a makeshift pass for four.

"Thanks, Jefferson," she said. "You're a real lifesaver."

"No, you're the real lifesaver. I'll never forget what you did for Nathan."

"He was a good patient," Sarah said, glancing over her shoulder to make sure Marshall had not heard. He and Jason were talking, so she felt safe. "Let's go," she said to her companions.

Marshall again took her hand as they walked into the stadium. Another attendant stopped them to look at the pass and waved them on. After climbing three separate levels of wide ramps, Sarah motioned them to turn left and go into the open air.

The sunlight was just fading, and the lights around the playing field and those in the stands had been turned on. The excitement in the air was contagious as the loud hum from thousands of conversations reached their ears. As if on cue, the loudspeaker began the introductions of the players. The foursome stood in awe for a moment, before Sarah urged them on down the steps toward the box seats. She kept glancing ahead for an empty box while she manipulated them past the people in the aisles. Why couldn't she see one? She checked the ticket again to make sure Jefferson had written the correct section number. He had. She stopped in the right spot and counted over three boxes.

"Oh, no," she gasped.

"What is it?" Marshall asked and grabbed her shoulders. "Are you all right?"

"This can't happen to me," Sarah said in a whisper, but Marshall was right beside her and heard even though the stadium thundered with applause for the players.

"My father's friends are in the box. He must have given them the tickets since he couldn't use them."

She watched disappointment wash over Marshall's face then saw it quickly replaced by a forced smile.

"Well, we can always go to a movie," he suggested.

"No. Let's find Jefferson." She did not know what he could do, the game was a sellout, but she needed to make some effort to get herself out of this mess. She closed her eyes briefly to gain her composure.

"What's going on?" Maggie asked as Sarah turned to lead them back up the steps to the platform where they had entered the arena. They moved against the traffic flow and were making slow progress when the national anthem began. Everyone stood and faced the flag flying over the scoreboard. Some rock star Sarah could not identify belted out his own rendition of "The Star-Spangled Banner." Before he reached the last two lines, the crowd cheered, including Sarah and Marshall, Jason and Maggie.

As the roar died down, the umpire called, "Play ball," and the four reached the exit and were about to begin their descent when Marshall stopped to look back at the first batter. As he swung and missed, the home crowd cheered and the Royals were off to a good start.

"So, what's going on?" Maggie demanded again.

Sarah explained.

"Well, we can't just stand here and watch the game," Maggie said.

"Why can't we?" Sarah asked, suddenly believing that that was exactly what they could do. "People are in the aisles all the time, going to the restrooms or to the concession stands. If we get in the way, we could always walk on up the aisle, as if we're going to our seats."

Maggie leaned over and whispered in Sarah's ear. "And you said you couldn't act like a dumb blond."

Sarah ignored her. "It'll work, won't it, Marshall?" She turned beseeching eyes to him.

"I don't see why not," he assured her. "You don't get the chance to see the play-offs very often, and we're already in here."

Maggie took Jason's arm. "I could use a hot dog. Why don't we head for the concession stand?"

"It might be better if we split up," Marshall suggested. "We'd be less conspicuous that way. When the game's over, why don't we meet you at the gate where we came in?"

"Fine," Jason agreed. He and Maggie headed for the refreshment area.

Marshall put his arm around Sarah's shoulders. "Don't worry. This will be fine. I've been sitting all day. I need to stand for a while, and I'd hate to miss this game."

They leaned, side by side, against a concrete pillar beside the arena's entrance and watched the game. Marshall hailed a peddler and bought them each a hot dog and a soft drink, which they demolished quickly.

"Every half inning, let's move to another section," Marshall suggested. He placed his hands on her shoulders and steered her through the crowd to the concession area.

They decided they would stay in the general vicinity of the box, so they would have it as an excuse if they were stopped. Marshall kept a hand on Sarah, either on her shoulder, around her waist, or just held her hand. When he would pull it away to applaud or buy another cold drink, Sarah felt bereft until he touched her again. In the midst of thousands of strangers, she wanted his presence close.

As the game seesawed back and forth, the fans were on their feet most of the time, and Marshall and Sarah blended right in. During the seventh-inning stretch, they met Maggie and Jason as they strolled to another section. Jason gave the thumbs-up sign as they passed on the steps. Even Maggie seemed caught up in the fun.

At the end of the eighth inning, the game was tied at four to four. The Royals got the first three batters out in the top half of the ninth, and then took their turn at bat. The entire stadium was on its feet as the bases were loaded and two players struck out. The next batter came up and successfully bunted, and the runner on third slid on home. Safe!

The crowd roared. Marshall picked up Sarah and swung her around.

"Enough! I'm dizzy," she cried, and he set her back on her feet only to pull her close in a bear hug.

"Best game I've ever seen," he shouted over the thundering crowd.

No one was in a hurry to leave the stadium. The euphoria continued even after the field was cleared of players and excited fans. Finally, Marshall ushered Sarah toward the ticket gate where they were to meet Jason and Maggie. The other couple was waiting for them.

"Thanks for getting us in, Sarah." Jason gave her a big hug. "Terrific game."

"Yeah. It was fun," Maggie said. "Where shall we go to celebrate? Your place, Sarah?"

"How about a small get-together at a friend's house? I know you won't know anyone, but trust me, you'll like it."

Marshall tossed her the keys. "It's your friend; you drive us there. I can't take any more of your last-second directions like on the ride out here."

"Okay. That might be easier," she said with a laugh. "Where's the car?" she asked as the foursome walked out the gate, and she was answered with three blank stares.

"If we hadn't checked so many ticket lines, I would have remembered," Jason said.

Marshall shook his head. "I haven't a clue."

They retraced their route from ticket gate to ticket gate and finally Jason spotted the right area.

It took forever to get out of the parking lot, but Sarah finally maneuvered the car through the stadium gates and onto the road. Thirty-five minutes, later she pulled to a stop at the guardhouse at Lake Quivera.

"Hi, George," she called out her open window. "Don't have the pass with me."

"No problem," the guard said and waved them through.

"What kind of place is this? Trying to keep people in or out?" Jason asked.

"It's a secure village. And could be a bit of both," Sarah said and laughed. "My parents live here as well as otherretirees who play golf every day on the courses. A lot of younger people live here, too, if they can afford it."

"And your friend can afford it?" Marshall asked.

"Yes, he can afford it."

"He?" Marshall did not like the sound of that. But she would not take him to a boyfriend's home, would she? He had not asked her if there were anyone special in her life. She had told him the doctor he had met last night meant nothing to her, but was there anyone else? He would have to straighten that out.

"He's my parents' neighbor," Sarah explained.

She followed the road that twisted around a couple of wooded hills, then crossed the bridge over Lake Quivera. After another few blocks, she turned into the wide driveway of a modern, glass-and-wood house.

"Looks like your friend's not here," Marshall said.

"This is my parents' home. My friend lives around the corner, although you can't see his house from here. All the homes must be sited so they can't be seen from other houses. The view's important." Sarah urged her companions out of the car and used her key to let them into the house.

"I thought we'd have coffee here. My friend was at the game, too, and will be just a little longer getting home."

"Your parents live here alone?" Jason asked. "Or do they keep an extra ten people around to fill the place up?"

"It's large for two, but they entertain quite a bit," Sarah said. "Maggie, show them around while I fix coffee."

"This is quite a place," Jason said a few minutes later when the men and Maggie joined Sarah in the sitting area. "Just what does your father do?"

"Dr. Stuart Madison, surgeon, now retired," Sarah answered.

"So you got your interest in medicine from him," Marshall said.

"What do you mean?" Maggie asked and cast a sharp glance at Sarah.

"Sarah's volunteer work at the hospital," Marshall answered.

"Oh, that," Maggie said, nodding in agreement.

Sarah sent a chilling look Maggie's direction. "I believe I'll phone my friend and see if he's home yet." She excused herself and returned a short time later. "He's there," she announced. "Let's go."

The foursome trouped over to Arlie's house where music poured from every window. A couple of cars were parked in the driveway.

"Looks like the party's in full swing," Jason said.

"Yes. It's a celebration because the Royals are going to the Series." Sarah marched them up to the front door, knocked once, although she was sure it would not be heard over the loud music, then opened the door without waiting for it to be answered.

She obviously knows this guy well, since she just walks right in, Marshall thought. He'd only known Sarah one day. Surely he couldn't be feeling even the tiniest bit jealous? He shrugged that thought off immediately.

"Sarah, you made it," a deep masculine voice yelled over the rock music. A man in his late twenties, with babyish good looks that were slightly familiar, hugged Sarah and spun her around. Marshall did not like it one bit. "What did you think of the game?" the man shouted.

"Wonderful, just wonderful," Sarah shouted back, laughing up at him. "Arlie, I'd like you to meet my friends. Marshall Adams, Jason Bradford, Maggie Gale, this is Arlie Gilbert."

"Arlie Gilbert? The shortstop?" Jason gasped, sticking out his hand and pumping Arlie's hand up and down.

"One and the same." Sarah watched Marshall shake hands with Arlie and laughed out loud at the look of excitement on Marshall's face.

"Come, meet my friends," Arlie said and led the small group into the large living room where three other ballplayers and their wives had gathered to celebrate the victory and rehash the details of the game.

❦

It was almost two in the morning when Sarah drove Marshall's car back to the Missouri side of Kansas City. She dropped Maggie off at her apartment building first. Jason walked his date to her door and took a long time saying good night.

"Perhaps we'd better say good night here, too," Marshall suggested, "while we have a bit of privacy." He shoved the armrest up out of his way and pulled her over toward the passenger side and into his arms.

"I had a wonderful time, Sarah. Couldn't have been any better even if we'd had box seats," he said, grinning that boyish grin she had seen at the game and at Arlie's party.

"I'm glad you enjoyed it. I did, too."

"Good. We have that out of the way. Now let's get down to some serious good-nighting."

"Good-nighting?"

"Yes. It goes like this." His lips met hers in a kiss that made the ones the night before pale in comparison. He kissed her again as the back door of the car was being opened and, with the sound, Sarah pushed away from Marshall, ending the contact.

"Excuse me," Jason said. "Should I come back later?"

"Yes," Marshall said.

"No," Sarah said at the same time.

"Which is it?" Jason asked, still standing outside the car with the door open.

"Get in, Jason," Sarah said and laughed.

"Give her the keys to a car and the power goes to her head," Marshall teased, but he let her scoot over behind the steering wheel.

"Did you get your car fixed?" Marshall asked.

"No. Well, yes, but I was too late to get it this afternoon. I'll have to take a cab to work again tomorrow."

"You can use my car," Marshall offered. "I don't need it at the hotel. I'll catch a cab over to your house tomorrow evening, pick up my car, and take you out to dinner. There's a fleet of cabs parked outside the hotel, so it'll be much easier for me to get one than for you to get one early in the morning."

"Oh, Marshall, that's unnecessary."

"I insist. Now, chauffeur us to the hotel, please."

Sarah dropped them at the front door, and Jason quickly jumped out.

"Thanks for a wonderful time, Sarah," he echoed Marshall's earlier words.

"You're welcome," Sarah called to his retreating back.

"I think he wants us to be alone," Marshall said.

"I don't think the car waiting behind us wants that."

Marshall turned in his seat and looked back. He sighed. "Okay, but tomorrow night just you and me. Seven?"

"Perfect. I'll see you then."

He gave her a quick peck on the lips and climbed out of the car. "I had a great time," he said before he slammed the car door closed and gave it a slap, as if sending a horse on its way.

Jason, who had been standing by the door, walked back to where Marshall was watching Sarah drive off. "How much did you pay for that car?" he asked his friend.

Marshall's eyebrows rose in reaction to the odd question. "Somewhere around thirty thousand."

"You just let a woman you've known for twenty-four hours drive off in your thirty-thousand-dollar car. Are you nuts?"

Marshall's eyebrows shot up again. "I guess I am. I hadn't thought of it like that. But I trust her. I don't know why, but I do."

4

$\mathcal{M}$arshall was a morning person. He had been an early riser all his life and, although he had gotten to bed late, his internal alarm buzzed him at six.

He turned over, knowing he should catch more sleep, but years of habit kept him from dozing off again. Instead, he gave up. Propping his pillows against the headboard, he leaned back and reached for the remote control that was securely fastened to the bedside table. The television sprang to life with the push of the button, and he flicked from channel to channel to find something interesting. He settled for an early morning business report on the falling value of the dollar. The newscaster droned on and did not hold his attention. When a cute, blond analyst came on the screen, she reminded him of Sarah and his thoughts never returned to the falling dollar.

Sarah was something special and he knew it. Jason may have thought it crazy that he had sent her off in the car he had had only two months, but he knew it was a simple matter of trust. There was something about her that defied easy explanations. She was classy, no question about that; she had been raised that way. The stately old house where she lived spoke volumes. And that she would not give up her childhood home, but bought it instead of looking for a modern glass-and-chrome place, told him about her sense of loyalty. He had not been in her home long the night before. Tonight he would get a tour and notice all the little touches that made it fit her personality.

The sound of downtown traffic reached his ears even though it was still early. City life. What a difference. His thoughts drifted to the Valley, his home in the country.

In the twenties, the story went, gangsters and underworld figures

363

from Chicago wanted vacation getaway places in the Ozark Hills. The Valley was started as such a place. The steep hills had been terraced and, from a distance, resembled stair steps for giants. A huge resort was planned, but only the first home was built before something happened to halt the project. Some said a gangster was gunned down and his widow would never return to the hills where he had been killed. Others said the developer went bankrupt. Marshall preferred the first story.

The original place had fallen into disrepair. All the glass had been broken out by vandals long before Marshall had been born. The first time he had seen it, the roof had already caved in. But he had fallen in love with the feeling of the Valley and when, years later, he had returned to Neosho as a doctor, he immediately inquired about the place.

Buying it was a lengthy process; the title was still held by someone in Chicago. But eventually it was his. The rotten timbers of the old place were bulldozed out and his A-frame home was built on its old foundation, nestled in a valley and surrounded by the terraced hills.

What would Sarah think of his home? She would like it; he knew she would. She might be a city girl, but she would fall in love with the country and be happy there.

What was he thinking? Sure, she might seem like the woman of his dreams, but he had known her only a short time. He did not even know where she taught or much else about her. She had certainly been embarrassed last night when the box seats had been taken, but she would not confront her dad's friends. She had carefully avoided being seen by them. He liked that. She would not put them in an awkward position because she had misunderstood about the tickets.

He might not know much about Sarah's everyday existence, but he knew her inner qualities. And he liked them. Couple them with her stunning appearance, and it seemed an unbelievable combination.

She had called Arlie and arranged the meeting with the ballplayer so that Marshall could have a special night. Arlie had pulled him aside at the party and had given him a friendly warning about her.

"Treat her right or answer to me," he had said in a joking way, but Marshall knew he meant it.

He would treat her right, and he wanted to talk to her. Glancing at his watch on the bedside table, he saw it was not quite seven. Too early to call. But then, she had said she had an early morning. If she were not up already, she should be, he decided.

There was no listing for Sarah Madison in the phone book, but there was one for Dr. S. B. Madison at Sarah's address. Obviously she had not been in the house long since the phone was still listed in her father's name. He hoped it was the right number. With a quick shrug, he poked the numbers and waited nervously as it rang once, twice, three times.

"Hello," she answered.

"Good morning, Sarah." It was wonderful to hear her voice. It sounded huskier than usual.

"Marshall?"

"Yes. Did I wake you?"

"No. I was about to have breakfast."

"I was wondering if there was any place special you would like to go tonight and if I needed to call for reservations."

"Let me think. Wednesday. It seems there was something . . . Oh, I know. Tonight is the opening of a new exhibit at the Nelson Art Gallery. Since it's a 'must' for tourists, and I had planned on going before I had the good fortune to meet you, why don't we take it in? Then go to the Savoy for a late dinner."

"Sounds wonderful. Reservations?"

"Be best. Probably around nine."

"I'll take care of it. And I'll see you at seven."

"That would be perfect. Oh, Marshall. The event is formal. Black tie. Is that a problem?"

Of course it was a problem. He had not packed formal gear to bring to a convention of doctors. The banquet Saturday night required a suit, but not a tux.

"Oh, that'll be fine. I'll see you tonight, Sarah."

She said good-bye, and he sat on the bed, holding the phone for a moment.

"No problem. Hah!" he said aloud. He flipped through the yellow pages until he found the rental places. He had no idea which one to call, and besides it was way too early. Best to shower and shave, then get advice from the hotel desk. They could tell him a good florist, too, so he could send roses to Sarah. Oh, no! He had forgotten to ask her where she taught. Well, tonight he would find out all about her.

❦

Sarah hung up the phone and smiled to herself. Marshall was a dear, sweet man like her father, and not at all like most doctors she had met. Why was it some doctors felt as if they were godlike? They had studied plenty, that was true, but it wasn't as if they could cure people by themselves. They relied on treatments, medicines, operations, things that other people had developed. And ultimately the outcome was in God's hands. Doctors were merely practitioners, like lawyers or architects, practicing what had been taught to them.

Hal Mosley was a perfect example of the typical doctor. If a patient got well, he took all the credit. If the patient died, there was nothing he could have done for him, he was too far gone before Hal saw him. It was not his fault.

Marshall did not seem that way. He seemed to be the type who tried hard, no matter what the odds, and who would mourn with the family of the victim. Marshall had talked little of his profession, but she had picked up bits and pieces. She had overheard him tell Jason that he called in every day to make sure his patients were doing all right. When she could finally tell him about her job, they could exchange their philosophies of healing, and she was sure they would be the same.

On reflection, it might be a good thing she could not tell him she was a doctor. She was getting to know him for herself, as a woman, and not as a professional. Yet she felt instinctively that he would respect her as a professional, too.

Jeff had not. They had met her senior year in college, then she had gone on to medical school. He resented the hours she spent studying and at the hospital; he never saw her enough, he had said. She should not have been surprised when he started seeing other women. Although she had thought she loved him, she would have survived it better if he had been honest and had said he thought they were too different to ever make a lasting commitment.

Instead, he had played her along as a sucker. One evening after a long day at the hospital, Sarah had dropped by his apartment, something she had not done before. One of the patients had died and she needed to see him, needed to be held, needed to know that life went on. Another woman had answered the door. She was petite and brunette, her opposite, but Sarah had not stuck around long enough to find out if the woman threatened Jeff on an intellectual level.

She found that out later when Jeff came pounding on her door. She had stepped outside and talked to him, or rather listened, as he ranted about how cold she was, how she thought she was so much smarter than he was, and how she would never be the woman Melinda was.

Stunned through and through, Sarah had somehow managed to maintain a stoic composure as he told her what he thought of her.

"Good-bye, Jeff," she had finally said when he had exhausted his supply of words. Then she had stepped back into her apartment and locked the door.

She had never seen him again and thought she had learned the lesson he had taught her. But later she had dated Troy, and he had been turned out of the same mold. Men liked intelligent women as friends, but not as marriage material. Male had to be macho to prove their masculinity, and they did not like intelligent women in a relationship.

But she might have been too hasty in drawing that conclusion. Marshall did not seem to fit that pattern at all.

He had a rugged look, high cheekbones, and a strong nose. Years of that wonderful grin had formed crinkle lines around his eyes. But it was more than that. It was the look in his eyes that said he was not surprised by much and that he was prepared for anything.

But his personality was not rugged in the typical sense of the word. He was polished and sensitive. And she would get to see him tonight. Too bad he was leaving in a few more days.

Oh, what was she thinking? Her life ran smoothly as it was and she was happy. She did not need a man complicating it. Long ago she had concluded that she was meant to remain single. She had seen how hard it was for doctors to combine family life and all those hours at the hospital. Her father had juggled as best he could, but there were times when he did not make it home. Her tenth birthday party came to mind and she quickly dismissed it. She understood now.

She sat at the kitchen table and thanked God for a new morning and a new beginning, then she quickly ate a piece of toast. Her thoughts had slowed down her normal brisk morning routine, and she was running late. Annoyed with herself for dallying, she rushed out the kitchen door that led to the garage and stopped short, staring at Marshall's car. She had forgotten that she had not picked up her car yet.

"I don't have to pretend to be a dumb blond," she said aloud. "I am one."

Sarah climbed behind the wheel of Marshall's car and drove to work. As soon as she entered the hospital, she began her rounds. Although the nurses took vitals and kept the charts current, she checked each patient three times a day. Even with a disease like leukemia, the look in the eyes and the color of the skin were indicators that were not easily communicated on a chart.

First stop was to see Andrea, who was still sleeping. Her mother sat beside her bed, holding the little girl's hand.

"Doctor?" Mrs. Garren's eyes pleaded for a word of assurance, but Sarah could give none.

"Stay with her," Sarah said. "I'll have the cafeteria send meals up for you. Your husband?"

"He went home for the night. He is going to work until noon unless I call him."

Sarah walked to the doorway and motioned for Mrs. Garren to join her.

"Call him," Sarah said in a low voice. "It may not be today, but her system can't fight it much longer."

Mrs. Garren nodded and, zombielike, walked to the bedside table. She reached for the phone, but fumbled the receiver, and it hit the floor with a loud clank. Andrea opened her eyes, bright with fever.

"Good morning, you little scamp," Sarah said tenderly. "Did you have a good night?"

Andrea smiled. "I dreamed about my new doll." She turned her head slowly on the pillow, as if her strength had been zapped. On one side of her was the new doll and on the other was the doll she had had for years. "I should put Sarah next to Tammy. They're sisters now," she explained.

Sarah placed the new doll next to Tammy. "I believe they like each other."

Andrea smiled again, but did not speak.

"Mrs. Garren, I'll make that call for you, if you'd like," Sarah volunteered. She did not want to talk to Andrea's father, but Mrs. Garren did not look as if she could handle it at the moment and certainly not in front of Andrea.

"Yes, please, Doctor."

"I'll be back later. Rest, honey," Sarah said and patted Andrea's foot.

At the nurses' station, Sarah had meals ordered for Mr. and Mrs. Garren and caught Mr. Garren just as he was about to leave his house. She explained the grave situation, then quickly made the rest of her rounds.

When she got to the lab, Dr. Lewis was already there, peeking through a microscope. He was a small man of around sixty, with gray hair and wire-rimmed glasses.

"We're losing Andrea Garren," he said without preamble.

"Yes, Doctor. I've called her family in."

He nodded. "You're good at that." At her look of disbelief he continued, "I know you hate it. Nobody likes telling parents their child is dying. But you're good at it. You let them know it hurts you, too."

"It does hurt me," Sarah whispered.

"I know. Fluconazole and itraconazole aren't fighting her infection." He deftly focused on their research. "Why does it help some and not others?"

"That's why we're here," Sarah answered. "We'll find out." She shrugged out of her white rounds jacket and into her lab coat and began examining blood samples collected earlier that morning.

An hour and a half later, Sarah reached for the ringing phone; she had a visitor in the lab station. Sarah pulled off her tight, disposable gloves and walked out to the lab desk. She recognized Maggie's red hair before her friend turned to face her.

"Hi, Maggie. I'd forgotten you were coming by this morning. Have you met with the auxiliary about the fashion show?"

"Yes. Those old gals drive me crazy."

"Keep it down, will you?" Sarah said. "Those women keep this hospital running. Research takes a great deal of money, and they raise a bundle."

Maggie looked around for any conspicuous pink jackets then whispered, "I still don't like working with them. Got time for a cup of coffee?" she asked in a more normal voice.

"A few minutes." Sarah led the way to the doctors' lounge and poured each of them a cup. They took a table by the window overlooking a water fountain, surrounded by bright flowers.

"So, what are you and Marshall doing tonight?" Maggie asked.

"We're going to the opening of the traveling Renoir exhibit at the Nelson. Then a late dinner at the Savoy."

"Wow. Fancy. If we tag along, Jason will naturally ask . . . to go with Marshall to the fashion show, if we set it up that we're a foursome. We'll come with you."

"No, you won't. I want to get to know Marshall without a crowd around."

"A double date is hardly a crowd."

"Too crowded for me."

"And what exactly is it you want to know about him you can't find out with an audience, Sarah?" Maggie asked.

"I just like talking to him alone. Why don't you go over to Ellen's and play games or something like that? But then, they'll probably be at the exhibit. There are a thousand other things around the city for you to do."

"Yes, but the art gallery on opening night sounds so sophisticated. I'll bet they'll have caviar."

"Probably. But it's black tie and by invitation, and you're not going to use me to succeed on your dare." Suddenly her heart sank. She would know several of the people there. She should never have invited Marshall. Now she would have to dodge people. Oh, she'd better call her brother. He would be there and could blow her bet if she did not warn him.

"Black tie," Maggie said thoughtfully. "Last night was fun. Even standing up, the game was exciting. How'd you get Arlie to invite us to his party?"

"Arlie wanted to meet Marshall. The victory made it a great party."

"I guess! It would have been a wake if the Royals had lost that game." Maggie downed the last of her coffee. "Well, I won't keep you. I know you're busy, and I've got to get downtown to deliver designs for next week's windows. We have a new window dresser who breaks an arm off mannequins by just looking at them." She stood up and tucked her envelope handbag under her arm. "Have you asked Marshall to the fashion show yet?"

"No," Sarah said as she walked Maggie toward the front entrance. "I was hoping to ask him tonight."

"I might mention the show. Lay the groundwork so he'll want to go. I like him, Sarah." Maggie did not explain who "him" was, but her soft tone said it for her.

"I know. Jason's a nice man. I like his friend," she admitted.

"We've found a couple of fine fellows, Sarah. Jason's had two failed marriages, and he's a little cynical, but the more I learn about him, the more I like him."

"Marshall thinks a lot of him," Sarah said. "And I trust his judgment. See you." Sarah waved as Maggie opened the outside door, then she walked purposefully to Andrea's room.

Mr. Garren sat beside his wife, his hands gripping the arms of the chair, his knuckles white. Andrea was asleep again. Sarah asked them to step into the hall.

"Has she talked in the last hour?"

Mrs. Garren looked up. "Yes. She's just now dozed off again."

"When she wakes, call a nurse. I'd like another blood sample," Sarah said briskly.

"Why, Doctor? If there's no hope?"

"What we learn from Andrea might save another little girl," Sarah said as matter-of-factly as she could, although she hated causing Andrea any more pain. She did not know how to act with families during the waiting period before death. Dr. Lewis might think she was good at it, but she knew she was awful.

"I'll be back later. Remember, call the nurse when she awakens again."

Sarah gave instructions at the nurses' station and returned to the lab. She met Hal coming out of his office.

"Glad I caught you, Sarah. Have you forgotten we were going over to the convention for the session on pediatrics?"

"It slipped my mind. Let me check out with Dr. Lewis." The renowned physician had asked her to call him Warner, but she could not bring herself to do it. Somehow it sounded disrespectful. She spoke with him briefly, then met Hal in the hall.

"Let's take my car," Sarah suggested. "Actually it's a friend's car. We can pick up my car at the garage on the way, and I'll leave his at the hotel."

"Let me guess. Dr. Marshall Adams?" Hal said as they walked to the parking lot.

"You have a good memory. Would you mind driving my car to the hotel for me?"

"Sure. Your friend was kind enough to let you borrow his until yours was fixed, right?"

"Something like that." She slipped behind the wheel and Hal climbed in on the passenger's side. He made no secret of the fact that he did not like being driven around by a woman.

"Relax, Hal. We're almost there." Almost to where Marshall was. Panic hit her briefly and she calmed herself. There were thousands at the convention and sessions going on in other meeting areas as well as at the main hotel. Marshall would not attend a workshop on pediatrics, or would he? He was a general practitioner, a much-needed family doctor, and a conscientious one. Wouldn't he want to learn what he could do for all of his patients, no matter what their age?

Hal had opened his leather-bound legal pad and flipped through some papers that were stuck under the flap on the left side.

"The session starts in ten minutes," he said, waving a schedule of meetings at her. "In the Maple Room."

"We'll make it." Sarah whipped the car into the garage parking lot. "Come with me, and we'll be out of here faster."

Inside the garage, Sarah scribbled a check to the mechanic and handed Hal the keys. The mechanic wanted to talk to her about the car, so Sarah motioned for Hal to go on and drive her car to the hotel.

"I'll meet you there," she called after him.

The mechanic explained what he had done to the car and kept Sarah a couple of minutes. When she pulled Marshall's car into the stream of traffic, her little Miata was nowhere in sight.

At the hotel, Sarah parked in the underground parking lot and took the elevator to the lobby. As she got off, the first person she saw was Marshall. He was talking to three men and a woman as the group walked away from the bank of elevators toward the meeting rooms. Sarah could see only the woman from the back, but quickly noticed how she walked closer to Marshall than was necessary down the wide halls. She wore a feminine, pink dress, had her long dark hair pulled back and tied with a pink scarf, and had on unnecessarily high heels for a casual session at the conference. Sarah's first reaction was to claw the other woman's eyes out. She was shocked that she could have such a violent response to the striking female. She was even more stunned that she thought of the woman in certain terms, and none of them were respectful

Marshall and his little group stood outside the Cedar Room, continuing their discussion. Instead of walking past him to her meeting room, Sarah ducked into the first door she passed. Unfortunately, it was a janitor's closet.

A single, white bulb hung from a cord in the center of the closet. A deep, white porcelain sink, bare pipes exposed below it, hung low from the wall. An assortment of mops and brooms hung from the opposite wall.

After a minute, Sarah peeked out. Marshall was still there. The men had disappeared, but the woman in pink remained, hanging onto every word Marshall uttered. He looked around as if he felt her eyes on him, and Sarah ducked back into the closet.

She waited another long moment. Then, as she was turning the handle to open the door, it was jerked open from the outside. Her heart jumped to her throat.

A young man in a janitor's uniform sprang back in alarm. Sarah put her finger to her lips is a request for silence. As soon as the man had his wits about him, his whole demeanor changed. A sly smirk told her he had misread the situation. Surely the man would not take her hiding in the closet as a come-on? And yet it seemed that that was exactly what he thought. He stepped into the tiny room and closed the door behind him. Sarah stepped back until she was against the wall. He moved closer, inching toward her in slow motion. Sarah suddenly gave him a hard push in the chest, which caught him off guard, and he sank down into the deep sink as easily as if he had sat in a chair, his legs dangling over the edge.

Rushing out the door, Sarah dashed down the now empty hall. The sessions had started. She found the Maple Room, opened the door, and slipped in. Hal was sitting in the back row with an empty seat beside him. Thankfully, she slid into the chair.

She did not hear a word of the talk by the famous television pediatrician. Was that episode in the closet really her fault? Had her signal for silence been misinterpreted? No, surely she was in the clear. That man had been a slimy worm. Maybe she should not have been in the closet, but he could have asked her why she was there instead of assuming the worst. He was lower than a slimy worm. Yet, he had not done anything to her. Maybe her imagination was working overtime.

By the time the question and answer period was halfway over, Sarah had calmed down. She borrowed a sheet of paper from Hal and wrote Marshall a note.

As the final applause died, Sarah jumped from her chair and started for the door with Hal in tow. Like a spy from a B-grade movie, she stuck her head into the hall and looked both ways before stepping out of the room. This time she was avoiding two men, or rather, one man and one worm. Hal, looking bewildered, followed her antics but Sarah ignored him. With a brisk pace, she marched to the check-in desk, asked for an envelope, wrote his name on it in her clear script, and tucked her note and Marshall's keys in it. She shoved the envelope back across the desk and asked that Marshall be notified that he had a message.

Sarah twirled away from the desk and immediately spotted the young janitor lounging at the entrance to a corridor a few feet away. She froze for a second, but his expletive, "Crazy woman!" said in a voice loud enough to carry to those around them, made her spring into action. She grabbed Hal by the arm and stalked to the stairs that led to the parking garage.

"Where are we parked?" she demanded.

"This way," he said. "What's wrong with you, Sarah?"

"Nothing," she snapped. "I have lots to do today. Covering for the other doctors so that they can lollygag at this convention is wearing me thin."

"Sarah, you agreed to cover so others could attend more sessions. And there are some top-notch physicians here. Didn't you listen to one word Dr. Alexander said today?"

"Of course, I did."

"Then you understand the importance of sharing information with each other. Sarah, you're in research. You know that."

"Yes, I do." She held out her hand. "Keys?"

"Your car handles well. I'll drive," he said.

"I'll drive my own car, thank you." She was startled by the force behind her words. Hal was her friend who had helped her out countless times. He was handsome and intelligent, and he had better shut up and give her the keys before she did something she could not predict.

Hal unlocked his door, handed her the keys, and climbed into the passenger's seat, slamming the door behind him. Sarah did the same on the driver's side.

What was wrong with her? She felt like calling Hal every name in the book. *Sanctimonious jerk* topped the list, and she wasn't even sure if *sanctimonious* fit. It sounded good in her mind, but she was too smart to say it out loud.

They rode to the hospital in a heavy silence, finally broken by Sarah.

"I'm sorry. I've got a lot on my mind. I didn't mean to take it out on you."

"What's wrong, Sarah?" Hal reached over and patted her hand, which lay on the seat.

She jerked her hand away to downshift and she turned the sports car into the hospital parking lot.

"I have a patient who's not going to make it."

"Sarah," he said as if talking to a child who had not learned her lesson in school. "Patients die here every day. We get the worst cases in this part of the state. You've got to learn to deal with that."

She nodded and bit her tongue to keep from yelling, "You sanctimonious jerk!" at the top of her lungs.

5

$\mathcal{M}$arshall smiled and nodded absently. Dr. Kerry Webster from Boston had leeched onto him early that morning in the hotel dining room before he had had his first cup of coffee. It was almost noon, and she was still beside him.

How could he get rid of her? The subtle approach had not worked; a ton of bricks probably would not do it, either.

They were strolling toward the lobby after a particularly long session. Marshall needed to slip out and run his errand to the tuxedo rental shop, but he did not want to be rude.

"Shall we have lunch downtown instead of here at the hotel?" Kerry asked in her honeyed voice.

Marshall looked closely at her. Kerry was soft looking. Her pink dress gave her a very feminine look, but her gray eyes revealed a streak of steel behind the womanly appearance. Rude was the only thing that would work with her.

"Sorry, I've already made plans. If you'll excuse me." Marshall spun around and walked the opposite direction. He had intended to inquire at the desk about a nearby shop, but he would ask the cab driver instead. He slipped out a side door and hailed a cab.

While the driver maneuvered through lunchtime traffic toward the nearest rental shop, Marshall sat back and thought about doctors in general and women doctors in particular. If Kerry was a typical woman doctor and, from his limited contact with female doctors he tended to think she was, he did not like them. Many men were in the profession for the money or the prestige. Women were in it for both those reasons and to prove they could tackle what was once an all-male profession. He knew there were some men, and begrudgingly he admitted some women, who were dedicated to healing, unconcerned with the perks of the job. He liked to believe he was one of them.

The cab pulled up to the curb, and the driver charged an exorbitant amount, but it had been a long ride.

The shop was not crowded, and Marshall was measured and fitted in a matter of minutes. Holding the hanger with two fingers, he slung the tuxedo bag over his back and began walking north, all the while watching for a cab.

There were not many events in Marshall's life that had called for a tuxedo. Mainly weddings. He smiled as he remembered one in Chicago when he was a groomsman. The church was not far from the hospital, and he had driven his motorcycle over and changed there, not thinking about the reception, which was scheduled for a posh country club. He was going on duty at the hospital and could not stay long at the reception, so he did not think he should inconvenience anyone by hitching a ride in a car. Instead, he had bundled up his regular clothes and tied them on his bike. He had thought he would be embarrassed, riding a motorcycle in a tux, but he had felt the most exhilarating high, as if he were defying convention, flaunting society. It was a feeling he liked, and he was not a rebel at heart. The motorcycle was not a statement against society; it was an economic move. His old clunker car had guzzled gas the way a teenager drank Coke. One dream, for when he got his own practice, was for a new car. He did not need a Mercedes or a Porsche, his Lincoln fit the bill. It was all the luxury he needed, and it was his third brand-new car.

He waited for the crossing light to tell him to walk, wishing he had his car right now. Maybe he had been foolish letting Sarah drive it to her house the night before, instead of putting her in a cab.

A cab. He waved with his free hand, and the approaching cabbie pulled up. Marshall climbed into the backseat and gave the name of his hotel.

The cabbie looked him over and said, "You're the boss. That tux heavy?"

"Not particularly," Marshall answered. Had he gotten one of those cabbies who would talk about anything? He settled back in his seat as the cab driver turned left and then left again at the next block.

"Here you are," the driver said.

Marshall was silent for a moment while he tried to get his temper under control. "You might say I've been taken for a ride. I asked another driver to take me to the closest rental shop, and he drove me around for twenty minutes."

"You just can't trust everybody these days," the cabbie offered his advice.

Marshall agreed and tried to think of something other than how he had been cheated. He did not like being taken for a fool. It was the worst feeling in the world. He had trusted someone who was untrustworthy, and he was usually a better judge of character than that. He should have watched the way the driver had gone, and maybe he would have noticed when he had doubled back.

Marshall paid the driver and carried the tux through the lobby to the stairs. He had found the stairs a good way to get some exercise while he was at the convention and a way to avoid offensive doctors. There were probably no more obnoxious people in his profession than in any other but, in his present mood, it seemed that way to him.

The moment he entered his room, he saw the flashing light on his phone. He called the front desk and was informed he had a note in his box. Once more he entered the stairwell, this time descending to the lobby. The clerk handed over the envelope, telling him a woman had left if over an hour ago.

Marshall climbed the stairs again and in the quiet of his room sat down and opened the envelope. His car keys fell out. He read the brief note from Sarah, then checked his watch. His car had been parked at the hotel the entire time he had been searching for a cab.

From there on, his day went downhill. His daily call to his office told him that one of his older patients, who should have been released from the hospital, had relapsed and had developed pneumonia. Although the doctor taking over his patients for the week was very competent, had it not been for Sarah, he would have packed his bags and left for home.

He did not feel he was getting out of this convention what he had anticipated. It was his first national convention and since it was so close to home, he thought he should attend it. Some new procedures and drugs were presented, and that was beneficial, but the event was more political than geared toward learning, and his attitude toward the people around him detracted from the informal sessions.

He did not know why he had such a bad attitude toward these other doctors. It was great seeing Jason again. Ed, he could take in small doses, and he had had enough already. Women like Kerry rubbed him the wrong way, too.

His growling stomach told him it was past time for lunch, so he walked to the mom-and-pop deli he had seen next to the hotel. He ordered pastrami on rye and iced tea and sat at a window table watching the traffic, both in cars and on foot. There was something lonely about seeing so many people and not knowing a single one. No one to say "hi" and call out his name.

The afternoon session was an election of national officers. It went on and on, like a political convention, with nominating speeches and acceptance speeches. Marshall was not a political animal; he did not seek the spotlight or awards that seemed shallow or insignificant. He felt like an outsider, but he was called upon to pass out and collect ballots, so he could not leave.

Later, dressed in the tux, he admired himself in the mirror. He was not vain, but he knew he was good-looking. Enough women had told him so. And tonight he was glad for he wanted to look good for Sarah. His spirits were beginning to climb as he drove his car out of the parking garage toward Sarah's home. He flipped up the armrest that divided the two front seats and discovered Sarah's checkbook caught underneath it. Her purse must have spilled while she was driving.

He pulled into her driveway, parked, and picked up the checkbook to return to its owner. Out of curiosity, he opened it to see which checks she had picked. Somehow he figured her for the standard, wavy blue-lined type, no fuss, no frills. Just class.

Instead, a family crest and the name of Dr. Harold C. Mosley jumped out at him. Sarah's friend he had met at the coffeehouse Monday night. What was Mosley's checkbook doing in his car?

Marshall poked the doorbell twice.

As soon as she heard the bell, Sarah opened the door with a welcoming smile. Marshall stood there resplendent in formal wear with a thunderous look on his face and a deep frown line between his blue eyes.

"I believe your friend left this in my car," he said without a word of greeting. He stalked into the large entry hall before Sarah could ask him in.

Sarah took the checkbook from his outstretched hand and opened it. A quick replay in her mind of the morning ride assured her Hal had dropped it when he was shuffling through papers searching for the location of the session.

"This morning Hal wanted to attend a session at the convention, so I persuaded him to go with me to the garage and drive my car to the hotel, while I followed in yours. I parked your car, got mine, and drove back to work. I'm sorry. I should have asked permission before driving your car so much."

"That's all right," Marshall said, waving his hand as if dismissing her apology. "But why Mosley? I thought he didn't mean anything to you." He was probably blowing it; he did not mean to sound jealous, but he was, and he knew it was showing.

"Hal was going to the hotel, and I was going to drop your car off there," Sarah explained. She hoped he would not ask how Hal planned to get back to the hospital.

"What were you doing at the hospital?" He seemed to be mollified by her answers, but he kept prying.

"Andrea Garren is a special little girl, and she's dying. I've become attached to her, and I wanted to see her."

How insensitive can I be? Marshall thought. He knew he could trust her, knew it instinctively, yet here he was giving her the third degree about nothing important when she was facing the death of a friend. That episode with the cab driver had him distrusting even her.

"Sarah, I'm sorry I've been such a bear. I've not had a good day, and I can tell that you haven't, either."

"What's gone wrong with your day?"

"Several things." He counted on his fingers. "I got cornered by a woman doctor and couldn't get rid of her. A cab driver took me ten miles out of my way so he could raise the fare. The session this afternoon was an absolute waste of time. I have an elderly patient at home who's developed pneumonia. That's enough. I won't bore you with the rest."

"You don't like women doctors?" Sarah asked. She was glad he had not wanted to be with the woman in pink, and she felt sure that that was the woman doctor he was talking about. "I guess you could say that," he said glumly. "Most of them are in medicine just to prove that they're just as smart as men."

"And aren't they?" Sarah's voice was rising. Her day had not been all candy and roses and she did not need the same song, different verse, from Marshall as she had had from Hal. And both were variations of Jeff's favorite theme.

"Well, I can see I'm not doing well here. Let's just say that at this conference I've had my fill of doctors, men and women. I'm not a chauvinist, Sarah, although I realize I sound like one. Let's forget this conversation and begin again. Okay?" He pivoted and walked back to the front door, opened it, and went outside, leaving an openmouthed Sara, standing at the foot of the oak staircase, staring at the door.

The doorbell rang, and Sarah smiled at his ploy. Again she walked to the door and opened it. Marshall stood outside with a wide grin.

"Good evening, Sarah. You look ravishing." And she did. How could he have ignored that fact before? Her navy blue beaded gown clung in all the right places and made the blond in front of him look magnificent.

"Thank you. You look very handsome. Please, come in." She was glad they had started over. She had spent more time than normal dressing up in her finery and had pulled her blond hair back on one side, securing it with a jeweled comb, to give her a more sophisticated look. She liked the way she looked and she liked the effect her appearance had on Marshall. She could see it in his eyes, the male appreciation, and not for a moment did she view it as a chauvinistic look. He looked at her as a man looked at a woman he admired and desired, and she knew she was looking at him in the same way. Marshall closed the door and immediately took Sarah in his arms. He held her close for a long moment, then he kissed her. One kiss melted into another.

Sarah was the one to break contact. "I think we'd better be going," she said.

Marshall continued holding her, although he did not kiss her again. He pressed her head to his shoulder and held her. Finally, he let her go.

"I'll get my purse," Sarah said and escaped up the stairs to her bedroom to repair her lipstick.

Left alone downstairs, Marshall wandered through French doors into the living room. The room was comfortable, dominated by a large, stone fireplace at one end. Bookcases on one wall held an assortment of books, mostly mysteries and lots of bric a brac. It was not the dime store variety of what-nots; it was classic stuff. An antique camera held the place of honor on one shelf, a bouquet of dried wheat on another. He stopped in front of a huge glass jar with a glass lid, which was full of hard butterscotch candies.

"Help yourself," Sarah said, as she entered the room.

"Don't mind if I do." Marshall lifted the lid carefully and picked out two of the cellophane-wrapped candies. He offered one to Sarah who immediately accepted it. "So, you have a sweet tooth," Marshall observed.

"No, not one. A whole mouthful." Sarah chuckled. "Don't warn me, doctor. I know the danger. I keep it around all the time and because it's here, I don't seem to crave it like I did when it wasn't available. Sounds crazy, doesn't it?"

"Not if it works." He pointed to a bust of a young girl, which was painted a fiery red. "Is it you?" There was a vague resemblance.

"It's me at twelve. My oldest brother made it in high school art class."

"I didn't know you had a brother."

"Two brothers, Matt and Joe, both older than me, and my younger sister, Annie. Matt will be at the exhibit tonight. Joe lives in Washington, D.C., and works for the diplomatic service."

"Impressive. Has he been out of the country much?"

"Many times. He speaks fluent Spanish so is in demand in the South American countries. Right now he's on R and R back in the States, but he's going to Argentina in February."

Sarah reached down and turned on a lamp. A soft puddle of light fell at her feet. "We'll leave this one on," she explained as she flicked a switch that turned off the wall lights. "Ready?"

"Yes. Lead me to another of Kansas City's wonders. But I don't believe it can top last night's," he warned as he followed her out to his car.

Sarah smiled to herself as she let Marshall hand her into the passenger's seat. She was glad he had enjoyed the ball game, but felt confident he would also like the Nelson Art Gallery. It was one of her favorite places, especially on a rainy Sunday afternoon. Tonight the mood would be different; a gala party atmosphere would fill the place. Sarah liked the special openings, too. Dressing up made her feel elegant and having a special man at her side was something she had looked forward to all day.

She gave Marshall directions, and soon they were entering the mammoth doors of the museum. Sarah handed her invitation to the doorman.

"This is an impressive building," Marshall observed as they wandered among a couple hundred other guests in the gigantic open lobby. Marble columns, three feet in diameter, reached to the ceiling three or four stories above them.

"As they say, you ain't seen nothin' yet," Sarah said with a laugh. "There are four wings to this building, which join to form a square. Inside the square is a garden, where they'll have refreshments. The exhibit of Renoir's work will be in the west part of this wing where traveling exhibits are displayed. Follow me."

"I'd follow you anywhere," Marshall said and winked at her.

Sarah took his arm. As they walked into the Renoir room, she was aware that many women turned for a second look at her escort, and her heart soared that she was the one with him.

It was not just his good looks that attracted her, although they certainly did not detract. It was his inner qualities. Oh, he had shown flashes of male chauvinism, but it would be hard to find a man who did not have a few of the characteristics that society had force-fed him. He was not like Jeff. Or was she wanting to believe that because she was falling under his spell?

They slowly toured the collection, pausing longer in front of a few paintings and passing quickly over others. Their tastes were similar and Sarah enjoyed discussing the paintings with Marshall.

"I don't know a lot about art," Marshall confessed. "Shall I say the cliché, which happens to be true? I just know what I like."

"I'm the same way," Sarah confessed. "I'd like to think I was a connoisseur of fine art, but that's not true. Some pictures make me feel a certain way and even if it isn't a feeling I like, if I feel an emotion, then I think it's good art."

"Sarah," a husky, masculine voice called, and Marshall cringed to think there was another male friend of Sarah's he would have to meet.

A portly gentleman, red-complexioned and with a thin mustache that looked incongruous on his large face, greeted Sarah with a hug. Marshall gave a deep sigh of relief, which was short-lived.

"Dewey, I'd like you to meet Marshall Adams. Marshall, Dewey Applebey. Dewey's a great patron of the arts and a longtime family friend." She doubted Dewey would give her job away. He liked talking about himself too much.

"For a moment there I thought you were going to say 'old' family friend," Dewey said as he shook hands with Marshall.

"Never," Sarah replied. "Should you live to be two hundred, you'd still not be old."

"I knew I liked this gal," Dewey said, placing his arm around Sarah's shoulders. "What sort of work do you do, Marshall?"

From the look in the man's eyes, Marshall decided Dewey was a lecherous old man—who had better get his hands off Sarah.

"I'm a doctor," Marshall answered.

"Ah. Keeping it in the family, huh, Sarah?" He squeezed her shoulder with his fat hand, and Marshall had to bite his tongue to keep from telling the man to leave her alone.

"Dad would like that," Sarah said, to cover Dewey's remark. She could tell that Marshall did not like Dewey, even though he was smiling and saying all the polite things. She excused them, saying they were headed to the garden.

The two men shook hands again, and Marshall escorted Sarah to the inner courtyard where a string quartet played.

"So, why don't you like Dewey?" Sarah asked after they had filled plates from the hors d'oeuvre table and found a bench in a corner.

"He's a dirty old man," Marshall said shortly.

"You're right. I don't know why my parents put up with him. He's been married four times, and each bride gets younger."

"Stay away from him," Marshall ordered, then realized by the little flare in her eyes and the lift of her chin that his tone of voice had not set well with her.

"I didn't mean that like it sounded. I just don't like that man, and I hope you don't have to be around him very much." Marshall hoped that would appease her. He had already been chauvinistic tonight, and his jealous words were giving away too much of his feelings toward her. And he did not even know what his feelings were.

He watched Sarah, who nodded acceptance of his words. "I'm very sensitive today. The least little thing tends to set me off. Sorry. I'll try to be more easygoing."

Sarah's eyes suddenly got large.

"What?" he asked immediately.

"Duck back here," she directed and stepped behind an oriental shrub.

"What is it?"

"It's who, not what. Maggie and Jason are here," she hissed. How had Maggie gotten in?

"So, why are we hiding?"

"Because," she started, then stopped. "Because I was hoping we could get to know each other better without them along," she blurted out. She could not tell him the truth, that she did not want Maggie using them as a constant foursome so Maggie could succeed at her dare. And yet, she had told a different truth by telling him she wanted to be alone with him. Things were getting very confusing, and she was not finding out much about him. He was sounding so typically male tonight, instead of understanding. All in all, it had been an upsetting day.

Marshall was smiling. "I want to know you better, too, Sarah. And you're right. They have been with us too much. If we're careful, we can avoid them. Where are they now?"

Sarah peeked through the leaves of the bush and spied Maggie's black dress and flaming hair by the hors d'oeuvre table.

"Oh, no, they're heading this way."

"Come with me," Marshall instructed and led her to a bench on the back side of another group of shrubs. "We'll be safe here. Too bad there aren't some big trees around."

"I know. Oriental shrubs are pretty, but not the hide-behind variety. Can you see them?"

"No, and I'm not going to look. If we stare at them, they'll sense it and notice us. So, let's sit here and get to know each other better. Although I'd hoped to get to know you in private, without several hundred people milling around," he teased.

His grin was infectious, and Sarah found herself grinning back. They were two against the world, well, at least two against two others, and it felt great to be lighthearted and adventurous instead of serious and responsible.

"What would you like to know about me?" Sarah asked.

"Some things I can't find out right now," he answered with a playful leer. "Like are you ticklish behind the ear? But I'll settle for where you teach."

6

*O*h," Sarah said, unprepared for that question. Where did she teach?

"Shh," Marshall warned, before she could think up something that was not a lie. "Listen," he whispered in her ear.

"There's quite a crowd here." Jason's voice carried to where they sat hidden from view. He was standing a couple of feet in front of their bushes.

"Yes, quite a crowd," Maggie agreed. "A lot of Kansas City's hotshots are here. You know, the big donors."

"Are you a patron?"

"Hardly. Not that I don't appreciate fine art," Maggie quickly added. "Actually, Sarah's a member of the Friends of Art or something like that. She got the invitation. We're her guests. She and Marshall should be here. Let's circulate and look for them."

Sarah wished she could see Maggie's face. Her guests! How had Maggie managed to get around the doorman?

"I have to see Sarah tonight to finalize some details for the fashion show I'm in charge of at the hospital. Most of those auxiliary women are a little hard to take. Sarah is the go-between." Her voice faded as the couple moved off.

"Whew! That was close," Sarah said.

"Did you invite them to the museum?"

"No, but I'm going to find out how they managed to get in. Maggie asked me what we were doing this evening, and I told her. I wouldn't be surprised if they showed up at the Savoy for dinner."

"Why do you think she wants to be with us?"

"Well, maybe she likes us. You'll have to ask her." Sarah weaseled out of the question. "There's my brother. Come on, I'll introduce you."

Together they walked toward her brother and his wife, depositing their plates on a waiter's tray as he passed. Sarah was glad she had remembered to call Matt at work. He would not disclose her secret.

"Hi, Matt, Jessie." Matt was two years older than Sarah, and they had always been close. His wife, Jessica, had grown up in their neighborhood, had played with them as children, and had carried a torch for Matt since she was fourteen and he was eighteen. But it was only after Matt had graduated from college that he noticed the little brat, who had tagged after him years before, had grown into a real beauty. Six months later, they had married.

Sarah introduced them to Marshall, and the two men shook hands, with Matt openly giving Marshall the once-over.

"In the absence of my father, I feel it's my duty to ask if your intentions toward my sister are honorable," Matt said, a twinkle in his eye.

"Matt Madison!" Sarah was aghast.

"That's a tough question. I do have intentions," Marshall said and slipped his arm around Sarah's waist in a possessive manner.

"Marshall!" Sarah exclaimed.

He grinned down at her. "I think I'm lucky your father's out of town."

"Speaking of Dad," Sarah said to change the subject, "have you heard from him or Mom since they've been gone?"

"Not a word," Matt said.

"Yes, we did, honey," Jessie inserted. "They called this evening while you were in the shower. We were running late, as usual, and I forgot to tell you. Your folks will be back Friday night. We're to pick them up at the airport."

"Ah, Jessie, did you forget we're to meet the Barlows at the lake Friday night?"

Jessie sighed. "I knew there was something, but I couldn't remember what. And we were so hurried tonight, it didn't even register that we'd already made plans."

"I'm free Friday night. I'll pick them up," Sarah offered. "Which airline? What time?"

Jessie gave her the details.

"What do you think of the exhibit?" Sarah asked.

"We haven't seen it yet," Matt answered. "We headed straight for the hors d'oeuvres. Lead the way, and we'll take a look."

The foursome wandered back into the exhibit area. Marshall saw Maggie and Jason first and steered his group to the opposite end of the huge room. Sarah and Marshall exchanged conspiratorial glances since Matt and Jessie did not realize they had been maneuvered across the room for a reason.

Marshall kept them moving until they paused too long in front of Sarah's favorite portrait of the girl at the piano.

"Sarah, Marshall," Maggie called out and covered the few yards separating them. "Hi, Matt. Hi, Jessie. How do you like the exhibit?" She gave Sarah a look that said, "I'm here, so make the best of it."

Sarah was sorely challenged not to be rude to her friend. This capped her day, but she smiled and admitted to herself that she had been beaten at the little game of hide-and-seek that they had been playing.

"Maggie, what a surprise to see you here." She could at least make Maggie squirm a little in front of Jason.

"I changed my mind about your invitation," Maggie said quickly. After Jason was introduced to the Madisons, she said, "Would you excuse us a minute. I need to discuss with Sarah a few things that I know would bore you." She took Sarah's arm and led her over to the viewing bench near the center of the room.

"How did you get in? Bribe the doorman?"

"Now, Sarah, don't get huffy. This seemed like such an uptown thing to do. Besides, I like dressing up."

"I'm still curious. How did you get in?"

"Simple. I told the doorman that we were your guests and that we were to meet you here since you'd been delayed at the hospital again. We were here when the door opened. I was hoping you'd be late, as usual."

"We were probably ten minutes behind you, maybe fifteen," Sarah admitted. "So, what are your plans for the rest of the evening?"

"We're going out to dinner."

"Let me guess where," Sarah said sarcastically.

"Well, face it, Sarah. How many places are there where we'd fit right in wearing formal dress? I didn't think you'd mind."

"Do you have reservations? It may be hard to get in without them."

"I had them change Marshall's request to a table for four."

"Maggie! I've got to hand it to you. You've got nerve. But tonight it might work out for the best. I've been snapping at Marshall, and another couple as a buffer may be what we need. But tomorrow night, don't come near us," Sarah warned.

"Not to worry. I have a fashion show at the Woman's Club, so I won't even be seeing Jason. Let's go back to the guys."

❧

Maggie and Jason had taken a cab to the museum, so they rode to the restaurant with Sarah and Marshall. Once inside the elegant old building, Marshall asked the maitre d' if his reservation for two could be changed to accommodate four.

Sarah exchanged a smug glance with Maggie, but the maitre d' was too well-mannered to tell Marshall that the change had already been made, and without comment he escorted them to their table in a corner.

"Isn't this cozy? Boy, girl, boy, girl," Maggie said.

No one commented, but studied their menus. After they had ordered, Marshall said, "Nice place. Do you come here often."

"On special occasions," Sarah answered. "My sixteenth birthday comes to mind. My boyfriend and my family came. I was embarrassed the entire evening. My brothers teased me unmercifully."

"I can believe that after meeting Matt tonight. Is Joe like him?"

"Worse. He teases in two languages."

"Joe is definitely worse," Maggie chimed in. "Remember that time we doubled and our dates took us back to your house since I was spending the night? Matt and Joe were home from college, and they met us outside the door. Wouldn't even let our dates say good night properly." Maggie laughed. "Those guys were so overprotective, they were a pain."

"I think I like your brothers," Marshall said.

"They're not overprotective now. Matter of fact, Matt and Jessie are always matchmaking. Luckily, Joe and Robin live too far away to set me up."

They had all ordered seafood, which was flown up from the Gulf daily, and as soon as the waiter set their plates in front of them, conversation dwindled for a few minutes.

"This is yummy. Have you tried some of the different restaurants in town?" Maggie asked the men.

"I ate at a little deli today," Marshall answered. "Good sandwich. We've been here since Monday, and that night we met you. Last night was a hot dog at the park, and tonight this."

"I wondered where you had disappeared for lunch," Jason said. "Uh, Dr. Webster came to the dining room alone and looked a bit put out. I knew you two had been talking earlier." He looked expectantly at Marshall.

Sarah knew from their exchange that Dr. Webster was the woman in pink.

"Kerry was so pushy. I tried politely to get rid of her, but she wouldn't take the hint. I finally had to be rude. Women doctors."

"You don't like women doctors?" Maggie asked with sudden interest, holding her fork halfway to her mouth.

Marshall looked at Sarah. She had objected to his opinion of women doctors earlier that evening, and he should have been smarter than to voice his opinion again.

"Oh, they're just like male doctors, some good, some not so good," he told Maggie.

"Really? For a moment there I thought you had some prejudice against them. You know, the old women-belong-in-the-kitchen routine."

"Oh, no. I believe a woman is as capable as a man."

"What about you, Jason? What's your opinion of women?" Maggie asked.

"I like them. There are basic differences between men and women, and I like that, too," Jason said with a wink.

"Oh, you," Maggie said and laughed. "Excuse us a moment," she said and motioned for Sarah to join her.

"Why do they always go in pairs?" Jason asked his friend.

"So they can talk about us, I imagine. Listen, I thought I'd invite Sarah to go to the banquet Saturday night."

"Me, too. Maggie has to work tomorrow night, but I thought we'd do something Friday night and make the banquet Saturday."

"They might find it boring."

"Not with us as their escorts," Jason said with a laugh.

"We can attend the banquet together, but this is the last double date, my friend," Marshall said.

"Fine with me. I'd like to be alone with Maggie, but she's keeping me at arm's length. I think she's been burned. She's told me a little about her ex, and he sounds like a real jerk. How are things going with Sarah?" Marshall did not want to answer that question. His relationship with Sarah was nothing he cared to discuss with anyone. He was not even sure what their relationship was.

"I like her," was all he said.

⤳

"Have you asked Marshall to the fashion show yet?" Maggie asked as she reapplied her lipstick.

"Not yet. But I will. I went to a convention meeting today and had to hide to avoid him. I want Ellen's money for research, but I'm not sure I know what we're trying to prove with this dare."

Maggie flipped her hair back in a fluffing gesture. "That we have different sides to our personalities than normally show. You're not to be a doctor or intimidate him with your intelligence. And I don't believe taking him to a museum fits that part," she said, turning from the mirror to face Sarah.

"He doesn't know I'm a doctor, but he likes intelligent women."

"Yeah, right," Maggie said as the two women walked back to their table.

Over dessert the conversation turned to the convention, and Marshall asked the women to the banquet.

"Sounds interesting," Maggie said. "Sarah and I were just discussing the fashion show at the hospital. It's at two o'clock Saturday afternoon."

This was her opportunity, Sarah knew. Maggie had set her up so she could do the asking, but would that matter if they both completed their dares? It was important that she win the money for research.

"Would you like to come?" she asked Marshall.

"Hey, I'll go," Jason said. "I'd like to see what you do for a living, Maggie."

"Sure," Marshall agreed. "You can show me around the hospital, Sarah. The closing speaker for the banquet is from there. I was reading the program this morning. Dr. Warner Lewis. Quite distinguished from the bio I read. Have you met him?" He rather doubted that she would have since Lewis was such an esteemed research doctor and probably did not mix with the volunteers.

"Yes. I know him. He's brilliant and quite down-to-earth, an unusual combination."

"Anyone want more coffee?" Marshall asked. No one did. "In that case, Jason, can we drop you somewhere?"

"Take us to Maggie's," he said. "I'll find my way to the hotel from there."

"Oh, well," Maggie began a protest. "It's already late. Perhaps it would be best if you dropped me off then took Jason to the hotel."

"Too much trouble," Jason said. Sarah could hear them discussing their destination as they walked out to the car.

"Marshall wants to be alone with Sarah," Jason whispered loud enough for Sarah to hear. That thought set her heart beating double-time. She wanted to be alone with him, too.

She caught the wink Jason gave Marshall and laughed to herself. Men were such boys sometimes.

As Marshall drove them to her house, Sarah made a sudden decision. She had intended to return to the hospital as soon as Marshall left her house, but she wanted him to stay a while. She had also promised Andrea that she would see her this evening, and the hour was already late.

"Would you mind if we checked on Andrea?"

"The little girl at the hospital?"

"Yes."

"Give me directions but with plenty of warning before the turns," he added with a chuckle.

She told him all the turns and had him park in the staff parking lot. The eleven-to-seven shift was already on duty, but there were plenty of parking places left. She would not tell him she was a doctor, so she could keep her word to her friends, but he would find out as soon as they entered the hospital. Besides, he had already agreed to attend the fashion show. She would argue the technicality with Ellen and Maggie later, but right now she needed to see a special little girl, perhaps for the last time.

Andrea's room was not far from the elevator. Sarah waved to a couple of nurses at the station, one on the phone and the other counting out medicine. She knew they were both checking out Marshall as they walked down the hall.

Outside Room 202 she paused before quietly opening the door. Mr. and Mrs. Garren sat side by side on the daybed that had been brought in for them. They were holding hands, but not speaking, their gazes focused on their daughter. Andrea lay asleep, her breathing labored.

Sarah glided across the room to them. "How long has she been asleep?" she asked in a hushed tone.

"About two hours. Dr. Lewis came in earlier this evening. He said it could be any time." Mrs. Garren was dry-eyed, but the puffiness around her eyes told that she had been crying.

Sarah laid her hand on Andrea's forehead. She did not need a thermometer to know the child was burning up with fever. Marshall crossed to the bed and felt Andrea's hand. His gaze met Sarah's and she nodded.

"Mr. and Mrs. Garren, this is Dr. Adams," she said simply. There was nothing she could do for Andrea and she knew it. "Is there something I can get for you? A cold drink? Have you eaten dinner?"

"We weren't hungry," Mrs. Garren said.

"Nevertheless, I'll have some sandwiches sent up."

"Mama." Andrea stirred. The voices must have disturbed her. Mrs. Garren was at her side instantly. Marshall moved away from the bed to make room for Andrea's father.

"How are you feeling, my little scamp?" Sarah asked.

"Hot. I'm hot," Andrea replied in a week voice. "You look beautiful." Sarah had forgotten she was in her beaded dress. "Where's my Sarah?" the little girl asked.

Mrs. Garren retrieved the doll from the table. "Here you are, darling. I moved her when you were rolling over on her. I'll put her here by Tammy."

Andrea smiled, then closed her eyes again.

Sarah could tell the Garrens needed time alone with their daughter. "I'll see you in the morning."

Mrs. Garren nodded. "Thanks for coming back tonight."

"You're welcome." Sarah took Marshall's hand, and together they walked to the nurses' station.

Marshall felt his fingers cramp with the tight grip Sarah had on his hand. She was hurting, but dealing with it the best she could. He wished some of the volunteers at his hospital showed as much compassion toward patients and especially toward their families.

"Mary," Sarah said to the plump nurse behind the counter. "Would you please see that the Garrens in 202 get sandwiches and cold drinks, in about twenty minutes?"

"I'll take care of it," Mary answered. "You look very nice tonight."

"Thanks." Sarah could tell that Mary wanted an introduction. "I'd like you to meet Dr. Adams. Marshall, this is Mary Hinman, the best night nurse in the hospital."

"That's high praise coming from Sarah," Marshall said. "It's nice to meet you, Mary."

"My pleasure," Mary said, extending her hand to shake Marshall's enthusiastically and nodding to Sarah in approval.

Sarah ushered Marshall out of the hospital, waiting for him to explode about her keeping her profession from him. But he seemed not in the least perturbed and did not mention it.

"What did you think of Andrea?" Sarah asked, wanting to get the subject out in the open.

"You were right; she's dying. Probably tomorrow. All the signs are there. Cancer."

"Leukemia. Acute nonlymphocytic. The odds were against her

from the beginning. Experimental treatments haven't worked." What was she doing? She sounded like Hal. It was not her fault that Andrea was dying. Although Sarah knew that was true, she did not want to sound as callous as Hal.

Marshall took her hand, giving her what comfort he could. Sarah's love for the little girl touched his heart. She had studied the doctor's diagnosis and had known all along there was little hope for this type of leukemia. She had probably researched it.

"You should have been a . . . ," he had started to say "nurse," but after his other chauvinistic remarks, he changed it to, "doctor. You care so much about the patients, don't you? I'll bet Andrea isn't an isolated case where you've become attached. Compassion is missing in lots of doctors, and I believe it's essential."

"Thank you, Marshall." Obviously he still did not know. Thinking back over the conversations at the hospital, she realized no one had called her Dr. Madison or Dr. Sarah, as she was known to her small patients.

A comfortable silence lasted until Marshall drove into Sarah's driveway. She had enjoyed having him hold her hand. His touch was not merely sensuous; it was much deeper than that. She felt a special kinship with this man.

Marshall took Sarah's key and opened her front door. He hesitated for a moment, thinking Sarah was not going to issue an invitation, but she must have thought it was understood, because she stepped into the entry and looked over her shoulder as if she expected him to follow. He immediately crossed the threshold.

"Coffee, Marshall?"

"Sounds good." He followed her to the kitchen.

Sarah filled the coffeemaker and puttered around the kitchen, setting coffee cups and saucers on a tray and adding a plate full of cookies she had taken from a tin.

Marshall looked around the kitchen, taking in all the little things he had promised himself he would notice about her house. The room was brightly colored, yellow daisies dominated the wallpaper, and the cabinets were a warm oak. She would probably be like this, warm and sunny in the mornings, puttering around the kitchen, fixing breakfast for him.

What was he thinking? It seemed he always thought of her in terms of the rest of his life, instead of until Sunday when he would leave to go back to Neosho.

"Shall we go into the living room?" Sarah asked, as she poured the coffee.

Marshall picked up the tray and followed her through the entry and into the living room. The lamp still poured its soft light, welcoming them back to the comfortable room. Marshall sat the tray on the coffee table and took his place on the couch beside Sarah. He handed her a cup and took a long drink of his own.

"This is good," he said to make conversation. He felt suddenly shy with this woman. As much as he wanted to hold her, he did not want to make a wrong move and alienate her.

"Thank you," Sarah answered politely. This was the moment she had been waiting for all day. She wanted him to take her in his arms and hold her, kiss her as he had on their two previous dates. Except this time there was not another couple with them or a cab driver waiting. This time they were completely alone.

Marshall studied Sarah over the rim of his cup. Unless his male instincts were wrong, and they were usually very reliable, she wanted him to kiss her. But what if he were wrong? Maybe he was rushing her. No, he was right. He knew he was right.

He set his coffee cup on the saucer with a clatter. He had not meant to use such force. Sarah took another sip, and set hers beside his, a bit more gently. With practiced ease, he put his arm around her and drew her close. She laid her head on his chest, and he could feel the tension ease out of her as he ran his fingers back and forth across the back of her neck. Little Andrea had her tied in knots, but he was going to make her forget, for a little while at least.

Sarah felt as if she had come home. The one place in the world where she belonged was in this man's arms. As he massaged her neck, she relaxed more and more.

"That feels wonderful," she told him. "I've been waiting for this all day." Oh, she hadn't meant to say that. It had slipped out.

"Me, too," he said and turned her in his arms so he could lower his mouth to hers and claim her lips.

His lips caressed hers as his hands slid down her spine and pulled her closer. He could not get enough of Sarah. He moved his left hand lower on her back when his cuff link got hooked on the beaded fabric. It took a moment for him to realize what had happened. Reluctantly, he slid his other hand to unhook the cuff link but, as it slid down, it snagged the dress, too.

"Sarah," he whispered, breaking off their kiss. "I'm stuck on you."

Sarah chuckled. "I'll bet you say that to all the girls."

"No, Sarah, I mean it. My cuff link is caught on these beads."

"Really?"

"Yes, really." He tried to wiggle his hands free, but only succeeded in tightening the hold her dress had on him.

"Don't tug, Marshall," Sarah instructed. "If we could stand up and move toward the light, I think I can get you loose without damaging my dress."

They struggled to stand. In a manner that the Three Stooges would have envied, they inched toward the light. Sarah had an attack of the giggles, which ended in outright laughter.

"I don't see anything funny about this," Marshall growled.

"No, I'm sure you don't," Sarah agreed. "But someday you'll look back on this less-than-romantic moment and laugh."

With his hands locked in place on her back, she wondered that she could see the humor herself, but dissolved into laughter once again when she thought of the ridiculousness of the situation. She took a deep breath, then another to control herself, and set to work.

Carefully, so as not to tear the threads that held the delicate beading, she managed to slip the first cuff link free from the small of her back. Now that he had a free hand, he could help with the one that was higher and impossible for her to reach.

"You'll have to work on this one," she said, turning her back to the lamp so he could get a better view.

She felt his free hand on her waist.

"Are you working on it."

"You bet I am. I'm even beginning to see some humor in this." He continued to move his hand slowly across her back.

"Marshall! Get busy on that cuff link," Sarah ordered.

"Okay, okay." He got it loose, but his hands continued to roam over her back.

Sarah twirled as soon as both hands began to move.

"Marshall!"

He caught her and held her close and kissed her as best he could, for she was choking with laughter again.

"Does this mean the mood is broken?" he asked, looking like a little boy who had just dropped his ice cream cone.

Sarah laughed so hard, tears came to her eyes. She leaned her head against his chest and placed her hands on his broad shoulders.

"You are good for me, Marshall."

"Ah, Sarah, you're good for me." He rested his chin on her head.

They stood like that for a long moment, then Sarah pulled back.

"I think we'd better call it a night, Marshall. It's late, and I'm usually not out every night during the week. I'm beginning to feel the late nights."

"What about tomorrow night? May I see you if we make it an early night?"

"I'd like that. In fact, I'd thought of showing you one more of Kansas City's attractions. The Gaslight Dinner Theater is performing a Neil Simon comedy I thought you might enjoy. But it probably will be just as late a night."

"That's okay. I'll go straight home afterward. Promise. What time should I pick you up?"

"Dinner's at seven, curtain at eight."

"I'll be here. It's not formal, is it?"

"No. A sports coat is fine."

"Good. No more cuff links."

Sarah laughed out loud. Marshall gave her a swift kiss. He put his arm around her shoulders, and she put her arm around his waist as they walked to the front door.

"Good night, Marshall."

"Good night, Sarah." He gave her another kiss, a definite good night kiss, long and lingering and leaving her wanting more.

"I'll see you tomorrow night," he said and with a wave of his hand, he was out the door.

Sarah leaned against the closed door and smiled. Marshall was a wonderful friend. He was more than a friend. If she did not watch it, she could find herself falling in love with this man, if she were not already in love with him. How had this happened so quickly? She tried to picture Jeff in her mind, remember the lesson she had learned from him, but she could not bring his image into focus. Instead, dark hair and the bluest eyes in Missouri crowded Jeff out of her mind.

Marshall certainly knew what to do to make her feel good. He understood her. She could hardly wait until Saturday when she could tell him about her profession and erase that secret from between them. She was still amazed that he had not discovered it for himself at the hospital.

That thought brought Andrea back to mind, and Sarah's up mood took a nose dive. She cleaned up the coffee cups, and as she climbed the stairs to her bedroom, she decided to set her alarm an hour earlier than usual so she could stay with Andrea awhile.

Sarah picked up her Bible from the night stand. It opened automatically to Ecclesiastes 3:1. "There is a time for everything, and a season for every activity under heaven." She knew the passage by heart. She read it whenever she was faced with losing a child. "A time to be born and a time to die." She closed her eyes and prayed.

7

The days of Indian summer would not last long, and Marshall was determined to be out in that early morning September sunshine. Although he was used to wearing ties, today he chose a short-sleeved plaid shirt and blue jeans.

Marshall was going to play hooky. He wanted to see more of the art gallery and decided to do some shopping at the Plaza, as well. There was also the War Memorial he had seen in a guidebook in his convention packet. He might check that out, too. And the huge old train station had been remodeled into shops and offices. He would like to see that. In short, he was going sightseeing. He would have loved for Sarah to show him around, but since she had to teach today, that was out of the question. Once again he had failed to find out where she taught. Odd, she had never talked about her job or her students. Of course, they had packed every minute pretty full and, at the moment, she was more concerned with Andrea than with teaching health. He knew she would be at the hospital after school and maybe during any free hour she had, so he would send roses to her there. This was one day he was sure she could use cheering up.

He could make the breakfast meeting this morning, but that was it. If he had been smart, he would have skipped yesterday afternoon's session. It was hard to tell which workshops would be good and which would be a waste of time. If he missed an exceptional one today, Ed could fill him in later. He would try to talk Jason into going with him.

Marshall took the stairs at a jogging pace. He needed to be outside getting some exercise; he missed his usual routine. All he had done since he had been in Kansas City was eat and sit. Time for some action as soon as the breakfast meeting was over.

He bought a newspaper from the machine at the front desk and leisurely walked into the dining room. It was still early. The meeting would not start for at least forty-five minutes, plenty of time for him to have coffee and read the paper.

He had made it through the front section, had chatted with an eager waitress, and had picked up the sports section to read about the Royals' chance in the upcoming World Series, when Ed joined him at the round table.

"How's it going, Marshall? How's your latest fling going."

"Fine," Marshall said shortly. He did not want to discuss Sarah with Ed.

"Didn't you take her out last night?" Ed asked. "I went by your room and you weren't there." Since Ed was intent on finding out about his date, Marshall was not going to give it more importance in Ed's eyes by concealing it. He waited until the waitress had poured Ed a cup of coffee before he answered. "We went to the Renoir opening at the art gallery and to dinner afterward. Jason and Maggie went, too."

"You're slipping, Marshall. Double dating didn't used to be your style." Ed laughed.

"It just worked out that way." He was going to say more, but at that moment Hal Mosley stopped by their table.

"Good morning, Dr. Adams. May I join you?"

"Of course." Marshall wondered at Hal's desire to join them. There were any number of tables to choose from and he wished Sarah's friend had picked one of them. Marshall introduced Ed to Hal and the two doctors shook hands.

"So, you and Sarah are old college friends," Hal started the conversation.

"What?" Ed said, obviously startled by that revelation.

"That's right," Marshall said smoothly. "By the way, Mosley, you left your checkbook in my car yesterday when Sarah gave you a ride. She's returning it to your office today."

The waitress had zipped over the moment Hal had sat down and looked him up and down as she poured his coffee.

"Thanks. It was nice of you to lend Sarah your car while hers was in the shop."

"How long have you known Sarah, Dr. Mosley?" Ed asked.

"Sarah and I have been seeing each other for over a year now," Hal explained to Ed, but his gaze was locked on Marshall.

"She's been seeing her old college friend this week," Ed said. "Every night." Ed was obviously enjoying this little show.

"Yes. I'm sure she and Dr. Adams have a lot to catch up on."

"Yes, I'm sure they do," Ed said and laughed.

Marshall had had enough of the inferences. Yet, he was male enough to stake his claim in this conversation.

"Sarah's very upset this morning about Andrea."

"You spoke with her this morning?" Hal asked, then looked as if he regretted his words.

"Yes," Marshall said. Well, it had been after midnight when he had left Sarah and technically that was this morning. Let Mosley draw his own conclusions.

"I know she's upset, but she has to learn that we get the ones who aren't going to survive. She gets too attached to them."

"This one seems special to her. We stopped by and saw her last night, and all the signs were there. I doubt she lasts many more hours."

"Sarah's known this was coming. She should have prepared for it. We talked about it yesterday. I'll have to console her again."

The way he said it told Marshall just exactly how he consoled Sarah. He did not believe it, not for a minute. This pompous man was lying about the woman Marshall loved.

What? He did not love Sarah, did he? He liked her; that much he knew for sure. And he respected her. But love? He had known her for only three days yet he had dreamed about her fixing breakfast for him and showing her the Valley.

Marshall's thoughts kept him silent. He did not know what to reply to Mosley's bomb so he contemplated the bottom of his empty coffee cup.

"Morning, doctors." Marshall looked up to see Jason, standing at their table.

"Morning, Jason. Join us," he said to his friend. He caught the eye of the waitress, which was not hard to do since she kept staring alternately at him and Hal, and motioned for more coffee.

Was Hal Mosley good-looking? He tried to see the doctor through the eyes of a woman and did not like what he saw. The jerk was athletically built and he obviously kept in shape. His blond hair was cut a little shorter than style dictated, but was full and shiny and, the way he combed it, it dipped over one eye. Hal must have felt Marshall's stare for he looked across the table at him. Gray eyes. Steel gray eyes and a firm chin. Since Marshall had not introduced Jason, Hal took the initiative, stood up, and introduced himself.

Ah-hah. Marshall smiled to himself. He was a good two, maybe three inches taller than Mosley. That should count for something. Of course, that still left Mosley at six foot, two.

The waitress hovered at their table. She poured Marshall another cup and brought a fresh one for Jason. She gave the newcomer the once-over, then returned to Hal and gave him a bright smile.

Okay, Mosley was good-looking but he was still a jerk. Marshall was sure that Mosley's relationship with Sarah was not what he had implied, but was a simple friendship. Well, maybe a bit more than that. She had told him that they went out, but she was obviously not interested in the guy, or why would she be spending every evening with him? And she surely was not going to be consoled by Mosley tonight. If there were any consoling to be done, Marshall would be doing it.

"How was your date last night, Jason?" Ed asked.

Marshall had expected Ed to get to that question. He listened intently for Jason's answer.

"Just fine. That's quite an art gallery you have here, Dr. Mosley."

"Call me Hal. And yes, it's a fine museum, known nationwide for its permanent exhibits. I go there often and rarely miss a traveling exhibit."

"You missed one last night," Ed said slyly.

"Yes. Unfortunately, I was on call at the hospital. And I needed to review the paper I'm presenting this morning."

"Oh. What topic?" Jason asked.

"Heart transplants in infants."

"Doctor Harold Mosley," Ed mused. "Not the eminent Dr. Mosley who performed the Baby John transplant?"

Marshall nearly choked on his coffee.

"One and the same, although I don't know that I consider myself 'eminent,'" Hal said modestly.

"Tell me about the transplant," Ed said eagerly.

Marshall glared across at Ed, the traitor. So Mosley was some hotshot surgeon. He tried to remember what Sarah had called him. Simply a cardiologist. She had not said he was a surgeon. Of course Mosley worked at Children's Research, so he should have put two and two together.

Turning to Jason, Marshall tried to block out the conversation between Ed and Hal. "I'm going to cut the meetings today and see some of the city. Want to come along?"

"Sounds good. But why don't we hear Hal's speech first, then go? His is the first session."

Marshall could not believe that his best friend had turned on him, too. Then he remembered that Jason had arrived after Mosley's comments about Sarah.

"He dates Sarah," he said half under his breath.

"No kidding? An interesting development. At least you know he has good taste," Jason said offhandedly.

"Right." Marshall wanted out of there, away from the wonderful Dr. Mosley. Yet, he would rather have Jason with him than sightsee on his own. He toyed with his coffee cup, deciding what to do.

"Good morning, Marshall," a soft, feminine voice greeted him.

Now what? he wondered. He looked up to Dr. Kerry Webster's hard gaze, then introduced her to Hal.

"Dr. Mosley, I'm looking forward to your talk," Kerry cooed.

Marshall thought he was going to be sick. He had decided to walk out, but the president called the session to order, so Marshall stayed and was herded through the breakfast line with the others.

Kerry managed to sit by Hal. They deserved one another, Marshall thought. Small talk and shoptalk ensued with Marshall contributing monosyllables. As soon as he finished eating, he excused himself.

At the front desk he inquired about a nearby florist and received directions to a shop within walking distance.

The fresh air felt good, and Marshall needed the exercise. He covered the four blocks in record time, ordered the roses for Sarah, and returned in time to see his little breakfast group standing together in the lobby. Kerry was hanging on every word Mosley uttered. Mosley stood tall in his dark, three-piece suit, looking more like a stockbroker than a doctor. Marshall looked down at his own clothes, shirt and jeans and wondered why he had picked today, of all days, to dress casually.

Jason walked over to him. "Coming to the first meeting? Then we'll go see the sights."

"I'll make some phone calls first, then be along."

He took the stairs two at a time, called his office, and was cheered with the news that his elderly patient was doing better. He walked slowly back down the stairs.

He did not want to go to Mosley's speech, but was drawn there like a moth to a flame. He wanted to see what this guy was like, to see what Sarah saw in him. The door to the meeting room was shut, but Mosley's voice carried into the hall. Marshall slipped inside and saw Jason sitting in the last row with his sports coat draped over the empty seat beside him.

"Thanks," Marshall whispered, as he handed Jason his coat. He settled down in a hostile frame of mind to listen to the eminent Dr. Harold Mosley.

An hour and ten minutes later, Marshall and Jason exited the underground parking lot. Jason sat in the passenger's seat, his hands full of brochures and a map he had taken from the hotel lobby.

"You've got to admit he's a good speaker," Jason said. He had been talking about Mosley since they had climbed in the car, and Marshall was sick of the subject.

"I don't have to admit any such thing," Marshall said belligerently.

"What's gotten into you?" Jason asked. "Oh, Sarah, huh? So what? The man dates Sarah."

"He hinted that they were more than friends."

"Marshall, did you ever consider that they might be? What do you expect of her? She's twenty-nine. Do you think she's been locked in an attic the last ten years?"

"No, I don't. And how do you know how old she is?"

"She and Maggie are the same age."

"Oh," Marshall said and after a couple of minutes of silence, returned to the topic at hand. "Sarah told me there was nothing between them, just an occasional date."

"And you believed her?"

"Of course. She wouldn't lie to me. There would be no reason to. We met him Monday night in the coffeehouse, and she pretty much told him to scram."

"You're dreaming if you think Sarah wouldn't lie to you. She's a woman, isn't she? You can trust me on this one, buddy. Women lie."

"Not Sarah. She's different."

"Right. They're all different," Jason said cynically. He flipped through the brochures he was holding and held one up. "Let's walk around the Plaza first." He found their position on the map. "At the next light, take a left."

❧

Sarah had pushed the alarm off as soon as the shrill sound had begun. Although she had been asleep only a few hours, she was wide awake with the first sound of the buzz. She needed to be with Andrea this morning.

After a quick shower and no breakfast, Sarah left for the hospital. It was not quite six when she walked into Andrea's room.

One look at the little girl's waxy skin and she knew Andrea would not make it through the day. The Garrens were stretched out together on the daybed. Mr. Garren was staring up at the ceiling as he held his sleeping wife close to him. He looked questioningly at Sarah. She motioned for him to stay as he was and not disturb his wife. The woman would need some rest to get her through the day.

Sarah walked to Andrea's side and touched her forehead. Andrea moved her head at the touch. So, she was still conscious. She could slip into a coma any moment now and in a couple of hours it would be all over. Sarah could hardly bear the thought that she would never see those bright, brown eyes again.

Sarah mouthed, "I'll be back," to Mr. Garren and went in search of Mary. She found the night nurse putting the morning medicines in little tablet cups.

"Is there coffee, Mary?"

"Just made a fresh pot. I figured you'd be in before I went off."

Sarah poured herself a cup of the strong brew. She did not have to ask before Mary answered her silent question.

"She's been pretty restless. Up every hour or so. She's been asleep since close to four, the longest nap she's had. That little girl's a fighter. She asked for you once."

"I'll bring the Garrens some coffee and sit with them until time to make the rounds."

Mary gave an understanding smile and nodded in agreement while she poured coffee for the Garrens and set the cups on a small tray.

Balancing the tray, Sarah walked slowly to Room 202. Mrs. Garren was awake when Sarah entered the room. She and her husband were still lying on the daybed, locked in a warm embrace. They were not kissing, just holding and comforting each other.

Mrs. Garren broke away from her husband and sat up on the edge of the bed. He also sat up and took the coffee Sarah offered. "Did you get some rest?" Sarah inquired softly and sat down in the padded, fake-leather chair at the head of Andrea's bed.

"Yes. Andrea was restless most of the night. Much like she was when you dropped in. But the last few hours she's slept and so have I."

"Good."

They all sat in silence for a few moments, their attention focused on the child in the bed. Andrea turned her head, as if feeling their stares, and opened her eyes.

"Dr. Sarah," she whispered. "I don't feel right."

"I know, honey," Sarah answered with a forced smile. "I see you still have your dolls in bed with you. They both have your brown eyes." Sarah was relieved to see the little girl awake again. She had feared Andrea would die before she had the chance to say good-bye. She would not say it out loud to the child, but in her heart, so she could stand this loss more easily.

Sarah moved from the chair so the Garrens could move closer to their daughter. If these moments were important to her, they would be precious to Andrea's parents. They would have to last a lifetime.

"Would you like a cold drink, Andrea? Maybe a Coke?"

"In the morning?" Andrea whispered, a spark of her old self in her eyes.

"I'll make an exception today. Be right back."

Sarah hurried off to get the Coke. She did not usually play waitress to her patients and their parents, but dying days were different. And Andrea deserved a Coke. They had often laughed about having Coke in the morning. Sarah told her she could have it only as an afternoon treat and then again in the early evening. Andrea had attributed drinking Coke as a sign of growing into the teenage years, and now she would never get to experience a first date or the high school prom.

Sarah carried the ice-cold Coke can back into Andrea's room, opened it, and slipped in a straw. She placed the straw in Andrea's mouth and watched as the little girl struggled to sip the cold liquid. She did not have much strength left.

"I've got to make rounds, but I'll be back pretty soon," Sarah told the child. She tried to make her voice sound professional, but it came out too soft for that.

Andrea looked straight into Sarah's eyes as if she were looking into her soul. "Good-bye, Dr. Sarah."

"Good-bye, my little scamp," Sarah said. She bent down and kissed Andrea on her forehead. "I'll see you later."

Sarah walked blindly out of the room. She took a deep breath and then another to gain control.

"Mary," she said as she came to the nurses' station. "Andrea knows. Her parents chose not to tell her, but I just did."

"Dr. Madison," Mary said with a mixture of surprise and concern, "what did you say?"

"I asked her if she wanted a Coke in the morning. It was a joke between us. She always had one as an afternoon treat, something to look forward to."

"She probably already knew," Mary said in sympathy.

"Maybe," Sarah answered. "She didn't seem distraught." She took a deep breath. "I'm going to make early rounds this morning so I can get to the lab and then back to Andrea. Where's Lorraine?" she asked about the nurse who usually accompanied her on rounds, then immediately understood her mistake. "Of course she's not here if you're here, Mary." She glanced at her watch. Fifteen minutes till seven. "I'll start alone. When she comes in, have her join me."

Sarah went from room to room, checking on her patients. The normalcy of routine settled around her until she checked the chart of Joey Garrison. The blood count was all wrong. The experimental treatments were not controlling the leukemia. With no further evidence, no proof at all, she knew without a doubt that Joey would be the next Andrea on the list. Her heart broke. She faked a smile, patted Joey on the foot, and told him she thought she heard the breakfast cart coming down the hall.

"I'll be back pretty soon and we'll talk," she said and made a hasty exit.

Sarah had finished her afternoon rounds and was in the leukemia lab again with Dr. Lewis. She had checked on Andrea four more times and the little girl was holding her own, in and out of a light sleep. Sarah had not told Dr. Lewis about her slip with Andrea. She did not know how to broach the subject. The Garrens had said nothing about it and acted as if nothing was different. Maybe she had imagined Andrea's response.

"I'm going down to check on 202," Sarah said offhandedly, in an effort to make her frequent trips seem normal.

Dr. Lewis was not fooled. "Andrea's special, isn't she?"

Sarah studied the brilliant doctor. He had heart. He was not a research scientist lost in another world, but a truly caring person.

"Andrea's special," she agreed. "I'll be right back."

"Wait. I'll go with you," the older man said. He took off his plastic gloves and walked with her down the wide corridor.

They had just reached the door to Andrea's room when the call light above the door lit up. Exchanging a lightning-quick glance, they rushed into the room to find Mrs. Garren leaning over Andrea and Mr. Garren shouting into the intercom.

Sarah moved quickly beside Mrs. Garren. She heard the death rattle in Andrea's breathing and when Mrs. Garren started to move back to give her more room, she stopped her.

"Stay with her. Hold her hand." Mr. Garren, on the opposite side of the bed, took his daughter's other hand in his large one and held it up by his cheek.

Within two minutes it was over. Sarah watched the little girl gasp for breath and then give up the struggle. Automatically she glanced at her watch. 3:42. She had to force herself not to call for the respirator, but the Garrens had made the decision not to prolong the inevitable and to let Andrea die in peace.

The parents, two doctors, and the nurse who had answered the call, stood in silence for a moment. Sarah knew she should move in and listen for the heartbeat that she would not be able to find, but she could not move. To do so would be to announce to the Garrens that their daughter was gone. She felt Dr. Lewis's gaze on her, and she looked back at him with tear-filled eyes.

Dr. Lewis was the one to step forward and try to find a heartbeat, signifying the end.

"I'm sorry," he said to Andrea's parents.

The anguished sob from Mrs. Garren and the answering one from her husband, tore at Sarah's heart. She could not stop the tears that rolled freely down her cheeks.

Dr. Lewis stepped back from the bed and walked over to Sarah. Mr. Garren moved to his wife's side. They stood with their arms around each other, staring at their dead child.

"Can you take care of them?" Dr. Lewis asked Sarah in a hushed tone.

"Yes," Sarah whispered. Dr. Lewis patted her on the arm and left the room, taking the nurse with him.

Sarah let the Garrens cry for a few minutes while she gained control herself. In the best professional manner she could muster at the moment, she stepped to the intercom and called the nurse back in.

"We have things to do," she said in a choked voice to the Garrens. "First, is there someone I can call who can drive you home? A relative or a friend?"

Mr. Garren gave her a name just as the nurse walked in, and Sarah instructed her to make that call and another to the funeral home the Garrens had chosen.

She wanted to get the parents out of the room, but they were not ready to leave their little girl. Instead, she helped Mrs. Garren gather up Andrea's things. There were her clothes, several pairs of pajamas, coloring books and crayons, a deck of Old Maid cards, and Andrea's two dolls.

Mrs. Garren held out the newer doll to Sarah. "Dr. Madison, she would want you to have the doll she named after you."

Sarah felt the tears forming and blinked them back. She could not start crying again. The Garrens were over their first bout of tears and were in the numbed, shocked period when everything seemed like a bad dream. She did not want them feeling again until they were safely home.

"I will treasure this always," she told Andrea's mother, as she took the doll.

She had to get the Garrens out of the room. The hearse would be there soon, and they did not need to see it take their daughter away.

Sarah ushered the parents into a private waiting room and stayed until their friend arrived. She walked them to the main door, listening to the friend talk about getting the Garren's car later. The Garrens wore blank expressions and looked at the friend as if their car were the last thing in the world that mattered.

At the door, Mrs. Garren turned to Sarah. "Dr. Madison, thank you for caring about our little girl. She loved you, too." She hugged Sarah then walked through the door her husband held for her. He looked back at Sarah and said a quiet thank-you.

She watched them walk out to the car and stood at the door long after the car had disappeared from view.

Cradling the doll in her arms, much as she would have a baby, Sarah walked back to the elevator. She did not wait for it but climbed the stairs and walked quickly to Room 202. Stopping in the doorway, she stared at the housekeeping staff, who were stripping the bed and cleaning the room.

Andrea was already gone.

Sarah stood sightlessly for a moment, looking inward, remembering the bright child who was no more. "God, please take care of her," she whispered.

Then, with a resolute squaring of her shoulders, she turned and walked purposefully toward Joey's room.

8

Marshall and Jason walked through the lobby from the parking garage.

"I'm beat," Jason said. "Maybe it's a good thing Maggie has to work tonight. Think I'll take a shower, call room service for dinner, and watch a movie in bed. Don't get that sort of luxury very often."

"No, such leisurely nights are few and far between," Marshall agreed. He stopped at the desk and asked if there were any messages for him. He had the feeling Sarah might have called to thank him for the roses.

"Yes, Dr. Adams." The desk clerk handed Marshall a note and flicked a switch that turned off the flashing light on the phone in Marshall's room.

"Well, did she get the flowers?" Jason asked as they walked over to the elevators.

"I don't know," Marshall said, rereading the terse message. "She can't make our date tonight. One of the patients at the hospital where she volunteers must have died. If that's the case, Sarah wouldn't be in the mood for a comedy at the theater."

The elevator arrived, and the two men stepped inside.

"Want to have dinner together?" Jason asked.

"Thanks, but I think I'll order room service, too. Sight-seeing is exhausting."

Jason got off on his floor and Marshall rode on to the fifth floor and reread the desk clerk's version of Sarah's message one more time.

Sarah Madison called. She is sorry, but will not be able to make your date tonight.

After a long shower, Marshall stretched out on the bed. He turned on the TV and flicked from one station to another, but nothing held his attention. His thoughts were with Sarah. The note did not say for him to call her back, but nothing kept him from doing it. He should have thought of that before.

The phone rang six times before she answered, and at first he thought he had dialed a wrong number, because her voice sounded so different.

"Sarah, it's Marshall. Is it over?"

"Yes," Sarah said in a low voice. "She died at 3:42. I'd just walked in the room, and a couple of minutes later she was gone." Her voice cracked.

"I'm sorry, Sarah," Marshall said softly.

There was a long silence on Sarah's end, then in a muffled voice she said, "I can't talk now, Marshall. I'm sorry about tonight. Goodbye."

Marshall lowered the phone after he heard the click. That conversation had not gone at all as he had planned. He prowled the room and finally decided to go downstairs for something to eat.

He did not feel like sitting down at a table in the hotel restaurant. A couple of tacos sounded better. With that decision made, he took the elevator to the garage. He felt as if he had walked over half of Kansas City and he did not need the exercise the stairs offered.

The fast-food Mexican place he had remembered seeing was a short drive away. He carried his food to a table by the window and stared out as he ate. What would Sarah be having for supper? Why wouldn't she talk to him? Was it because she was too upset? Or was it because there was someone else there? His mind flew back to the morning conversation with Hal Mosley. Was he there with her now, consoling her? Marshall stuffed the paper trash from his meal into a huge garbage can and stalked out to his car. He started the engine, but instead of turning back toward the hotel, he went in the opposite direction. He told himself it was stupid, that he was acting like a teenager with a crush but, nevertheless, he drove over to Sarah's house.

There were no lights on and no car parked in front of her house. Marshall slowed down but had to drive on past it because of a car tailgating him. He swung around the block and made another pass in front of Sarah's house. Of course, her car would be in her garage, but surely Mosley's would be visible if he were there. There were no lights to be seen from this angle, either, but it was not dark yet. What was she doing in there? Determined to find out even if he made a fool out of himself, he parked and walked to the front door. He rang the bell, but there was no answer. Trying the knob, he was surprised to find it unlocked. He stood uncertainly on the porch with his hand on the doorknob, then opened the door and stuck his head inside.

"Sarah," he called into the empty hall.

He thought he heard a noise and closed the door behind him before walking from the entrance to the living room. The draperies were closed, allowing none of the last rays of the sun into the room. In the dimness he made out Sarah, huddled on the couch.

"Sarah?" he said softly. "Are you all right?"

"Marshall?" she said and sniffed.

"Yes." He reached for the light switch on the lamp, and the room filled with soft light. Sarah blinked. Her eyes were red rimmed, and it took no detective's mind to see that she had been crying.

Marshall walked swiftly across the room and sat down beside her. Without hesitation she moved into his arms, her head resting on his wide chest. She cried; huge, wrenching sobs shook her slender frame. Marshall murmured soft reassuring words and held her close. When the crying subsided, he handed her his handkerchief, then stood and pulled her to her feet.

"We're going for a walk," he said, his voice brooking no argument.

He led her out the front door and walked with his arm around her down the street toward a wooded park area she had pointed out to him before.

"When one of my patients dies," he said, "I always go for a walk in the hills to remind myself of all of God's nature around me. I see His hand in every flower and every leaf. And I see His plan of spring and renewal and fall and quietus."

" 'To everything there is a season,' " Sarah whispered.

"Exactly. Death is the natural result of living, and we shouldn't fear it but rejoice that God has promised an even better life than the one on earth. That doesn't mean I don't grieve for the one who's died, but I'm really grieving because of the void left in my life by the person's death. Am I making any sense?"

She nodded and he continued.

"Everyone has his own way of dealing with death. Mine is to walk. I think of the person who's died, all the good things I knew about that person, characteristics I liked and that I should imitate."

They had reached the park, and Marshall paused to read the wooden sign that declared the area a nature haven in memory of Millie Rawlings.

"What a wonderful monument to a person." He led Sarah through the woods. Many of the leaves had already changed colors, announcing that autumn would end soon and winter begin. But spring would follow. The changing of seasons, as old as time, would still go on.

They walked the length of the park in silence and turned to retrace their steps. Dusk had settled, the western sky painted pink and orange by the setting sun. Within minutes the color would disappear and darkness would fall.

Marshall hurried their pace so they could reach Sarah's home before the light was gone. At home he liked walking after dark, but he did not know these woods or the slope of the land.

When they reached the sidewalk on Sarah's street, he slowed their steps. They had their arms around each other as they walked.

"What did you like about Andrea?" he asked softly.

She was silent a moment. "Her bright eyes, her sunny disposition. I know she's with God now, and I do rejoice in that for her. And I've been thinking back over the times she's been in the hospital. She knew she was dying, Marshall. She knew all along. Her parents couldn't bring themselves to tell her, but she knew, and she wasn't afraid. She was sharp. She watched what went on around her, and she sorted it out for herself. That was why she didn't seem distraught when I told her she could have a Coke this morning. It told her that today was her last day, but she knew that."

"Wait a minute. You've lost me. What about a Coke?"

As Sarah explained about her early morning visit, she withdrew her arm from around him and began wringing her hands together.

Marshall understood. She felt she had betrayed Andrea somehow. It was his experience that patients knew if they had an incurable disease. Parents were fooling themselves if they thought their children could not read their moods and see their fear and agony and correctly interpret it.

It must have been a horrible day for Sarah. To have the guilt she had laid on herself for the Coke episode and then to go to the hospital after school and arrive just as Andrea died would be a lot to handle. He doubted that Sarah had ever been with anyone else who had died. And to have her first time be with a special little girl must have been heartbreaking.

"Have you had anything to eat?" he asked as soon as they walked back into Sarah's house. At the negative shake of her head, he pushed her in the direction of the kitchen.

"I'll fix you a gourmet meal," he said. "Point me in the direction of the canned goods."

Sarah smiled, the first smile he had seen all evening, and pointed to a door.

Marshall found a well-stocked pantry, but decided she would eat only a little, so chose a can of chicken noodle soup. While it heated on the stove, he checked the refrigerator and found two French rolls. He sliced them in half, spread them with butter, and sprinkled Parmesan cheese on top before sticking them in the oven under the broiler. He poured two glasses of iced tea, ladled up the soup, and placed the toasted bread in a basket he found on the counter.

"Your dinner is served," he said with a flourish.

Together they sat down at the round kitchen table.

"It looks delicious," Sarah said and started on her soup. Marshall watched her eat and helped himself to a couple of slices of bread. She finished the bowl of soup, but declined a refill. While she sipped her tea and munched on bread, Marshall cleaned up the kitchen.

"Shall we take our tea to the living room?" he suggested.

She nodded. She had smiled a couple of times, had made small talk over supper, but she was not her old self yet. She still needed to talk, to get her grief out in the open.

She sat on the couch, and Marshall walked over to the fireplace. Inside it, wood was laid up for a fire. It was not cold and they did not need a fire for warmth, but the crackling sound and the glow of the flames would lend a cheery atmosphere to the room.

"Do you mind if we have a fire?" She shook her head. "I like fires," he said as he struck a long match from the holder on the mantel and turned on the gas starter. He watched it until the kindling caught, then turned off the gas.

Time to get Sarah talked out, he decided, as he sat down beside her. He placed his arm along the back of the couch, his hand resting on her shoulder.

"How did Andrea's parents handle it?"

"As well as could be expected. She is, was, their only child." The way she said that, as if they would suffer this only once, while she suffered over and over, gave Marshall sudden insight into Sarah's deep depression. She was not grieving for Andrea alone, but for all the children she had known who had died.

"You see a lot of children die at the hospital." It was not a question, just a statement, but she nodded in response.

"The next one will be Joey. He's the same age as Andrea. The one before Andrea was Eric. The one before that was Taryn. It goes on and on. It never stops."

"Perhaps you should consider quitting at the hospital. Find another hospital for your work, but not one strictly for children. Death is hard to accept any time, but when it strikes children repeatedly, it's especially hard." He felt sure she would be welcomed at any hospital where she chose to volunteer her time.

"You might have something there," she said thoughtfully.

"You know the Serenity Prayer, Sarah?" He did not wait for an answer, but began and Sarah's voice joined his. "God, give us grace to accept with serenity the things that cannot be changed, courage to change the things which should be changed, and the wisdom to distinguish the one from the other."

"Amen," Sarah said and felt a peace settle over her. They sat in silence for a moment, then Sarah said, "Oh, thank you for the flowers, Marshall. I appreciate them." She gazed across the room at the vase of roses on a side table. Marshall had failed to notice them until now.

"I'm glad you like them. The night we met, you left your rose in the cab, and I've been enjoying it in my room." He had not meant to say that, to tell her he prized anything that reminded him of her, but she did not have the triumphant look of a woman with the upper hand. She must not have read the correct meaning into his remark.

"I like it when you hold me," Sarah said softly, catching him off guard. He immediately settled his arms around her and she snuggled to fit her soft curves against his hard frame.

"I like it, too," Marshall murmured into her hair. He understood her need. He had experienced it many times himself. Being close, touching someone, renewed the sense of being alive. And after losing someone, it was necessary to have that feeling. They sat that way for a long time.

Finally, Marshall turned her so he could kiss her lightly on the forehead. It was all he meant to do, but a couple of kisses there led to a kiss on each eye and then to the tip of her nose and her cheek, and then her lips beckoned him. He kissed her again and again.

Sarah nestled closer to him. He knew she was vulnerable tonight, and he did not want to take advantage of that situation. He needed to go. He needed to go because he loved her. And he knew she loved him. He felt it in his heart.

"May I see you tomorrow night?" he asked.

"I'm picking up my parents at the airport tomorrow night. Remember? And this evening I talked to Mom, and she asked me to spend the night out at Lake Quivera with them."

"Could I go to the airport with you? I want to meet your folks."

"That's a new twist," she said. "Most guys shy away from the meet-the-parents routine. Be here at seven."

Marshall grinned again. "Seven." He pulled her into his arms and held her close. He did not want to let her go, and she would never understand what it cost him to leave her. He gave her a quick peck on the cheek and walked out of the house.

He loved her, his heart sang. He had found the woman of his dreams. A warm, loving, intelligent, sensitive Christian woman. She would say yes when he asked her. And she would love the Valley as much as he did. Sarah Madison Adams. Sarah Adams. Dr. and Mrs. Marshall Adams. He liked the sound of that.

9

*S*o, you've both got the men coming to the fashion show to-morrow," Ellen said. She sat in the doctors' dining room with Sarah and Maggie. "Sarah hasn't told him she's a doctor, but she sure hasn't played down her intelligence," Maggie said. "She took him to the museum, if you can believe that."

Ellen turned to Sarah, her eyebrows raised in a silent question.

"He likes intelligent women. He told me the first night we met. And I also took him to a baseball game."

"And what a game." Maggie took over the conversation and told Ellen about the mix-up with the box seat tickets and the four of them standing the entire game."

"The fans were on their feet most of the game anyway. And the men did enjoy it," Sarah inserted.

"And the museum?" Ellen asked. "Kent and I attended but we couldn't make it until late. I'm sorry we missed you."

"Maggie failed to mention that she and Jason crashed that museum party and also attached themselves to us for dinner," Sarah said. She looked at her watch. "We'd better finish up. I need to be back in the lab by one-thirty."

Maggie cut another bite from her chicken breast. "How come we haven't ever eaten in here before? I didn't know you had gourmet dining."

"The hospital treats us right. If the doctors used the cafeteria, families would besiege us, and we wouldn't get to eat." She rarely stopped long enough for a complete meal, but today Ellen had insisted they meet before tomorrow's fashion show and having them come to the hospital was easier for Sarah.

"Now," Ellen said, "we've covered Tuesday and Wednesday. What did you do last night?"

"I'm totally innocent," Maggie announced. "I worked. Big show at the Women's Club. What about you, Sarah?"

"One of our little girls died yesterday and I was upset. So, I called Marshall and canceled our date, but he came over anyway. We went for a walk, and he fixed me dinner. He was very understanding about not going to the theater."

"Did you tell him about the little girl? About being a doctor?" Ellen asked, waving her fork at Sarah.

"He doesn't know. He thinks I'm a volunteer. I told him when I met him that I spend a lot of hours here without getting paid. Which is true. I come in lots of times when I'm not required to."

"Hey, we're not questioning that, just making sure you haven't told him you work here," Maggie said.

"I want to tell him. I like him, and I want him to know the truth. I brought him over here late Wednesday night to check on Andrea, but he didn't find out. No one called me Doctor. Guess I'll have to work on the staff and have them show more respect for the title."

"Sarah," Maggie said. "Tomorrow is only a few hours away. Why ruin this little dare by telling him tonight?"

"But both men have agreed to come to the fashion show. Why carry this little charade further?" It seemed to Sarah that the purpose of the dare had been achieved. She had had fun, proved she had a different side to her personality and a balanced life, but now she felt as if she were trapped in a game. She still believed a doctor's life and a family did not mix, but she wanted to be honest with Marshall and be his friend. No, that was not true, a voice inside her said. There was more than friendship at stake here.

"A dare's a dare," Ellen said. "What's a few more hours?" Maggie asked.

"I suppose you're right." Sarah patted her mouth with her napkin. "Did I tell you Marshall sent me a dozen roses yesterday?"

"Well, well. A promising sign. Ellen, do you think this little experiment has changed Sarah?" Maggie asked.

"I think this little experiment has worked a little wonder," Ellen said with a knowing smile.

Sarah studied Ellen. What was she thinking? Ellen had always been able to discern her innermost thoughts. Perhaps she was right on target once again. Sarah had been more relaxed with Marshall than with any other man she had ever known, and that included Jeff. And she felt something special for Marshall that she had never felt for any other man. She respected him.

Maybe this little dare had helped her. If Marshall's not knowing she was a doctor in some way had helped her relax and be a woman with him, then this dare was worth it.

"I've got to run," Sarah said. "Are you two ready?" She could not leave them in the doctors' lounge by themselves.

"Okay. Tomorrow at two," Ellen said. "I'll meet the men you have maneuvered so skillfully. Let's plan on dinner afterward."

"Oh, Ellen, we failed to mention that the two men skillfully maneuvered us. We're going to the convention banquet with them tomorrow night," Maggie said.

Ellen had stood up to leave, but sat down again in a bout of laughter. "Oh, the games we play." She was still laughing when she was able to walk away, leaving Maggie and Sarah staring after her.

❧

"Hey, Marshall. Where were you this morning?" Ed's booming voice was loud enough for three tables around them to hear. Marshall pulled out a chair and sat down at the dining table with Jason and Ed. Here he was again, eating. He had probably gained five pounds this week. He ordered a chef salad, which was promptly placed in front of him.

"Well?" Ed demanded. "Where were you?"

"I went for a walk and went farther than I'd planned. Did I miss something important?"

"No. But this afternoon's session should be good. The drug companies are conducting seminars. I love it when they pay us to listen to their spiels."

Marshall was not surprised. Although he had to have plenty of money now, Ed's past still exerted an influence on him.

"So, what did you do last night?" Jason asked. "I called your room and you weren't in. The TV movie was lousy, so I thought we could check out a theater."

"I went over to Sarah's. She was feeling pretty low and we talked. I fixed a bit of supper for her."

"Then the little girl died?"

"Yes. Yesterday afternoon. Sarah had just walked into the room. Just came in from school, I guess, and she was there when Andrea died. It hit her pretty hard. Although she's in a hospital where they lose a lot of children, I doubt she's witnessed it before."

"Couldn't you console her like Dr. Mosley does?" Ed asked with a sly smile.

"Dr. Mosley insinuated something that isn't true. They don't have a relationship, just an occasional date."

"Let me guess. She told you that, and you believe her," Ed said. He exchanged a knowing look with Jason, who shrugged his shoulders.

Marshall already knew Jason's opinion, and he did not like having it seconded by Ed.

"Of course, I believe her. She's not the kind of person to lie."

Ed exchanged another look with Jason. "I believe there may be a little more here than I first thought. Are you hung up on her, Marshall?"

He did not want to answer that question. "I've known her only a few days. She's easy to talk to, that's all. She's a good listener and a good person. We might keep in touch after I go back to Neosho." He wanted to do much more than that. He wanted to show her the Valley, show her what his world was like. And he wanted her to love it, too, and be a willing part of it. But he could not confide in Ed and Jason.

"Oh, really?" Ed said.

"Yes, really. It doesn't mean anything," he said. "Just that we like each other's company. What about you, Jason? Going to see Maggie again after we leave Sunday?"

Jason looked a little sheepish. "I thought I'd invite her out to Denver. Maybe take her skiing over Thanksgiving."

"Well, well," Ed said, shaking his head. "So the old Adams charm is still there, and Bradford has some, too. Want to see the Foster charm?"

Ed pulled out his wallet and extracted a picture from the photo section. He handed the picture of a woman to Marshall, who looked at it, then handed it to Jason.

"You sure this picture didn't come with the wallet?" Jason asked.

As if anticipating the question, Ed handed a second picture to Marshall. The same brunette, Ed and two small children smiled at him from the photo. "She's quite a looker, Ed. How did you manage to catch her?" Marshall asked. He passed the picture to Jason, who gave a low wolf whistle.

"I guess you guys underestimate the Foster charm. And I am true blue to my woman."

Marshall studied his friend. Here was another side to the brash, loud, obnoxious man that he had not suspected. Ed's tone of voice even softened when he spoke of his wife.

"Needra's a wonderful wife and a good mother, too. She doesn't work," he told them, pride in his voice. "She stays home with the children. It was my lucky day when I met her."

"Your chauvinism is showing," Jason said.

"I don't care. My mother had to work, and I swore my wife would never have to. And she doesn't. Her job is to take care of me and our children."

That sounded wonderful to Marshall. What would it be like to go home at night to a warm house filled with the sounds of children's laughter and the smells of dinner cooking on the stove? And be greeted by Sarah at the door, a kiss on her lips just for him. Oh! He was at it again. His visions of the future always included Sarah.

"What are you doing tonight, Marshall?"

"What?" He had heard his name, but not the question. Jason repeated it.

He did not want to answer. He did not want to tell them he was going with Sarah to get her parents at the airport. That would open up more speculation.

"We're going for a drive," he said without mentioning the destination. He gulped down his last bite of salad and stood up to leave the dining room.

"Going with us this afternoon?" Jason asked.

"No. I need to call my office again, then I might run over to Children's Research to look around a big city hospital. It's been quite a while since our Chicago days, and I'd like to examine the differences, now that I've had experience in a small town."

"We'll be in the Cedar Room, if you change your mind," Jason said.

Marshall nodded and wound his way around the other tables and out into the lobby area. He climbed the stairs to his room and made his phone call, then wandered over to the windows looking down on the city street.

He had enjoyed his walk this morning. He had not intended to miss the morning meeting, but it was such a nice day to be outdoors. He had come to this conference with high hopes of being inspired to be a better doctor, to learn new techniques and procedures, and now he had skipped a day and a half of meetings. Perhaps he should go this afternoon, but these sessions were just live commercials.

On the other hand, the convention planners had scheduled alternative activities for the doctors. Golfing, boating, tours of Kansas City were all listed in the conference guide. All work and no play was not the rule for this convention.

If he went to the hospital, he might run into Sarah. He hoped he would see her as soon as her school day ended. But today she might not volunteer; she might not want to go back to the hospital just yet. Andrea's death was too fresh in her mind. A couple of days away would help her deal with things without so much emotional involvement.

Sarah, he thought. "Sarah," he said aloud. He would see her at seven o'clock. He remembered her sister-in-law telling Sarah that the plane landed at seven-fifty, which would not give them time for dinner. He called Sarah's house and left a message on her machine. He could come over earlier, and they could get a bite to eat before picking up her parents. He hoped she would call him back when she got home from school.

❧

Sarah punched the button on her machine as soon as she arrived home at five-thirty. It had been a rough week, and Dr. Lewis had insisted she leave on time for once. As soon as she heard Marshall's message, she called the hotel.

"Come on over," she told him. "We can pick up something to eat on our way to the airport."

Under the soothing spray of the shower, Sarah thought of Marshall's kindness last night. She had cried in front of him and responded to his kisses. Now she felt shy about seeing him again and at the same time impatient that it would be a half-hour before he could get there.

She showered longer than she had meant to, and then everything went wrong. Mascara caked on her lashes. She took it off twice before she was satisfied with the result. Then she smeared her lipstick. She tried on three outfits and discarded them in favor of a pair of peach-colored slacks and a white blouse. Since the day she had discovered Jeff was seeing other women, she had insulated herself from hurt. Now she realized she had also insulated herself from other feelings, as well. Her profession had helped. She blamed it on men not liking intelligent women. But time had healed the pain, and now she was ready for an emotional involvement—if it worked out that way. She changed clothes one more time and dashed in designer jeans and a sweater to the front door as the bell rang. She opened the door, and Marshall wasted no time in taking her in his arms and kissing her thoroughly.

"Are you all right?" he asked.

"I'm okay," she said. "I'll be just a minute. I need to stick a toothbrush and some pajamas in a bag. It's been a long time since I stayed at my folks'. Oh, Marshall, I just thought, we need to drive to Lake Quivera, so I can get Dad's car. Mine won't hold us."

"I'll drive," he offered.

"But I'll need my car to get back tomorrow. Would you follow me out there?"

❧

The drive to the Kansas side of the state line took longer than she had planned. Sarah locked her car on her parents' driveway and jumped in the car with Marshall.

"Did I tell you Jason and I went sightseeing yesterday?" Marshall asked.

"Really? You skipped meetings?"

"Yes. Well, we heard the esteemed heart specialist talk," he said, trying to keep the sarcasm out of his voice, but failing.

"How did Hal do?" She had meant to go hear him, but was glad she had not taken the time. She had heard him before.

"Fine. I imagine he's used to public speaking."

"He's had a lot of press lately. The Baby John transplant."

"Yes, I know. Hal had breakfast with me yesterday. I'm not his favorite person."

"Oh. Because of me?"

"Yes, dear, because of you." She seemed to digest that piece of information. Marshall did not think she knew how much Hal wanted her for his own. But enough of that. He did not want her thinking of Hal when he was with her. "I skipped this morning's meetings, too. This afternoon I thought I'd tour Children's Research, but I got sidetracked." He had been on his way out of the hotel when he had met another doctor from old school days, and they had renewed their acquaintance over coffee. He glanced over at Sarah and saw her take a deep breath. "Are you all right?" he asked.

"Fine," she said. What if he had walked in on her at the hospital? She needed to tell him about her job herself, in her own way, and explain the importance of the dare and the money for research. "Tomorrow after the fashion show, I'll show you around if you'd like." Then they would laugh about her deception and wonder that he had not found out from Hal or their earlier visit to the hospital.

After a hamburger stop, they arrived at the airport with only five minutes to spare. They rushed to the gate to find the flight was a few minutes behind schedule.

"So, tell me about your parents. Will your dad quiz me like your brother did?" Marshall asked as they settled in chairs for the wait.

"No. My brothers are much more forward than my dad. Mom might ask a few questions."

"Oh, no. Moms are worse than dads."

"Don't panic. I'm just teasing. My mom's a real lady. She won't quiz you about personal things. She's kind, getting more gray hair than she cares to have, and is a bundle of energy. Annie and I could never keep up with her. Now, Dad is sixty-six. He retired two years ago because his hands were beginning to bother him. Arthritis. They moved to Lake Quivera so he could play golf every day and keep his hands in shape. He was a brilliant heart surgeon, but the moment his hands started to go, he turned in his knife. Sometimes he teaches a seminar, or is a guest lecturer, that sort of thing, so he keeps up on what's new in O.R. I think he's content with his new life. He doesn't look back, just keeps looking forward."

At the roar from outside, Sarah peered through the windows at the lights of an approaching plane.

"They're on the ground," she said and glanced at her watch. Only ten minutes had passed. Sarah called to her parents as they walked out of the unloading tunnel.

"Hello, Sarah," her mother said, and they hugged each other.

"Hi, Dad." Sarah kissed her father on the cheek, then introduced Marshall.

They discussed the weather and the flight and Annie's new baby while they waited for the luggage to arrive. As soon as it started down the chute and filled the carousel, Marshall and Dr. Madison picked up the cases Caroline Madison pointed out.

"If you'd like to wait here, I'll get the car," Marshall suggested.

"If it's not far, we can carry the luggage," Dr. Madison said.

Marshall gazed at the two biggest pieces, but assured Sarah's father that it was not far. He started to pick up the two large cases when Dr. Madison stopped him.

"I'll get those, young man," he said and would not hear of Marshall carrying them. Obligingly, Marshall picked up the two smaller cases and led the way to the exit and outside to the car.

"What's he doing?" Sarah whispered to her mother.

"I believe your father is proving in typical male fashion that he's as fit as your young suitor. He feels threatened. His daughter turns up at the airport with a boyfriend who is obviously possessive of her."

"Mom, how can you tell that? We've only talked about the weather."

"Sarah, we've seen three other children go through this. And we were young once ourselves, you know. Besides, it's not in the conversation; it's in the looks and the way he had his arm around your shoulder."

Sarah stared at her mother. She had a keen sense of reading people. "He is special," she said softly.

Her mother smiled and nodded. The men had arrived at the car ahead of them, and Marshall already had the trunk open. Sarah climbed in the front seat and left the backseat for her parents.

On the drive home Caroline Madison asked how Marshall met Sarah, and then they discussed his hometown.

Sarah led the discussion to the fashion show the next day. She had not warned her folks not to mention she was a doctor, and she directed the conversation away from medicine. But as they crossed the bridge over Lake Quivera, her dad asked how things were at the hospital.

"It's been a trying week," Sarah admitted. She turned around in her seat so she could see her father better. He and her mother were sitting close together. "Did Mom tell you we lost a little girl yesterday?"

"Yes. How did you deal with it?"

"Not very well. Marshall took me for a walk, and it helped."

Her dad studied the back of Marshall's head, and Sarah suffered an uncomfortable moment. She had never seen her father like this before.

"I used to walk when I'd lose one," he said finally, a note of respect slipping into his voice. "What's your specialty, Marshall?"

"General practitioner. Although, since I practice in a small town, I'm really more of a family doctor." Marshall met Dr. Madison's gaze in the rearview mirror. Some of the initial hostility he had sensed from Sarah's father was beginning to vanish. Nevertheless, he breathed a sigh of relief when the house came into view. He parked beside

Sarah's little sports car, jumped out, and lifted the suitcases out of the trunk before Dr. Madison could climb out of the car.

"Can you come in for a while, Marshall?" Caroline asked.

He glanced at Sarah. "For a few minutes," he said, but wished he was back at the hotel that moment. As they walked to the house, Marshall carried one of the large bags and one of the smaller ones. Dr. Madison's load equaled his.

Marshall set his load down in the entry.

"Could I speak to you a moment?" Dr. Madison asked in a quiet but determined voice.

"Of course," Marshall agreed. He glanced at Sarah, who gave a small shrug, then he followed Dr. Madison into the kitchen.

"Now what's he doing?" Sarah asked in a low voice.

"I don't know, dear. Being with Annie has been hard on him. He wasn't expecting a C-section and seeing her in so much pain brought out all his fatherly instincts. My guess is he's still feeling protective." In the ensuing silence, Sarah could hear a low mumble of voices, but could not make out any words.

In the kitchen, Dr. Madison stood clutching the back of a kitchen chair. "This may be very premature, and I never thought I'd ever say this, but what are your intentions toward my daughter?"

Marshall held the doctor's gaze and answered in a straightforward fashion. "I've known Sarah only since Monday, but in that short time, I've grown to love her. I haven't asked her, and I'd appreciate it if you didn't mention it, but I intend to marry her, if she'll have me. I know that sounds sudden, but that's the truth."

Dr. Madison seemed to relax a little, but stood silent as if taking it all in. "I knew the first time I met Caroline that she was the one for me," he said softly. "But you may be fighting an uphill battle with Sarah. Her work at the hospital is very important to her."

"I know, but she could work at the hospital in Neosho. She's been around dying children so long, she may welcome the chance to see them get well." He believed it would be better for her, and he had given Sarah's job some thought as well. She would want to finish the school year in Kansas City. An eight-month engagement was longer than he wanted, but he could stand it if he knew she would be his wife in June.

"Marshall, forgive me for overstepping the line as Sarah's father. Her sister's just gone through a trying time, and it's hard on an old man to see his daughter in pain. I just want to protect Sarah from hurt."

Marshall smiled. "I understand, Dr. Madison. Sarah was wrong about you. She said Matt was a much tougher inquisitor than you, and she was wrong."

"Oh, when did you meet Matt?"

Marshall explained about the museum exhibit and then told Sarah's father about the baseball game and the mix-up with the tickets.

In the great room, Sarah was wringing her hands together. What were they talking about in there? If her father was grilling Marshall, she should go in and break it up.

A burst of laughter came from the kitchen. Sarah's gaze darted to her mother. A moment later, the two men joined them.

"Walk me to the car?" Marshall asked Sarah.

"Of course," she said.

Her parents shook hands with Marshall, and then the young couple walked outside.

As soon as the door shut behind them, Sarah asked, "What did he want? I've never known my dad to act like that."

"Just man talk," Marshall said with a smile.

"You're not going to tell me?"

"No."

"You're really not going to tell me?" Sarah was amazed.

"No."

"You go in the kitchen with my father, and the hostility could be cut with a knife, and you come out ten minutes later laughing and patting each other on the back. And you're not going to tell me?"

"That's right. Oh, maybe someday I'll let you in on it, but not now."

"Could you at least tell me what you were laughing about?"

"That baseball game we went to."

"That's it?"

"Yes. Now, kiss me good night, then you can enjoy your evening with your folks." But he could not let her go after one kiss. Two and then three melted into four and five.

"I should go back in," Sarah said when he released her mouth for a brief moment.

"I know," he said then hugged her closely.

"I'll see you tomorrow," she whispered in his ear. "Remember, the fashion show at two."

"I'll be there," he promised, then he kissed her once again.

10

*M*aggie, where do you want the microphone?" Sarah called. She was standing beside the maintenance man who was waiting impatiently for the redhead's answer.

"Put it by the entrance door," Maggie called across the large cafeteria. Late-lunch diners turned their heads to watch the action.

The fashion show would start in an hour, and all the last-minute details had yet to be attended to.

"Dr. Madison," a volunteer asked, "do you think these flowers should go on the piano?"

"That would be lovely," Sarah answered. She had her hands full with the custodian, who was being contrary about leaving his regular work to tend to this function. The models were still arriving, all of them members of the Ladies' Auxiliary, and some of them near panic, now that the time had come to walk out in front of a crowd.

"May I have your attention?" Maggie shouted over the din of raised voices. She moved to the microphone and finally got quiet from the group. "We have too much confusion here. You two," she pointed to two women, "finish putting the flowers on the tables. We'll close the cafeteria in ten minutes and begin charging an admission fee," she directed toward the diners. "Models, follow Dr. Madison down this hall to the room where you will be dressing. The clothes are there and numbered. A corresponding numbered list of models is taped to the wall. Check it and go ahead and change into your first outfit. Is the woman here who's going to narrate?"

Heads turned, looking about. "Fran's not here yet," someone said.

"Who's in charge of refreshments?" Maggie asked. She looked at the woman who raised her hand. "Is everything under control there?"

"We'll be setting things out by one-thirty, so the guests can be served as they walk in."

"All right, fine. Does anyone here not know her job?" Silence. "Good. Let's get things finished up."

Sarah gave her friend the okay sign, thumb and index finger forming a circle, then led the models to the area designated as the dressing room. It was actually the doctors' lounge, and a volunteer had posted a sign that directed the doctors to a conference room for lunch.

The models began changing clothes, and a few minutes later Maggie appeared, looking a little frazzled around the edges, but still in charge. Sarah admired her friend. At times she appeared scatterbrained, but she knew her business.

"Do you all know the route you take around the tables? Remember, pause at each one when you are asked to. We're here to sell these clothes and make money for your hospital."

As soon as she quit speaking, the chatter rose to a fever pitch. Maggie grabbed Sarah and took her over to a corner away from the center of the noise.

"Where's Fran, the narrator?"

"I don't know."

"I told her to be here at one."

"I'll go call her. Is the pianist here?"

"Yes. She's getting set up. Pull that scarf over to the side," Maggie directed one of the models.

"I'm out of here," Sarah said, glad to escape the chaos. She walked briskly toward the nurses' station to use the phone, but ran into Fran before she had gone many steps.

"There you are. Maggie's been asking for you," she said as she ushered the woman toward the dressing room.

"Dr. Madison," Fran whispered. "I've been practicing so much, my voice is gone."

Just what they needed. One more thing to deal with. "Oh. Well, let's find Maggie." Sarah pushed open the door and motioned for Maggie to come out in the hall. "Go on in," she told Fran.

"What?" Maggie barked as she joined Sarah.

"You've heard of hysterical blindness?" Maggie nodded. "Our narrator has a case of hysterical dumbness. She can't talk. My diagnosis, without a thorough exam, is a temporary case of stage fright."

"I knew working with these amateurs was going to be a real pain."

"Calm down, Maggie. You've got a script. It shouldn't be hard to find another reader."

Maggie shot her a sly look. "No, it won't be hard. Come here." She picked up a script and thrust it at Sarah. "You've been to my fashion shows, and you got me into this. Read!"

"Now, Maggie, there's got to be someone else. You read it."

"Can't. I've got to make sure each model is decked out right and enters on cue. There's no other way, Sarah. Those women are basket cases. They'll need me to tell them every step to take."

"Well, surely—"

"No, Sarah, there isn't time. Now take this and go over it so you're familiar with the terms."

"But I was going to sit with Marshall."

"That's too bad. Ellen can baby-sit him." Maggie glanced at her watch. "Twenty-four minutes until curtain. The show must go on and all that stuff."

"All right, all right. But I'll get you for this, Maggie."

Sarah took the script and got a cup of coffee from the volunteer in the cafeteria. The place was beginning to fill, so she took a seat at an empty table by the microphone and skimmed the script. She could do this, but she was getting butterflies thinking of Marshall watching her.

"Sarah." She looked up to see Ellen. "Is this the best table in the house?"

"No. I'm the new narrator. Would you sit with Marshall and Jason?"

"Of course," Ellen said. "I've been waiting to meet those men."

"I've got to go over this." Sarah motioned to the papers in her hand. "When the men come in, I'll introduce you. Be nice to them, and don't tell Marshall I'm a doctor. I'll do that in private after the show. Do you have the check?" After her mental anguish over this dare, she wanted to make sure the end and the reward were in sight.

"Right here," Ellen said and patted her pocket. "Don't worry about the men. I'll take care of them." She found a table near the center of the room. Within ten minutes the men arrived, and Marshall made a beeline for Sarah. She explained the situation, left the men with Ellen, and hurried to the dressing room.

"Five minutes till show time," Maggie was telling the models. "Are you ready?" she asked as soon as she saw Sarah. "Are they here?"

"Yes, on both counts. Ellen is with Marshall and Jason. Are we starting on the dot of two?"

"Unless people are still paying to get in."

It was ten after by the time Sarah stepped in front of the microphone. She looked out on a packed house, said a quick prayer for courage, and took a deep breath. "Good afternoon, ladies and gentlemen." She glanced at Marshall and Jason, two of about ten men in the crowd. "Ambassadors and the Ladies' Auxiliary of Children's Research Hospital present a 'Step into Fall.' Our first model, wearing . . ."

For an hour Sarah read and the models turned and walked and twirled. As the models strutted out for the finale, Sarah glanced at Marshall's table. She had been sneaking looks every chance she had, at risk of losing her place in the script. He did not look bored, but rather was very attentive. She saw him stop one model and ask a question. The pianist kept playing and audience conversations could not be heard. Too bad she could not read lips, for Marshall's table was carrying on quite a low-pitched conversation.

The fashion show was over, and it was not as bad as Marshall had anticipated. Ellen had kept a quiet conversation going. She knew quite a bit about him, and asked about the museum and the ball game.

"Did you talk to Sarah this morning?" Ellen asked.

"No. She spent the night with her parents after we picked them up from the airport."

"You met Sarah's parents?" she asked, her eyes wide.

"Yes, they seem quite nice," Marshall said, although that had not been his first impression of Dr. Madison.

"Hal's never met her parents," Ellen announced.

"Is that right?" Marshall asked, glad to hear that the esteemed Dr. Mosley did not know Sarah nearly as well as he had implied.

"You've met Hal?" Ellen asked.

"Yes. And I don't like him," Marshall said with a smile.

"Me, neither," Ellen agreed. "You and Sarah are much better suited."

"Thanks. I couldn't agree more." Marshall wondered just how much she knew about his relationship with Sarah. "Are you going to see Sarah after tomorrow?" Ellen asked.

"I hope to." Marshall had had enough of the quiz. "What did you think of the show, Jason?" he asked in an effort to change the subject from himself and Sarah.

"Interesting. Where's Maggie?"

As soon as he asked the question, the models filed into a straight line at the front of the room, and Sarah called Maggie into the cafeteria. A young girl handed Sarah a bouquet of roses, which she presented to Maggie amid applause from the models and the audience.

"Maggie's a nice person," Ellen said as soon as the noise died down.

"Yes, she is," Jason agreed. "And yes, I'm going to see her after I leave. I hope she'll come to Denver for a few days."

"Is it that obvious that I'm trying to find out how things are between you?" Ellen asked. "I don't mean to pry, but I'm interested in their welfare."

"You have nothing to worry about," Marshall said. "They're both in good hands. If you'll excuse us, we need to be getting back to the conference." That was not entirely true. Oh, there was one last workshop going on, but he did not intend to sit in on it. What he needed was to get out of this crowd of women and the inquisition.

Other guests were milling about, admiring the dresses on the models and the ones that were wheeled in on a long rack. Marshall and Jason made their way to where Sarah and Maggie were standing. Although Sarah had offered to give him a tour of the hospital after the show, Marshall was feeling uncomfortable with all these women around. The high-pitched chatter nearly deafened him, and it looked as if Sarah could be tied up for some time.

"Nice job," Marshall said. "We've got to be going, but I'll see you tonight."

"Can't you stay?" she asked, then was immediately besieged by auxiliary women.

"No. I'll take that tour tomorrow before I head to Neosho, so you can enjoy your friends now." He found it hard to stand next to her and not touch her. Yet this was not the place for holding hands or putting his arm around her and pulling her close.

"Marshall, I'll meet you at the hotel," Sarah said.

"Oh, I can pick you up," he said.

"No. I can come with Maggie and you can take me . . ." Her voice trailed off as she turned to acknowledge the woman who had grabbed her arm and in a loud voice congratulated her on a magnificent show.

Marshall took her free hand and squeezed it. "I'll see you at the hotel at six-thirty," he said and turned to leave. He stopped by the table at the exit and talked to the woman taking dress orders and asked that Sarah pick out a dress as a gift from him. He quickly wrote out a check.

"Nice gesture," Jason said as they walked outside.

"It's for the hospital," Marshall said and shrugged. He took a breath of fresh air. "Good to be out of there."

⸻

Sarah did not normally resort to violence, but she wanted to smack the loud-mouthed woman who had hold of her arm. Instead she thanked her for coming, then turned to the other well-wishers. "I didn't get to tell him," she said to Maggie.

"You can tell him in privacy in three hours. Be better that way than here."

Maggie could have a point. Telling him at the hospital might be a bit of overkill. Still, she wished she had that moment of telling him she was a doctor behind her.

"Okay, Ellen. The check, please," Sarah said.

Ellen made an elaborate gesture and reached into the pocket of her suit jacket. "Fifty-thousand dollars to the leukemia lab at Children's Research Hospital. This dare was worth every penny of it."

"Good," Sarah said as she stuck the check in her purse. "We'll stretch every penny as far as it will go." And, she thought, it was worth every effort she had made in not revealing her profession to Marshall.

"Dr. Madison," one of the volunteers called to her from beside the clothes rack.

Sarah walked over to the area where the guests were going through the clothes. It looked as if quite a few outfits were gone, a good sign for the fund-raiser.

"Dr. Marshall Adams," the volunteer read from the check, "bought you a dress. Which one would you like?"

"Oh," Sarah said. A pleased smile settled on her lips, and she was touched by his thoughtfulness.

"Did I hear right, Sarah? Marshall bought you a dress?" Ellen asked. "I like the red one, and I sure like Marshall. You should snap him up."

"Thanks, I might. The red one's pretty. I'll try it on."

"Try this black one, too," Maggie said. "It'll set off your hair and be perfect for tonight."

"It will, won't it? Be right back."

Sarah modeled the dresses for her friends then glanced at the price tag of the black one. "Oh, this is too expensive."

"He paid more than that," said the volunteer. "The rest was to go to the hospital.

"You'd better grab him, Sarah," Ellen said. "Or I'm going to invite all my single friends over to meet him."

"Don't send out invitations yet," Sarah said with a laugh. "Give me tonight to make an impression on him."

It was after five by the time Sarah made it home. She showered, washed her hair, and was putting the finishing touches on her makeup when the phone rang. "Dr. Madison, this is Nurse Richardson. Dr. Lewis has broken his leg," she said in a matter-of-fact tone. "He's asking for you to come see him immediately."

"Is he all right?" Sarah asked, concern in her voice.

"He will be after it's cast. Right now he demands to talk to you before he lets them knock him out and set it."

"I'll be right there."

She slipped on her new dress and checked the clock. Six. She called the hotel. Marshall did not answer, and the desk clerk came back on the phone and asked if she would like to leave a message.

"This is Sarah Madison. Tell Marshall Adams that I'll be late, but I'll be there. Thanks."

There really was no time to explain. She might try to reach him again from the hospital once she knew how late she would be. She was thankful that she had changed her mind and decided to drive herself to the hotel instead of riding with Maggie. She raced for her car and automatically headed for the hospital.

～❧

Marshall saw the flashing light on his phone as soon as he walked into the bedroom from the bathroom. He had shut the door or he might have heard the ring over the shower.

The desk clerk informed him that Sarah would be late. But there was no explanation. What had happened? If she had been hurt, surely she would have said so. He hung up the phone, then picked it up and punched in Sarah's number. It rang eleven times before he hung it up again.

He pulled his navy blue, three-piece suit from the closet. No way was Hal Mosley going to show him up tonight. The intellectual side of his brain told him that Hal was no threat to his relationship with Sarah. However, his emotional side was afraid of Hal. Afraid of his reputation and his long friendship with Sarah.

He was tying his tie for the second time when Ed knocked on his door.

"Come on in," he invited after Ed had already entered the room. Marshall buttoned his vest and slipped on his suit jacket. "Sarah's going to be late. Come on, we'll wait in the lobby." For once he did not mind his friend's companionship. Talking with him would make the time go faster while he waited for Sarah.

The elevator took the men down to the lobby. Ed and Marshall got off as Maggie got on.

"Sarah's going to be a little late," Marshall told Maggie before the elevator door closed. "Save a place for us if you and Jason go in first."

❧

When the hotel desk came back on the line again, Sarah asked for Jason's room. Maybe Marshall was there. But he wasn't.

"Please tell him to go on into the banquet. I'll be there. And, Jason, tell him to trust me. There's been an emergency, and I'll explain everything when I see him. I know it will confuse him, but I can explain." Sarah felt as if she were babbling. She did not want to tell Jason about the dare, but she was worried about Marshall's reaction once he learned she was a doctor. And he would learn it shortly, and not in the manner she had planned.

"I've got that, Sarah. I'll see that he gets the word. See you later," Jason rang off.

Sarah replaced the receiver and smiled across the small room at Dr. Lewis, who lay on a hospital bed. He was pale, and she could tell he was in pain.

"My notes are here, Sarah. You won't have any trouble reading them. I had Lorraine type them up."

"I'm sure I can read them just fine," Sarah said and smiled reassuringly at her boss. "Why don't I call the bone setter in and get you all fixed up?"

"Don't try that patient talk on me, Sarah. I know your style. They're going to hurt me, and you know it. Just think, I'll be the oldest patient at Children's Research."

"If you don't behave and let them get to work, I'll have you transferred to Mercy. And you won't get all the special pampering you've been receiving from our nurses." She said it with a laugh, but shook a finger at him. He needed that leg set now.

"Now, Sarah. Just give the speech one time so I can answer any questions you might have. Then I'll let the quacks at me. I was so honored to be chosen for the closing address," he mumbled. "And this had to happen. I'm such a klutz."

On his way to the hotel, he had stopped by the lab to check an experiment, had spilled some water, and then slipped in it.

Sarah read the speech out loud, stopping several times for Dr. Lewis to clarify points. It was after seven when they finished.

"How about one more time, Sarah?"

"No. You promised you'd let them work on your leg, and you're going to. I'll read it again before I go on stage. I'll do the best I can."

"Oh, I'm not worried about that. You'll do a better job than I would."

"Thanks for the vote of confidence. I need it." Sarah pushed the button for the nurse to come in. "What time were you scheduled to go on?"

"After eight."

A nurse walked in, followed closely by two more nurses. "About time," she grumbled. "We've been ready for an hour."

"Take care," Sarah said and patted the doctor on the hand. "I'll check back in with you after the speech. Oh, and Dr. Lewis, I have something to show you." She smiled apologetically at the nurses for the delay and dug in her purse. She handed Ellen's check to her boss.

"I don't know how much we made on the fashion show for the hospital, but this check is just for our lab."

"Why did Kent Crawford give us this money?" he asked.

"Actually it's his wife, Ellen, who's behind it. It's a long story, and I'll tell you after your leg is set."

He handed the check back to her. "All right then, let's go," he directed the nurses. "Have that story ready," he said to Sarah before he was wheeled out into the hall.

"Good luck," she called after him. Sarah gathered up her notes. She felt sure that Dr. Lewis would be fine; she had seen the X ray as soon as she had walked into the hospital. Because of his age, it would take some time to heal, but it was a clean break. He had had some medicine for pain before she saw him, but until after he saw Sarah, he had refused the medicine that would make him drowsy. He was tough. She admired that streak in him. She admired everything about him, but he had surely put her in an awkward situation.

❧

On the way to the hotel, Sarah tried to go over the speech, but without the notes in front of her, her mind refused to think along those lines and instead focused on Marshall. What would his reaction be when he saw her on stage? Maybe she could pull Marshall out of the banquet so she could talk with him before she gave her speech. She certainly could not tell him in front of a table of people; she discarded that idea. There was no time; she needed to go over that speech again. At ten minutes before eight, she arrived at the hotel. The master of ceremonies had been informed that she would be replacing Dr. Lewis, and a hotel employee had been dispatched to tell him Sarah had arrived. Sarah paced the hall, waiting for the doctor to come out of the banquet room.

"Would you like to come to the head table?" he asked when he appeared. "There isn't time for you to eat, but we can arrange for something afterward."

Something to eat was the least of Sarah's worries. She was soon to face a mob of doctors who had been practicing medicine many more years than she. And Marshall was in there, too. "I'd like to reread this speech before I go in," Sarah said.

"Fine. When I introduce you, enter from the side door, which is right beside the head table." He took her down another hall and showed her the door.

"I'll send someone out right before we're ready for you."

With that he slipped back inside the banquet hall.

There was no chair around, and Sarah did not dare go hunt for a place to sit. A dim light fixture provided her only light. Obviously the hall was used for employees and not guests of the hotel. Sarah stood under the light and studied Dr. Lewis's notes, talking aloud in a quiet tone.

All too soon a man of about fifty came out into the hall. "We're ready for you." He kept the door open a crack, and Sarah heard the master of ceremonies tell a joke and the audience respond appreciatively. She hoped they would be as receptive to her. She strained to hear her introduction.

"Our closing speaker was to have been Dr. Warner Lewis, noted research scientist from Children's Research Hospital right here in Kansas City. Due to an accident, Dr. Lewis is at this moment having his broken leg set. In his place he sent his assistant. He assured me that she knows every bit as much as he does and is prettier, besides. Please welcome Dr. Sarah Madison."

11

*M*arshall stared at the stage in shock as Sarah walked out, looking as calm as if she gave speeches every day of her life, which as far as he knew, she just might. He knew his mouth was hanging open, but he could not take it all in. So this was the meaning of her cryptic message to Jason. She would explain everything later. She was a doctor, not a high school health teacher. Why had she lied? Maggie reached over the empty seat that separated them and patted his hand. "She'll explain everything, Marshall. She wanted to tell you, but we wouldn't let her."

"You wouldn't let her?"

"Well," she hesitated. "She'll tell you when she's finished. Let's listen."

Marshall nodded and sat very still, but he did not hear a word of Sarah's address. He watched her every move, her every gesture, but did not listen to what she said. His head was spinning. He had trusted her. Both Jason and Ed had laughed at his blind trust, and he had been blind, all right.

She was wearing one of the dresses he had seen at the fashion show. The one she had probably bought with his check. He felt used. He felt foolish. But most of all he felt betrayed. Tonight was the night he was prepared to declare his love. And what was she thinking? That tonight was the night she would laugh at Dr. Marshall Adams? The twenty-five-minute speech lasted half a lifetime. As soon as it was over, Marshall scooted into the empty chair by Maggie's and demanded the story.

"I can't tell you," she whispered. "But she really likes you, Marshall. Don't be mad at her."

"Don't be mad at her? She lied to me. I trusted her and she lied to me. And you say don't be mad? She said she taught health."

"She teaches interns. She said she wouldn't lie to you; she would just avoid the truth." Maggie bit her lip as if she had said too much. She turned away as the master of ceremonies introduced the conference chairman.

Marshall looked around at the people at his table. From their expressions, Jason and Ed had not known that Sarah was a doctor. But the thorn in his side, Dr. Hal Mosley, was sitting across from him and leaned forward to make a comment.

"Sarah's very good, don't you think?" Hal said proudly. "She's an excellent doctor, but she gets too involved sometimes."

That was the last straw. The pompous Dr. Harold Mosley had known about Sarah's little joke all along. What an idiot Marshall was. Dr. Mosley had sat at breakfast with him only two days ago, making ownership statements about Dr. Sarah Madison, and now he knew they were true. Mosley had never once let on that Sarah was a doctor. If he hadn't been in on the joke, he would surely have said something that would have told Marshall that Sarah was a doctor. And tonight Hal purposely sat at their table so that he could watch Marshall's reaction.

Marshall stared at Sarah. She was seated beside the new president of the AMA and had her head inclined his way to hear what he was saying. But her eyes were searching the audience. For him? Probably. She wanted to see the effect of her little joke on him. He knew she could not see him. His table was at the back of the room and the house lights had been turned off with only lights on the dais to spotlight the head table.

Sarah peered through the darkness that engulfed the audience. She could make out only the shapes of tables and bodies. The lights shining down on her were too bright for her to see through the dimness that hid Marshall.

What must he be thinking? She tried tactfully to hush the man beside her, for he was making small talk, and she thought he could at least give the chairman of the conference the courtesy of listening.

The traditional thank-yous that ended the convention took forever. Finally it was over, and Sarah stood as soon as the lights in the banquet room were turned back on. The men at the head table grouped around her and shook her hand, congratulating her on a fine job on such short notice. She brushed their praise aside and stepped off the dais, making a beeline for Maggie. Her friend's red hair had been a beacon and she homed in on it. Marshall stood with his back to her. She came up behind him and took his arm, leading him a few steps away from the others.

"Marshall, I can explain," she said.

"Please do," he said coldly, his arms folded across his chest.

He was furious and she did not blame him. This was not the way he was supposed to find out. She took a deep breath and began.

"I took a dare at that restaurant Monday night that I could get you to the fashion show this afternoon. My friends said I'm usually too serious, so I promised not to tell you I was a doctor, so I wouldn't intimidate you and scare you off. We didn't know you were a doctor, too. I got you to the show. I wanted to tell you several times. I'm sorry, but it was important. You see—"

"Sarah, you did a magnificent job," Hal said as he came up beside her and gave her a congratulatory hug. "How's Warner doing?"

"He'll be all right. It was a clean break," Sarah answered and pulled away from him.

Marshall positively glowered.

"Marshall didn't tell us you were a doctor," said the chunky fellow who was with Marshall that first night in the restaurant. He stood behind Marshall. Jason and Maggie joined him.

"Well, I am," Sarah said.

"Marshall didn't know," Jason explained. "There was some sort of dare that Sarah could get him to go to a fashion show."

Sarah glanced at Maggie, who shrugged. Obviously, she had filled Jason in on the bet.

"And did you?" the fellow asked.

"Yes," Sarah said, watching Marshall's explosive expression.

"You took a dare about him and he took a dare about you." The fellow laughed. Sarah stared at him.

"That's enough, Ed," Marshall cut in.

"No, it isn't. What dare?" Sarah demanded.

Ed looked from one to the other and shrugged. "Ah, you acted like a glacier in that restaurant. We dared him to melt the iceberg and get you to go out with him. Prove that the Adams charm was still strong.

Sarah felt as if she had been hit in the stomach. She turned her head and closed her eyes. So this whole week had been a charade.

Hal stepped in for her. "Of all the sophomoric pranks! Come on, Sarah, I'll take you home."

Sarah did not answer, but turned and walked out of the banquet hall with Hal following. She crossed the lobby and strode out the door to the parking garage.

"Sarah," Hal called to her from the door. "Wait, Sarah!"

She did not want to talk to anyone and certainly not to Hal. But by the time she had her key out of her purse and had unlocked the car door, he was at her side.

"Sarah, let me drive you." He put his arm solicitously on her shoulder.

"Leave me alone, Hal," she said and moved away from his touch.

"I know you're upset about that silly dare. And I don't blame you. The man's obviously a cad. I never did like him."

"You don't know anything about it, Hal. So just keep quiet."

"Well, at least nothing happened between you two that you would regret later. He may be a smooth operator, but you shot him down."

"Shut up, Hal." She pulled the door open and sat down but Hal held the door. "Get out of my way. I mean it. Stay out of my life now, and stay out of it later!"

He turned loose of the door and she slammed it. "You don't know what you're saying, Sarah." She could hear his loud voice through the closed window.

"Oh yes, I do." With Hal standing inches from the car, Sarah surged out of the parking space. As she moved forward, she had the grace to look in her rearview mirror to make sure she had not run over his foot. Not that she cared. She had told him to get out of the way. She drove home in record time, pulled into her garage, and rested her head on the steering wheel. She was weary. The stress of giving the speech and the fear of Marshall's reaction to her deception had drained her. Still, she was angry and hurt that he had asked her out on a dare. Was that his sole purpose in pursuing her and why he was so persistent? That was why he had introduced himself to her that first night at the restaurant. She had thanked God that he had approached her instead of her having to ask him out. Now she understood why.

Sarah lifted her head from the wheel. She was tired. She had not slept well at her parents' house and she needed some sleep. Then she would sort through all that had transpired in the last hour.

How fast her future had disintegrated. She pushed the remote control button to close the garage door and climbed out of the car. The house seemed empty as she dragged herself through the kitchen door and found the strength to put on the kettle for a cup of soothing tea. She had had no dinner, but the thought of food turned her stomach.

Two nights ago in this very kitchen, Marshall had fixed her soup and toasted bread. He had been so kind, so understanding. Was that an act? The kettle whistled and Sarah mechanically made a cup of tea. She carried it into the living room and collapsed on the couch, her mind whirling. Something did not add up. If they had merely dared him to get her to go out with him, he had accomplished that on Monday night.

Before she lost her courage, she dialed the hotel. There was unfinished business between them, and she wanted it settled.

"Marshall Adams's room, please," she said to the desk clerk.

"I'm sorry. Dr. Adams checked out a few minutes ago."

So this was it. She would never see him again. They had deceived each other with dares, lies, and manipulation. The love that she had felt withered inside her.

"Thank you," she finally mustered, and hung up the phone.

So he was gone. And why would he leave, if he had nothing to hide himself? If only Dr. Lewis had not broken his leg.

Her sense of responsibility took over, and she reached for the phone and dialed the hospital.

"How's your most famous patient?" she asked the head nurse.

"Dr. Lewis is a real grouch. He wouldn't take general anesthetic. Gave him a local. He told me to put you through as soon as you called."

Sarah talked to her boss for a few minutes. His voice was groggy, and he spoke slowly. As soon as she assured him the speech was well-received, she felt he would quit fighting the medicine and go to sleep.

Ten minutes later, from her bedroom phone, Sarah called the nurse back and found that Dr. Lewis was sleeping. She unzipped her new dress that Marshall had bought for her. He had surely paid a premium price for the time they had spent together. That thought made her feel bought, and she hung the dress out of sight at the back of her closet.

She had been bought. She had allowed Ellen to buy her honesty for fifty-thousand dollars. Every person has his price, didn't the old saying go? Who would have thought she was worth only fifty-thousand dollars? She was so confused. One minute she was furious with Marshall, and the next she was missing him and wondering how he was feeling and where he was.

Maybe he would come to his senses and call her. Of course, that's what he would do. He was not the type to run from a confrontation. Actually, she was the one who had fled the banquet hall. He would give her time to cool off, then he would phone. After donning her nightgown, she lay down on the bed to await his call.

She stared at the ceiling for the longest time, watching the patterns that car lights made as they drove by on the street below. After a while the lights became more infrequent.

"Dear God," she prayed, "I've really messed things up. What do I do now? What do I do?"

When the phone rang at midnight, she was still awake. It had to be Marshall. He had gotten over his initial anger and wanted to talk.

It was Maggie. "Are you all right, Sarah?"

"No, I'm not all right, but I'll survive."

"I've told Jason everything, all about my dare, too. And you know what? He loves me anyway. He's asked me to go to Denver next weekend, and I'm going. We'll see each other as often as we can and get to know each other. We want to be sure that this relationship is right for both of us."

"That's wonderful, Maggie," Sarah said and meant it. At least one of them had come out ahead on this dare. "I'm happy for both of you."

"Sarah, about Marshall. I told him you wanted to tell him about being a doctor, but we wouldn't let you. I tried to smooth it over, but he was angry."

"What exactly did he say?" Sarah asked. She could barely breathe, and her heart was beating double time.

"He said he'd trusted you, but you lied to him. That's about all."

"I see. Well, that's that." Sarah tried to sound as if it did not matter. It was not Maggie's fault that she had let herself be talked into the dare. She had thought it would be an experiment to see if all men were like Jeff and felt threatened by an intelligent woman. Well, she had her answer, or did she? She was too confused to even think about that angle.

"Sarah, about Marshall's dare. He'd been talking about how women were after him because of prestige and money. Then you showed up, and they thought you looked glacial, and Jason and Ed dared him to see if the Adams charm was still there without a woman knowing he was a doctor. It's really no big thing. He told you he was a doctor as soon as you agreed to a cup of coffee with him. Now he's upset because he thinks you lied to him."

Sarah stifled a sob.

"Call him, Sarah," Maggie urged. "Just a minute." Sarah heard mumbled voices in the background. "Jason said Marshall cares about you. He's just upset and hurt."

"I see."

"Sarah, if you want me to come over—"

"No," Sarah cut her off. "I'm fine. I'll probably call him and get this worked out. 'Bye."

She hung up an instant before tears poured down her cheeks again. She was in the right, and he was in the wrong. Or was it the other way around? Her mind spun and the tears continued to fall.

12

Marshall turned into the driveway of the Valley. As he followed the winding lane to the house and parked his car in the detached garage, the clock on the dashboard read 1:03. He had run into such hard rain, he had had to pull over to the side of the road and wait for the thunderstorm to move on.

As exhausted as he was, he was still furious with Sarah. During the long drive home, he had replayed the entire week in his mind. She was some actress.

His house had that musty, closed-up smell. He walked around opening windows, then fixed a cup of coffee and sat in the huge, brown, overstuffed chair that faced the fireplace.

He felt empty inside, and his thoughts were racing a mile a minute back to Kansas City.

The whole week had been phony. He reexamined their initial meeting. At the time, he had been amazed at how quickly Sarah had agreed to have coffee with him. Now he understood. What would her approach have been if he had not taken the initiative? The conversation about intelligent women played in his mind. Maybe there was a bit of honesty in her. At least she did not follow through on that routine. Astrological signs! Hah! The ball game, the museum. Were Sarah's brother and sister-in-law in on the big joke? And what about her father? Had Marshall actually told the man that he was planning on marrying his daughter? She was an excellent actress, he thought again. He had trusted her. She had said she taught high school health. No, she had said she taught health, but never said where. He had assumed it was in a high school, but he had never asked her. If it had not been for Hal Mosley, he might think there had been some horrible mistake. She had wanted to meet him before the banquet. Maybe she was going to tell him then. Maggie had said she wanted to tell him, but the dare would not let her. She had not planned on giving that closing address. Dr. Lewis' breaking his leg was an accident. But what if she had not planned on telling him at all? Why did she take the dare? She did not seem like the type of woman who went around taking crazy dares.

The late hour and the strain of the trip home were undermining his desire to stay awake and sort through his relationship with Sarah one more time.

Did he love Sarah? Yes. Although all evidence pointed otherwise, he could not bring himself to believe that Sarah was capable of leading him on so callously.

He shook his head to clear it. His heart was overruling his head, and he had to make order of it. He should never have left Kansas City without talking to her, hearing her side of the whole affair. He kept coming back to Hal Mosley. Marshall thought of himself as a fair man, but he hoped Mosley would drop off the face of the earth. And he really did not know the man. He set his cup down on the table next to the chair, closed his eyes, and took a deep breath. He should have followed her home instead of coming back to Neosho.

So, she was a doctor instead of a health teacher. Big deal. Maybe she had a good reason for taking the dare. Maybe she needed to be known for herself instead of her profession. He had felt that way before, wanted people to think of him as a man instead of a doctor. He thought about the women who were so impressed with his credentials.

He sat up straight. He had forgotten about his dare. She had stormed out before he could explain it was not a big deal, and he had been too angry to stop her. It had started as a fun event, just as Sarah's dare had that night in the restaurant. But she did not know that. What must she be thinking about him? He was a fool, and it was none of Sarah's doing. He had felt inferior to Mosley. A general practitioner could not compete with a heart surgeon. But Sarah did not care about his profession. Hadn't Maggie said that Sarah did not even know he was a doctor when she had accepted her dare? He had to talk to her.

Should he call her? No, he needed to see her reaction as they talked. He would go back to Kansas City. Yes, that was what he would do.

Several hours later, the sun streaming through the open window woke him. He stretched to ease the cramped muscles that came from sleeping in a chair.

It was after nine. He felt better after his sleep, and his first thought was that he would return to Kansas City as soon as he had seen his patients. He walked outside on the porch. It was cool this morning, a definite nip in the air. It was always cooler in the Valley than it was in town. He looked across at the giant steps on the terraced hills. He loved this place. It gave him a sense of well-being. Everything would work out, one way or another, and he felt hope again. If Sarah rejected him, he would be hurt, but at least it would be out in the open and settled without this awful unfinished feeling. And he could come to grips with it. But if they worked things out, if they could find a way to merge their complex lives. . . . He smiled. She would find a sense of place here, too.

❧

Sarah carried a cup of coffee into Dr. Lewis's room. He was propped up in bed for breakfast with his newly cast leg lying outside the covers to dry.

She had awakened by six, and although she was still tired, she opted for action instead of analyzing things gone wrong. Dr. Lewis would need her. And she needed to check on Joey.

"Sarah, you work too much," Dr. Lewis told her. "You should be out having fun instead of baby-sitting an old man with a broken leg."

Sarah took a big gulp of coffee. She was getting the same song, second verse, from her boss as she had had from the Fab Five.

"I probably need more balance in my life," she said. "And I'm working on that."

"Good. I've been worried about you. Have you ever thought about getting out of clinical research and setting up your own practice?"

He had read her mind. In the night she had examined not only her failed relationship with Marshall, but her life's goals and expectations, too. Even when Marshall thought she volunteered time at the hospital, he had suggested she find another place to give her time, such as a hospital where children got well instead of died. A person could take only so much pressure, and she had had her limit.

"I've given it some thought lately," she said. "But I don't want to give up on the children."

"You wouldn't be. You'd be helping in another way. We don't know what causes leukemia, but keeping children healthy and discovering the disease early if it struck could give children a happy ending. Now, tell me the story behind the check you showed me last night."

Sarah finished relating the tale in a dispassionate voice then left for early church. She thought more about opening her own practice as she drove to her church.

As she studied the smiling faces in the children's choir, she imagined what it would be like to see children on a regular basis for healthy checkups instead of saying a final good-bye to them as she had Andrea.

She returned to the hospital a little after nine as she had promised Dr. Lewis she would check on him again. Besides, what else could she do with her Sunday? She did not want to be alone and let her mind focus on Marshall.

"Dr. Madison, you've had a message." A nurse stopped her at the main desk and handed her a phone slip.

Could it be that Marshall called at last? She was disappointed to read her parents' number on the message. With a heavy heart, she called home.

"Sarah, I knew you'd show up at the hospital," her mother said.

"Dr. Lewis has a broken leg and is our oldest patient now," she explained.

"Yes, I heard. A friend of your dad's called after your speech last night. He said you were fabulous. We're so proud. Are you working today?"

"No. Just checking on things."

"Good. If you and Marshall have no other plans, we were hoping you'd come out for Sunday dinner."

"Thanks, Mom, but Marshall has already gone back to Neosho."

"Oh, that's too bad. I was hoping to get to know him better. Well, next time he's up you could bring him out."

"There won't be a next time," Sarah admitted. She did not want to explain everything, but she did not want her mother harboring any false assumptions.

"What's wrong, Sarah?"

"We had a disagreement." That really simplified what had happened, but she could not tell her mother about the dare.

"Don't worry, dear. He'll be back. He's already told your dad that he plans to marry you if you'll have him."

"What?" Sarah could not believe what she heard. "What did you say?"

"Oops. I guess Marshall didn't get around to asking you before this little disagreement."

"He told Dad he wants to marry me?" Sarah had to have it exactly.

"Yes. That's what they were discussing in the kitchen Friday night. So, don't be too upset about your little spat, Sarah. It'll all work out, if you love him." Sarah could hear the question in her mother's voice.

"Yes, I do," Sarah said softly, and began unwinding the telephone cord she had twisted into a knot. "I know this seems sudden to you—"

"Not at all," her mother interrupted. "I knew I wanted to marry your father the night I met him. Some things are just meant to be. And I think you and Marshall make a strong couple."

"Yes, we do," Sarah agreed. "Thanks for the dinner invitation, but I think I'll decline. I need to talk to Marshall."

"Good idea, dear. Good luck."

"Thanks, Mom." Sarah hung up the receiver with a lighter heart. Surely Marshall would not have told her father he intended to marry her if he did not mean it.

With new hope, she fairly skipped to Dr. Lewis's room.

"Is there anything I can get for you, Doctor?" she asked.

"No, Sarah. Will you be back today?"

"Probably not. I'll be out of town most of the day." It all depended on Marshall. She could not discuss everything with him on the phone. She needed to see his eyes, read his expressions.

"Take care, Sarah. He'd better treat you right."

"What?"

"You came in here earlier like a whipped pup. Now your eyes are sparkling again. One plus one equals a man in your life and my guess is he's the one who attended the fashion show."

Sarah laughed. "You missed your calling. You should have been a detective." She sobered a bit. "I'll let you know how it works out." With a smile and a wave, she left the room and strode down the hospital corridor, and the minute she stepped outside, she ran for her car.

Pulling out a Missouri map from the glove compartment, she studied it a moment. Four lane highway most of the way. Her gas gauge registered full. She drove the most expedient route out of town and within minutes was on the highway heading south. She checked her watch. Nine-thirty exactly.

Marshall walked around the house and checked to see that no damage had been done to his house from wind or rain while he had been gone. Everything looked the same. The hills beckoned to him. He wanted to climb them, but time marched on.

It was ten-thirty before he had unpacked his luggage from the convention, showered, and driven to the hospital. His patients were all doing well. Even the elderly man with pneumonia was much better. Marshall read his latest X rays and agreed with Dr. Pierce's diagnosis. Only a slight shadow darkened one corner of one lung. The pneumonia was almost gone. Relieved that his patients were doing well, he now could turn his thoughts toward Sarah and get things straightened out with her.

He strode purposefully out of the hospital and headed his car for the open road.

Sarah had no idea where the Valley was. Marshall had said it was west of town. Finding the town was easy. Crisscrossing the country roads on the west side was making her more and more nervous about the coming confrontation with Marshall.

She did not know how she would start the conversation and hoped he would help her out. She would be honest and answer any questions he had about the dare. And she had a few questions of her own to ask, too.

She had not passed a farmhouse in the last quarter-mile and was ready to turn back and try another road when she saw the terraced hills ahead. He was right they did look like stairs for giants. A stone arch announced the entrance, right beside it stood a rural mailbox that read: ADAMS, ROUTE 3, BOX 14A.

She had found it! She followed the drive at least an eighth of a mile till she saw the house nestled in the Valley. It belonged there. The A-frame fit in with the terraced hills and tall trees that surrounded it.

She saw no movement anywhere. After parking her car in the graveled area beside a detached garage, she walked to the front porch, which held two rocking chairs at one end and a porch swing at the other. She stood in front of the door, took a deep breath, and rang the bell. No answer. She punched the doorbell again and waited.

He was not home. Where could he be? At the hospital? She walked dejectedly back toward her car, then veered to the garage. There were no windows in the garage door, but two high ones on the side. The window at the rear of the garage revealed a workshop, complete with table saw. Other woodworking tools sat neatly on shelves that lined the one wall she could see.

She did not know that Marshall liked to work with wood. It did not surprise her, though, that he would make things with his hands. But it did point out that there were many things she did not know about him.

The second window was just as revealing. The space for his car was empty. She had hoped he was walking around the hills, as he had told her he liked to do. Now what? Should she wait and hope he would return soon? Should she go to the hospital and try to catch him there? What if he never came home at all? She glanced at her watch. Twelve-thirty. Her stomach told her it was much later, since she had not eaten since a quick lunch the day before. She was finally hungry. No, she was ravenous.

For absolutely no reason, except frustration, she marched to the porch and rang the doorbell again. Reaching for the doorknob, she gave it a quick twist and was amazed when the door opened.

"Marshall?" she called before she stepped inside. She knew he was not there, but she called his name again anyway.

Feeling a little like Goldilocks, she looked around guiltily before she entered, searching for clues to Marshall's personality.

The living room looked neat, but unbalanced. A stone fireplace dominated the room and provided the focus for the conversation area. Instead of the couch facing the fireplace with chairs on each side, the couch was on the side with a big, brown, stuffed chair facing the fireplace. This must be his favorite chair. The ottoman was scooted out a ways from the chair, as if he had gotten up suddenly without pushing it back in place.

She moved quietly to the chair and sat down where he had been, how many hours ago? She knew he had been here the night before. The windows were opened, and the house had the faint smell of coffee. Climbing out of the deep chair, she walked to the kitchen. On the stove sat a skillet and spatula. Inside the dishwasher were dirty dishes from his breakfast. The refrigerator held the usual assortment of condiments, but lacked the perishables: milk, bacon, and so on. He had not gone shopping since he had been back. Maybe he was doing that now.

The stairs led to a loft with two bedrooms. One room served as a study. The other was his bedroom with the bed neatly made. The bathroom yielded more information. A towel, hanging next to the shower, was still damp from recent use.

The pieces of the puzzle were fitting together for Sarah, who thought Dr. Lewis was not the only one who could have been a detective. Marshall had come home and sat in the brown chair. He had taken a shower and had coffee and fixed something to eat in the skillet for breakfast. Probably an egg.

Eggs sounded pretty good to her right now. Not hesitating more than a moment, she descended the stairs to the kitchen.

Marshall stopped at the traffic light and turned right instead of going straight on the road that led to the highway. What had he read on his flip-a-day calendar that very morning while he was eating breakfast? "Sunday clears away the rust of the whole week." If ever he needed the rust cleared, today was the day. The digital clock on the dashboard told him it was past eleven. Church would have already started, but he turned back anyway and pulled into the parking lot five minutes later. He found a seat in the back pew and listened to the triumphant singing of the choir.

No soft hymns today, but loud alleluias and amens made the windows rattle. He felt his spirits being lifted with the music. When the last strong chords faded, the minister addressed the congregation. The sermon droned on and on, going well past the noon hour, but Marshall did not know what the minister had said. His heart and mind were talking to God about Sarah.

When the service ended, he felt more at peace. And he knew he needed to talk with the woman he loved. But he needed to tackle this in a systematic way. Instead of traipsing all over Kansas City looking for her, he would call first and tell her he was coming. This time when he reached the stop light, he turned toward home to call her. If she was not at her house or at the hospital or at her parents' home, he would head north anyway and have Maggie help him find Sarah. His arched entrance came into sight, and he felt a great relief. Why? He could not explain his feeling. He drove down the lane to his house, and as soon as he saw her car, he knew. God had answered his prayer to work things out with her. She was here, and he also knew everything would be wonderful between them. She would not have driven down here to gloat about the dare.

The front door stood open; he must have left the door unlocked, which he sometimes did. He did not worry about prowlers in the country. She must be inside, but he thought she would come out when he pulled up. He turned off the engine and heard music pouring from the open windows and door.

He smiled to himself. She was making herself right at home. Good. She might like it well enough to want to live here.

His shoes made a sharp tapping sound on the wooden planks of the porch, but still Sarah did not appear. He walked through the open doorway and into the entry. At first he did not see her, then he caught movement in the kitchen. He walked quietly toward her and stood beside the bar and waited.

Sarah had her back to him and was stirring something on the stove. Scrambled eggs. He could smell them now.

Suddenly, she stiffened. She had felt his presence. A whispered, "Marshall," escaped her lips as she turned around.

For a long moment they stared at each other across the room. "Sarah—"

"Marshall, we need to talk."

"Yes, we do," he agreed. "But first I suggest you take care of the eggs."

"Oh, no." The acrid smell of burning eggs reached her nose the second he mentioned them. She turned back to the stove, but it was too late. The eggs were scorched on the bottom and still raw on top. "Too late," she said as she carried the smoking skillet to the sink and deposited the mess in the garbage disposal.

"Too late for the eggs, but not too late for us." Marshall took her by the hand and led her to the living room. "I stopped to call you before I headed back to Kansas City. I wanted to talk to you in person."

She smiled as he motioned for her to sit in the big brown chair. He scooted the ottoman farther out and sat down facing her.

"Now," he said. "Let's hear about the dare."

"I can explain it all, but I'd like to hear about your dare, too."

He grimaced. "I figured you would. I guess we both have some explaining to do."

Sarah talked first and told him how many times she had started to tell him the truth about being a doctor. "When I took you to the hospital to see Andrea, I thought you'd find out without me telling you. I'm still amazed that no one called me Doctor."

"Why did you take the dare?" Marshall asked.

"I earned fifty-thousand dollars for leukemia research."

"Wow! I had no idea there was incentive like that. I'd have taken the dare myself." He reached for her hand and held it. "I thought it was a joke on me. After much thought, I knew there had to be more to it. That's why I was headed back to see you." He wanted to know one more thing and was apprehensive about bringing it up. If this were going to be an honest relationship, he had to be up front about anything that bothered him. He plunged ahead.

"What about Hal Mosley?"

"What about Hal?"

"Did he know about the dare? He hinted that you two were . . . more than friends."

"Why that jerk!" Sarah was indignant. "You pegged him right the night I introduced you. I've always known he's wanted more in our relationship than I was willing to give. He's a friend, although pompous at times, and he treats me in a condescending manner sometimes. But he knew nothing about the dare. I'm surprised he didn't give me away. Trust me, there's never been a relationship other than friendship between us."

Marshall sighed his relief. "That's what this whole misunderstanding is all about, isn't it? Trust. I'm sorry I didn't follow you home so we could explain everything in Kansas City instead of rushing back here like a hurt fool."

"You aren't a fool, but I know you were hurt."

"Devastated. I couldn't put the whole picture together. I knew you'd lied to me, and I thought the whole week was phony, yet I couldn't believe you were like that. The Sarah I know and love is warm, caring, sensitive, and has a wonderful sense of humor."

"A sense of humor? Really?" At his nod, she continued. "That's what started this whole bet. The Fab Five think I'm too serious and should let loose more. Now, let's hear about your dare," she said.

He stood up and crossed to the fireplace. "It started as a dare. I was attracted to you immediately, and the thought of spending time with you was more than appealing."

"By the way, there was a third dare."

His eyebrows shot up in question.

"We dared Maggie to get Jason to the fashion show without asking him. She used my dare to help her out. Sounds really juvenile, I know. She told Jason all about it."

"How did he take it?"

"The airlines are going to make a fortune on Denver-to-Kansas City airfares. They're going to take turns visiting each other while they get to know each other better. They've both had bad experiences, and they want to be sure before they make a permanent commitment."

"What about you?"

"Me?"

"Do you want more time to make sure, or will you marry me now?"

Sarah closed her eyes and leaned back in the chair. "There are lots of things I don't know about you, but I'm quite sure I want to spend the rest of my life finding out what they are."

"When, Sarah?" He took her hands in his and pulled her out of the chair and into his arms. They hugged each other, then Sarah lifted her face to receive his kiss.

The kiss was all she had hoped it would be. Anger was missing, but passion and love were in full force when his lips met hers. When he lifted his head, she withdrew slowly.

"Just name the day," he said.

"A month from now." That would give her mother time to arrange a small wedding and let her give notice at the hospital. "We have a few problems to work out."

"Problems?"

"Not major. Just logistics. I have a job in Kansas City, and you have a practice here."

"I'd like to keep my practice, but I could start over if necessary."

"I've been thinking about working in another hospital away from terminally ill children. I've reached my limit. When one of them dies, a little of me dies, too. For now I need to help children get well. Is there a pediatrician in Neosho?"

"You know," he said with a grin, "we don't have a children's specialist here."

"Good."

He kissed her again. When he finished the kiss, she pulled away and grinned up at him.

"Right now I'm so hungry I can hardly think. I haven't eaten since yesterday."

"Come to the kitchen, and I'll rustle something up. Then I'll show you around the Valley and the hills, starting with a tour of your soon-to-be new home. I think you'll love it here."

"Yes, I daresay I will."

A Class of Her Own

by Janice Thompson

This book is dedicated to my mother, Shirley Moseley, an amazing woman of God who, like the heroine in this story, has endured many hardships and come through them all a victor in Christ. In my eyes she will always be in "A Class of Her Own." I love you, Mom.

1

*L*aura Chapman stood at the kitchen table, anxiously wringing her hands. Something needed to be said, but could she say it? She fought to summon the courage. "I, uh, I'm—"

"What is it, Mom?" nineteen-year-old Jessica asked impatiently. "What's wrong?" She continued to clear the dinner dishes from the table, oblivious to her mother's struggle.

"Oh, nothing," Laura stammered, trying to compose herself. This shouldn't be so difficult. She had been through much tougher things than this, especially lately. "See, it's like this, Jessica." She drew a deep breath. "I'm going back to school." *There. No turning back.*

"What did you say?" Jessica looked shocked. The butter knife slipped out of her hand, clattering onto the oak table.

"I said, I'm going back to school." Laura Chapman spoke the words in her most determined voice, though she couldn't seem to hide the tremor. She had wanted to talk to her two kids about this for days. Time wouldn't allow her to wait any longer. If she didn't register by tomorrow, there would be no chance—at least not this semester.

"But Mom," Jess argued, "school?"

"Mom's too cool for school," fifteen-year-old Kent said, entering the room with music blasting from the earphones of his portable CD player.

"It's definitely not that." Jessica ignored his obvious attempt at sarcasm. "It's just that you're so, so—"

"So what?" Their eyes met for a showdown of wills.

"Well, you're so—" her daughter stammered, suddenly falling silent.

"Old?" Kent offered, turning up his music to deafen his mother's response.

"Thanks a lot." Laura felt an odd mixture of emotions rise within her as both kids shrugged their response. *I should have expected this.* She tossed her wavy brown hair defiantly, something she would have done at her daughter's age. "You think I'm too old?"

"It's not just that," Jessica argued. "You haven't been to school in, what's it been—nineteen years?"

"Twenty, but I'm sure I could do it." She needed a vote of confidence, a confirmation. For nearly three years since her husband lost his fight with colon cancer, Laura Chapman lingered on the verge of depression. They were cold, hard years, laced with self-pity and fear. But Laura refused to give in. She forced herself to get out of bed every morning, dragging herself back and forth to the bookstore where she worked, though it proved to be the toughest thing she had ever done.

When Greg passed away, something in her died too. She seemed to grow more numb by the day, unable to feel much of anything, unable to dream, to hope. Only in recent days had she begun to come alive again, started to view "tomorrow" as something more than an empty hole to be filled. Surely her children would understand and offer moral support when she most needed it.

"Mom, you just don't understand."

Help me understand. Laura looked into the deep green eyes of her eldest child, her beautiful Jessica—her jewel, her prize. The spitting image of her father, Jessica stood tall and slender, with sleek auburn hair and a light spray of freckles that danced across her cheeks. Her passionate interest in the arts seemed to grow daily, just as Greg's had. She had inherited both his ear for fine music and an eye for the artistic. A fine pianist, Jess always seemed to excel at everything she put her hand to. The grand piano in the living room reminded Laura daily of Greg. He had given it to their precious daughter nearly seven years ago as down payment on her future in the field of music. Now it stood as a reminder that things didn't always work out as planned.

Thankfully, Jessica reconciled herself to studying music at Wainesworth Junior College, a far cry from the university education the anxious teen had craved. She endured it all with little argument—just one in a long list of necessary sacrifices.

Greg would have made sure she received all she needed and more. Laura sighed as she reflected on her husband's great love for their family. A smile instinctively crossed her lips. Just thinking about him could transport her back to better times. Romantic and funny, he had been the perfect mate. There had been a sensitive side to him as well, one that many men did not possess. What amazing memories Laura held of their years together. Their God-given love had run deep. Greg had truly loved her as Christ loved the church, and being his wife had been an honor.

Lord, I miss him so much. No other man could come close to Greg. He'd given of himself day after day, working hard to provide for their family. He'd made himself available to the children and had been genuinely interested in their wants and needs. He'd planned so much for them, so much more than she could give them.

Her daughter's dancing green eyes proved to be a reminder of his spunk, his tenacity, and his undying love. Jessica was, in every way, Greg's child. And yet, Laura had to admit, her eldest also bore a determination that trickled down from Laura herself—a stubbornness that could only be traced back to her own side of the family.

"What don't I understand?" Laura asked, coming back to life again. Surely her daughter could come up with nothing that she hadn't already considered herself. She had argued the negatives and positives of this decision with herself for several nights as she twisted and turned in the sheets.

"Things aren't like they were when you were in school, Mom. They'll eat you alive in college." Jessica gave her a confident, knowing look, one that could not be ignored.

Kent added his two cents' worth. "Yeah, no kidding."

"Thanks for the vote of confidence." Laura's oversensitive heart felt the betrayal, but she bore it with a stiff upper lip.

"Anything I can do to help, Mom." Kent shuffled from the room, earphones still tightly attached and music blaring as loudly as ever.

Jess shook her head, obviously unwilling to give up the fight.

"Mom, you don't get it. The students are really crude, the professors are even worse, and the workload is a killer. I barely made it last semester myself. You see how it is. I had homework every night last year—hours of it. How would you make it with your job?"

"I can work part-time at the store in the afternoons and evenings, and take morning classes. Besides, if God is for me, and I'm convinced He is, who can be against me?"

"I'm not trying to discourage you," her daughter said with a shrug. "I just want you to be practical, that's all. One of us has to be."

"I am very practical," Laura argued. *I've got a solid plan, a good plan. It will work. You'll see.* "Lots of people do this."

"Young people," Jessica argued, lips tight. "Some of them don't make it when they're working and going to school. Remember Bridget Kester? She dropped out of college last spring because she couldn't seem to pass any of her classes. She tried to work at the health club and go to school at the same time. College is tough. And she's young. Bridget's my age."

"I know how old she is, Jessica." *Lord, help me keep my temper in check.* "But you're not giving me much credit. It's not like I haven't been to school before." Laura felt her zeal begin to wane.

"Twenty years ago."

"What difference does it make, really? Besides, we're only talking junior college here—not graduate school. I want to get my associate's degree. That's all. I've wanted it for years. I gave up college when you came along, so I never had the chance to—"

"I know, Mom. You've told me a hundred times." Jessica's face twisted slightly, an indication she already carried the guilt of this situation.

Oh, but it was worth every moment just to be with you. Don't you realize that? Haven't I told you enough? Laura carefully reworded her story. "Jessica, I went to college for one year before I married your father. The second—well, the second year was tough. When you're a new bride, setting up house and caring for your husband feels like the most important thing. Marriage can be a little distracting when you're in school." She smiled, remembering those early days—how torn she had been between schoolwork and decorating their first little apartment. Greg had been so proud of her as she chose fabrics and stitched curtains herself. He lovingly helped her hang them, commenting on their beauty. They'd ended up in each other's arms, curtains hanging lopsided from the rod above.

No, there hadn't been much time left for schoolwork. Not then, anyway.

Laura composed herself, continuing on. "At the beginning of the next semester, I found out you were coming. I just couldn't make myself go back. I never could."

But there were no regrets anymore, not about school anyway. Ever since the catalog had come in the mail three weeks ago, Laura had been making her plans, calculating, counting the cost. She would go back to college, and nothing would stop her.

"It's your decision, Mom," Jessica said, clearly exasperated. "Even if it's the wrong one."

Laura shook her head in disbelief. "I love you, Jess. And I want the best for all of us." She turned toward the bedroom, hoping a few minutes alone would put an end to her frustration. She headed to the vanity, where she sat gazing long and hard at her reflection. "I look as tired as I feel." Her weariness would surely increase as she took on the added responsibility of school on top of a job and child rearing. *I need Your strength, Lord.*

Though she fought to remain strong, her faith had weakened over the last three years, truth be told. Still determined to remain close to Him, Laura found herself calling on the Lord more as the months crawled by. Her moments with Him brought genuine comfort. *"I will never leave you nor forsake you."* The familiar Scripture ran through her mind. Laura contemplated the words. *Lord, why can't I feel Your presence like I used to?*

Everything felt different now that Greg was gone. He had been such a good spiritual leader—making sure everyone went to church on Sunday, teaching Sunday school, praying with the kids before bed. Lately, she couldn't even seem to get out of bed on Sunday mornings. Her church attendance had wavered over the last few months. It seemed she found an excuse to stay home nearly every week now. *It's just so much easier.* Facing those happy, carefree people proved far too difficult.

Laura ran a brush through her wavy hair, trying to style it in several different ways. No matter how long she messed with it, the stubborn stuff would only do the same old thing it always had. Her waves cooperated in one direction and only one. She tossed the brush down onto the vanity, ready to admit defeat.

Laura sighed, gazing at the mirror. *Who are you?* she asked the face staring back at her. *I don't really know you anymore. Can you be more than a wife and mother? Can you be a student too?* An uncomfortable silence lingered in the air.

Reaching over to the bedside table, she picked up the catalog one last time before turning in for the night. In order to obtain the associate's degree she craved, a serious workload lay before her. But, after all she had been through in the last year, it should be a piece of cake. She ran her fingers over the cover, her index finger tracing the letters "Wainesworth Junior College."

Laura caught a glimpse of her own smile in the mirror. *Nothing to be ashamed of. I have a perfect right to smile. After all, this marks the beginning of a brand-new adventure for me.*

∿

Professor Andrew Dougherty sat at his computer, scrolling to an American Revolution Web site with renewed zeal. The red, white, and blue background held his interest for awhile, though his computer seemed to be dragging tonight. "Too many graphics," he observed.

A history buff, Andrew had much to glean from the Web. With only a few days before school began, he certainly didn't have much time to put together a comprehensive list of applicable sites for his students. He sat back, rubbing at his eyes. The monitor had really done a number on his vision. The flag's colors were all melting into one rather lackluster shade of gray.

Andrew glanced at the clock on the computer—2:45 A.M. "No way." Had he really been on-line that long? Where had the time gone? Too many nights he seemed to sit alone in this chair, wasting the hours. They always managed to slip by like minutes.

Too much time on the Web, old man. Not that he was old, and not that he had much else to do with his time. Still a bachelor at forty-seven, Andrew found himself completely disinterested in things that had appealed to him in his younger years. The Internet had become a friend and companion, filling his evenings with unspoken words and genuine satisfaction. With so many sites to see, chat rooms to visit and E-mails to send out, he could easily waste a full evening. Most nights were spent browsing the Web, when he wasn't up to his ears with papers to grade.

Andrew sighed, thinking about his upcoming classes at the college. He leaned back so far in the chair that it almost toppled over. "Careful now!" He nervously typed in the address to a familiar site. He had heard about it through a chat room he frequented—a computerized dating service. "$29.95," the header read. "Money-back guarantee." Andrew had, for some time, toyed with the idea of actually filling out the form and entering a credit card number. It was a game he played with himself quite often these days.

But how would he put it? His mind began to wander. "Charming middle-aged man—" No. That wouldn't work. Middle-aged would be a definite turnoff. "Charming, academic forty-something." Nah. But what could he say? How could he possibly begin to describe himself? How did people do that?

His fingers began to trip nimbly across the keys—his heart suddenly releasing him to be free with his thoughts. "Ready for love."

Had he really typed that? After fifteen years of dealing with a broken heart, the time for a change was rapidly approaching. His last relationship had left him wounded in a way that he never wanted to repeat.

Smiling, he continued on. "Romeo is ready to meet his Juliet. Tall . . ." Hmmm. A bit of a stretch, perhaps, since he stood at five-nine. "Tanned." He'd be sure to visit a tanning booth as soon as possible. "Blond, wavy hair." "Sandy" would have been a better word, but who cared? And "unruly curls" might have been a more accurate description, but did it really matter? It wasn't like he was actually going to send this thing off, anyway.

Andrew stared at the screen, facing the next question with some scrutiny. Hobbies. They wanted to know what he did for fun. In all honesty, he sat at the computer and scrolled the World Wide Web for fun. But that didn't really sound right. "Romantic walks on the beach," he typed, smiling. South Texas beaches seemed tolerable enough, he supposed—as long as people weren't crammed onto every square inch of them. Besides, that's what ads like these were supposed to say. "Books." That much was true. "And movies." That one wasn't far off either.

There. All done. Andrew's heart pounded in his ears. His palms grew sweatier with each keystroke. The undeniable had occurred. He had actually completed the form. A first. All he needed to do was pull out that credit card and—

"Wait a minute!" he said, startled. "Just what do you think you're doing?" He quickly closed out the site, turning off the computer with a vengeance. This time he had come too close for comfort.

No need to worry about that. The peace and quiet would end soon enough. Within days, his hours would be filled with the usual hustle and bustle of college students entering and exiting his classroom. He felt his pulse slowing as his mind shifted to the thing he loved most. American history. A subject I can handle. No great risks there.

There seemed to be a certain comfort to teaching history at Wainesworth Junior College. So what if his classroom had a revolving door? Students enrolled, came, then left quickly. Lazy. So many of them just don't know what it means to earn their grades. So he might be a little tough. There were far worse things a teacher could be accused of. No shame in admitting he made his students work hard. Most lived easy lives—too easy, to his way of thinking. His college professors had been plenty tough on him, preparing him for life. These students needed to be just as prepared. He would give them all a fresh dose of reality.

Laura tossed and turned in the bed, trying to sleep. Her excitement wouldn't allow it—at least, not yet. She made out the glowing yellow numbers on the clock: 2:34 A.M. Even if she managed to doze off, she would only get in five hours. I don't want to run the risk of getting off to *a bad start. Not on such an important day.* Laura propped herself up on three pillows, thinking through her class schedule once again.

Her thoughts held her captive, as they so often did these days. Laura had far too much on her mind to sleep. What would she say to Greg, if she had the chance to talk to him? How would she explain her decision about going back to school? She could see his smiling face in front of her, nodding as she explained herself away. His auburn hair shimmered in the afternoon sunlight as he listened intently, and his cheeks held the color of a healthy man.

But she would never talk to Greg again. She would never know how he might have felt about this. As difficult as it might be, she had to begin making her own decisions and sticking with them.

Laura listed the courses in her head again, just to be sure she hadn't forgotten anything. Tomorrow would be a critical day, and she didn't want to risk anything going wrong.

$\mathcal{E}$xcuse me. I wonder if you could direct me to the admissions office." Laura's voice trembled with a mixture of nerves and excitement.

The woman in front of her looked too young for college. *"You think you're getting old when high school students start looking like kids, but you know you're getting old when college students look like kids."* They were Greg's words. She remembered them as clearly as if he had just spoken them.

The girl turned, looking at her curiously. "Up those stairs," she said in a cheery, youthful voice. "Take a left at the first hallway, then follow it all the way to the end. Turn right and go about twenty feet, and then take another right. About three hallways up on the left you turn again. You should see admissions directly in front of you. There's a bright blue sign just above the door."

Laura couldn't be sure she had absorbed the directions, but she didn't ask the young girl to repeat herself. *This is all so embarrassing, and I feel so out of place.* "Oh, uh, thank you." She found herself distracted by the girl's eyeliner. It was a little too thick on the right eye and smeared a little on the left, a sure sign of puberty. Her skirt was short—a little too short, to Laura's way of thinking.

"Are you registering a son or a daughter?" the girl asked.

How embarrassing. How totally, completely embarrassing. Of course, Laura couldn't blame her for making the assumption. If she had a lick of sense, she would turn around and walk out the door. Instead, Laura shook her head. "I, uh, I'm signing up. I mean I'm going to start classes here." She spoke the words half ashamed, half proud.

"Really?" A sudden look of interest filled the girl's dark brown eyes. "Well, I'm happy to hear it. We need more people your age. I'm Kaycie Conner, head of the English Department."

"What?" Laura tried to decipher this new information, to work it into the equation, but it just didn't seem to compute. *No way.*

"I, uh, I'm Laura Chapman. I'm hoping to get my associate's degree." Her ability to speak coherently seemed to be slipping away more with each passing moment.

The woman nodded and smiled. "Well, good luck to you. Let me know if there's anything I can do to help."

Laura focused on the young woman as she walked away, unable to speak a word. She began to walk in the direction Ms. Conner had pointed, hoping she'd heard correctly. Her heels clicked against the white tile floor, creating a melancholy echo. The sound seemed to scream out, "Look at me," when she really wanted to disappear into the woodwork. At the end of the hallway, Laura turned and headed up the stairs. Which was it again? Right, left, left, right—or left, right, right, left?

Gratefully, at the top of the stairs, an "Admissions" sign pointed to the left. She followed a trail of clues until she reached the proper office. Finally. The big blue sign. She breathed a sigh of relief, happy to be at her destination. Not that it made much difference. The line went on forever.

Laura took her place at the end of the line, feeling like a wall flower at a junior high school dance. She half-listened, half-ignored a host of young students as they rambled on and on about this professor and that, griping and cursing. Their language proved to be almost as unforgivable as their attitudes. Jessica had been right about one thing: Teenagers were different these days. Crudeness seemed to be the rule of the day. This amazed yet frightened her.

Off in the corner, a couple stood with their lips locked. *Best to ignore them.* Laura pulled out her catalog for one last excited look at her possibilities. There would be no room for mistakes. She had to get this right. She thumbed through the book, closing it willfully. Her mind drifted ahead, into the vast unknown. *Perhaps someday I'll own my own bookstore. It might be a dream but not an unrealistic one.* She would have not only the courage to achieve it but the wherewithal to accomplish it. She would be bold, confident, daring . . .

"Next."

Laura looked up, shocked to find herself at the front of the line. She gazed into the eyes of a young man, about twenty-one or so. He looked tired and irritable.

"Can I help you, Ma'am?" His curt words startled her. "We're about to close."

"Uh, yes. I—"

"Are you here to sign up for classes?" he snapped, glancing down at his watch.

"Yes, I am. Am I too late?"

"That depends. Have you seen a counselor?"

"Yes," Laura spoke quickly. "He gave me this." She pushed a card across the counter, smiling in his direction.

His face softened a little as he read it. "Ah. Working on your degree, huh?"

"Yes." Laura smiled, energized at his sudden interest.

"Don't sweat it, Sister," he said. "I'm in the same boat. Most of these kids are."

"Really?" *Not that I'm your sister. And not that I'm a kid.*

"Toughest thing is American History, at least for me. Looks like you're gonna end up with Dougherty. He's the only one still taking students." At that, he let out a whistle.

"What? What's wrong with Dougherty?"

"Harsh guy. He makes his students work twice as hard as the others. But you'll make it. You look pretty tough."

Tough? She suddenly didn't feel very tough.

❧

Andrew entered the empty room with a large cardboard box in hand. He always loved this part of the year—setting up his classroom. He looked forward to it with an unashamed vengeance. American history would soon come alive for a new group of students. He would see to it. On the other hand, if it didn't come alive to them, he would see to a few other things—like a few extra assignments, for example.

Excitedly, the professor began pulling maps from the box. One by one, he secured them to the wall. Lovingly, he ran his fingers across the brightly colored map of North America, tracing the path he had taken from Florida, the place of his birth, to Texas, where he found himself planted. Hot and muggy, it certainly hadn't proven to be the location of his dreams, but at least he could work in the one field that made him happy. Not everyone could say that.

Andrew backed away from the wall, looking at it carefully, curiously. There seemed to be something missing, but he couldn't quite put his finger on it. *Ah, yes.* He groped through the box, searching for his prized copy of the Declaration of Independence that lay inside.

"There you are," he said with a proud smile. "Thought you could hide from me, eh?"

He unrolled it carefully, reading as he went along. The edges were frayed and the printing worn, but the words still captivated him, kept him locked in their grip—even after all these years. The founding fathers had worked diligently on the vital document so that he could have freedom, so that he could one day live out the American dream. Just the idea brought a rush of patriotic pride.

"Better get ahold of yourself," Andrew said, shaking his head. "People might start to think you've got a screw loose."

Ah, let them talk. Folks already thought he was an oddball, anyway—forty-seven and still single. They had their probing speculations, to be sure, though he did his best to ignore them. Why bore them with the details, anyway? His heartbreak fifteen years ago wasn't any of their business. They didn't need to know the one woman he had ever given his heart to jilted him.

No, no one at Wainesworth Junior College would ever have to know.

❧

Laura left the crowded college bookstore with five minutes to spare. Her arms were loaded with textbooks in varying shapes, sizes, and colors. They had to be carried out to the car—which was parked over a half mile away in the farthest parking lot. The momentous stack of books blocked her vision, and her arms ached already.

Laura turned the corner and ran headlong into a tall man with sandy-colored hair. Her books tumbled to the tile floor with a crash, scattering about in every conceivable direction. Her purse flew from her arm, hitting him squarely in the belly. He doubled over instinctively.

"I'm—I'm so sorry!" Laura said, dropping to her knees. *I won't look into his eyes. I can't. This is so embarrassing.* "Really, I just wasn't looking where I was going." Her heart beat loudly in her ears. She found herself eyeball-to-eyeball with a man, a nice-looking man, and it scared the living daylights out of her.

"No problem." He reached down to help her pick the books up. "But that purse of yours packs a pretty heavy punch."

Laura groaned loudly. "I'm sorry. I really am."

"You might want to invest in a backpack before classes start next week," he said with a grin. "That's what most of the students carry. You are a student, aren't you?"

Laura looked up at him, grateful for the acknowledgment. "Yes, I am." Frankly, she was so relieved to see someone her own age, she hardly knew what to say. *Hopefully, he's a student too.* His curly hair was a little unkempt, but not unforgivably so. Their eyes met in an embarrassed glance. The gentleman placed her American History book on top of the pile, looking at her intently.

"Are you taking American History?"

Why is he staring at me? Laura wondered, fighting to balance the stack of books.

"Yes, I just signed up, but I'm not looking forward to it." She shuddered, remembering what the young man at registration had said.

"Why is that?" The stranger reached to catch the history book as it slid from her grip again.

"Oh," she said, clutching it tighter. "It's not the class. It's the professor."

"Really?" He looked at her curiously. "Who do you have?"

"Dougherty. I hear he's tough. Really tough."

"Tough, huh?"

"Yeah," she said with a sigh. "Hope I'm up for it. What about you?"

"Me?" he said with a look of chagrin. "Me? I'm late for a meeting. Have a nice day." He turned abruptly and walked in the opposite direction.

$\mathcal{L}$ aura buzzed around the kitchen in happy anticipation. Once the registration process drew to its logical conclusion, she finally enjoyed a good night's sleep. The world suddenly seemed a much brighter place. *I'm going to make it.* Laura took a sip from her cup of coffee, glancing out the kitchen window. The yard needed mowing, but even that didn't deter her this morning.

Kent, walked in, yawning. "Morning, Mom." He looked groggy. "What's for breakfast?"

"I signed up for classes yesterday," Laura said excitedly. It wasn't exactly "bacon and eggs," or "good morning," but it seemed to be the only thing that would come out of her mouth. She didn't even try to disguise her zeal.

"Yeah, Jessica told me," he replied with a shrug. "She's pretty bummed."

Immediately, Laura felt her expression change. Jessica must really be upset if she took the time to talk to her brother about it. She rarely talked to Kent about anything.

"It's cool, Mom," Kent continued, pulling open a loaf of bread. "You do what you have to do. Don't let her get to you. I know I never do."

"I won't." Laura said the words but didn't really know if she meant them—at least not yet. Truth was, Jessica did get to her. She always got to her.

"When do your classes start?" Kent reached to stick two pieces of bread in the toaster.

"Next Monday." Laura took another sip of her hot coffee, deep in thought.

"Doesn't seem fair," he said, frustrated. "We've already been in school a week."

"I know. But I'm sure you'll have an easier time than I will."

"That's putting it mildly," Jessica said, entering the room. "What classes did you sign up for, anyway?" She sat at the table, reaching for the nearly empty box of cereal.

Ah. So you're speaking to me, eh? Maybe this wouldn't be so bad. "I'm taking Algebra, English, and a fitness class," Laura said. "Oh, and I managed to sign up for American History. That's the one I'm worried about."

"American History?" Jess looked concerned.

"What's wrong, Honey?" Her heart began to pound, dreading a confrontation.

"Nothing. At least not yet." There was an undeniable edge to her voice. "Who's your professor?"

"Dougherty."

Jess turned white. "Not the one-fifteen class."

"Well, yes," Laura said. "Why?"

"I already told you, Mother." Her daughter's voice was laced with anger. "I told you I had an American History class at one-fifteen."

"But you said your professor's name was Miller—or something like that. It's not like I planned this. In fact, I was very careful to avoid this situation."

"When I went to sign up, Miller's class was full," Jess explained. "And I got stuck with Dougherty. Trust me, he's the last one on the planet I ever wanted."

"What's wrong with him?" Laura asked, more than a little curious. "Surely he can't be as bad as everyone makes him out to be."

"He works his students to death, and I've already got too many other classes to worry about. But I had made up my mind to get through it somehow. If I had known . . ."

"Neither of us could have known," Laura argued. "I guess it just couldn't be helped. He was the only professor still taking students at that time."

"I know, I know. But can't you take history at another hour?"

"No, I really can't." Laura couldn't possibly adjust her schedule.

Everything had been carefully arranged. She needed to be at work by three in the afternoon.

"Mother, you don't understand. I *have* to take an American History class. It's required."

"And you don't seem to understand. I *have* to take it just like you do. I'm working on my degree too."

Shaking her head in defeat, Jessica turned and left the room.

Andrew sat at the small, round breakfast table, swallowing a fried egg and two pieces of bacon. His morning routine hadn't changed in decades. He carefully wiped the edges of his mouth, feeling the draw of the computer. *I've probably got just enough time to check my E-mail before heading up to the college.* Andrew hoped to find something special today—a letter from a colleague with important news.

He placed his plate in the dishwasher, realizing it would be several more meals before he had enough dishes in there to actually warrant turning the dumb thing on. Sooner or later, the plate would get washed. Living alone had its benefits. Anything beat a sink full of dirty dishes and toys lining the stairs. That would be awful. Probably.

Using an antibacterial spray, Andrew wiped down the counter meticulously—not just once but twice. He couldn't be too careful. With school starting in a few days, there would be enough germs to battle in the classroom.

He made his way into the small cubbyhole he called an office and turned on his computer. Barely three months old, it flew on with great speed. Andrew enjoyed investing in the latest technology. He had to keep up with the times, especially today. What else did he have to spend his money on, anyway? *It's not like I have a wife and kids to support.*

"Snap out of it," he said aloud, shaking his head. He didn't need a reminder about marriage, at least not yet. He sat in silence as the computer booted up, then raced to sign on-line. *Today's the day.*

The familiar "You've Got Mail" rang out, creating a little stir. He scrolled through the pieces of E-mail, mostly junk. No letter. He sat back in the chair, feeling the rejection intensely. Hadn't Joe said he would write back today with news of . . .

Aw, what difference did it make anyway? No woman on the planet would be interested in him, blind date or otherwise. Andrew snapped the computer off, not even bothering to shut it down in the usual fashion. He stared at the black monitor, deep in thought.

Karen. He thought about her every day. She was the first thing to cross his mind in the morning, and the last thing he reflected on at night. His Karen.

Just out of graduate school, Andrew had met Professor Karen Norris at a dinner for incoming staff. Of course, that had been light-years ago, in a completely different state. But he had noticed her the minute she walked in the room—dark hair, slim figure, deep brown eyes. Perfect in every way. Karen.

Well, almost every way. They had connected on more than an intellectual level. He fell head over heels for her, and she had for him—at least, that's the way it looked and felt at the time. Their years together escalated into plans for matrimony, a state he had grown to desire. They planned, plotted, and strategized. The future looked like a field of endless possibilities.

And then . . .

Andrew pushed himself up from the chair. *I won't play this game today. Thousands of times I've thought about her, and where has it gotten me?*

No. Today the whole world lay at his feet.

⚓

Laura threw a load of clothes into the washer, thoughtlessly tossing in a cupful of detergent. She missed the mark only slightly—about half of the detergent landed on the washer and the other half in it. "What are you doing?" Scolding herself, she swept her hand across the gritty stuff, brushing it into the machine. She slammed the lid shut, turned the button on, and leaned back against the washer to think.

Lord, this isn't working out like I need it to. Show me what to do, Father. Her mind couldn't seem to release the earlier conversation with

Jessica. Going back to school might be impossible. Doing so would humiliate her daughter. That much had been made painfully clear.

The hum of the washer coursed her thoughts along. She had already invested so much money into the venture. She couldn't possibly stop payment on the checks she had written. That would be impractical, and she would end up feeling foolish about the whole thing.

Laura turned to look at the kitchen table, piled high with textbooks. She sighed deeply, making her way over to them. She had really looked forward to the fitness class, and the English class too. Algebra would be a challenge, but her determination could see her through that, even if it meant spending extra hours in the math lab. But American History—that presented a completely different problem, one she couldn't seem to find an answer to. Laura ran her fingers over the cover of the American History textbook. A picture of the Liberty Bell adorned the front of the book, pealing out the message of freedom, liberty, and failure.

Was this really all that divided her from Jessica—a crazy American History book? Irritated, Laura tossed it on the floor.

$\mathcal{L}$ aura picked up the telephone to call her mother for a heart-to-heart chat. Somehow, with all she had been through in the last few years, she craved her mother's companionship most. Perhaps the fact that her mom had already walked this road ahead of her drew them together.

Laura's own father passed away in his forties, the victim of a massive heart attack. Her mother limped through the grieving process and somehow managed to come through it a stronger woman. She managed to transition from victim to victor. Her great faith pulled her through. She'd never let go of the Lord's hand. Her marriage to Buck a few years later led to many happy, comfortable years. Buck was wonderful for her mother. His personality proved to be as refreshing and down-to-earth as his name.

"Mom?"

"Laura? I was hoping you'd call today. I've just got a few minutes. My quilting club meets in half an hour at the church." Somehow just hearing her mother's voice sent a wave of happiness through her. Her mom reflected such joy—and peace. She always seemed to ride a wave of tranquility. Laura needed that.

"I know, Mom. I just needed someone to talk to for a couple of minutes."

"What's up, Laura?"

She felt the familiar knot in her throat. "I went to the college yesterday." She tried to keep her voice steady.

"Good for you." Her mother's voice rose in pitch. "Just what I wanted to hear. Well, how did it go?"

"Not bad, really," Laura said, dabbing at her eyes with a tissue. "But I've upset Jessica."

"Jessica?" Her mother's voice changed slightly. "What's wrong with our girl?"

"She doesn't want me to go to school with her, and I'm not so sure it's the right thing anymore."

The silence on the other end startled her. When her mother finally spoke, the voice seemed exceptionally stern. "You mean to tell me you're going to let your nineteen-year-old daughter control your chances for happiness?"

Wow. Quite a comment from a woman who prides herself on her soft, gentle nature.

"I wouldn't go that far, Mom," Laura said, choosing her words carefully. "She's had such a hard time since Greg died—in some ways, even harder than Kent. And she's enjoying college so far. I don't want to ruin that experience for her."

"Listen to me, Laura Marie," her mother said, suddenly sounding quite motherly. "Once upon a time I almost let you do the same thing to me, remember?"

Laura did remember, and the memory still carried the guilty sting of a teen who had treated her mother badly. *I was so young then and so selfish. If I had it all to do over again, I would . . .*

"There was a time many years ago when I almost stopped my relationship with your stepfather before it started."

Laura remembered all too well. She had behaved very badly. But Buck hadn't seemed right for her mother—at least not at first. Of course, time proved differently, and the guilt she carried over her childish behavior still plagued her from time to time. *We make mistakes when we're young, but time has a way of teaching us the lessons we need to learn.*

"I had just met Buck," her mother continued, "and he invited me out to dinner. You told me, quite bluntly, if I recall, that if I went out to dinner with him, you would never speak to me again."

The knot in Laura's throat began to grow. "But I didn't mean that, Mom. It was just the grief of losing Daddy speaking." Twinges of guilt gnawed at her again.

"Same with Jessica," her mother said firmly. "Just listen to me. I went on and defied you, taking the risk you wouldn't speak to me. Oh, I knew you would eventually, but I really worried my decision might cause a rift in our relationship. I went ahead and did what my heart told me to do."

"And it's all worked out for the best, hasn't it, Mom?" Laura knew she spoke the truth. No doubt about that. Buck had turned out to be the best thing that could have ever happened to her mother.

"All for the best," the older woman said confidently. "But not without a lot of prayer on my part. Maybe that's what's missing here, Laura. Have you really prayed about your decision to go back to college?"

"Yes, Mom. I've prayed about it for weeks." *I've asked for direction from the very beginning.*

"How do you feel when you've prayed?"

Laura thought about that a moment before answering. Except for the small jittery moments, she had been comforted by an incredible amount of serenity about the decision. "I've had peace," she said, "until now."

"So what you're telling me is you're going to let Jessica disrupt the one decision that has brought you peace?"

"Well, when you put it that way . . ." Laura felt a resurgence of energy. She'd been excited by the idea of going back to school from the very beginning. It seemed so right.

It *was* so right. Suddenly everything became very clear. "Mom, you're a miracle worker."

"All mothers are. Just keep your wits about you when Jessica gets her skirts all twisted up in a knot. Don't let her control you. Stop it before it starts. You do what's best for you."

"I love you, Mom." The words were heartfelt, genuine. Laura only hoped someday she might be half as amazing as her own mother.

❧

Andrew yawned, carefully folding the evening paper. Politics—the usual rhetoric. That's all he encountered as he glanced through the pages. "Not much worth reading about." But what else could he do? He could squander a few minutes going over notes for his first lecture on the Vikings' exploration of America, but he'd given that lecture dozens of times before. Nothing new there. What would be new was the much-awaited E-mail from colleague Joe Morris about the promised blind date. He leaned back against the couch cushions, trying to imagine what she might look like.

Funny, the only face that flashed before him was that of the woman in the hallway at school—the one with the American History book. Andrew suddenly found himself irritated. *I felt sure she would be a great student, a hard worker. But it looks like she's going to turn out to be just like so many of the others.*

Lazy.

❧

"Jess, you're home!" Laura looked into her daughter's eyes. They were red and swollen, along with the tip of her nose—a sure sign something was amiss. "What's wrong?"

"Nothing." Jessica headed toward her room, focus shifting down toward the floor.

Something was wrong, all right. "Jess, tell me."

"It's nothing, Mom."

"Well, I need to tell you something." Laura heard the quiver in her voice as she spoke. She didn't want to hurt her daughter but had to speak these words.

"What, Mom?"

"I've decided I'm going to go—"

Jessica's bloodshot eyes looked directly into hers.

"I'm going back to school, Jess—even if you don't understand. I have to. It's the hardest thing I've ever done, but it's the right thing for me—for all of us."

❧

Andrew tossed and turned in the bed, a Technicolor dream enveloping him. He stood near the door of his car, just about to step inside when a beauty with dark brown hair walked up to him.

"Have you got the time?" she asked, eyes glowing. Her soft, pretty face captivated him. Her hair, tied back with a yellow ribbon, flowed down to her waist.

"I've got nothing but time," he answered, swinging the door open. His voice remained rock-solid, his hands steady.

She looked at him with a smile, and his heart began to beat wildly. She clearly seemed interested in him. He would do his best to impress her. "What've you got in mind?" he asked, trying to look casual.

"I was just thinking . . . ," she said demurely.

"Yes?"

"I was just thinking," she said with a smile, "that if you've got the time—you might want to get that tire checked." She pointed to his left rear tire. Flat. The sound of her laughter echoed through him to the very core of his being. She disappeared into the mist.

Andrew groaned in his sleep, twisting among the covers until they caught him in their embrace.

Laura bowed her head to pray, feeling the weight of the day's decisions slowly lifting. Her heart spoke the words that needed to be voiced. The prayer was deliberate and sweet, not so much a prayer of frustration as one of praise. Funny how much better things suddenly seemed. She hadn't been avoiding the Lord—not really. More like holding Him at arm's length.

I should go back to church on a regular basis. Greg had served as Sunday school teacher for nearly twenty years at their local congregation, and she loved the people, but just the thought of attending sent a shot of pain through her heart. The memories were too fresh, too deep. How could she go from being a wife, seated next to her husband in the pew, to a widow, seated alone?

Everything was different. There would be no more couples' parties, no more camping trips with friends. Somehow, when Greg passed away, Laura lost far more than just her relationship with him. She lost everything.

5

*L*aura nervously entered Room 314. Her first three classes had gone far better than expected, but she genuinely dreaded this one. American History. If it proved to be even half as bad as everyone predicted, she needed to be on the ball before the ball even got rolling.

Laura intentionally arrived early, choosing a desk near the front. She hoped this move might win her a little favor with the slave-driving professor she'd heard so much about. She glanced about the room, surprised at its appeal. *He sure takes a serious interest in the subject matter.* She focused on the Declaration of Independence, which hung on the wall.

A familiar figure stood near the door. Laura smiled as she gazed at the gentleman with sandy curls who had helped her with her books. For some inexplicable reason, her heart skipped a beat as she saw him. "Hey, it's you!" she said with a smile. "Have you recovered?"

"I've recovered," he said blandly. His answer was cool—a little too cool. Laura waited for him to take a seat nearby, but he did not. He milled about the room, looking at the walls. Other students entered the class, most sitting as close to the back as possible. Laura watched and waited.

Just as the bell rang, Jess entered the classroom. Laura glanced at her wistfully, hoping, at the very least, for a nod or a whispered hello. It never came. She turned her attention to the door once again.

Where is this professor I've heard so much about? What does he look like? Will he really turn out to be as tough as everyone says? Her heart raced with anticipation. Biting her lip, she pulled out a notebook and began to write . . . *American History, August 26.*

The sandy-haired gentleman hadn't yet found a seat. Laura wondered at his boldness, his apparent lack of fear. *Isn't he as worried about Dougherty as the rest of us?* His eyes met hers for a brief moment before he moved toward the blackboard at the front of the room.

"What in the world . . . ?" she whispered.

He began to write slowly, in large, concise letters . . . M-R. D-O-U-G-H-E-R-T-Y.

Everything after that became a blur.

✒

Andrew turned to face his class, letting his gaze fall on the middle-aged woman who sat squarely in front. Her skin had drained of its color; her gaze remained fixed to the board. *Good. Let her suffer a little. If her words last week were any indication, she's just as lazy as the young ones. She probably never had to work a day in her life—just sits at home, watching the soaps and doing her nails. Well, I'll light a fire under her. She's about to find out what real work is all about.*

"My name is Andrew Dougherty," he said finally, pointing to the board. "You can call me *Mr.* Dougherty." The woman's glance shifted to the desk, a clear sign of defeat. *Good. I've got her under my spell.* "I would like to welcome you all to American History—one of the most exciting and difficult classes you'll ever take."

A groan went up from the crowd. This he had grown accustomed to, but it remained part of the drama—and no one could accuse him of not acting his part.

"Oh, I know what you're thinking," he said, sitting on the edge of his desk. "You're thinking, 'I'll transfer out of here and sign up for another class.' "

Another stirring from the troops.

"What sad news I have to convey," he said dramatically. "All of the other classes are full. But I promise you this—if you work hard, and if you take great notes, you just might get out of here alive."

✒

Laura managed to keep her emotions in check in the classroom, but once released to the freedom of the hallway, she felt like collapsing. "That class is going to kill me," she said, leaning against the wall.

"I tried to tell you that," Jessica said with a shrug. "But you had your mind made up. Remember?"

All Laura could seem to remember was her run-in with Professor Dougherty in the hall last week. What was it he had said as he reached down to pick up her books? _"Are you taking American History?"_

"Yes, but I'm not looking forward to it." Had she really put it quite like that?

"Why?" It had been a logical question on his part.

"It's not the course," she remembered saying, _"it's the professor."_ Laura shook her head, the memory lingering. If only she could take those words back. She had not only judged him—she had accused him right to his face. _I'm going to reap the consequences of that. I can just feel it._

Jessica's voice interrupted her thoughts. "Mom?"

"Yes?"

"You didn't answer me."

"Oh, I'm sorry," Laura turned to look at her daughter. "What did you say?"

"I said, Nathan's going to be picking me up after math and driving me home. Is that all right?"

"Oh, sure, sure—"

"I just don't understand you, Mom." Jessica shook her head. "There are other people in this world who have problems too. I have my piano auditions tomorrow and I'm scared to death. Did you remember that?"

Laura shook her head in shame. As hard as this was, it was just as hard on Jessica.

Father, help me to concentrate. I need to stay focused!

"I'll talk to you later."

Laura watched as she headed off to another class. Her gaze remained on Jessica, but her mind drifted elsewhere. Frustrated, she turned toward the car. She had only taken a step when she ran directly into someone, her books taking another tumble onto the floor.

"Oh, I'm so sorry," she said, looking up apologetically at the gentleman. "I . . . ."

Could things possibly get any worse than this?

❧

Andrew chuckled all the way to the cafeteria. He had won round one in the great contest he had started with this woman. He could hardly wait for round two. If she survived that, perhaps he would reward her with a pop quiz over chapter one next week. He entered the crowded lunchroom, looking for a place to sit. Nothing. He made his way up to the counter to order, fighting to get through the mob of teenagers.

"What'll it be, Professor Dougherty?" A plump, dark-haired woman with a friendly face and welcoming voice called out to him from across the counter.

"Well, if it isn't Regina Torres, the best cook in all of Houston," he responded with a playful smile.

"It's Regina Leal now," she said, showing him her wedding ring. "Remember?"

He remembered. "I'm just giving you a hard time. So, how was the wedding?"

"Amazing. But you weren't there! Why didn't you come? I sent you an invitation."

Andrew didn't answer. He had no excuse. It wasn't that he didn't like Regina. Few people at the college treated him with such generosity and kindness. She always made the lunchroom a brighter place with her broad smile and cheery greetings. Her good humor warmed him on days when the cold shoulder from his students left him chilled. No, it had nothing to do with Regina. It was just that the idea of going to a wedding conjured up too many memories of days gone by. It would have been too difficult, far too difficult.

Better to change the subject. "You're back at Wainesworth. I didn't think you'd be working this year."

"Who, me? Leave this place? I could never leave."

"I thought you said that new husband of yours was going to take you off on a cruise or a six-month vacation or something like that."

She shrugged. "Aw, come on, Mr. Dougherty. You know better than that. He works for the cable company. We won't be seeing any European vacations for a long, long time."

Her broad smile cheered him, as always. "Why aren't all women as wonderful as you are?" he asked, his minding shifting immediately to Laura Chapman.

"I guess when the good Lord made me, He broke the mold," she said. "What sort of woman trouble are you having, Professor?"

"Trouble?" he stammered. "No trouble. "It's just that most of the women I meet are so . . . so . . ." He wasn't sure what they were.

"It's the women, eh?" Regina said. "Couldn't be the problem's on the other end?"

"I'll have a root beer and a bag of pretzels," he said curtly, reaching for his wallet.

"Great combination. What did you do—skip lunch again today?"

He shrugged. "Yeah. I didn't have time between classes—not today, anyway. Talk about swamped."

"You better take care of yourself," she said. "Stay in good shape for that wife we're gonna snag for you this year."

"I beg your pardon?" He looked at her curiously.

"I'm just saying—with the two of us working together . . ."

"Regina, my love life is none of your business."

"What love life?" she asked, practically tossing the bag of pretzels at him. "When was the last time you were on a date?"

"For your information, I'm about to go out on a date."

"Today?"

"No," he said, shaking his head. "But soon."

"With who?"

"A girl named Judy. My friend Joe is fixing me up with her." His heart raced, just thinking about her. *She's the one. I just know it.* After all of these years, it would be so amazing to walk headlong into a romantic relationship. *If anyone deserves it, I do.*

"What's wrong with her?" Regina asked, lips pursed.

"What do you mean?"

"I mean, if she has to be fixed up on a blind date . . ." Regina's eyes reflected her thoughts on the matter.

"There's nothing wrong with her, just like there's nothing wrong with me. Not everyone is blissfully in love like you are. So just let me have my date, and I'll report back to you when it's over. Who knows? She just might be Ms. Right."

"Well, hallelujah to that!" Regina said triumphantly. "Maybe I won't have to play matchmaker after all."

"Matchmaker?"

"I had my mind made up I would find you the perfect wife this year. It was sort of a challenge—almost made coming back worthwhile."

"Very funny."

Her face suddenly took on a serious expression. "Don't you worry, Mr. Dougherty. I've got my eyes wide open. I'll let you know when I meet the girl of your dreams."

"Gee, thanks, Regina." He popped open the root beer. "Keep me posted. I'm on pins and needles."

He turned to leave, feeling a little better about his life. As usual, she had managed to put a smile on his face. There were a few nice women in the world, after all.

❧

Laura opened the car door, deep in thought. How could her day have ended this way? Just when she had to face a full afternoon of work, she had *him* on her mind. Professor Andrew Dougherty. He had proven to be every bit as tough as everyone said he would be.

No—worse. He had given the class two chapters to read for homework, along with a work sheet and a biography on Christopher Columbus. *How am I going to get all of this done and still have time to work at the store? Lord, I'm going to need more help than I thought.*

Laura climbed into the car, pulling out of the familiar parking lot. Try as she might, Laura could not stop thinking about what had happened in the hallway. She did her best to forget it, but how could she?

Lost in her thoughts, she drove to the Bookstop, hoping to make it in time for her shift. How could she possibly handle all of this—classes in the morning, working the afternoon? "I must be crazy." She drove on in absolute silence, her thoughts overwhelming her. By the time she arrived at the store, exhaustion had completely consumed her.

Laura fretted and fumed as the hours rolled by at the bookstore. She found herself pacing around, frustration growing. She couldn't focus on her work because of Professor Dougherty. She could see him now with his cocky expression, walking toward the board, spelling out his name: D-O-U-G-H-E-R-T-Y . . . very slowly, for effect. His cool eyes had stared into hers as he turned back toward the class. His motives were unmistakable. *Well, I won't let him interfere with my work here. I can't. I need this job too badly.*

"Excuse me?" An elderly woman spoke, interrupting her thoughts. She looked a little lost.

"Yes?" Laura responded quickly, pulling herself out of the daydream.

"Could you please tell me where I can find the biographies? I just love to read about people's lives."

Biographies. *Reminds me—I need to look through some books for information on Columbus.* "Sure," Laura said. "We have a great biography department. Just follow me." She wound her way through fiction and around the children's area to the nonfiction books. *Dougherty would really love it here in this section.* There were biographies galore from his precious American history. She could just see the excitement on his face.

"Oh, thank you, Sweetie," the older lady said with a smile. "Just what the doctor ordered. You know, you can learn a lot about a person from one of these books. It always fascinates me to know what makes folks tick—what makes them happy, sad, angry . . ." She rambled on and on, but Laura stopped listening at some point. *There's no way he can expect us to get through two chapters, complete a work sheet, and write a biography in two days. That's ridiculous.* She realized exactly what must be done.

He gave us his number in class, said to call if we had any problems. Well, this is a problem. I'm going to call Mr. Dougherty and give him a piece of my mind.

Andrew buzzed around his apartment in happy anticipation. The long-awaited phone call from Joe had just come in. His blind date, Judy, would be waiting at the Happy Oyster on Highway 290 and Mangum Road. He had just enough time to get there if nothing went wrong. He slipped on a navy shirt, accidentally tearing a button off as his anxious fingers fumbled with it.

"Oh, man!" He pulled the shirt off and reached for another—a gray-and-white stripe. It wouldn't look great with his dark blue sweater vest, but what did it matter, really? *If she's really interested in me, clothing won't be an issue, anyway.* He pulled the vest on, followed by the jacket. *There. Nearly ready.*

He glanced in the mirror for one last look at his hair. *Curly. Too curly.* He rubbed a little hair gel between his palms and spread it all around. No change, but nothing could be done about that. Andrew sprayed some cologne on with a smile. *I'm going all out for this one.* She would be worth it. He could just feel it.

He grabbed his car keys and raced toward the door, double-checking to make sure he hadn't forgotten anything. Just as his hand hit the doorknob, the telephone rang.

"Forget it," he said, looking back. "Let the machine get it." But something in him wouldn't allow it. It could be Joe with a change of plans. Or maybe, just maybe, it was Judy, herself. Andrew dropped his jacket on the bench in the front hall and reached over to grab the receiver.

"Hello?"

Nothing could have prepared him for the voice on the other end of the phone.

❧

Laura's voice shook almost uncontrollably as she spoke the words. "Mr. Dougherty?" She stressed his name, envisioning how he had so carefully spelled it on the board.

"This is he. With whom am I speaking?"

"Laura Chapman," she said, trying to keep her voice steady. "C-H-A-P-M-A-N."

"Very funny. What can I do for you, Ms. Chapman?"

"I'm just calling to make sure I got the homework assignment right. Did you really say chapters one and two, along with the work sheet you handed out?"

"That's right. And don't forget—"

"The biography." They spoke in unison.

"That just seems like a lot of work for two days," she argued. "It's just . . ."

"Just what, Ms. Chapman?"

"Well, I thought maybe I had misunderstood. It just seemed like a lot, that's all."

"Look, Ms. Chapman," he said, sounding exasperated, "I know your type. You come into a class like this expecting to breeze through, then reality slaps you in the face. Am I right?"

"Well, actually—"

"Why don't you do us both a favor and drop my class while you can still get a refund? It's obvious this is going to be too much for you." Sarcasm laced his voice.

"Too much for me?" A renewed zeal kicked in. "Who said that?"

"You've done everything but say it. I'm a firm believer in excellence, Ms. Chapman."

"So am I," she echoed, more determined than ever. "In fact, you just wait and see, Mr. Dougherty. I'm going to be the best student you ever had." She meant it with every fiber of her being.

He laughed so loudly, she had to pull the receiver away from her ear.

"I'm not kidding!" she hollered into the phone, then abruptly hung up.

❦

Andrew doubled over with laughter. *How delicious!* He dropped down onto the couch, trying to calm himself. He began to picture in his mind the infamous Ms. Chapman—what she must have looked like as she spoke with such energy. What a scene she must have created. A smile crossed his lips as he remembered their first encounter. This woman seemed destined to make him a little crazy.

But wait. Another woman waited for him now. Andrew glanced down at his watch and groaned. He would be late, even if he drove like a maniac. Once again, Ms. Chapman had run him down, though she didn't even know it.

❧

Laura shook violently as she placed the phone back on the hook, but she felt an overwhelming sense of satisfaction. "I guess I told him!" she said, forcing back a laugh. "Let's just wait and see who he thinks he's messing with." Returning to her work, she found herself energized by an undeniable surge of excitement and hope.

Of course, she had made a rather hefty promise. *I'm going to be the best student you ever had.* She would keep that promise if it took her all day and all night to do so. What did losing a little sleep mean, anyway—as long as she accomplished her goal?

6

*P*ut your books away, and take out a piece of notebook paper and a pen." Andrew spoke the words with a sense of sheer delight. The gaze of every history student locked firmly on him. "We're going to have a pop quiz."

A groan rose from among them, giving him great joy. *Ah! I live for moments like this!* One student in particular held his gaze. Her eyes were unmistakably laced with frustration, but they refused to concede.

"Ms. Chapman," he said, feeling a surge of sarcasm, "I noticed from your records that your maiden name is Eriksson." She nodded as he continued. "Our quiz today will cover the journeys of the Viking, Leif Eriksson. No doubt a relative of yours—a great-grandfather, perhaps?" He couldn't resist the temptation.

The roar of laughter that went up from the class convinced him he had accomplished his goal—humiliating her in front of the group.

With the coolness of a cucumber, she replied, "An uncle."

Her response startled him a little. The class erupted, their laughter suddenly focused on him. His ears began to burn, as they always did when turning red.

"This quiz will be worth 10 percent of your overall grade," he announced. "You can leave as soon as you've completed it." The students began to murmur, and rightfully so. *So I'm a little irrational. So what?* Laura Chapman had judged him, slam-dunked him, and all but ruined his date the other night. She wasn't going to humiliate him in front of his students. He wouldn't allow it.

Laura struggled through the pop quiz, amazed at the unfairness of the questions. *"What were the names of Eriksson's children?"* Were they even mentioned in the book?

"Larry, Mo, and Curly," she wrote, lifting her pen with a dramatic flair. If she couldn't beat the professor at his own game, she could surely join him in the lunacy of it all.

The pen slipped from her hand, rolling halfway down the aisle before it stopped. She felt Mr. Dougherty's gaze on her as she crept down the aisle to pick it up.

"Having a problem, Ms. Chapman?"

She glared her response and sat back in her seat, her hands still shaking with anger. She looked down at the pen, noticing ink all over her fingers. "Great." She made her way up the aisle to his desk.

"Can I help you?" he asked, his eyes peering directly into hers.

"My pen broke. Do you have one I could borrow?"

"Certainly." He reached into his top drawer for a black ink pen. "Don't forget to give it back after class."

Laura turned, gripping the pen as she headed back to her seat. She would overcome this—all of this—if it was the last thing she ever did. She sat with a defiant thud, focusing on the paper once again. Question number two seemed worse than the first one. Number three didn't look much better. She took a deep breath, beginning to write. She would give this an honest effort, regardless.

One by one, the class began to empty. Out of the corner of her eye, she could see students marching back and forth to Dougherty's desk to place their papers in the appropriate basket. Each one left with a sigh. As she passed by, Jessica cast her mother an accusing glare.

Laura sat scribbling, marking through, scribbling, marking through. She had read the chapters. Several times, in fact. It was just that these questions were so poorly worded.

She looked up, finding the professor's eyes clearly focused on hers, an undeniable look of satisfaction on his face. *You're insufferable. Nothing like Greg.*

Wait a minute. Where did that come from? Snap out of it. The pen slipped from her fingers once again, hitting the desk and bouncing off to the floor below. It rolled all the way down the aisle, landing just in front of Dougherty's feet. Laura's head dropped to the desk instinctively. *This is partly my fault, Father! I've let my anger overwhelm me. Help me. . . .*

There were still two unanswered questions on the quiz. She couldn't possibly complete them without getting up for the pen. She stood, making her way up the aisle one final time.

"Time's up," Professor Dougherty said sharply.

⟨ ⬥ ⟩

Andrew spoke the words with complete satisfaction. Laura Chapman had to face the music. Thanks to her, his date last night had been a complete fiasco. He arrived at the restaurant fifteen minutes late, much to his own chagrin. Judy, it turned out, wasn't a very patient sort. She wasn't a very intelligent sort either. She had the looks, no questioning that—a redhead with the appearance of a model but few brains to match. A trip to the dentist would surely have been more pleasant. She spent most of the night whining about everything from his tardiness to the nail fungus under her phony red fingernails. It sickened him.

Andrew looked again at Laura Chapman as she made her way to the front of the class. She didn't have Judy's figure, and her haircut couldn't compete, but it always seemed to catch his eye. Still . . .

Wait a minute, man. What are you doing?

He forced his attentions back to the where they should be, pushing thoughts of women behind him. They simply weren't worth the trouble.

His eyes met Laura's as she dropped the paper onto his desk. He had clearly frustrated her, but that had been his intention, after all.

Right?

She left the class in a huff, pulling the door shut behind her. He observed the color in her cheeks as she gave him one last angry look.

Andrew glanced through the papers quickly, looking for her quiz. With great satisfaction, he skimmed the page. "That's wrong." He struck a red line through her first answer. "And that's wrong." He added more red to the page.

A sea of crimson ink covered the page before he had finished. Andrew leaned back in his chair, a wicked smile crossing his lips. *I'm perfectly content and completely justified.* She got exactly what she deserved, and he couldn't be happier about it.

"Well, Ms. Chapman," he spoke aloud to an empty room. "Looks like you didn't do very well on your first American History quiz. But don't worry—you'll have plenty of others in the weeks ahead. I'll make sure of that."

He gathered up the stack of papers from his desk, preparing to leave. He had one last stop to make—the lunchroom. He hadn't eaten all day. Again.

He made his way across the crowded campus to the familiar hub at the center. Teenagers surrounded him on every side. He felt his age more acutely than ever in this place. He worked through the maze of kids to the lunchroom inside, where a familiar face greeted him.

"So," Regina said as he approached the counter, "how was your— uh, your 'date?'"

"My date?" He tried to act innocent.

"Yeah," she reminded him. "Remember? You said something about a girl named Judy. How did that work out?"

"Oh, well, you know," he mumbled, looking past Regina at the food choices. "I'll have some cheese curls and a bag of those oatmeal cookies—and a chocolate milk."

"Are you sure about that?" she asked, looking at his midsection. "We're never gonna get you a wife if you keep eating like this."

"Regina," he said, his lips tight, "I told you, I don't need any help. I'm perfectly capable of—"

"Sure you are, sure you are." She collected his food and placed it on the counter. A silence fell between them, lingering in the air for a moment before Regina finally broke it. "By the way, I heard about that pop quiz you gave today." She let out a long whistle.

"What? What did you hear?"

"A killer. That's what I heard."

"Who said that?" he asked, growing angry.

"Who didn't?" came her swift reply. "It's all over campus. You're a legend, Mr. Dougherty. You know that. But they're saying this one really took the cake."

He shrugged. "It wasn't so bad."

"Well, all I'm saying," she leaned toward him, whispering, "is it sounds like you're mighty frustrated with something and taking it out on these poor kids. Why don't you give them a break and let me help you find a wife?"

"The last thing on earth I need," Andrew said forcefully, "is a wife. I'm perfectly happy with me, myself, and I."

∾

"Laura, it's not that I'm complaining," her boss, Madeline, spoke hesitantly. "It's just that a couple of our customers have asked about you—wondering if you were okay."

"What do you mean?" Laura looked into the worried gray eyes of her boss. Madeline wasn't the type to mince words. All business, she prided herself on running the bookstore like a well-oiled machine. This showed in the way she dressed, the way she spoke, even in the way she wore her hair. Never married, Madeline couldn't begin to understand the issues of balancing a home and career.

"Well, they seem to think you're a little . . . distracted."

The understatement of the century, Laura had to admit. She had been here only in body. Her mind and her emotions had been divided between her children and her classes. Factor American History into the equation and, well—there just wasn't a lot left to bring into the workplace.

"I'm sorry, Madeline," she said, feeling the weight of her own words. "I've been distracted. I know it. But it's only because I'm trying to get used to my schedule, and I've had a little bit of trouble at school. I can handle this. I really can." She sounded like a kid, trying to convince herself.

"What sort of trouble?"

Laura shrugged, not wanting to get into it. "It's really nothing.

Nothing I can't handle, anyway. Everything is going to be fine. Just give me awhile, okay?"

"Oh, speaking of trouble," Madeline interjected, "I hate to be the bearer of bad news, but you had a call from Kent's school just before you got here."

"Kent's school?" Laura asked nervously. "What did they want?" *Lord, keep him safe!*

"He's fine. Something about an incident on the bus."

Laura felt the usual twisting in her chest. Her son had spent much of last year in trouble at the junior high. He really seemed to be slipping since Greg's death. But they had talked about it—at great length—just weeks ago. He had promised this year would be different. They had both hoped for a fresh start. Surely he wouldn't blow it this quickly.

"What sort of incident?"

Madeline shrugged. "I told them you'd call as soon as you got in, but you're already late. Make it a quick call."

"I'm sorry." Laura walked behind the counter and picked up the phone, thumbing through her pocketbook for the tiny phone book she always carried. She located the number for the high school and began to dial.

"Carter High School," a cheery voice rang out on the other end.

"I need to find out about my son. I understand he was involved in some sort of an incident on the bus this morning."

"Ah. You must be Mrs. Chapman." Laura's heart sank instantly. "We've been trying to reach you for hours. Can you come up to the school?"

"I just got to work," she said, "and I can't leave."

"It won't take long, Mrs. Chapman, and we really need to talk to you."

"Where is Kent?" She asked the question carefully, dreading the woman's answer.

"He's here in the office, sitting across from me as we speak."

"You mean he's been there all day?"

"Yes."

"I'll be right there." Laura spoke the words, hoping that Madeline would understand. She hung the phone up, heart racing.

"Please let her understand," she whispered the prayer on near-silent lips, then turned, facing her boss.

"They need me to come to the school."

"Now?"

"It's some sort of emergency; at least that's what they said."

"How long will you be?"

"I don't know," Laura whispered hoarsely, feeling the lump in her throat growing. "But I'll come back just as quickly as I can, I promise."

Madeline sighed. "Do the best you can," she encouraged, turning to take care of a customer.

Laura turned at once and headed for the door.

7

*L*aura sat in the courtyard of the college, battling with her emotions. *September 28. Our anniversary. Today would have made twenty-two years.* She wiped away a tear, reaching for her American History book. *Distracting myself is the best thing. I can get through this.* She thumbed through the text frantically, looking for the right chapter. *I've got Dougherty completely figured out. At least I think I do. I can predict there will, without any question or doubt, be another pop quiz today.* His demeanor in the last class left no uncertainty in her mind.

Staying focused seemed difficult these days. Problems at home escalated daily, causing Laura to be even more distracted than before. She suffered from lack of sleep. Night after sleepless night, she promised herself things would be different, but nothing appeared to be changing. She managed to stay awake reading, studying, writing, or worrying.

Things with the kids weren't much better. Jessica remained in a foul mood much of the time, and Kent had been suspended from school for three days because of his fighting incident on the bus. *When Greg was here, things were so different, so much better—in so many ways.* Kent had always been close to his dad, but now . . .

Now everything felt different. Her son grew angrier with each passing day, and it showed in a variety of ways. Looked like they were in for a rough year.

She needed to remain focused on school things. Despite all of her gloating, Laura's grades were slipping dramatically in History. A sixty-two on the first quiz set the ball in motion. She hadn't done much better on last week's paper. Her best hope lay in the essay she would turn in today on the Declaration of Independence. She'd spent a great deal of time on it. Of course, Dougherty would find plenty wrong with it. He always did.

Why this particular professor had singled her out remained a mystery to Laura. Surely he couldn't still be holding a grudge after all of this time. There must be something more. But what? Did he hate women in particular, or just her?

Sighing deeply, Laura closed the book. Studying seemed to be pointless. His pop quizzes defied logic, anyway. She made her way toward the class, wondering about Jessica. How would her daughter treat her today? Would it be the cold shoulder, or a friendly hello?

Will things be like this forever, Lord?

Somehow, in the midst of the battle, it seemed they would.

⁕

Andrew watched Laura Chapman carefully as she entered the room. His disappointment in her had diminished greatly over the past month, replaced with a growing amazement at her tenacity and charm. He hadn't shown that, of course. Andrew looked forward to this class on Tuesdays and Thursdays above all others. All of these changing emotions perplexed him, but not overwhelmingly so. On the surface, she seemed just like any other woman.

Or did she? He looked at her with curiosity. Today she wore a pair of jeans and a soft blue sweater—quite a sight for his sore eyes. Her hair had a shimmer that held him captivated. *She's really very pretty. And maybe she's not as lazy as I made her out to be. She seems to be trying.*

He quickly changed gears, hoping not to attract her attention. "Class, please turn in your essays on the Declaration of Independence." He watched as she rose, stepping into the aisle with paper in hand. His gaze never left her. She carried herself with grace. Andrew hadn't yet figured out her story. Was she divorced, widowed? No wedding ring adorned her left hand, and yet she had a daughter, Jessica.

Ms. Chapman placed her paper on the desk—typed, double-spaced—just as he had requested. She certainly seemed to be doing everything in her power to conform. Perhaps the time had come to declare a peace treaty. Enough damage had been done. Clearly she struggled, not just in this class, but with deeper issues. Her eyes were often weary, and her shoulders down. He would change that. He would be a better man. He would step up to the plate.

"Ladies and gentlemen," he said to the class, "today we're going to have an open discussion on the Declaration of Independence. Whom did the authors intend to include? Whom did they exclude? How do you feel about the men who signed, etc.?"

The class erupted into a lively discussion—everything from the lives of the men who had framed the document to those excluded from the rights of the Declaration because of the issue of slavery. He kept a careful eye on Ms. Chapman, who never stirred once during the entire discussion. She seemed frozen in place. Finally, when he dismissed the class and the other students left, he approached her. "You were unusually quiet today, Ms. Chapman."

She shrugged her response.

"Nothing to add to the conversation?"

"Since you brought it up," she said, looking at him quizzically, "what about a woman's right to independence—and, in particular, her right to vote? No one even touched on that subject."

"What about it?"

"I mean, for all the good it did, the Declaration of Independence still didn't provide for the women of those original thirteen states. It excluded them, didn't it?"

"Well, to some extent, perhaps," he said frankly. "But women were viewed differently in those days." *Things are about to get touchy. I can feel it.*

"How so?"

"Well," he said hesitantly, "they were viewed much more as . . ." How could he put this? "They were viewed more as possessions than as thinking people. When a man took a wife, she became his property."

Laura had taken to staring, her jaw hanging open in surprise. "Isn't that how most of you still feel?"

"Of course not." He felt a little twitch of irritation. "Though how I feel is irrelevant, I think that women are completely entitled to their right to vote, as are all American citizens of voting age." He did. No question about that.

"But . . ." Laura looked at him intently.

He chose his words quite carefully. "Well, it's just that some of the women I know aren't exactly nuclear physicists, if you get my drift." Visions of his blind date danced in front of his eyes. Judy's nail fungus had been far more important to her than political matters, that was for sure. Of course, she wasn't like many of the woman he had known, so he couldn't judge them all by the way she'd acted.

"You mean, 'men are smarter than women,'" Laura argued.

Andrew noticed how pale her face had become. It intrigued him but worried him as well. He certainly didn't want to create an even larger rift between the two of them. "Well, no," he stammered, trying to make the best of this. "We're not all smarter . . ."

"All?" Her eyes began to sparkle with anger. Had he said something wrong? No. Every word he had spoken could be backed up with intelligent and accurate statistics.

"Men, as a rule, have a higher intelligence quotient than women," he argued, "but that's because we've been privy to a history of learning, whereas women have only been allowed full access to all of the academic opportunities this country has to offer for a short time. We've got several hundred years of university education under our belts." There. That should satisfy her.

Apparently not. She stared at him in silence—deafening silence.

"What I mean to say," he stammered, "is that you—I mean, *women*, haven't had the same access to a college education. You've missed out on many years of possibility." Could he get any plainer than that?

"Are you really saying what I think you're saying? You honestly believe men are smarter than women?"

Her words were heated, and they stirred something in him. She didn't seem to understand where he was coming from. Her stubbornness wouldn't allow it.

"That's not what I . . ." he tried to interject another explanation. He found himself completely frustrated with the direction of the conversation. *How can I turn this around?*

"All you have to do is look around you, Ms. Chapman. You'll find a good many women here at Wainesworth your age but not many men. I'm sure Jessica's father, if he didn't have his degree yet, would head to a major university to obtain his bachelor's or master's. That's true of most men. But you're going to a junior college. See what I mean?" He smiled in her direction.

"I think it's time for me to go," she said, turning to leave the room. Her eyes widened with his last comment, a sure sign she had misunderstood his words. Laura disappeared down the hallway, never looking back. Andrew sprinted after her. He needed to say something to her—obviously something more carefully thought-out than his last statement.

"Ms. Chapman," he called out her name, but she kept walking. "Ms. Chapman." Nothing. "Laura!"

At this, she turned and looked at him, ashen-faced. "There is one thing you should know, Mr. Dougherty, one very important thing."

"What?"

"My husband died nearly three years ago after a terrible battle with cancer. Does that answer your question about why I'm struggling? He never cared if I had a degree or not. He didn't put a lot of stock in things like that. He loved me for who I was. He respected me. He would have been proud of me for going back to school—even if it was only a junior college."

Andrew swallowed hard, and his heart pounded in his chest until he felt like it would explode. "I'm so sorry. I . . . ."

"Except for my kids, I'm alone. Up 'til now, I've been doing the best I could to get by, no thanks to you. I may not be the smartest woman in the world, but until today, I've given this my best shot. Apparently my best wasn't good enough for you."

Andrew's heart sank to his toes. How could he begin to redeem this? "I'm a tough teacher. Maybe a little too tough; I don't know. But I'm really sorry if I've said anything to hurt you. We can work this out."

"I don't want to work it out. I'm tired of trying. So I'm dropping your class, Mr. Dougherty. Isn't that what you wanted? You've won." Defeat covered her like a shroud.

I haven't won. Neither of us has won. I've caused this—caused her to fail. But how can I stop her? "Laura, please don't."

"That news should make you happy. I'm not going to be around to make fun of anymore."

He never had a chance to respond. She turned to walk in the opposite direction.

꩜

Laura made her way to the car, jaw clenched. *I just want to get out of here and never come back.* She couldn't blame it on the school. Her other classes were going well. Even the younger students all treated her with respect and dignity. It was only *him*—only that professor. *Why do I let him get to me? What is it about him that bothers me so much? He's not worth it. The class isn't worth it.*

Laura climbed in the car and rested her head on the steering wheel in defeat. "Now what?" she asked herself. She knew the consequences of dropping the class. It meant she couldn't possibly get the degree within the two-year period. It messed up everything. *He* messed up everything. Her thoughts deepened from melancholy to hopelessness. Without a degree, she would never make it out of her dead-end job. *Unless they fire me, of course.*

September 28. Looks like I might not make it through the day, after all. The tears began to flow. Frustrations were mounting. And now, thanks to Mr. Dougherty, the sky was falling.

$\mathcal{C}$ ome on, Matt—just tell me," Andrew coaxed the young man in the admissions office. "I just need Laura Chapman's work number so I can call her about something that happened today after class."

"Why are you so hard on everyone?" Matt asked. "Why don't you just give this one a break?"

"Is that what everyone thinks—that I'm too hard on people?"

Matt smiled. "Well, yeah."

Andrew shook his head, miserable. "I really need to apologize, but I can't if you won't give me the information."

"You're gonna humble yourself and do the right thing, eh?" Matt said. "Think you'll regret it?"

"Probably not." He couldn't possibly regret anything more than he did the mess he'd gotten himself into already.

Matt typed a few words into the computer. "Here you go," he said finally. "She works at the Bookstop on Tully. The number's right here."

"She works in a bookstore?" Interesting.

"Yeah. Do you want the number or not?"

"Sure. Sure." Andrew quickly scribbled down the number, but he'd already decided on a better plan. A bookstore. What a logical place for a college professor to turn up. Nothing contrived. He would simply be one in a number of shoppers, especially in a store the size of the Bookstop. Maybe, just maybe, he would find her there.

❦

Laura drove up to the store, anxious to get inside and start working. The harder she worked, she reasoned, the quicker she could put this afternoon's incident out of my mind. And that's exactly what she had to do in order to maintain her sanity.

"Laura, everything all right?" Madeline asked.

"Yeah. Rough day," she said, deciding not to elaborate. "But I'm fine. Really. I want you to know things are going to be better, Madeline. With me, I mean."

"What do you mean?"

"I mean," she said, with a look of determination, "I'm going to drop a class or two, and that should relieve my schedule a little." *Madeline will appreciate this news. She, of all people, knows how stressed I am.*

"But your plans . . ."

"Never mind my plans," Laura asserted, putting on her best face. "I'm going to be fine; just wait and see. Now, what needs to be done?" There would be no time to dwell on the day's events if she had her mind on her work.

"Well, I've been thinking of revamping the inspirational section," her boss said. "That area's not getting a lot of business, and I think maybe it's because of the way we've got it set up."

Laura nodded. "Sounds great." Just the titles alone in the inspirational section would cheer her up. She moved forward, into a newer, brighter day. She would put Mr. Dougherty and this whole fiasco out of her mind.

❧

Andrew pulled up to the Bookstop and anxiously looked toward the door. He glanced at his reflection in the rearview mirror before getting out, wet his fingers, and ran them through the lopsided curl in the center of his forehead that never seemed to lie down. *Useless.*

He made the short walk to the entrance of the large store. A poster in the window advertised Grisham's latest book. Looked like they were also having a sale on art books. None of that interested him at this moment. Only one thing captivated his mind: He had to find Laura Chapman.

❧

Laura pulled books off the dusty top shelf with a little more force than usual, placing them onto the cart in front of her. She looked around her, trying to imagine what this section would look like in a few hours. With her help, it could be a showcase. This area could be improved in so many ways. What they needed were posters and promos, drawing people to this corner of the store. Perhaps a center table with inspirational best-sellers available at a glance.

Laura thumbed through a few of the books on the cart. Some of them looked a little dull, but others really caught her eye. One in particular stood out—*Put Your Troubles in the Blender and Give Them a Spin*. She didn't recognize the author's name, but she could certainly relate to the title. Who would have thought inspirational books could be humorous? She gave it a once-over. The text was clever, funny— yet packed a real punch in the emotional department. *Lord, are You trying to tell me something?*

❧

Andrew wound his way through the bookshelves, nervously looking for Laura. He rehearsed the words over and over again in his mind— what he would say when he saw her. He would start with a practical apology. He owed her that. He would then shift into a reasonable explanation of why he had said what he had. He would do his best not to further damage his case. Rather, he'd try to make himself look like the reasonable man that he was. Being a reasonable woman, she would respond in kind.

At least he hoped she would. He rounded a corner, practically running into a cart full of books. *Looks like I've found her. Now who's running into whom?* He smiled warmly, attempting to regain his composure.

Laura glanced his direction, her face falling. "What are you doing here?"

"Me?" He tried to look calm. "I come here a lot, actually. Interesting you should work here."

"Very."

"Laura—"

"Ms. Chapman." She stressed the words.

"C-H-A-P-M-A-N," he said, trying to be funny. She didn't smile. "Look, Ms. Chapman, I really felt like we needed to talk. Do you have a few minutes?" His heart pounded in his ears, making it difficult to hear her response. He watched her lips as she spoke.

"I think we did all the talking today that needed to be done, don't you?"

She has a point, but won't she even give me a chance? "I just wanted to say how sorry I am."

A baffled look crossed her face as he forged ahead. His gaze shifted to the ground. "I'm so sorry. I don't want you to quit the class. I really don't." He meant it. He hated to see any student give up, truth be told, but there was something special about this one. She needed to get through this—for psychological reasons as well as any other.

"I have to work and I really don't have time to deal with this. I'm going through enough at home and here at the store."

"What do you mean?" Nosiness kicked in. There seemed to be so much he didn't know about her, about Jessica.

"Never mind," she said, moving toward the door.

Just be direct. Get to the point. "So, will you come back?"

"Why should I?"

"I just hoped—" No, he wouldn't go that far. He didn't want to let her know that he had grown accustomed to seeing her, looked forward to every class with her.

"Can you give me one logical reason why I should come back to your class, Mr. Dougherty?" Laura asked, her face set.

Should he tell her that he enjoyed seeing her there, that she brought a smile to his face with her wit and her persistence? Should he let her know how impressed he was by the effort she took to raise her kids, work, and go to school? "I, uh . . ." He started, then hesitated slightly.

She shook her head in disbelief. "I thought so."

Laura watched as Dougherty sauntered out of the door, making his way to an old sedan with worn black paint. The car suited him—outdated and not terribly pretty. He deserved a car like that. She watched as he pulled out of the parking lot and sped down Tully with tires squealing.

Laura immediately set her mind back on her work. So much needed to be done, and she had lost time—thanks to him. He had quite a way of spoiling things. She quickly moved back toward the inspirational section, ready to dive in headfirst. She picked up a Bible to place it on the cart with the others. Her fingers lingered across the cover. It had been weeks since she picked up her own Bible to read. Somehow, just holding one now made her feel better.

She turned it open to the New Testament, her fingers racing along the words. They were as familiar as an old friend, and yet stirred an emotion in her she was unprepared for. Her index finger rested on a verse in 2 Corinthians that startled her. She had never read it before.

"If anyone has caused grief, he has not so much grieved me as he has grieved all of you, to some extent—not to put it too severly. The punishment inflicted on him by the majority is sufficient for him. Now instead, you ought to forgive and comfort him, so that he will not be overwhelmed by excessive sorrow."

"Forgive and comfort him?" She spoke the words softly, struck by their simplicity. But it couldn't be that easy! Laura closed the Bible quickly, placing it on the cart. Surely she wasn't supposed to comfort a man like Professor Dougherty. He was beyond help.

But, then again, why had he come here? Her mind began to drift to their conversation. Did he really feel bad about what he had said, or were there darker forces at work?

Madeline walked up.

"I guess you pretty much figured out who that was," Laura said.

"The infamous professor. Yeah, I've got it—and I hope you don't mind my saying this, but he doesn't seem like the ogre you made him out to be. He's a cutie."

Laura groaned—loudly, for effect.

Madeline grinned. "What did he want, anyway?"

"Actually, he wanted to apologize and asked me to come back to the class."

"Are you going to?" A smile made its way to her boss's lips. "I mean, I'm just saying if I had a professor who looked like that, I'd go back."

Laura thought carefully about her words before answering. "If I do, it won't have anything to do with him. I'd be going back for myself."

"Good girl. I'm proud of you."

"You are? I thought you didn't like the idea. Balancing work and school is a real pain."

"Like the idea? I'm so proud of you, I could burst! You make me want to go back myself."

"I do?"

"You do."

"Well," Laura said with a sigh, "it's a lot tougher than they make it out to be. I'm not sure how I'm ever going to get through this American History class if I do go back."

Madeline's eyes began to sparkle immediately. "Oh, Laura," she said, grabbing her hand and squeezing it tightly, "I have the most amazing idea!"

9

*L*aura sat in the college cafeteria, clutching her colorful American History book. She slowly worked her way through a chapter on indentured servants, fascinated by the material. She glanced up occasionally, slightly distracted. She looked back and forth—from her book, to her watch, to all of the people. The noisy room provided some degree of comfort—trays clattering, soda cans popping open, students chattering incessantly—these were all things she had grown to love. Even so, Laura found it very difficult to focus. It was nerve-wracking, especially under the circumstances.

"Come on, come on."

He should be here soon. She took a bite of her sandwich, chasing it down with a mouthful of soda. She glanced at her watch nervously. *Not much time left. He'd better come quickly, or there really won't be much point to all of this.* She tried to keep her attention on the chapter but found it extremely difficult. She stared at her watch as the minutes ticked by. *He should definitely be here.*

"Are you Laura Chapman?" A deep voice rang out.

Laura looked up into the twinkling eyes of a gentleman with peppered hair and a well-trimmed gray beard. "I am," she answered. "And you must be Richard."

"Dick DeHart," he responded, extending his hand for a firm handshake. "Madeline says you need some help in history."

"Help is an understatement," she confessed. *How much should I confide in him?* Then again, it might be better to let him know what he was up against. She spoke hesitantly. "If I don't pass this course, I might as well drop out of school."

"Well, we can't have that, can we?" He sat next to her, pulling a chair close. "You've come to the right place."

She couldn't help but notice his dimples, not hidden in the slightest by his beard. He was a nice-looking man, just as Madeline had said—probably fifty-two or three, somewhere in that neighborhood. Not that it mattered. It was just that Laura had looked for a tutor in her own age group, not from among the students at Wainesworth. Things were rough enough this way.

"I don't know what my sister told you about me," Richard explained, "but I used to teach here at the college until about three years ago. That's when my wife passed away."

"I'm so sorry," Laura said. "I'm a widow, myself. In fact, my husband has been gone three years too."

"Really?" He looked more than a little interested.

Laura immediately grew nervous.

"I think I've seen you at the store a couple of times. I've been doing a lot of research."

"What sort of research?"

"History, naturally," he said excitedly. "I've taken to writing college textbooks since I left the teaching profession."

"That's fascinating." Madeline had simply described him as a history buff.

"In fact," Richard said, pointing to her American History text, "I had a hand in writing that book."

"You wrote this textbook?" she asked, turning to the cover for a quick glance. Sure enough, *Richard DeHart & Jonathan Frisk* jumped off of the cover at her. "For heaven's sake."

"I had a particularly tough time with that chapter you were reading when I walked up," he said, reaching for the book. "You're just starting the unit on slavery, right?"

"That's right," she said, looking at the open book with new admiration and respect. "Why did you have a tough time?"

"There's a shortage of documents concerning slave groups brought over from the Caribbean." He frowned. "I wanted to include a well-researched section on their story, but I couldn't track down everything I needed. What you're reading there is just a shell of what I had hoped to include."

"Looks pretty thorough to me," Laura observed.

"Still, we may have to do a second edition. There's just so much material to cover."

"If you don't mind my saying so, there's plenty of material in this book as it is. Getting through it in one semester is going to be rough. And Dougherty—well, he's not making my life any easier."

"Professor Andrew Dougherty?"

Laura nodded.

Richard let out a whistle, shaking his head.

"You know him?"

"Know him? We used to be archenemies—seemed to be an ongoing battle over who could be the better teacher. Also, there was that *dean* issue."

"Dean issue?" She grew more curious by the moment.

"Well, yeah," he said, "but I hate to talk about it. I was named dean of the History Department here at Wainesworth about five years back. Apparently Dougherty felt I had one-upped him. I don't know that he ever quite forgave me."

"Sounds like he carries a lot of grudges," Laura said. "Actually, that's part of my problem. . . ."

"Got on his bad side right away, did you?" Richard laughed.

She nodded, embarrassed. "Yeah, but it really wasn't my fault."

"It rarely is. Dougherty's got a real chip on his shoulder. But you're barely two months into the school year. There's plenty of time left in the semester to make things even worse."

"Very funny. But I'm serious. He hates me."

"Hate is a pretty strong word," Richard said, suddenly looking serious. "Besides, I think he's just covering for something."

"Covering for something?" He must know quite a few things about Andrew Dougherty that she didn't. Not that she cared.

"I think he must have had his heart broken somewhere along the way," Richard said with a sly grin. "At least that's what I've gathered."

Really. Interesting tidbit of information. For the life of her, Laura couldn't imagine any woman entering a relationship with a man like that.

"Well, let's forget about our dear Professor Dougherty, shall we?" Dick asked, pulling his chair even closer. "Looks like we've got our work cut out for us."

"Yes, we do." She tried to sound confident, but the smell of his cologne distracted her. Greg had worn the same brand in their earlier years together. Somehow, just the aroma made her feel a little out of sorts.

"I think we should go over this unit before you head into class today." He pointed to the book.

"You're right." She turned her attention to the chapter on slavery. It looked, for once, like she had come up with a logical, workable plan.

❧

Andrew entered the cafeteria, hoping for a quick bite to eat before teaching his last class of the day. *What a madhouse.* The sights, sounds, and smells were dizzying, making him claustrophobic and completely uncomfortable. He needed order, control. What had made him think grabbing a baked potato and soda would be easy? Nothing proved to be easy here.

He forced his way through the mob, heading to the counter. "Oh, excuse me," he said, bumping into the back of a chair. He looked down instinctively. Only then did he realize Laura Chapman's eyes gazed directly into his. "Laura . . ."

She didn't respond immediately. Instead, her gaze shifted to the man sitting next to her. *Richard DeHart. What's he doing here?* He hesitantly extended his hand. "DeHart."

"Professor Dougherty." Dick shook it with a firm grip.

"What are you doing here?" It was a fair question. After all, the man didn't teach at the school anymore.

"Ms. Chapman has asked me to tutor her."

"In history?" Talk about throwing a kink into his plans to offer to help Laura. This guy had no business . . .

"Naturally," Richard said. "What did you think?"

Andrew looked back and forth between Laura and Richard. Something about the combination almost made him feel sick. He sought out Laura's eyes. "How did you two meet? If you don't mind my asking."

She looked up at him with a confident smile. "Richard's sister is my boss, Madeline."

"That's right," Dick said. "She told me about Laura's plight, and I rushed right over."

Laura's plight? What is that supposed to mean? Andrew's heart quickened a beat, looking at the two of them together. Not that Dick DeHart was a bad guy. He was great. Maybe a little too great.

Laura observed the look of confusion on Professor Dougherty's face. "Richard tells me he wrote our text," she said, closing the book and holding it up under Andrew's watchful eye.

"Yeah. Knew that."

Great show of support for his colleague. "We were just discussing this week's chapter. I'm finding it very enlightening." *That might be stretching it just a bit.*

"Are you?" He didn't sound very convinced.

"We were just about to enter a lively discussion on indentured servants," Richard added. "Would you like to join us, Dougherty?"

"No, thank you," he said, looking at Laura but speaking more to Richard. "I, uh—I've got a ton of other things to take care of. And then I have to teach a class. I still do that, you know."

They stared at each other until Laura grew uncomfortable. She turned her glance to the textbook in question, trying to change the direction of the conversation. "This is so well written," she commented, pointing to a particular passage. "How did you ever think to phrase it that way?"

Richard's eyes beamed. He spoke in earnest. "I just felt passionate about the subject matter and wanted to express it in the most ardent way I could so that the reader would be drawn into the discussion. That's all."

"Good grief." Andrew turned on his heels to leave.

"Sure you won't join us, Dougherty?" Richard called out, a smile crossing his lips.

"No, thank you." He turned to walk in the direction of the counter, leaving her to face Richard DeHart alone.

❧

"That's the one," Regina said, looking Andrew in the eye.

"I beg your pardon?" He followed her finger until his gaze fell on Laura Chapman.

"That's the one I've got picked out for you."

"Oh, no, not that one. Anyone else but her!"

"Why not?" Regina asked, insulted. "Not good enough for you?"

"It's not that. She's just—well, she and I don't exactly get along."

"I'm sure it's your fault. She seems like a nice enough lady."

"Thanks a lot."

She smiled. "Even though your heart is in the right place, your people skills are a little lacking."

"Meaning I'm not really the tyrant everyone thinks I am?"

"Of course not. But you've changed the subject. I want to talk about finding you a wife. Thank goodness you have me; otherwise I don't know what you'd do."

"I don't need a wife," he said defiantly.

"You don't need all that butter and sour cream, either," Regina said, pointing to his baked potato, "but I notice you're still eating it."

❧

Laura looked up from her conversation with Dick DeHart, her gaze resting on Andrew Dougherty. He remained deep in conversation with a woman across the counter. She had dark hair and complexion and looked to be in her early forties. *A real beauty.* Not that it made a difference.

Laura noticed they had been talking for quite awhile. An odd mixture of emotions shot through her. More than anything, she found herself extremely intrigued by the woman. How could any female on the planet look that comfortable with Andrew Dougherty?

10

*A*ndrew passed out the exams, pausing as he placed one on Laura Chapman's desk. Nearly three weeks had passed since that awful day when she threatened to quit his class. Each day he breathed another sigh of relief when she walked in the door. However, he had mixed emotions when it came to her sudden and obvious association with Richard DeHart. *I can't stand that guy. What a lady's man.* Laura Chapman certainly didn't need that in her life. *Wait a minute. I've got no right analyzing what Laura Chapman does and doesn't need. It's none of my business.*

Still . . .

He glanced down at her wavy hair, his hand accidentally brushing against it as he handed a paper to the girl on her left.

"Sorry," he said quietly. Truthfully, he wasn't sorry. One touch had been enough to send sparks through him. Just the thought of it scared him to death.

❧

Laura reached up instinctively, her fingers pushing through the spot where the professor's hand brushed against her hair. It had been an accident, surely, but his lingering gaze left her more than a little curious. Irritated, she turned away from him. She was about to prove a point—a very strong point.

"You may begin." Professor Dougherty gave the go-ahead.

Lord, help me. She turned the paper over and began to read through the questions—first, with fear; then with overwhelming relief. She knew this stuff. A couple of questions might present a challenge, but they were essay questions. Surely she could come up with something for those. As for the multiple-choice questions, they would be a piece of cake.

Laura looked up at Andrew's desk, where he sat silently grading papers. He seemed lost in his work. She turned back to the questions, breathing a huge sigh of relief. At one point, she glanced across the room to where Jessica sat, stone-faced, staring at her exam paper. Try as she might, Laura had not been able to get her daughter to study with her.

She focused on the test, answering questions rapidly and accurately. A short time later, she walked to Professor Dougherty's desk and dropped the exam into the appropriate basket with a smile. She had a lot to smile about. For once, she'd actually accomplished her goal. She'd proven, at least to herself, that she could excel. Soon enough, he would know it too.

The professor looked confused. For a moment Laura felt a twinge of guilt, though she couldn't quite figure out why. She had nothing to feel guilty about. *I've done all of the right things, so why do I feel so bad?*

Dick DeHart had turned out to be a regular Romeo. Picking up on the fact that he seemed interested in far more than her mind, she carefully chose when and where they would meet to study. *I could never be interested in a man like him.*

Her gaze fell on Andrew Dougherty once again. His rumpled hair stuck up on his head. He wore a mismatched shirt and tie, and his pants had gone out of style years ago.

Still . . . he did have a certain charm about him. He looked up at her with a smile and she almost returned it. Almost.

❧

Andrew waited until the classroom cleared before shuffling through the stack of exams to find the one he was looking for. "Miller, Johnson, Tanner, Breckenridge . . . Chapman." Ah, yes. Laura Chapman's exam. He scanned it quickly and made it to the bottom of the first page. No errors so far. He turned to page two. Flawless. A little glitch in an essay question on page three—worth about two or three points at most, but page four appeared to be perfect. She'd aced the exam. Aced it.

Amazed, he checked it once again. Only one conclusion could be drawn: Her study sessions with DeHart had been effective. Very effective. That confirmed something he'd worried about for days. She and Dick DeHart must have spent a lot of time together.

A twinge of jealousy shot through him, stirring up an odd mixture of emotions. *I'm so proud of her. She's turned out to be a much harder worker than I gave her credit for.* But on the other hand, how could she give so much of her time and attention to someone as unscrupulous as DeHart? He struggled with the thought. *Maybe she hasn't figured him out yet. Maybe someone needs to warn her.* Andrew tossed ideas about, clearly confused over the whole thing. If her academic performance improved with Dick's help, how could he possibly go about approaching her now?

❧

Laura turned the key in the front door, hearing the ringing of the phone. "Come on, come on," she said, struggling with the key. By the fourth ring, she made it into the living room. "Hello?" She dropped the armload of books, still panting.

"Ms. Chapman?"

A man's voice—probably one of those annoying telemarketers. They called a lot. She glanced at the Caller ID. "Unavailable."

Oh, why did I even pick it up? "Yes?"

"I was hoping to catch you." Why did the man's voice sound so familiar? "I've been meaning to talk to you about your work in my class."

Bingo. Andrew Dougherty. What in the world did he want with her? Her hands began to tremble. Clutching the receiver, she forced her voice to remain calm. "What about my work?"

"I'm really pleased with it. In fact, I just graded your exam."

"So soon?" Something must have happened to prompt this.

"Uh, yes. You got a 97."

97? That's awesome! And yet, she wouldn't let her jubilation show.

She couldn't. "Well, thank you for letting me know," she said, trying to keep her voice on an even keel. "Though I'm not sure why you took the time to call. You could have just told me in class."

"I'm pleased with your grade," he continued, "but . . ."

"But what?"

"Well, to be honest, I was hoping to talk with you about Dick De-Hart and the role he's playing in your education."

What? That's none of his business! "I'm not sure where you're headed with this, Professor Dougherty."

"I just think you need to know that DeHart has a . . . well, a past." He seemed to be choosing his words very carefully.

"A past? What does that have to do with anything?" Laura grew angrier by the moment. "This is really none of your business."

"I just thought you might like to know."

"I'm not interested in gossip, Professor. In fact, I'm stunned that you are. To be perfectly frank, if I had anything to say about Mr. De-Hart to you, it would all be good." Granted, Dick DeHart acted a little too close over the last couple of weeks, but she certainly wasn't ready to admit that to Andrew Dougherty. "He's gracious and kind," she continued, "and seems to see something of value in me. It's clear he has my best wishes at heart."

"Among other things."

"I beg your pardon?"

"His reputation precedes him, Laura."

"Ms. Chapman."

"Ms. Chapman," he said slowly, deliberately, "I've got your best interest at heart. Really, I do."

"Well, thank you just the same, but—"

"If I were you—"

"Well, you're not," she said emphatically. She had just about reached wit's end with this guy dabbling in her personal life. She wouldn't allow it. "Besides, this is really none of your business, Professor."

"Fine."

"Fine," she echoed. "Was that all you were calling about?"

"That's all."

"Well, if it's all the same to you, I really need to hang up. I've still got to work today. Good-bye, Mr. Dougherty."

"Ms. Chapman."

With a click, he disappeared. Laura still clutched the phone in her sweaty hand. She slammed it back down, shifting her gaze to the books she'd carelessly tossed on the coffee table. The American History book sat at the top of the stack, a grim reminder that this battle had just begun.

Irritated, she shoved the book to the bottom of the stack.

❧

Andrew stared at the receiver, dumbfounded. *There's no winning with this woman.*

Yet he couldn't get those amazing eyes and wavy brown hair out of his mind.

11

*Y*ou want to what?" Laura turned to face Dick DeHart, who had come into the store for a visit.

"I want to take you out to the movies this Saturday night," he said, slipping his arm across her shoulder.

"But I . . ." Uncomfortable, she pulled away from his embrace. Laura couldn't seem to get the professor's words out of her mind— something about Richard DeHart's past. She had no idea what he meant, but she wasn't taking any chances.

"There's a great new movie out on the Civil War," Dick said, trying to look convincing. "We could look at it as an educational date."

"I'm not sure I'm up to any kind of a 'date,'" Laura said. "I'm just not ready for that yet."

"Well, we don't have to call it a date, then," he argued. "We could go to dinner afterwards and have a, uh—a study session."

Laura had seen just about enough of his study sessions already. She spoke very candidly. "I don't think so, but thanks for the offer."

"Aw, come on, Laurie," he wooed.

"It's Laura."

"You know you want to spend time with me. I'm irresistible."

"Is that what you think?" she asked incredulously. "You think I'm that easily swayed?" *He's got to be kidding.*

"You're a woman." He shrugged. "That about says it all, doesn't it?"

Laura's blood began to boil. She couldn't stand men with an attitude like this. She hadn't tolerated it in the professor, and she wouldn't in this man either.

"I may be a woman," Laura said, trying to keep her voice steady, "but that doesn't mean I don't know how to use sound judgment and reason. I'm perfectly capable of doing that."

His expression never changed. "Aw, come on," he coaxed. "I didn't mean anything by that comment. Let's go out Saturday night and have a good time. We'll paint the town red. I promise to have you back home before you lose your glass slipper."

"I don't think so," Laura said, turning back to her work. "In fact, I don't think I'll be needing any more tutoring sessions either. I'm doing pretty well on my own."

"Sure you are. Just like you were before I came along."

Laura stared at him in disbelief. *This guy is too much.*

"You'll change your mind." He turned to leave. "And when you do—call me."

She wouldn't call him. She would never call him.

~❧

Andrew signed onto the Internet and scrolled through his E-mail—junk mail, a letter from a colleague, and a quick note from his friend, Joe, asking if he'd be interested in going to a high school football game Saturday night to watch his son play.

A high school football game? Andrew barely tolerated sports, and the idea of sitting out in the cold to watch a bunch of kids toss a ball around sounded anything but inviting. Still, Joe was his friend, and he owed him for the blind date thing. Might as well balance the scales by going. "Why not?" Andrew said aloud. He had little else to do, anyway.

~❧

"Mom, Saturday night's homecoming," Kent said nervously.

"Do you have a date?" She looked into his eyes as she asked the question. He looked too young to even consider dating, and yet the inevitable seemed to be upon her.

"Yeah, I'm going with Mandy. The dance is after the game. That's what I wanted to talk to you about."

"She needs a mum, right?" It wouldn't be the first red-and-white mum she'd made over the years.

"Yeah." He looked like a nervous wreck. "I need it by Friday morning."

Laura smiled, realizing this would be Kent's first school dance. Her heart began to ache, realizing that Greg wouldn't be here, snapping pictures as he had so often in the past as Jessica headed out the door.

"You'll have it by Friday morning," she promised.

"Great. But that's not all."

"What else?"

"The band is playing at the game. Are you coming?"

A football game? *Lord, you know I can't stand football. Surely You wouldn't ask me to do that.* "I don't know, Kent . . ."

"Aw, come on, Mom," he argued. "You go to all of Jessica's piano recitals."

He had a point there.

"I guess so, but I might leave after halftime. I have a lot of homework this weekend."

"That's cool." Kent smiled. "Just as long as you watch me play the trumpet, you can go whenever you want."

He bounded from the room with his usual zest, and she was left alone with her books and her thoughts. Not that she minded. It had been a long day, and the silence felt just right.

Andrew slipped into bed for the night, television still running. A sappy love story played itself out on the screen. Whether he meant for it to happen or not, he found his attention glued to the set.

"Aw, don't do it, man," he said to the character on the screen. "Don't give your heart away to her. She's not worth it."

He stared in disbelief as the man in the movie told the young woman that he loved her. She responded by slapping him in the face.

"I tried to tell you," Andrew said, shaking his head. "But you wouldn't listen."

What's wrong with women these days? That's all Andrew really wanted to know. What did they want? And how in the world could any man ever succeed in being everything they expected him to be? He quickly snapped off the TV, determined to put females out of his mind. Unfortunately, when he closed his eyes, all he could see was Laura Chapman's face. She had an amazing smile—when she bothered to smile—and the cutest dimples he'd seen in ages. How could he possibly go about winning a woman like her? He didn't stand a chance in the world.

Andrew wrestled with the sheets, trying to get comfortable. Would there ever be someone—anyone—to call his own? Perhaps some people just weren't meant to have love in their lives. Maybe that was part of some sort of master plan. Who knew?

His mind reeled back to Karen instinctively. She had been so ideal, so perfect. And yet she hurt him. Terribly.

"We all make mistakes," he whispered to himself, remembering some of the words he'd spoken to Laura in those first few days of school. He had been deliberately cruel. Even Karen, in breaking his heart, hadn't acted maliciously. She simply followed her heart.

Suddenly, lying in the stillness of his room, Andrew Dougherty managed to forgive the woman who had broken his heart fifteen years ago. For the first time, he felt completely free to love again.

12

*L*aura put the finishing touches on the red-and-white mum, then handed it to Kent.

"Looks great, Mom." He held it gingerly, as if afraid it might break.

"It ought to," she responded. "I had to mortgage the house to buy all that stuff." *A slight exaggeration—but only slight.* "What time is the game tomorrow night? I'm hoping Jess and Nathan will want to come with me."

"Seven-thirty," he said, biting into a muffin. "You gonna leave after halftime?"

"It depends on how the team is playing," she said with a chuckle. "Nah. If I leave, it will only be because I've got a lot of—"

"I know," he interrupted. "You've got a lot of homework. Trust me, I understand."

"Just promise me this." Laura looked at her son tenderly. "Promise me you'll do your best not to get into any trouble."

"It's cool, Mom. I'm fine."

"I sure hope so." She gave him a peck on the cheek. "Get on out of here. Go to school." He headed out the door, whistling as he went.

Thank You, Lord. He's doing so much better! As he left with the mum in hand, she couldn't help but think of the one she'd worn her senior year in high school, so many years ago. It had been blue and white, a gift from Greg. His mother had worked diligently on it. To this day, it hung in her closet, though the cloth flower had faded over the years.

"Mom?" Jessica's voice sounded surprisingly sweet.

She turned to face her. "Good morning, Jess."

"Mom, I was wondering if you'd like to go to breakfast with me."

"Breakfast?"

"Yeah," Jess said with a smile. "I need to talk to you and thought I might do it over breakfast. Sound good?"

Laura smiled, in spite of herself. Jessica wanted to spend time with her. A first—in quite awhile, anyway. How could she turn that down?

"I'd be delighted. Where do you want to go?"

"Your choice, but this is my treat. I've still got a little birthday money left from Grandma."

"Okay then," Laura said, standing. "Pancake House on Wilson. Their waffles are incredible. Blueberry pancakes—"

"With blueberry syrup," Jess added with a smile. "I know. I remember."

"Why the celebration?"

"You'll see, you'll see. Go get dressed and let me get you out of here for a little while." Jessica looked anxious. Something must be up. Suddenly Laura knew the answer. It had something to do with the piano scholarship. Jessica had gotten the news she'd been waiting on and wanted to share it with her.

"Are you sure?" Laura asked excitedly.

"Yep. I'm sure."

Laura bounded off to her bedroom, erupting five minutes later in a sweater and slacks.

"Better?"

"Much better," her daughter said, smiling.

Fifteen minutes later, they sat in a corner booth of the Pancake House, sipping cups of hot coffee. *What a wonderful treat!* Laura hadn't felt this spoiled in ages.

"Mom, I need to tell you something." Jessica looked serious for a change.

Laura's heart began to pound instantly. *Why do I always assume the worst?*

"Don't look so scared."

"What is it?" *Whatever it is, I can take it.*

"Well, you know that I planned to audition for the piano scholarship, right?"

545

"Planned to?"

"Well, I . . ."

"What, Honey?" Laura asked. "You can say it."

"I couldn't do it, Mom. I was too scared to go in and play."

"You what?" Laura felt stunned. "But you've waited for that audition for weeks. You didn't even go in?"

Her daughter's beautiful face fell immediately. Laura knew she should try to be more understanding, but once the words started, she just couldn't seem to help herself.

❧

"She can't stand me," Andrew said, sitting across from Regina in the nearly empty lunchroom. With no classes scheduled today, only faculty and staff drifted in and out. Regina took advantage of the break, plopping down onto the chair across from him at the lunch table.

"Oh, pooh!" Regina said. "She just doesn't know you yet."

"No, she knows me. And she really can't stand me." Andrew sighed deeply. "I tried to call her."

"You called her?" Regina asked excitedly. "To ask her out?"

"No, of course not. I just wanted to talk to her about her grades."

"Oh." Regina's face fell. "Well, that was a romantic touch."

"You don't understand." He felt his shoulders sag in defeat. "It's not that easy for me. I don't know how to talk to a woman."

"You're talking to me."

"That's different." Surely she could see that.

She gave him a look. "What's that supposed to mean?"

"I mean, you're like a sister to me—not like a woman."

"Well, thanks a lot."

"I can't say anything right."

"I sure hope you do a better job than that when you're talking to her, or the game will be over before it even starts."

"It's already over," he said, standing. "And we're not even in the second quarter yet."

❧

Laura struggled through the afternoon at work, her thoughts in a jumbled mess. *Jessica didn't get the scholarship.* The words went round and round in her head, disappointment filling her.

"I, uh . . ." Laura shook her head, not wanting to talk. The knot in her throat wouldn't allow it anyway.

"That's all right," Madeline said. "I'm just worried about you, that's all. This doesn't have anything to do with my brother, does it?"

Laura laughed, in spite of herself. "No," she said, grateful for the relief the laughter brought. "Nothing to do with your brother."

"That's good," her boss said. "Because I thought for a minute there, I was going to have to hurt him. You just let me know."

Let her know? Should she let her know her brother had one thing, and only one thing, on his mind—and it wasn't American History?

"Would you mind taking over the register?" Madeline asked. "I need to check a new shipment that just came in."

"No problem." Laura headed to the cash register, her mind still reeling.

Jessica didn't get the scholarship. The words still tossed themselves around in her head. She shouldn't be this disappointed, but money didn't grow on trees, and with two of them in college, things might get tight by the spring.

"Uh, umm . . ." A man in front of her cleared his throat, trying to get her attention. "Are you going to wait on me or not?"

"Oh, I'm sorry. My mind is on other things."

"That's obvious."

"Will this be all?" She glanced down at the book he'd placed on the counter: *One Hundred Ways to Become a Better Person.* Intriguing title. She would have to remember to look at it later.

"Yeah, that's all," he said, pushing the book toward her. "My wife says I have to read this."

"Really." She didn't mean it in an accusing way, but he glared at her, just the same. "Well, I hope you enjoy it. That will be $22.95 plus tax—a total of $24.78."

"That's a lot of money just to become a better person," he grumbled, reaching for a credit card.

"I'm sure you're worth it, sir."

He smiled warmly—for the first time. "Yeah, I guess I am. Who knows? Maybe this book will help."

"If it does," she said, "come back in and let me know so I can buy a copy for myself."

The gentleman headed toward the door, his expression totally changed from when they had begun.

"Looks like you had a nice effect on him," Madeline said, returning with a tracking slip in hand. "He's one of my worst customers. Comes in here every few months to buy another self-help book his wife has recommended."

"I've never seen him before. But he wasn't so bad, really. Sometimes people just . . ." She glanced at the floor. "Have a rough day." She smiled lamely at her boss, hoping for a positive response.

"Laura," Madeline said, looking at her intently, "it seems like nearly every day has been a rough one for you lately, but you're going to get through all of this. I know you are. You're a lot stronger than you think."

"Then why don't I feel it?"

"It doesn't matter what you feel. You just have to begin to act on it." Laura smiled warmly at her boss, thankful for the encouragement. *I sure hope you're right.*

13

$\mathcal{K}$ent bit into an apple, then spoke with his mouth full. "You didn't forget about the game tonight, did you, Mom?"

"No." She glanced through the refrigerator for something that might resemble lunch. There wasn't much to choose from—a stale package of bologna and a half-eaten can of sliced peaches. Neither sounded appetizing.

"You're gonna freeze to death if you stand there all day." He reached around her to grab a half-gallon of milk.

"Yeah, I know." She closed the door, opting to skip the food idea. *It's not like things aren't already cold enough in this house already.* Ever since her breakfast with Jessica yesterday morning, little more than a word or two had been spoken between them. *I need to apologize.* But every outward sign convinced her Jessica wasn't ready to hear it yet.

Kent poured a tall glass of milk, leaving the carton standing open on the counter. "Is Jess coming with you?"

"I don't think so."

"Bummer." It was only one word, but it genuinely reflected her feelings.

❧

Andrew pulled his jacket out of the closet and slipped it on. For late October, today proved to be particularly chilly. *I don't know why I'm going, anyway. I've got no interest in football. What an illogical game.* Then again, Joe had been a good sport about the whole "Judy" thing, and his eldest, Jonathan, was like a son to Andrew. For that reason alone, Andrew would go. He would endure the crowd and the noise. He

549

would put up with their lousy band and their childish bantering back and forth.

Andrew made the drive to the stadium with the radio playing softly in the background. A love song streamed from the radio. For some reason, a picture of Laura Chapman came to mind immediately—the way her hair framed her face, the richness of her smile every time she received a good grade. She seemed to be receiving a lot of those lately. Just thinking about her made him smile.

～❧

Laura made her way through the crowd, shivering. Already, she regretted her decision to wear a lightweight sweater instead of her heavy coat. She gazed out onto the field where cheerleaders excitedly warmed up. They leaped about like gazelles, ready for the game to begin.

It feels so awkward, coming here by myself. Almost as bad as sitting in a pew alone. She hadn't managed to do that for quite some time either. Her mind began to wander back to another game, just two years ago, when Jessica had been nominated for homecoming queen. *Greg would have been so proud.* Though their daughter hadn't won the coveted crown, she had certainly excelled above the other girls in Laura's eyes. *In every conceivable way, she was a queen that night.*

Just the thought of her daughter caused Laura's brow to wrinkle. The strain between them grew more with each day. The gap seemed wider than the football field below, and there didn't appear to be a way to narrow it.

"Andrew, over here!" Behind her, a man's voice rang out, almost deafening her. Laura looked up to find Professor Andrew Dougherty waving from a distance. Their eyes met. She immediate dropped her gaze to the ground. *Great.*

～❧

Andrew's heart skipped a beat the minute he saw Laura. She looked beautiful in her soft peach sweater. With her hair pulled back like that, she almost looked like a teenager. In fact, she looked remarkably like Jessica tonight. Should he tell her so? Would that be inappropriate? He made his way up the steps to her row, pausing momentarily to nod in her direction. She nodded back with less enthusiasm.

Joe acted a little more interested. "Glad you could make it," he said as he reached out to shake Andrew's hand. "I was starting to think you'd changed your mind."

Thank goodness I didn't. "Oh," he said finally, "I, uh . . . I got caught up in traffic." He sat quickly, gaze fixed on the back of Laura's head.

Truth was, he had pulled his car off the road to listen to the love song on the radio. It sparked something in him that he hadn't felt for some time. And now, the very one he'd been thinking about sat directly in front of him, completely alone. *This has to be more than coincidence. I'm not that lucky.*

Joe slapped him on the back. "You look like you're a million miles away tonight. Rough day?"

"No, not at all."

"Well, I hope you're ready for a great game. I hear they're playing a tough team tonight."

"Really? That's nice."

Joe laughed, slapping him on the back once again. "You're a laugh a minute. No wonder Judy never asks about you anymore." He erupted into laughter, and Andrew did everything in his power to change the subject, hopeful Laura hadn't heard.

"Who did you say they were playing again?" he asked, looking toward the field.

"Westfield High. They're a tough team."

"Oh, yeah. I've heard that." Not that he cared. Football was a sport he deliberately avoided.

"We'll whip 'em." The proud papa beamed.

"Speaking of 'we,' where's Jolene?" Andrew asked, looking around. He still chuckled, thinking of their names. Joe and Jolene. The all-American couple.

"Oh, she's at the junior high tonight," Joe answered with a shrug. "Kelli's in a play of some sort. You know how it is when you've got a houseful of kids. You have to divide your time."

No, I don't know. Andrew often wondered if he ever would. He turned his attention back to Laura's hair. A soft breeze played with her tiny ponytail, causing the peach ribbon to dance around in the wind. He stared at it, fixated.

The field below came alive as the game got under way, yet Andrew just couldn't seem to concentrate on it. Laura's perfume pulled at him in a way that boggled his mind. *What is that smell—some sort of flower or something else?* He couldn't quite put his finger on it, but talk about alluring. *And that hair of hers—that amazing, wavy brown hair—it's making me a crazy man.* He wanted to run his fingers through it, to nuzzle close and smell it. *What's come over me? Is Laura Chapman some sort of unattainable dream? Do I really need a woman in my life?*

"Snap out of it!" he whispered to himself, shaking his head. *What am I doing, thinking about her that way? She's certainly not making any moves to communicate with me.*

Perhaps she had plans to meet someone. A fear gripped him as he considered the idea. Maybe Dick DeHart would take the place on the bench in front of him. Maybe he was already here. Maybe . . .

"Andrew, are you listening to me?" Joe's voice shocked him back to reality.

"I, uh . . ."

"Are you okay, man?" His friend looked concerned. "You're not acting like yourself."

"Yeah, yeah . . ."

"You're sure acting strange," Joe said. "I know what you need. You need food. I'm gonna go get a hot dog and a soft drink. You want the same?"

"Oh, sure," Andrew said, fishing for his wallet. "Whatever you say."

"What I say is, you're in need of some serious help, my friend." Joe flashed him a grin as he left. Andrew sat in silence, trying to decide what to do next. *Should I talk to her?*

❧

Laura watched in silence as the professor's friend left the stands, realizing he sat alone behind her.

Please don't let him talk to me. The words flashed through her mind like an alarm going off. She couldn't bear another confrontation tonight. She'd been through enough over the last few days.

His voice interrupted her thoughts. "Laura, how are you?" *The moment of truth.*

"Fine," she said, glancing at him briefly. She deliberately looked back down at the field, hoping he would take the hint. He didn't.

"I didn't realize you still had children in high school," he commented, moving to sit next to her. *That took some nerve. What does he think he's doing?* Laura knew she should say something to him—make him go back to where he came from. She turned, prepared to do battle—but no words came out. Something about the way he wore his hair tonight seemed a little different, but she couldn't quite put her finger on it.

"Uh, yes," she said finally. "Well, just one. My son Kent is in the band." She pointed to the section below where red and white reigned alongside silver and gold instruments. Suddenly the cold air gripped her. She began to shake, and goose bumps made their way up each arm.

"You're cold!" Andrew pulled off his jacket. "Please, put this on."

"Oh, no, I couldn't," she argued. He draped the coat over her shoulders and she instinctively pulled it tight, grateful for its warmth.

"Kent, did you say?" the professor asked with interest. "Which one is he?"

"He plays the trumpet. He's the one with the brown hair on the end of the fourth row." *Why are you so nosy?*

"Ah. He looks like you," the professor said with a nod. "Same hair."

She shrugged, still shivering. "I guess so."

"No, it is," he said firmly. "Your hair is brunette, just like his."

Brunette? It was brown—plain dull, boring brown. She'd never thought of it as anything else. Somehow "brunette" made it sound more intriguing.

"His hair looks a lot more like yours than Jessica's does," Andrew observed. "Her auburn hair isn't anything like yours."

Had he actually spent time thinking about this? The notion blew her away. "She takes after her father. Greg was a redhead." She inwardly scolded herself for talking about her husband to a man she barely knew.

"Ah, that would explain the temper too," he said with a laugh.

"You think Jessica has a temper?" Her own quickly rose to the surface.

"And you don't?"

He has a point. Jess had even used that temper in his class a time or two to gain attention from him.

"I'll bet you're really proud of her."

"Sure. I'm proud of both of them." He had struck a nerve—flattering her kids. Was he serious or just trying to smooth things over with her?

"No, I mean the news . . ."

"What news?"

"I just found out yesterday afternoon myself," he continued. "Of course, it's all over campus."

"What are you talking about?"

"The scholarship," he said, looking at her incredulously. "The music scholarship."

Laura's heart began to race. Something must be wrong here—very wrong. Just yesterday morning, Jessica sat across from her at breakfast, telling her that she *didn't* get the scholarship.

"That's not right," she said, shaking her head. "Jess didn't get the music scholarship. She didn't even audition. I know all about it."

He looked at her in disbelief. "Sure, she did. Her vocal coach, Barbara Nelson, is a friend of mine. We talk about Jess all the time. She's doing really well in her voice lessons."

"*Voice* lessons?" Laura struggled to maintain her composure. There must be some mistake here.

"Sure. They say she's a natural. Haskins was anxious to hear her the other day. From what I heard, she really knocked his socks off. He said there was something about hearing that hymn sung with such depth that almost brought tears to his eyes."

Haskins? Hymn? Laura's head began to spin. She started to tremble uncontrollably but not from the cold. Her emotions were in a whirlwind. This made no sense at all. *Jessica is a pianist. She went to audition for a piano scholarship. When did she start taking voice lessons?* To be honest, Laura had been so busy, she wasn't sure what classes her daughter had signed up for.

"Haskins?" she stammered.

"Sure. The choral director. He was very impressed—said she sounded like she'd been singing for years."

"Singing for years . . ." Laura's voice trailed off. *This is awful.*

"That Haskins really knows his stuff, so she must be good. He told Barbara that he might be willing to commend Jess for the Houston Grand Opera's Youth program if she continues to work hard. He feels she'd be an asset to their program."

"An asset to their program . . . ," Laura stammered.

"I'll bet you're really proud," Andrew said with a smile.

"Really proud . . . ," she echoed softly. Laura nodded numbly, not knowing what to say next. *Jess won a scholarship. That's what she was trying to tell me yesterday morning.* Laura had been so impatient, she hadn't even waited to hear the news. Shame suddenly flooded her heart. *I'm a terrible mother. The absolute worst.*

⚭

Andrew watched as Laura's eyes filled with tears. *What did I say?* Something had gone terribly wrong, but what? "Laura, is there a problem?"

She nodded, biting her lip. "I, uh . . . I have to go." She stood abruptly, trying to step across him, the jacket dropping down onto the bench below.

"But your son . . . He hasn't even played yet."

"I know, but I have to go."

She looks almost frantic. What did I say?

She made her way down the steps, disappearing into the crowd below. Andrew wasn't sure what he'd done, but somehow he had done it again.

⚭

Laura pulled the car up the driveway, relieved to see Nathan's car parked there. *Father, for once let me get this right. Help me to lay down my crazy, foolish pride and show my daughter the kind of love she needs and deserves. Help me to use the right words.* She bounded up the walk to the front door, knocking instead of reaching for her keys. Jessica answered. Nathan stood just behind her.

"We just got here, Mom, I promise," Jess said defensively. Apparently she had prepared herself for an argument.

"I trust you, Jessica, but I really need to talk to you. Do you mind, Nathan?"

"Of course not," he said, reaching for his jacket. "Should I go?"

"No, please stay," she said. "I want you to hear this too." She stood silently for a moment, trying to decide what to say and how to say it.

"What is it, Mom? Are you gonna stand there all night?" Jess's voice had a sarcastic edge.

"Jess, I'm so sorry." Laura's mind shot back to one of Greg's favorite Sunday school expressions—the twelve words to heal any relationship: *"I am sorry. I was wrong. Please forgive me. I love you."* She would say them all before this conversation ended, no matter how difficult.

Jess looked at her dubiously. "Sorry about what?"

"About getting angry. About the scholarship. It was really wrong of me. Why didn't you tell me?"

"Tell you?"

"About the vocal scholarship."

Jessica's expression changed immediately. "You know?"

"Yes," Laura explained. "I just found out."

"Who told you?"

"Professor Dougherty."

"What? When did you see him?" Jessica looked stunned.

"He was at the game tonight."

"You're kidding. What's he doing—following you?"

"Of course not. It was just a coincidence, but I'm glad he was there. He told me what a great job you did and how proud your vocal instructor is. He told me that you got the scholarship."

"That's what I've been trying to tell you for days, Mom."

"I know that now," Laura said, reaching out to embrace her. "Jessica, I'm so proud of you."

"Right." Her daughter pulled away.

"I am, Honey. I really am."

"Well, anyway," Jess said, "it's five hundred dollars. That part should make you happy. I'm going to be less of a burden in the spring than I am now, I guess."

"Jess, please don't talk like that."

"Isn't that what you're thinking?"

"No, it's not what I'm thinking at all." Laura felt a knot in her throat. "What I'm thinking is how very proud I am of you—and how much I would love to have your forgiveness."

Jess shrugged.

"And something else too," Laura continued. "I love you. I hope you know that."

Her daughter moved toward the door, shaking her head. "Sorry, Mom. Nathan and I were just about to leave. We're going to a nine o'clock movie. Maybe later."

Nathan glanced in Laura's direction, then looked at Jessica. "We don't have to go. This is important. You guys need to talk this out."

"We don't need to talk," Jessica said, glaring at him. Laura couldn't help but see her own reflection in her daughter's countenance.

Nathan shrugged. "Whatever," he said. "But I really don't feel like seeing a movie anymore. I think I'd better go home."

"But—" Jessica never had time to finish her sentence.

Nathan gave her a quick kiss on the cheek and headed to the door. "See you tomorrow," he called out. The door shut behind him.

Jessica's eyes sparkled with anger. "Do you see what you've done? Do you see?"

"What I've done? I just wanted to ask you to forgive me and to tell you that I love you. I've been so wrong about so many things. I'm so sorry."

"Don't you get it, Mom?" Jessica said angrily. "You ruin everything for me. Everything!" With that, Jessica stormed into her room and slammed the bedroom door behind her.

Unwilling to let it go at that, Laura followed closely behind her, speaking through the door that separated them. "You can shut me out of your room, but you can't shut me out of your life."

Silence.

"I'm going to make mistakes, Jess. Lots of them."

"No kidding." Her daughter's voice sounded muffled.

"I'm human. But I don't ruin everything for you, and I won't stand by and let you say such a thing. You have no idea what it's like to be in my position. Someday, when you have kids . . ."

"That's what all mothers say." Jess opened the door abruptly. "I can't wait until then to understand what makes parents tick. I know that you're so stressed out about everything that you don't even have the time to spend with Kent and me like you used to. You're no fun anymore, Mom."

Laura looked down at the floor, unable to respond past the growing lump in her throat. "All I can say is I'm sorry, Honey. I'm doing my best." A lone tear rolled down her cheek. She brushed it away, embarrassed.

Jessica's face softened slightly. "Mom, I didn't mean to make you cry. I do love you, but I miss things being the way they were. I miss it so much."

"Me too, Honey." Laura reached to give her a hug. "Me too." They held each other for a few moments before Jess backed away and disappeared into her room.

Laura headed off to the privacy of her own bedroom, her thoughts rolling. She pulled on her flannel pajamas, then reached over to slam the closet door. Greg's suits still hung in the closet, just where he had left them. The time had come to give them away, to put them and the pain of losing her husband behind her. But she couldn't seem to do it. They had remained in the closet this long. They could stay a little longer.

Just looking at Greg's suits reminded Laura of Andrew, of the jacket he so carefully placed across her shoulders earlier this evening. Was it an attempt to reach out to her? To be nice? If so, did she feel ready for that?

Laura tossed herself across the big queen-sized bed for a good, long cry. Her heart hurt so desperately, she hardly knew how to begin mending it. Perhaps it couldn't be mended. The hole left by Greg's death had grown to immense proportions. No one, nothing, could ever fill it. Not now. Not ever.

"Surely I am with you always . . ." The words from the Scripture came to her mind. What brought them there, she could not tell. *"Surely I am with you always. . . ."*

"Who?" she cried out to the stillness of the room. "Who is with me always?" Greg certainly wasn't here. She couldn't wrap herself up in his arms and ask him to make everything all better. She had no one to fill the emptiness she felt. There would never be another human being loving enough to fill that hole, no matter whom she turned to.

What she needed to fill the gaping hole in her life, no human could fill, no mortal man could conjure up. She needed God's assurance. She needed His peace, His strength. She needed Him to move in and take over the loneliness and become the lover of her soul, to be more than just Someone she called out to in her moments of extreme need.

Problem was, she couldn't seem to let go of the pain long enough to allow Him to do that. Maybe she never could.

❧

Andrew drove home in silence, contemplating what had happened at the game. He wanted to call Laura right away, as soon as he arrived home, but he didn't have the courage. What would he say, anyway? Clearly, she hadn't wanted to share her thoughts with him. Maybe she never would.

J did it again," Andrew said.

"Did what?" Regina's eyes were more curious than accusing.

"I blew it." He looked at her for some show of support, hopeful her response wouldn't be negative. He needed a pat on the back, needed someone to tell him he wasn't a total and complete failure.

"Tell me what happened," she said soulfully, taking a seat. "I don't have to be back behind the counter for fifteen minutes. Will that give you enough time?"

He nodded lamely. "I think so."

"What happened—and be specific."

"I was at the ball game the other night with Laura—"

"You were?" Regina squealed excitedly, causing a lunchroom full of students to turn and look at them. "You asked her out? Well, it's about time. I knew you would. I just knew it."

"No. No, I didn't," he said, trying to quiet her. "I didn't ask her out."

"But you said—"

"I said I was at the ball game with her," he tried to explain. "I didn't say I asked her out."

Regina looked confused, but he plowed ahead. "Anyway, we were sitting there and I don't know what I said, but she just jumped up and ran off."

Regina let out a whistle.

"What?" he asked, avoiding her eyes.

"Must have been pretty awful. What'd you say?"

"That's just it. I didn't say much of anything. I was congratulating her on the music scholarship her daughter just received, and before I knew it, she jumped and ran."

"Maybe her pumpkin was waiting." Regina smiled. "She didn't by any chance drop a shoe when she ran off, did she—'cause you know . . ."

"I'm trying to be serious here," he interrupted, getting irritated. "You're supposed to be cheering me up. That's what you do. I come in here and whine, and you cheer me up. That's your job."

"And it's what I'm trying to do, but this time, I think I'm really on your side. Doesn't sound like you did anything wrong. Did that ever occur to you?"

He shrugged.

"Maybe she had something on her mind. Could have just been a bad day. That happens to other people too, you know. You don't need to take everything so personally."

"I know." He had already considered that possibility. But why had Laura run off at that very moment—just when he brought up Jessica?

"Professor," Regina said, looking at him seriously, "I'm going to give you some sage advice."

He looked into her eyes. If anyone could give advice worth taking, Regina could. She had a depth that seemed undeniable.

"I think it's time to back off and just let nature take its course."

"Let nature take its course? In that case, I might as well forget the whole thing."

"I said, 'back off,' not drop out of the race. There is something you could be doing in the meantime."

"What's that?"

"I'm just wondering. Are you a praying man?" She spoke the words quietly, but with an assurance that seemed to come from deep within.

"A what?" How in the world could he go about answering a question like that?

"A praying man . . ." She said it again, this time looking him right in the eye.

His gaze shifted immediately. It wasn't that he never prayed; it was just that he hadn't for awhile—a long while—say five, ten years. "I suppose."

"Well then, why don't you stop all your whining and just get down on those knees of yours," Regina said, "and get busy praying? She'll come around if it's God's plan."

God's plan? "Are you saying I'm supposed to pray for a wife? Is that how desperate I've become?"

"No, of course not." She stood. "You've always been that desperate. You just never knew what to do about it."

"Regina, I never know how to take you. You're kidding, right?"

"No, I'm not. That's how I found my Daniel. I prayed for a godly husband, and before I knew it, Daniel Leal just waltzed into my life. And now that we've already got this woman picked out for you . . ."

"Picked out? Regina, you are too much."

❧

"What are you talking about?" Laura asked the man at the front door. "I paid the electric bill last week."

"Better check again, lady," he said, placing a slip of paper in her hand. "According to the office, they never received a payment."

She shook her head in disbelief. "I thought I paid it." *Of course, with everything going on in my life, I could have forgotten.* "Could you wait just a moment while I check?"

"Won't make any difference. I can't take a payment at the door. I'm just here to shut you off."

"But . . ." *This is crazy. I know I paid that bill.*

"You could make a payment on-line, but they usually take a couple of days to post."

Is he kidding? This house is all electric. We'll freeze to death in here.

"If you want your power turned back on by tomorrow, you could go to one of our payment centers. There's one about five miles from here, on Robinson."

"You look like a very understanding man." She forced a nervous smile. "Would you really do this to us three weeks before Thanksgiving?"

He shrugged, a look of compassion crossing his face. "I just do what they tell me, Mrs. Chapman. You understand."

Within minutes the house sat in cold, stony silence. The rattle of the dishwasher no longer hung in the air. The gentle flow of warm air no longer emanated from the vents. The refrigerator ceased to hum. Laura would have missed them all, if she had let herself. But the anger was far too hot in her heart for that. *I know I paid that bill. I remember writing the check.* She thumbed through her checkbook until she came to the one made out to the electric company. *I forgot to mail it. I can't believe it. I've never done anything like that before.*

A surge of emotion raced through her. "It's not fair!" she shouted, though no one was close enough to hear. She leaned against the wall as her knees gave way. Everything seemed to be crumbling around her, and she couldn't do a thing about any of it. Nothing had prepared her for this. Nothing.

She gave herself over to the tears without a moment's guilt. They were long overdue. She had played the role of valiant widow long enough. She couldn't keep the game going any longer. Her heart ached with a fierceness she hadn't known in all of the time since Greg's passing. The full gamut of emotions tore through her. Anger. Pain. Fear. Loneliness.

This can't go on, Lord! I'm asking for Your help, Father—but more than that, I'm asking You to forgive me for not trusting in You. Increase my faith. Give me courage. I love You, Lord!

$\mathcal{L}$ aura shuffled back and forth between the bookstore and home, working until her body passed the point of exhaustion. For over a week, she had covered both Madeline's hours and her own. It couldn't be avoided. Madeline had been sick with the flu and someone needed to fill her shoes. Laura was the logical candidate. Unfortunately, she had missed several classes along the way.

The lights might be back on at home, but everything else remained in the dark. Jessica hadn't spoken to her in days. Laura managed to get a few words out of Nathan—something about Jess moving out—but there had been no sign anything like that was actually going to happen.

I'll show her the same patience You've shown me, Lord.

On top of everything, the car broke down. One evening last week, it just wouldn't start. A dead battery would have been bad enough, but the source of the problem turned out to be an alternator. As usual, when it rained, it poured—at least in her life. But something felt different. Somehow, in the middle of her turmoil, Laura found peace. In the very middle of her storm, she felt anchored.

Her only real regret was being away from school. She had missed two days this week—Tuesday and Thursday. Any more, and she might never get caught up. Her English teacher had been amiable, even offering to e-mail her assignments. Her math homework would have to wait. And American History—well, there just didn't seem to be much hope that she would ever catch up in that class, so why bother trying?

Andrew sat at the dinner table, listening to his fellow professors drone on about unimportant things. He was up to his ears as they rambled on about economics and politics. To be honest, he didn't give a rip about the latest stock market analysis. He had far more important things on his mind.

Laura Chapman. He couldn't release himself from the image of her wavy hair and silly smirk . . . her soft, smooth skin that carried the bold pink hue of a hot temper when she got riled up . . . her voice, trembling with anger as she spoke. Her "I told you so" smile when she proved him wrong. He missed those things, and so much more. Laura had been absent for the last two classes. With only two weeks before Thanksgiving, he started to worry that she might not come back at all. Truthfully, he missed her. There didn't seem to be any other way to put it. He missed the look of anger in her sparkling eyes. He missed her furrowed brow as she leaned over those unreasonably hard pop quizzes he gave.

For nearly two weeks, he had thought of little but her. When she ran off from the football game that night, she left behind far more than the scent of her perfume. The undeniable lingered in the air. Regina had been right all along. Andrew didn't hate Laura. He liked her—maybe a little too much. What he had grown to feel couldn't be explained without some amount of stammering on his part.

Did he really have room in his heart for someone like Laura Chapman? He hoped so.

"Andrew, are you with us?" Sociology professor, Mack Brewer, asked.

"Yeah, yeah . . ."

"We were just asking about your position on yesterday's big story out of Washington. Where do you stand?"

"Oh," he said, trying to focus. "I think it's awful, but I've got faith in our leadership. I'm sure they'll bring us through it all in fine style— if we don't mind hanging in limbo until then."

"What are you talking about?" Mack laughed. "I was asking your opinion on the renovations taking place at the National Art Gallery. What were you talking about?"

"Oh, I, uh . . . ," Andrew stammered. "I'm sorry. I guess I wasn't paying attention."

"Well, that's obvious. But at least we're all aware of your political views!"

Those at the table had a good laugh at Andrew's expense. He turned his attentions back to Laura, completely oblivious.

꙳

Laura tossed and turned in the bed, unable to sleep. She reached across the sheets. In that moment, Laura felt a sudden breeze blow through the room. She gazed at the window. *Surely no one would have opened it in the middle of November.* No, thank goodness, it was closed. But the breeze . . . Where had it come from? She lay, transfixed, watching, wondering. She began to sense an undeniable warmth, a somber satisfaction.

"Surely I am with you always." There was that Scripture again. God was taking the time to call out to her, to let her know He was still here. He hadn't gone anywhere. Greg's spot in the bed might be vacant, but she didn't have to be empty.

"Lord, I'm here. Please don't leave me."

"I will never leave you nor forsake you." Another of her favorite Scriptures came to mind almost immediately, doing its work to fill the void within. She was not forsaken! God hadn't left her at all. He hadn't been far off. In fact, He was so close, she could almost reach out and touch Him. Laura's heart began to dance within her. She was almost giddy as the words tripped across her tongue, "Thank You, Lord! Thank You!"

Suddenly everything became clear. She had been walking through the valley of the shadow, where the darkness had all but overwhelmed her. But this was a new day. *I'm going to be just fine.* God, the very lover of her soul, was there to remind her of that—and what a sweet reminder!

Emotion gave way to exhaustion and a peace like she hadn't felt in quite some time. Laura fell into a deep, well-deserved sleep.

16

"Ms. Chapman?"

Laura looked up from the bookshelf into the eyes of Professor Andrew Dougherty. Her heartbeat immediately quickened. *What's he doing here?*

"Professor . . ." She said the word slowly, hesitantly.

He took a step in her direction. "Can you call me Andrew?"

"Mr. Dougherty," she said, looking the other way. "Is there something I can help you with?"

"I was going to ask you the same thing."

"What do you mean?"

"Well, we've missed you in class this past week, and I thought maybe you'd like your assignments."

Is he actually here on a goodwill mission? "I'm . . . I'm sorry. I've been working a lot of extra hours."

"That's all right. I understand completely. I just wanted to make sure you weren't staying away because of me."

Interesting remark. Laura looked into his anxious eyes. "No." Had he really been worried about her? Was that possible? "It doesn't have anything to do with you." She straightened the books as she spoke.

"That's good." He sounded relieved. "When you left the game last Saturday night, I felt sure I'd said something wrong. You may recall that I'm pretty good at putting my foot in my mouth."

"I do." She smiled, in spite of herself. "But you didn't do anything wrong this time. To be honest, I didn't know about Jess auditioning for the vocal scholarship. I guess I felt a little left out. I don't know."

"Oh, I'm sorry."

I can't blame him. It's certainly not his fault. "You were just happy for

567

her—which I should have been—but wasn't because we had spent the whole weekend not speaking to each other." Suddenly Laura felt a release to talk, to really talk. For the first time in a long time, it felt great to have someone to share with, even if it was Professor Andrew Dougherty.

❧

Andrew stood, mesmerized, listening to Laura speak. He learned much about her family during those precious minutes—far more than he had counted on. *She's a beautiful woman, inside and out. I can't believe she's taking the time to share all of this with me.*

His heart beat in his ears as he tried to work up the courage to ask her the question on his mind. "Do you get a break anytime soon?"

"I have been here all day, but I haven't gone to lunch yet. Why?"

Why? Because I have plans, if I can just work up the courage to implement them! "There's a deli a couple of doors down," he said nervously. "Have you ever been there?"

"Sure."

"Well, I was thinking maybe I could take you to lunch." *I can't believe the words are coming out of my mouth. Then again, it's not as difficult as I thought it would be.*

She hesitated for what seemed like an eternity. "I, um . . . I'll have to check with Madeline."

He followed her to the front of the store, where her boss's broad smile let him know instantly that she could go. *I can't believe it. I'm actually going out to lunch with Laura Chapman.* Try as he might, he couldn't wipe the silly grin off his face.

❧

Laura's hands shook as she reached behind the counter to pick up her purse. *What am I doing? I can't stand this guy, right? Of course he does seem easy to talk to. And he's been so understanding about the classes I've missed. Maybe I've misjudged him. Maybe he's not such a bad guy after all.*

"Are you ready?" she asked, looking into Andrew's eyes. For the first time, she noticed what a remarkable shade of blue they were. Not that it mattered. She just hadn't taken note of it before.

"I'm ready." He pulled the door open for her. They stepped out onto the sidewalk, then turned in the direction of the deli.

"Laura, is that you?" She heard the voice, somewhat familiar, and turned. Richard DeHart stood just behind her.

"Dick?" *Talk about lousy timing.*

"I was just coming in to ask you to lunch." He frowned. "Am I too late?"

Andrew jumped in quickly. "We're just headed out—the two of us." His voice sounded strained.

"I'm so sorry." Laura looked from Dick to Andrew and back.

"No problem." Dick reached out to take her arm. "You're both hungry. So am I. What do you say we all go together?"

Laura's eyes searched out Andrew's. She hoped he would say something. *He's obviously upset. So am I, but what can I do about it? I don't want to be rude. Maybe he doesn't either.*

"I don't think—" Andrew began.

"You're right," Dick said. "I don't think it's such a bad idea either."

&

Andrew's pulse quickened. *Dick DeHart is the last man on the planet I'd want to go to lunch with.* He watched out of the corner of his eye as Dick patted Laura's arm. *This guy infuriates me. I should do something about this.* He looked at Laura intently, hoping for some sign of her feelings. Her face looked slightly flushed, but she didn't seem to show the same level of anxiety he felt. Either that, or she was better at hiding it. Worse still, maybe she wanted to go to lunch with Dick DeHart.

"We're just headed down to the deli," Laura said. "I really don't have long, anyway."

"Well then," Dick said, "I'm awfully glad I got here when I did. Talk about great timing."

Yeah. Talk about great timing.

&

Laura sat at the table between the two men, completely confused and frustrated. Andrew's ears grew redder by the moment. Dick—well, Dick was content to barrel away, pounding Andrew into the ground with his expertise on early American presidents. She could slip away, and they would probably just go right on bickering. She tried, at several points, to enter into their conversation, but they seemed to be talking around her, not to her.

"So," she said finally, "I guess you'll both have to agree to disagree." They'd argued about the difference between the administrations of John Adams and John Quincy Adams for the last ten minutes.

"Are we boring you?" Andrew looked her in the eye.

Boring? Are you kidding me? She was half-asleep already. She shrugged, unwilling to speak her mind. She felt bored, yes, but more irritated than anything—like a third wheel, stuck directly between two flat tires. "I have to get back to work." She stood, relieved to be leaving.

"So soon?" Dick looked at his watch. "We're just getting started."

"Well, I'm sure the two of you will have a lot to talk about once I'm gone." She turned quickly and noticed Jessica, who stood just outside the window.

Oh, dear. Just when I thought things couldn't possibly get any worse.

❧

Andrew stood, pulling out Laura's chair. *She looks frustrated. I don't blame her. This isn't how things were supposed to work out at all.* He had planned a long, lingering lunch over an exhilarating conversation—just between the two of them. *Leave it to Dick DeHart to mess things up.* "Are you sure you have to go?" He gave her his most imploring look.

She turned away from him as she spoke. "I'm already late."

"Would you mind if I stopped by the store in a few minutes?"

"Whatever."

Is she disinterested or just plain mad? Laura quickly moved toward the door, taking his hopes with her.

"Looks like it's just the two of us," Dick said with a sly grin.

"Great." Andrew reached to take another drink of his soda. "Just what the doctor ordered."

❧

"Jess, what are you doing down here? Is something wrong? Is Kent in trouble again?"

"Mom, calm down. Kent's fine. Everything's fine. I just wanted to talk to you."

"Talk to me?"

"Yeah, is that so surprising? But it looks like you already have enough people to talk to. You certainly don't need me." She turned abruptly.

"Jessica," Laura said sternly. "This is not what it looks like. Professor Dougherty came by to . . . well, to talk to me about school stuff. He offered to take me to lunch. On the way out the door, we ran into Dick DeHart, and then things got complicated. I just couldn't seem to get rid of him."

"Whatever."

"Jess, stop it. Besides, it's not like I was having a good time." She waved her arms toward the deli to indicate her frustration. "They're both so egotistical and self-serving, they never even saw me."

A faint smile crossed Jessica's lips, the first sign of compromise. She gazed into the window of the deli. Both men seemed to be engrossed in conversation.

"Despite what you might think, I don't like either one of them. I really don't. I wouldn't go out with Dick DeHart under any circumstances, and the professor . . ."

"Yes?" Jessica asked. "What about the professor?"

"Well, he's a nice guy, but . . ."

"Not your type?"

Laura hesitated slightly. "To be honest, I'm not sure what my type is anymore." She gazed through the deli window at Andrew, who looked miserable sitting next to Dick DeHart. *I almost feel sorry for him.*

"Look at them," Jessica said with a smirk. "They're two peas in a pod."

"Aren't they? Let's get out of here and leave them alone." That thought seemed very appealing to Laura.

She and Jessica walked toward the bookstore, laughing and talking about the professor, the tutor, and her daughter's apparent misunderstanding. Laura didn't mind being misunderstood, as long as things were made right again. Within moments, they chatted like youngsters. For the first time in a long time, Laura felt comfortable around her daughter.

They stopped just outside the door of the Bookstop. Jessica's expression changed abruptly. "Mom, there's something I need to talk to you about. That's why I came down here in the first place."

Laura nodded, waiting for her daughter to continue. No one ever wanted to "just talk" anymore, especially not Jess. "What is it, Honey?"

"It sounds stupid now, after just blowing up at you. In fact, I've been doing that a lot lately. I can't seem to control my emotions. But that's why I'm here. I, uh . . . I just wanted to apologize."

"For what, Honey?"

"Mom," Jessica said tearfully, "I'm just so sorry about everything that's happened this whole semester. I feel like I've ruined everything for you. I should have been more supportive when you told me you wanted to go back to school. You've been through so much these last couple of years, and I couldn't even give you any support at all. I'm selfish. There's no other way to put it." At that, Jessica burst into tears and buried her face in her hands.

"Jess," Laura said softly, reaching to put her arms around her precious daughter. "We've all been through a lot. Ever since your father passed away . . ." The tears filled her eyes as well. "Ever since your father passed away, I've had to become mother and father. Nothing in life prepared me for that. It's hard enough just being Mom. I don't have any idea how to be Dad too."

"You don't have to be." Jessica lifted her head. "Don't even try. We'll be fine with just you."

The words were freeing. Laura began to weep uncontrollably. Customers passed by. Many gazed at her oddly, but she didn't care.

"I just don't want to get in the way," Jess continued.

"You're not in the way. You never were, and you never will be."

"But I'm such a pain in the neck."

"Yeah," Laura said with a smile. "But aren't we all, sometimes? I mean—I'm a pain too. Don't you think?"

"Do you really want me to answer that?"

Laura shook her head. "Not really, but we're all grieving, Jessica. And the way you've felt—about the music, about my going back to school, about Nathan, even . . ."

"What about Nathan?"

"I know things have been tense between the two of you," Laura said. "It's pretty clear."

"I don't know what to do about that either. I don't know what to do about anything."

"I think it's time for a fresh start," Laura said firmly. "For all of us. Time to start everything over again."

"How? How do we do that?"

Laura suddenly came to life. "Well, for one thing, I think we need to go back to church on a regular basis. None of this in-and-out stuff."

"I know I could use it," Jess agreed. "My spiritual life has been, well, almost nonexistent."

"I'm sure we could all do with a little spiritual help. Besides, I miss being in Sunday school and singing in the choir. Most of all, I long for the closeness I used to feel when we were there together as a family."

"Yeah," Jess responded. "To be honest, I've really missed being in the youth group and all that. Heaven knows, Kent could use it."

"True."

"But, Mom," Jessica said suddenly, "there's something else I want to do. It's actually the reason I came down here."

"What's that?"

"I want to come to work for you."

"What do you mean?"

Determination etched Jessica's face. "I mean, I want to work some of your hours here at the shop so you can get back into your classes and finish the semester."

"But—"

"I've got it all worked out, Mom. I can give at least two or three hours a day and still keep my schedule at the school. I've even talked to Madeline about it. She's totally cool with the idea. I'll have to miss a couple of history classes, but I'm okay with that. I haven't missed any until recently."

"Madeline wants you to take some of my hours?"

"That's right," her boss said, appearing behind her. "I think it's a great idea, don't you?"

To be honest, Laura didn't know what to think.

17

"Hey, you!"

Regina's voice rang out, waking Andrew from his lethargy. He had been grading papers—one after another—and welcomed the interruption. Regina stood in the doorway of his classroom, looking as nervous as a cat.

"What's up?"

"Just wanted to come by and let you know something." She walked into the empty room. "I've got news."

"Me too," he said excitedly. "But you go first. What's up?"

"Nope. You first. Is it something to do with the infamous Ms. Chapman?"

"Maybe."

"Well, come on. Spill the beans. I don't have all day."

"You'd be proud of me," he said with a smile. "I took her to lunch."

"You did! You actually did it?"

His gaze shifted to the ground as he spoke. "Sort of."

"Sort of? Tell me."

"I went to the store where she works to talk to her, and there was this deli next door—"

"Good boy, good boy."

"So I asked her if she wanted to go and talk for awhile."

"And she said yes?" Regina's voice reflected her glee.

"Uh-huh."

"Andrew, that's great! Then what happened?"

He felt his face fall. "Then DeHart walked up on us."

"Oh, no. That weasel."

"Yeah."

"I hope you got rid of him."

Andrew shrugged.

"Don't tell me . . ." Regina stared him down.

"He came to lunch with us."

Regina slapped herself in the head. "I'm about to give up on you, Professor Dougherty. In fact, that's what I came to tell you. You're on your own after today."

"What do you mean?"

She hesitated slightly. "I, uh . . ."

"Spit it out." *She's obviously got something on her mind.*

"Today was my last day in the lunchroom."

"You quit? Why?"

"Had to," she said. "I'm just too tired."

Don't tell me she's sick. Bad things don't happen to great people like Regina. If anyone deserves a break, she does. "Tell me about it," he said finally. "I mean, if you want to." *I don't want to get too personal.* She stepped toward his desk, half-sitting on the edge. He waited for her explanation.

"It's like this. I . . . I'm going to have a baby."

He shot out of his seat instantly. "A baby? Are you serious?"

"I'm serious. But my husband says he wants me off my feet. I'm no spring chicken, you know. Turned forty last month."

"You don't look a day over twenty-nine."

She gave him a thankful smile. "Well, anyway, I just wanted to come over and say good-bye, wanted to make sure you could handle this romance business without me. You're really not very good at it, you know."

"I'm not so sure about that, but I'll do the best I can." He reached over and gave her a playful hug. "Congratulations, Regina." He felt a lump in his throat. "I'm very happy for you. Please tell Daniel for me."

"I will." She returned the hug. "In fact, he's waiting for me in the car. We're both tickled pink." She paused. "Better make that blue. He's holding out for a boy."

⁓

Laura entered the American History classroom, struggling with her emotions. She wanted desperately to be here and yet felt terrified at the same time. As she came through the door, she saw Andrew with his arms wrapped around the lady from the lunchroom in a warm embrace. Laura stood, transfixed. She couldn't seem to move forward. She didn't want to go backward.

"I'll see you later, Andrew," the woman said, passing by her at the doorway. Laura noticed the woman stared at her. A twinge of jealousy shot through her, though she wasn't sure why.

"Mr. Chapman." She looked up into the eyes of Andrew Dougherty, amazed at the twinkle she found there. "You're back?"

"I'm back," she said, trying not to let her emotions show. "I've got to get through these last few weeks somehow."

He smiled a warm, inviting smile. "It's going to be just fine, and I'm going to help you."

~❧~

Andrew's heart pounded so hard, he could scarcely breathe. Laura had returned. His trip to the store must have made the difference. He looked at her inquisitively. Was she here because she really wanted to be? Did it have anything to do with him at all?

"My daughter is going to miss class today," Laura explained. "She's taken some of my hours at the bookstore."

Ah. So, Jessica made all of this possible. Well, thank goodness for Jessica! "I'll be glad to send her work home with you."

"Thank you—for everything." She smiled at him warmly.

Andrew fought to keep his composure. He wanted to know what made her tick, what gave her such tenacity. He wanted to take back everything he had ever thought about her being lazy. Laura Chapman had turned out to be one of the hardest workers he'd ever come across in his years as a teacher. Should he tell her, give her some sort of confirmation she would make it?

Andrew watched as she sat at her desk, pulling open the textbook. He turned his gaze to the board, where he wrote questions from today's lesson, then turned slightly to see if she had watched him. No, her head remained buried in the book. She seemed to be lost in her own world.

She probably thinks I'm going to give another pop quiz. Well, not today. No, he would take it easy on his students for a change. For some reason, he felt like a new man, invigorated, alive. As the rest of the students entered and took their seats, he made a silent pact with himself to go easier on them today.

"Welcome, everyone." He turned to face the class. "I trust you all managed to get through the work sheet I gave you when we met last."

A slight rumble went up from the students, who reached for their papers.

"Well, let's forget all about that and take a look at something else." They looked up at him, obviously startled.

"You mean we don't have to turn them in?" one of the boys asked.

"Not this time."

A look of relief flooded several faces. Still others looked puzzled. "Are you feeling all right, Professor Dougherty?" one of the girls asked.

"Never better." He turned his attention to an enlightening discussion on the Industrial Revolution, trying to remain focused. The students chimed in, creating a lively discussion. From the front of the room he kept a watchful eye on Laura. What was she thinking? Had he said anything to offend her?

No, she appeared to be smiling, enjoying the conversation as much as the others. All through the class, Andrew couldn't seem to take his eyes off of Laura. She seemed different, somehow—more peaceful than before. The angry edge was gone, replaced with the closest thing to happiness he had observed in quite awhile.

His heart continued to race as he concluded the class. Andrew hoped for a way to keep Laura after class, to ask her . . .

What he really wanted to do was ask her out, but he couldn't even say the words to himself. A date. He wanted a real date with her. But would she? She certainly hadn't shown interest in him at the deli the other day. Then again, that was Dick DeHart's fault. He had ruined the afternoon entirely.

Andrew dismissed the class, waiting to see if she would linger behind the group. Their eyes met for a brief moment. He turned his gaze to the papers on the desk, embarrassed that she had caught him looking at her. He looked back up again, disappointed to find she had slipped out of her seat and was headed toward the door.

"Ms. Chapman?"

"Yes?" She turned, looking at him.

"I wonder . . . I wonder if you could stay after class for a few moments," he said, feeling his hands begin to shake.

"Why?"

"Well, I, uh . . ." The other students disappeared down the hallway, leaving them alone.

"I want to tell you how happy I am to see you. I'm glad you're back."

She looked startled. "You are?"

"Certainly. Haven't you figured that out yet?" He fought to continue. "I enjoy your company, Ms. Chapman." Andrew searched her eyes for a response.

Her face flushed as she whispered hoarsely, "Call me Laura."

"Laura." His hands shook uncontrollably now. "That's why I wanted to take you to lunch the other day. I'm so sorry about the way everything turned out."

"Me too."

"I wanted to spend some time alone with you, to get to know you. I wanted to make up for the time I've spent poking fun at you or making assumptions."

"It's all in the past. I hope you can forgive me for the day we met."

He smiled, remembering. "Done." He paused slightly. "Do you still think I'm so tough?"

"In a good way. Most of these kids need a little push. I know you've made me a better student."

"I have?"

"If nothing else, you motivated me, made me want to be the best I could be. That's what every good teacher strives to do, right?"

"Right." Andrew stared at her in disbelief. *She's so giving.* "Look," he said, feeling strength well up in him, "I've been trying to work up the courage to ask you something."

She looked up, their gazes locking. "What is that?"

"This probably isn't the right time or place . . ." He looked toward the door. Any moment now, students from his next class would be arriving. It was now or never. "I've been wanting to ask you out on a date. A real date. Just the two of us."

"Are you serious?"

"Never more serious."

She bit her lip before responding. "I'm not sure if I'm ready for that yet."

His heart twisted inside him as he took her hand. "Will you let me know when you are? I don't want to rush you, but I'd love to spend some time getting to know you better."

She nodded silently. "I'll do that."

His heart swelled. "That would be great." Just then, two students barreled through the door, laughing at one another. Laura quickly pulled her hand from his and moved toward the door. "I really need to get to work. Jess has been so good to cover for me, but I'm sure she's ready for a break." She smiled, then left the room in a hurry.

Andrew turned toward the board, erasing the notes from the last class. His heart soared as he contemplated her words. "Andrew Dougherty," he whispered, "I do believe you're making progress."

18

"Kent? Jessica? Are you guys ready?" Laura called out, trying to rush them. "We're going to be late to church." Something about the words reminded her of when they were children. Many a Sunday morning had been spent looking for missing shoes or socks or arguing over appropriate church attire. She and Greg had always managed to get them out the door and to church in time for Sunday school.

Kent appeared at the top of the stairs, still in his pajama pants and T-shirt. He stretched, letting out a loud, rehearsed moan. "Mornin'."

"What are you doing, Kent? I told you to get ready nearly an hour ago."

"I fell back asleep," he said with a yawn. "Just go on without me."

"Go to church without you? But—"

"Aw, give me a break, Mom. I've had a tough week at school. I'm beat."

Laura felt the disappointment deeply. *I wanted this to be a family affair. Well, at least Jessica will go with me.*

"Jess?" She called up the stairs. Her daughter appeared, dressed in a dark green suit.

"You look great."

"Thanks." Jessica smiled. "So do you."

"Did you say Nathan wanted to sit with us this morning?"

"He's meeting us there. He always rides with his parents, anyway." She pulled the door shut behind them, and they headed out to the car. The air outside felt crisp and cold. Laura shivered, pulling her jacket tightly around herself. Doing so reminded her of the night at the football game when Andrew pulled his jacket over her shoulders to keep her warm. *Andrew*. Thinking of him brought an unexpected smile. *Is it possible I'm beginning to have feelings for this man?*

"It's almost Thanksgiving." Jessica interrupted her thoughts as they climbed into the car. "Can you believe it? It seems like the semester just started."

"Seems more like an eternity to me, but I'm happy the holidays are coming. It means I'm one step closer to being done with my first semester."

"You've done a great job, Mom. I'm really proud of you."

Laura felt her heart swell. "I never thought I'd hear those words—not from you, anyway."

"Well, just like you've been saying—today's a new day."

They drove to the church, chatting about everything from Christmas gifts to Thanksgiving dinner. It was a truly wonderful trip.

❧

Andrew changed the channels on the TV, frustrated. *Church services.* He certainly wasn't interested in any of those . . . or was he? One, in particular, caught his eye. It was a room full of people, singing, worshiping. They seemed to be happy, in an odd sort of way.

"What phonies. Like anyone could be that happy in church."

And yet, he couldn't seem to change the channel. Something about those people held him captivated—something in their expression intrigued him. They didn't look like they were faking anything. In fact, they looked perfectly natural, genuinely comfortable.

"Comfortable in church. Now that's something I've never felt." It wasn't like Andrew had never been to church. He had been raised in one. His strict mother had pulled him out of the arms of his agnostic father every Sunday until Andrew turned about twelve or thirteen. That's when he rebelled—started staying home with his dad for one-on-one conversations about the things that really interested him—explorers, navigators, maps, and so much more. That's where the fun had been. He certainly never experienced any joy sitting in a pew.

Joy. There seemed to be so little of it in his life. His passion for teaching brought him joy, but not the kind that really lasted. Those people on the television looked like they had something that superceded what he felt in front of the classroom. Their joy seemed to come from something inside, something he couldn't quite understand. "I don't get it," he whispered, "but I'd sure like to figure it out."

He watched as the pastor brought the congregation to laughter with a joke about children. "No, I never went to a church like that." He spoke to the empty room. "But maybe someday I will."

～❧

"Turn with me to Colossians, chapter three," the pastor said. "Verses twelve through fourteen."

Laura turned through her worn Bible until she found the passage. She had always loved this one, but somehow, in the middle of things, she had simply forgotten about it.

The pastor's voice rang out against the silence. " 'Therefore, as God's chosen people, holy and dearly loved, clothe yourselves with compassion, kindness, humility, gentleness and patience.' "

Kindness? Patience? Laura had shown little of these traits over the last several months, in spite of her good intentions.

" 'Bear with each other,' " the pastor continued, " 'and forgive whatever grievances you may have against one another. Forgive as the Lord forgave you.' "

She had forgiven everyone, hadn't she? After all, she excused Jessica for giving her the cold shoulder. She pardoned Kent for complicating their already complicated lives with his shenanigans. She had forgiven Greg . . . Wait a minute! Greg hadn't done anything wrong. Why should she have to forgive him? Could she possibly be holding him in unforgiveness—after all this time?

The pastor continued on, oblivious to her inner turmoil: " 'And over all these virtues put on love, which binds them all together in perfect unity.' "

Love. She and Greg had been in love—the kind that surpassed romance. The kind that could have lasted forever—at least that's what she always thought. Gentle tears began to course down Laura's cheeks. She reached for a tissue but found none. Jessica quickly handed her one, then reached out to touch her arm.

"It's all right, Mom," she whispered, eyes glistening. "I know how you feel."

The pastor went on to talk about the steps to mend broken relationships. Laura took notes, scribbling down as many words as she could on the back of an offering envelope. Jess handed her the church bulletin, pointing to a blank spot on the back. "There you go, Mom," she whispered.

Laura reached to pat her hand, a gesture of thanks. *Lord, thank You so much for sending Jessica with me. I love spending time with her.* She paused from her note-taking, content to sit with her hand wrapped around her daughter's. She could go on sitting like this forever.

The service ended some time later, but Laura couldn't seem to pull herself from the sanctuary. Even after most of the others left, she remained. She slowly made her way up to the front, a place she had often visited as a child. Funny how the altar still cried out to her. Jess had disappeared to the foyer with Nathan, so Laura took advantage of the situation by kneeling for a few moments alone.

"Lord, I'm here," she whispered. "I made it. And I'm back to stay this time. I'm not going anywhere." She felt the presence of God overwhelm her. "How did I stay away so long?" She spent a few more minutes opening up her heart to her Father. How wonderful it felt to be back in this place, the very place Greg had loved so much.

"Greg." No sooner did she speak his name than she realized what she must do. "I have to forgive him, Lord. Help me."

Her daughter appeared behind her. "Mom, is there anything I can do?"

"No, Jess." She looked up with a smile, dabbing at her eyes.

"I'm worried about you."

"No need to worry. This is a good thing."

"Are you sure?"

Laura nodded. "Yes, but I'm not sure I can explain what I'm feeling right now."

"Could you try?" Jessica knelt down beside her.

Laura took her hand and clutched it tightly. "When your father died . . ." That was all she got out before the tears came again.

"Tell me, Mom."

Laura took a deep breath. "When your father died, I blamed God. I didn't realize it until months later. I was so angry with Him that I never wanted to come back into a church again. In fact, I even told Him that."

"You did?"

"Yes, but it was wrong of me. I knew that, after awhile. That day—when you came up to the store—I realized then that I was also angry at you kids."

"At us? Why? What did we do?"

"It wasn't anything you did, exactly. The situation I found myself in had reached a crisis point. Don't you see? I've been completely responsible for the two of you with no one to help me. Since I had locked God out, I sure couldn't look to Him for help. That left me on my own. But that day you came up to the store, God began to show me this."

"Really?"

"Yes. He showed me that unforgiveness is like a prison. It holds us in its grip until we can't breathe. Eventually we become so bitter, we're no fun to be around. I don't want to be like that!" At that, Laura began to cry unashamed. "Can you ever forgive me, Jess? I'm so sorry about everything!"

"Mom, of course I do, and I know Kent will too. But you have to forgive us, too. We haven't exactly made things easier." They embraced for what seemed like an eternity.

"There's something else," Laura said finally. "And this is the worst part. I didn't realize it until just this morning. I really didn't."

"What, Mom?"

"I've been angry with your father." She spoke through the tears. "I've been so angry with him, I couldn't think straight. He left me. He abandoned me."

Jessica held her tightly. "I do understand, Mom. More than you know. I've been mad at Daddy too. I've been so mad, sometimes I fight with him in my dreams."

"You what?"

"I dream about him," Jessica explained, "and we always end up fighting. I argue and argue but never seem to win. He always wins. But then I wake up and realize what's happened—that it's just a dream— and try to put it out of my mind. But the dreams don't go away."

"Jess, I never knew."

"I know," she said sadly. "I never told you. I just wake up in a bad mood and take it out on you and Kent. I have a feeling things are going to be better after today, don't you?"

"It felt really good to go back to church," Laura said, smiling through the tears. "I mean, it was hard—seeing all of those women sitting there with their husbands beside them, but it still felt wonderful."

"I thought so too. I missed having Daddy next to me, trying to sing bass."

"He had a terrible voice," Laura said with a smile. "Do you remember?"

Jess laughed. "How could I forget?"

He hadn't been the best singer in the world, but he had certainly made up for it by being the best husband.

"Jess, would you pray with me before we leave?"

"Here?" Her daughter looked around. "Out loud?"

Laura nodded. "If you don't mind."

Jessica began to pray aloud, hesitantly at first, then gaining strength as she went. Her prayer was passionate, heartfelt. As she continued on, Laura's heart swelled with joy inside her. She had truly come home.

❧

Andrew paced back and forth across his tiny living room, the words from the television still on his mind. Something the TV pastor had said intrigued him. He couldn't seem to shake it: " 'Be transformed by the renewing of your mind . . . ,' " or something like that.

"Transforming your mind." He repeated the words. Andrew understood the concept of strengthening his mind by gaining knowledge, of bettering himself. That's why he had spent so many years in college, and why he felt driven to teach.

But this idea of transforming his mind . . . Now that was certainly something new, something to think about.

"Does he mean I should gain more knowledge?" he asked, pacing across the room. "Or is there something more?"

He headed to the computer, rapidly signing on-line. "Surely there's got to be some sort of Bible on-line I can read," he spoke aloud. "I'll get this figured out."

Before he knew it, three hours had passed. Bleary-eyed, Andrew reached to shut the computer down, his mind reeling. If the Scriptures he'd read were true, bettering his mind didn't have anything to do with education.

It had everything to do with inspiration.

❧

"I'm sorry . . . what did you say?" Laura felt sure she had heard the voice on the other end of the phone correctly, but she didn't want to believe it.

"This is Officer Meyer with the Harris County Sheriff's Department. Your son was in an accident on Interstate 45 about half an hour ago and has been taken to Northwest Hospital."

Please, God, no! "I'm on my way," Laura spoke, suddenly feeling faint. She hung the phone up, trembling as she called, "Jess!"

Her daughter appeared quickly, a look of fear crossing her face when she saw her mother. "What is it?"

"It's Kent."

"What about him?"

"He's been in an accident."

"What? What happened?"

"I don't know. They didn't say."

"Where is he?"

"Northwest. Can you drive?"

Jessica nodded, taking the keys from her hand. "Of course. You just get whatever you think you'll need. Do you have his insurance card?"

Laura nodded lamely, letting her daughter take charge. If nothing else, it felt good to have someone else in control—at least for the moment.

Laura felt numb as they made their way outside.

"When we get there, I'm going to let you off at the door," Jess explained as they got into the car. "Then I'm going to park. Getting a parking space at Northwest isn't easy. Did they say where to go? Is he in the Emergency Room, or have they moved him?"

"I . . . I don't know." Laura tried to speak over the lump in her throat. "I forgot to ask."

"Well, we'll start there. Don't worry, Mom. I know he's going to be all right."

Laura nodded numbly, trying to collect her thoughts. She hadn't asked for any information at all. *I don't know who was driving, how many other people were injured, or if Kent was badly hurt. I only know that he needs me—and quickly.* The ride to the hospital seemed to take forever. *Are they ever going to finish these interstates? This construction is ludicrous.* "Take the back way."

Jessica followed her instructions, and they quickly reached the hospital. "Just stay calm, Mom. Don't let Kent see you upset. You need to be strong."

Laura didn't feel strong. She felt completely unprepared to face whatever lay on the other side of that door, but she had to put her best foot forward—for Kent's sake.

"I'm Mrs. Chapman," she said to the first official-looking person she came in contact with.

The elderly woman nodded compassionately. "They've taken your son into surgery."

"Surgery?"

"Yes, Ma'am. The doctor will tell you all about it when they're done. In the meantime, a police officer is here, waiting to speak with you." She pointed to her right.

Laura made her way to the officer, who sat filling out papers. "I'm Laura Chapman. Could you tell me what happened to my son?"

"Officer Meyer." He stuck his hand out to grasp hers. "Nice to meet you. I'm sorry it has to be under these circumstances."

"Please tell me something."

"Your son was in a major collision on I-45," the officer explained. "Apparently, a friend of his was driving under the influence."

Driving under the influence? "Who? What friend?"

"We're still trying to determine that, Ma'am. He came in without any ID, and your son was in a state of shock—unable to identify him. The doctor will give you details when he comes out of the operating room, but I can tell you Kent's in pretty bad shape. A paramedic mentioned the possibility of internal bleeding. We had to Life Flight him here."

Laura spoke over the knot in her throat. "How did you know to call me?"

"Kent had his permit in his wallet," the deputy explained. "Wish the other boy had."

"But you're sure Kent wasn't driving?"

"We're sure. The other boy is pretty cut up—took some damage from the steering wheel and the air bag. He didn't have a seat belt on."

"Oh, no . . ."

"Would you please come and have a look at him for us? We're really hoping you can help identify him."

Laura followed him to the room where the boy lay unconscious, hooked up to various machines. He was almost unrecognizable—the cuts on his face and head were bandaged, covering much of his face.

"I know him," she whispered. "His mother is a good friend. His name is Josh. Josh Peterson. He's just a kid. . . ."

"An intoxicated kid who lost control of his car and hit the railing on the interstate. He managed to hit two other cars."

"Did he hurt anyone else?"

The officer shook his head. "No, not this time. But we need some information on Josh. Do you have a phone number? We'll need to contact his parents."

"Is he going to be alright?" she asked, quickly scribbling the number on a piece of paper and handing it to him.

"He looks bad, but the doctors say his wounds are superficial. If I were you, I'd focus on Kent. In fact, I'll ask an aide to walk you down to the surgical waiting area so you're there when they finish with him."

Laura followed the aide down the long hallway, a prayer on her lips the entire way. *Father, I'm asking You to guard the surgeon's hands as he operates on Kent. He needs Your healing, Lord. Help him. Help Josh. Help us all.*

Laura collapsed numbly into a chair in the waiting area. Jessica arrived, breathless, a few minutes later.

"That parking garage is a madhouse," she said, panting. "What did they say? Is he here?"

"They've taken him to surgery," Laura said, giving way to the tears.

"Surgery? Why? What's wrong with him?"

"I don't really know. The doctor will tell us when he comes out. I guess we'll just have to wait and see."

"Wait and see?"

"There is something you can do, Jess," Laura said, gathering her strength. "I need you to call Grandma, and I need you to give the Petersons a call, just to make sure they got the message."

"What message? What do the Petersons have to do with this?"

"Josh was driving the car. He was . . . the policeman said he was intoxicated."

"No!"

"That's what he said. But please, just make the calls. Don't tell them that part—at least not yet. Just make sure they come. I've got to go in and see Josh again, make sure he's okay. I feel like someone needs to be in there with him." She reached out to embrace her daughter, squeezing her tightly.

"I know everything will be okay. We'll get through this. If God is for us—"

"Who can be against us," Laura finished the Scripture with her daughter's hand tightly clutched in her own.

19

*A*ndrew stood in his classroom, silent after a long day's teaching. He'd just received the news that Laura's son had been in an accident, and Andrew found himself torn. *Surely I should do something, but what? Send flowers? Drop off a card?*

Did he dare go up to the hospital? Would that be too forward? Andrew paced nervously to the board, erasing all that had been written there during the last class.

I should go. I should. It didn't take much more to convince himself.

❧

"Mom? Are you all right?"

Laura awoke suddenly, fearfully, looking toward the hospital bed. An immediate fear gripped her. "Kent?"

"No, Mom. It's me, Jess. I didn't realize you were sleeping. I didn't mean to wake you."

Laura's nerves calmed immediately. She turned to face her daughter, who stood in the doorway. Just the tone of Jessica's voice soothed her. "Oh, that's okay. I shouldn't have been dozing."

"Why not? If anyone deserves to rest, you do. You've been shut up in this hospital room for three days now."

That was true, though Laura wouldn't have had it any other way. How could she possibly leave Kent's side? He was still not out of danger. Though the surgery to remove his lacerated spleen went well, there was still the broken arm to contend with. The orthopedist insisted Kent needed to stabilize before he could surgically repair the fracture. That surgery had taken place just this morning. It didn't matter how long any of this took. Laura would stay regardless of how much it taxed her.

"He's been sleeping for hours." She yawned loudly.

"You need a break," Jess said. "I thought I'd stay awhile."

"I could stand some food." Laura felt a surge of strength rise within her. "Maybe I could go down to the cafeteria. Have you eaten?"

"Yep. Stopped off at the cafeteria after class."

Laura's heart twisted within her as she thought about the classes she had missed. "How was school? Were you able to make it to all of your classes?"

"Yep. Everything at school is fine." Her daughter reached into her backpack to pull out some papers. "These are from Dougherty. He said he hopes to see you soon—whatever that means."

"Did you tell him?" Laura didn't know why it seemed important that he know . . . but it did, somehow.

"Yeah." He looked pretty shook up but said not to worry about class, that everything would be fine. He knows you're a good student."

"Humph. Don't know about that."

"Well, anyway. I told him you were shut up here with little to do, so he sent some work over. Hope that's all right."

"Sure. Whatever. I need something to pass the time." While she had been intent on staying by Kent's side, there had been little to do but watch TV, chat with the doctor about his condition, and pray. Laura had done a lot of praying over the last few days.

"Anything else?"

"I talked to Madeline. She also said not to worry—you've got several sick days coming to you."

"Yeah, but the day after Thanksgiving is the busiest day of the year," Laura said nervously. "I know she'll need me then."

"Let's just take this one day at a time, Mom."

Laura nodded. She was right. Besides, Laura couldn't do anything about it, anyway. "Anything else going on that I need to know about?"

"Nope."

"Well, in that case, I'd love to get some coffee and something to nibble on." Laura looked around the room, still feeling a little unsure about leaving.

"Go on . . . ," Jess urged.

"I'll be in the cafeteria if anyone needs me. And I may stop by the chapel for a few minutes afterwards." *I've meant to do that for days.*

Jessica nodded. "Go on, Mom. Get out of here for awhile. I'll hold down the fort."

Laura nodded, turning to leave the room. As much as she hated to go, she felt she had to get out for at least a few minutes. She made her way down to the cafeteria, finding a spot at a table where she could be alone to drink her coffee and nibble on a banana. She then headed back toward the room, walking slowly through the now-familiar halls of the first floor of Northwest Hospital.

Laura paused at the chapel door. *I should go inside.* To be honest, she had avoided it for days, though she couldn't put her finger on a legitimate reason. A hospital chapel shouldn't frighten her. She tiptoed into the empty room, making her way to the altar where a Bible lay open.

Quietly she sank to her knees, though doing so felt a little awkward. Once there, the tears began to flow. She hadn't planned them. They just seemed to erupt from a deep place within her—a place that needed comforting. Where the words came from, she wasn't quite sure, but they began to flow too.

"Father, do You ever get tired of hearing how much I need You? If it's a lack of faith on my part, then give me more. I need You more than ever. I don't know how to make it through this alone. I can't do it on my own. Take care of Kent, Father. Heal him. Mend his broken heart so he can let go of the anger he's been holding onto. Lord, I pray that Your work would be complete, not just in Kent, but in me. Take away the things in my life that aren't pleasing to You. Make me the woman you want me to be. Help me to know how to show Your love to the people You've placed in my life."

Laura poured her heart out to the Lord, begging Him to spare her son, and asking Him to forgive her for every conceivable thing she could think of. Somehow, at the end of it all, she felt the burden lift.

✒

Andrew Dougherty stood outside the chapel of Northwest Hospital, listening. Jessica had said he might find Laura here, though he was completely unprepared for the way he found her. She was praying, actually praying out loud, and on her knees.

As a child, he had spent many hours on his own knees—punishment from a stern mother who used prayer as a means to an end: to bring him to repentance for his thoroughly wicked deeds. He had spent more time daydreaming than praying back then, but if he had known prayer could be this simple, he might have tried it.

Andrew had never heard anyone pray like this before. Laura's words were genuine, heartfelt. They spoke volumes. He felt like a traitor as he strained to hear each and every word. They weren't his to hear, and yet somehow they sounded as comfortable and comforting as anything he had heard in a long, long time.

"Be transformed by the renewing of your mind. . . ." The Scripture ran through his head once again. For the first time in his life, he began to understand just how possible that could be. *Lord, is it really that easy? Do I just talk to You like she's doing? Can it be that simple?*

Relief flooded his soul. Perhaps this wasn't something he would have to earn. Maybe it wouldn't require a huge amount of study on his part. Perhaps all he had to do was just believe.

✒

The sound of a man's cough at the chapel door roused Laura from the altar. She wiped at her eyes, trying to get control of her emotions. She didn't want anyone to see her like this, even a stranger. Laura reached for a tissue but couldn't seem to find one.

"Are you looking for this?" A man pressed a tissue into her hand.

She didn't dare look up. "Thank you."

"I hoped I'd find you here," he said softly.

Laura suddenly recognized the voice. She turned, finding herself face-to-face with Andrew Dougherty. Instinctively, she reached out to take the hand he offered, letting him pull her to a standing position.

His arm slipped around her shoulder in a warm, sincere hug. There was nothing uncomfortable or awkward about it.

Wrapped in his embrace, she felt completely free to let the tears flow. Her face found its way to his shoulder, where she buried it, sobbing uncontrollably. He wrapped both arms around her, whispering gentle words of reassurance. "It's going to be okay," he said softly, running his fingers through her hair. Laura found comfort in his touch. He had come at just the right moment. She needed someone to be there just then. She'd longed for it for quite some time, though she hadn't realized just how much.

But Andrew Dougherty?

Funny. His touch was tender, loving, nothing like she would have expected. He caressed her hair with his fingertips, pausing to brush it from her eyes. None of this made sense, and yet she couldn't deny the feeling of peace and satisfaction she felt wrapped up in his arms. The whole thing felt perfectly natural. It felt good.

Too good.

After a few moments she pulled away, looking in the other direction. Embarrassment filled her. "I'm so sorry. I don't know what came over me."

❧

"Please, don't be sorry." Andrew felt his heart swell. "I wanted to be here for you. It's the least I can do."

Laura Chapman had felt good in his arms. So very good. The scent of her shampoo lingered, dizzying him. It had been years since he had been close enough to a woman to smell that. His fingers had run through her hair with a mind of their own. That lustrous hair of hers had always been a temptation for him. Andrew's arms ached to reach for her again, to wrap her up into them and whisper comforting words to her. It felt so right.

Andrew could no longer deny his feelings for Laura Chapman. He desired to know her as a friend and as much more.

He spoke softly. "That prayer of yours . . ."

"You heard me pray?"

"Yes. That prayer was beautiful. I haven't heard anything so incredible since I was a kid in Sunday school."

"You're making fun of me."

"No, I'm not." He meant every word of it.

"You were a Sunday school kid? That's hard to believe."

"I know, but it's true," Andrew said with a sigh. "Somewhere along the way, I turned my back on God. When I got to my teens, I guess. I remember accepting Christ at an altar when I was nine. It seems like a lifetime ago. But I never learned to pray like that. Never."

"It's pretty simple. You talk, He listens. He talks, you listen."

Andrew shook his head in disbelief. "In the academic world, everything has to be earned—every grade, every promotion. Everything. Nothing comes easy."

"Prayer should."

"I can see that. Now. I'm not sure what I've believed about God since my days in college. It's like I put Him away on a shelf and forgot about Him."

"What about now? What do you believe?"

"I believe . . ." Here Andrew hesitated. He wasn't completely sure how to go about saying what was in his heart. "For years, I've been frustrated. So many things have happened to make me give up on God and on people—mostly women."

"Women? Why?"

How could he begin to explain why? "I was engaged once, but something happened on the way to the church."

"She broke your heart?"

Andrew nodded lamely. "Yeah."

"I figured as much."

"What do you mean?"

"It wasn't so hard to figure out that someone must have hurt you at some point along the way. Is that why you're so angry with God?"

"What do you mean? Who said anything about that?" He would admit to a lot of things but not that.

"Isn't that what this is all about?" Laura asked. "I know I've had to struggle with that. Ever since Greg died, I've been so mad at God, I hardly knew how to function. But admitting it is half of the battle. It gets easier after that."

Andrew laughed, shaking his head in disbelief. "You are something else. Just about the time I think I've got you figured out, I find out that there's so much more."

"I'm not such a bad person," Laura said with a smile. She looked down at her watch and gasped. "I have to get back up to the room. Jessica is up there alone with Kent, and I need to be with her."

"Would you mind if I came along?" He almost dreaded her answer.

To his relief, she shrugged. "No, come if you like. I'm sure Jess would be glad to see you."

He walked beside her, chatting all the way. What he wanted to do—what he longed to do—was to pull her close to him and tell her everything would be all right. Would she think him awful if he reached for her now? No, that wouldn't be the appropriate thing to do. What had happened in the chapel had been perfectly natural, perfectly comfortable, but anything more would spoil an otherwise perfect moment.

Andrew continued to ramble on about everything from the weather to his latest history quiz. Truth be told, he was so nervous, much of what he said didn't make a lot of sense. Not that she seemed to notice. Laura's mind appeared to be a million miles away.

$\mathcal{H}$ ello there."

     Laura looked up as Andrew peeked in the door of the hospital room. Her heart skipped a beat as their eyes met. His visit yesterday had been unexpected, but today she had secretly hoped he would come. He stood in the doorway, clearly hesitant.

Laura laid down the magazine she had been reading. "Well, hello."

"How's our patient today?" he whispered, turning his gaze toward the bed, where Kent lay sleeping.

She smiled, feeling relief wash over her. "Better. But they are keeping him pretty sedated. He's been sleeping most of the day."

"What about you?" Andrew took a couple of steps into the room. "Have you had any sleep?"

She shrugged. "A little." An embarrassing yawn worked its way to her lips.

He pulled a small bouquet of flowers from behind his back. "I thought these might cheer you up."

Yellow roses. I love yellow roses. "Are they for me or Kent?" She suddenly felt like a shy schoolgirl.

"They're for you." He handed them to her. She clutched them tightly, suddenly unable to breathe correctly.

"I actually have something else for him, when he wakes up, that is." Andrew reached inside his coat, pulling a small package from the pocket.

"What is that?"

"It's a cassette tape. Dizzy Gillespie. He's a trumpet player."

"Dizzy Gillespie? How in the world did you know—"

He laid it on the bedside table. "The football game, remember? After you left, I stayed to watch Kent play. I don't know much about trumpets or trumpet players, but he looked like he knew his stuff."

Laura nodded, stunned. She couldn't seem to get past the fact that Andrew had handed her three yellow roses, which she still held tightly. They smelled incredible.

"I wanted to get it on CD, but they were out of it. Hope someone at your place still has an old-fashioned cassette player."

"We have one." Laura carefully ran her finger over one of the blossoms. "And I'm sure he'll love it. It was very thoughtful of you." *Very thoughtful.*

"No problem. I enjoyed shopping for it. I'm not much of a contemporary music person, but I love to browse through the old stuff." Kent stirred slightly in the bed. "Sorry, I guess I'm too loud," Andrew whispered.

"No, trust me. Nothing could wake him." Laura stood, carrying the roses toward the bathroom. "I need to get these in some water." As she crossed in front of Andrew, their eyes met. He held her captive for a moment with his smile, and her heartbeat accelerated slightly. Laura glanced at the ground nervously, then chose to keep walking.

"I'll just be a minute," she said, entering the bathroom. She quickly turned on the tap water with one hand, unwrapping the roses with the other. She glanced around for something to put them in. The only thing she could find was a small glass. "This will have to do." She broke the stems off at the bottom, then placed them in the glass, which she filled with water. They leaned a little too far to the right.

"I think I'll put them on the windowsill." She walked past him once again, feeling his eyes on her hair. *Why am I so nervous? It's not like I've never been alone in a room with him.*

"I was hoping you might be able to take a little break."

"A break?"

"Yeah. I thought we might grab something to eat in the cafeteria."

"I don't know." Laura looked nervously at Kent, who lay in a sound sleep. "He might need me." She yawned again. "I am hungry. And I haven't been out of this room all day. Maybe I could just stop by the nurses' station and tell them where I'll be."

"Sounds good."

She went to Kent's bedside, stopping to brush a kiss across his forehead. Her heart twisted as she gazed at him. *I won't do it. I won't get down about this. The doctors say he's going to be fine. I can be strong. I will be strong.*

She turned to face Andrew, immediately relieved by his presence. "I think I'm ready now."

He smiled and led the way out of the door.

❧

Andrew sat across the table from Laura in the hospital cafeteria, mesmerized by her conversation. "And then what happened?"

"Then I told the kids that they were never allowed to eat peanut butter and jelly again—at least, not in the living room!" She chuckled merrily, then sighed deeply. "It feels good to laugh. It really does."

"You've got a great laugh."

"What do you mean?"

"Oh, come on. You know. Some women have those really high-pitched, annoying laughs. They hurt your ears. And some have that terrible snorting laugh. That's the worst."

"And I'm neither of those?"

"No, you have the perfect laugh."

"You can't imagine how long it's been since I've felt like laughing. Lately it seems like my life is just this never-ending cycle of . . ."

"Stuff?"

"Yeah."

"I can relate to that," he said, feeling it was safe to open up. "I keep pretty busy with all of my students."

"What about your family?"

"My mother passed away three years ago," he explained.

"Oh, I'm sorry."

"I am too. She was a difficult woman, but I still miss her keenly. I spent a lot of time trying to figure her out. She was always so bitter, so frustrated. I never really knew why."

"Some people get like that as they age. Life doesn't go the way they expected it to, and they can't seem to gauge their reactions."

"She always took everything to heart. Wore her emotions on her sleeve. Guess that's why it bothers me to see women like that."

"What about your father?" Laura took a bite of her sandwich.

"My dad died when I was in my late teens." Andrew's heart ached with the memory. "He was such an amazing man. He knew everything there was to know about history, about everything."

"Everything?"

Not everything, Andrew had to admit. His father had been very well schooled, had learned much about the world he lived in. But he had never really cared to learn about the things that seemed important to his mother—church, faith, the Bible . . .

Maybe that's why she was so bitter.

"Andrew?" Laura gave him an odd look.

"Oh, I'm sorry. I lost my train of thought. I was just remembering how my dad treated my mom. He didn't care for her religion."

"She was a religious woman?"

"Oh, very."

"What do you mean by religious?"

Andrew shrugged. "She went to church a lot. Took me for years. Like I said, I was a Sunday school kid. She preached at my dad a lot, always tried to get him to go with her. But he wasn't interested. After a few years, I wasn't either. It just seemed like my dad was more exciting. He was so smart, one of the brightest men I ever knew."

"If you don't mind my asking, how did your father . . . I mean, how did he . . ."

"How did he die?" Andrew began to tremble slightly, remembering. He took a deep breath before continuing. "It was a couple of days before my seventeenth birthday. My dad was late coming home from work. My mom got supper ready, as usual, but he just never came. Finally, after a couple of hours, she started making calls. In the middle of all of that, there was a knock at the door—a police officer."

"He'd been in an accident?"

"His car was struck by an eighteen-wheeler," Andrew said, shaking his head. The memory still carried the pain of a seventeen-year-old boy's broken heart. "When my dad died, something in me just sort of gave up too."

"I can understand that," Laura said softly. "When my husband passed away, I felt like I couldn't go on. He was so much a part of me. Or vice versa. I don't really know how that works, but it hurts so terribly when they're gone."

Andrew looked at her tenderly. "I'm so sorry."

"So your mom was a widow at a young age."

"Yeah, I guess you could say that. She was in her forties when he passed away." Andrew suddenly realized what he was saying and how closely it paralleled Laura's story. "Oh, Laura."

"I think I can understand where some of your mother's bitterness came from. I've struggled with it since Greg died. But last Sunday . . ."

"What about last Sunday?" His curiosity grew.

"Last Sunday, something happened at church. I'm not sure if I can explain it exactly, but God did something in me. He . . . He . . ."

Andrew's heart raced. *Last Sunday. Something was stirring in me too.*

"I spent some time at the altar Sunday morning after everyone else left the service. I think, for the first time, I was really able to deal with my unforgiveness."

"Unforgiveness?"

"Remember I told you the other day in the chapel that I had been angry? Angry at Greg?"

He nodded.

"I needed to deal with that. It's one thing to carry around anger and frustration. It's another thing to get rid of it, to give it to God."

She makes it sound so easy.

She glanced at her watch, suddenly coming to life. "Oh, no. We've been gone nearly thirty minutes. I really need to get back to Kent. He might be waking up, and I want to be there for him." She rose abruptly, wiping crumbs from her blouse.

Andrew stood to join her. "I should probably go, anyway." They stared at each other in silence for a moment before either spoke.

"Thanks for the roses."

His heart leaped as she reached to squeeze his hand. "You're more than welcome," he said, not wanting to let go.

$$\widehat{21}$$

O n Thanksgiving morning, Andrew visited the hospital once again.

By now, Laura had grown accustomed to seeing him. He had become as familiar as the flowers from friends at church, which lined the windowsill. However, she hadn't expected him today. *Not on Thanksgiving.*

She stood as he entered the room. "Why are you here?"

"I just had to see for myself. Jess told me he was up walking around this morning."

"Jess? You've talked to Jessica?"

Kent groaned loudly, interrupting them.

"Looks like he's awake, all right."

"I can use all the sympathy I can get." Kent struggled to roll over in the bed. "My arm is killing me." He let out a dramatic moan.

"I'll bet," Andrew said with a laugh. "But this too shall pass. I'm Andrew Dougherty," he said, nodding in Kent's direction.

Laura watched for her son's response. "Kent Chapman." There was an extended pause as he looked Andrew over. "So you're the infamous professor. We meet at last. Thanks for the tape, by the way."

"You're welcome. But I see my fame precedes me."

"Oh, yeah." Kent nodded. "I'll say."

"I'm not sure how to take that," Andrew said with a laugh. "So I'll just take it as a compliment."

Kent looked up his mother. "He's not half as bad as you said, Mom. He actually looks like a pretty nice guy."

Laura groaned loudly. "Kent . . ."

"So," Andrew said, looking her in the eye, "what has your mom been saying about me?"

Laura's heart hit the floor. She sent a glaring look Kent's way, but it didn't seem to phase him.

"She says you're tough as nails." Kent looked up at her curiously. "What's that other name you use so much, Mom?"

Laura's gaze shifted to the floor. *Slave driver.* But she couldn't force herself to say it. Why did she suddenly feel like such a heel?

"Hateful?" Andrew guessed, looking at them both.

"Nah. That's not it." Kent shook his head. "It was something else. . . ."

"Prideful?"

Laura looked up on that one. He had been prideful, though she had never said so.

"No," Kent said. "I think it was . . ." He lost himself in his thoughts for a moment before answering. "Slave driver. She said you were a slave driver."

Andrew shook his head, then gave Laura a nod. "Can't argue with that one," he said, almost playfully. "Looks like she hit the nail right on the head."

"Well, anyway," Kent said, "you don't seem like such a bad guy. I don't know what she was talking about."

"Thanks, Kent," Andrew said. "I'm glad someone in here sees me for who I am."

Laura groaned aloud at that one.

"So, what are you doing here, anyway?" Kent's question was blunt, but frankly, Laura had been wondering the same thing. Why did Andrew keep showing up day after day? She looked up at him. Just a few short months ago they had felt so differently about each other and now . . .

Now she didn't know what to think. He had become a regular member of the family.

"I'd do the same for any of my students," Andrew said, his eyes looking straight into Laura's eyes. She felt her face flush.

"Sure you would," Kent said.

"Anyway, Jess said to tell you 'hello.'" Andrew reached over to straighten up the flowers in a nearby vase.

"You've seen Jessica today?" Laura asked incredulously. How could that be? Her daughter hadn't been up to the hospital since early morning, and it certainly wasn't a school day.

"Yeah. Well, I took a turkey over to your place before coming here." He spoke the words with a slight tremor in his voice. His focus shifted up to her face.

"You did what?" She couldn't believe it. He had actually been to her house. "How do you know where I live?"

"Oh, well, I . . ."

Ah. Of course. His friend in the registrar's office. *I'll have to remember to report him later.*

"Jess says she wants you to come home and have Thanksgiving dinner with her," Andrew explained. "She misses you."

"I have to stay here. Kent needs me." As much as she would love to go home for a few hours, she simply couldn't. Her conscience wouldn't allow it. How could she leave Kent alone?

"Aw, Mom, I don't need you. I'd feel better if you went home and had Thanksgiving with Grandma and Buck."

"My mother and stepfather are coming over later this afternoon," Laura explained. "In fact, my mom plans to bring a turkey too, I think."

"Well, there should be plenty for all, then," Andrew said with a laugh. "So why don't you go on home, and I'll stay here with Kent?"

"You would do that? Why?" Why would he make such an offer?

"Sure. Why not?"

She stood for a moment, contemplating his offer. Maybe she could go home for a few hours. Kent didn't seem to mind, and she would love to take a shower and get cleaned up before coming back to the hospital for the night. A Thanksgiving dinner certainly wouldn't hurt either.

"Are . . . are you sure you wouldn't mind?" Laura asked, looking back and forth between Kent and the professor.

"I don't mind if he doesn't mind," Andrew said.

"Get out of here, Mom. You deserve a break."

"I won't be gone long. Maybe a couple of hours."

Andrew dropped into a chair. "Take your time. We can play cards, or watch TV, or something."

Laura looked intently at him, hardly recognizing her own voice as she spoke: "Well, maybe you could . . . maybe you could join us for Thanksgiving dinner in about an hour and a half. That is, if Kent doesn't mind staying here alone for awhile."

"I told you, Mom, I don't need a sitter. Go home and eat until you're sick. Just bring me some turkey when you're done. And some sweet potatoes."

"You've got a deal," she said, heading for the door. She turned back, looking at Andrew once again. "An hour and a half?"

"Great," he said, then directed his attention to Kent.

She left the room, headed out into the hallway. It was only when she was about halfway to the car that she realized what she had done. "The professor's coming to my house for dinner."

She thought about him as she made the drive home. She'd grown attached to him over the past few days and had come to rely on his visits. Beyond that, she had learned to enjoy his company, really enjoy it. He was a good man, a kind man.

Is that wrong, Lord? Are my feelings wrong?

She prayed as she drove, trying to come to grips with her changing emotions. By the time she reached the house, she could no longer deny the obvious. "I think I'm falling for this guy." How or why it had happened, she couldn't be sure, but she was sure of one thing. She liked him. A lot.

Laura approached the house with a smile on her face, anxious to see her family. "Is anyone home?" she called out, opening the front door.

"We're here, Mom." Jessica exited the kitchen wearing a flour-covered apron.

"What in the world?"

"I'm helping Grandma. We just finished rolling out the home-made biscuits. I mixed them myself." Jessica threw her arms around her, planting a floury kiss on her cheek.

Laura acquired a noseful of the white, powdery stuff and sneezed. "Uh-huh. I can see that. How long 'til dinner's ready?"

"A little over an hour," Laura's mother said, popping her head out of the kitchen door. "And don't be late."

"That gives me plenty of time for a shower." She headed for her bedroom. "I feel grungy."

"Well, we certainly can't have that at the dinner table. Go take your shower, Mom. We can smell you from here."

Moments later, Laura relaxed under the steady stream of warm water. It felt like heaven. Every time she closed her eyes, she saw herself, head tightly pressed against Andrew's shoulder in the chapel of the hospital. He certainly hadn't seemed to mind. She hadn't either. In fact, she had enjoyed the moment, more than she would have admitted just a few short days ago.

"This is so crazy," she said, leaning against the shower wall. Laura's mind drifted to the smell of his jacket, a brand of cologne she hadn't recognized. Nice. Not too strong, not too light. It suited him.

"Is my heart ready for this, Lord?" she whispered.

The peace that followed suddenly motivated her. Laura reached for the shampoo bottle, pouring a large dollop of the golden liquid into her palm. "The professor's coming to my house, and I'm standing here as nervous as a schoolkid."

Energized, she flew into action.

❧

Andrew nervously knocked at the door. Jessica answered with a shocked look on her face.

"I'm here."

"You're here," she echoed. "Uh, come on in." She hesitantly opened the door.

Awkwardness kicked in. "Didn't your mom tell you I was coming?"

"She must have forgotten that, but she's been a little preoccupied lately."

"That's understandable."

"Please come on in. I'm sure she'll be out of the shower soon. We're having dinner in about thirty minutes. Are you hungry?"

"Starved."

"Well, have a seat." She gestured to the couch.

He sat reluctantly.

"You the fellow who brought the turkey?" An elderly man entered the room.

Andrew rose, extending his hand.

Jessica made the introductions. "This is my grandfather, Buck Timmons. I'm sure he'll keep you occupied 'til dinner's done."

"Guess she thinks I've got a big mouth," Buck said, "but that ain't true. I like to talk with the best of 'em, sure, but I know when to quit. What is it you do for a living again, Mr. . . . ?"

"Andrew. Andrew Dougherty. I teach at the college. In fact, Jessica and Laura are both in one of my classes."

"Well, I don't know anything about your teaching skills," Buck said, joining him on the couch, "but you sure know how to pick your turkeys. I just carved your bird, myself."

"I'm glad to finally have an excuse to cook it," Andrew felt the weight lift off of his shoulders. "To be honest, someone gave it to me awhile back, and it's just been taking up room in my freezer. I don't have any family in the area, so I started to think it would stay in there forever."

"No family, eh?" Buck gave him a wink.

"Uh, no, Sir."

The elderly man dove headlong into a discussion about the merits of family. Andrew sat quietly, listening as he rambled on and on about every conceivable thing. Their conversation transitioned from families to the battles Buck fought in the Korean War. "You fight in 'Nam, Boy?"

"No," Andrew said, looking down. "I missed it by six numbers."

"Probably for the best. I tell ya, fighting for your country can be a blessing and a curse all at the same time. Wait. Didn't I hear someone say you taught history?"

"Yes, I teach American History," Andrew said, smiling.

"Well then, if anyone knows your battles, you do."

The older man transitioned into another story about his journey across the Pacific on a battleship as Andrew politely listened. He found himself slightly distracted by the photos of Laura and her husband on the wall across the room. Another smaller snapshot of the whole family sat on the end table next to him. Without thinking, he reached to pick it up and ran his finger over Laura's brown hair.

"That Laura . . . ," Buck exclaimed. "She's a pretty filly, ain't she? I always said she was the spittin' image of her mother. They both just get prettier every day."

Andrew nodded, not sure how to answer. He found himself captivated by the face next to Laura's. This had to be her husband. He had been a handsome man—light-skinned, with auburn hair and an inviting smile. His eyes glowed with a warmth that spoke of friendship.

"Greg was a great man. Did you ever meet him?"

Andrew shook his head, suddenly apprehensive.

"A great man," Buck repeated with a sigh. "Just about the best father a kid could ever have. And so good to Laura. They were still very much in love, just like young kids. It like to broke her heart when he passed, it really did."

Andrew set the picture back down, not wanting to hear anymore. Suddenly he felt like a stranger in this place, a man who didn't belong. He could never fill the shoes of the man in this picture. Why would he even try to? He stood suddenly, knowing he must leave. He had to back out of this thing before it was too late, before . . .

⤜⤜

Laura stuck her head out of the bedroom door, shouting, "Jessica, could you get my jeans out of the dryer?" She had tossed on an old terry-cloth robe and wore a towel around her head but didn't figure her mother or Buck would mind. "Jess?" No answer. Laura stepped out into the living room, hollering a little louder. "Jess!"

"Laura?" She looked up at the sound of Buck's voice to find herself face-to-face with Andrew Dougherty.

"Oh, my goodness," she said, clutching at her robe. "I'm, I'm so sorry. I didn't know you were here. You're early." For a moment, Laura felt a familiar frustration rise up within her. Then, just as suddenly, it was replaced with an odd sense of satisfaction that he had come. *I can't let him see me like this.* She backed toward the bedroom.

"Kent fell asleep," Andrew explained, "and the nurse said she didn't see any point in my staying. His medication should keep him out like a light for a couple of hours—at least, that's what she said. I just came on over. I'm sorry. I should probably go."

But I don't want you to. She gave him an imploring look. "No, please don't go. If you'll excuse me, I'll just be a minute." She backed into the bedroom, overcome with embarrassment. "Jess!" she called once more, peeking her head out of the door. She watched as Jessica raced across the living room, a pair of jeans in her hand.

"I'm coming, Mom. I'm coming." She practically knocked the professor down as she passed by him. She entered the bedroom, closing the door behind her.

Laura trembled as she pulled the towel off of her hair. "Help me, Jess," she whispered, flipping on the blow-dryer and running a brush through her hair.

"What's wrong with you, Mom? What's got you so shook up?" Jess teased.

"Nothing. Just help me." Laura fought with her brush until her hair was nearly dry. She grabbed her jeans, struggling to slide into them. Her hands shook so hard, she could barely get them up.

"Mom . . ."

"I don't have time, Jess."

"Mom, you're putting your jeans on backwards."

"Oh." She turned them around and tried again.

"Much better," Jessica said. "What'll you wear with them?"

"Get my peach sweater out of the closet." Laura put on a pair of earrings.

"You mean your 'special occasion' peach sweater?"

"It's Thanksgiving, Jessica. That's a special occasion, isn't it?" Her hands still trembled as she fought to put her earrings in.

"What's wrong with you, Mom? You're acting like a giddy school-girl with a crush."

"That's crazy." Laura tried to avoid looking her daughter in the eye. Why was it so hard to admit she actually liked this man? *I do like him, very much. More than I could admit to Jess or anyone else.*

She quickly applied some lipstick and blush, then ran the brush through her hair one last time. "Do I look okay?" she asked, turning for Jess's approval.

"You look great, Mom. Now get out there and knock him dead." Jessica clapped her hand over her mouth, realizing what she had said. "I'm so sorry. I didn't mean . . ."

Laura grinned a silly grin. "It's okay. It's about time we got back to joking around here. You just be yourself and everything will be fine."

~❧~

Andrew tried to compose himself as Laura entered the room. Keeping his emotions in check proved to be very difficult. Her hair was still slightly damp, but it carried the familiar aroma of flowers. She wore the same sweater she had worn at the game—the one he remembered so well. She completely took his breath away.

"I hope you didn't mind waiting," Laura said, looking as nervous as he felt. "I just had to change before going back up to the hospital. You understand."

Of course he understood. He would have understood if she had decided to paper and paint the living room before going back.

"Everything smells great, Mom," Laura said, giving her mother a hug. "Professor Dougherty, have you met my mother, Violet Timmons?"

"Just call me Vi," the older woman responded.

He shook Violet's hand firmly and smiled, knowing from her easygoing smile she would be easy to like.

"Well, why don't we all go on into the dining room," Vi said, leading the way, "before everything gets cold."

~❧~

Laura watched Andrew carefully as he made his way into the dining room. Buck pulled out the seat that had always been Greg's and gestured for Andrew to sit down. Immediately, Laura's heart began to twist inside her. *Greg's chair. No one else should sit there. No one. Not yet, anyway.* She reluctantly sat across from Andrew, unable to focus.

"Let's pray, shall we?" Buck said, looking around the table.

Laura glanced in Andrew's direction, trying to read his reaction. How would he feel about this? Would he be offended, or . . . She was relieved to see that he bowed his head reverently and closed his eyes. She did the same. Buck began to pray a deep, genuine prayer, thanking God for Kent's recovery and for the food provided. He added a special prayer of thanks for Andrew's gift of the turkey, but Laura barely heard it. Her eyes were once again fixed on Greg's chair.

Heads lifted, and the food began to make its way around the table. Everyone chatted and laughed as if nothing in the world could be wrong. But something felt wrong, very wrong.

"Laura, honey, would you pass the potatoes?" She numbly passed them to her mother, trying to focus.

"I'll have the dressing, Laura," Buck said, reaching out for it. She nodded but never touched it, her focus drifting once again to the chair.

"Mom, are you okay?" Jessica asked, looking at her curiously.

"Oh. Yeah, sure." *I'm not.* A war had suddenly and inexplicably risen up inside of her. There was no logical reason why she should feel this sudden anger, but she couldn't seem to stop it.

"I'll take a roll," Andrew said, looking directly at her with a smile. She picked up the basket, clutching it tightly. She couldn't seem to release it.

"Mom?" Jessica gazed at her with a worried expression.

"Oh, I—" She passed the rolls without further explanation, turning her attention to her own plate. She could do this. She wouldn't humiliate herself or anyone else. Not today, not when everything was so perfect. She looked up again, and a very clear picture of Greg seated in the chair greeted her. Suddenly, Laura could take it no more. "I . . . I have to get out of here," she said, standing.

"What do you mean?" her mother asked.

"I . . . I have to get back to the hospital. I'm sure you all understand. Kent needs me."

Andrew stood immediately. "Maybe I should leave. It's getting late, anyway."

"No, please don't go, Mr. Dougherty," Buck said. "You're our guest. You just sit right down and eat."

"Really," Laura said, trying not to look at him. "Just because I'm leaving doesn't mean you have to." She practically ran to the front door, throwing it open. "If anyone needs me, I'll be at the hospital."

She stepped outside into the cool autumn air and leaned back against the house, where her tears flowed freely.

❧

Andrew stood up from the table, excusing himself. He needed to catch up with Laura before she left. He had so much to say to her. She couldn't just slip away—not this time. He had lost her this way before, and he wasn't about to let it happen again.

He opened the front door, expecting to find her in her car, but she was propped up against the side of the house, sobbing.

"Laura?"

She looked at him tearfully. "I'm . . . I'm sorry. I have to go."

He reached out to take her arm, but she eluded him. "Laura, please wait. I need to talk to you."

"I can't talk to you right now, Andrew," she said, turning away from him.

"I just want to tell you something. Please." He felt like his heart would burst if he didn't say it.

"Can't it wait?" she asked impatiently.

"No, it can't. I can't." His ears were ringing now. *Just get through this.*

"What's so important?" She took a few steps toward her car, obviously trying to avoid him. He followed her closely.

"You remember that conversation we had in the hospital cafeteria yesterday?" he asked breathlessly. "Something really, I don't know . . . amazing happened to me when I got home last night. For the first time in years, I found myself able to pray."

She looked up at him with tears in her eyes. "Really?"

"Yes. I asked God to forgive me for being so angry with Him. That happened because of you, Laura." He reached to take her hand. She let him hold it for a moment, then pulled away. "Don't you see? I would never have had the courage to face the truth if it hadn't been for you."

"The truth . . . ," she stammered. "It's the truth that's killing me right now. The truth of how I felt about Greg. The truth about how scared I am when I see someone else sitting in his chair."

"So that's what it is."

"Yes." Tears filled her beautiful eyes again.

Andrew reached out to brush them away, but she pushed his hand away. "Can't we at least talk about this?" he implored. "Please?"

"Maybe someday," she said, opening the car door.

"When?"

"I don't know," she spoke through the emotion. "I just can't right now. I can't." She jumped into her car and sped away, leaving his heart in a state of chaos. With his head hanging, Andrew climbed into his car and drove away.

*M*om, it's been two weeks, and you haven't even spoken a
word to him. That's not fair."

Laura did her best to ignore her daughter. Frustration
overwhelmed her these days. She seemed to always be in a bad mood
at home. She had thrown herself into her work with a vengeance. "I
don't expect you to understand, Jessica," she said finally. "I'm just confused, that's all. I need time. Space."

"Confused about him?"

"Him who?"

"You know who, Mom. The professor. The one you've been avoiding for the last two weeks."

"I haven't been avoiding him," Laura argued. "I've been going to
class, haven't I?"

"Yes, but you haven't said a word to him," Jessica commented
"Everyone's noticed. The whole class is talking about it."

"The whole class?"

"Yes."

"What are they saying?"

"They're just wondering what's up. The kids loved the bickering
that went on between the two of you, and now it's just nothing but silence. It's boring. You're boring."

"Thanks a lot."

"No, I mean it, Mom. You've got to snap out of this. Whatever he's
done, you need to forgive him. Remember, we talked about that. Forgiveness is everything."

"It's nothing he's done, Jessica. That's the problem."

"What do you mean?"

"I mean . . ." Laura hesitated. "I mean, he's not your father. He never will be. There will never be another man like your dad." Surely Jessica would understand that.

Her daughter looked her squarely in the eye. "You're right, Mom. He's not Daddy. But did you ever consider the fact that God might be bringing you something—someone—completely different?"

"He's different, all right." Laura smiled.

"Maybe you shouldn't be looking for someone like Daddy at all. Maybe you should just be open to any man God might bring into your life, no matter how different he is."

"What?" Laura was stunned at her daughter's tenacity.

"No one can ever take Daddy's place—that's true. But you don't have to worry that we'll forget him, Mom. He's always here, in my heart." Jessica's voice trembled with emotion as she continued. "But you've got things all confused where the professor's concerned. Maybe all he needs to do is just be himself."

"You're right, Jess. I know you are," Laura said softly.

But what could she do? There were too many bridges crossed, too many things left undone.

·❧·

Three weeks and counting. Andrew paced around his classroom, tormented by the struggle that ensued in his heart and his head. His head convinced him he should give up—not pursue any type of relationship with Laura Chapman, friendship or otherwise. His heart cried out for more, much more. As the semester came to a close, he faced an inevitable deadline. Grades for American History had just been averaged. Laura's good, solid A had been earned without any assistance from him. She had aced his class. Not many people could boast of that.

Of course, it might not have happened if Dick DeHart hadn't gotten involved. Andrew's skin began to crawl. The idea of any other man looking at Laura—his Laura—made him so angry, he could hardly see straight. *But she's not my Laura. She doesn't want to be with me. She made that abundantly clear on Thanksgiving.* It had started . . .

when had it started, again? *Ah, yes. When I sat in that chair.* A light tap on the door distracted him. He looked up, shocked to see Jessica standing there with a concerned look on her face.

"Professor Dougherty," she said hesitantly. "Can I come in?"

"Sure, Jess. What's up?"

She looked a little nervous. "I just wanted to talk to you. Of course, my mom would kill me if she knew I came."

"What do you mean?"

"I mean," she said, "I think you need to know that she's, she's just——"

"Just what?" He waited anxiously to hear the rest of the sentence.

"Scared," Jessica said finally. "She's scared to death."

He dropped into a chair, his forehead breaking out in a sweat.

"You don't look like you're in much better shape than she is," Jessica said with a laugh. "This is really pathetic."

"I'm not very good at this."

"I'll say. That's why I'm here to help you."

"Help me?" *She's just a kid. How can she help me?*

"Yep. My mom's at the Bookstop, and I want you to go there to see her."

"She's back at work?"

"Has been for a week and a half. Kent's back in school, doing great," she explained.

"That's good."

"Yeah. Well, anyway, she's back at work; but her mind isn't on her work, I'll tell you that much."

"It's not?"

"No, it's not."

"If you don't mind my asking——" he stammered.

"She can't stop thinking about you," Jessica explained. "I know because she talks about you all of the time. She's scared of how she feels, that's all."

"I can relate to that," Andrew said, looking at the ground. "I'm pretty, well, I mean—I'm a little scared too."

"You two are like a couple of kids," Jessica said finally. "But don't you worry. Just leave everything up to me."

Andrew's heart beat so fast, he could barely breathe. "Are you sure about this?"

"More than sure," Jessica said.

He suddenly knew what he had to do. He would go to her. Somehow, someway he would communicate his love for her in a way that wouldn't threaten the memory of her husband. He could do that. With the Lord's help, he could do that.

"Can I ask you a personal question?" Jessica looked him in the eye.

"Sure. Why not?" Everything he had ever kept hidden had already come out over the past few days.

"Do you pray, Professor Dougherty?"

He paused before answering. "If you had asked me that question a few weeks ago, I would have answered so differently. But I do pray, Jessica. Believe it or not, I've been spending a lot of time in prayer over the past few weeks." He had felt years of coldness toward the Lord melt away in the process.

"Well then, if you want to see those prayers answered, get on over there to the bookstore and tell my mom how you feel. If she's half the woman I know she is, she won't break your heart. At least, I don't think she will."

The words "at least" nearly drove a stake through Andrew's fragile heart, and yet they propelled him to his feet. "I'll do it," he said, suddenly energized. "It may seem crazy, but I'll do the impossible."

"Professor," Jessica called out to him as he bolted through the door. He turned and looked at her one last time.

"Yes?"

" 'With God all things are possible.' "

" 'With God all things are possible.' " He repeated the words, feeling the smile return to his face. "Thanks, Jessica. Thanks for everything."

"Hey," she hollered, as he sprinted down the hallway toward the parking lot. "Does this mean I get an A in your class?"

Andrew didn't answer. After all, he didn't want to spoil what had suddenly become a perfect moment.

◦◦

Laura passed through the inspirational section of the bookstore, taking another look at the book that had long captivated her attentions: *Put Your Troubles in the Blender and Give Them a Spin.* She stood in silence, thumbing through the book. Funny in some places, it struck a serious nerve in others. Many of the situations in the book were not unlike her own. Somehow this author, also a woman, had triumphed over her tragedies and turned them into victories using humor.

"It should be so simple," Laura mumbled, placing the book on the shelf.

"So, what do you think, Madeline?" Laura asked, clutching the book in her hand. "Do you think I should or I shouldn't?"

"Should or shouldn't what?" the woman asked.

"Should I or shouldn't I . . ." Laura's heart beat so hard, it took her breath away. It had been many, many years since talking about a man had made her this nervous. "Take a chance," Laura stammered finally. "With the professor." She looked nervously at Madeline. What she found there was warmth and understanding.

"I've been hoping for quite some time that you would find someone."

"Really?"

"Yep."

"I wasn't even praying for this," Laura said with a sigh.

"Don't you see?" Madeline interjected. "That's exactly what makes it so special. God knew what you needed and wanted even before you did. Besides, it's about time you had a fella in your life. To be honest, I had hoped my brother would be the one, but . . ."

"I'm so sorry, Madeline, but Dick just wasn't my type." She said the words firmly. Perhaps a little too firmly.

"I know. He's a Romeo, that's for sure," Madeline responded. "It may make you feel better to know he's already dating someone from the university."

"Good grief." Somehow knowing that did make her feel a little better.

"So do you think I should go up to the school and see Andrew?" Laura asked. "He's probably still there. I think so, anyway."

"I wouldn't waste another minute. You get in that car of yours and make haste all the way down to the college. Go. Don't worry about the shop. I'm here."

"Are you sure?" Laura's heart raced, making it difficult to breathe.

"Completely sure," Madeline said. "Get out of here."

Laura sprinted to the door. "See you later, Madeline." She raced toward the car, turning the key in the ignition. *I can't believe I'm doing this! I'm actually going to tell him how I feel.*

❧

Andrew drove like a maniac along the interstate, fighting traffic all the way. "Come on . . . ," he grumbled at the cars in front of him. They crawled along, ignoring his pleas. "Just a couple of miles. It's not that far." He had already decided what he would say. He would tell her exactly what he felt, what his intentions were. If she rejected him this time, he would give up. Plain and simple. Andrew reached the exit for Tully, pulling off onto the feeder road. In just a couple of minutes he would see her.

He would tell her.

23

*I*s Laura here?" Andrew asked, his eyes bearing down on Madeline's.

"Oh, dear. Oh, dear," she said, looking as nervous as a cat. "I'm so sorry."

"She's not here? Where did she go?"

"Well, actually, she went to the college to try to find you," Madeline explained.

"To find me? Why?" *This is too confusing.*

"She wanted to . . . ," Madeline stammered. "She was going to . . . It's like this . . ."

"Could you please just say it?" Andrew hollered, feeling his face go hot.

Madeline stood frozen, saying nothing.

"Fine," he said, turning toward the door. "You say she's at the school? I'm going back to the school." Andrew groaned loudly as he headed back to his car.

❧

Laura paced back and forth in the empty classroom, her heart feeling as if it would break.

"Where is he?" The door stood wide open. He never left it open unless he happened to be nearby, but he didn't appear to be anywhere.

She plopped down onto the edge of his desk, deep in thought. Her eyes traveled the familiar room, drinking in the things that Andrew loved. American history. She had somehow managed to make it through his course with flying colors, with or without assistance from Dick DeHart. If nothing else, she could be very proud of that.

But something else captivated her mind, something that wouldn't rest. She had to talk to Andrew, had to tell him how she felt. She did have feelings for him, she had to admit—strong feelings. Her conversation with Jessica had convinced her of that. God had arranged all of this. But she had treated Andrew so badly on Thanksgiving. Would he forgive her?

Laura's thoughts shifted, wandering back to the day when she had walked in on him in this very room—a day when a dark-haired woman sat in the very spot she found herself. Was it possible? Was Andrew involved with her, the girl from the cafeteria? They had been seen together on more than one occasion, deep in conversation.

And yet Andrew had swept her into his arms with such tenderness that day in the chapel. The look in his eyes spoke of more than friendship.

Laura stood and walked across the room toward the door. She gave the walls one last glance as she left, running her finger across the Declaration of Independence. She pulled the door shut behind her, realizing it could very well be the last time she would ever step inside this room.

~&

Andrew raced back out to his car, immediately climbing inside. "Please be there," he whispered as he turned the key in the ignition. So many unanswered questions lingered in his mind. *Why did she go back to the school? Is it possible . . . ?*

Moments later, he entered the interstate, accelerating much faster than usual up the entrance ramp. He raced along, honking his horn at any driver who had the nerve to drive the speed limit. Finally he arrived at the school. Anxiously, he turned into the parking lot.

He raced from the car to the history classroom. *Please be here.* He made his way up the hallway, quickly opening the door to his classroom. *Empty.* Andrew made his way to his desk, dropping into the chair. He buried his head in his hands. "This is too much. I can't do this anymore."

"Well, what happened?" Jessica appeared at the door.

"She wasn't there. Madeline said she was on her way here. Have you seen her?"

"Nope. I've been waiting in the cafeteria with my nose buried in a book. I had a feeling you'd come back here afterward."

He sighed deeply. "This is such a mess."

Jessica plopped down in a chair, staring up at him. "I'm really sorry about all of this."

"It's okay. I should probably just go home and sleep it off. Maybe I can try again tomorrow."

"Well," Jessica said, "I have this one little problem."

"What?"

"I need a ride home. You don't really mind, do you?"

Mind? Of course he didn't mind. He lived for days like this. "Come on," he said, reaching for his keys once again. "Let's get out of here."

❧

Laura climbed into the shower, talking to herself. "What's wrong with me?" she mumbled, letting the water run over her hair to cool her down. "Andrew Dougherty probably thinks I'm the biggest flake on the planet."

She pulled out her favorite shampoo, working it into lather. Scrubbing her head vigorously, she continued the conversation with herself. "I'm crazy to think I need a guy in my life. I don't need anyone. I don't."

She leaned against the shower wall, tears cascading down her face. Her heart began to beat so hard, she could barely breathe.

"I may not need him," she whispered to herself. "But I love him."

She stepped out of the shower, agitated. "Of course he wasn't at the school," she grumbled. "Why should he be at the school just because he teaches there?" She wrapped herself in her bathrobe, still upset. "Where else would he be? He probably doesn't want to talk to me, anyway."

Frustrated, she pulled a towel up around her wet hair and looked in the mirror. "It's not like I'm pretty," she said, staring at her reflection. "I'm not even close to pretty." What Greg had seen in her, she had never understood. A solemn reflection met her gaze—an ever-present reminder of the fact that she was average, ordinary.

Laura reached up into the medicine chest, pulling out a container. "Not that this will do much good." She smeared the gooey mask all over her face. When she finished, the only things left visible were her mouth and eyes. "Anyway, it's not like he's such a great catch," she reasoned with herself. "He doesn't even know how to dress. His clothes are wrinkled, and his ties are older than my children. He's as hopeless as I am."

Laura made her way across the bedroom, still talking to herself. Somehow, it made her feel better. "And his hair," she continued. "It wouldn't hurt the man to use some hair gel. It wouldn't wound his ego that much, would it?"

Frustrated, she pulled the bedroom door open, feeling the mask begin to harden. A cup of hot chocolate would make everything better. It always did.

"Men," she exclaimed, stepping out into the living room. "They don't know what they're missing, anyway."

"Mom?"

"Yeah?" She didn't even look up, still lost in her private conversation.

"Uh, Mom?"

"What, Jessica?" she asked, exasperated.

"I just thought you might want to know we have company."

Laura turned abruptly, finding herself face-to-face with Professor Andrew Dougherty. Her heart leaped into her throat. Suddenly she wasn't sure whether to throw her arms around him or to turn and run.

Andrew took one look at Laura and started laughing. He couldn't seem to control himself. Whether the laughter came from the sheer relief of finding her at last, or the fact that her face was covered in the thick green mask, he couldn't be sure. How comical, yet how endearing. He had never seen anything like it on any woman, let alone the one he now found himself helplessly, hopelessly in love with. "Laura?" It was more question than statement.

She instinctively put her hands up over her face, clearly embarrassed. "Oh, no. . . . Not now. Not like this!"

"Please don't hide your face," he said, reaching for her hands. "It's beautiful." His hands trembled uncontrollably as they clutched hers.

"You're making fun of me," she pouted, backing toward the bedroom.

Andrew's heart pounded loudly in his ears, which were heating up more with each passing moment. He could hardly breathe, let alone think or speak like a rational man. "Laura, the last thing on earth I want to do is make fun of you. I think you're beautiful—green face and all."

"You do?"

"I do." He spoke the words almost prophetically. There would be no more broken hearts in his world. He had waited for Laura Chapman all of his life, and she was well worth the wait.

She continued to take tiny, nervous steps backward until she ran smack-dab into the living room wall. Jessica stood off to one side of the room, giggling helplessly.

Kent stuck his head in from the kitchen, his jaw dropping. "Mom?" He looked more than a little surprised.

"Kent," Andrew said, turning toward him, "your mother and I are having a little conversation. You don't mind, do you?"

"Not a bit," Kent said, heading back into the kitchen.

"Jessica," Andrew said firmly, turning to look at her. "I think your brother needs your help in the kitchen." He gave her a look that could not be misunderstood.

"Whatever you say," Jessica agreed. "You're the teacher."

Laura looked up into the sparkling eyes of this man who had captivated her. How clear everything suddenly seemed.

"I feel like I've known you forever, not just a few months," he said, reaching to run his fingers softly through her hair.

Months? It seemed she had always known Andrew, always felt drawn to him as she did now. It was true that he could never take Greg's place. But, then again, maybe he wasn't supposed to. Maybe, like Jessica said, he only needed to be himself.

But how could she begin to break through the layers of unspoken words that had traveled between them over the last several weeks? Laura had rehearsed the prepared speech in her head so many times. She would tell him how she felt, what her heart had been longing to say. And yet, no words seemed to come at all. She found herself completely and utterly speechless. Part of that, she had to admit, came from the fact that the mud mask had completely hardened, leaving her with little or no facial movement.

"Ms. Chapman," Andrew said, moving closer to her. She looked up into his eyes. They were kind eyes, loving eyes. They seemed to reach into the very depths of her soul and touch a spot that had not been touched for a long, long time. For the first time, she saw herself in their reflection. It was wonderful, amazing.

"Yes, Professor Dougherty?" She fought to form words through tightened lips. The "professor" part was just for emphasis, but it seemed to work like a charm. A grin spread across his face. She struggled to catch her breath with the reality of the thought. . . . *I love this man. I love him!*

"Your very wise daughter asked me today if I was a praying man."

"What did you tell her?" Laura spoke slowly, forcing the words.

"I told her that I was," he answered. "I've taken to praying quite a bit these past three weeks."

"You have?" She tried to smile, but her cheeks refused to cooperate.

"I have, and I can say I'm a firm believer in the power of prayer." A look of determination filled his eyes—a fiery look.

"Really? Is that what you came to tell me?" she asked, half-teasing.

"I came to tell you that you aced my class," he said, moving closer still, his fingers sweeping through her hair.

"I did?" She asked breathlessly, cradling her head in his hand. "I got an A?"

"You got an A," he said, coming so close that her heart began to race. "But that's not the only reason I came."

"It isn't?" Her knees suddenly grew weak, and she felt a little dizzy. The only thing that kept her standing was the wall itself, which she had firmly pressed herself up against.

"Nope," he said, slipping both arms around her neck and pulling her to himself. How right it felt to be in his arms, how totally and perfectly right. "I came to tell you, Ms. Chapman, that, no matter how many students I have, you're absolutely in a class of your own." His breath lingered warm against her lips.

She looked up at him, wanting like crazy to smile, but unable to with her face frozen in position by the mask. "Does that make me the teacher's pet?" she whispered, feeling her heart about to break wide open with the joy that consumed it.

Andrew never took the time to answer. His lips spoke more than words could ever say.

*E*PILOGUE

*L*aura sat alongside her fellow students, anxiously waiting her turn. Any moment now, she would hear her name. She glanced across the large auditorium to where her family sat in the stands. Kent waved frantically, his new girlfriend, Courtney, joining in. They had only been dating a few weeks, but Laura loved her like a daughter. She was a strong Christian and had made quite an impact in Kent's life. In fact, just this morning Laura had heard the two of them discussing plans to work in the youth ministry at church. *God is so good.*

Her eyes traveled to her mom, who sat at their right. As usual, Buck was with her, a broad grin on his face. They smiled and waved, and Laura's heart began to race in anticipation of what was about to take place.

She glanced to and fro, looking for Andrew. *Ah. There he is, seated just behind them, with a fistful of yellow roses. I'm so glad he's here. He's my biggest fan.* She grinned at them all, waving madly. He blew her a kiss in response. She pretended to catch it, nearly knocking the cap off of the boy sitting next to her.

"So sorry."

"No problem."

She turned her attention to Jessica, who sat on her left. "It's almost our turn," she whispered.

"I know, Mom. I know." Her daughter looked nervous.

"Are you going to be all right?"

"Uh-huh."

Laura turned her attention back to the speaker at the podium, trying to concentrate. He spoke of hope, of potential, of possibilities.

They were words she fully understood. In fact, she appreciated them now more than ever.

Laura's two years at Wainesworth Junior College had paid off, and then some. With her associate's degree in hand, she had transferred to the university a couple of years back. She would cross the stage to accept her bachelor's degree in Business Management any moment now.

The whole thing had been her husband's idea, really. Laura looked up at Andrew once again, a smile instinctively spreading across her face. His sport jacket and tie were terribly mismatched, and his rumpled hair desperately needed combing. Not much had changed over the years.

She hoped it never would.